PRAISE FOR THE COREAN CHRONICLES

Soarer's Choice

"The characters have become more fascinating with each novel; moreover, this one includes even more action than either of its predecessors . . . which contributes mightily to bringing the adventures of Dainyl, Alector of Corus, and Mykel, an officer in the native military corps, to a stunning conclusion while leaving enough unanswered questions for many more Corean stories." —*Booklist* (starred review)

"I especially enjoy the way Modesitt writes characters. The details that he shares create believable characters that are both powerful and flawed." —*SFRevu*

Cadmian's Choice

"Vividly imagined . . . well-crafted fifth volume of [Modesitt's] Corean Chronicles." —*Publishers Weekly*

"Dedicated Modesitt fans will anxiously await the next installment." —*VOYA*

Alector's Choice

"Modesitt's fourth entry in his Corean series (after 2004's *Scepters*) contains plenty of fine world-building and intelligently developed magic. Modesitt fans, knowing what they're in for, will find reaching the end of the challenging fantasy well worth the effort." —*Publishers Weekly*

"Corus is a fascinating land, full of both new and ancient magic, and the inhabitants are possibly the most fascinating of all, with complex motivations underpinning their every action." —*Romantic Times BOOKreviews*

Scepters

"In the trilogy . . . Modesitt has portrayed Alucius's development as both man and soldier and created a world original in its details but familiar in the cussedness of its inhabitants, human and nonhuman. It's a notable achievement." —*Booklist*

Darknesses

"A superb fantasy . . . a strong epic fantasy that will have the audience wondering where the author will take them next."
—*The Midwest Book Review*

Legacies

"L. E. Modesitt, Jr. uses his fabulous world-building skills to introduce a new fantasy world of ancient magic. Strange creatures or supernatural beasts are glimpsed but not yet explained. . . . An intriguing study in contrasts with its elements of talented vs. normal, female vs. male leadership, prosperity vs. poverty." —*Romantic Times BOOKreviews*

SOARER'S CHOICE

TOR BOOKS BY L. E. MODESITT, JR.

THE COREAN CHRONICLES

Legacies
Darknesses
Scepters
Alector's Choice
Cadmian's Choice
Soarer's Choice

THE SAGA OF RECLUCE

The Magic of Recluce
The Towers of the Sunset
The Magic Engineer
The Order War
The Death of Chaos
Scion of Cyador
Ordermaster
Fall of Angels
The Chaos Balance
The White Order
Colors of Chaos
Magi'i of Cyador
Wellspring of Chaos
Natural Ordermage

THE SPELLSONG CYCLE

The Soprano Sorceress
The Spellsong War
Darksong Rising
The Shadow Sorceress
Shadowsinger

THE ECOLITAN MATTER

Empire & Ecolitan
(comprising *The Ecolitan Operation* and *The Ecologic Secession*)
Ecolitan Prime
(comprising *The Ecologic Envoy* and *The Ecolitan Enigma*)

The Forever Hero
(comprising *Dawn for a Distant Earth, The Silent Warrior,* and *In Endless Twilight*)

Timegod's World
(comprising *Timediver's Dawn* and *The Timegod*)

THE GHOST BOOKS

Of Tangible Ghosts
The Ghost of the Revelator
Ghost of the White Nights
Ghost of Colombia
(comprising *Of Tangible Ghosts* and *The Ghost of the Revelator*)

The Hammer of Darkness
The Green Progression
The Parafaith War
Adiamante
Gravity Dreams
The Elysium Commission
Octagonal Raven
Archform: Beauty
The Ethos Effect
Flash
The Eternity Artifact
*Viewpoints Critical**

*Forthcoming

SOARER'S CHOICE

The Sixth Book of the Corean Chronicles

L. E. Modesitt, Jr.

A TOM DOHERTY ASSOCIATES BOOK
NEW YORK

SOARER'S CHOICE: THE SIXTH BOOK OF THE COREAN CHRONICLES

Edited by David G. Hartwell

A Tor Book
Published by Tom Doherty Associates, LLC
175 Fifth Avenue
New York, NY 10010

www.tor.com

ISBN-13: 978-0-7653-5559-1
ISBN-10: 0-7653-5559-0

First Edition: November 2006
First Mass Market Edition: November 2007

Printed in the United States of America

0 9 8 7 6 5 4 3 2 1

For Ben Bova,
who offered the first opportunity, and the key advice

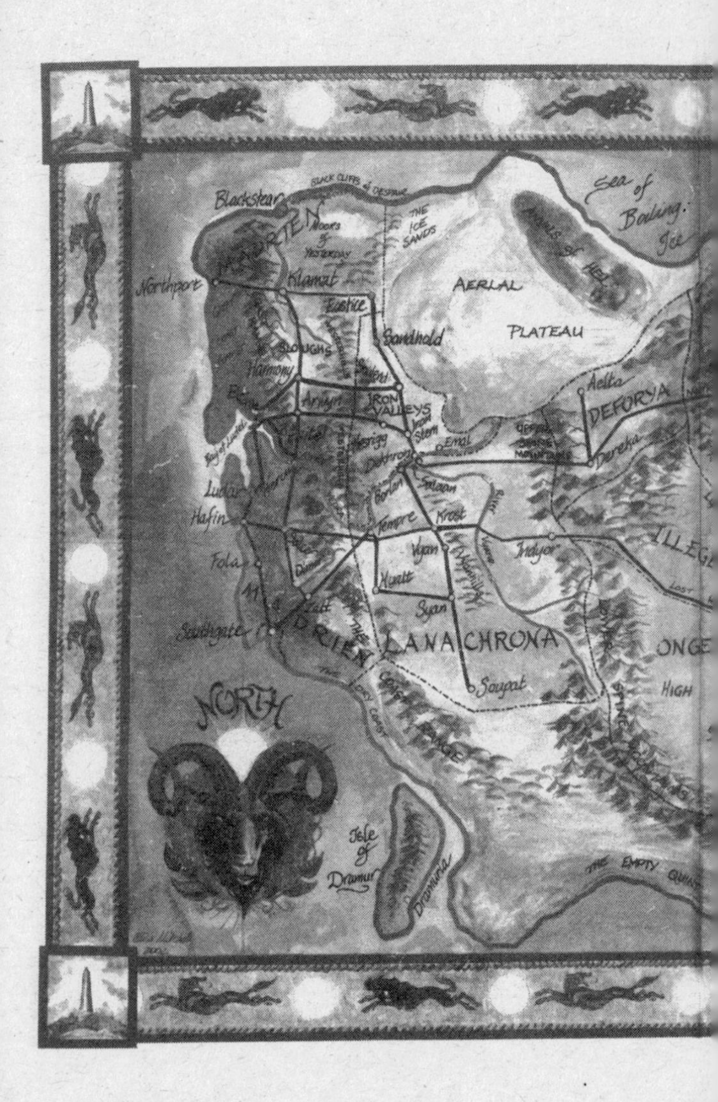

BLACK CLIFFS of DESPAIR
Sea of Boiling Ice
Moors of Yesterday
THE ICE SANDS
Northport
Klamat
Eastice
AERLAL
PLATEAU
Sandhold
Harmony
IRON VALLEYS
Iron Stem
Emal
Aelta
DEFORYA
Dereka
Ludar
Hafin
Tempre
Krost
Vyan
Indyor
Fola
Hiatt
Syan
Southgate
LANACHRONA
Saugat
HIGH
NORTH
Isle of Dramur
Dramuria
THE EMPTY

Frozen Headland
Scien
Norda
Inknyt
Cape Allure
Passera
Fordall
THE SPINE of CORUS
Coren
Vysta
LUSTREA
GREAT MARSH
Prosp
HIGHWAY
SOUTH PASS
GELYA
Flyr
Lysia
Dulka
STEPPES
Sudya
Tyjora
Sinjin
CORUS

ALECTORS OF ACORUS

KHELARYT	Duarch of Elcien	
	ZELYERT	High Alector of Justice
	CHEMBRYT	High Alector of Finance
	ALSERYL	High Alector of Transport
SAMIST	Duarch of Ludar	
	RUVRYN	High Alector of Engineering
	JALORYT	High Alector of Trade
	ZUTHYL	High Alector of Education
BREKYLT	High Alector of the East [Alustre]	
ASULET	Senior Alector—Lyterna	
PAEYLT	Senior Engineer—Lyterna	
SHASTYLT	Former Marshal of Myrmidons	
DAINYL	Marshal of Myrmidons—West [Elcien]	
ALCYNA	Submarshal of Myrmidons—East [Alustre]	
NORYAN	Majer of Myrmidons, deputy to Alcyna	
LYSTRANA	Chief Assistant to High Alector of Finance	

Table Cities
[Recorders of Deeds]

Elcien [Chastyl]	Lyterna [Myenfel]	Norda [Dubaryt]
Ludar [Puleryt]	Tempre [Chyal]	Prosp [Noryst]
Alustre [Retyl]	Hyalt [Rhelyn]	Blackstear [Delari]
Dereka [Jonyst]	Soupat [Nomyelt]	Faitel [Techyl]
Lysia [Sulerya]	Dulka [Deturyl]	

Green towers rise against a setting sun,
proud monuments to choices ill-begun,
spare spires of eternal stone to stand
and long imprison spirits of the land.

Alectors' choices fell on friends and foes.
They struck with force, righteousness, and woes.
Heeded not good or grace when day was done,
and greater powers had turned stars and sun.

1

Dainyl sat behind the wide desk in the large study in headquarters. On the desk were stacks of reports. To his left on the polished wood was a shorter stack—the immediate orders he had written for the Myrmidons in an effort to undo the worst of his predecessor's plotting. Outside, the morning sunlight of late harvest warmed the courtyard and the blue-winged pteridons of First Company—those that were not flying dispatches and undertaking other duties. The solid granite of the courtyard and the walls sparkled in the bright sun, clean and crisp.

He'd permanently reassigned the Seventh Company of Myrmidons to Tempre from Dulka to keep them from being suborned by Quivaryt, the regional alector in Dulka, and clearly the tool of Brekylt, the Alector of the East in Alustre. After that had come the cover letter forwarding copies of Dainyl's appointment as marshal to each of the eight Myrmidon companies spread across Corus. Beside those lay the draft of his report on what he had done to quash the "revolt" in Hyalt and Tempre. Of course, he couldn't tell the entire story, because his superior, the High Alector of Justice, the most honorable Zelyert, had firmly ordered him to treat the matter as a local revolt, rather than the first thrust of a conspiracy masterminded by Brekylt. To make matters worse, and more delicate, Dainyl suspected that Brekylt was being quietly urged on by Samist, the Duarch of Ludar.

Dainyl looked up from the various papers and back out through the window at the nearest pteridon in the courtyard behind the headquarters building, standing on its wide raised stone square and stretching its blue leathery wings. The long crystalline beak glittered in the sunlight. After a moment, Dainyl's eyes dropped back to the papers before him.

Despite the proclamation that lay on his table desk and the green-edged gold stars on the collars of his blue and gray shimmersilk uniform that attested to his rank, Dainyl still didn't feel like the Marshal of Myrmidons.

Add to that the fact that he was dreading the translation trip to Alustre, but the longer he waited, the more dangerous the situation became, and it wasn't something he could delegate. For one thing, he didn't have anyone to whom he could delegate the task. He'd been the submarshal in Elcien, and Colonel Dhenyr, who had been the Myrmidon operations director, had attempted to kill Dainyl when Dainyl had discovered Dhenyr's treachery. Dainyl was the only senior officer left in headquarters. The other submarshal, Alcyna, was stationed in Alustre, the width of the continent away. For years, she had directed Myrmidon operations in the east, and she was one of the reasons Dainyl had to go to Alustre—and before long.

He took a deep breath and reached for the next document on the top of the taller pile. In less than a glass, he was due at the Palace of the Duarch in Elcien, to meet with Duarch Khelaryt to brief him personally on all that had happened in Hyalt and Tempre. He assumed that he would also be asked for his plans for the Myrmidons. That possibility worried him far more than explaining the past, because he doubted that it would be wise to reveal the reasons behind what he planned until he had a better idea of what the Duarch—and those around him—already knew.

Still, he needed to finish catching up on the other Myrmidon and Cadmian operations, or as many as he could, before he met with the Duarch. He began to read the report from Colonel Herolt, commander of the First Regiment, Cadmian Mounted Rifles.

When he finished, Dainyl couldn't help but frown. Except for Second Battalion, every battalion in the First Regiment was understrength, and the colonel was reporting that matters were worsening. And why in the Archon's name had a battalion been sent to Soupat? The mines there were marginal. At least he thought so, but it wouldn't hurt to ask Lystrana. As a chief assistant in the Palace of the Duarch, his wife might know the trade and finance background.

Slowly, he got up and headed for the records chamber.

Doselt, the squad leader in charge of records, then jumped to his feet. "Yes, Marshal?"

"Would you find me the records of and the orders to the First Cadmian Regiment that deal with the deployment of its Sixth Battalion to Soupat last season?"

"It might take a bit, sir."

"Just bring them to me. If I'm not here, leave them on the corner of my desk."

"Yes, sir."

Dainyl moved down the corridor to see if Captain Ghasylt was in his study. Dainyl needed some help, and he needed it now. Ghasylt might be out in the courtyard—he spent more time flying or with the pteridons than did many company commanders. Dainyl was fortunate. The captain was standing by his desk, holding a report, looking at it quizzically.

He dropped it on the table. "Sir?"

"Ghasylt . . . you know that we have no operations director . . ."

"Yes, sir." Ghasylt swallowed. "No, sir."

"No, sir?" Dainyl couldn't help smiling.

"I'm a flier, sir. I can't do operations and scheduling and paperwork."

"Your reports are excellent," Dainyl pointed out.

"That's because I don't do them. Undercaptain Zernylta does. She has for years."

Dainyl laughed. "I might steal her, then."

"She writes well, sir. I'd hate to lose her, but she'd do better than I would."

"Where is she?"

"She's on the dispatch run from Ludar. She won't be back until late."

"Would you leave word that I would like to see her?"

"Yes, sir." Ghasylt sounded disconsolate.

"If she works out, she won't get jumped three ranks to colonel," Dainyl said. "She'll be a captain and assistant operations director." Of course, there might not be an operations director for a while, but Dainyl needed the job done. "And you could still make majer . . . without doing much paperwork." He grinned. "If you can find another undercaptain who can write."

"Ghanyr's not bad. Chelysta's nearly as good as Zernylta, but don't steal her. She's the best squad leader in the air."

Dainyl made a mental note to jot that down when he got back to his study. He could never tell when he might need another good company commander. He'd also have to check on Ghasylt. He might be able to promote him to majer anyway. The commanding officer of the Elcien company probably ought to be one, and Dainyl needed a good flying commander and loyalty as much as he needed an operations officer. "I appreciate the information, and even more, I appreciate your honesty and loyalty. These days, it means a great deal."

Although Ghasylt's expression remained politely attentive, Dainyl sensed the concealed surprise—and gratitude.

"We need to talk, before too long, about what may lie ahead for you and First Company."

"Yes, sir."

Dainyl nodded, then turned and headed back toward his study. He didn't make it.

"The duty coach is ready, sir!" That was Undercaptain Yuasylt, the duty officer.

"I'll be there in a moment." Dainyl paused. There was nothing he really needed in his study. He turned and headed toward the archway to the front entrance.

Outside, waiting with the coach, was Wyalt. As always, the duty driver had a smile on his face when Dainyl strode out of headquarters. "Good morning, Marshal."

"Good morning, Wyalt. The Duarch's Palace."

"Yes, sir."

Dainyl stepped up into the coach and closed the door.

Once the coach began to move, he concentrated on how best to brief the Duarch. Some of that would depend on whether Khelaryt wanted a private briefing or one that included other High Alectors.

As the duty coach neared the Duarch's Palace, Dainyl looked out at Elcien, a city built on an isle, of stone and tile and gardens and trees, orderly and vibrant, with stone-walled dwellings set on tree-lined streets, shops with their perfect tile roofs set around market squares that held everything produced on Acorus. Goods shipped from across the world flowed from the wharves and docks on the southern shore into endless warehouses and to everyone in Elcien, alectors and landers alike.

His eyes lingered on the twin green towers flanking the Palace, soaring into the silver-green sky, gleaming and glittering in the midmorning sunlight, symbolically crowning the accomplishments of the alectors of Acorus, who had turned a freezing and dying world into a place of life and achievement. Even as he marveled at the towers, Dainyl recalled the words of the ancient soarer. *You must change, or you will die.* That seemed so unlikely, yet the ancient had been so certain . . . and so melancholy in saying those words.

The coach slowed and came to a halt under the portico at the main entrance to the Duarch's Palace. Dainyl stepped out.

"I'll be waiting for you, sir," Wyalt called down from the driver's seat.

Dainyl almost told him to return to headquarters because others might need him, but cut off the words before he spoke. There wasn't anyone there who would need the coach, not without a submarshal or an operations director. "Thank you. I don't know how long I'll be."

"I'll be here, sir."

Dainyl made his way in through the archway, past the pair of guards armed with lightcutter sidearms. He did not recall the slender alector who met him inside the main foyer of the Palace, although his face was vaguely familiar, but it was clear that the functionary knew Dainyl.

"Marshal, the Duarch is ready to see you. If you would accompany me." He turned down the high-ceilinged hallway, flanked by goldenstone marble columns that led to the east wing of the Palace.

The hall was floored with the traditional octagonal tiles of green marble, linked by smaller diamond tiles of gold marble, and dark green velvet hangings between the goldenstone columns were trimmed in gold. The sound of Dainyl's boots hitting the octagonal- and diamond-shaped marble floor tiles was lost in the expanse of the corridor.

Near the end of the corridor, the alector turned to his right and knocked on a door. After the briefest of moments, he opened it, and motioned for Dainyl to enter, then followed the marshal into the chamber. It was the same small library, six yards wide and twelve in length, where Dainyl had met with the Duarch on the one previous occasion he had briefed Khelaryt. The inside walls held oak shelves filled with volumes, while the outside wall contained smaller sections of shelves. The narrow floor-to-ceiling windows between the built-in bookcases overlooked the southern sunken garden.

The Duarch rose from behind his desk. This time, unlike the last, it was almost empty, instead of being stacked high with books. Standing, he was an immense presence, close to three yards tall, with shimmering black hair and deep violet eyes dominating his alabaster face. He radiated Talent.

"Thank you, Bharyt." The Duarch's voice was deep but warm. He turned from the aide to Dainyl and gestured to a chair set across the wide desk from him. "Please, Marshal."

Dainyl bowed and seated himself. Behind him, the door clicked shut.

"Dainyl. First, let me offer my congratulations and my gratitude." With the words came a feeling of warmth.

Dainyl did not trust that feeling entirely, because he had no idea whether it was genuine. The Duarch was so accomplished with Talent and shields that he could conceivably project the feeling without revealing what lay behind the projected emotion.

"I understand from what the High Alector has said," continued Khelaryt, "and from what he has refrained from saying, that the incidents in Hyalt and Tempre were far more than the minor revolt that is the official description. I also understand that you had anticipated this . . . possibility . . . and were ordered not to act until actual misuse of lifeforce energies occurred."

Dainyl waited. He had not been asked a question.

"You are deferential, Marshal."

"As I should be, sir. Would you like a fuller explanation of the events?"

"I will request two explanations. The first will be a complete one, and that is for me alone. The second one will be for several other High Alectors—those of Finance and Transport, and the High Alector of Engineering from Ludar. You will not tell them everything, and based on what you tell me, I will suggest what should go no farther. You may proceed."

"Yes, sir." Dainyl cleared his throat. Even though he had planned what to say, carefully, he was still less than sanguine about briefing the Duarch, because he knew that, despite Khelaryt's immense Talent, the shadowmatch conditioning of a Duarch resulted in blind spots and seeming irrationalities. "It began in early spring when I visited Alustre, under the orders of Marshal Shastylt and the High Alector of Justice. There I discovered a number of patterns, small things, seemingly, that suggested all was not as it should be. . . ." He went on to tell about Brekylt's comments, what he had discovered about the "substitution" of key Myrmidon personnel, and then about the attacks on him, both by the regional alector in Dulka and by the then-commanding officer of the Seventh Myrmidon Company. He also mentioned the diversion of engineering resources at Fordall, and the mysterious deaths used to cover up the details, as well as some of the attacks on him by the Recorders of Deeds, but only those that had taken place in the Table chambers, and not those occurring while he had been in transit between Tables. Those incidents would have revealed far too much about his own abilities. ". . . and when Rhelyn complained about a wild lander Talent in Hyalt, but declined firmly any Myrmidon assistance, it was clear to me that we needed to move against Rhelyn before matters became even worse."

"This was when Marshal Shastylt ordered you to await further developments? Was that because Rhelyn was regional alector and Recorder of Deeds in Hyalt?"

"I assume so, sir. Shastylt told me that to act immediately would be unwise."

"What prompted him to change that decision?"

"That happened some weeks later when I received a copy of a report from a Cadmian battalion commander in Hyalt suggesting that road-building equipment had been constructed and modified to be used against both Cadmians and Myrmidons."

"You received a copy directly? Is that not . . . unusual?"

"It was very unusual. The majer had sent the original to his commander, as per regulations, but a copy to me. It was clear he feared that too much delay in relaying what he discovered would be unfortunate. When Marshal Shastylt read the report, he ordered me to proceed. . . ." Dainyl went on to describe the use of Fifth Company pteridons out of Dereka, rather than First Company from Elcien.

"You did not trust your own officers, Marshal?"

"I trust First Company totally, sir, but it was clear to me from the beginning that Colonel Dhenyr was someone's tool. I had absolutely no proof, and frankly, I was less than certain about what Marshal Shastylt was doing."

"As you unfortunately had every right to be."

"The other aspect of the matter that was especially troubling were the weapons that were used by the forces of Regional Alector Fahylt. He had created his own regional force of armed and mounted rifles, using landers and indigens, and a smaller force of alectors armed with lightcutter sidearms. The mounted rifle companies even had unmarked Cadmian weapons. Those I left in Cadmian custody, but the lightcutters were sent under seal to High Alector Zelyert."

Dainyl could sense the Duarch's surprise even before Khelaryt spoke.

"How did that come to pass? Arming steers for use against Cadmians, and alectors with lightcutters?" The sudden chill in the library matched the coldness of the Duarch's voice, and the Talent force of the Duarch felt strong enough to shake the entire Palace. Belatedly, Dainyl realized that might have been a projection of an illusion, although he wasn't so sure of what had been real Talent and what had been illusion.

"That I do not know. I suspect that the lightcutters came

from Fordall, and might be another aspect of the engineering problems that resulted in Zestafyn's death. Fordall was certainly where the lightcannon used in Hyalt originated."

"How do you know those did not come from Faitel?"

"I don't, sir. But if they did not come from Fordall, why did someone go to the extremes of creating mishaps and deaths and trying to cover up the use of additional resources in Fordall and why were there no such diversions in Faitel?"

"Why indeed? Please continue."

"It's likely that the unmarked rifles did come from Faitel, if Shastylt's and High Alector Zelyert's assurances to me about the source of the unmarked rifles happened to be correct."

"They were correct, and there were far more unmarked rifles produced than were initially accounted for. So you are doubtless correct in that supposition."

"Whether the lightcannon and the lightcutters came from Fordall or Faitel, then their presence, and that of the rifles, suggests that either the High Alector of Engineering or someone high in engineering was involved."

"That is doubtless correct, but you will not mention that in briefing the High Alectors. Only note that the rifles and lightweapons were present in large numbers in the hands of indigen steers who were rebels."

"Yes, sir."

"Pardon me, Marshal. Please continue." A smile followed the words, dispersing the sense of doom and chill.

"There isn't much more to add. When I returned, Shastylt was so shocked that it led to his death, as I told you earlier, and Colonel Dhenyr was so upset when I suggested that I now had proof of his treachery that he attempted to kill me on the spot with his sidearm."

"Did you threaten him?"

"Only with the fact that I had proof. I did raise my shields."

"And he added to your proof. Fatally." Khelaryt laughed deeply and warmly. "Did Shastylt say much before his unfortunate . . . shock?"

"He said it would be easy to prove that Submarshal Alcyna and I were planning a coup."

"He told me that you had gone to Hyalt without orders, and he was concerned. That seemed unlike you."

Dainyl wasn't at all surprised at that revelation. "He was the one who ordered me to keep everything secret." That wasn't quite true. So had High Alector Zelyert.

"Why did you?"

"Because not doing so would have endangered the Myrmidons and Cadmians involved far more."

"So you put your people ahead of other considerations?"

"No, sir." Then Dainyl shook his head. "Not exactly, sir. What I meant was that I might not have had the resources to deal with each problem had they occurred at once, which was likely if information leaked out before I could get the Myrmidons from Fifth Company to Hyalt. We were able to isolate Hyalt. That meant the Cadmians did not have to fight the mounted rifles from Tempre while guarding the perimeters and that Fifth Company did not have to deal with the misguided orders of Seventh Company while subduing Hyalt."

"Put that way, your actions are commendable. How do you propose to keep such . . . misunderstandings from occurring in the future?"

"I had thought to promote Submarshal Alcyna to headquarters—immediately— with a personal visit to Alustre."

"That might be for the best, under the circumstances." The Duarch tilted his head to the side, and a humorous smile appeared. "From what I have gathered, when one of the Fifth Company Myrmidons was killed, you took his pteridon and led the attacks. You were also instrumental, I understand, in keeping the casualties to a minimum in persuading Seventh Company that their orders were . . . misguided. You also came up with a novel means of dealing with command in Seventh Company."

How had the Duarch known that? Dainyl did not reply for a moment, then managed to smile but slightly as he realized the source, belatedly recognizing a certain resemblance. Yet, if the Duarch were conditioned against receiving or reading any communications from his daughters . . . It had to be Undercaptain Asyrk, acting under Captain Lyzetta's orders. He risked a guess. "She is exceedingly courageous, sir, but I would not have guessed her heritage."

"Say no more, Dainyl. Your thoughtfulness and courage are greater than any marshal in generations. Let us trust that they are sufficient for the challenges ahead, and that they will help us bring the Master Scepter to Acorus." The Duarch's face froze, if but for the tiniest fraction of an instant, Dainyl could sense that conflict between what Khelaryt almost knew, and was not allowed to accept.

Even knowing that, Dainyl barely managed not to betray his total shock.

"You look concerned. Is it not best that the Master Scepter be transferred here?"

"I am concerned, sir. I have done my best, but even so, much lifeforce was squandered in the process, and you had told me earlier that the decision was close and hinged on the surplus of lifeforce." That wasn't quite what the Duarch had said, but what he had implied, and it was the best Dainyl could offer.

Abruptly the Duarch nodded, as if he had heard enough. "You did manage to minimize the loss of lifeforce, especially by destroying hundreds of the rebel alectors from Ifryn, who had no authority to be on Acorus."

Dainyl kept his expression pleasant and waited.

"All is judged on lifeforce mass, yet today's measurement does not always reflect what it will be tomorrow or next year. Nor what a world will be or could be."

"Yes, sir."

"As always, as with all those who serve the Duarchy and the Archon, you have not told me everything, have you?"

"No, sir. As I told you the last time you requested my presence, we would be here for days were I to do that. I will be happy to answer any questions you may have, now or in the future, or to provide more details about anything."

"That you will." Khelaryt laughed, not quite harshly, but the laugh was followed by a sense of warmth. "How is Lystrana faring with your child?"

"She fares well."

"That is good. She is one of the best chief assistants to any of the High Alectors."

"So I would believe, sir, although I am less than unbiased. She would do well at anything."

"You think so?" Khelaryt asked, almost jokingly.

"She has excellent judgment and can see much of what others do not." All Dainyl wanted to do was plant the germ of an idea.

"And we are fortunate that she does." The chill feeling returned to the library. "Continue to be careful in what you believe of Zelyert, Dainyl. He sees both more and less than he thinks he does. Be most careful." Another smile appeared, this one rueful as he rose again from behind the desk. "It is time for you to brief the others."

Dainyl followed Khelaryt out through the library door and down the corridor.

Four alector guards appeared, two walking beside him and two beside the Duarch, escorting them to a conference room, scarcely larger than the library, but containing only a large circular table with comfortable chairs—and three alectors in shimmersilk greens.

Walking into the conference room was like flying into the eye of a storm. While the chamber was calm, Dainyl was all too aware of the Talent forces that circled around him, yet the only one he truly feared for might of Talent was the Duarch. The other three alectors who stood waiting around the Table exuded Talent, but individually not that much more than did he, and he doubted if any had shields as strong as his. Still, he certainly could not have prevailed against any two together, or the Duarch alone, not that he ever wished to be in such a position.

Dainyl had seen all three High Alectors at functions, but only from a modest distance. Chembryt was the High Alector of Finance, for whom Lystrana was the chief assistant. Alseryl was High Alector of Transport, and Ruvryn was the High Alector of Engineering. Dainyl had to wonder why Ruvryn was even in Elcien, since he was based in the southern capital of Ludar and reported directly to the Duarch Samist.

"Before we have our meeting," Khelaryt said quietly, "I have asked Marshal Dainyl to brief you on the recent events in Hyalt and Tempre." The Duarch seated himself, as did the other High Alectors.

Dainyl hoped he was to remain standing. It seemed appropriate, and no one had motioned for him to seat himself. He cleared his throat and started. "There have been many rumors and stories, so I've been told, about what happened in Hyalt. I doubt that we will ever know all the reasons for what happened, but the Myrmidons were drawn into the situation when we began to receive reports of strange events in Hyalt. Then we received a documented report from a Cadmian officer that verified that there were alectors in uniforms testing and practicing with lightcannon . . ." Dainyl made the summary as brief as he dared, concluding less than a quarter of a glass later, ". . . the entire complex at Hyalt will require rebuilding, but there was little damage in Tempre. Paradoxically, the Table damage in Hyalt appears far less grave than that in Tempre."

"Does anyone have any questions?" asked the Duarch.

"I presume the Myrmidons will supply immediate transport for Table engineers from Faitel and Ludar," Ruvryn stated bluntly.

"Second Company in Ludar should be able to transport any engineers from Ludar, and First Company will transport those from Faitel. As soon as you inform me of the numbers and any limited supplies, we will make arrangements."

"You should have those within the next few days, Marshal." Chembryt smiled at Dainyl.

Dainyl could sense the thrust coming, but not at him.

"You had mentioned that the alector rebels in Hyalt possessed lightcannon," began Chembryt, "that the alector rebels in Tempre had Myrmidon-type hand sidearms, and that the mounted rifles of the former RA in Tempre had Cadmian rifles. Did you verify this?"

"Yes, sir. The lightcannon killed three Myrmidons from Fifth Company, and two pteridons and two Myrmidons from Seventh Company. The lightcutter sidearms were collected and are now under seal and custody of the High Alector of Justice. The Cadmians took custody of the rifles. I personally inspected all three types of weapons."

"Do you have any ideas as to their sources?" Chembryt did not even glance toward Ruvryn.

"The rifles were identical, in every particular, with the exception of serial numbers, with the Cadmian weapons. There is no doubt that they were manufactured either in Faitel or Fordall, but I have no way of knowing which it might be. As for the other weapons, I lack the engineering skills to determine where they may have been built or originated, save that there were no facilities at either Hyalt or Tempre where that could have been accomplished."

"Thank you."

Ruvryn did not smile as he looked at Dainyl. "Marshal . . . were you aware that proceeding without written orders from Marshal Shastylt or the High Alector of Justice verges on breaking the Code, and that could have created an even greater instability and loss of lifeforce?"

"I had thought of that, sir. But I was ordered to do so, and insubordination is definitely against the Code."

After the brevity of Dainyl's reply, there was silence, but only for a moment, when Alseryl coughed slightly.

"I don't believe you mentioned exactly how many rebel alectors there were, Marshal."

"We can't be absolutely certain how many there were, because some may have escaped, one way or another. We did find the remains of more than three hundred."

"Three hundred. You killed three hundred alectors?"

"Yes, sir. My orders were to put down the revolt. When I attempted to visit RA Rhelyn, even before I could dismount from the pteridon, we were attacked. There was never any attempt to communicate with us, and they refused to consider surrendering."

"That was in Hyalt. What about Tempre?"

"What were the casualties among the mounted rifle companies of the so-called Alector's Guard?"

"Did you attempt to avoid the initial conflict between Fifth and Seventh Companies?"

Dainyl answered questions for another quarter glass before the Duarch raised a hand.

"I think the marshal has been forthright. He has done his

best to preserve lifeforce and to ensure that Acorus is prepared to receive the Master Scepter. Thank you, Marshal. You may go."

"Yes, sir." Dainyl was more stunned by the total lack of reaction, even hidden, to the Duarch's statement about the Master Scepter than by his abrupt release. Even so, he bowed slightly and stepped to the door, letting himself out.

Another pair of alector guards escorted him back to the entry foyer, with its high arched dome. He was more than glad to step out into the rotunda and walk toward the waiting duty coach. What awaited him back at headquarters seemed far more manageable than what faced Khelaryt.

2

Under a clear silver-green sky, the late morning sunlight fell across the low rise to the north of Hyalt. From the saddle of the roan, Mykel surveyed the nearly completed Cadmian compound, standing out amid the tannish grasses of the grazing lands to the north. While he'd been occupied in fighting the rebel alectors at Tempre—and then recovering from his injuries—all the walls had been completed, and the paving of the interior was a third done. That included the areas around the gates, which could now be hung and secured in place. Both the barracks and the stables looked finished, on the outside, anyway. Work was beginning on digging out the roadbed south of the gates so that a stone-paved road to the high road could be built once the interior paving was finished.

"You've done wonders, Rhystan." Mykel turned to the senior captain mounted beside him. The captain's aura remained a deep brown, so deep it verged on black, but showed no sign of the green streaks that indicated the possibility of possessing the same Talent as Mykel did—and as did almost all alectors. In convalescing, Mykel had finally made the connection between what the soarer had told him a year before and what the one alector at Hyalt had called him in trying to kill him—a wild Talent. The soarer had told him to find his talent, but he hadn't realized that the alectors' term for his emerging abilities was Talent.

"How did you manage it?" Mykel asked.

Rhystan offered a sheepish grin. "Well, Majer . . . I kept telling the craftmasters that it wouldn't be all that long before you got back, and I really didn't want to have to explain why things weren't farther along."

Mykel forced a smile, and a chuckle. "You're a scoundrel." Behind the expression, he was both bemused and appalled. "I suppose Troral pressed you on the blankets?"

"No, sir. Not once."

"How are things going with Cismyr? Do you think he'll be able to handle the compound once we're sent back?"

"He's been very attentive. He has asked a few questions about you, indirectly."

Mykel wasn't sure he wanted to know. "Such as?"

"Whether you were the son of an ancient?"

"What?" Mykel shook his head. "My father's a tiler in Faitel, and my mother was a weaver before they married. Why would he ask that?"

"One of the Hyaltan Cadmians swears he saw you with an ancient, up on the hillside by the old garrison." Rhystan raised his eyebrows. "You have to admit, Majer, that more than a few strange things have occurred around you."

Mykel had been afraid he'd been observed, but it meant that the ranker who had seen him had some of the same Talent he did. Otherwise, the man would have seen nothing. "Many of them would have happened to you if you'd been in charge."

Rhystan laughed, shaking his head. "I don't think so, sir."

Mykel shrugged, then smothered a wince. His back was still tender, and doubtless would be for days more. Then, if it hadn't been for Rachyla, he probably would be in far worse condition—if he were still even alive. Had it been a mistake to give her the dagger of the ancients? What else could he have done? He'd tried kindness, understanding, and she'd still insisted he was her enemy.

Mykel *knew* they were somehow tied together, but Rachyla's

attitude had varied from grudging respect to outright hostility, all of it bordered with a large amount of condescension. When he thought about it, Mykel wondered why he cared—except that he had the feeling that she was caught in what amounted to an invisible prison and that she would be a far different person were she not. But was that only wistful thinking?

Rhystan eased his mount up beside Mykel. "Sir . . . I haven't asked, not where anyone could overhear, but what did happen in Tempre? There's all sorts of rumors from the factors, and the men have picked them up. They said that a building fell on you, and you walked away from the rubble, and that you'd killed two score alectors—the rebels, that is—by yourself."

The last part was all too close to the truth, but it wasn't something Mykel wanted spread about, particularly among his Cadmian rankers. He shook his head. "There was an explosion of some alector device they'd hidden in the lower level of the regional alector's headquarters. I got flattened by some of the stones. The building is very much intact, except for part of one door and a doorway. Altogether, the three companies did kill close to two score of the rebels, but that took all three companies—and you've seen the casualties."

Rhystan snorted. "You lost sixty-three men in Tempre out of slightly less than three hundred. Against irregulars and Reillies that would be on the high side, but not by that much. Losing that few against alectors armed with those lightcutters is unbelievable. It takes five to ten shots—unless they're head shots—just to knock them down."

Mykel was grateful Rhystan didn't mention the other exception besides head shots—that Mykel was doing the shooting. "I kept the men behind stone walls, and the rebel alectors didn't seem to have much sense of tactics. I don't think any of them had ever been in a real fight."

"Probably not."

"Then . . . there was something else." Mykel frowned. He'd thought of it earlier, and was having trouble recalling what it had been.

Rhystan waited.

"Oh . . . their weapons. They're all the kind that are designed to kill—usually instantly."

"So will a rifle bullet," replied Rhystan dryly.

"It's not the same thing. A Myrmidon fires one of those skylances, and anything in its path is gone, up in flame. With those uniforms that they wear, they'd have to have weapons like that, but how many times do they use them?"

After a moment, Rhystan nodded. "I see what you mean. All their battles tend to be shorter. Even when they did a siege of the regional alector's compound here, the actual battle took less than half a day. Most of that was sniping and preparation. The heavy fighting when they broke in was over in less than a glass."

"I'm guessing, but I think one reason why we won in Tempre was that . . . well . . . they ran out of ammunition. Or whatever passes for ammunition, and there was no one to resupply them."

"You realize, Majer, that you're a very dangerous man to the alectors?"

"Me?" Mykel had his own ideas as to that, and they concerned his Talent, but he wanted to hear what Rhystan had to say.

"You're among the few that know what their vulnerabilities are, and how to fight them successfully. You've figured out what weapons we could make that would be effective in taking them out, and at least some of them respect you, and I would not be surprised if some were not afraid of you."

"That's absurd."

This time Rhystan shrugged. "The word's out how you backed down a Myrmidon captain or undercaptain, and how the submarshal of Myrmidons made a special trip to see you when he discovered you were wounded. I don't know of any time ever when a Myrmidon officer checked on a Cadmian—let alone the number two man in all the Myrmidons."

"I'm sure he was only after information."

"Fabrytal said that he didn't ask anything except about your health and how you knew the rebels were rebels—and that was because Fabrytal couldn't tell him."

Mykel shifted his weight in the saddle. "I never thought

about it that way." And he hadn't. But then, he had not been in the best of shape when Submarshal Dainyl had sought him out at Rachyla's. He forced a grin. "You're just as dangerous. You know everything that I've figured out. In fact, some of it you worked out before I did."

"I've thought of that," Rhystan replied. "That's one reason why I'd rather remain a captain for a while. No one pays much attention to Cadmian captains—unless their commander is an idiot like Vaclyn . . . or Hersiod."

Although Mykel hadn't thought about Hersiod for months, Rhystan's comment jarred his memory. He managed not to swallow. The purpleness that had tinged Hersiod—that was what happened to people who spent much time around alectors. But could that also mean that somehow the alectors had used their abilities on the majer, making him intransigent like Vaclyn had been? Mykel wondered if Vaclyn had been influenced by the alectors. He'd met with them, and he'd said he'd only had a short meeting, but the reports Mykel had gotten had suggested a far longer meeting.

But why would the alectors influence Cadmian officers?

"Majer . . . sir? You have that look again, the one that means trouble."

Although Rhystan's tone was humorous, Mykel could sense the concern behind the humor. "I was wondering if Hersiod spent any time with the Myrmidon marshal."

"Of course he did. He and the colonel were briefed personally about the Iron Stem problems."

"Can you think of any reason why the Myrmidons would want Hersiod and Vaclyn to act stupidly?"

Rhystan's face hardened. "Frig! They both meet with Myrmidons, and they both started acting like ill-tempered asses, instead of the simple asses they were before. I should have seen it!" He shook his head. "But it doesn't make sense. If the alectors wanted to screw things up, it didn't work. You and Dohark are far better commanders than Vaclyn was. I'd bet that the senior captain in Fourth Battalion is better than Hersiod."

"Who would know that? In the Myrmidons? And whom did they meet with?" countered Mykel. "The submarshal is the one who promoted me and Dohark. Hersiod and Vaclyn met with the marshal . . . and we had a rebellion of alectors here in Hyalt and in Tempre."

"You're suggesting that the submarshal and the marshal are on different sides, with different agendas?"

"I don't know . . . but it's something to keep in mind. From what I've seen, I'd trust the submarshal more, but I'm not sure any of them are looking out for us."

"Sometimes I wonder if any of the senior officers do."

"They have their own ideas." Mykel smiled faintly.

"And it doesn't seem to matter what it costs us."

"Has that ever changed?"

"No." Rhystan studied the compound for several moments before speaking again. "Do you know where we'll be posted after we finish here?"

"Unless we get different orders, we report that we're ready to turn the compound over to Cismyr and Matorak. Then we get specific orders from the colonel as to how we're to head back to Northa. The way things are going, we may have to ride the whole way." Mykel snorted. "If we're lucky, we could ride to Tempre, and take a barge or a boat down the Vedra. That'd make more sense."

"Don't count on it, sir."

"I won't." Mykel urged the gelding forward. "I need to take a closer look at the compound."

3

Dainyl did not get home until far later than usual, because he'd discussed with Ghasylt the need for another Myrmidon to succeed Wyalt in training as duty driver and flier, as well as catching up on the problems of First Company. Then he had waited for Undercaptain Zernylta to return from her dispatch run from Ludar. Dainyl had asked her to try the position as assistant operations director on a temporary basis—without giving up her pteridon—to see if she would be happy with it.

She'd agreed, with reservations. "The writing part doesn't bother me, sir, and I've been doing most of First Company's scheduling for the captain, but . . . for all the companies?"

"In practical terms, right now you'd be mainly scheduling First Company, and occasionally Seventh Company out of Tempre."

"Tempre, sir?" Zernylta's black eyebrows lifted.

"They've been transferred there from Dulka. Why don't you give it a try, and we'll talk at the end of next week. If it works, you'll be promoted to captain."

Dainyl hadn't mentioned that she and Ghasylt would be the senior officers in headquarters anytime he was absent—at least until he dealt with Alcyna.

By the time he left headquarters, he was a good glass and a half late, and he didn't feel that badly about using the duty coach. It didn't hurt that Wyalt was cheerful.

When he walked in the door, Lystrana was waiting in the foyer. Her frown vanished, and the relief in her deep violet eyes was obvious.

She stepped forward and embraced him. "I was worried. I heard from Chembryt that you'd had to brief the High Alectors and the Duarch. And when you weren't here . . ."

"I had to wait for Zernylta to return from Ludar. I twisted her arm a bit to get her to try being assistant operations director."

"There isn't anyone else, is there?" She took his arm. "Dinner is waiting."

"I'm sorry."

"I think I'll be getting used to it."

"How is Kytrana?" His eyes dropped to the slight swelling of her abdomen.

"She was a bit upset when I got worried. She can sense that."

"That's a sign of Talent. Were you like that?"

"Why do you ask?"

"Because I certainly wasn't," he replied with a laugh, reaching out and tousling her shimmering black hair, cut short, just above her elegant neck.

The sun was so low in the west that while the sky was still light, both the dining room and the sunroom were shadowed by the courtyard walls. Both Zistele and Sentya—the blond lander serving girls—were already setting the platters on the table when Lystrana and Dainyl entered the room.

He looked through the archway into the sunroom and to the courtyard beyond, with its garden and fountain, then turned to the girls. "Do we have any ale?"

"Yes, sir," replied Sentya. "Would you like some?"

"Please." Dainyl sat slowly.

"Your stomach is a little uneasy?" Lystrana settled herself across from him.

He nodded. "It's been a long day."

"I hope the fowl isn't too dry. There is a cream sauce. I had Zistele make it to go with the noodles."

"You didn't get home all that early yourself, did you?"

She grinned at him. "No. We had some problems. I'll tell you later . . . when you tell me about your day."

"Here is your ale, sir." Sentya placed a pitcher and beaker on the table, not quite beside the pitcher of cider for Lystrana.

"Thank you so much." Dainyl served Lystrana and then himself. He took two small swallows of ale before he began to eat.

"The weather has been wonderful. I hope it stays this warm into fall."

"So do I," he replied.

As was their custom, neither talked of their work while they ate, nor until they retired to their bedchamber on the upper level—and the girls had gone to their quarters on the lower level.

Lystrana had slipped into a gown and robe and stretched out on the large bed while Dainyl slowly disrobed and hung up his blue and gray shimmersilk uniform.

"How did it go with Khelaryt?"

"I briefed him first, and gave a shorter presentation to the three High Alectors. I don't know why Ruvryn was there. He didn't look that happy, and he asked a few sharp questions."

"He was there because he'd been summoned by both Khelaryt and my Highest about more irregularities in the engineering accounts. I'll tell you about them when you're done."

"I was a little nervous. I've briefed the Duarch before—once—but never any of the High Alectors, except Zelyert—and he wasn't there."

"I'm sure he felt he knew what you had to say."

"He knows more than I said, and he may not have wanted to reveal anything." Dainyl paused. "It's worse than I thought. Everyone just nodded at the story of the limited revolt. It's as though no one wants to admit that there's a bigger problem. At the end, Khelaryt commended me for limiting lifeforce losses and my efforts to make sure that the Master Scepter comes to Acorus." He shook his head. "I really thought he understood that it's effectively been decided that it's going to Efra. But it's as if all the High Alectors know, and not a single one of them will point that out to him."

"Would you?"

"With his Talent-strength? That would be dangerous, but . . . they've all worked with him for years and years. With the shadowmatch conditioning, I don't think he can ask the right questions. And all those around him know it, and unless there's something else I don't know, they don't want to tell him what he doesn't want to hear."

"Did you really expect it to be much different, dearest?"

"No . . . not about them not wanting to tell him unpleasant news, but I had thought he could entertain the idea that the Master Scepter would not come to Acorus." Dainyl sighed, then offered a wry smile. "But it's clear he cannot even do that." After a moment, he added, "I can't believe how much Talent he has."

"That's why he's Duarch. With the way everyone plots and schemes, no one without that kind of strength could survive."

That certainly made sense. "Oh . . . I had another question. What do you know about the copper and tin mines around Soupat? I'd always thought they were marginal."

Lystrana inclined her head, concentrating for a moment. "They're not the most productive, but there's been more demand for copper in the west from the engineers for work in Faitel. Why did you want to know?"

"One of Shastylt's last acts, while I was in Hyalt, was to deploy a Cadmian battalion there to protect the mines against mountain brigands. There's nothing in the records to indicate why."

"I don't know about that. I do know that Ruvryn was insistent that he needed more production, especially of copper."

"Copper?" Dainyl didn't like that at all. Copper tended to be used more in crystal-based weapons—such as Myrmidon sidearms. "That makes the kind of sense I don't like."

"Weapons and road-building equipment?"

Dainyl nodded.

"That only confirms what you already know about him."

"All too true." He paused. "Speaking about what I already know and can't bring to light, I'm going to go to Alustre tomorrow. I can't put that off any longer."

"I worry about that, too."

"Try not to. If not for yourself, for the little one." Dainyl pulled on his robe and sat on the corner of the bed, facing her. Neither had lit the lamps, but with alectors' night vision, no lamps were necessary.

"Are you certain that you want Alcyna as submarshal here in Elcien?"

"Unfortunately, yes. What else can I do? Her official record is outstanding. She sent Seventh Company to attack me and Fifth Company in Hyalt, but those orders were never put in writing, and the officers who received them are dead. Even if there were some documentary proof, she'd claim that all she knew was that the regional alector was under attack."

"In your command area," Lystrana pointed out.

"She'd already sent a protest about my actions, but she was clever enough to say that Shastylt sent me without justification, and Shastylt's dead."

"You really want to deal with her on a daily basis?"

"I'd rather do that here, than have her keep working with Brekylt in Alustre. By removing her . . ."

"But you'll have to promote Noryan, and he's from Ifryn."

"He's a bull, and strong-willed, but he's not so devious. He'll do what Brekylt tells him, but what else can I do?"

"You can hope she'll attack you, or Brekylt will."

"You have great confidence in my shields, dearest."

"I do, but don't let your guard down, especially when they're not around."

Dainyl laughed, then eased up beside her.

4

An alector who wishes to be a responsible administrator must always keep in mind the difference between expectations based on facts and careful analysis, and expectations based upon a desired outcome.

All beings capable of some degree of thought speculate upon outcomes—those that are most probable, those that are least probable, those that are most desired, and those that are least desired. A truly intelligent individual first gathers all facts and all manner of knowledge that may affect an outcome, even such knowledge of the sort that cannot be quantified in numerical or objective terms. Then the intelligent alector assesses that knowledge and constructs a probabilistic analysis of the possible outcomes, weighing all the factors on as objective a basis as possible.

Subjective factors can and must be analyzed objectively, and this is one area where even the most rational of alectors can mislead himself. Just because an alector does not allow excessive emotion to affect his choices and decisions, that does not mean that steers or less perceptive alectors will not be affected by emotional factors. In addition, positive influences that cannot be quantified affect outcomes, such as a desire for excellence.

Even when both objective and subjective components are factored into the assessment of an outcome, however, an alector who must make a decision may be influenced by the desire to see a particular outcome. Usually, this outcome-influence results in the decision-maker weighing the component factors in such a fashion as to produce a prediction of the desired outcome. If the alector in question dislikes an outcome that will likely occur if subjective factors are weighted correctly, then the subjective factors will be dismissed or denigrated because they cannot be accurately quantified.

In similar fashion, when quantifiable factors truly outweigh the subjective factors, the alector who favors a subjective-influenced outcome will tend to minimize the impacts of the quantifiable factors, often on the basis that beliefs or feelings have a stronger impact than can be accurately assessed.

In the end, the judicious alector must work to assure that his expectations do not influence his analysis, but that accurate analysis and study form the basis for his expectations.

Views of the Highest
Illustra
W.T. 1513

5

Quattri morning found Mykel in what would be the quarters of the senior visiting Cadmian officer in the new compound. For now, he was that officer. Officially, Captain Cismyr, the commanding officer of the First Hyalt Company, was the commander of the compound.

Mykel's quarters were on the upper level of the main barracks, but at the rear. All the officers' quarters were accessed by an outside stairway. The space was empty, except for a bunk and a thin pallet mattress. The companies were scheduled to move from the old garrison to the new compound on Sexdi—if all went well, and the weather continued dry. Mykel would have liked to have moved everyone sooner, but the interior of the stables needed work, and he really wanted more of the courtyard paved.

Mykel sat on the bunk, using a square of wood balanced on his knees as a writing desk, trying to complete the last few lines of his report to Colonel Herolt. From through the open window, he could hear the sounds of clay being tamped in place, and rock chunks, gravel, and finally sand, as a base for the redstone paving for the courtyard. Farther away was the rhythmic droning of a saw, cutting planks—or timbers for the roofing of the headquarters building, the last structure in the compound to be completed. He'd made arrangements with craftmaster Poeldyn for the stone paving of a narrow road from the compound to the high road, although most of that work beyond the area immediately outside the south gates would have to wait until the stone work in the compound was completed.

Finally, Mykel put aside his makeshift desk and the completed report and stood. He still had to make a copy for his personal files, but the harder work of drafting a report that was complete—without disclosing matters that would create trouble for himself and without revealing that there were such omissions—was done. He had another day to make the copies he needed before the biweekly sandoxen coach made its next trip through Hyalt.

He walked to the half-open window and looked out. The barest breath of air wafted past him. For an early morning late in harvest, it was already hot. Styndal was directing a windlass crew and a crane in placing the last of the roof beams on the headquarters building. Mykel nodded. He had to admit that the Hyaltan crafters had done good work, better than he'd seen in a few places. But then, he reflected, Hyalt was a town that had come on hard times, and the workers were eager for work—and good pay.

His eyes lifted above the walls to the west, but he could not make out the regional alector's complex from the new compound, not that there was much to see, according to Rhystan. Submarshal Dainyl's pteridons had flattened and burned the one outbuilding and used some sort of fire to gut the interior of the tunnels and chambers cut into the rock of the cliff.

Mykel took a deep breath and stretched, before heading for the door and down to the half-paved courtyard.

Troral, the head of the council in Hyalt, as well as the largest cloth factor in the area, was due to arrive any moment to discuss the delivery of blankets and other needs for the compound. After that, Mykel needed to observe a drill involving both Hyaltan companies. In a sense, the exercise was a formality. Both companies had performed well in the actions in Hyalt and Tempre, although Second Company had seen more action in Tempre than First Company had in Hyalt.

Mykel had no more than stepped away from the barracks when Captain Cismyr appeared and rode toward him. "Good morning, Majer. We stand ready for the exercise and evaluation."

"I'd guess about half a glass, Captain. Don't head out to the exercise area until then." Mykel offered a wry smile. "I have to meet with Troral first—about some supplies for you and your men, like blankets for the winter. Is there anything else you need beside what we went over yesterday?"

"No, sir. Matorak couldn't think of anything, either."

"Good. At least, I hope that's good." Mykel smiled. "If it's likely to be much longer than half a glass, I'll send a messenger. It's too hot for men and mounts to wait in the sun."

"Yes, sir."

Cismyr turned and rode back toward the main gates. From what Mykel could sense, First Company had drawn up in the shade of the outside west walls.

Mykel walked toward the headquarters building, staying well back, but watching as Styndal's crafters fastened the last of the roof beams in place.

The telltale creaking alerted Mykel, and he turned and waited as a cart, pulled by a single horse, eased through the open main gates on the south side of the compound. Troral drove the cart, which held a load piled high and covered by tarps carefully fastened in place—blankets, no doubt. The factor eased the cart to a halt short of the front of the new barracks.

"Good morning, Troral," Mykel called cheerfully as the factor climbed off his cart.

Troral finished tethering the leads to a stone post not intended for that purpose and walked toward Mykel. He stopped a good yard away. "Good morning, Majer." Although the factor looked up at the taller lander, Troral's eyes did not quite meet Mykel's.

"I see you brought the blankets."

"You did say you'd be wanting them once the barracks

were done, and I heard that you'd be moving here in the next few days. That'd be telling me the barracks were done, or near enough."

Mykel caught, not with his eyes, but with his senses, feelings of absolute fear that even permeated the yellowish brown aura of the mastercrafter. Was it still his reputation as a dagger of the ancients? "Near enough. I'll write out the authorization. You'll have to draw the golds against the Cadmian letter of credit."

"I figured as much, what with you being in Tempre so long. True that you had to lay waste to the place?"

Mykel laughed gently. "Not even close. We did kill a number of rebels, but there was only a little damage to one building. I doubt that most people even lost a copper or more than a little sleep."

"Said you wiped out companies and companies of the regional alectors' mounted rifles." Troral's tone was dogged.

"We did wipe out three companies, but that fight took place outside Tempre."

"I figured you weren't the type to do that—hurt folks not involved, I mean—but people were saying . . ."

"We didn't have much choice. They attacked us in the middle of the night." That was a slight exaggeration. It had been two glasses before dawn, but Mykel didn't want to get into details. "How have things been here?"

Troral shook his head. "Weren't for you Cadmians, times'd be terrible. After what those rebels did . . . be months, seasons maybe, before anyone will be able to sell anything to the regional alector again. Terrible mess out there."

Mykel wondered if the Duarches would even bother to replace the regional alector, and if so, when. "I can see that will be a problem." He smiled politely. "I do have a list of other goods that we'll be needing for the compound."

Troral did not look pleased, merely less unhappy. That didn't surprise Mykel. In more than two seasons of working with the factor, he'd never seen more than a momentary smile.

Mykel handed Troral the list. "If you could give me a bid in the next few days . . ."

"That I can do, Majer. That I can." Troral folded the paper and tucked it away. "Now where do you want the blankets?"

"In the barracks here, in the front bay for now." For all the factor's outward cheerfulness, Mykel could still sense the man's fear, and it was clearly a fear of Mykel. Yet Mykel had never ever threatened anyone in Hyalt, even indirectly.

Mykel had the feeling the day was going to be very long.

6

Dainyl had requested that Wyalt pick him up at the house with the duty coach at a glass before dawn. While he hated losing that much sleep, or causing the duty driver to do so, the sun rose a good four glasses earlier in Alustre, and leaving even as early as he planned would put him in Alustre in very late midmorning. He still disliked using the duty coach to take him to and from his house, but at such early hours, since he'd neglected to make advance arrangements with his usual transport, the hacker Barodyn, his choices were to use the duty coach or to walk.

When Dainyl stepped out through the gates of his front courtyard on Quattri morning, he wore the traveling uniform of a Myrmidon officer—a blue flying jacket over a shimmercloth tunic of brilliant blue, both above dark gray trousers, with a heavy dark gray belt that held his lightcutter sidearm. On his collar were the single green-edged gold stars of a marshal. Inside his uniform tunic were two envelopes—one containing Alcyna's promotion to submarshal in Elcien, and the second containing Majer Noryan's appointment and promotion to submarshal in Alustre.

Wyalt was waiting. "Good morning, Marshal. The Hall of Justice, sir?"

"There's nowhere else in Elcien I'd be headed this early." Dainyl climbed into the coach.

Wyalt swung the coach back around a side street and then turned west on the boulevard, the main thoroughfare that ran down the middle of the isle from the bridge in the east to the gates at the Myrmidon compound at the west end of the isle. As they passed the public gardens of the Duarch, Dainyl glanced out, but in the predawn darkness only the outlines of the elaborate topiary were visible, and the life-sized pteridon looked to be next to the long hedge sculpted into the likeness of two sandoxen and a set of transport coaches, when in fact they were separated by a good fifty yards. Beyond the gardens were the Palace of the Duarch on the south side of the boulevard and the Hall of Justice on the north. The Hall's golden eternastone glowed to Dainyl's Talent, even in the darkness.

Wyalt brought the coach to a smooth stop at the base of the wide golden marble steps of the Hall of Justice.

After emerging from the coach, and nodding to the driver, Dainyl hurried up the steps and through the goldenstone pillars that marked the outer rim of the receiving rotunda. From there he crossed the green and gold marble floor of the rotunda, the sound of his boots lost in the stillness before dawn. At a pillar beyond the dais where, later in the day, petitioners would assemble, he cloaked himself in a Talent-illusion, out of habit, since no one was nearby. Then he turned the light-torch bracket, and the solid stone shifted to one side, revealing an entry and a set of steps leading downward and lit by light-torches. He closed the entry behind himself and made his way down the steps, turning right at the bottom to follow a stone-walled corridor.

Before he reached the doorway to the Table chamber on the north side, a sleepy-eyed young alector appeared.

"Oh . . . Marshal . . . I had not heard you would be here so early. Let me tell the guards."

"Guards?"

"Yes, sir. We now have our own guards here. We've been getting too many wild translations, and more than a few renegades from Ifryn. Oh . . . when do you expect to return?"

"If all goes well, later today."

The aide to the High Alector stepped forward and released the hidden Talent lock, then stepped into the foyer, lit by a single light-torch. Before opening the second door, he called out, "It's Cartalyn." After speaking, he released the Talent lock on the second door and stepped into the Table chamber.

Dainyl followed him, raising his Talent shields.

The Table chamber walls were of white marble, the floor green. Two sets of double light-torches set five yards apart in bronze brackets on the side walls provided the sole illumination to the underground chamber. Unlike other Table chambers, there were no furnishings at all. The Table itself looked like any other Table—a square polished stone pedestal in the center of the room that extended a yard above the stone floor. The stone appeared black on the side, but the top surface was mirrorlike silver. Each side of the tablelike pedestal was three yards. The other aspect of the Table, perceived only through Talent, was the purple glow that emanated from it.

Two guards in dark purple sat on stools beside the doorway, facing the Table. Each carried a lightcutter sidearm. Dainyl recognized one of them, a former Myrmidon who had served fifty years before requesting a stipend.

"Marshal, sir . . . congratulations."

"Thank you, Tregaryt. Have you had any problems on this watch?"

"No, sir. Had a wild translation yesterday. Vrityst had to cut down a fellow with a Myrmidon guard blade on Duadi."

Dainyl shook his head. "I'll be back later today. I'd appreciate your being a bit careful." Never before in the history of Acorus had guards been stationed—or necessary—inside a Table chamber. Even before now, Dainyl had not taken Table travel casually, not when some of the Recorders of Deeds had backed Brekylt and tried to create fatal "accidents" for Dainyl when he had been translating. Now he also had to worry about emerging from a translation and being "accidentally" shot if he did not maintain Talent shields every moment.

With a smile at the guards, Dainyl stepped up onto the Table, immediately concentrating through his Talent on the darkness beneath and within the Table. He dropped through the silvered surface and into . . .

. . . *the intense chill of purplish blackness that permeated every span of his body, despite his uniform and flying jacket. Although he saw, not with his eyes, but his Talent, he extended his senses toward the dark gray locator, bordered in purple, that identified Alustre. He ignored the stronger and closer locators of Tempre, bright blue, and the crimson-gold of Dereka, instead pressing himself toward the more distant wedge of dark gray.*

Other locators swirled by—wedges of amber, brilliant yellow, green, gray . . . Well beyond stretched a distant purple-black wedge—the long translation tube back to Ifryn, the tube that all too many Ifrits were bribing and forcing their way into, knowing that Ifryn was dying and that there was too little time remaining.

With the usual suddenness that ended all translations, the silver barrier seemed to flash toward Dainyl, hurling him through it.

Dainyl stood on yet another Table in another windowless chamber. He had made the translation so swiftly that only the slightest hint of frost had appeared on his flying jacket and uniform, before vanishing.

Dainyl held his Talent shields, but the pair of guards in black and silver uniforms waiting and watching did not even move as he descended from the Table. Unlike the Table chamber in Elcien, a set of black-and-silver-bordered hangings adorned the walls, and each hanging contained a scene featuring an alector. A long black chest stood against the wall opposite the single entrance—a square arch, in which a solid oak door was set, and on each side of which sat a guard.

A younger alector in the purple-trimmed green of a Recorder of Deeds stepped forward. "Marshal Dainyl, welcome to Alustre. We had not expected you, but you are more than welcome anytime. I am Retyl, Zorater's successor." Behind Retyl's modest shields lay apprehension.

"Thank you, Retyl." Dainyl smiled politely. "I appreciate your thoughtfulness. As a dutiful recorder, I'm more than certain that you will do your best to maintain the stability of the grid, unlike the late recorder in Hyalt."

"Absolutely, sir."

Dainyl could read the consternation behind the calm expression on Retyl's face, but only continued to smile as he walked to the chamber door.

On each side of the arch in the hallway outside were another pair of alectors, also wearing black and silver uniforms. They did not speak as Dainyl departed, walking to the end of the corridor and up the stairs to the main level.

From there, he took the main corridor leading to the west portico. The passageway was floored in a shimmering silver-gray marble, the octagonal tiles outlined with thin strips of black marble. Silver-and-black-bordered hangings decorated the walls. The portico was not paved in marble, but white granite, and the columns were smooth circular white granite pillars.

Dainyl had not expected a duty coach to be waiting, and indeed, one was not. While he waited, he occasionally looked at the residence and headquarters of the High Alector of the East. It was a long and solid white granite structure, with three stories showing above ground level and two wings angling from the central rectangular core, and the stone sparkled in the late-morning sun. He also looked at the cloudy sky, hoping that it didn't rain before he found transportation.

He had to wait a quarter of a glass before a free hack arrived, but the indigen driver was more than pleased.

"The Myrmidon compound? Yes, sir. Be half a silver."

"That's fine." Dainyl swung up into the coach.

As the coach carried him away from the parklike grounds surrounding the residence and along the divided boulevard that ran from the hilltop residence overlooking Alustre itself to the ring road that encircled the main sections of the city, Dainyl considered what lay ahead of him. Alcyna was supposed to be in Alustre, but whether she was or not . . . that was another question. Still, the last thing he would have wanted to do was to announce when he was arriving.

After a time, he looked out at Alustre, a city far more spread out than either Elcien or Ludar. The sole compact area was around the wharves, packed with warehouses and factorages. Most of Alustre stretched east of the river and north of Fiere Sound.

The walled eastern Myrmidon headquarters dominated the larger bluff east of the city proper and overlooked both the river and the ocean, but the driver pulled up outside the gates, since no non-alectors were permitted within.

Dainyl got out, handed the driver a half silver and three coppers, and walked through the unguarded gates toward the headquarters building, also constructed of perfectly cut and fitted white granite, with blackish green roof tiles.

The duty officer bolted into the entry corridor within moments after Dainyl stepped through the arched doorway into the building.

"Marshal Dainyl . . ." There was a long pause. "Sir . . . no one knew."

Dainyl had met her before, but her name escaped him. "No one was supposed to know." He smiled politely. "Is the submarshal in? In her study."

"Yes, sir."

"Good. Thank you." With that, holding full Talent shields, he turned down the corridor, his boots clicking faintly on the green marble, and walked to the very end of the hallway, where he stepped through the open door into Alcyna's study, a space a good third larger than his spaces as marshal in Elcien.

As before, not that he would have expected any change, the walls were bare except for a single depiction of the city of Alustre—in black ink on white paper and framed in black and silver. Alcyna glanced up from the wide ebony table desk and froze—if for only a moment.

Then she laughed. "Marshal . . . you have just demonstrated why you succeeded Shastylt."

Dainyl had to admire her recovery. He doubted that he could possibly have made such a rapid adjustment. "And you have proved why my trip here is both worthwhile and necessary." He gestured at the circular ebony conference table, with five wooden armchairs set around it, all finished in silver. "If you would join me."

Alcyna rose gracefully from behind the table desk. "How could I refuse such a request?"

Dainyl seated himself so that he had a view of both the Sound through the wide south window and of the still open door. "I believe I said this before, but you do have a lovely view of the Sound."

"It is lovely." Alcyna took the other side of the table, from where she could watch him and the doorway as well. "Might I ask why you are here, sir?"

"To offer you your due—as submarshal in Elcien and as my designated successor."

"Marshal Dainyl, you're more devious than Shastylt." She laughed, and her laugh remained warm, so at odds with the coldness he sensed within her. "And I thought you were so simple."

"I'm very simple, Alcyna. I don't want you plotting against me. The best way to assure that is to give you what you want. You want power. You also want some assurance that you won't be removed or cast aside. I'm the most trustworthy alector you'll ever find, so long as you don't plot against me." He shrugged. "You're also extremely good at organization and delegation. There isn't anyone better left in the Myrmidons. I need that excellence. Despite the situation here, you can do better, and with less risk."

Alcyna just looked at Dainyl.

He let her Talent probes wash over him.

Abruptly, she straightened slightly in her chair. "How did you manage Hyalt?"

"As well as I could."

"Seventh Company, I meant."

"Simple. I took out Veluara, and then Klynd, and then Weltak, and disarmed Lyzetta, and threatened to take them all out, one at a time."

"As a passenger?"

"No. Once Rhelyn's men killed one of the Fifth Company Myrmidons, I took it."

"A High Alector flying and leading a company . . . I doubt that's ever happened."

"There wasn't much choice if I wanted to stop Myrmidon from fighting Myrmidon."

"If . . . *if* I accepted the position in Elcien, who would you name as submarshal here?"

"I'd thought Noryan. Do you have a better idea?"

Alcyna nodded slowly. "Why are you doing this?"

"I told you."

"There's more."

"There is. Ifryn is far closer to collapse than people know. Without a united Myrmidon command, matters will be far worse. Personal allegiances will change like the wind, as one High Alector or another finds his allies have other needs."

"Do you trust Zelyert?"

Dainyl had considered that, long and hard, but what he felt wasn't necessarily what he wanted to answer. "He is my superior. So long as he follows the Code and his responsibilities as High Alector of Justice, I see no reason not to trust him."

"Sir, that's scarcely an enthusiastic endorsement."

"I find, Alcyna, that I have become far less enthusiastic in recent times."

"When do you want me in Elcien?"

"Tomorrow, or as soon after as you can manage." Dainyl withdrew the envelope with her name written on it. "Here is your appointment." He took out the second envelope. "Here is Noryan's. If you would tender it to him . . . I do not intend to remain long in Alustre, and he owes the appointment to your training and supervision."

"What would you have done if I had declined?"

"Torn them up."

"I should be able to manage arriving in Elcien by next Duadi. It will take a few days to brief Noryan—especially since he will have to fly here from Norda."

Dainyl smiled. "Is Brekylt here in Alustre?"

"He actually is. He hasn't been using the Tables as much recently. You seem to be one of the few High Alectors who is unworried by all the instability. Do you plan to see him?"

"I had thought to convey your promotion, and that of Majer Noryan, to him personally."

"You think he will react in a way similar to Kelbryt?" Alcyna's words were casual.

"One never knows, but I'd be most surprised."

"We can walk out, and I'll make sure Undercaptain Bryanda summons the duty coach."

"She's from Ifryn, too, isn't she?"

"Of course. As you are discovering, Acorus has too small a number of alectors to supply the intelligence and ambition for all the leadership needs." Alcyna stood.

"I can see that, but how could you be sure that you got the best from Ifryn?" Dainyl rose, his attention on her.

"I can't answer that, sir, but if I had to speculate, I'd guess that the worst were sent to other duties and locales."

Dainyl held in a shudder. Alcyna and Brekylt had basically culled the survivors of the unauthorized translations from Ifryn, taking the best for the Myrmidons, and sending the others to Hyalt and Dulka as disposable troops—and Dainyl had conveniently disposed of half of them.

"How else would things have worked out as they did?" she asked. "It did force Zelyert and Khelaryt to accept your abilities, and that wouldn't have happened otherwise."

"They didn't have any choices left," Dainyl replied. "Shastylt was trying to blame you and me for staging a coup. I think he may even have contacted Brekylt."

For another brief moment, something too quick to identify flashed behind Alcyna's shields. She spoke quickly, but softly. "Your meeting with Brekylt will be interesting." She walked toward the doorway and the corridor beyond.

Dainyl joined her, and the two walked without speaking for a moment, as Alcyna gestured to Undercaptain Bryanda, who smiled and nodded back. "Bryanda already has the duty coach waiting for you."

"As with so many of your officers, she's perceptive."

"Now that Dhenyr has . . . departed, I imagine yours in the west are also perceptive."

"That could be."

"Brekylt will be relieved to see you come to Elcien, I suspect," offered Dainyl as they neared the entry foyer.

"He may at that. Or he may surprise you."

"I'm rarely surprised," Dainyl said wryly. "I don't know

enough to create expectations, and surprise comes from having one's expectations upset."

"That may be one of your great strengths, Marshal, because it is so rare among alectors."

"The illusion of alector impartiality," he said with a laugh, stepping through the archway and out toward the duty coach. He did not recognize the driver. Granyn had already become a flier, and perhaps Olyssa had as well.

He stopped short of the coach and turned. "I'll expect you on Septi."

"Yes, sir. I'll be there."

Dainyl could sense, perhaps for the first time in dealing with Alcyna, what amounted to a feeling of respect. That worried him more than her past attitude of near-contempt, because it suggested matters were even worse than he'd thought. He nodded and stepped up into the coach.

On the ride back to the eastern residence, he considered the possibilities for dealing with Brekylt, but the only one that made sense was the polite and direct approach. Dainyl had never been good at intrigue and playing people off against each other, and now was no time to start.

Dainyl stepped out of the carriage on the upper drive of the residence.

"Marshal, sir, would you like me to wait?" asked the driver.

"No, thank you." One way or another, it wouldn't be necessary.

He turned toward the entrance, noting that one of the guards in black and silver had vanished, but that mystery resolved itself when the guard reappeared almost instantly with an alectress. Dainyl had never seen her, but the darker purple sheen of her aura told him all too clearly that she was a recent arrival from Ifryn, despite her shimmering silver and black uniform.

"Is the High Alector expecting you, Marshal?" She bowed deferentially.

"I'm certain that he is not, but then, I could be wrong." Dainyl laughed politely. "He will wish to see me."

"Yes, sir. I have no doubts about that. If you will follow me . . . he is in his study."

Dainyl walked beside the alectress along the colonnade and past two lander guards in black and silver stationed before the vaulted archway. The guard on the left opened one of the double doors for the two. As Dainyl recalled, she continued through a high-ceilinged entry hall that held black marble columns spaced at four-yard intervals along the white walls. The floor of the entry hall was composed of black octagons set in white granite. Beyond the entry hall, the corridor narrowed, and at the end was another set of golden oak double doors, guarded by a young alectress in the black and silver.

"Coromyn, if you will inform the High Alector that Marshal Dainyl is here."

"One moment, Marshal, if you will." The guard slipped through the door, returning within moments. "The High Alector will be pleased to see you immediately." She held the door open.

Dainyl walked through the door alone, seeking anything untoward with his Talent-senses and raising full Talent shields. He took the archway to the right and the next hallway to the first doorway on the left. The door to Brekylt's study was open, and Dainyl entered.

The inner wall of the study was lined with shelves of books, while the shelves on the outer wall were limited to narrow stretches between the floor-to-ceiling windows, except in the middle of the wall, where there was a set of open double doors.

Brekylt sat behind the table desk before the full wall of books and gestured to the two armchairs in front of his desk. "Please do have a seat, Marshal."

"Thank you." Dainyl eased into the armchair on the left.

"What brings you to Alustre? Certainly not your health." Brekylt's wide and expressive mouth offered a wry expression that was not quite a smile.

"Myrmidon matters. I find that I have little time for anything else."

"Ah, yes. When are you planning to return Seventh Company to Dulka?"

"Not for a while. There appears to be a need for the Myrmidons in Tempre."

"I must congratulate you on your handling of that minor uprising in Hyalt."

"Thank you."

"I don't believe you mentioned why you were here."

"Since I was in Alustre on other matters, I thought I would pay a courtesy call on the Alector of the East. It seemed only fitting."

"Dainyl," said Brekylt with a single laugh, "you do nothing without purpose. That might be your greatest weakness."

"I am certain that I have others." Dainyl offered a faint smile in return. "As you may know, there is currently no submarshal of Myrmidons in Elcien. Since the most able and qualified individual for that position is here in Alustre, I came here to offer the position to her, and I am fortunate that she agreed to accept. Noryan will replace her as submarshal here."

Only the slightest hint of a pause suggested any thought considered by Brekylt. "That is interesting."

"Necessary, as I am sure that you understand. It's similar in a fashion to gardening."

"I'm certain you had hoped that I would attempt something foolish, Marshal. I assure you that I will not. At my advanced age one learns which battles to fight, and I will leave you to fight those you must." He smiled. "Now that you are marshal, you will find there are more than you ever believed possible."

"That is something I've already discovered."

"Do you really think you can manage Alcyna?"

"No. I have never had that illusion."

"Then why . . . ?"

"I need excellence even more than loyalty, Brekylt, especially in these times."

"You will pay a high price for that excellence."

"Excellence always has a high price, as does everything of value, according to what I have seen, as well as the *Views of the Highest*." What Dainyl didn't say was that the price for not paying for excellence, in some fashion, was even higher.

"You quote the Archon well, Marshal."

"It is a useful skill." Dainyl smiled and inclined his head. "I had not meant to take any more of your time, but I did not wish for you to find out about these changes in the Myrmidons from anyone else."

"I do appreciate your courtesy, Dainyl, and you are always welcome in Alustre."

"Thank you." Dainyl stood and bowed slightly.

He held his shields at full strength all the way back down to the Table chamber.

7

Retyl bowed as Dainyl stepped into the Table chamber in Alustre. "Marshal, we wish you the best."

Dainyl doubted that, but he only smiled as he stepped up onto the Table. "Thank you." While he wanted to get back to Elcien quickly, he held his shields, even as he concentrated and . . .

. . . slipped through the Table and into the blackness beneath—where he found himself in a turbulence that he'd never encountered before. The entire translation tube felt as though it were undulating its entire unmeasurable length, rippling from a nexus of green somewhere beyond the tube and near—yet lost in the distance. For all that, the blackness beneath the purple darkness of the tube seemed unmoving.

Whatever was happening had to be the doing of the ancients . . . somehow and in some fashion.

For a long moment, Dainyl did not even seek out the brilliant white locator of Elcien. Then, he reached out with Talent, but found the seemingly shifting nature of the tube made concentrating on the locator difficult. His Talent probe vanished as if he had never extended it.

He tried again, conscious of the chill seeping into him, but just as his probe seemed to touch the locator, the tube twisted.

Dainyl jabbed quickly a third time and linked with the Elcien locator.

Even so, he felt as though he tumbled through the rapids of an unseen river before he flew through the silver-white barrier.

He avoided stumbling over his boots as he emerged on the Table at Elcien, but staggered in trying to regain his balance. Both guards had their weapons aimed, and Dainyl strengthened his shields before even completely recovering his balance.

"No! It's the marshal!" Chastyl looked up at him from the end of the Table.

Dainyl jumped off the Table and stood beside the Recorder of Deeds. "What's happening with the Tables?"

"I don't know, sir. Everything . . . it's strange. We've had three wild translations in the last glass, and the whole grid . . . it was pulsing." The recorder extended a Talent pulse into the Table. "It peaked a little while ago, and it's beginning to subside."

"Do you know what caused it?" While Dainyl certainly had his own ideas, he wanted to know what Chastyl thought. Dainyl had the feeling that Retyl had known there was some sort of difficulty and had refrained from warning him.

"No, sir. It just . . . happened."

"Has anything like this happened before?"

"I don't know of anything like that. It might be because the Tables in Tempre and Hyalt haven't been repaired yet."

Dainyl didn't know what else to say about the translation tube. "Thank you for warning the guards not to shoot me."

"Oh, you're welcome."

Dainyl nodded and turned toward the door. He noted that there were now no Talent locks in place, and that made sense, given the guards inside the Table chamber.

He was halfway down the corridor to the steps up to the open section of the Hall of Justice when Zelyert stepped out of his private study.

"Dainyl . . . a moment of your time, if you would."

"Yes, sir." Dainyl turned and headed into the High Alector's study, one of the more spartan he had ever seen, with little more than an ebony table, two chairs, and two bookcases, all lit by light-torches on the windowless stone walls. He closed the door.

Zelyert seated himself and motioned to the other chair.

Dainyl took it and waited.

"I heard from Khelaryt that you were impressive in your briefings, and successful in conveying a veiled message to High Alector Ruvryn."

"I doubt it was that veiled."

"That is not of the matter. He will report what happened to Samist. How did your visit to the submarshal in Alustre go?"

"I offered her the position as submarshal here in Elcien. She had several questions, but after I answered them she accepted."

"What did you promise her?"

"Nothing. I did mention that Shastylt had told me that she and I were planning a coup."

"So she is aware that Brekylt intended to betray her to save himself, if necessary?"

"She was doubtless aware of that all along. Brekylt was her only way to power. I have offered her a way that seems less fraught with danger."

"You phrase that in an interesting manner, Dainyl."

Dainyl shook his head slightly. "Any way to power is dangerous."

Zelyert smiled faintly. "Now that you have dealt with the . . . difficulties in Alustre, I would trust you will not be away from Elcien so much."

Dainyl smiled politely. "That will depend, sir, on what future difficulties arise."

"You will have a submarshal."

"That is true, and Alcyna is a superb administrator."

Zelyert offered a smile even more faint than the last. "You intend to continue to travel?"

"Only as necessary, sir. I have little love of travel for the sake of travel. Nor do I like spending time away from my wife."

"How did Brekylt take your visit?"

"He intimated that I would have great difficulties in controlling Alcyna. He said he would not do me the favor of attempting to attack me, and that I would learn which battles to fight and which to avoid."

"He has always operated in such a fashion," replied Zelyert. "How did you respond?"

"I told him that was something I had begun to discover."

"What do you think he believes about Alcyna?"

"That she will cause us great difficulty, and that will make his efforts to gain control of the east of Corus that much easier."

"You are assuming a great deal, Dainyl, and not wisely."

"I do not believe it is unwise to assume that Brekylt seeks power. He has attempted to control or suborn the recorders and regional alectors in the east—as well as a few in the west. His actions indicate that he is clearly of the opinion that the Master Scepter will go to Efra, and not come to Acorus, and that the Duarches will be unable to rule as they have. I am not assuming he will be successful in his efforts, but to disregard what he has done and the implications behind those actions would also be unwise."

"You suggest an unlikely set of probabilities."

Dainyl did not think so, but he smiled. "Brekylt's motivations come from seeking power. I defer to you in his likelihood of success, but that probable lack of success does not mean he will not create great difficulties in the near future, and I would prefer to be prepared for whatever efforts he may undertake . . . or cause others to undertake."

"Being prepared for such efforts is wise, so long as it does not take excessive resources."

"I believe I understand that as well, sir."

"So long as you do." Zelyert stood. "I wish you the best, Marshal."

Dainyl rose easily, but not abruptly. "Thank you."

"And, Dainyl, remember that even the most able of indigens and landers are only steers, to be used as necessary."

"Yes, sir." Dainyl could feel Zelyert's eyes on his back as he left the High Alector's study.

Outside, on the boulevard on the south side of the Hall of Justice, Dainyl managed to find a free hacker in less than a tenth of a glass.

When he returned to headquarters, he was pleasantly surprised to find a complete proposed schedule for both First and Seventh Companies for the next month, with a cover note from Undercaptain Zernylta, politely requesting his review and any suggestions for improvement, since she had not prepared a report for him before.

He read through the schedule, and made a note to tell her about the need for a designated standby on Decdi, in case the duty flier was sent on a long run, and the need to schedule transport for the Table engineers from Faitel to Hyalt.

She had also attached the latest report from Colonel Herolt on the First Cadmian Regiment, with a written question as to whether he wanted the reports forwarded to him with any comments she might have or without comment. Dainyl shook his head. Dhenyr had never even considered written comments. Dainyl would have to see how she handled other matters, but from what he was seeing, Zernylta was well suited to handling operations and scheduling.

He picked up Colonel Herolt's report and began to read. For all the battalions—except Fourth Battalion—little had changed. All but Second Battalion were understrength, but no significant new casualties had been reported. On the other hand, with the reporting delays, Dainyl probably knew more about what had recently happened with Third Battalion than did the colonel.

He concentrated on the Fourth Battalion report:

> Fourth Battalion, Majer Hersiod commanding, is currently deployed to Iron Stem, based out of the Cadmian compound there. In the last few weeks of summer and early harvest, the battalion has encountered increasing attacks from irregulars believed to be Reillies and from packs of the large predators termed sandwolves by the locals. Limited injuries have also occurred from several horned creatures similar to sheep. Despite increasing casualties, the battalion continues to provide support to the local Cadmian forces in maintaining order at the iron and coal mines, and the ironworks . . .

Dainyl shook his head. What was it about Iron Stem and the Iron Valleys? For two years, the place had created problem after problem. Now . . . another new creature? Should he send a squad from First Company? Perhaps Undercaptain Chelysta and fourth squad—Ghasylt had certainly recommended her highly enough. If more support were needed, he might be able to detach a squad from Seventh Company in Tempre, although Captain Lyzetta was operating at close to twenty percent understrength.

He needed to send a message to Asulet in Lyterna. As the senior alector in charge of lifeform management, Asulet might be able to provide more information. And, in addition to the problems in Iron Stem, Dainyl still had no idea what was happening in Soupat.

8

In the darkness a good glass after sunset, Mykel walked slowly uphill away from the old garrison that Third Battalion and the two Hyaltan Cadmian companies had used for the past two seasons and would be leaving permanently in the morning. The night was dark, because Selena—the brighter moon—had already set in the west, and the smaller green moon—Asterta—was but a crescent in the east. Even so, Mykel had little trouble navigating through the darkness that seemed little more than early twilight with the night vision that had accompanied the development of his Talent.

Just short of the jumble of rocks where so much had happened over the last season, Mykel halted. There were no ancient soarers around, and he hadn't expected any. He certainly hadn't sensed them, but they had appeared to him a number of times, and only in particular places, always on hills. There had to be some reason why the soarers had appeared on this particular hill, and nowhere else around Hyalt, at least not that he knew.

When he had finally connected himself to the world where

he was—and not from where he had been born—he had sensed a certain darkness that lay beneath. But did that lie beneath all the earth . . . or just beneath the hillside?

He stood in the night, looking westward, letting his senses extend from him, especially trying to feel what lay beneath.

In time, he began to sense the blackness he sought, almost like a river, or a high road, well beneath the surface of the ground, arrowing westward from where he stood, toward the battered and half-destroyed compound of the regional alector. He could also sense his own lifethread extending downward through the very soil and rocks into that blackness.

There might have been a few streaks of purple as well . . . he concentrated—and the blackness vanished. After forcing himself to relax, to experience everything around him, he once more began to gather in the blackness beneath, as well as something else—a line of purplish mist that lay right above the darkness.

Slowly, he turned, until he faced the garrison, looking eastward. To the east, the blackness angled more deeply into the earth, until his senses could trace it no farther. He turned back to the west until he looked into the night, once more in the direction of the regional alector's compound. The purple mist had something to do with the alectors—perhaps their Tables?

He shook his head. If he had studied the Table in Tempre more closely, he might well have a better idea . . . but he had not.

After another quarter glass or so, he began to walk down the gentle slope, back toward the garrison.

Rhystan was waiting outside the west gate.

"Majer?"

"It's me, Rhystan."

"Who else would it be at this time of night?"

"You worried that I might get hit by alectors' lightning again?" Mykel chuckled.

"When you go off in the night, it's not always good." Rhystan shook his head.

"I needed to get away to think."

The captain laughed softly. "I can barely see, and you're walking around as if it were broad daylight."

"I've always had good night vision. You know that."

"You have lots of talents, sir. Could be that you have too many."

Mykel understood what Rhystan meant. "What am I supposed to do? Let my men die because captains—or majers—shouldn't do certain things?"

"In some ways, Majer, I'm glad that I don't have to make those choices."

There was a silence.

"Fabrytal said that seltyr's daughter helped nurse you back. How did she get to Tempre?"

"Women in Dramur can't inherit. Her brothers died, and Vaclyn killed her father. Her cousin got the lands. She was sent to Southgate to her mother's brother or cousin, and he sent her to run his nephew's household in Tempre—at least until he finds a wife. I'd asked her for some information, and Fabrytal pressured her into taking care of me. He worried about me being unconscious too close to the regional alector's headquarters."

"That was smart of him, but how did he get her to agree?"

"I don't know." Mykel laughed. "I wasn't awake enough to listen."

"Seems sort of strange, the way she keeps turning up."

"More than a little, but sometimes things happen that way." Mykel didn't believe that for a moment. All he knew was that, in some fashion, he and Rachyla were linked, but he couldn't have explained why or how.

"Which way do you think the colonel will send us?" asked Rhystan. "Back to Northa, I mean?"

"I'm not sure he will," replied Mykel. "Sixth Battalion was sent to Soupat. Fourth Battalion is still in Iron Stem, and Fifth is up north dealing with Reillies. Troubles seem to be happening faster than they can be put down."

"That's true, but it doesn't make sense."

"It might, if we knew more," Mykel admitted, "but no one tells Cadmian majers and captains that much."

"Not until they've fouled up and want us to fix things."

Mykel agreed with that, too. He only wondered what else was likely to go wrong—or already had.

9

Quattri had been a very long day for Dainyl, and he was more than glad to retire with Lystrana to their bedchamber almost immediately after the evening meal. He'd undressed and pulled on a robe. Lystrana stretched out on the smooth white cotton spread that covered the deep blue wool blankets, propped up against the headboard by three pillows.

Even sitting on the high stool away from the foot of the bed, Dainyl could sense the separate essences of both Lystrana and Kytrana.

"You still have some of that greenish force around your shoulder," Lystrana mused. "It's as if it's diluting itself through you, rather than fading away."

"I'm turning green?"

"Just a faint tinge. Most people won't sense it. Do you think that it's just the result of your wound or something the ancients did?"

"Both, I think." He shook his head. "I wouldn't have survived without their aid."

"Why would they want to help you? Do you think it's some sort of subterfuge?"

Dainyl frowned. "Some sort of Talent-spread illness that will infect others? Do I feel ill or unhealthy? To you, I mean? I certainly don't feel that way."

Her forehead furrowed. After a moment, she replied, "You seem strong and healthy, but I don't understand why they would help you."

"They said that they owed us a debt for saving the world,

but that if we did not change, we would destroy it. The old one also said that the sword with which Rhelyn wounded me was their responsibility and that I would have died had I not reached them."

"They do not use Tables, either, do they?"

"They have the mirrors, but they seem to be able to translate to other places where there are no mirrors."

Lystrana tilted her head. "Do you think we could?"

"The only times I've managed anything like that, I had to use . . . counterfeit, in a sense, their greenish Talent."

"I don't like that."

"I didn't either."

"No," she said slowly. "I meant that it suggests there is something more powerful about their Talent."

"There is. Shastylt and Asulet both noted that the ancients were the only force able to destroy pteridons." Dainyl chuckled wryly. "Lightcannon will as well."

"You're tired."

"The translation back from Alustre was hard. I think it was because the ancients were doing something. The entire translation tube was undulating, like you might do to a heavy rope or a cable, if you whipped it up from one end. Chastyl said that they'd received three wild translations, and one of the guards in the Table chamber in the Hall of Justice was ready to cut me down. . . ."

"Guards in the Table chambers? Here on Acorus?" Lystrana frowned.

"It's something that the recorders are doing now, over the past few days. All sorts of translations are arriving from Ifryn."

"That sounds like Ifryn is collapsing—or close to it—and that the ancients know it and are preparing to attack in some way. If they keep doing that to the tubes, not many will translate successfully from Ifryn here. Guards in the Table chambers." Her frown was far more expressive than any headshake could have been.

"I couldn't prove it." Dainyl stretched, stifling a yawn, "but I think the ancients' power is limited. Their technique with the green Talent is better, but there can't be that many of them."

"There aren't that many of us," she pointed out. "And there won't be many more if the ancients keep the successful translations low. Do you think you should tell Asulet, or the Duarches?"

"How can I tell them much? I can mention the sense of greenness in the last translation to Asulet. I've already sent him a message about another new creature around Iron Stem. So I may have a reason to go to Lyterna before long. But if I say much more, then I risk being destroyed because I haven't been truthful. I couldn't tell Shastylt everything. He would have used it against me."

"So would Zelyert," added Lystrana sadly. A quizzical expression followed. "What new creature?"

"I don't know, except the Cadmian reports say that it is horned and similar to sheep, and that it's caused casualties—and that's not like any sheep I ever heard of."

"Doesn't it strike you as strange that all of this is happening now?"

"Strange? No. It's predictable. We're likely to be more vulnerable, at least during the transfer of the Master Scepter, and the ancients have to know that more alectors are coming to Acorus. There's been a rebellion and unrest as alectors seek to change who holds power on Acorus. At the same time, we've seen new predators, or a resurgence of old ones and greater efforts by the ancients against the pteridons. To me, it all follows. They'll strike at us now because we're not really unified and because, if they don't, we will get stronger and wipe them out."

"And yet they saved you."

When Lystrana put it that way, Dainyl didn't care for the implications at all. Had he somehow, even without his own knowledge, been subverted to the goals and desires of the ancients? And if he had not, why had they not only spared him when he'd been in their power, but actually saved him?

He stifled another yawn.

"Dearest . . . you need some sleep. It will all make more sense when you're rested."

She was right about his needing sleep, but Dainyl had the feeling that what the ancients had in mind would not be any clearer in the morning or, indeed, at any time until it was too late for him to do anything about matters.

10

With all the details and difficulties involved in moving Third Battalion from the old Hyalt garrison to the new compound north of the town, it was the following Londi before Mykel felt matters were settled enough for him to take Fabrytal and Fifteenth Company on an armed reconnaissance of the half-destroyed regional alector's complex in Hyalt. He had wanted to get there before the alectors returned, but not before he had the companies relocated in a more defensible position. Still, as of Decdi evening, the squads maintaining the security perimeter around the area had not reported any activity.

Mykel had not seen any reason to take the more circular patrol route to the north. Instead, he had ordered the company along the main route to the compound. For the first vingt away from the square in Hyalt, the way was paved, but after that it deteriorated to a packed clay and gravel road that circled around low hills covered with the brush and junipers that seemed ubiquitous west of Hyalt. The road was wide enough for easy travel with two mounts abreast, and hard-packed enough that where ruts existed they were shallow.

Despite the haze that created an even greater silver sheen across the otherwise cloudless green sky, the morning sun was warm on the back of Mykel's gray and maroon Cadmian uniform tunic. He shifted his weight in the saddle, gingerly, in order not to jolt his still-tender shoulder.

"You think we'll see any strange creatures, Majer?" Fabrytal rode to Mykel's right.

"These days, I'm not certain what we'll see or where we'll encounter it. We might see anything, and we might run into nothing." Mykel glanced ahead, his eyes on the scouts a good half vingt out, moving out of sight where the road curved south and then west again. He did not sense anything untoward, but he had not forgotten there were some alectors and landers that he could not sense.

His lips curled into a faint smile. One of those was Rachyla. That should not have surprised him, but at the time he had discovered that it had. He felt that there was so much more to her than he could sense.

Less than a glass later, a half squad of Cadmians appeared on the road, formed up and apparently waiting for Mykel and Fifteenth Company. Once they neared the patrol squad, Fabrytal halted Fifteenth Company, and the two officers rode forward to the Cadmian in charge.

"Majer, sir, no intruders sighted this watch." The squad leader was from First Hyalt Company, and Mykel did not recall the man's name.

"Any sign of anyone in the compound?"

"No, sir."

"We're going in to take a closer look. I'd appreciate it if you'd continue your patrols. If you see anything strange, or any pteridons flying in, send a messenger."

"Yes, sir." The squad leader nodded emphatically.

"Thank you." Mykel eased his mount westward.

"Fifteenth Company! Forward!" ordered Fabrytal.

Neither officer spoke as they rode away from the patrol and led Fifteenth Company up the last section of the road, a long gentle slope, at the end of which Mykel could see the redstone cliffs that held part of the compound. The packed dirt and clay of the road had turned a redder shade, and there was more sand in the loose dust and dirt, and more space between the clumps of harvest-tan grass. The wind had picked up, hot and dry out of the south, carrying fine dust that stuck to the sweat on the back of Mykel's neck.

"Why do you think they haven't sent anyone to repair things here?" asked Fabrytal.

"I imagine Tempre is a higher priority. It takes longer to transport men and materials here. They've all got to come by the high roads. It's close to seven hundred vingts by road from Faitel to Hyalt. That's after they decide how they want to rebuild."

"If they want to."

"They will," predicted Mykel. There had to be some reason why the alectors had built in Hyalt in the first place. He just didn't know what it happened to be.

When Fifteenth Company reached the level section of ground that stretched eastward from the line of cliffs, Mykel studied the area with both his eyes and other senses. What remained of the outbuilding was a heap of redstone, discolored by soot and ashes. A stone archway and recessed entry provided the access to whatever chambers and passages had been cut into the redstone cliff. Higher up, he could see scorched and blackened patches.

"Burned it good," murmured Fabrytal.

"I don't think they had much choice. How else do you get people out of a stone redoubt without losing all sorts of men?"

"They don't mind losing our men."

"Some don't, and some do. The submarshal doesn't like wasting men. He kept the Cadmians here out of the direct fighting, and he ordered us not to deal with the rebel alectors in Tempre directly unless absolutely necessary."

"Majer . . . sir . . . he's about the only one I ever heard who thinks that way."

"You may be right. We'd better hope nothing happens to him."

As they drew nearer to the ruined outbuilding, Mykel could make out black lines across the sandy soil, and there was still the faintest odor of smoke and burned wood. Although he saw no bodies, and no crows or other carrion eaters, a sense of death permeated everything.

Mykel reined up a good twenty yards from the stone archway that framed the recessed entry into the cliff. Smoke had stained the stone, and a faint odor of brimstone lingered. "I'll want to inspect the tunnels."

"Yes, sir. I'll send a squad out first, just in case." Fabrytal turned in the saddle. "First squad, dismount! Rifles ready! Second squad, take their mounts!"

Mykel did not protest. From what he could sense, there

was no one present. Even if there might be someone undetected by his Talent, that was infrequent, and a single individual could only inflict limited damage.

"First squad! Check out the chambers and report!" Fabrytal rode to the side. "Fifth squad! Rifles ready! Watch for intruders!" Then he rode back and reined up beside Mykel.

As they waited, Mykel kept his senses alert, but could only detect Cadmians.

"Do you have any idea why the alectors here rebelled against the Myrmidons, sir?" Fabrytal finally asked.

"No. That's not something they tell Cadmian officers." It likely had to do with which alectors wanted to control Corus, Mykel reflected, but he still had no idea which side Submarshal Dainyl was on or whether that might be the best side. But then, Mykel was having doubts as to whether any "side" was good for most people.

"When do you think we'll get orders from the colonel?"

"It could be anytime, or it could be weeks." Mykel grinned. "And, no, I don't have any idea whether we'll be sent back to Northa or to some other place."

"Ah . . . yes, sir."

Another quarter glass passed before first squad returned and Gendsyr reported. "No one there, Majer, Undercaptain. There must be hundreds of those silver and black uniforms in a big hall carved into the stone—and boots and clothes, but there's no one in any of the tunnels and chambers. Some places, things are burned pretty bad. Other places . . . there's not much damage."

"Thank you." Mykel turned to Fabrytal. "I need to check it out."

"Gendsyr, a five-man detail to accompany the majer," ordered Fabrytal.

"Yes, sir." The squad leader turned. "Shenylt, Noart . . ."

Mykel dismounted and handed the roan's reins to Bhonat, one of the first squad members who was not in the detail, then took his rifle from its holder, and walked toward the archway. As he stepped into the tunnellike entry, he raised his own shields with as much strength as he could offer them. The only sounds were those of the hot wind outside and the crunching echo of his boots on the marble floor tiles. The smell of brimstone was far stronger, so strong that it must have been overpowering during the attack. Behind him followed the five rankers.

Once past the door, swung back to the left in an alcove, he could see a pile of metallic pieces and parts of a cart—probably the remnants of one of the light-weapons he had seen earlier. Had it been destroyed in the fighting, or later?

Another few yards along was an archway to the right. Mykel stopped and looked through it into an enormous chamber with a stone ceiling that soared into darkness—except for a small area that had been a skylight of some sort before it had been blocked with large stones. The far side of the chamber was filled with ashes. Along the near side were stacks and stacks of the black and silver shimmersilk uniforms worn by the rebels, along with other items of clothing—all folded carelessly—and rows of boots. All had once been worn.

Mykel turned and continued along the passageway, trying to follow his senses toward a faint sense of purpleness. The corridor to the left ended abruptly, after a number of vacant rooms. He retraced his steps and made his way back to the main underground hallway, lit by the strange crystal lamps in their brass wall brackets. Since he'd only seen lamps like those in the lower reaches of the alector's building in Tempre, he assumed that they were used only by alectors.

He walked along the curved corridor, knowing that the Table had to be somewhere near. He could sense a faint purpleness, but was having trouble determining from where it was coming. A knot of purple Talent appeared ahead, on his left, head-high, on what appeared to be a blank stone wall.

Mykel stopped, turned, and studied the wall.

After a moment, he tried to recall exactly what he had done in Tempre, the puzzlelike untwining of the Talent energy. It took him three tries before the knot of purple force unraveled and then a section of stone slid back, leaving an opening little more than a yard wide.

". . . how'd he do that?"

Low as the whisper was, Mykel caught the words. He decided to ignore them. "Stand by out here."

He stepped through the opening into the oblong chamber. Outside of a single black chest set against one stone wall, and the Table itself, there were no furnishings in the windowless space. Several sets of clothing lay on the floor, as if the alectors had died there and vanished. Most had been in silver and black, but one had worn green shimmersilk trimmed in purple. Mykel stepped around and over garments and boots.

Five of the crystal lamps provided a gentle but indirect illumination. There was but a residual sense of the purpled force buried deep within the Table. While the surface still held a mirror finish, it felt dead, compared to the Table in Tempre before Mykel had disabled it.

He walked around the Table to the chest-high cabinet and pulled out the top drawer. It was empty, except for stacks of blank paper of various sizes. The second drawer held purple-trimmed green tunics and trousers. The third held various writing-related implements—marksticks, pens, styli, blotting powder—and something else. Mykel lifted the folded item. It felt like stiff fabric, but unfolded to reveal a map of Corus, in brilliant color on a glossy finish unlike anything he had seen. He debated returning it, then slipped the map inside his tunic, and closed the last drawer of the chest.

Then, he turned back to face the Table. He concentrated, letting everything fall away from him, trying to sense beneath and beyond the Table. He couldn't help smiling as he gained the impression of the wider and deeper blackness that lay beneath the Table, on top of which rested a narrower purplish mist. Somehow, he knew, the Tables used the purple tube and the blackness as their basis for what they did. He also had the feeling that where the soarers appeared had more to do with the black than the purple, although that was even less certain.

Now what that understanding gained him he had no idea, but perhaps in time he would. He nodded, then turned and left the chamber. He left the door open, since he assumed that the alectors would return before long, and he preferred to leave as little trace of his own Talent as possible.

"There's nothing in there, except a few uniforms and boots. We'll head back, now. There's nothing else we need to see."

As he walked back through the tunnel, he half smiled as he picked up the murmurs behind him.

". . . he *knows* things . . ."

". . . what officers are supposed to do."

"Not like that."

Mykel felt as though he had found various pieces of a gigantic puzzle composed of various intricate and strange shapes, but that he had no idea how to assemble those pieces or what they might look like once he did. Even so, he felt that it had been important to see the Table in Hyalt, and he definitely wanted to study the map he had removed—but in private.

11

On Duadi morning, less than a glass after morning muster, Captain (acting) Zernylta stood before Dainyl's desk in headquarters. Her fingers were slightly ink-stained, and several strands of her black hair, short as it was, had drifted down across her forehead. Dainyl had been standing at the window, looking at the morning clouds outside, when she had appeared. He had turned to invite her in and had remained on his feet beside the desk, which he had just cleared of reports—finally—shortly before she had arrived.

"Sir, you had said that the High Alector of Engineering would be wanting pteridon transport for some engineers."

"He's requested more than we can supply from Elcien, I take it." Dainyl had no doubts that High Alector Ruvryn would be difficult, not after what Lystrana had told him and after his own briefing of the High Alector.

"Yes, sir. He wants three squads for a full week, starting on Sexdi. He says that they'll need to transport three tonnes of equipment and supplies and five engineers, first to Tempre, and then to Hyalt."

Dainyl frowned. He had his doubts whether Ruvryn's engineers needed all that equipment, but he couldn't very well question an engineer about engineering equipment, especially when he wasn't supposed to know about Table maintenance and internal operations—and when he'd been the real cause of the failure of the Table in Hyalt. He still wondered what had caused the Table failure in Tempre, but pushed that aside to consider Ruvryn's "request."

For long distances, a hundredweight was generally the most a pteridon could carry without extreme lifeforce use. At ten hundredweight to a tonne, that amounted to thirty round-trips from either Faitel or Ludar, and a day each way for each trip. If some of the equipment had to go to Tempre first and then to Hyalt, or the other way around, that could add another ten or fifteen trips.

"He can have one squad from here—either second or fourth—and two from Seventh Company in Tempre, whichever ones Captain Lyzetta thinks will do best."

"Seventh Company isn't all that heavily tasked, sir. I have been giving them the long runs to Dereka and Lyterna, but . . ."

"I understand, but remember, Seventh Company is short three pteridons. If you need to, you can bring in one of Seventh Company's squads for dispatch runs from here, but I want one of First Company's squads there supporting the engineers, and I want a full report on what they're asked to do."

"I'd say fourth squad then, sir."

Dainyl had thought that might have been her recommendation, based on what Ghasylt had told him earlier. "Write up a concurrence on those terms, and I'll look it over, and sign it. Then you'll need to send a dispatch to Captain Lyzetta. We'll need to know where they want the pteridons on Sexdi, and we'll need to know no later than tomorrow night. Someone may ask why, and the answer is because Tempre has no Table, and we'll need to fly a dispatch there, and that takes a day, and a day to fly to where they want the equipment picked up. So every day they delay in telling us past tomorrow is a day later before they can start."

"Sir . . . ?"

"Yes, Captain, there are some assistants to High Alectors who honestly do not think such matters through. They're used to instant travel by Table, and it doesn't occur to them that logistics take more time. You wouldn't think it, but . . ." Dainyl shrugged. "Write up the concurrence for me to sign first. Then work on the other dispatches and the supporting details."

"Yes, sir."

"Oh . . . how are we coming on getting the transfers from the sandoxen drivers to Seventh Company?"

"Two of them are in Tempre. Two more should be detached before long, but the chief assistant to the High Alector of Transport said to tell you that it will be hard to get any more for another few months. Usually, the Myrmidons only need five or six new fliers every year."

Dainyl was well aware of that—and the fact that his operations against the rebels in Hyalt and Tempre had resulted in the loss of more than that in the last few weeks alone.

"Be nice. Tell her we understand. Also tell her that I said times are changing and that we'll likely be needing more this year."

Zernylta smiled. "Yes, sir."

After she had left, Dainyl turned back and looked out the window to watch one of the dispatch pteridons land on the flight stage in the courtyard. The clouds were moderately high and not too dark. Over the end-days, nothing had happened. Dainyl corrected himself—no news of anything happening had reached him. He and Lystrana had enjoyed the time together, although it had rained most of Decdi, foreshadowing the cold rains of fall, and the snows that would follow the icy rain all too soon.

He turned at the knock.

"Marshal?" Wyalt, acting as duty messenger within headquarters, stood at Dainyl's study door, holding an envelope. "This came in for you on the dispatch run."

Dainyl took the envelope. "Thank you."

"Yes, sir." Wyalt bowed, turned, and departed.

The envelope bore Dainyl's name and title. He opened it and began to read.

> Congratulations, Marshal. We wish you the best.
>
> The creature about which you wrote is best discussed here in Lyterna, at your convenience. We look forward to seeing you whenever you appear.

The signature was Asulet's.

Dainyl smiled. As time went by, Asulet's mannerism of insisting that any information Dainyl needed required a trip to Lyterna was tending toward becoming wearing—except that Asulet dared not leave Lyterna, not while his rival Paeylt waited for him to make an error. And some of the information Dainyl had learned from Asulet was not to be entrusted to ink.

He had best get to Lyterna—and return—quickly, before some other trouble appeared, and before Alcyna arrived on Septi. In fact, there was no reason not to go within the glass—right after he signed the concurrence Zernylta was drafting.

Because everything took longer than he'd anticipated, Dainyl did not leave headquarters for close to a glass and a half. By then the clouds had darkened, and a light rain was falling, turning the stone-paved streets liquid silver as the duty coach carried him to the Hall of Justice.

When he got out of the coach he ordered Wyalt back to headquarters, since he had no idea how long he would be in Lyterna and since the driver would be needed to carry Zernylta's messages to the Palace and the Hall of Justice.

"You sure, sir?"

"I'm sure. I'll see you later."

Dainyl had to be more circumspect in entering the lower chambers, using his Talent earlier to conceal himself as he crossed the main hall where Zelyert himself was on the dais receiving petitions from unhappy landers and indigens. Few decisions of local justicers would be changed, Dainyl knew, but there was always the chance that an injustice had in fact occurred.

When he reached the Table chamber, the guards nodded. Dainyl nodded back to Tregaryt.

"Do you expect to return today, Marshal?" asked Chastyl.

"I do, but . . ." Dainyl shrugged.

The recorder nodded knowingly.

Dainyl stepped up onto the Table, squared his shoulders, and concentrated on the purpled darkness beneath, sliding through the mirrored surface easily and . . .

. . . into the chill beneath. Unlike his last translation, the tube was still. Dainyl thought he could sense hints of greenish ripples around the hazy perimeter of the tube, but he concentrated on the pink wedge locator that was Lyterna . . . and found himself hurling through the silvered-pink barrier . . .

. . . and standing on the Table in Lyterna.

Myenfel—the Recorder of Deeds for Lyterna—stood watching him. Beside Myenfel were two white-haired alectors in gray—both with lightcutters and concentrating on the Table.

"Is every Table in Acorus guarded, Myenfel?" asked Dainyl as he stepped off the Table and onto the marble-tiled floor.

"So far as I know, Marshal. Several recorders have had to request alectors be added to their staffs."

"Places like Prosp and Blackstear?"

The recorder nodded. "Now that your Seventh Company is in Tempre, once a new regional alector is appointed and the Table is repaired, you may be requested to supply Table guards there." His voice turned dry. "Particularly since there are so few alectors remaining in Tempre."

"I doubt that the new RA would wish to employ any such as those who died in Tempre," Dainyl said.

"That might depend on whom the Duarch Samist appoints."

Myenfel had a point. Dainyl was more convinced than ever that Samist and Brekylt were working together against Khelaryt. "I'm here to see Asulet."

"He said to expect you. Can you find your way?"

"By now I had best be able to." Dainyl smiled, then turned toward the door.

The stone-walled corridor outside was empty, but well lit by the light-torches on the wall. At times, Dainyl found himself amazed that all of Lyterna had been carved out of solid rock literally hundreds of generations earlier—yet it did not look ancient. He began to walk more quickly, along the corridor to the first cross-corridor toward the stone staircase to the next level.

At that moment, a hidden doorway on the left opened, and an alector garbed in gray and black stepped out and waited as Dainyl approached. His uncharacteristic gray eyes radiated friendliness, as did his Talent. Beneath the outward friendliness was the cold precision of a lightcannon. "Marshal Dainyl. I had heard you came to Lyterna often. I do not believe we have met. I'm Paeylt."

"The engineering master? I've heard much of you and your skill." Dainyl stopped and nodded politely. He also maintained his Talent shields while assessing those of the engineer—strong, but apparently not quite so strong as his own. Still . . .

"Really? Those are among the more flattering words I've heard in years." Paeylt's voice was a warm, soothing baritone.

"I doubt anyone would slight your skills as a master engineer or as a planner of cities."

Paeylt laughed, also warmly. "Already, I see why you are Marshal of Myrmidons."

"I was fortunate." And he had been, if not in the manner the words connoted.

"Indeed you were, but you are more than that, and you will have to be even more, especially bearing the shade of the ancients." He paused. "I assume you are here to see Asulet, and I will not keep you, but I did wish to see you for myself." After a polite nod, he stepped back into the doorway.

The stone door slid shut, silently, but not before Dainyl got a quick glimpse of a large space filled with equipment he could not recognize or identify in the time before the opening closed. He continued along the narrow corridor until he reached the staircase up to the main gallery east of the so-called Council Hall. From there he walked past the grand pteridon mural of a battle scene that never had been—not until a few weeks ago, hundreds, if not thousands of years after the mural had been painted. Two more turns, and another narrow hallway carried Dainyl out into the gallery holding the niches with the ancient specimens of life on Acorus—and the spare pteridons—all preserved in time against a future need.

Dainyl turned right and made his way to the first door.

Asulet was waiting in his oak-paneled, windowless study, with its entire wall of bookshelves and the painting—or plan—of Dereka as it had been planned to have been built, with twin green towers.

"I thought you might be here today." The elder alector stood beside a wide table desk of ancient oak. He gestured to one of the two oak armchairs, while taking the other.

"I only received your message this morning." As Dainyl sat, he could feel the airflow from the wall air ducts.

"Would that others took my communications with such care and haste," Asulet began. "While I would be among the first to offer my congratulations, Marshal, your success indicates the perilous situation in which we alectors of Acorus find ourselves, as well as the perilous situation that faces you personally."

Dainyl suspected he knew what Asulet meant, but decided to let the elder alector explain. But when Asulet did not speak, Dainyl asked, "That a Myrmidon perceived to have so little Talent is marshal?"

"You have disabused those with any intelligence of the idea that you are weak in Talent. No, I was referring to the fact that you now carry the tinge of the ancients."

"The green? That was Rhelyn's doing. He attacked me with one of the weapons of the ancients." Dainyl went on to explain, finishing up with, ". . . and it seems to be fading."

"That never fades. At best you can keep it in check." The older alector shook his head. "You may be strong enough to do so, but you must watch yourself all the time, in how you use your Talent and for what."

"Why is the green such a danger?"

"When one becomes totally green, one ceases to be an alector, and . . ." Asulet shrugged.

While Dainyl thought he understood what Asulet meant, he could see other possibilities. "An ancient? Could an alector truly become one?"

"*That,* to my knowledge, has never occurred." Asulet frowned, then fingered his chin, as if debating how much more to say. "All intelligent life that lives on the same world must, by nature, share physical similarities, and more than that. The ancients appear to be more like pteridons in that they are Talent creatures, if of a differing kind of Talent. It *might* be possible to transform an alector into an ancient. Certainly, Table travel can twist the less Talented into all manner of Talent creatures." He shrugged. "But who would wish such? I was referring more to the danger of becoming less of an alector."

That was what Danyl had surmised, but the other question had intrigued him because of what he had already experienced among the ancients.

"Another and greater peril faces us all. For now, in order to preserve what we have created, we must guard the Tables day and night to keep from being swamped."

"What else can be done? It is clear to all who can see that the Master Scepter will shortly be transferred to Efra, and yet Khelaryt cannot see that."

"No . . . he cannot," said Asulet sadly, "for many reasons."

"Why doesn't anyone tell him?"

"Did you?"

"No . . . I didn't realize he didn't know—or couldn't accept that knowledge until I was in a situation where I could not say anything. Why doesn't anyone tell him?"

"Because once he is forced to admit that Acorus will not receive the Master Scepter, he loses much of his power, and divided as the High Alectors are, they do not wish to see even greater conflicts break out."

Greater conflicts?

"That is why he favors you," Asulet went on. "You kept the revolt small and crushed it." His eyes glinted, but Dainyl wasn't certain whether the expression was humor or something else, and he could not Talent-read what the old alector felt. "How you did so is a mystery and should remain so. Those who seek to overthrow the existing way are always more awed by what they cannot understand."

"At times. At other times, they merely ignore it."

"Like Paeylt. I understand he deigned to greet you."

Dainyl should have felt surprise, he supposed, but he did not. "You watch him closely."

"I have him watched. For the moment, that is best." Asulet cleared his throat. "First . . . the creature you wrote about. It is another animal out of the past, and its presence in the Iron Valleys bespeaks change. It grazes on plants that are rather rare—quarasote, we called them. They actually take up quartz into their shoots. When grown, these bushes are sharp enough to rip through leather. The nightsheep usually graze in the area of the ice sands. That's why few alectors even know about them. They can only be controlled by Talent, and their horns are sharp enough to cut through even thin sheets of metal. They're inedible, of course, because of the quartz and mineral intake. They tend not to be aggressive unless strongly provoked. Something must have pushed them south. That is far more troublesome than the creatures themselves, although I would not advise indigens or landers to approach them closely."

"Because only Talent can control them?"

"Exactly. I'd judge that the ancients are behind this, but why I could not say."

"You're telling me because Zelyert would ignore the signs and Khelaryt can do little."

Asulet laughed gently. "Sulerya thinks highly of you, and each time I speak with you I see why."

"I think highly of your daughter."

"There is another matter, as well," Asulet said after a moment of silence. "That is the growing cooperation between Paeylt and Ruvryn. As relatives, they once exhibited some rivalry, but that has now passed."

Just as Dainyl thought he had some inkling of who was plotting with whom, someone else came up, not that it was surprising, he reflected, that two disgruntled engineers might conspire for mutual benefit.

"Paeylt has decided he cannot oust you from here or gain control of Lyterna directly," volunteered Dainyl. "So he is passing information to Ruvryn, or to engineers that work for him. Is that it?"

"You knew of this?"

"No. But it fits. Shastylt mentioned special weapons being fabricated at Faitel. With what you have said, I have to question whether he was part of that alliance."

"That is possible. I had not heard of that complication. Shastylt did say weapons?"

"He did."

"Too much deviousness always leads to ruin. You might remember that, Dainyl."

"I will." Dainyl had already discovered that. "What else is Paeylt plotting?"

"He thinks he should be the Duarch of Ludar, but he would be willing to let Samist remain as Duarch of Elcien."

"Why can't anyone think about holding Acorus together until after the succession of the Master Scepter takes place, and then worry about who has power?"

"Because," Asulet replied dryly, "whoever is ready to take power immediately after the transfer is likely to keep it."

"Is that because of what will happen when the transfer takes place?"

Asulet nodded.

"What will happen?"

"Both Duarches will have their powers limited, if it does not happen sooner for other reasons."

"How . . . ?"

"That I cannot say, but it will happen." Asulet rose. "I should not have said even that, but you are trustworthy and should know such. You probably need to get back to Elcien, Marshal."

Dainyl stood. Once more, the older alector had said what he would say, and nothing Dainyl could do would be likely to elicit more information. "Thank you, Senior Alector."

"My thanks to you."

Dainyl felt watched as he retraced his route back to the Table chamber, and he wondered if there happened to be any High Alector who was not involved in plots and schemes of some sort. Probably not, because those who were not initially involved would have had to build their own alliances and allies to protect themselves, as he had with Asulet and Sulerya—and Lystrana, of course. Zelyert might not be an enemy, but Dainyl certainly couldn't count the High Alector of Justice as an ally, either.

He stepped through the door of the Table chamber, closing it behind himself, and checking the chamber, which still held the recorder and the two older guards in gray, then approached the Table.

"Have a good translation, Marshal," offered Myenfel.

"Thank you." Dainyl started to step onto the Table, when someone appeared on the mirrored surface.

Chill billowed away from the figure, a tall alectress clad in the green and gray of a Myrmidon captain of Ifryn. Her form held a strange greenness, somewhat like that of the ancients, but not exactly. Her lightcutter flashed at the guards, cutting one down immediately.

Dainyl clamped his own shields around her as she triggered the lightcutter.

The bluish light flared, reflected from Dainyl's shields back across her abdomen, and she toppled, slowly, hitting the Table with a dull *thud.*

He dropped his shields and lifted his own lightcutter, sensing another welling of Talent, this one twisting and uncontrolled.

The next appearance was that of a wild translation—half wild sandox from the neck up, a wide triangular head with a glittering horn, and crystalline blue eyes, and Myrmidon-clad below. Like the captain who lay on the Table, beginning to turn to dust, the second translation held a lightcutter sidearm.

Dainyl shot the beast through the chest, right below the neck. The wild translation collapsed. Unlike that of the dead captain, the translation's body remained solid.

"Thank you, Marshal," Myenfel said, from beside the collapsed gray uniform of the dead Table guard. "I'd suggest you hasten your translation."

Dainyl stepped onto the Table, but bent and dragged the dead form of the wild translation off the Table, and then the collapsed uniform and equipment of the dead Myrmidon captain—if indeed she had even been such. He straightened and concentrated on the darkness beneath the Table . . .

. . . and the purpled darkness rose up around him with its

chill. He began to search for the brilliant white locator of Elcien, but as he did, lines of green coruscated along the purple translation tube. So bright were the lines of green that he had difficulty discerning any of the locator wedges.

One green beam struck his shoulder, and a combination of pain and . . . something else—something that felt welcoming and familiar before it faded—knifed through him. Another seemingly knocked his feet from under him, and that was nonsense, because no one really stood in translation. There wasn't the same physical reality.

Dainyl struggled, but the locators were gone—or blocked out for the moment.

There was one green diamond in the distance, and he reached for it. Better to be somewhere *than end up dying nowhere or becoming a wild translation himself.*

He flashed through a green-silver barrier and . . .

. . . stood bent over in a narrow tunnel, one so low that his hair still brushed the roof. Warm air flowed toward him.

Where was he?

He glanced toward the light . . . and swallowed. Outside he could see a small flat area, surrounded by rugged boulders. He recognized the place. He was in the mountain cave of the ancients in Dramur.

He forced himself to ignore the absolute impossibility of his location and eased back until he stood—even more hunched over—on the silver rock mirror at the back of the unnatural cave. There he concentrated, seeking not the purpled blackness of the translation tube, but the plain and deeper blackness he had latched on to before.

His efforts seemed hard, and to take far longer, but . . .

. . . he was in a dark chill, if not so chill as a translation tube.

This time, he had decided to look for the locator wedges from outside the purpleness of the translation tube. He sensed another of the amber-green squares, but decided against trying that. He didn't want another encounter with the ancients.

Then, through the flashing green beams and the darkness that alternated with momentary green brilliance, he began to make out the locator wedges—except they were more like cylinders, as if a triangle had been rolled so that the vertex touched the base. That wasn't quite it, because each side of the wedge had been rolled, yet there was only one cylinder.

Dainyl shook off his bemusement, and Talent-reached for the cylinder wedge that he hoped was Elcien, and he found himself back in the purpled translation tube with the whiteness of Elcien speeding toward him.

Passing through the white-silver barrier was like passing through a mist of tiny unseen knives.

He stood on the Table, throwing up his shields full—barely before the bluish beams of lightcutters flashed across him.

"Stop! It's the marshal."

Dainyl waited, then stepped off the Table.

"I'm so sorry, Marshal. I'm so sorry, sir," babbled the recorder. "It's just that we've had wild translation after wild translation for the past half glass. We lost one guard already."

Dainyl sensed both the truth of Chastyl's words, and his sincere regret.

"You've got some of that Talent-green on you . . . like all the wild translations did," the recorder added.

"That's from the ancient weapon the rebels used on me. It will take a while to wear off," Dainyl explained. He had grave doubts that was the full explanation, but it was easier and more appropriate for the moment. "I need to get back to headquarters."

He also needed time—that he was running short of—to sort matters out, if he could.

12

In the darkness just after twilight, Mykel and Rhystan sat at the single long table in the small room that was the officers' mess in the new compound—or would be. The single bronze wall lamp cast but a haze of light that scarcely reached the end of the table and the two officers.

"I have to say that it's good to sleep on a real bunk again," offered Rhystan. "How long that will last . . ." He shrugged and looked at Mykel. "Have you heard from the colonel?"

"Not a thing, but I'd judge he only got my report within the last day or so—and that's no guarantee that he's read it."

"You've got a feel for these sorts of things. How long do you think we'll be staying here?" Rhystan took a last sip from the beaker of ale he had been nursing along.

"I don't see us being sent off until the alectors return to their compound. The two Hyalt companies can't really provide perimeter security there and handle road patrols against brigands. When the alectors start rebuilding the compound—or if they make a decision not to—they'll want us out of here pretty quickly, especially if they rebuild. There really aren't enough supplies and provisions for us and for rebuilding and repairing their compound." Mykel also doubted that the submarshal wanted a Cadmian battalion around that had learned it could kill alectors.

"Majer . . . we killed alectors. We got a few here, and you took out more than that in Tempre."

"I know. I worry about it. The alectors went to great lengths to create the impression that they are unkillable. My guess is that we'll be sent somewhere out of the way, and somewhere that will cost us a lot of men. I'd thought about resigning, or leaving, but . . ." Mykel shook his head. "It's too late for that."

"If you do, more will die," Rhystan pointed out.

"No officer is indispensable, as much as I'd like to think otherwise."

"I didn't say you were indispensable. I said more men would die. That's because you see things others don't." A twisted smile followed Rhystan's words. "That's only true if you don't go off alone and get yourself killed, like you almost did here in Hyalt and again in Tempre."

"In Tempre, I had no idea that the lower level of the alector's building would explode."

"Maybe not, but everything was fine until you went first.

You've led from the front for enough years that the men won't mind if you do something to assure that you stay alive. The squad leaders and junior officers might even prefer keeping their commander."

Mykel winced. "It's hard. I'm not trying to be a hero or anything. I just don't like asking them to do what I won't."

"Majer . . . look at it this way. You've done more than any of them have to lead from the front. You've been wounded something like five times—if not more—over the past two years. You've also proved that you lose fewer men in fights. So . . . they know you're willing to put yourself on the line. Now, they'd prefer that you stay alive so that you can keep more of them alive." Rhystan paused. "Probably not all the newer Cadmians know that, but all the senior rankers and squad leaders do, and they're the ones who count."

Mykel looked down at the still polished wood of the new table, then finally lifted his eyes. "It makes sense, but it's hard."

"Mykel . . . there are all kinds of courage. Sometimes, it takes more courage to let someone else lead, especially if you're the kind of commander who feels for his men. And you are." Rhystan stood abruptly. "By your leave, Majer?"

Mykel looked at the older man, then smiled. "Good night, Rhystan . . . and . . . thank you."

"Thank you, sir."

Mykel sat alone in the officers' mess for a time, thinking.

Why had he had such a hard time seeing what Rhystan had pointed out? The older officer had earlier hinted at what he had said so bluntly, and Mykel had thought he had understood, but he'd still risked himself at times that he should not have. There were other times when there had been no real choice. At the very least, he needed to make those distinctions.

But . . . how could he truly know whether he was making an accurate assessment, or deluding himself? Had he really needed to lead the way down to the Table in Tempre? No. Had he needed to scout out the rebel alectors in Hyalt? Probably. Should he have led the charge against the rebels in Tempre? No. In fact, he might have saved more of his men by holding back and shooting more alectors.

Then there was Rachyla. Had he acted fairly and honestly in giving her the dagger of the ancients? Or had he done so out of mere desperation, because he was drawn to her, and knew he had to do something extraordinary to reach her?

For those questions, he had no answers.

Finally, he stood, crossed the small room, and blew out the lamp. He walked slowly back up to the visiting officers' quarters he had taken.

Once inside, he lit the sole lamp, then sat on the bunk and pulled out the map of Corus he had taken from the black chest in the alector's Table chamber. He opened it carefully, feeling the smooth surfaces. When he laid it out across his knees and thighs, there were no creases where it had been folded. He took a corner and flexed it. While he did not actually try to rip the corner, he could sense that it would take tremendous pressure to tear or cut the map. The map was not drawn on paper, or not on any paper Mykel knew, and yet it was not cloth, either. Nor was it imbued with the lifeforce essence that Mykel had sensed in the Myrmidon uniforms or those of the rebel alectors.

He studied the depiction of the continent carefully, deliberately, but what he saw was certainly not any different in outline or overall shape than any map he had seen before. He continued to peruse the map, noting that fourteen cities all were marked with tiny green octagons. Each octagon was framed by a colored border edged in purple. Two of the octagons were Tempre and Hyalt. Others were Elcien, Ludar, and Alustre. That suggested that each octagon had to be the location of a Table. The one in Tempre was blue edged in purple, and the one at Hyalt was bordered in amber.

Mykel had to wonder at the placement of the Tables—if indeed that was what the octagons signified. Some—such as those in Ludar, Elcien, Alustre, and Faitel—clearly made sense. But why were there Tables in some isolated places, such as Hyalt and Blackstear, and not in others, such as Sinjin and Southgate? And the other thing was that the closest Table to the Aerlal Plateau was the one in Dereka—and it was still some 250 vingts away.

13

The rest of Duadi had been a blur for Dainyl. He and Zernylta had gone over the pteridon schedules for the next two weeks, and that had gotten more than a little complex because Dainyl had insisted on keeping close to two full squads of First Company in Elcien. Then he'd gotten a dispatch from Captain Elysara in Lyterna. A landslide into Lake Vergren had sent a wave of water down the river that had washed out the main bridge on the high road through South Pass. That meant the high road through the Northern Pass was the only land route open to the east for at least a month—and possibly until late in the following spring if the winter snows were heavy. The pteridons out of Lyterna would have to be tasked with helping with the repairs—and that rebuilding effort would be overseen by the chief engineer of Lyterna—Paeylt. And that meant that the high-powered road-cutting equipment—even more powerful than the lightcannon Rhelyn had used at Hyalt—and the insulated suits to protect the engineers would be in Paeylt's hands. That concerned Dainyl, but there wasn't anything he could say or do about it.

Dainyl had sent back a message agreeing to the use of Sixth Company pteridons, with the stipulation that no more than two squads were used at any one time. He'd also had to respond politely to the High Alector of Transport about the need for more flier trainees from the sandox coach drivers, because Zelyert had requested that Dainyl personally answer Alseryl's charges that Dainyl's requests for trainees were unreasonable and that Dainyl's strategies had been exceedingly wasteful of alector personnel when Cadmians were available.

All in all, after those incidents and his normal reports and budget preparations, Dainyl felt he had been fortunate to arrive home only a glass and a quarter late.

"You look weary, dearest." Those had been Lystrana's first words to him.

That was one way of looking at it. Exhausted, furious, and frustrated at having to explain what should have been obvious was another. He could see her own tiredness, however, and he smiled. "I think you had a day every bit as long as mine. I'm sorry I'm late."

"We should eat."

He offered Lystrana his arm, and they walked to the dining room, where Sentya and Zistele were already bringing out the platters. The meal was chiafra—mint-minced beef mixed with creamed white cheese and parsley, rolled in thin pastry tubes and covered with a rich brown sauce—accompanied by steamed snap beans and heavy sweet brown bread.

Dainyl had a second helping, not realizing that he was so hungry because he'd had nothing to eat since his early breakfast.

Lystrana ate more sparingly, looking up after a time. "How long will the rain continue?"

"The dispatch fliers say that the skies to the west of the bay are clearing, but that there's snow on the higher reaches of the Coast Range peaks to the north. The ice is beginning to close in on Blackstear."

"An early winter, then."

"In the north, it would seem. It's warmer than usual in Soupat and Southgate." Dainyl finished the last of his bread and looked toward the kitchen. "Sentya, Zistele . . . it was a wonderful supper. Thank you."

"It was the alectress's recipe, sir."

"We just followed it."

Dainyl smiled at the murmured demurrals from the kitchen. "It was still excellent."

"Thank you, sir."

After the girls had cleaned up the supper and retired,

Dainyl and Lystrana settled into the front room with the two corner chairs.

"You still look tired, Dainyl. What happened?"

He leaned back in the chair and took a small sip of the Vyan Grande brandy. "You first."

Lystrana put her feet on the stool. "Chembryt's worried. Tariff collections are falling off, and they shouldn't be. We need more golds, not less. The engineers need more materials and more fabricators. The Myrmidons have built one new compound and enlarged another, and there are two new Cadmian compounds, one completed and the other under construction. Those don't include the costs of the repairs at Hyalt or Tempre. Or the need for more guards for the Tables by all the Recorders of Deeds."

"Why are tariffs falling off?"

"Most of the tariffs are assessed on goods being produced for sale. People—especially the landers and indigens—aren't buying as much. And prices for coal and coke and iron are higher because of the problems at Iron Stem, and that means fewer people are buying iron, except for the engineers, and they're buying more, which costs the Duarches exactly at a time when we have less revenue."

"Maybe people are worried. People don't buy nearly so much when they are."

"Why would the landers and indigens be worried?" she asked. "Tempre is the only city where there have been real problems, and what you did didn't affect anyone except a handful of alectors. Hyalt's too small to make a difference."

"It could be that they feel that trouble is ahead." He paused. "What else?"

"Chembryt got a message from Ruvryn. He destroyed it. He only said that the High Alector of Engineering was acting as if he were the Duarch, rather than a subordinate who served at the Duarches' pleasure. Then he asked me to draft a polite note to Ruvryn for him to sign. The note said that, unfortunately, even the High Alector of Finance could not create golds by fiat, not without ruining the patterns of trade and commerce, and that any decision to raise tariffs would have to be approved by both Duarches."

"Someone's pressing Ruvryn to fabricate additional equipment."

"It sounds that way." Lystrana sighed.

"Oh . . . I have more bad news. Have you heard that a cliff or something fell into Lake Vergen and created a surge downstream that wiped out the high road bridge in the South Pass—and that part of the high road to Lustrea is likely to be closed for months?"

"Why now?" She shook her head. "That will only make matters worse."

"Is there that much trade that travels that far?"

"Not that much. It's generally unique goods, but they do bring in good tariffs. We'll lose many of those, or receive them later, and that's in addition to the repair expenses . . . on top of everything else." She forced a smile. "That was my cheerful day. What about yours?"

"Interestingly enough, mine also began with a request from Ruvryn." Dainyl smiled wryly.

Even in the dim light, Lystrana caught his expression, and a smile of ironic bemusement crossed her lips.

"He demanded three pteridon squads for a full week, to transport more than three tonnes of equipment, material, and engineers from Ludar and Faitel to Tempre and Hyalt—to repair the Tables in both places. That will require something like between thirty-five and fifty round-trip flights. It also means burning a great deal of lifeforce. If we use First Company, it means leaving no Myrmidons to speak of in Elcien."

"And?"

"I'm going to have Seventh Company do most of it."

"Is that wise?"

"Well . . . Seventh Company's captain is Khelaryt's youngest daughter. I don't think Ruvryn knows that."

"I didn't know that," Lystrana said.

"I thought I told you. She was the one who brought up that Asyrk was senior, because she wanted me to know that he was one of Alcyna's plants from Ifryn."

"That, you did tell me, but not that she was his daughter."

"I'm sorry. I thought I had."

"How do you know she's Khelaryt's daughter?"

"By what he revealed when I briefed him. Lyzetta got Asyrk—or someone—to write him. She can't because part of his shadowmatch conditioning—"

"—blocks it. That's why Captain Sevasya can't contact him." Lystrana shook her head. "You didn't know that when you gave her command of Seventh Company?"

"No. I had no idea."

"That must have amused Khelaryt."

"I suppose so. He didn't say anything. He couldn't even say she was his daughter. He did acknowledge that she was of his heritage, and there is a resemblance. The rest I could sense."

"It makes sense. Where else would they be safer?"

Dainyl took another sip of the brandy.

"So you minimized the danger from Ruvryn's engineers—if they are indeed engineers. What else happened?" asked Lystrana.

"I had to go to Lyterna to see Asulet, and he warned me about the dangers of the green, as if I didn't have enough to worry about . . ." Dainyl recounted his visit and his difficulties with the return translation. ". . . and I was in Dramur . . . and there's no Table there."

"Yes, there was. Didn't you say that there was an ancient mirror Table there? When our Tables were blocked, you used theirs."

"It still bothers me—and just when I thought all that green Talent was fading, I've got another dose of it, and Asulet tells me that I'm supposed to keep it in check."

"Dearest, don't complain . . . You're alive and well."

"There's too much going on with the ancients—and with all the wild translations."

"Ifryn is coming apart, and it's bleeding over into Acorus."

"I don't understand why the Archon doesn't move the Master Scepter before things get even worse."

"Maybe he can't for some reason."

That made sense. At least, Dainyl thought it did.

"Besides," added Lystrana morosely, "would you really want him to condemn all those on Ifryn to die any sooner than absolutely necessary?"

"I have to wonder about that. What would happen if he transferred the Master Scepter earlier?"

"All the Ifrits would die."

"But so long as some lifeforce remains, the indigens wouldn't, would they?"

Lystrana was silent for a moment. "A few might survive. For a while."

Dainyl looked down at his empty brandy snifter.

14

Dainyl had barely looked over the morning muster reports from Captain Ghasylt on Tridi morning when Wyalt knocked at his half-open study door.

"Another urgent message, sir." Wyalt appeared apologetic, his eyes not meeting Dainyl's, as he stepped into the study and handed the large envelope to the marshal.

"You don't have to look that concerned, Wyalt. You didn't create the problem, whatever it is."

"No, sir . . . I just . . . well, I've liked being part of First Company and headquarters."

"You're leaving tomorrow, aren't you?"

"Yes, sir."

"You'll do fine with Seventh Company. Captain Lyzetta is a good commanding officer. She comes from a fine heritage, and she's a solid Myrmidon officer. And you'll get to fly far sooner this way."

At that reminder, Wyalt smiled, if faintly. "I'd thought of that, sir."

Dainyl grinned. "Whoever your lady friend is, Tempre isn't that impossibly far away, and it's likely that Seventh Company will be based there for a time." That was stretching matters, he realized, since Tempre was close to seven hundred vingts. But considering that Dulka, where Seventh Company had been based, was more than two thousand vingts in a straight flight, Wyalt's lady love could at least reach Tempre by sandox coach in a few days.

The messenger flushed, if but briefly. "Yes, sir. Thank you, sir."

Dainyl watched as Wyalt left. While he would have liked Wyalt to remain in Elcien, with the shortage of Myrmidon fliers, especially in Seventh Company, Lyzetta needed Wyalt as a new flier far more than Ghasylt and headquarters needed a messenger and driver.

Finally he opened the envelope. The dispatch inside was from Colonel Herolt, commander of the Cadmian Mounted Rifle Regiment based at Northa, immediately east and north of Elcien. Dainyl skimmed the salutations and concentrated on the body of the dispatch.

> Fourth Battalion, commanded by Majer Hersiod, has been deployed to Iron Stem and based out of the Cadmian compound there. The battalion's mission has been to provide support to the local Cadmian forces in maintaining order at the iron and coal mines, and the ironworks. Battalion patrols have also provided security against large local predators. Over the past week, concentrated assaults by local Reillies and other irregulars, possibly including disgruntled and disguised miners, have resulted in casualties totaling more than half the battalion. These armed assaults occurred in coincidence with an unprecedented series of attacks by giant sandwolves and other creatures . . . Majer Hersiod and two captains are among the fatalities . . .

Dainyl looked at the dispatch. Behind it, there was another report as well. He laid aside the Fourth Battalion dispatch and began to read the second dispatch.

> Three companies of Fifth Battalion, commanded by Majer Druvyr, had pursued a Reillie irregular company and backed them into an indefensible position at the base of the northern cliffs of the Aerlal Plateau some thirty vingts east of Eastice. While the majer prepared for an attack, a section of the cliff

broke away, and both the Reillies and all three Cadmian companies and their officers were annihilated by the mass of ice and rock. Two Fifth Battalion companies remain largely intact. Twenty-third Company remains on station in Klamat, while Twenty-sixth Company continues to patrol sections of the high road between Klamat and Northport . . .

After rereading both dispatches once more, Dainyl set them on the desk, then looked out through the window at the empty stone flight stage in the courtyard. According to Asulet, the recently rediscovered creatures, the nightsheep, while somewhat dangerous, tended not to be aggressive unless attacked. The sandwolves were dangerous, but not to a well-armed and prepared Cadmian force. Had the attacks been accompanied by the other predator, the one that Asulet said had only been glimpsed in the past?

If so, why were all these attacks and strange occurrences happening now? They bore the mark of the ancients, although Dainyl doubted there was any concrete proof of that. If the ancients had been responsible, surely they knew that the problems they had created were minor and would change nothing. Yet the ancient who had spoken with Dainyl had been absolutely certain that unless any alector changed, and linked directly to Acorus, he would perish.

He looked down at the dispatches. There was little to be done, not immediately, about Fifth Battalion. All companies of the battalion had been scheduled to be withdrawn to their headquarters within weeks. Fourth Battalion was another matter. More than ever, the Duarchy needed iron and coal.

Slowly, he nodded.

Third Battalion. If anyone could deal with the ancients, Majer Mykel could. And, Dainyl told himself, that assignment would also keep the majer away from other alectors. He pulled a sheet of paper toward him, then began to write the orders to Colonel Herolt that would send the majer and his battalion to Iron Stem.

He hadn't quite finished when Wyalt reappeared, this time bearing a smaller envelope.

"Sir . . . it's from the Highest."

Dainyl nodded. "If you'd set it on the desk, Wyalt, please."

Dainyl finished drafting the Cadmian orders before he lifted and opened the envelope. The message inside was simple. He was to report to High Alector Zelyert no later than a glass before noon. Somehow, that was typical of Zelyert. Either he didn't care what Dainyl was doing, or he knew Dainyl was at headquarters.

That gave Dainyl a glass to hand off the Cadmian orders to Zernylta in order to have copies made for dispatch to the colonel and to take the duty coach to the Hall of Justice.

He stood, shaking his head.

Three-quarters of a glass later, he stepped out of the duty coach outside the Hall of Justice. "Wyalt, today, you'd best wait for me."

"Yes, sir."

Dainyl made his way through the Hall of Justice, avoiding the larger than usual crowd of petitioners lined up before the dais, where one of Zelyert's assistants was sitting to receive them. Few would receive what they wanted, Dainyl knew, because neither alectors nor landers nor indigens really wanted justice. They just wanted matters to favor them.

Cloaking himself in a Talent shield, he vanished to their sight and opened the hidden entrance to the chambers below.

Zelyert was waiting in his small and spare study. He did not stand when Dainyl entered and closed the door.

"Marshal . . . always punctual. I trust you will keep that habit. A number of your predecessors became less than responsive once they became marshal."

Dainyl inclined his head before taking one of the two chairs before the table.

"First, Chastyl asked me to convey his apologies for the inadvertent firing at you in the Table chamber yesterday."

"No apology was necessary. I was fortunate to have been holding full shields. I can understand the confusion with all the wild translations from Ifryn occurring across Corus."

"That is unfortunately quite true." Zelyert leaned forward slightly. "I would be interested to know where you had been to return tinged with a Talent-green that has not yet faded."

"That is no secret. I had received a report last week about

yet another ancient lifeform that had appeared in the Iron Valleys, a large horned and dangerous variant on a sheep. I sent an inquiry to Asulet. His response was that he couldn't provide such information by message." Dainyl shrugged helplessly. "So I went to Lyterna and was returning. The entire translation tube held streaks of green. Chastyl told me that everything coming onto the Table was tinged green."

Zelyert nodded. "He had mentioned that, as I now recall. What did you discover from Asulet?"

"He said that the new creature was not all that new, that it was a nightsheep, and that while they were dangerous to landers if provoked, they were amenable to Talent control. He was more worried about what that signified. As I discovered just before I received your message, he was correct. Half of the Cadmian Fourth Battalion has been killed by a combination of rebellious miners, sandwolves, and another ancient predator, presumably the most dangerous and elusive creature of the ancients. In addition to that, three out of five companies of the Cadmian Fifth Battalion were wiped out when they cornered armed Reillies beneath the Aerlal Plateau, and a section of the cliff and the ice above fell on them."

"Such occurrences are unlikely to be coincidences." Zelyert's deep voice was mild.

"That was my thought," Dainyl replied.

"The ancients have begun to act. What do you plan to counter them?"

"For the moment, I am sending the Third Cadmian Battalion to Iron Stem. That battalion is the only one with experience in dealing with Talent creatures."

"No Myrmidons?"

"No. Not at this time."

Zelyert nodded. "You think these are diversions?"

"That I do not know, but it is unlikely that any ancient activity near Eastice can harm us, and the main problems in Iron Stem lie with indigens, not ancients." Dainyl paused momentarily before going on. "Shastylt once mentioned 'special weapons' being ordered from Faitel. If matters worsen, with greater ancient activity near Iron Stem, could those be used there?"

"That would be overkill, Marshal."

From what he had seen and sensed of the ancients, Dainyl had his doubts about that. "I watched them destroy two pteridons, sir. We have weapons that are that powerful as well. I am assuming those were developed by the Engineers' Guild."

"It is true that the engineers have certain . . . capabilities . . . and those have been employed, shall we say, unwisely, in the recent past. The lightcannon are an adaptation version of road-cutting equipment, and I understand that there is a weapon that creates and fires hundreds of crystalline spears every instant. The problem with them is that prodigal as pteridons are of lifeforce, the most terrible of the engineers' weapons are even more so. They are best kept in reserve for eventualities we hope never to see."

Considering how wasteful of lifeforce pteridons and skylances could be in battle, in principle, Dainyl had to agree with the High Alector. At the same time, he wondered if the eventualities Zelyert alluded to were the same as those Dainyl feared.

"Did Asulet mention anything else of interest?"

"No, sir. Nothing else. I wasn't there long before he sent me off again."

"Does he have guards at the Table there? Have they had difficulties?"

"Yes, sir. Just before I arrived, they lost a guard to a wild translation of some sort. I asked if all the Tables had guards, and his recorder indicated that they did."

"That will get worse in the season ahead."

"You anticipate that the actual transfer of the Master Scepter is near at hand?"

"One never knows what the Archon will do—or when he will do it. I doubt that Ifryn will be inhabitable for Ifrits for more than two seasons, certainly not more than three, but we are making that judgment on the basis of those who survive the long translation—and the majority of those who arrive here in these times are not placed so well as to have the most accurate of information. That being said, matters will get worse until the transfer occurs. After a period of quiet, there will be more disruption." Zelyert stood. "Please keep me informed about the progress of restoring order in Iron Stem. High Alector Ruvryn is likely to become more unsettled if the supply of coke and iron does not remain steady and eventually increase."

Dainyl rose. Zelyert had said what he would say. "I certainly will, sir." He inclined his head. "Good day."

On his way back up the stairs to the upper and public level of the Hall of Justice, Dainyl considered the implications of Zelyert's inquiry and words. He also couldn't help but worry about the Highest's observations about the green cast to his aura.

15

Under a hot midafternoon harvest sun, Mykel slowly rode back along the track of the road that was to be paved from the high road to the new Hyalt compound. The shoulders of his tunic were sticky and damp, and on hot dusty days such as this Quinti, he almost was ready for fall and the cooler winds. Almost.

The planned road had been marked roughly with stones, redstone chunks that sometimes were hard to pick out against the reddish soil between the clumps of tan grass. Captain Cismyr rode beside Mykel.

"They'll need to angle this section to the west a little higher on the hill," Mykel said to the captain, gesturing to the southeast. "If you get heavy rains, the way this is laid out now, that little stream there will rise to cover the road. I'll tell Poeldyn, but you may have to follow up on it, if we get sent orders before they finish paving the compound courtyard."

"Yes, sir. Do you know when you'll be getting orders?"

Mykel laughed. "Tomorrow, next week, next season . . ."

Cismyr chuckled politely.

"Don't be in too much of a hurry to get rid of us, Captain," Mykel pointed out. "My letter of credit is far more ample than yours, and I'm trying to build up your equipment and supplies. Also, yours doesn't take effect until I leave."

"What about the paving? We can't . . ."

"I've made arrangements for that. It's a separate agreement. You'll get extra golds until the end of fall." Mykel eased the roan up and around the sand, gravel, and crushed rock road base below the recently paved causeway outside the main south gates. The completed portion of causeway extended a good twenty yards on a gentle slope down from the gates, and the next section had a base in place, but no more would be done until the interior courtyard paving was finished.

Once past the road base, Mykel turned his mount onto the paved section of the causeway and rode through the gate. Ahead, he could see the last roof tiles of the small headquarters building roof had been put in place.

He'd finished stabling and grooming the roan and was heading to inspect the interior progress of the headquarters building when Undercaptain Matorak walked swiftly toward him.

"Undercaptain, how is Second Company?"

"We're doing well, sir." Matorak stopped, paused, then cleared his throat. Finally, he spoke. "Majer, I've had two squads on quarry duty today, and we've had quarry duty for a time, and we will for a while, I understand. Until there's enough stone to pave the road from the compound, anyway." He paused again. "Well, sir, I've noticed something."

Mykel was afraid of what might be coming next. When undercaptains noticed things, it usually meant trouble. "Yes?"

"Sir, we haven't spied one of those strange cats in weeks. I checked with Captain Cismyr and the other undercaptains from Third Battalion, and none of them have seen any, not since the Myrmidons came down and destroyed the buildings of the alectors' place."

"You're sure of that?" Mykel hadn't seen any references to the giant cats in any of the reports he'd received since he'd returned from Tempre, and his Talent-senses told him that Matorak was telling the truth with great certainty. Still, he had to ask.

"Yes, sir."

"That's interesting—and important. It could be that the cats were connected to something those rebels were doing. I'll pass that along. Thank you." Mykel smiled. "How are your men doing with the road patrols to the east?"

"There's not much traffic, sir, but we've scared off a few brigands. They were across a gully, and we couldn't reach them, but we haven't seen them since."

"That's one of the things you'll have to keep doing." No matter how many the Cadmians caught or shot, there would always be some brigands. Someone always wanted to take, rather than grow or build or create. That wouldn't change soon—it hadn't in all the long centuries of the Duarchy.

After Matorak turned and headed toward the stable, Mykel considered the disappearance of the giant cats. Had they really been tied to something that the rebels had been doing? He frowned. There had been reports of problems with the creatures going back at least a year. Had the rebels held the compound for that long? Or were the creatures linked to something else—like the alector's Table? Or the alectors themselves?

Mykel fingered his chin. He'd have to consider how much to tell the two Cadmian officers who would be in charge of the compound . . . and he'd need to do it carefully.

Like everything else. He laughed softly.

16

Slightly past midmorning on Septi, Undercaptain Yuasylt knocked on the door to Dainyl's study. "Marshal, sir . . . we got a message that the submarshal has arrived at the Hall of Justice. I dispatched the duty coach, but I thought you'd like to know."

Dainyl looked up from the ledgers he'd been studying, trying to get a better sense of what resources were where. "Thank you, Yuasylt. The senior officer's visiting quarters are ready for her, but I'll see her as soon as she arrives."

After the duty officer left, Dainyl glanced out the study window. The day was gray, and the usually clear silver-green skies of harvest had been replaced by haze and high clouds, a harbinger of the colder weather of fall that was only a week away. It still gave him a start when people referred to "the submarshal," and he realized they weren't talking about him.

His eyes went to the ledger, but he closed it and picked up the draft flight schedules Zernylta had left for him. About a quarter glass later, Dainyl heard measured and quick steps on the stone of the corridor, and sensed a strong Talent presence—Alcyna. He laid aside the draft flight schedules and waited.

"Good morning, sir. I'm reporting for duty as requested," Alcyna said brightly, stepping into Dainyl's study and closing the door behind her.

Beneath her Talent shields, she seemed cheerful and amused, Dainyl sensed. He gestured to the chairs. "Please sit down."

Alcyna slipped gracefully into the chair from which she could watch Dainyl and the door.

"How was the translation?" asked Dainyl.

"I had Retyl monitor Table traffic, and then left when things looked empty." Alcyna shuddered, and her shimmering black hair, short as it was, rippled. "I'd just as soon not do too much Table travel anytime soon. They've had to kill more than a half-score of wild translations in the last two weeks, in Alustre alone. We've accepted five unauthorized translations and had to execute ten criminals trying to escape Ifryn."

Dainyl wondered how she knew they were criminals, since criminals would either have been restrained or executed on Ifryn. Or were the recorders deciding anyone who couldn't prove usefulness was a criminal? If the twelve functioning Tables were receiving similar translations—that was close to 150 alectors a week trying to flee Ifryn.

"I can't say I like the idea of guards in the Table chambers, either," Alcyna went on. "Some High Alector will be shot by mistake before it's all over."

"It's already happened," Dainyl said. "Fahylt was killed several weeks ago in Ludar."

"He wasn't that good on the Tables, and he didn't have

strong shields. He wouldn't even have been an RA if his wife hadn't been a cousin of Samist."

While Dainyl hadn't known that, it didn't surprise him in the slightest. He laughed, softly. "Who are you related to, Alcyna? Or are you?"

"No one that important anymore. Weylt was my mother's cousin."

Weylt had been Tyanylt's predecessor as submarshal, a good ten years back. He'd vanished, supposedly, in translating from Dulka, as Dainyl recalled. "He got you into the Myrmidons and promoted to undercaptain, and the rest was up to you?"

"Something like that. Not quite as laudatory as your background. He didn't think I was cut out for the Myrmidons, but my mother badgered him until he supported me. I still spent three years as a sandox driver on the Alustre to Coren run."

"That's a long run," observed Dainyl. "Have you heard that Alseryl is complaining that we want too many of his drivers for trainees?"

"You were a bit hard on Fifth and Seventh Companies, sir." Alcyna's voice was light, just short of brightly ironic.

"Rhelyn was hard on Fifth Company. I was hard on Seventh Company. By the way, they'll be based at Tempre for now. They're supporting Ruvryn's engineers in rebuilding the Tables in Hyalt and Tempre."

"I can see why you would feel that necessary."

"Wouldn't you, in my position?"

"Yes, sir." Alcyna laughed warmly. "Even as submarshal I see the necessity. Brekylt did ask me, before I left, if I thought that Seventh Company would return to Dulka soon. I told him that I thought it was unlikely to occur anytime soon. Was I wrong?"

"We'll have to see." Dainyl paused. "Can you tell me what Brekylt really has in mind? Does he want to replace Khelaryt, or merely gain greater control over Corus east of the Spine?"

"He has never said, not directly. He did suggest that the

Myrmidons in the east should be a separate command and controlled from Alustre."

"With you in charge, I presume?"

"Of course." A warm and humorous smile followed her words. "He will say what he thinks needful to obtain the ends he wishes."

As will you, thought Dainyl. "It would seem that he wants power without controls."

"Would not anyone seeking power?"

"What will he do next?"

"Very little, I would judge. He will wait for events to unfold, and for others to make mistakes. He did say that Shastylt had gravely misjudged you."

"Oh? In what fashion?"

"He said that you were as much a son of Acorus as of Ifryn, and that Shastylt did not understand that."

That was an odd comment, reflected Dainyl, since it was patently obvious. Dainyl had been born on Acorus of parents also born on Acorus, and those facts had been one reason—not the only one, but one—why his advancement in the Myrmidons had been so slow.

"Sir . . . if I might ask . . . your shields and your Talent are tinged with green, a green similar to the ancients . . ."

Dainyl laughed, shaking his head ruefully. "Rhelyn attacked me with a weapon of the ancients. My entire arm was green, but after I recovered, the greenness dispersed through my system and began to fade." He paused briefly, sensing what he thought was deeply concealed shock and surprise, before continuing. "Then, a few days ago, in returning from Lyterna, I was in translation when the ancients filled the tube with green. Chastyl—the recorder in the Hall of Justice—said that they had gotten wild translations that ended up on the Table all Talent-green as well. He assured me that it will fade as well . . . assuming something else doesn't happen."

Alcyna nodded, a trace stiffly.

Dainyl had to wonder why the greenness and his story had bothered her. Because it suggested he could survive aspects of the ancients' weapons? Or because she'd been involved with Rhelyn's weapon? "I don't know if I mentioned the weapon Rhelyn used. I had thought it was a dagger, but it turned out to be a sword of the ancients, the kind that bleeds lifeforce. I was fortunate that he barely cut me."

"I suspect you were. What happened to the weapon?"

"It's been removed. No one will ever see it again. I have no idea where it is."

Dainyl could not help but catch the slight relief within Alcyna. "Where did you find it?"

She laughed, harshly. "Brekylt said Shastylt underestimated you. I think he has as well."

"Near Scien?" Dainyl asked.

She shook her head. "Buried near one of their mountain places along the Northern Pass. Years ago. It disappeared a year or so ago. I'd never shown it to anyone."

For the first time since she had entered his study, Dainyl sensed no evasion or equivocation. "Brekylt gave it to Rhelyn, then."

"I don't know. I would judge so."

"You may be fortunate that he gave it to Rhelyn before I chose you for submarshal," suggested Dainyl.

"That is very possible."

For a moment, neither spoke. Dainyl saw no point in pursuing the circumstances surrounding the weapon's disappearance.

Finally, he spoke. "The best quarters for visiting senior officers have been prepared for you, and they're yours for so long as you may require them. I have a large stack of reports and materials waiting for you on your desk, but I'm going to go over briefly the most pressing problems with you here, first."

She nodded.

"The ancients appear to be getting ready to attack in some fashion. It appears as though they dropped a cliff on a Cadmian battalion and that they unleashed some new Talent creatures against another battalion in the Iron Valleys. . . ." Dainyl went on to outline the situations and the initial steps he had taken in response. "What I'd like you to concentrate on are three matters—following the progress of the Table repairs in

Tempre and Hyalt; seeing what you can find out about what really happened up in Eastice; and working with Alseryl's chief assistant on the matter of getting more trainees from the sandox drivers."

"You think we'll lose more Myrmidons?"

"The Third Cadmian Battalion has had better fortune against Talent creatures than any other Cadmian unit, but it's a question as to whether they can deal with what the ancients may do. I'd rather not send Myrmidons there unless we have to."

"And not immediately, not while you're worried about what Brekylt will do?"

"That's right." Dainyl smiled. "I almost forgot. Lystrana has asked that you join us for supper tomorrow night."

"That would be delightful. I've heard so much about her. All of it good, of course."

Dainyl stood. "I'll show you your study, and you can get to work."

17

Late on Octdi, Alcyna sat across from Dainyl in the duty coach as it carried them eastward on the boulevard from Myrmidon headquarters toward Dainyl's dwelling. Both wore their duty uniforms of blue and gray.

Dainyl glanced forward in the direction of the new duty driver. "It didn't take you that long to get a replacement for Wyalt. How did you manage that?"

Alcyna smiled. "I just suggested to Alseryl's assistant that morale among sandox drivers might suffer greatly if it became known that the High Alector was refusing to allow drivers to become Myrmidon trainees, and that, in these times, it would be a shame if the High Alector had to explain that to either Duarch, especially if you had to brief the Duarch Khelaryt about it."

"And?"

"She left to consult with Alseryl. When she came back, she said that there would be no need for matters to go that far." Alcyna shrugged. "I pushed a bit. I asked if she were certain that you didn't need to brief Khelaryt. She was quite definite that it would not be necessary."

"They don't want me near the Duarch, that is."

"No more than absolutely necessary, I'd judge."

Alseryl's reaction seemed excessive to Dainyl, but he decided to mull that over, rather than comment further. "Sharua seems pleased to be with First Company and headquarters."

"Very pleased." Alcyna smiled. "So are the junior rankers who might have had to do time as duty drivers."

The coach drew to a halt.

"Marshal, sir?" called Sharua. "Is this your dwelling?"

"This is it." Dainyl opened the coach door and nodded for Alcyna to precede him. Then he stepped onto the still damp paving stones of the small front courtyard. "Thank you."

"My pleasure, sirs." The driver inclined her head.

Dainyl took the steps and opened the door.

Lystrana was waiting in the foyer.

"Alcyna, I'd like you to meet Lystrana," Dainyl said politely.

"It is good to finally meet you," offered Alcyna. "I've heard so much about you."

"And I, you," replied Lystrana politely. "I'm glad you arrived in Elcien safely. You accomplished much in the east, Dainyl said, and there's doubtless much he has not mentioned."

"He has mentioned very little about you, Lystrana, but I've heard much from others, and all of it is impressive."

"All of it is doubtless overstated," demurred Lystrana. "If you would care for some wine . . ." She gestured in the direction of the dining room and the sunroom beyond.

Dainyl and Alcyna followed her into the sunroom.

Dainyl poured two goblets of wine, and then added less than a finger full to the third goblet. After extending the near-empty goblet to his wife, he offered the tray with the two full goblets on it to Alcyna. "It's a Vyan Argentium, not quite up to the standards of the Argentium Grande from Elcadya, but very nice."

Alcyna laughed. "He forgets very little."

"Very little," Lystrana agreed, "but unlike many, he's not a slave to his memories." She settled into a straight-backed chair.

Dainyl let Alcyna have the settee and sat in the other straight-backed chair, the one that left his back to the window out into the courtyard.

Alcyna sipped the wine. "It is quite good."

"We enjoy it, but one has to be careful on a Myrmidon's pay, even when he's married to an important special assistant."

"You two are a remarkable pair," said Alcyna. "How did you meet?"

Dainyl and Lystrana exchanged glances. Lystrana raised one eyebrow. Dainyl nodded, almost imperceptibly, before taking a sip of the Argentium.

"At an administration of justice." Lystrana offered a smile somewhere between mischievous and amused. "He was an undercaptain and had the guard detail. I was the most junior assistant to the High Alector of Trade at the time."

Alcyna glanced from Lystrana to Dainyl. "That *is* unusual. What else is there that no one knows?"

"I'm sure that there's a great deal," Dainyl replied, "as there is for most pairs. We like gardens and flowers, and neither one of us is that good a cook—and my mother decidedly approves of that. Cooking turns the brain to mush, she once said."

"Your mother is Alyra, isn't she? The one who turned down the post of—"

"Everyone's heard of that, I think," replied Dainyl, with a tone of humorous resignation. "Arts administrator of Elcien, the post was titled. She said no one could or should administer the arts, and then she proceeded to do so for fifty years, without the title and only a minimal stipend. She thought that I had so little artistic ability that I might as well become a Myrmidon. I think I had one of the least rapid rises in Myrmidon history."

"That may have provided you with great advantages," suggested Alcyna.

He shrugged. "For a long time, no one paid any attention. That is useful, especially if one has a great deal to learn."

"I hope you like fowl," said Lystrana, looking at Alcyna. "I've had the girls prepare a family recipe, cider and honey-roasted, with nut-crusted long beans . . ."

Dainyl got the message—no more about Myrmidons or anything serious.

18

After morning muster on Londi, Mykel sat at the table in the officers' mess, the only large table in the compound besides those in the main mess, writing up his weekly report to Colonel Herolt. He had another day and a half before the next sandox coach run through Hyalt, but he hated to wait to write his reports. He'd always disliked leaving things to the last moment.

Rhystan stepped into the room. "Majer?"

Mykel looked up. "We don't have any orders yet, Rhystan."

"Yes, sir. That wasn't why I came in. There's a Myrmidon captain, landed on the pteridon square—the new one they just finished. She's asking for you."

"Frig . . . that can't be good news." Mykel slipped the sheets of paper into his leather case, then stood, and tucked the case under his arm.

"They can't always bring bad news, sir."

"Close enough." As he left the mess, Mykel strengthened his shields, in an effort to conceal his Talent from the Myrmidon, although he did not know how much Talent the officer might possess.

The pteridon squares were in the open area of the courtyard at the far north end, and Mykel walked quickly across the newly paved area. Only a small section in the northwest corner of the compound remained to be paved, but Poeldyn's men had stopped working and were watching the Myrmidon and the pteridon. A faint haze covered the southern third of the sky, and a hot breeze blew out of the southeast, suggesting even warmer weather to come later in the day, and possibly for several days to come. Mykel found himself blotting his forehead with the forearm of his tunic.

Several of the stoneworkers glanced at Mykel as he approached, but their eyes returned to the pteridon square.

"Majer Mykel? I'm Captain Lyzetta, Seventh Myrmidon Company out of Tempre." Standing beside the pteridon, the captain looked tall, even for an alectress. "The Marshal asked me to deliver your orders to you personally." She extended an envelope.

Mykel inclined his head politely. "Thank you."

"I also thought I'd let you know that you no longer need to provide perimeter security for the alector's compound west of Hyalt. We'll be bringing in engineers and personnel to rebuild."

"When do you want me to pull the patrols?"

"At dawn tomorrow, unless someone returns with a change."

"You'll have perimeter patrols until dawn tomorrow."

"Thank you, Majer." Captain Lyzetta swung up into the silvery saddle and fastened the riding harness with quick and practiced movements.

Mykel stepped back from the square, joining Rhystan. The two Cadmian officers watched as the pteridon spread its wings and sprang skyward. Again, Mykel sensed the burst of purpled Talent energy required for the creature to become airborne.

"Wonder what it's like to fly on one of those?" asked Rhystan.

"I'd just as soon not discover," replied Mykel. "Let's go back to the mess and see what the Marshal of Myrmidons has in mind for us. I'd feel slightly happier if the orders came from the submarshal." He paused. "Only slightly."

Rhystan glanced toward the departing pteridon once more.

"I have a few concerns when we get orders directly from the Myrmidons, rather than from the colonel."

So did Mykel, but he said nothing as he walked back toward the barracks. Once inside the small mess room, he opened the envelope and took out the papers inside. He began to read.

> The Third Battalion, Cadmian Mounted Rifles, Majer Mykel commanding, is hereby ordered to proceed immediately to Iron Stem. The commanding officer, Third Battalion, will assume full command of all Cadmian forces in the Iron Valleys, including but not limited to command over Fourth Battalion. He will take any and all steps necessary to restore complete civil and military order and will eliminate as necessary all predators and disturbing influences. . . .
>
> In proceeding to Iron Stem, Third Battalion will proceed by mount and wagon to Tempre, and take barge transport from Tempre to the river port of Dekhron . . .

Mykel finished reading the orders and instructions, then looked back at the title and signature under the orders proper: Dainyl, Marshal of Myrmidons.

"What is it, sir?"

"Submarshal Dainyl is now the marshal. The orders are from him." Mykel laid the orders on the mess table. "We're headed to Iron Stem. Half of Fourth Battalion was wiped out."

"Majer Hersiod isn't much better than Vaclyn. If you're junior to him . . ."

"He was among the casualties. We're in charge of all Cadmian forces in the Iron Valleys," Mykel replied. "And we have to deal with strange creatures like sandwolves, rebel miners, and predators supposedly nastier than anything we've faced yet."

"I think you were telling me that Marshal Dainyl was better than his predecessor." Rhystan raised his eyebrows.

"Well . . ." Mykel drew out the word. "He did put us in charge from the start."

"When do we leave?"

"Immediately. We'd better plan on Tridi morning. We'll take all the wagons and as many supplies as we can. We're to ride to Tempre and take barges upriver to Dekhron. Have you been there?"

"Years back. It gets cold in the winter, and the women aren't that friendly. The miners don't like anyone, and the holders north of Iron Stem are wealthy and arrogant. The garrison there isn't that big, either. Oh, and the air stinks from the ironworks."

"You're so cheerful, Rhystan."

"I'm only telling you what to expect, sir."

"I know. That doesn't even take into account the problems we're being sent to fix." Mykel had no doubts as to why Third Battalion was being sent. None at all, but he couldn't very well tell anyone, either, although Rhystan would certainly suspect those reasons. "We'd better tell the undercaptains, and see what supplies we can get from the locals."

Rhystan nodded as Mykel picked up the orders and tucked them into his leather case.

19

Dainyl looked at the message from the High Alector of Justice again, reading over the key phrases.

> . . . all unnecessary uses of resources by Myrmidon companies and associated units and activities should be deferred or minimized to the greatest extent possible . . . Likewise, use of pteridons and skylances should be restricted as much as possible to allow lifeforce on Acorus to increase in the immediate seasons ahead. . . .

Zelyert was all but admitting that the transfer of the Master Scepter was imminent, but that he didn't know exactly when it might occur. He folded the note, then laid it on the floor, extending a flash of Talent. Only fine ash remained.

His eyes drifted to the window, closed against the cold and damp wind blowing in out of the northwest. Londi had been warm enough, but from early on Duadi morning, the day had gotten progressively colder. Now, by midafternoon, high dark clouds had appeared in the west, and outside it was positively chill.

As he watched, a pteridon alighted on the flight stage. The flier carried a dispatch pouch, which she handed to Sharua. The duty messenger hurried toward headquarters, the wind blowing her hair around her face. Shortly, there was a knock on Dainyl's door.

"Marshal, sir, there's a dispatch from Captain Lyzetta. It came in marked urgent."

"Bring it in, Sharua." The last thing Dainyl needed was another urgent problem, especially one from Lyzetta.

The new duty messenger practically tiptoed into Dainyl's study, handed him the thin envelope, and quickly retreated, even before Dainyl could finish saying, "Thank you."

He opened the envelope and began to read.

> Marshal—
>
> I felt you should know about some other matters, as well as the progress of the rebuilding efforts. Rains have been extremely heavy for late harvest, and for some reason, the water level of the River Vedra has risen suddenly. East of Dekhron, the River Vedra is at flood stage already. The bridge at Emal has been destroyed. So have the barge piers at Dekhron. The late field crops in the area north of the River Vyana may all be lost.
>
> We have completed all of the initial transport required by the engineers, and all of the material and equipment was first carried to Tempre. We have since made some ten trips to Hyalt, and another ten remain. The engineers are asking for a pteridon to make small equipment flights every other day. Seventh Company can do so, but I told the engineer in charge that continuing flights would have to be approved by the marshal . . .

I would also note in passing that, as you instructed, I conveyed the orders for Third Battalion to Majer Mykel personally and relieved the Cadmians of the duty of guarding the perimeter around the regional alector's compound. The majer is highly skilled, and if not for his lander heritage, might well pass for an alector in all his capabilities, and I thought you would best be able to decide how to deal with his future assignments in that light.

Dainyl shook his head at the last paragraph. He would have to write an acknowledgment to Lyzetta, along with the background of the majer's next assignment. When he had promoted her to commanding officer, he had not realized her parentage, and that might have been for the best, but it was likely to cause additional problems for him in the troubled times ahead.

He took out paper and began to write, while he still had a few moments before something else transpired.

Captain Lyzetta—

I appreciate your dispatch and thorough report. You may supply pteridon transport to the engineers for another two weeks on an every other day basis. If more use of Seventh Company pteridons than that is required, please inform me, and I will take the matter up with the High Alector of Justice.

In regard to the other matter you mentioned, and for which I appreciate your diligence, Third Battalion is being transferred to Iron Stem to deal with certain problems created by the ancients, including the loss of more than half of the Fourth Battalion, Cadmian Mounted Rifles. I am certain that the majer's capabilities will prove useful in that unsettled locale. If necessary, and assuming that he has some success there, we will review his future options.

Dainyl remained torn about the majer. Talented landers were a great danger, and should be eliminated, but the unspoken policy did not indicate an absolute timing, and he did owe his life to the majer. Since the majer was in the field, and since he had neither wife nor any apparent close female ties, he was thus less likely to have offspring immediately. If Zelyert discovered the majer's abilities, and that seemed unlikely immediately, Dainyl could justify using Majer Mykel's Talent against the creatures of the ancients, rather than risking Myrmidons far from Elcien. Lyzetta's indirect communications with her father might be a greater danger, and that was why Dainyl had taken pains to spell out his rationale to a junior Myrmidon captain.

Because Dainyl needed to inform both the Duarch and High Alector Zelyert about the loss of the iron and coal loading piers in Dekhron, he immediately drafted a short message. While it would have been easier to send a copy of Lyzetta's message directly to them, he did not wish the second part of the message going anywhere. Quickly, he finished both copies. While he could have asked Doselt, the administrative clerk, to copy the second one, Dainyl could write out a second copy in less time than it would have taken to explain what he wanted.

With both copies in hand, he then headed to the administrative spaces.

"Doselt?"

"Yes, sir?" The squad leader jumped to his feet.

"Here are two reports. They need to go to High Alector Zelyert and the Duarch immediately. Please take care of it."

"Yes, sir."

Dainyl also needed to talk with Alcyna to discover what she had found out about the troubles in Eastice and to update her on the Table repairs. He turned from the records room and walked back down the corridor to Alcyna's study. Her door was ajar.

"Alcyna?" He stepped inside, but did not bother to close the door.

She looked up, then stood. "Yes, sir?"

He motioned for her to sit down and took the chair across from the desk that had once been his. "Have you found out anything new about what happened to the Cadmians in Eastice?"

"Some, sir. I went to the Hall of Justice, and had the recorder show me the site in the Table. A whole chunk of the cliff did give way. Chastyl pointed out that there were some silvery-green sparkles in the image, and that suggested the use of Talent. The green component . . ."

"The ancients helped it happen," Dainyl said.

"That would be my judgment. It was Chastyl's as well."

Dainyl fingered his chin. "I could see it if they had attacked Myrmidons—or engineers—but why the Cadmians? They're no threat to the ancients."

"What are you doing with the Cadmians, sir? Where are you sending Third Battalion?"

Dainyl laughed ironically. "You're suggesting that they're sending a message—that the Cadmians can't stand up to them. Is that a tactic to make us use Myrmidons?" He frowned. "It well could be. They don't operate far from higher locales."

"That would be my best guess," replied Alcyna.

"We'll have to see, then."

"You intend to wait and see what Majer Mykel can do? He's the one who handled the rebel alectors, is he not?"

"He is."

"It's said that he can recognize Talent and avoid it."

Dainyl wondered where she'd picked that up. It certainly wasn't in any of the records, but then, Alcyna had probably been the one to suborn the late Colonel Dhenyr, and she doubtless had her own sources. "He has some abilities, and he is a good, if not an excellent, field commander. It seemed prudent, in many respects, to send him and Third Battalion to Iron Stem. We will have to see what happens." He paused, then continued. "We haven't any updates on the Sixth Battalion in Soupat, either. Oh . . . and Captain Lyzetta just sent a message saying that the River Vedra is flooding in Emal and Dekhron. That may cause some delays in getting Third Battalion to the Iron Valleys. It will likely also cause delays in getting coke and iron to Faitel. I've taken steps to inform the Highest and the Duarch."

"You think the ancients know you're sending the Cadmians?"

"They might. It also might not matter to them. They could have their own agenda directly aimed at us."

"How intelligent are they, Marshal?"

"I would judge they are highly intelligent. At one time, they had a city where Dereka now stands, and they built the aqueduct to serve it. They created metals that are as hard as anything we can forge. They can destroy pteridons."

"Then why do they not control Acorus?" Alcyna's question mirrored curiosity, rather than exhibiting challenge.

"I would guess that they do not have many offspring and that they could not increase their numbers quickly when we began to warm the world. We also had the indigens to help."

"You're worried, aren't you?"

"I have to say that I am," Dainyl admitted. "The flooding and the cliff have to be their doing. The rains aren't heavy enough to create those floods by themselves, not in fall. And I don't like the possibility that they stole the skylances from Fifth Company in Dereka."

"You honestly think that?"

"It's a real likelihood. The lances are useless without a pteridon. That's why Rhelyn built lightcannon."

"But why . . ."

"What if they wanted to analyze them?" asked Dainyl.

Alcyna was silent for several moments. Then she said, "You've been studying the ancients, haven't you?"

"As I can," Dainyl replied. That was certainly truthful, if misleading. He stood. "Whenever you find out what's happened to Sixth Battalion, let me know."

Alcyna nodded.

Dainyl smiled pleasantly, then turned and left her study.

20

When Third Battalion had arrived in Tempre late on Novdi afternoon, Captain Lyzetta had immediately informed Mykel that the River Vedra was running too high and too turbulently for safe barge transport for the battalion, but that the water levels were expected to drop to near normal within the next few days. For that reason, Third Battalion would be staying at the compound with Seventh Company. Certainly, there was enough space. The compound had been built to hold more than a battalion of Alector's Guards, and a Myrmidon company only had twenty-one alectors, and the pteridons did not use the stables.

Even so, Mykel didn't like the idea of spending too much time around the captain. She did not have the Talent-strength that Submarshal—Marshal, Mykel corrected himself—Dainyl had, but Mykel suspected she was every bit as sharp. Still, there was little enough he could do about it.

On Londi, a glass after morning muster, Mykel crossed the compound courtyard, the cool breeze out of the northwest ruffling hair that needed to be cut. He'd just completed an informal inspection of the stables and the barracks and was enjoying the hazy sunshine and cooler weather in Tempre, a relief after the hot harvest days in Hyalt.

"Majer!" called Captain Lyzetta, stepping into view several yards ahead of him.

"Captain," returned Mykel pleasantly, tightening his shields and walking toward the tall alectress, stopping a yard or so short of her.

"I thought you would like to know that it's likely the river will return to close to normal levels within the next two days. Our scouts have observed that the rains have stopped and the stream levels to the east are dropping quickly. Submarshal Alcyna sent word that you should expect to embark on the barges at noon on Tridi."

"Thank you. I'm glad to know that." Mykel had no idea who Submarshal Alcyna was, except that the name indicated an alectress was Dainyl's successor as Myrmidon submarshal. "We've appreciated your hospitality while we've been delayed."

The captain smiled. "You were the one who turned the compound over to us in such excellent condition."

"We did the best we could on short notice."

"It was appreciated. Our move to Tempre was also on rather short notice." She paused, then asked, "You were with the marshal in Dramur, weren't you?"

"All of Third Battalion was, Captain."

"How did the difficulties in Tempre compare to those in Dramur?"

Mykel smiled, as pleasantly as he could. "You can't compare them. They were very different deployments. In Dramur we faced large numbers of local troopers, who had been hidden from both Cadmian and alector authorities, as well as a number of escaped rebellious miners. All had Cadmian rifles obtained in a manner against the Code. The actual fighting went on for close to two seasons. We were outnumbered, but better trained. The real fighting in Hyalt and Tempre was very brief. In Hyalt, Third Battalion was only slightly involved, primarily for scouting and perimeter patrols. In Tempre, we were attacked by a group of mounted guards who were of equal numbers and weapons. Their training was inferior, and we prevailed. Later, when we were guarding the regional complex"—Mykel nodded to the west—"we were attacked by rebel alectors with superior weapons but lesser numbers. We lost two squads in less than several glasses, but we had position, marksmanship, and numbers, and more ammunition, and in the end we reclaimed the building for the rightful administrators."

"We have not seen any trace of those armed Alector's Guards," Lyzetta said. "Could you tell me why that might be?"

"We killed over two-thirds of them, and the others scattered. Since having such a Guard is against the Code, and since the regional alector who created them did not return, I imagine that none of us will see the survivors. Not in uniform."

"Did you surprise them? Is it not unusual to gain such an overwhelming victory with equally sized forces?"

"Actually, Captain, they attempted a predawn attack. Most of my men were sleeping. We had less than half a glass notice."

Lyzetta nodded politely. "I won't keep you. Good day, Majer." She stepped back.

"Good day." Mykel was equally polite and pleasant, then continued across the courtyard to his quarters, where he intended to finish his report to Colonel Herolt because the sandox coach came through Tempre on Duadi morning.

As he made his way to the visiting officers' quarters,

Mykel pondered about the alectress captain. He could sense that she was intensely curious about him, as well as extremely wary and polite, and that she seemed to study him. He had not felt any Talent probes, but she merely might be waiting to catch him off guard.

Once back in his quarters, he used the small writing desk to finish a brief report to the colonel, brief because, fortunately, the battalion had seen no action. After that, he found his eyes going to the narrow window and his thoughts elsewhere.

Should he pay a call on Rachyla? How could he, after giving her the dagger of the ancients? Yet . . . He shook his head. One fact was simple. He wanted to see her. The other fact was that he didn't know what to do about her. He'd gone over their previous conversations and meetings, and it seemed as if she held two entirely different views of him. At times, she had been pleasant and at other times, sardonic and distant. Yet she had been truly concerned when he had been wounded, both in Dramur and Tempre, much as she had tried to conceal that concern.

Or was he seeing what he wanted to see?

What man did not?

Still, he had duties to see to, and he wanted to check on exactly how the battalion would be taken on the barges and what supplies would be necessary. Since Lyzetta had not known those details, he would have to ride to the piers and talk to the piermaster, or to someone there.

Finding out what he needed, in addition to arranging for equipment and other items, and finding a factor who would honor his letter of credit, took most of the rest of the duty day. Then he had spent another glass working out the arrangements for logistics with Bhoral, who, as battalion senior squad leader, had the duty of coordinating logistics.

Because Third Battalion was not heading back to Elcien, he wrote a quick letter to his parents, explaining that he was headed to Iron Stem. That would cost him a half silver to get delivered, but they would certainly pass the word to his brother and sister, although Sesalia was doubtless occupied with her five children. As for Viencet, who knew what he might be doing now that he'd finished his formal schooling?

Mykel feared that Viencet would continue to try to avoid real work, while finding excuses, and blaming others, as he had all too often in the past.

After that, even while he was telling himself he was being a fool, he finally rode out of the compound once more, taking the roan southwest along the Silk Road.

The guards at the gate to Amaryk's villa glanced at him, at his uniform. Then one spoke. "You're Majer Mykel?"

Mykel merely nodded as they opened the gates. He rode down the narrow drive to the courtyard off the small rotunda. There the doorman with the double daggers at his waist immediately tugged on the bellpull before Mykel announced himself and dismounted, walking up the steps to the small covered rotunda, but stopping well short of the doorman.

Shortly, the door opened, but only a fraction, although Mykel caught enough of a glimpse to know that Rachyla was behind the heavy oak door.

"Majer Mykel, Chatelaine," murmured the doorman.

After another moment, Rachyla stepped out, just beyond the archway. She wore dark gray trousers and vest, and a deep green shimmersilk shirt whose color matched that of her eyes.

"I had thought not to see you again, Majer. You did declare me your enemy . . . as I recall from our last meeting."

Mykel bowed and smiled politely. "Lady Rachyla, I never said you were my enemy. I recognized that you held me as your enemy. That was an accession to your views, a reluctant one, not a statement of mine."

"For a Cadmian officer, you are eloquent." For the briefest of moments, Rachyla hesitated before she continued. "There is little more to say, then. I'm sorry you traveled all the way from Hyalt for nothing."

"I was sent to Tempre en route elsewhere. Third Battalion is being dispatched to the Iron Valleys."

"By the great and glorious submarshal or by your own colonel?"

"Submarshal Dainyl has now become Marshal of Myrmidons. How that occurred, I have no idea, but the orders came from him."

"That is not all that surprising. I would suggest that he has yet another task for you. An unpleasant and difficult one. You are a useful tool, Majer. It is too bad that you cannot be more than that."

"We all do what we can with what we have, Lady—"

"I have told you that salutation is incorrect and improper."

"Since you hold me as your enemy, Lady, I believe I can address you as I see fit, so long as the salutation is one of respect, and I do believe that 'Lady' conveys respect. I have always respected you, although that is not why I am here. I thought it might be of some minor interest to you to know that we will be taking barges to Dekhron, once the river flows finish subsiding."

"Are you then off to slaughter more innocents, Majer?"

"If there is to be slaughter, it will not be of innocents. More than half of Fourth Battalion has already been destroyed."

"How fortunate for you that the marshal needs your services, Majer." Rachyla's voice remained cool.

"As you once observed to me, Lady, while one lives, there is always hope of improvement."

"Hope is a slender reed, Majer. It is best employed with children, who do not know that the faults, the status, and the reputation of their parents can often blight an otherwise bright future."

"Children have the right to their own future, and that does not always rest on their parents." Mykel wondered why he bothered . . . except there was an undercurrent behind Rachyla's words, one he had not identified.

"Perhaps in the north, Majer, but not in Dramur or Southgate, or even in Tempre. There, and here, position counts for more than ability or ambition. Or hope."

"But hope bends with winds that will destroy more rigid trees."

"Even you will not rely upon hope alone, Majer. Do not declare bootless hope and empty words."

"Neither my words nor my hope are empty." Mykel inclined his head politely. "Nor are yours, for all your deference to the past." He had to break through that coolness.

"You would speak to my hopes, now, Majer?"

"How could I not?"

"Do you not think that I might find that presumptuous?" She raised her eyebrows.

"You might indeed, but my presumptions are out of concern and respect. They always have been, despite your words and denials."

"I will admit that even with the restrictions placed on you in your position as a comparatively junior Cadmian officer, you have behaved with honor and respect, Majer. I might wish that circumstances were different, but as a landless daughter of a dead seltyr, I can only grant you respect."

That was a major concession, Mykel realized. He inclined his head in reply. "For now, Lady, I can ask no more. Again, I would thank you for your past kindness in restoring me to health."

"That was the least I could do for one who was an honorable enemy of my father." The faintest smile crossed Rachyla's lips. "You had best return to your duties, Majer. Perhaps I will see you again. Say, when you become a colonel."

Mykel wasn't about to accept that limitation. "The future will bring what it will, Lady, to both of us."

"That may be, Majer, but mastering the future is difficult and requires more than hope. Great power and substance are required. As of the present, you have neither." Her deep green eyes fixed on him, almost challenging.

"As of the present," Mykel acknowledged. "As of the present."

She nodded. "Then, there is little more to be said." She extended her hand, as if in dismissal. "I will wish you safe travels."

Mykel's fingers touched hers, lightly. He could sense . . . something. Fire? Hope? His fingers squeezed hers, ever so gently.

Hers tightened around his, almost imperceptibly, trembling, before she withdrew her hand. "Good day, Majer."

"I will not keep you. Good day, Lady Rachyla." He bowed again, then turned and walked back down the steps, where he untied his horse, and mounted.

Rachyla still stood outside the archway, but said nothing. Her eyes were bright.

Mykel inclined his head to her a last time, then eased the roan around and rode back up the narrow drive. He could feel her eyes on him, as well as another pair—those of Amaryk? With the factor watching, he dared not glance back. Even the hand touching could have endangered her.

He had conveyed his feelings. That he knew, but could he ever do more? What would it take to free her from her family in a way acceptable to her . . . and them? She had made it clear that she would not trade the prison of privilege for the prison of poverty—or what would be poverty to her.

Once outside the gates, he turned the roan back toward the stone compound.

21

As Mykel rode out of the undersized Cadmian compound on the eastern edge of Dekhron on Septi morning, he reflected on the previous three days. Proceeding from Tempre to Iron Stem had been anything but pleasant, what with further delays with the barges and the tugs, the lack of stalls or containment for the mounts, the rough water of the river, the heavy coal smoke, and the continual drizzle that had soaked everything.

After two and a half long days on the river, they had arrived in Dekhron, only to find that the piers had been washed away, and that the horses had to be walked down ramps into the water and led through frigid waist-deep water, and in places around blocks of rose-colored stones that were all that remained of the river piers.

Uniforms and mounts were wet and smeared with coal dust, and they were a sorry sight as they entered the Cadmian compound in Dekhron at midnight on Quinti. It had taken all of Sexdi to get dried out and reorganized—thankfully with a welcome sun. Mykel wasn't so certain that he wouldn't have preferred to ride the high roads from Tempre to Dekhron—except that more than eleven days on the road would have been even harder on the mounts.

On Septi morning, the battalion was cleaner, fed, and more rested. They rode out of the compound and followed the eternastone road westward through the center of Dekhron and then north, through what looked to be the less affluent areas. For all that Tempre was larger than Dekhron, the river town looked and felt far older than did Tempre. The larger streets leading off the eternastone main boulevard had been paved many years before, and now held grooves and chips in the stone, as well as off-colored replacement stones, and in some places, packed clay. The side lanes were dirt.

Mykel noted more than an occasional set of deserted stone walls and vacant lots filled with rubble between buildings. A large number of dwellings, at least those bordering the main boulevard that was the high road, were roofed with old and faded slates or cracked tiles. Early as it was, less than a glass past dawn, few people were on the streets, but even had it been later, Mykel had the feeling that there would not have been that many about.

For the first glass, Sixteenth Company led the Third Battalion, and Rhystan rode beside Mykel. Neither officer said much until they were several vingts north of Dekhron and the early sun fell full upon them.

"Good thing it's sunny," observed the captain. "Cold and damp on the river."

"I'm glad to be away from Hyalt—and Dekhron," Mykel said. "If it weren't for the mounts, I'd rather not have traveled by barge, though."

"It'll give the men something to talk about, and no one got hurt."

Mykel managed a smile. He had no desire to travel by barge again.

"That Myrmidon captain . . . she spent a lot of time looking at you, sir."

Mykel had spent more than a little time in Tempre avoiding Lyzetta. "Why do you think she was?"

"She's worried about you. She kept watching you the way my little brother used to look at snakes. Da said that he couldn't try to kill them, and to keep away. Williet would have tried anyway, if he hadn't been afraid of the whipping more than the snakes. That Captain Lyzetta had that same look."

"Who'd whip a Myrmidon captain?" Mykel knew, but he wanted Rhystan's reaction. "And why?"

"Marshal Dainyl, Majer. To me, that says that what we faced in Dramur and Hyalt will seem easy compared to what's up the road in Iron Stem."

"That could be. Or it could be that Hersiod was influenced by the former marshal, the way Vaclyn was, and now the new marshal needs us to clean up the mess."

"That's not much better, sir."

"I know." Mykel chuckled. "But we can always hope." *Just so long as we don't get deluded by that hope.*

22

Dainyl had already been restless before Zernylta brought in the report from Captain Lyzetta. It was already Septi—a week after Alcyna had arrived—and he'd heard nothing about any of the problems he'd faced then being resolved . . . or even showing signs of improvement. About the only positive event had been the return of the River Vedra to near-normal flows.

After Zernylta handed him the report and left, Dainyl slowly began to read what the junior captain had written.

> . . . repairs to the Table in Tempre have been completed, and the Table engineers report that the Table is fully functional . . . The Table in Hyalt was easier to repair, according to the engineers. It will take several weeks' more work before the cliff-tunneled section is again fully habitable. The engineers have recommended to their High Alector that the

> freestanding structure not be rebuilt at this time, unless the High Alector of Justice can fund the rebuilding. . . .

In short, thought Dainyl, the Myrmidons were being blamed for the destruction, as if there had been any other way to defeat Rhelyn's forces. Whether Zelyert knew or not, Dainyl needed to tell the High Alector before he was summoned before the Duarches to explain.

Dainyl forced himself to finish reading the rest of what Lyzetta had written.

> The Cadmian Third Battalion arrived safely in Dekhron and is proceeding to Iron Stem. There was some delay because of the river flooding and the slowness in unloading mounts in Dekhron without piers . . . Tempre remains with limited alector supervision . . .

That meant Duarch Samist had not named a regional alector to replace Fahylt, or that if he had, it had been recent enough that no one knew.

Dainyl folded the report and tucked it into his uniform tunic, then stood and hurried out of his study and down the corridor. Alcyna was out, supposedly dealing with Alseryl's assistants over the matter of younger sandox drivers being transferred as Myrmidon trainees, as well as discovering why the South Pass bridge could not be repaired more quickly.

Captain Zernylta was the headquarters duty officer—that was one responsibility that continued over from her previous position as squad leader. Saddling the other junior officers with extra watches would not have been a good idea.

"Zernylta, is the duty coach back?"

"Yes, sir. Sharua was about to pick up the submarshal at the Palace."

"She can take me to the Hall of Justice, and then pick up the submarshal and swing back to the Hall and wait for me. I need to see the Highest." If Zelyert weren't there, Dainyl would leave word with one of his assistants, but he needed to make the effort.

On the coach ride to the Hall, he couldn't help but worry

that he wasn't making much progress as marshal. That feeling continued, even as he made his way into the Hall and down to the lower levels, where he rapped on the closed door.

"Come in, Dainyl."

Dainyl stepped inside and closed the door behind him.

"You're obviously seeking me out, Marshal, and you look less than pleased. What is it that you feel I should know? Before you do, however, thank you for the information about the piers in Dekhron. It was useful to be able to point out to Ruvryn that some problems are not caused by Cadmians and Myrmidons."

"You sound as if you may already know what I wanted to tell you. The tables in Hyalt and Tempre are both functioning again, but it took more than two weeks' support by most of Seventh Company. That meant a great amount of lifeforce usage, and High Alector Ruvryn will attempt, if he has not already, to have Justice pay for rebuilding the freestanding structure destroyed in the conflict with the rebels in Hyalt."

"He has not said anything yet." Zelyert looked directly at Dainyl. "Why was destroying the structure necessary?"

"As I indicated when I first returned from Hyalt, the question was how many Myrmidons would be killed by the methods we chose. I chose the method that would produce the fewest Myrmidon casualties. Had I chosen a method that spared the structure, Fifth Company would possibly be at as little as half-strength. I suspect that was in fact what Brekylt had in mind, and that we would use First Company. We have barely been able to replace the seven Myrmidons lost from Seventh and Fifth Companies. It is unlikely that we could replace any significant number more for at least several months. The High Alector of Transport is less than pleased at our request for more trainees. The submarshal has been spending much of her time on placating Transport and seeking more trainees."

"Myrmidons are not supposed to be killed by rebels." Zelyert's tone was mocking. "That is exactly how Duarch Samist stated his objections last week."

"We have not lost a single Myrmidon to landers or indigens. We lost every single one to other alectors, a number to lightcannon that should never have been built." Dainyl did not mention that he had been forced to kill three of the rebel-suborned officers of Seventh Company. "That suggests that the High Alector of Engineering has been rather lax in his oversight, if not tacitly in support of the rebels."

Zelyert laughed, a low rumbling sound. "I can only suggest laxity in oversight at the moment. That should be sufficient." He paused, then asked, "Has anything new happened in the Iron Valleys?"

"Third Battalion should be there tomorrow. They were delayed by the floods and the loss of the piers at Dekhron. There is no sign of adverse action by the ancients."

"Not that you know about."

"That is true, sir."

"You may be requested to brief the Duarch on that—and to explain again the reason for your tactics in Hyalt."

"I will be happy to do so, sir." Dainyl had very conflicted feelings about that, especially about explaining again what he had already explained.

"Is there anything else, Marshal?"

"No, sir."

Zelyert rose. "Then I need to depart for the Palace. The Duarch is greatly concerned about the number of criminals fleeing Ifryn and translating to Acorus. Even if they are executed immediately, the translation tube linkage creates a life-force loss. For a handful, that is not a problem, but we're seeing more than handfuls."

Dainyl stood. "That suggests that order on Ifryn is breaking down and that it will not be long before the Master Scepter is transferred." He paused. "Is it possible that some of those translating here have been tacitly encouraged and allowed to reach the Tables in order to reduce the pressure on Efra?"

"There's no doubt about that," returned Zelyert, his tone ironic, "but it would do little good to tell the Duarch so."

"Because we can't do anything about it but accept alectors or kill them?"

"I don't see any of us trying to translate to Ifryn to complain to the Archon." Zelyert gestured to the door.

"Until later, sir." Dainyl took the hint, bowed, and departed.

As he headed back up the steps to the main level of the Hall, Dainyl could not help but shiver slightly at what he knew was occurring all across Acorus. The world was a refuge for alectors, but a refuge that could only hold so many. If too many flooded through the Tables . . .

He shook his head.

23

The sun hung low over the Westerhills, and a cool breeze threatening chill blew out of the northeast, seemingly straight from the towering cliffs that marked the Aerlal Plateau some forty vingts away. Third Battalion had ridden all Septi, with minimal breaks, and Mykel's shoulder and back had begun to ache, reminding him that he was not quite healed from his injuries.

Not long after he saw the waystone announcing Iron Stem was but three vingts ahead, Mykel ordered the battalion off the road to allow another heavy black wagon, bearing iron pigs, drawn by eight dray horses, to rumble past them, heading south for Dekhron. Mykel had not told any of the drivers that the loading piers had been destroyed. Either the iron would wait there, or the piermasters would find some way to transfer it to the barges for the trip down the Vedra to the engineers and forges of Faitel.

While Mykel could not see the town ahead, only a scattering of cots and outbuildings amid the rectangular fields and oak forests whose leaves had begun to turn, he could make out a reddish glow coming from the north, somewhere to the west of the high road.

"That must be the ironworks," he said to Culeyt, captain of Sixteenth Company, who rode beside him.

"Sir?"

"There's a glow up ahead on the left."

"You must have better eyes than me, sir. I can't make it out."

"It's there."

From somewhere in the Cadmians riding behind them, Mykel caught the murmurs.

"Majer sees stuff vingts before anyone else . . ."

". . . hears things, too," came the unmistakable tone of a squad leader.

There were no more murmurs for the moment.

Another quarter glass of riding brought Mykel and the vanguard to where they could make out the rough outline of the town ahead. In the twilight, a haze enveloped the dwellings and buildings, a haze that almost glowed.

Before long, the high road had become the main north–south avenue of Iron Stem, with modest dwellings and occasional shops fronting it. Most of the structures were of brick or stone, with split slate roofs, and all seemed modest. Ahead lay the town square, a stone-paved area empty except for the granite pedestal with the statue of the Duarches in the middle. On the south side was the town fountain, and two stone troughs for watering mounts and dray horses. The east side contained a cloth factor's, adjoining a weaver's. An old two-story inn dominated the west side. It had been constructed completely of brick and stone, which dated it back centuries, to the time before timbering had been permitted from the forests to the west and south of the town.

On the north side of the square were four shops, side by side and seemingly identical, except that the shutters and doors had been painted differing colors, with each set of shutters matching that shop's door. The colors might once have been bright, but even in the fading light of the day, it was clear that the soot and grit from the ironworks had grayed and dimmed them. Even the windowpanes looked gray. Although the inn had wide covered porches, supported by brick columns, not a single person stood outside. Even so, the windows on the main level were bright and cheery, but the clicking of hoofs on the stone echoed emptily across the square.

As the battalion continued northward, the very air Mykel inhaled felt dry, thin, and each breath burned with the mixture of fine dust and smoke and vapor. By now, all the Cadmians could see the stone smokestacks and the high walls of the ironworks ahead and to the left of the high road, looming over the tiny dwellings between the main avenue and the works.

A wide short stone way led from the high road to the works, and some fifty yards to the west of where Mykel rode was a loading yard. Late as it was, a crew was working the winches powering the crane that lifted the iron pigs onto one of the black transport wagons. Another winch and crane stood idle, and the iron pigs were stacked on the loading dock waiting to be loaded into a second empty wagon behind the first.

The overseer shouted out orders, but the roaring of the furnaces drowned out the man's orders. Hot and acrid air swirled around Mykel, mixing with the cool northeast breeze.

Mykel pulled his gaze to the road ahead.

Immediately north of the ironworks were shops and buildings so dingy that in the twilight Mykel could not determine what they might be. Farther along were small houses, little more than huts bathed in soot. The few curtains that did hang in windows, those that were lit by lamps inside the poor dwellings, looked to be various shades of gray.

Even more to the north Mykel could make out the green spire of a Duarchy tower, supposedly beyond the Cadmian compound. "That's where we're headed."

"Mean-looking town, sir," observed Culeyt.

"Hard-looking town, that's for sure."

Third Battalion covered another vingt and a half before reaching the Cadmian garrison, or compound, at the north end of the town, separated from any dwellings by a quarter vingt of open space. The walls hardly qualified as such, standing little more than two yards high, constructed of but a single course of stone in thickness. The main gates were only iron grills, and Mykel thought that they were rusted open. To the north was the green stone tower, its iron-bound door locked, as were those of all Duarchy towers. Mykel wondered, not for the first time, why such towers had been built all across Corus when they never seemed to be used.

The single guard took one look at the riders and bolted for the small headquarters building that stood in front of a long and close to ramshackle stone barracks.

As he rode past the two-story barracks toward the stables, Mykel noted that some of the roof tiles were askew and others badly cracked. He had barely dismounted outside the stables when a short and muscular Cadmian officer hurried across the courtyard. Mykel turned, and the officer stopped, taking in the majer's insignia.

"Captain Hamylt, sir. I'm the senior officer left here, commanding Nineteenth Company and what's left of Fourth Battalion."

"Majer Mykel, Third Battalion. We've been ordered here by the Marshal of Myrmidons."

"Yes, sir. Ah . . ."

"We've come directly from Hyalt. Once we get the men squared away, Captain, I suggest we meet and discuss what's happened here, and what the marshal intends. If you'd also notify the cooks. In the mess in around a glass?"

"Yes, sir. Majer Hersiod's quarters—they were his—they're at the end of the barracks on the upper level on the north side. The other officers . . . well, there are two bunks to each junior's room."

"Good." Mykel gestured. "Bhoral?"

The battalion senior squad leader eased his mount forward.

"Captain, this is Bhoral, the battalion senior squad leader. If you would introduce him to whoever is in charge of billeting . . ."

"Yes, sir."

Mykel led the roan into the stable and took the first open stall that had an officer's mark on the post beside it. He finished grooming the roan and, gear on his shoulder, was checking how many of the mounts were double-stalled when Bhoral reappeared.

"Majer . . . there aren't enough bunks, or pallets. We'll have to double up . . . some of the men will have to use bedrolls," Bhoral said.

"There's no help for it. Tell the company officers, and do the best you can."

"Yes, sir."

Mykel's next stop was the main mess. The local cooks

might have been unhappy with preparing a second meal for over four hundred hungry troopers, but they had managed.

Mykel made his way back to the kitchen area and located the head cook. "I wanted to thank you. This is one of the few hot meals the men have had in days."

"Yes, sir . . . if we'd had more notice . . . it's dried mutton and sauce and potatoes."

"I'm sure they're happy to get a decent hot meal."

From the kitchen Mykel headed to the officers' mess, a narrow room with two tables. Three of Third Battalion's officers had arrived—Fabrytal, Culeyt, and Loryalt.

Hamylt was waiting, standing in the corner. "Majer."

"Let's step outside," Mykel suggested.

"I've been using the majer's study, sir. It's not far."

"That will be fine." Mykel followed Hamylt across the short stretch of paved courtyard between the mess hall and the headquarters building and then down a narrow corridor.

Hamylt lit a single lamp in a wall sconce, then turned. "Yes, sir?"

"Just so we're perfectly clear," Mykel said quietly, handing a copy of his orders to the captain, "I'd like you to read these." He remained standing, watching with his sight and senses.

Captain Hamylt paused after the first paragraph, then kept reading. Finally, he looked up. "The marshal is very clear. You're in command of all Cadmians. Wasn't he the submarshal, sir?"

"He was, but after the operations in Tempre and Hyalt he became marshal. Some alectors rebelled. The marshal, two Myrmidon companies, and Third Battalion destroyed them. The Myrmidons took care of Hyalt. We took care of Tempre."

"Against alectors, sir?"

"Against most of a battalion of mounted rifles created by the regional alector, and against somewhere around forty alectors with lightcutters. We killed two-thirds of the mounted rifles and the rest scattered. The alectors attacked later. We lost two squads. They lost everyone." That was true, if slightly misleading. Mykel could sense both apprehension and caution from Hamylt. "Now . . . tell me exactly what happened . . . and what you've done since."

"Yes, sir. We've been here since late spring. Majer Hersiod had to discipline the garrison here. The iron miners had shut down the mines. Then coal miners joined them. They said conditions in the mines were killing too many miners. The undercaptain said he wasn't about to shoot miners, not until he had orders from the High Alector of Engineering or whoever was in charge of the mines. The majer—he disagreed. I didn't see what happened between the two of them, but there was some sort of argument, and the undercaptain walked out. The majer sent troops after him, and they brought him back, and there was a court-martial. The undercaptain was found guilty of five charges."

Mykel could see how that could have happened with Hersiod. "What was the sentence?"

"Death, sir. By firing squad."

"He didn't send the sentence to the colonel for review?"

"He didn't have to, sir. He said Iron Stem was a combat zone."

That was certainly true now . . . but at the time, there had been no combat, only miners who refused to work. "Were the miners armed?"

Hamylt offered a puzzled frown. "No, sir. Except with shovels and picks, that sort of thing."

"All right. How did Fourth Battalion lose half its men?"

"It wasn't like that, sir. Except for the last . . . I wouldn't call it a battle, except I guess it was . . . except for that, we lost a man here and a man there, but it happened almost every time there was a patrol."

"What were you patrolling for, or against?"

"The local herders, the ones who live within five vingts of town, they started losing livestock, cows and sheep, to the wolves. Some call them ice-wolves, and some say they're sandwolves, but whatever they are, they're nasty beasts. Close to three yards long, and they can run down a mount at a full gallop. They've got teeth like crystal knives a span long and sharper than a razor. Unless you get a bullet in their brain, maybe two, nothing seems to stop them."

"When do they attack?"

"Anytime, but mostly in the day, because the herders lock up their stock at night. We'd send out a squad and end up losing a scout or a flanker . . . no ranker wanted to ride those positions . . ."

As Hamylt continued, Mykel listened. He hoped he could learn enough to piece together what had really happened.

". . . and last month . . . that was when the majer got word that the miners had gathered in the hills north of the mines . . . decided that he'd put a stop to it all. Took the whole battalion out . . . except there weren't just miners there . . . a bunch of Squawts and Reillies and when the shooting started, the sandwolves showed up and then the sander things . . ."

"Sander things?"

"They're creatures that look like a clay figure of a man made by a child. You can hardly see their eyes, and their skin is colored like tan sand, and it sparkles. They touch anything, and it dies, just like that. There were even things with wings that glowed green and flew, some of the men said. I never saw one, but . . ." Hamylt shrugged. "Anyway . . . what with one thing and another, we lost over two hundred rankers right there . . . killed a third of the miners, I heard, but once the majer went down, I tried to hold things together and get what was left of the battalion out of there."

"What have you done since then?"

"Mainly routine patrols against the sandwolves. The miners went back to work, those that were still alive."

"Just like that?" asked Mykel.

"Seems strange," admitted Hamylt, "but that's the way it is, and I'm not one to go stir up trouble after all that's happened."

Mykel knew he was tired, especially after the long ride from Dekhron, and he should have had more questions, but he needed to think things over. He nodded. "It is strange, and we'll talk more later after I've had a chance to go over matters. Thank you."

"Yes, sir. Will that be all, sir?"

"For now, Captain. I'll see you in the morning."

"Yes, sir. I'll have my gear out of here before muster tomorrow."

"I'd appreciate that." Mykel smiled politely.

After he left Hamylt, Mykel crossed the dusty paving stones to the barracks building and quietly climbed the outside stairs to the officers' quarters in the upper level, quarters that Majer Hersiod had occupied not so long ago.

From the paved area below, he heard voices, and he listened from back in the shadows.

"Third Battalion? Majer Mykel? They sent the Dagger? May the ancients save us . . ."

Mykel smiled sadly at the juxtaposition of the terms. The ancients were the reason he was called the Dagger.

24

Early on Octdi, right after morning muster, Mykel took over the study used by Hersiod and then Hamylt. He ordered Hamylt to continue what he'd been doing with his patrols for the next day. Then he began to study the maps of the area to get a better sense of where the events related by Hamylt had taken place. Mykel wasn't about to send any of Third Battalion's companies off anywhere until he had a better grasp of the situation. Once he finished looking at the maps and reports, such as they were, he wanted to look over the records of the court-martial—although he had his doubts about their accuracy.

A glass later, he'd finished with the maps and was halfway through the reports.

"Sir?" Bhoral knocked on the side of the open study door. "There's someone to see you. Gosyt says he's one of the big landholders north of Iron Stem."

That was another complication Mykel didn't need. "I'll see him. Do I need to come out?"

"Ah . . . no, sir."

Even before Bhoral finished speaking, a tall lander appeared.

"How kind of you to condescend to see me, Majer."

Mykel stood slowly and looked hard at the holder, a man a good ten years older than Mykel, about the same height, but more heavily muscled, and with a tanned, weathered, and clean-shaven face.

After a long moment of silence, Mykel replied coolly, "I don't condescend, and I don't care much for it from others." He gestured to the chair in front of the writing desk, then sat without waiting for a response from the holder. "I'm Majer Mykel. I didn't get your name."

"Croyalt." The holder sat easily in the chair.

"What can I do for you, Croyalt?" Mykel managed to sound pleasant, although he could sense anger from the holder.

"You can take your troopers and leave. Everything here was just fine until you Cadmians arrived."

"That's a pleasant thought," replied Mykel. "But as I understand it, the additional Cadmians weren't sent here until after someone cut sections of forest against the Code, and some of the miners used explosives to collapse one of the shafts in the coal mines."

"That didn't have anything to do with the herders and holders. That was between the alectors and the miners and the local building crafters."

Mykel offered a puzzled expression. "I'm not certain I understand what your point is, Holder Croyalt. There were two significant violations of the Code before Fourth Battalion was sent, and yet you claim that there were no troubles."

"The marshal sent some Myrmidons, and before long, everything was under control. It was after they left."

"What happened then?"

"The iron miners—the malcontents—they said that it was easier to top the hills than to tunnel, and they claimed miners had died because of that. The coal miners said that the lower tunnels were unsafe. All the miners refused to work. The local Cadmian officer claimed he wasn't going to shoot men for that."

"So he was replaced by Majer Hersiod?"

"That bastard Hersiod came in, trumped up some sort of trial, and executed the undercaptain for some charge and then sent the two squad leaders who objected to his actions off to the mines as malcontents."

Mykel managed to avoid wincing.

"Then he threatened to take over the stead of any outholder who objected."

"Outholders are those farther from Iron Stem?"

"More than ten vingts. So we all avoided Iron Stem much as we could." Croyalt snorted. "Soon as Hersiod gets himself killed, we get another Cadmian battalion."

"How did he manage to lose so many men?"

"Stupidity. Those little rifles you Cadmians use aren't that effective against sandwolves, and if you don't have a lot of men firing at them . . ."

Mykel managed to keep his expression pleasant. Croyalt was implying that the outholders not only had rifles, which was generally against the Code, but that their weapons had far more stopping power. "Did Hersiod know you'd developed bigger bore rifles?"

"How would he? He never listened to anyone."

"Does anyone use them except outholders?"

Croyalt frowned. "There's no reason for anyone else to."

"I can see that." Mykel nodded. "How long have you had to deal with the sandwolves?"

"They've been here as long as there have been outholders. Seems like there have been more this year and last, but we don't really keep count."

"Majer Hersiod reported that they were attacking livestock of the local holders and that they were a new threat in the area closer to Iron Stem. Was he mistaken about that, too?"

Croyalt tilted his head. "That might be true. Usually the sandwolves avoid people, unless they can catch them alone." He grinned. "Could also be that they found Cadmian patrols easy pickings."

"Do you know how Hersiod lost so many men against the miners?"

"He didn't. Murderous bastard killed more than half the ones that were gathered out on the hill. They were just having a meeting. All the killing drew the sandwolves and the sanders . . ." He shook his head. "Don't want to mess with sanders. Don't see many, but you see one, and you head the other way. If you want to stay alive, anyway. They'll chase livestock, but not people."

"How would you suggest we handle the sandwolves?"

"If you have to patrol, with lots of men throwing lead."

"What else should I know?" Mykel asked. "Besides the fact that my predecessor was stupid, didn't listen, and didn't have the right equipment and tactics?"

Croyalt grinned once more, then stood. "That's about it, Majer. Except that you still ought to leave well enough alone."

Mykel stood as well. "The Marshal of Myrmidons ordered us here directly. That means I can't very well leave, but I do appreciate your coming in."

Croyalt nodded brusquely. "Don't envy you, Majer. Not at all. Could be a long cold winter. Good day." He stepped out of the study.

After Croyalt left, Mykel began to search through the file cases. It took him half a glass, but he finally found the record of the court-martial of Undercaptain Emolart, such as it was. Emolart had been charged with three counts of failure to carry out the orders of a superior officer, disrespect to a superior, and striking a senior officer. He'd been shot by a firing squad the night of the court-martial.

There was no transcript, and only a brief summary of the alleged events. After having known Majer Hersiod and almost suffering the same fate as Emolart, except at the hands of Majer Vaclyn, Mykel had no doubts that Croyalt had been basically accurate in his assessments.

Mykel replaced the files and closed the box. He just stood there and looked at the wall.

Why had the previous marshal wanted both Hersiod and Vaclyn to do stupid things? It was as if he'd wanted to destroy the effectiveness of the Cadmians. But for what reason? If Rachyla were right, that the Cadmians were the alectors' sheep dogs, what purpose was served by destroying them?

Then, too, there were the outholders. They were breaking the Code with their heavier rifles. But Croyalt had been telling the truth about the sandwolves, and that meant that the outholders had been using heavy rifles against the sandwolves for generations—despite Hersiod's report that the sandwolves were a "new" predator.

Had the alectors ignored the Code-breaking? Or had the outholders kept it secret? Had there been some sort of tacit agreement? Had the alectors decided to break that agreement, or had they only just discovered what the outholders had been doing? Given the Talent skills of the alectors and their Tables, Mykel doubted that the heavy rifles had been unknown to all alectors.

Then, there were the questions surrounding the miners. From what Mykel had discovered so far, over the past two years, the miners—mainly malcontents sentenced to terms in the iron and coal mines—had been forced to work longer and harder for reasons that no one had spelled out anywhere. More had died, so many that the survivors had risked death to try to change matters, except . . . if Croyalt happened to be correct, Hersiod had decided on his own to teach them a lesson. That didn't make sense, either, because dead miners didn't mine anything.

Uneasy as he had been before, Mykel was feeling even more so with every glass he spent in Iron Stem.

25

Midmorning on Londi found Dainyl in the Hall of Justice, sitting across the small table from the High Alector.

"I must say, Dainyl, that your handling of the Third Cadmian Battalion is masterful," Zelyert observed with a broad smile. "You did not let them return to Elcien, but immediately dispatched them to Iron Stem. That way, there is far less chance of contamination once matters are resolved."

"That seemed to make the most sense." How much did Zelyert know? "I did worry about them realizing their effectiveness in dealing with the rebels in Tempre."

"Shastylt would never have considered that. He had a tendency to underestimate all those below him—as you well know."

"I've discovered that some of the Cadmian officers are quite resourceful," Dainyl temporized. "That can resolve immediate difficulties, but . . ." He shrugged.

"Exactly. There is a balance involved. We need resourceful monitors to control the steers, but monitors who understand and accept that they are indeed our monitors, working under our guidance." The High Alector of Justice smiled coolly. "What do you intend to do with Majer Mykel?"

"Nothing—not until I find out what really is happening in the Iron Valleys. He is most resourceful. Everything I have seen suggests that the ancients are planning something there. It is in his self-interest to oppose whatever they have in mind. I would prefer using him rather than hazarding Myrmidons, or removing them from Elcien, especially since there are indications of growing . . . mutual interest between Ruvryn, Brekylt, and the Duarch Samist."

"Do you think Submarshal Noryan will follow you and Submarshal Alcyna, or High Alector Brekylt—in a case of divided loyalties, shall we say?"

"That will depend on the circumstances. Noryan is a very direct officer."

"You know he is not who everyone thinks he is, yet you think he will oppose Brekylt?"

Not only had Dainyl never mentioned Majer Mykel's abilities to Zelyert, but he had also never revealed Noryan's false identity to anyone besides Lystrana except to Shastylt and Captain Sevasya. As Khelaryt's daughter, Sevasya was highly unlikely to have told Zelyert, and Shastylt was dead. Although Dainyl couldn't have verified it in any way, he doubted that Shastylt would have told Zelyert about Noryan. "I don't know. Under certain circumstances, it might be possible." Dainyl offered an ironic smile. "I'm not counting on such. That is one reason why Seventh Company has been relocated to Tempre."

"That was another good move. It limits the scope of

Brekylt's possible influence." Zelyert steepled his long fingers. "Still . . . I think you should give a full account of the latest developments to the Duarch directly. I've made arrangements for you to see him tomorrow morning, at the third glass of morning."

Dainyl almost protested. Not that much had happened since he had last briefed the Duarch. "What else would you like me to convey?"

The High Alector offered a deep, warm, and rumbling chuckle. "Any reaction the Duarch might have, especially to the . . . positioning of Seventh Company."

"If he has one, sir."

"That will be a reaction as well. You might also mention that the number of attempted long translations from Ifryn is continuing to increase."

Although Zelyert's words suggested Dainyl had an option, it was clear that the High Alector wanted Dainyl to deliver the general news about the long translations before Zelyert provided actual numbers. That meant the increased numbers were very bad. "Should I know actual figures?"

"You continually amaze me, Dainyl. I don't know whether that's always good. No. You shouldn't, and I won't tell you. Khelaryt could read any deception on your part."

With the amount of Talent the Duarch possessed, Dainyl knew that was certainly true.

"One other thing," said Zelyert. "How long before the ancients act?"

Dainyl hadn't the faintest idea, although it would not be that long, and would depend on the timing of the transfer of the Master Scepter. "I have no indication. You might have a better idea than I do."

"They cannot know when the Scepter will be transferred. So . . . it is likely to be sometime after that."

Dainyl nodded. "What will happen to the translation tubes to Ifryn?"

"The one linking the Master Scepter to the dual scepters will shift from Ifryn to Efra. The one between Efra and Ifryn will vanish."

That made an unfortunate kind of sense.

"And . . . what will happen on Ifryn?"

"With the higher lifeforce dwindling, most alectors remaining there will soon die. The few that survive will wish they had not. The less intelligent indigens will revert to their sources. Other life on the world will survive, but it will not be fit for intelligence for eons, if ever."

The thought of all the glorious cities on Ifryn standing as lifeless monuments, slowly decaying as even the lifeforce in the eternastone bled away, chilled Dainyl.

"We cannot dwell upon the past, Marshal. We can only build the future."

But what kind of a future, and who was really building it?

"Yes, sir." Dainyl smiled politely.

26

Under a cool noonday sun that filtered down through a hazy fall sky, Mykel rode westward along the narrow stock trail that arced gradually toward the southeast through the low rolling hills that held spiky bushes and intermittent clumps of irongrass. Undercaptain Loryalt rode beside him and Seventeenth Company behind them, with four scouts half a vingt ahead. For the past four days, he'd gone on patrols with various Third Battalion companies, without even a glimpse of the fearsome sandwolves. All he'd seen besides the livestock of the local inholders were the smaller local animals like the grayjays and the rodentlike scrats.

Mykel wondered if he should have spent more time at the garrison. But then, despite what Croyalt had said about there being no real problem outside of Iron Stem, Mykel had definite concerns about predators that had wiped out half a battalion.

As he rode, he was all too conscious of the massive ramparts of the Aerlal Plateau rising to the east, even more impressive when he considered that they were some thirty vingts away. A wall against the sunrise, he reflected, or perhaps one to hold back night. He'd heard how the stone cliffs rose some six thousand yards near-vertically, but hearing and seeing were two different things.

"Hate to try to climb those," offered Loryalt, gesturing eastward.

"I don't think you could, not if all the sides are that sheer." Mykel stiffened in the saddle. He sensed something—a grayish violet and then a reddish violet that seemed to come and go—but what he felt came from behind the column. Were the sandwolves stalking the last squad?

"Rifles ready," Mykel ordered, turning to Loryalt and adding in a lower voice, "You're in command here. I'm heading to the rear of the column."

"Rifles ready!" echoed the undercaptain. "Pass it back." After a moment, he asked, "Do you know what kind of trouble?"

"Not yet." Mykel turned the roan out to the right, avoiding the prickly-looking bushes whose lower shoots could rip through flesh and leather, and then began to ride back west, paralleling the column. He eased his rifle from the holder.

"Trouble . . . Majer's got that look . . ."

"Rifle out, too."

"Don't see anything . . ."

Mykel was only halfway back along the column, passing third squad, when a dark form charged from what seemed open ground, yet Mykel had not seen it a moment before. His rifle was up, and he fired immediately, willing the shot toward the creature.

The sandwolf shuddered, and slowed, but only for a moment.

"Column halt! Fire at will!" Mykel followed his own orders with another shot, as did several of the rankers in fifth squad.

The creature collapsed less than a handful of yards from the last rider, but more than a score of the sandwolves appeared on both sides of the column, converging on fifth squad. Not only could he see them, but he could sense their gray-violet auras as clearly as he could the auras of either alectors or the rankers around him.

Even as Mykel aimed, and fired, aimed and fired, taking

down one sandwolf, and then another, he could sense something else, the reddish violet auras, but those were coming from the front of the column. He could only hope that Loryalt could handle whatever menace had appeared there.

The short and continuous barrage of fire that had flowed from fourth and fifth squad died away as the remaining sandwolves broke off their attacks and then seemingly vanished. Mykel thought he had sensed one death, but for all he knew that could have been one of the sandwolves. He could see one trooper having an arm bound.

"Reload and keep a sharp eye out!" Mykel turned the roan and reloaded once more while he rode forward, back toward the head of the column.

Ahead of him, scattered shots continued for several moments before becoming intermittent and then ceasing.

Loryalt and first squad had ridden forward toward where the scouts had been. As he neared the undercaptain, Mykel saw two mounted scouts and two riderless horses ahead of Loryalt. When he had ridden within thirty yards of the scouts and Loryalt, he could make out two Cadmians sprawled on the sandy soil, one on each side of the trail. They were dead. Neither had an aura.

Mykel reined up beside Loryalt. "What happened?"

"I . . . I never saw anything like it, sir." The undercaptain gestured to the unmoving forms. "Two creatures like stocky little men appeared out of the ground. Each of them dragged a trooper right off his mount. They held them for a moment, and then they vanished. I think the men are dead."

"You're right." Mykel managed not to swallow. He'd seen the creatures before—in Dramur. He just hadn't equated them with the sanders that Croyalt had mentioned.

"What were . . . those things, sir?"

"They're called sanders. Outholder Croyalt warned me about them. They killed a lot of troopers in Fourth Battalion. He said they were best avoided. We didn't seem to have that option today." He paused. "Strap them over their saddles."

"Yes, sir." Loryalt turned. "Mysaelt, Sedryk . . . get them over their saddles." He looked to Mykel.

"Once we deal with the casualties, we'll follow the trail around to the northeast road back to Iron Stem," Mykel said. "That's quicker than retracing the way we came."

"Sir? In the rear?"

"Oh . . . sandwolves. More than a score. I didn't wait to learn casualties, but I got the impression that there were more wounds than fatalities."

"There aren't even any livestock near here." Loryalt sounded almost aggrieved. "We didn't attack anyone."

"We're interlopers," Mykel pointed out. *Both to the sandwolves and the outholders,* he thought. "Get a report on casualties, and let's get riding."

"Yes, sir." Loryalt turned his mount. "Company, order! Squad leaders, report!"

Mykel glanced out over the low rolling hills toward the plateau, then to the southeast along the stock trail.

Had the sanders set the sandwolves on the rear of the column to draw Mykel away? Or was that a coincidence? How smart were the manlike creatures? Or had both been directed by the soarers? But why? The soarer had as much as told him that the alectors were the enemy of landers and indigens and especially of the soarers. Cadmians weren't an enemy of the soarers. So why had the soarers let the sanders attack the Cadmians? Or were there tame sanders and wild sanders?

27

Power as wielded by an alector comes in many different forms. There is the power of a weapon, a skylance or a lightcutter. There is the power of law, as enforced by the High Alectors of Justice. There is the power of structure, as demonstrated by the cities created and ruled by the Archon. There is the power of example, and the power of tradition.

Whatever the form of power, it can be used only in two fashions, either as a tool for creation or preservation or as a means of destruction. The forms of power can be employed constructively in a myriad of fashions, as all intelligent alectors should know, but the most dangerous and self-deceptive use of power consists of those instances where an alector employs power for the sole sake of demonstrating that power.

If a demonstration of power is required, then the alector who conducts or orders such a demonstration has already failed in the constructive use of power, or he is attempting to create an image of greater power to the end of instilling fear or greater respect from others. Those who are weaker will indeed bow to that demonstration of power—but only so long as they are weaker—and those who are more powerful will act to reduce the power of one who undertakes such a course.

Demonstrations of power are useless. A demonstration that does nothing constructive and is undertaken for display wastes lifeforce, energy, time, and resources. Better to plan a constructive use of resources that will herald power and accomplishment.

If destruction of an enemy is necessary, do so without warning. If such is impossible, an alector should not posture, but bide his time until he can act. Posturing can only reveal weakness and invite contempt and attack. . . .

Views of the Highest
Illustra
W.T. 1513

28

Sharua slowed the Myrmidon duty coach well before the team reached the entrance to the portico at the Duarch's Palace, then brought the coach to a gentle halt opposite the passenger mounting blocks.

"Very smooth," observed Dainyl as he stepped out.

"Thank you, sir. You'll need me to wait for you?" asked Sharua, looking down from the driver's seat.

"If you would, please. It shouldn't be that long." Dainyl

hoped it wouldn't, but he had no idea how many questions the Duarch might ask or where they might lead. He hoped that Khelaryt didn't press him on the green shading to part of his aura.

"I'll be waiting, sir."

Dainyl strode past the columns of the portico and through the archway, past the two armed guards. Once more, the slender Bharyt stood waiting.

"Marshal, it's good to see you."

Dainyl thought the feeling behind the words was genuine, but in the Palace of the Duarch, who could tell? "You're looking good, Bharyt." He smiled. "You always are pleasant. Don't you ever get tired of escorting alectors to see him?"

"Some days are longer than others, sir, but serving the Duarch is a pleasure."

Bharyt meant that, also, and Dainyl hadn't sensed any Talent restraints.

"We'd best go, sir." Bharyt started down the hallway between the goldenstone marble columns.

Close to the end of the east wing corridor, Bharyt halted and knocked on the study door.

"Have the marshal come in, Bharyt."

Faint as the words were, blocked by the heavy oak, Dainyl could make them out, but he waited for his escort to open the door. This time, Bharyt merely stood outside and closed the door behind Dainyl.

Khelaryt was standing beside his desk and had apparently been studying the books on the inside wall shelves. "So many volumes, it seems, and yet they are but a fraction of what has been written and lost. It represents the tragedy of alectors, in a fashion. We seek knowledge and strive for beauty, and in our striving, must leave behind so much of what we have created, time after time."

"That is a tragedy," admitted Dainyl, not knowing what else he could have said.

The Duarch turned directly toward Dainyl, radiating, as always, his Talent with such force that it was almost a pressure. His deep violet eyes were friendly. "We should sit."

Dainyl waited and then took the corner seat after the Duarch had settled himself.

"The High Alector of Justice was insistent that you brief me on recent developments, Marshal. Most insistent."

"He was rather insistent," Dainyl replied dryly.

"That is less than favorable, and it would be wise to ask what agenda he pursues."

"His agenda is always to have someone else do what is difficult, whenever possible."

"You sound critical of your High Alector. So soon after you have become marshal?"

"I did not say that it was necessarily a bad strategy, sir, but for me not to recognize what is almost invariably leads me to greater self-deception."

"So practical you are, Dainyl. Do you believe in nothing of a higher nature? Destiny? Fate?"

"I'm not certain either destiny or fate, should they exist, represent a higher nature."

Khelaryt shook his head slowly, but a faint smile appeared. "What are you here to tell me?"

"First, that the Cadmian Third Battalion has reinforced Fourth Battalion in Iron Stem, and that they did so by moving directly there from Hyalt without returning to Elcien. Their commanding officer may have latent Talent, but given the difficulties with the ancients and the Reillies, it seemed best to exploit that possibility, rather than remove Myrmidons from Elcien." Since Khelaryt might well have received information indirectly from Captain Lyzetta, Dainyl felt that there was less risk in addressing the issue. It also meant that Zelyert could not use the information against him. "Second, I have transferred Seventh Company from Dulka to Tempre, at least for several seasons, in order to preclude any more Myrmidon officers being suborned by the High Alector of the East."

"I had heard of the majer's possible Talent," replied the Duarch. "Even a latent lander Talent can be dangerous. They can breed like rodents," Khelaryt pointed out. "Are you willing to take that gamble, on behalf of all alectors?"

"He is a young majer, and correct in his manner. He has

neither wife nor lady friends and is unlikely to produce offspring in the next season or so. That, I would judge, is a lesser risk than employing Myrmidons. There is also the possibility, since he tends to lead his men, that he may not survive this deployment. If he does, then I will deal with the situation." Exactly how, Dainyl didn't want to dwell on, not yet.

"You like this lander. That is dangerous."

"I cannot say that I like him. I respect him, and he has been effective—extremely effective—when other officers have not. I do not feel that I can sacrifice effectiveness on the grounds that he *might* develop full Talent and have offspring."

"You're flying close to the storms, Marshal."

"We all are, sir."

The Duarch glanced toward the study door, then back at Dainyl. "What else are you to convey?"

"The High Alector also said to mention that the numbers of unauthorized long translations from Ifryn continue to increase."

"By how much?" The very air around the Duarch seemed to darken.

"He would not tell me. He said he would have exact figures for you shortly."

"No wonder he was insistent." Khelaryt's laugh was grim. "Is that the real reason he wanted you here?"

"Knowing that he thinks of multiple uses for everything and everyone, possibly, sir."

"In this time when we await the arrival of the Master Scepter, that is not totally undesirable," mused the Duarch, his face twisting slightly, as if he were being precluded from thinking or considering some aspect of the Master Scepter.

Dainyl swallowed. He might not have another opportunity, and he would not refuse to say what was obvious to all any longer. "It would appear that the Master Scepter is being transferred to Efra, sir."

Talent surged and solidified. Darkness swirled around the Duarch. "That cannot be. It must not be." A blast of Talent flew toward Dainyl.

Somehow, he deflected it, but that deflection shredded his shields down to nearly nothing.

"From those fleeing Ifryn," he said quickly, hoping to forestall another Talent blast, "we have learned that many of those closest to the Archon have already translated there. The guards at the Tables on Efra are slaughtering scores every day—"

Even with all his remaining Talent in his shields Dainyl found himself flung against the inside wall bookcases.

"You *dared* tell me this?" demanded Khelaryt, striding from behind his table desk.

Yet as Khelaryt advanced, Dainyl sensed that the Duarch's Talent had diminished. He was probably more Talented and stronger than Dainyl, especially with the punishment Dainyl had just taken, but he was no longer the colossus of Talent that he had been.

"No one else would," replied Dainyl, straightening himself and standing, facing what might well be his end.

Khelaryt halted and offered a sad smile, so at odds with his rage of a few moments before. "They did not dare. Not for the reasons you might think, however."

"The artificial infusion of Talent?" guessed Dainyl. "Was it tied to the shadowmatch only until you knew where the Master Scepter would be transferred?"

"That was part of it."

"And no one wanted to reduce your power because they feared each other?"

"And Samist," pointed out Khelaryt. "If I could, I would make you the next Duarch, just to watch how you would handle such fighting. I cannot, and that means I will likely have to remove one of the High Alectors, if only to prove that I can." Khelaryt was still an impressive alector, but the huge mass of Talent that had surrounded him and radiated from him had dissipated. "For what you have done, Marshal, there is a price."

"Sir?"

"I am dispatching you immediately to deliver the same message to Duarch Samist. You *will* deliver that message." A cold steeliness filled his words.

Dainyl understood.

The Duarch walked to a small side table and opened the single drawer. From it, Khelaryt extracted a purple sash trimmed in green, with the eight-pointed star of the Duarch emblazoned in gold on the section that would cross the chest. "This will allow you entry to Samist directly. If anyone would deny you, it provides you the justification to do what is necessary to speak to the Duarch of Ludar. You may have to destroy even a High Alector to reach the Duarch. Do not hesitate to do so, or all of Acorus may be lost. You are to go to the Hall of Justice and translate immediately to Ludar. Do not let anyone delay you for any purpose. Is that clear?"

"Yes, sir."

"When you return—if you return—we will discuss what must be done next. Return here. Do not speak to anyone except Samist, and especially do not speak to Zelyert." Khelaryt extended the sash. "Put it on now."

Dainyl took the sash and donned it.

29

As Mykel rode out from the garrison on Duadi, a cold breeze blew out of the northeast, even though it was close to midmorning. The penetrating chill of the wind suggested that the coming winter would be anything but mild in Iron Stem. He turned the roan southward on the eternastone high road, with the green tower behind him, heading toward the ironworks.

The first structure south of the open space that surrounded the Cadmian garrison was a small school, set on the east side of the road, with battered brick walls that had once been whitewashed, but now held only scattered and peeling white remnants of the wash. Immediately south of the school was what passed as a green or a park, bordered by low stone walls, but Mykel saw only a few patches of grass and no bushes. There were stone benches, set almost at random.

South of the park were dwellings, small houses with narrow windows that ran for nearly a vingt before giving way to shops and dingier buildings. As he continued south, the ironworks loomed larger and larger on the west side of the road that had become the main north–south street of Iron Stem. Here and there, women, small children, and old men hurried through the chill morning, bundled in faded and heavy woolen coats. None looked in Mykel's direction.

The closer he got to the ironworks, the more each breath he took burned, as the air itself became acrid with-a mixture of fine dust and smoke and vapor from the ironworks. Just ahead of him, one of the short black wagons, bearing iron pigs and drawn by eight dray horses, groaned as the teamster eased it onto the high road, heading south for Dekhron.

Mykel turned the roan up the paved way leading to the works. In the loading yard to his left, on the south side, he counted seven mals working two of the winches that lifted the iron pigs onto the transport wagons. Three armed guards, wearing gray, watched from the loading dock, their iron-tipped staves casually ready. Mykel rode on, up to the compact brick building that Hamylt had said held the works' supervisor's spaces. There, he tied his mount to the iron hitching rail and dismounted. The door lever was coated with grime, but Mykel opened it anyway and stepped inside.

"Sir?" A narrow-faced young man, barely more than a youth, looked up from a stack of papers he appeared to be sorting on the table before him.

"Majer Mykel to see Supervisor Curosyn."

"Yes, sir." The young clerk hurried to the half-open door on the left. "Sir, it's the new Cadmian majer to see you."

"Have him come in." The tired voice barely carried to Mykel.

The lander who stood behind a table desk piled with stacks of papers was probably only five years older than Mykel, but his forehead was already heavily lined, and his eyes were slightly sunken in a pallid face. "Curosyn, Majer. Welcome to the ironworks. Such as they are."

"You're in charge?" asked Mykel. "Of both the mines and the ironworks?"

"For the moment. Since the end of harvest. I'm really an assistant mining engineer, but Miramyn and Faosyr left town once Majer Hersiod started trying to find ways to execute anyone who disagreed with him. That was the story, anyway. No one has seen them since." Curosyn shook his head. "I'm the acting supervisor. I report to the High Alector of Engineering in Ludar, or rather to some alectress who's his assistant." Belatedly, he gestured to the single chair in front of the table desk. "How can I help you?"

Mykel took the chair. "Why did the miners refuse to keep mining?"

Curosyn took a deep breath. "Every year we've had to go deeper to follow the coal seams. Every year we've lost a few more miners than the year before. Then when the old barracks burned, things got worse. Miramyn couldn't get brick or stone, and he finally worked out something for timber. I guess it was against the Code, because the Myrmidons showed up, and they had the forester flogged. Someone took a shot at one of them with a crossbow . . . and one of them flamed some loggers. That got back to the miners, and a bunch of the mals broke out and headed out to join up with the Reillies . . ."

Mykel listened, intently, concentrating on both what the engineer said and how he said it, but he could detect no sense of untruth. The longer he listened, the more he was convinced that some alector, perhaps the old marshal, had deliberately set things up to go wrong. No matter what the dispatches and records had reported, he couldn't believe that anyone who had been thinking clearly wouldn't have seen what had happened. But then, it could be that the missing engineers had seen things clearly, and had been quietly removed and replaced by an assistant so overwhelmed that he could barely keep things together. Why someone wanted matters to go wrong was another question, and one for which he had no answer. Not yet.

He let Curosyn talk, before finally asking, "What are your production levels right now? What they used to be? Three-quarters of that? Half?"

"A little more than half for the coal mines . . . we're still working on trying to clear one of the main shafts for number two. You can't operate a blast furnace without coke, and you can't make coke without coal. We're only at three-quarters production on the iron ore, but I'm having them stockpile the ore we can't process now. Once coal production is back up, we'll run through the backlog pretty quickly. The iron's playing out, though. I reported that more than a year ago. The alectress just told me to mine as much as we could as fast as we could for as long as we could." Curosyn shrugged, then sighed. "You do what you can."

As much as possible as quickly as possible—someone had wanted as much iron as they could get. The High Alector of Engineering? "Did anyone say why they needed all that iron?"

"No, sir. I asked once in a dispatch, indirectly, of course. I never got an answer, and I didn't want to press."

"I heard that the miners were gathered peacefully, and Majer Hersiod rode up and shot them down. Is that true?"

"You've been talking to the outholders. It wasn't that simple. Some of the Squawt and Reillie hotheads were there, too, and they were trying to get the miners to take up weapons. That was because Majer Hersiod rounded up some of them to work in the mines. That didn't work. They either escaped or got shot. So when the Cadmians showed up, some of the Squawts and Reillies fired at them. They thought it was another roundup. That's how that all started."

That, unfortunately, made more sense . . . but raised another question. "What were they doing out there? I thought the mals were confined to the compound."

Curosyn's laugh was short and bitter. "What compound? The walls are maybe two yards high. We never did get the timber and brick to rebuild the burned barracks, so the mals are jammed in at night in the newer ones. We're short of guards, and we can't get the golds to hire more. The only reason most of them stay is that they've got no coin and they get fed, and they have nowhere else to go. The townspeople would just as soon gut 'em as talk to them, and the women here are as tough as the men, sometimes tougher. We lose a miner to them almost every week, dumped in the streets behind the brothel. No one ever knows anything."

"They could go to the Reillies."

Curosyn laughed. "You have to survive in the wild for a week before they'll even talk to you. Most mals are townies."

Mykel shook his head sympathetically. "You've got your hands full."

"I'd just as soon leave, but there's nowhere to go these days—except as a laborer—and I'm not that desperate."

When he left the ironworks supervisor, Mykel walked slowly to his roan and mounted. Iron Stem was a side of Corus he hadn't seen before, and one he almost wished he hadn't. How could the alectors have let the situation get so far out of hand? Or didn't they care?

As he turned the roan northward and rode back toward the garrison, he reminded himself to pass the word about the women in Iron Stem to the rankers. He wasn't about to put the town off-limits, not yet, not unless the townspeople started killing Cadmians.

30

"Don't wait for me this time," Dainyl told Sharua as he left the duty coach outside the Hall of Justice, straightening the sash he had gotten from Khelaryt. "I'll be a while." And that would be if he were skillful and fortunate.

"Yes, sir."

Under a cloudy sky that promised a cold rain long before he returned from Ludar, Dainyl hurried up the stone steps, then skirted the main area of the receiving hall, where, for once, Zelyert himself was listening to the petitioners who assembled. Grateful that he would not have to explain anything to the High Alector immediately, Dainyl made his way through the concealed entrance and down the steps to the lower level.

"Good day, Marshal," offered one of Zelyert's newer assistants, who peered out of her study as Dainyl approached the closed door to the Table chamber. Her eyes widened at the sash he wore.

"Thank you." Dainyl opened the door to the foyer, closing it behind him before opening the inner door and stepping into the Table chamber.

One of the gray-clad guards glanced toward Dainyl but for a moment before returning his attention to the Table itself. There stood a blocky and muscular alectress in a purple coverall, her squarish face intent on Chastyl, who stood at the end of the Table.

Dainyl caught a glimpse of the figure of an older alectress, her dark hair streaked with silver, sprawled beside the Table, just before her figure disintegrated into dust.

"You . . . killed her . . ." stammered the alectress on the Table.

"Do you have a pass from a High Alector on Ifryn?" Chastyl's voice was almost bored.

The blocky alectress laughed bitterly. "At my age . . . with my figure?"

"What skills do you have?"

"I was an assistant to the concertmaster of Cheutorl."

"Doing what?"

"Whatever he wanted."

"Do you play an instrument?"

"No . . . I—"

Chastyl nodded to the guard. The lightcutter flared, and the alectress toppled off the Table, her body beginning to disintegrate even before it reached the stone floor.

"She was one of the older ones, hanging on," Chastyl said to Dainyl. "They're too much of a drain on lifeforce unless they have special skills or they're pregnant. She didn't have any real skills, no abilities. We tend to forget that there are alectors who aren't much better than steers, particularly on Ifryn." He took in the sash. "To Ludar? Give my best to Puleryt if you get the chance. You better translate before we get another batch."

"Have there been that many?"

"Four this morning. A half-score yesterday. The numbers are going up."

If the other Tables were getting those numbers of long translation attempts, that was another indication of how bad conditions were on Ifryn and how order was breaking down.

"That's a sign of more trouble to come." Dainyl stepped up onto the Table and concentrated, dropping through the silvered surface and . . .

. . . into the chill purpled darkness beneath. He immediately pressed a Talent link toward the brilliant yellow locator that was Ludar. Still . . . in the timeless instants in the darkness, he sensed strong purple lines and wavering ones, and an occasional flash of brilliant green.

The entire translation tube shuddered, pulsing and contracting. Was that because something was happening on Ifryn—or even Acorus—or because so many Ifrits were trying to leave Ifryn?

Pushing away his unease, Dainyl focused on the Ludar locator, sweeping through the silver-yellow barrier, and . . .

. . . holding his shields firm as he emerged on the Table in Ludar. Although there were five armed guards in gray watching the Table, none lifted a weapon. The chamber was quiet as Dainyl stepped down off the silvery surface of the Table.

Puleryt—the Recorder of Deeds at Ludar—gaped momentarily at Dainyl and the sash. Finally, he spoke. "Marshal . . . you have an urgent message for the Duarch?"

Dainyl nodded.

"Derai will escort you to the coach."

A slender alectress appeared, and Dainyl followed her out through the foyer. Behind him, before the door closed, he caught part of what the recorder said.

"When a High Alector wears that sash, don't get in his way or be around when he delivers the message."

The corridor outside the Table chamber was walled in green marble with a gray granite floor. While Dainyl knew the Table was in the Hall of Trade and Engineering, he'd never translated to Ludar before. He followed Derai to the circular staircase that spiraled upward, and emerged in a hallway lit by expansive clerestory windows.

"The portico is this way, sir."

The area held but a single coach—gray with red trim.

The driver took in Dainyl's uniform—more than the sash, Dainyl thought—and leaned down and opened the door. "Sir."

"Take the marshal straight to the Duarch's portico, Geram," ordered the alectress.

"Sir . . . right away."

Dainyl slipped into the coach and closed the door. No sooner had it closed than the driver eased the team into motion. Once clear of the roof over the coach area, Dainyl leaned forward to get a better view. Although he had flown over Ludar in the past, especially years back when he had done the dispatch runs, he had never traveled the distance between the Trade and Engineering Hall and the Duarch's Palace on the ground.

If Elcien was the city of spires, then Ludar was the city of arches and domes, its structures lower, more rounded, with more distance between them, the space filled with wide lawns, hedges, and flowers, even in late fall. But then, Ludar was more than two hundred vingts south of Elcien and on the warmer and more sheltered end of the Bay of Ludel.

As the coach passed the gardens of the Duarch of Ludar, Dainyl noted that they, too, were spread more, with the hedges lower, and the flower beds wider. There was also no topiary, and he could smell the lingering fragrance of the autumn lilies. Those in Elcien had faded weeks earlier.

Geram turned into a narrower lane at the west end of the Palace, a structure that was but two stories in height and extended more than half a vingt from the west end eastward. The coach halted at what was clearly a private, or at least restricted, entrance. Two guards in green and silver stepped forward, then, once they saw the uniform or the sash or both, stepped back. Dainyl walked quickly through the archway toward a single door that opened inward as he neared.

The functionary who met Dainyl just inside the entryway took one look at the sash, then nodded, although Dainyl could sense the alector's dismay. Was the sash only used for urgent and terrible news?

"The Duarch is in the music room, Marshal, and he doesn't like to be disturbed there, but there's no help for that. This way, sir."

Given the extent of the Palace, Dainyl was braced for a long walk, but he had gone less than sixty yards when his guide stopped at a door, knocked, and opened it. "Here, Marshal."

Not without some trepidation, Dainyl stepped through the doorway as the sounds of a violin swept around him, music he did not recognize.

The music-room door clicked shut behind Dainyl. The chamber itself was twice the size of Khelaryt's study, and floor-to-ceiling windows comprised the entire outer wall. At the north end was a series of oversized shelves built into the paneled wall, filled with thin books and folders, possibly bound sheet music. A table desk with its top in the shape of a semicircle was placed before the music shelves.

Standing between the desk and Dainyl was a tall alector, who had been playing the violin. As the echo of the sweet notes died away, the Duarch turned to face Dainyl.

Samist looked to be fractionally shorter than Khelaryt, but that still left him a figure who would tower over most alectors. Like Khelaryt once had, he embodied Talent that surrounded and infused him, power enough to take down a half-score of High Alectors. He was dressed in a sleeveless tunic, with a clinging undertunic, both of purple. He held a violin and a bow.

"You know," he began, then broke off the words as he saw Dainyl and the sash. "It must be urgent for Khelaryt to turn the Marshal of Myrmidons into a messenger."

"Yes, Most High."

With a weary smile, Samist carefully laid the violin and then the bow on the music table. " 'Sir' will do."

"Yes, sir."

"What is it?"

"It's simple enough, sir. From what we have learned, the Master Scepter will be or is already being transferred to Efra—"

The unseen darkness of anger and Talent shrouded the Duarch. Unlike Khelaryt, Samist did not lash out with Talent at Dainyl.

Even so, Dainyl could feel the enormous force of Talent rising, ready to strike.

"Stop!" demanded the Duarch.

Dainyl waited, unsure what to do with Samist reacting so differently. Still, he held his shields as strongly as he could.

The Duarch shuddered. Talent swirled around him like a storm before vanishing, leaving the Duarch standing before the table that held the violin and bow, his Talent reduced to that of an extremely powerful alector. "Now . . . please repeat what you said and go on."

"From what we have learned, the Master Scepter will be or is already being transferred to Efra. Those fleeing Ifryn who have reached Acorus are confirming that many of those closest to the Archon have already translated to Efra. The guards at the Tables on Efra are slaughtering scores every day—"

"They have been so kind as to tell you that?" Samist's sardonicism was spoken gently, but Dainyl could feel the Duarch's probes.

"The information was sent back to the recorders on Ifryn to warn people not to try the long translations without authorization. Several Table functionaries have made their way to Acorus and reported this. The Table in Elcien alone has received a score of refugees in the last day."

Samist laughed. "Oh, how Khelaryt misjudges me."

Dainyl wanted to ask how. He did not.

"Deep within I have always felt that the Master Scepter would not come to Acorus, yet I could say nothing, only find ways to encourage, or not discourage, those who were more realistic. Khelaryt was the idealist and thought I was trying to thwart the transfer here, rather than recognizing what could not be. You are here only to break the shadowmatch so that my Talent will not surpass his. Is that not so?"

"He did not say, sir, but I would judge so."

"Poor Khelaryt." Samist laughed once more. "If he could only see what must be, but that is not his role."

"What might that be, sir?" Dainyl wanted to change the subject, and quickly.

"Khelaryt's role was his to choose. Not so Acorus. It will always be the violated handmaiden. How else could it be?"

"Because of the ancients, or because it is so cold?"

"Both . . . and because it is where those who displeased the

Archon were sent." Before Dainyl could say another word, Samist went on. "You have released me from bondage, so to speak, Marshal." Samist laughed once more. "You have done so early enough that all may not be lost for what I would have done. What favor would you wish? To become a High Alector? To replace Zelyert?"

"No, sir." Dainyl paused briefly. What did he want? Dare he ask?

"Then what do you wish—assuming that you live long enough for me to offer a favor? You must know that Zelyert will be less than pleased with Khelaryt's loss of the shadowmatch and the associated Talent-strength."

"I am certain some will be displeased and others pleased."

"You sound much like your predecessor."

"I am not much like Shastylt, but I know little of those around you, or of any around Duarch Khelaryt, except for High Alector Zelyert."

"A cautious marshal, yet one who flew against an entire company."

Dainyl offered a polite smile.

"Speak."

"I understand you have not yet named the regional alector for Tempre."

"You would wish that?"

"Not for myself, but for my wife. She is a most capable administrator."

The Duarch of Ludar laughed once more. "That she is, and she would make a very capable RA. It would also handicap that idiot Chembryt, who could do little without her." His long fingers intertwined, and he nodded. "I cannot make her RA of Tempre, but Yadaryst suffered a wild translation several days past. Would you consider . . . would she consider becoming RA in Dereka?"

"I think she would, although that would have to be her decision."

"If she would, that would resolve many . . . difficulties . . ."

Dainyl was both elated and dismayed. He was anything but certain that Lystrana would wish to leave the beauty and glory of Elcien for Dereka. Yet he harbored the growing sense that Elcien would not be the best place to be after the Master Scepter was actually transferred. "I can only ask her."

"Do that, Marshal. If she is willing, have her translate here to see me to receive the appointment. No later than Septi." A sad smile crossed his face, a visage slightly too long to be ideal for an alector, especially for a Duarch. "If that is all, I would like to return to the violin."

Dainyl bowed, still wary, still holding full shields. "That is all. By your leave, sir."

"By my leave."

After another nod, Dainyl turned and left the music room.

Once he closed the door, he thought he heard the Duarch resume playing, but he wasn't sure. Playing the violin . . . after losing so much Talent? Was Samist that composed? What did that say about Khelaryt? What did Dainyl face on his return to Elcien?

"This way, sir."

Dainyl followed the functionary.

31

Dainyl found the coach and driver still waiting outside the Palace of the Duarch in Ludar. After a quick trip back to the Table chamber in the Hall of Engineering and Trade, he stepped toward the Table, but had to wait as one of the guards folded a set of clothing around a pair of boots, then added the bundle to the short stack in the corner of the chamber before resuming his position at the corner of the Table nearest the door. The air held a sickly sweet odor that threatened to turn Dainyl's stomach, a stench that reminded him too vividly of what had happened in Hyalt.

"More wild translations?" Dainyl asked Puleryt.

"Unacceptable translations, sir. He was a street poet from Yarat. He demanded artistic asylum."

"Why did he need asylum?" Dainyl couldn't imagine a street poet anywhere on Ifryn being a danger to anyone.

"He didn't say. He only said that the Archon had forbidden all dissident artists to translate from Ifryn. He begged. He even groveled."

"And the guards shot him?"

"Orders from the Archon and the Duarch, sir. No one, except pregnant alectresses, who does not have a pass order-sealed by a High Alector is to be accepted. We would be overwhelmed."

Although he knew logically that what the recorder said was true—he and Lystrana had actually worked out the lifeforce-carrying ability of Acorus a year earlier—the thought of killing people whose only offense was a desire to live added to the nausea he already felt. He nodded politely, swallowed, and stepped up onto the Table. Concentrating, he felt himself sliding through the silvered surface and . . .

. . . into the purple-shaded gloom of the translation tube. All around him flashed streaks of purple, but he concentrated on the brilliant white locator of Elcien, simultaneously trying to hold and rebuild his shields before he appeared on the Table there.

The silvered-white barrier flashed toward him . . .

. . . and he had to take a quick step to balance himself.

"It's the marshal!" called out Chastyl.

Dainyl quickly cleared the Table and made his way out through the foyer and into the corridor, conscious that most eyes had been on him.

An assistant whose name did not immediately come to mind stepped toward him. "The Highest will be down from the Hall shortly."

"The Duarch insisted I return to report to him immediately," Dainyl demurred, glancing down at the sash across his chest. He recalled the alector's name. "I am certain that the High Alector will understand that, Cartalyn."

"I will tell him, Marshal." Cartalyn's words suggested Zelyert would not understand at all.

"You can tell him I'll return once the Duarch has dismissed me."

"Yes, sir." Cartalyn sounded barely mollified.

Dainyl hurried up the stairs and out through the concealed entrance. The rain he had anticipated before he left had begun to fall, but as a chill drizzle that, under the dark clouds, turned all Elcien gray. He found a hacker almost immediately, although he could have walked the distance, had it been necessary, but he preferred not to arrive at the Palace soaked.

Even so, his tunic was still damp in places as he followed Bharyt along the corridor back to the Duarch's study. Dainyl was not looking forward to the reception he would receive once he reported back to Khelaryt. He only hoped that he had Talent-read the un-shadowmatched Duarch correctly.

Khelaryt was standing at the study windows looking out into the rain. He turned as Dainyl entered, but waited until Bharyt closed the door. "You told him?"

"Yes, sir. I did."

"And he let you leave?"

"He offered me a favor for freeing him of the shadowmatch," Dainyl volunteered. "I think he already suspected that the Master Scepter would go to Efra and was having great difficulties with the shadowmatch."

"If he suspected . . ."

"No one would tell him, either," suggested Dainyl. "Suspicion, or even announcement, without proof was not enough—as you discovered, sir."

"You offered little proof."

"You truth-read me, sir, and that was enough, combined with what you already knew."

"Did you accept his favor? What was it?"

"Not for myself. No. For Lystrana and our daughter." Before Khelaryt could object, Dainyl went on. "I asked that she be named RA in Tempre. He refused, but offered her the position in Dereka. I told him I could not accept for her. She has until Septi to decide."

Khelaryt laughed—and kept laughing.

Dainyl waited, wondering exactly what Khelaryt found so extraordinarily amusing.

Finally, the Duarch wiped the tears of laughter from his face. "He thinks that by removing Lystrana from Elcien he will weaken Chembryt and strengthen his own position. Without your wife as chief assistant, Chembryt will turn to me more than before. Only her insight allowed him independence. She has all my support to become RA in Dereka—provided you remain as marshal."

"I had not thought otherwise, sir, but I do serve at the pleasure of you and the High Alector. Also, I do not yet know Lystrana's decision."

"She would be foolish not to become RA—even in Dereka."

Dainyl wasn't about to volunteer an opinion on that. Lystrana had a definite mind of her own.

"Is there anything else, Dainyl, not that I can imagine much?"

"Were you aware that the Archon has ordered the execution of anyone fleeing here without a pass ordersealed by a High Alector?"

Khelaryt frowned, clearly concentrating. "That is true, but as Duarch, I can countermand such as I see fit." He paused. "Dainyl . . . even without the restraint of the shadowmatch, I cannot allow everyone who wishes to flee Ifryn for Acorus to come here. If I do, within a handful of years, or less, Acorus will spiral down into the same fate as Ifryn, and no one here will have anywhere to go. I have told the recorders who heed me to spare the best, and those bearing a child. That is the best that I can do."

Dainyl could sense that Khelaryt truly believed that. What was worse was that he suspected that the Duarch's assessment was accurate.

"You have one more task, Dainyl."

"Telling Zelyert? He already knows that you sent me to Ludar. I had planned to tell him, unless you had an objection."

"Very wise of you. You can tell him that I insisted you report to me first on your return." Khelaryt smiled. "I would judge that you already did."

"I left word that I had to report to you first, and left the Hall before he could get to me."

"Creative avoidance. He won't care for that."

"You would have cared less for the alternatives, sir."

"You might be right at that. You'd best go." Khelaryt paused. "The sash, Marshal?"

"Oh, yes, sir." Dainyl eased it off and handed it to the Duarch. "By your leave?"

Khelaryt nodded.

Even before Dainyl opened the study door to depart, he could see that the Duarch had turned back to the windows and the rain.

Dainyl had to walk through the increasing drizzle back to the Hall of Justice. His uniform was thoroughly damp by the time he stepped into Zelyert's private study on the lower level. He closed the door behind him quietly.

Zelyert stood and did not sit or motion Dainyl to do so. "You were rather arrogant in dismissing my request to remain, Marshal."

"No, sir. I was under the direct orders of the Duarch to go to Ludar and then return immediately to him after completing the task he assigned me."

"As an urgent envoy? What message were you required to deliver to the Duarch Samist?"

"The message was that it was highly likely that the Master Scepter would be transferred to Efra and not to Acorus."

"You . . . you told him." Zelyert shook his head. "I would say that telling Khelaryt was one of the most foolish acts possible, but you knew I would say that. With his Talent diminished, what is to stop the other High Alectors from combining against him? Why . . . why did you do that?"

"He is still strong enough to stand against any two," Dainyl pointed out. "If you stand by him, or Chembryt does . . ."

"How can you say that?"

"Because he said he might well have to remove one of his High Alectors, if only to prove he could."

"With the shadowmatch lifted, he is thinking more clearly. Whether that is for the best remains to be seen." Zelyert leaned forward.

"Besides," Dainyl said calmly. "That is what you wished, except that you never wanted to say so."

Zelyert looked hard at Dainyl. "That is rather presumptive on your part."

"No more so than your sending me to deliver news you did not wish to impart." Dainyl held his shields, even though he knew he was far from full strength.

"You see too much, Marshal, and someday, perhaps soon, that will be your undoing." With scarcely a pause, Zelyert asked, "What will happen in the east?"

"At some point, Brekylt will attempt to establish himself as Duarch of the East."

"What would you suggest we do about that?"

"Nothing."

"Nothing? How can you watch Acorus fragment?"

More easily than watching alector fight alector, and pteridon fight pteridon. "I would rather not see that happen, but to send the Myrmidons against Brekylt at this time, or even as soon as he rejects the unity of Acorus, will only ensure greater fragmentation."

"Don't fight, in order to preserve the Myrmidons so that we can pull the pieces together later. Is that what you're suggesting?"

"For the moment," Dainyl admitted. "I may change my mind if Brekylt acts in a different fashion. We have no reason to act now, in any event."

"That is true, unfortunately." Zelyert gestured toward the door. "I think it best that you depart, and we reflect separately."

"By your leave, sir."

Zelyert's nod was abrupt.

Dainyl nodded more politely in return and stepped back, then departed, taking the lower corridor to the stairs.

Once outside the Hall of Justice, he waited until a hacker appeared through the cold rain that had replaced the earlier drizzle. As he sat in the coach headed toward Myrmidon headquarters, he reflected.

Beneath his calm exterior, Zelyert had been furious, angrier than Dainyl had ever sensed, yet Dainyl was convinced the High Alector's anger was not because Dainyl had revealed what was to happen with the Master Scepter. The other possibilities were far worse, because they suggested Zelyert had hoped Dainyl would not survive the events of the day—or that he was increasingly concerned that Dainyl was too accurate in his assessments of the High Alector. The other mystery was why neither Duarch had commented, even in passing, on the green tinge of the ancients that Dainyl still bore. Khelaryt knew about the initial cause, but had someone told Samist? Khelaryt remained a mystery. Even with the shadowmatch removed . . . something foreign was there . . . and Dainyl could not determine what it was, let alone what it might mean.

He made his way from the coach into headquarters quickly, although some rain got on his uniform. As he passed Alcyna's study, he stopped and knocked on her door, then opened it.

She was alone, reading through a stack of reports.

"If you'd join me in my study in a moment?"

"Yes, sir."

Dainyl continued down the corridor and into his own study. Several reports had been carefully placed on the left side of his table desk. He ignored them for the moment. Instead, he glanced out his windows into the rain, now falling in sheets so heavy that the midafternoon appeared more like twilight, before settling into the chair behind the desk. He sighed, glancing once more at the reports, but not picking up either.

Alcyna appeared within moments. Her eyes went to Dainyl's face, and she closed the door behind her.

"Submarshal . . . please sit down."

Alcyna eased gracefully into the chair at the corner of the desk. "You have very bad news. You're always quietest when matters are worst."

"The Master Scepter is likely going to Efra." Dainyl paused. "Both Duarches know it, as does the High Alector."

"When did they discover this?"

"This morning. Most of the High Alectors have known for

a time, but no one wanted to tell either Duarch. I would not be surprised if Brekylt has known as well."

"He had hinted that he thought Efra was more likely well before I left Alustre. That was certainly what he was planning for."

"How do you think this will affect the Myrmidons?" Dainyl watched her closely, with both eyes and Talent-senses.

"He will certainly try to place the companies in the east under his control. I don't think Noryan would like that, but whether he would oppose Brekylt I don't know."

"When might he act?"

"As soon as he is certain that the Duarches cannot do anything to oppose him."

Dainyl considered. He had now met both Duarches and Brekylt. With the loss of the Talent that had accompanied the shadowmatches, he would have judged Khelaryt to be the strongest of the three, then Samist, and then Brekylt, who appeared to have about as much Talent-strength as Zelyert.

"How close are Brekylt and Samist?"

"Brekylt has occasionally met with Samist. They could have met more often than that. Brekylt does not care for Khelaryt. So far as I know, they have not met in years."

"What do you recommend we do?"

"Wait." Alcyna shrugged. "Brekylt will do nothing overt, but there may be signs of what he intends. Your wife or the other assistants may see signs well before anything affects the Myrmidons."

"The signs may already be there, and we may not understand what they portend."

"That is always possible, but without some clear evidence, what can we do?"

"Nothing . . . yet. I'd like you to draft up a promotion for Captain Sevasya to majer. Then draft orders deploying Fourth Company to Lysia and placing Captain Josaryk under Majer Sevasya. Then deploy Third Company back to Norda to deal with the difficulties raised by the ancients. I'd like to see those sometime in the morning. I'd appreciate it if you didn't mention the specifics to anyone."

"Yes, sir." Alcyna smiled. "You think . . . ?"

"I think Majer Noryan is a good Myrmidon, whatever his background, and I know Majer Sevasya is."

"It might work."

Dainyl hoped so.

32

Dainyl did not arrive home on Duadi evening until almost a glass later than usual because Alcyna had wanted to review the orders he had asked her to draft.

Lystrana hurried toward him even before he stepped through the doorway out of the continuing chill rain and into the foyer. "Are you all right?" Her eyes and Talent scanned him. "You've been hurt . . ."

"Call it Talent-diminished," he said. "Things have gone from bad to worse, and then back to only bad." He closed the door.

She put her arms around him, and Dainyl could feel the gentle swell of her against him and could sense the strengthening lifeforce that was their daughter.

"I heard that Khelaryt sent you as a privileged envoy to Samist. I've been so worried." She stepped back, but took his hand. "After the girls fixed supper, I sent them off for the evening. We can eat, and you can tell me about it."

"There are a few things you should know," he said, following her out of the foyer and to the dining area.

"Only a few?"

"More than a few," he admitted.

"Just sit down." Lystrana pointed to the chair at the end of the dining table, then half filled a goblet from the carafe. "I'll bring out supper."

"You should be the one sitting down."

"I didn't have the day you clearly did," she called back over her shoulder on her way to the kitchen. "Besides, when I'm active near the end of the day, Kytrana sleeps more at night, and that means I sleep better."

Dainyl took a sip of the wine, a white from the Vyan Hills, he thought. Within moments, Lystrana was back, carrying a covered dish and a basket of bread, still faintly warm.

"It's only a fowl and noodle casserole, but I thought it would be warm and filling on a chilly damp day like this." She ladled a healthy helping onto his plate and another onto hers before seating herself.

"It smells wonderful." Dainyl took a mouthful, then another.

"I was worried when I heard that you'd had to go back to report to Zelyert after returning from Ludar."

"Do you know everything?" he asked with a grin after swallowing.

"Only everything that happens in the Palace," she replied, trying to hide a smile. "What did you have to tell Samist?"

"That it was most likely that the Master Scepter would go to Efra. You were right. Khelaryt and Samist both were Talent-magnified by their shadowmatches."

"Were?" Lystrana raised one eyebrow in the gesture that Dainyl had often wanted to emulate, but had never mastered.

"Once they learned where the Master Scepter was headed, they lost shadowmatches and the extra Talent. As you thought, their native Talent was artificially enhanced somehow through the shadowmatches."

"No wonder Khelaryt dispatched you to Ludar immediately. Did you have to tell him?"

"No. He couldn't ask about it, but when Zelyert dispatched me there to tell him that Seventh Company had been transferred to Tempre and—by the way—that the number of refugees flooding the Tables, not to mention the wild translations, were growing all over Corus . . . it was clear he'd be sending me time and time again until I revealed it inadvertently. So I told Khelaryt. When I told Zelyert that, he reprimanded me. I suggested that he shouldn't be disturbed because I did what he'd wanted. He tried to hide it, but he was as cold and as full of suppressed rage as I've ever seen."

"That's because he was setting you up to reveal the Master Scepter's fate later, and your acting too soon spoiled some scheme of his."

"He doesn't like my seeing through him and telling him."

"No one likes that, Dainyl."

"Even wives?"

"Especially wives. What was Khelaryt's reaction?"

"Absolute rage. Even somewhat restrained, he almost shredded my shields, and he threw me into the wall. Then he recovered and sent me off to tell Samist, with my weakened shields and all. When I got there Samist was playing the violin, and playing it well. That surprised me. I've never met him personally, and I'd never thought of him as a musician. Then, when I told him, he wasn't nearly so upset as Khelaryt had been. It was as though he had expected it all along."

"That's the way he has been acting—or letting those who serve him act."

Dainyl took yet another mouthful of the casserole, some bread, and then another sip of the wine. "Good wine."

"I'm glad you like it. I wish I could have more than a sip or two." She broke off some of the bread. "Samist thanked you and sent you back? That was it?"

"Ah . . . actually, he even asked what favor he could grant me. I asked about the RA of Tempre. He demurred, but offered Dereka."

"Do you really want to be an RA?"

"I asked for you."

"What! Are you . . . why would you even think that? Why did you think that we should leave Elcien for a Talent-impoverished place like Dereka?"

"Because, as I said, matters have gone from bad to worse . . ."

"But Dereka? Why? Why there?"

"As I told you, I tried to bargain for Tempre for you, but Samist said that wasn't possible."

"You still haven't answered why you want to leave Elcien."

"I don't, and I'd still have to be Marshal of Myrmidons, but I can get to Dereka easily enough by Table. I'm worried about what's likely to happen."

"You want to shove me out into the high and cold hinterlands?"

"You don't have to accept," Dainyl said. "You have until Septi to decide."

"Four days to decide whether to change everything?"

"You'd see less of my mother."

"Dainyl . . ."

"There haven't been any alectresses who have been RAs. You deserve it more than anyone."

"And I won't get it except through you?"

What could he say to that? "You might. I wanted to hurry things."

"You don't think so. Not really." She set down the wine goblet that had held less than a finger of the white and looked at him. "I know. You're trying to help. You want my abilities recognized."

"And you want them recognized without my help," he said quietly. "Then refuse. Blame me for being impulsive."

"It's not that simple."

"Nothing ever is. If you decline, people will say that you're afraid you can't handle it. If you accept, they'll say that you got it because of me. Others will say that it's about time your abilities were recognized, and some of them will say that it's a shame that it didn't happen sooner. I don't think any of that is the question."

"Oh?"

Dainyl ignored the anger beneath her calmness. "I've listened to you for more than thirty years. I've changed what I could and tried to modify what I could not. Most of Elcien knows I would not be where I am without you. I can't provide that kind of help to you, not in the way you did. I did have the chance to provide this. Tell me what the difference is. In either case, neither of us would be where we are without the other." He looked at her, evenly, directly.

"It doesn't feel the same."

"It's not. You helped me in little bits for years. That's harder, and it's more work, and you'll never get the credit you deserve."

"Dainyl . . . why do you want me out of Elcien?"

He forced himself to look directly at Lystrana. "I'm worried. I don't think it's going to be safe, and I can't give you reasons, or tell you why or how. I don't know. All I do know is that we're getting more and more refugees, and they're shooting them, like rodents, or . . . Have you been in a Table chamber lately?"

"Not for nearly two weeks."

"Every one has at least four and sometimes six guards. They have orders to execute anyone without a pass, or skills, or pregnant alectresses. In the last two days, they've killed close to fifteen refugees here in Elcien. That doesn't count wild translations."

"That's hundreds across Corus. That's terrible. It's . . ." She shook her head.

"Khelaryt says there's no choice. Without the killings, in something like three weeks we'd be at the optimum lifeforce-carrying capacity of the entire world."

"I know . . . but it's different when you think of real people dying."

"When I talked to her months back, Sulerya pointed out something else. Every Ifrit translating from Ifryn takes four times the lifeforce of those born on Acorus. So every refugee means three fewer children that can be born here, or that much less time before we exhaust this world. That means that the refugee situation is going to get worse. Then there are the ancients. I can't forget the way the one told me that unless we changed we would perish. It wasn't a threat, or a promise, but a wistful and sad certainty."

Lystrana looked oddly at him.

"What?"

"I can't help but feel that you're tied in some way to them, and not just because of the wound you got from their ancient weapon and their healing of you. Except they wouldn't have healed you without a reason."

"I know that. They want me to change, to somehow become . . ."

"It's more than that."

It doubtless was, but Dainyl couldn't do anything about it. "There's another thing. It's already getting dangerous to use a Table. That bothers me. You'd have to use a Table to get to Ludar to accept the position and then come back and then translate to Dereka."

"I'm not escaping Tables one way or another. Chembryt wants me to go to Alustre at the end of next week. He's still worried about the overages in the Engineering accounts."

Dainyl winced. "Brekylt might not do anything by then."

"Let me sleep on it, dearest."

Dainyl couldn't disagree with that, especially since he could sense that she was truly torn between Dereka and Elcien.

33

Dainyl picked up the slender volume from the corner of the desk, turning it in his hands. He'd made it a practice to read *Views of the Highest* regularly, if only so that he could quote from it when appropriate. Yet . . . the more he read, the more he felt that appropriate as much of what those views might be, the alectors he knew observed the wisdom more by ignoring it.

He flipped through several pages before stopping and taking in several lines.

> Just as the laws of the universe are simplest in explaining the everyday functions of the worlds we administer, so are the motivations of steers and alectors. The most common motivations are desire, pride, and contempt. Desire can be praiseworthy when it serves honest ambition, as can pride when it fuels the need for worthy accomplishment, but both have their unworthy sides, as seen in political machinations among alectors and unbridled greed for goods and wealth among steers. Moreover, those who exhibit these deplorable perversions of motivation are often impelled to hide their unworthiness from themselves by burying it within a welter of complexity. . . .

How guilty was he of the same base motives? Desire to prove himself worthy, pride at having become marshal, and contempt of alectors such as Shastylt? Why had he pressed for Lystrana to obtain the position of RA? Because he truly believed Lystrana deserved it and because he worried about the increasing dangers in Elcien or because he had power enough to break the old prejudices against alectresses in high positions?

His eyes went to the flight stage behind headquarters, outlined in cold sunlight that seemed more like winter than fall. For the moment, it was empty of pteridons.

That morning, he had not pressed Lystrana on her decision, knowing that asking her would merely make matters worse. She would decide, and she would tell him, probably when he got home. He thought she would decide to accept and go to Dereka, but he was far from certain.

He turned from the window and settled himself behind his table desk. To his right were copies of the orders Alcyna had hand-carried to Noryan in Alustre. He expected she would return before too long—at least he hoped she would.

On the left were the latest reports from the Cadmian regiments. He picked up the top report, the one from Colonel Herolt in Elcien, and began to read. The colonel's prose was even more tortuous than usual, or his own attention was lagging, because even skimming through the words was difficult.

> . . . Second Battalion, Majer Wekeryt commanding, stands ready for deployment . . .

> . . . Third Battalion, Majer Mykel commanding, has reached Iron Stem and has taken over duties previously handled by Fourth Battalion . . .

> . . . Fourth Battalion, Captain Hamylt acting in command, remains currently deployed to Iron Stem, under the overall command of Majer Mykel, as ordered by the Marshal of Myrmidons. . . . Casualties reported to date exceed sixty percent of the battalion's initial cadre, including Majer Hersiod and two other officers . . .

> . . . Fifth Battalion, Captain Josult acting in command, has begun a return from Northport to Elcien for the winter. . . .

As reported earlier, personnel losses extraordinarily heavy, totaling three hundred ten fatalities and twenty-three nonfatal casualties over the entire deployment . . .

. . . Sixth Battalion, Majer Juasyn commanding, remains deployed to Soupat to defend tin and copper mines in the area against Ghourat mountain brigands. Continued scattered skirmishes have resulted in significant casualties, currently totaling sixty-one fatalities and twenty-eight nonfatal casualties . . .

After finishing the reports, Dainyl looked up and back out the window at the chill light of afternoon. Even with Second Battalion at full strength, First Regiment, Cadmian Mounted Rifles, was overall only slightly above sixty-five percent of full complement—and that was the status two weeks earlier. He could not imagine how matters could have improved . . . or that they would.

Should he have dispatched a Myrmidon squad to Iron Stem once more? He doubted that the Myrmidons would have been any more effective against the ancients than Majer Mykel, and he still had the feeling that he was going to need all the Myrmidons he could muster before long.

He went from the Cadmian reports to Zernylta's schedule. There, at least, something had worked out. She'd finally agreed to become the permanent assistant operations officer, with the promotion to captain, and that had removed one headache. She was already far better than Dhenyr had been.

He had just finished checking over the schedule when Alcyna stepped through his door and closed it behind her. Her face was pale—even for an alectress.

"Are you all right?" He gestured for her to take a seat.

"Thank you for asking, Marshal." Alcyna sank into the chair, then caught herself and straightened. "Are you aware of what's happening in the Table chambers?"

"The killing of refugees without skills or abilities needed here?" Dainyl nodded. "Is it happening in Alustre as well?"

"If anything, it's worse there. Brekylt's guards are killing children in arms. I saw that on the translation out." She shook her head. "I didn't really even see it. I saw the clothing and asked Retyl. He said that children born on Ifryn were the greatest problem. They'd live the longest and draw the greatest Talent."

"Ifryn is collapsing. I don't see why the Archon hasn't transferred the Master Scepter. The longer he waits, the worse the chaos will be."

"That's what he wants. Here on Acorus, anyway. Isn't it obvious? Rather than telling people that they have no hope, he provides false hope. It's clear that the recorders on Ifryn have been ordered to let hundreds of Ifrits try to translate here. It could be even a thousand. Who knows how many are perishing in the long tubes between worlds? They're told to come here and warned that they'll be killed on sight if they emerge on Efra. That way, the Archon doesn't have to spend the resources to enforce order on Ifryn. It also allows a more orderly translation to Efra and bleeds Ifryn to the last to allow lifeforce to build or not decline on Efra . . ."

Dainyl swallowed. He should have seen that. Perhaps he hadn't wanted to see it.

"You look truly appalled, Marshal."

"I am. I know the lifeforce requirements here and on Efra, and we cannot take but a fraction of those Ifrits living on Ifryn, but . . ." He was the one to shake his head. "Knowing something and seeing the results of what you know are not the same. Yet . . . I don't know what else can be done." He gestured in the general direction of the Palace of the Duarch. "I asked Khelaryt about the guards and the rules, and he pointed out that letting everyone come would destroy Acorus in a few years. He didn't say how many, but I tried to work it out. Less than twenty years—that was what my calculations showed."

"There's no good answer, it seems."

"Except to use lifeforce more sparingly in the future," Dainyl suggested.

"How would you propose to implement that?" Alcyna asked dryly. "How many more alectors would the Duarches have to kill to make that work? How would we maintain control over the steers without using lifeforce, either through the pteridons or the Tables or the other technologies that elevate us above them?"

"That's a good question," temporized Dainyl.

Alcyna laughed harshly. "You don't have an answer to that, either."

Dainyl shrugged. He didn't, and there was no point in saying that he did. "How did Noryan take the orders?"

"Like a good submarshal. He did suggest that he deploy Josaryk first, and then follow with Third Company to Norda in a week or so. I thought that was acceptable. Was it?"

Dainyl had wanted Noryan away from Alustre as soon as possible, but Alcyna had been there, and had a better feel for matters. "If you thought so, it's probably for the best that way."

"We talked it over. Brekylt is arming all his personal guard with lightcutters, and he has over two hundred in Alustre alone. Even Noryan is concerned. Pulling both companies at once might push Brekylt into acting immediately, and the Myrmidons do have families there. There's no way to move all of them."

"Once the companies are gone, he could only use the families for retribution, and that wouldn't give him control—just more determined enemies."

"I'd have to agree. Brekylt's out for power, and alienating other alectors, even lowly ones, won't add to his control." She smiled, faintly. "One of Retyl's assistants let something slip. He wanted to know if the messenger from Ludar had returned. I didn't look back, and I don't think they know I heard."

"So Samist or his High Alectors are dealing with Brekylt."

"More directly since he has been freed of the shadowmatch."

Had that been a mistake? Should he have waited? Dainyl still didn't know. There was so much he didn't know, even now, Marshal of Myrmidons or not.

34

Lystrana was standing in the foyer when Dainyl stepped out of the cold wind and closed the door behind him. He stepped forward and put his arms around her. For a time, they clung to each other.

Then Lystrana stepped back. "I translated to Ludar this afternoon. You knew I would, didn't you?" Her voice was low, subdued.

"I had thought you might," replied Dainyl cautiously, "but it was your choice."

"I was in the Table chamber in the Hall of Justice, getting ready to translate. They killed a father and his daughter. Even Chastyl had tears in his eyes." Her voice dropped to a murmur. "It's inexcusable! The Archon is sending people here with false hope, just to make it easier for him and his cronies. Acorus can't take them, and he knows it. He has to know it."

"That wasn't why you decided. It might have made it easier." His smile was lopsided. "Or harder."

"You. That was why I decided. You risked everything to ask for that. You wouldn't do it if it didn't feel right. And for Kytrana, too."

"But does it feel right to you?" Dainyl asked.

Lystrana nodded. "Especially now. The translation upset Kytrana, especially coming back. She was afraid."

Dainyl had no idea how an unborn child would be afraid, but it had to be something that intruded upon their daughter's growing Talent. Could she sense the turmoil in the tubes? Or the green streaks and flashes that were the ancients? "These days, sometimes I'm afraid."

"I said I'd go to Dereka immediately. I can use the quarters in the regional headquarters until I find something else."

"When do you leave?"

"Quinti morning. I don't want to make any more translations after that anytime soon. With Kytrana, once I'm there, I can plead pregnancy. I don't think that will bother Samist, or Khelaryt."

"Did you tell Chembryt?"

"He seemed resigned. He said I deserved it. He did ask if whoever he selected as a new chief assistant could come to consult with me." Lystrana smiled. "I agreed to that."

"Did anything else . . . happen?"

"Khelaryt sent me a note congratulating me. He even put a phrase in it requesting that I exert my influence to keep you from moving the Myrmidon headquarters to Dereka."

"That's safe enough. He knows I wouldn't." Dainyl shook his head. "I'll be happier when you're settled."

"I do have one favor to ask, dearest."

"What is that?"

"You translate with me, so that you can carry everything I'll need."

Dainyl repressed a frown, although he knew Lystrana would sense his concern anyway. "You're as worried as I am."

"The next month, the next several months, will be very dangerous."

Dainyl had come to believe that, and certainly he and Lystrana had talked about it, but she had said little before tonight. "Is that because of the Table chamber?"

She shook her head, then nodded. "More because of what's happening there, and the fact that no one is even considering it in the Palace. I mentioned it to Chembryt. His response was that it was regrettable, but that none of them had wished to chance the long translation when almost anyone was allowed to make it."

"That was never true. Alectors still had to obtain permission." He stopped. "The rationalization, the willful ignorance of what's happening—that's what you meant."

She nodded again. "Enough. We can talk later. We shouldn't be talking here, anyway, even in whispers. Dinner should be ready." She held out her hand.

Dainyl took it, then offered his arm.

35

A good half glass before sunrise on Quattri, Mykel seated himself in the small officers' mess and took the first sip of a cider that was bitter and turning. The egg toast was brown and already congealing into a leathery mass.

"Majer! Sir!" Wyorst—the duty squad leader from Fourteenth Company—stood in the mess doorway. "Sir . . . Captain Culeyt would like to see you, sir. He's out by the north gates. Fifty yards to the north, by the green tower."

Mykel rose quickly. Culeyt wasn't one to waste his time. "Did he say why, Wyorst?"

"No, sir. He said to get the majer."

Mykel hurried out of the mess and across the paving of the courtyard through an icy wind. In the gray-shaded light that preceded dawn, he saw Culeyt standing to the east of the eternastone pavement beside the dry ditch for drainage from the high road, but one that had never held water in the time Third Battalion had been in Iron Stem. With the captain was a town patroller, in brown and gray. Both were looking down at the ditch.

Culeyt turned as Mykel approached. "Sir. I thought you'd want to know." He gestured toward the figure lying in the ditch faceup.

Mykel looked down at the almost innocent face of the young ranker, then at the blood-smeared tunic with the slash across the abdomen, and a deeper thrust up under the ribs.

"Kersion didn't report back last night, and Wyorst couldn't find anyone who knew where he'd been. Some of his squadmates said he'd left early, wanted to get some sleep." Culeyt shook his head. "He'd have been better staying and drinking with them."

The hard-faced town patroller looked at Mykel. "Look close at the dust. Someone dragged him here from maybe around the gates."

Mykel looked at Culeyt. "Did anyone report anything last night?"

"No, sir. I checked that when Wyorst reported Kersion missing."

"I'd like to see whoever was on guard duty last night right after we finish here."

"Yes, sir."

Mykel turned back to the patroller. "What do you think happened?"

"Simple enough, Majer. The dusters'll do anything for coin. It's a couple of silvers for a little sniff. Your boy didn't let him off, one of them anyway. Wrenched the knife away from him and slashed his throat and wrist. He made it another two hundred yards north, still trying to get out to pay for another sniff. Found him by the road. Someone came along and robbed him, too. Later, probably."

That Kersion had made the duster pay was no consolation to Mykel.

"I'll take care of it from here, sir," said Culeyt. "I thought you should see."

Mykel nodded. "I'll be in my study. I'll see the duty guards once you round them up."

"Yes, sir."

Mykel walked back to the compound. He couldn't believe that the guards hadn't heard something, and if two dusters were involved, why would one drag Kersion's body away while the other one was dying. The surviving duster might have wanted what little remained in Kersion's wallet, but Mykel still had trouble believing that a duster cold enough to leave a companion to die would have cooperated in the first place. Where dreamdust and dusters were involved, anything might be possible . . . but he wanted to hear what the guards had to say.

Rhystan was waiting outside Mykel's study. "I just heard about Kersion."

Mykel gestured. The two walked into the small study.

Rhystan closed the thin door, so old that all the panels were cracked.

"There's something strange about this," Mykel said. "I

asked Culeyt to round up the guards who were on duty last night. They should have reported something. They didn't."

"Ah . . . I think they were from the garrison here, sir. They've been handling gate duty. It seemed only fair, with our men taking the casualties."

"From now on, one of ours with one of theirs. I'll tell the other officers." Mykel sighed.

"Are you going to put the town off-limits?"

"Do you think I should? We've already warned them about the women. I don't like the idea of keeping them cooped up here. That's trouble of another kind. I'd like to require them to go in pairs, at least. Will that work?"

"It might," Rhystan replied. "Especially if you tell them that you'll restrict everyone for a week for every time you find out that someone went out alone."

"I'd like to try that."

Rhystan nodded. "You going to eat?"

"Not till later. Go ahead."

With a nod the senior captain opened the door and left, closing it behind him. Mykel walked to the desk and picked up the duty rosters, leafing through them.

"Sir?" Culeyt's voice came through the thin door.

Mykel stood, walked to the door, and opened it.

Two Cadmians Mykel did not recognize—clearly from the local detachment—stood before Culeyt.

"Shymal." Culeyt inclined his head to the brown-haired taller Cadmian. "Frejyl." The second Cadmian was not quite rotund and far older, his black hair shot with gray.

"Captain, I'd like to talk with each one separately. I'll start with Shymal."

"We'll wait down the corridor, sir." Culeyt clearly understood what Mykel wanted.

Mykel gestured for the younger ranker to enter. "Take a seat, Shymal." After closing the door, Mykel slipped behind the small desk and seated himself.

The thin-faced ranker sat. His eyes did not meet Mykel's.

"You were on duty for the four glasses before midnight?"

"Yes, sir." Shymal shifted his weight in the hard wooden chair. "Me and Frejyl."

"Most of the men come back just before the eighth glass, don't they?"

"Guess so, sir. I mean, that's when they're supposed to be back, two glasses before midnight."

"Did you hear or see anything strange before that?"

"It's pretty quiet, sir, least until a quarter before the glass."

Mykel could sense Shymal's unease. "Why don't you tell me about it?"

"Sir?"

"About what happened. You're not sure about it, but something did happen. When did it happen?" Mykel waited.

The ranker looked at the floor planks, worn and battered under the latest coat of oil and wax. "Didn't think it was all that much, sir. A couple of fellows were talking. Far enough away that you couldn't see. Just heard it. Frejyl told me to wait. He'd go over and quiet them down. He was gone for a while. Not long, less than a quarter glass. He said it was two dusters, and he got them on their way."

Shymal was telling the truth, but he was still uneasy, Mykel sensed. "It didn't feel right to you, did it?"

"Lots of stuff hasn't felt right lately, sir."

"You didn't want to say anything because you didn't want to get into trouble."

"I didn't see anything, sir. Just didn't think Frejyl shoulda been away from the gate that long."

"Why not?"

"He just shouldn't. We're supposed to be guarding the gates, not talking to dusters."

"Did you hear him talking to someone?"

"No, sir. Well, yes, sir. I heard him talking, but I couldn't make out what he was saying. Then he stopped talking."

"For how long?"

"I don't know. It was a while before he walked back. He said everything was settled, and there wouldn't be any trouble."

Mykel asked questions for another quarter glass, but Shymal's story and reactions remained constant. Finally, he stood and walked to the door, opening it and calling for Captain Culeyt.

Culeyt reappeared with the other ranker.

"Shymal can go back to the barracks. He's not to leave the post until I finish looking into this. I'll need to speak to you after I talk to Frejyl here."

"Yes, sir." Culeyt nodded.

Mykel could sense a vague puzzlement from the captain, but he only smiled. "If you'd come in, Frejyl, and take a seat."

"Yes, sir."

Mykel closed the study door and seated himself. "Did you hear or see anything strange last night?"

"No . . . not really, sir." The older ranker shifted his weight on the armless oak chair, so old that the wood was deep golden brown, and black where it had been nicked or scarred.

"That's odd." Mykel smiled politely, waiting. "Are you sure?"

"There's always stuff out beyond the gates, sir. Always has been. Out a ways, maybe half a vingt or so is where the dusters get their sniffs. Dusters come by here all the time."

"Maybe strange isn't the right word." Mykel managed a pleasant smile. "Did you see or hear any dusters last night?"

"There was one. He was louder than most. I told Shymal to watch the gates. I went out and told him to be quietlike."

Despite Frejyl's calm outward appearance, Mykel could sense the fear and guilt. "Had he already stabbed Kersion? Or did you help with that, too?"

"Sir?"

"You were involved, Frejyl. The only question is how much."

"Sir, that is not true."

"Don't lie to me. You were gone a quarter glass, long enough to drag Kersion's body north and into the ditch where it wouldn't be found immediately. The only questions are whether you were the one who stabbed Kersion and the duster and where you put the coins you took."

"Sir, I'd never stab another Cadmian. No, sir."

That particular sentence rang true, even to Mykel's Talent.

"What about the duster?"

Frejyl shook his head. "No, sir."

"So what did you do? Let Kersion die and then take his coins?"

"No, sir. He was almost gone when I got there. The duster, he tried to take the knife to me. I used my rifle to knock it out of his hand, and he started running . . . well, he was stumbling. I let him go. Kersion was dead by then, and his belt wallet had been cut away."

Mykel had noticed that. "Go on. What happened then?"

"I went after the duster. He was lying on the side of the road. Figured I might as well take his wallet. Suppose I shoulda said something, but it wouldn't have brought the boy back."

"Why did you drag Kersion out of sight?"

Frejyl looked at the floor.

Mykel waited.

Finally, the ranker looked up. "No one was going to believe me. Not you. Not anyone. Figured I might as well keep the coins and let the dusters take all the blame."

Unfortunately, it all made sense, especially after the low level of discipline in the Iron Stem garrison, followed by Hersiod's actions. Mykel suppressed a sigh.

"You'll face a court-martial for theft, Frejyl." Mykel stood. "Culeyt!"

The captain opened the door. "Sir?"

"Cadmian Frejyl is being charged with theft. We could also charge him with lying, but I don't see much point in that."

"He didn't kill Kersion?"

"No. The patroller was right. The duster did. Frejyl happened on the crime and made off with the coins. Find somewhere to lock him up. We'll convene the court-martial first thing tomorrow."

"Yes, sir."

Mykel stood alone in the study after Culeyt marched Frejyl off.

He supposed that such matters occurred at every post, now and again, but he was in charge, and it bothered him. He'd still implement the pairing rule, because what had happened to Kersion likely would have been prevented if there had been at least two rankers together. Beer and spirits were bad enough, but from what he'd heard and seen, the dreamdust from the dustcats was even worse, and now he had to deal with dusters in addition to the local women, the ancients, the sandwolves and other predators, and unhappy miners and workmen, not to mention hotheaded Reillies and Squawts. Two or three silvers for a sniff of the dust? That added up to a lot of golds, but for whom?

He sat down at the desk, and with frequent references to the last set he had written, in Hyalt, he began to write out the court-martial orders. The first page was easy enough, and he set it aside to dry.

There was a knock on the half-open door.

"Sir?" offered Chyndylt, the senior squad leader for Fifteenth Company, who was the duty squad leader for the day. "There's a letter for you. Came with the sandox coach. Driver said that you could pay later." He extended the missive.

"Thank you." A letter? From whom? It certainly couldn't be from Rachyla, much as he would have liked that. He doubted he would ever get a letter from her, but then, from the beginning, Rachyla had always confounded him, perhaps because he had never been able to read her, or understand truly the culture from which she had come. Yet . . . there was something there, something that he could not deny, as well as something she could neither deny nor acknowledge except in ways that no one else could see. She was held in a shimmersilk prison, and Mykel could only hope that a dagger of the ancients could prove sharp enough to free her.

Mykel rose and took the envelope, then smiled as he saw the careful script that was his mother's. He set it on the narrow desk, opening it only after Chyndylt had left.

Dear Mykel,

We were all so pleased to get your letter. You write so seldom. We had hoped you would be coming back to Elcien. That way you could visit sometime over the end-days. Sesalia had hoped you would be able to see little Mykela. She and Bortal hoped you would be pleased they named her after you.

Things are getting harder here. The alectors are requiring longer hours in the mills and manufactories. They removed all landers from one place. No one knows why.

There was enough work that no one was put out. They went to work in the steel mill.

Viencet spent the summer working as a gardener's assistant for Cymeryl. He's a spice factor. His house is like a palace. It is in the hills to the northeast off the old mill road. Viencet could work in the steel mill, but he is looking for something else. Your father says he should work there until he can find another place, but Viencet says he won't ever find another place. He's not working now, and he avoids your father as much as he can.

We got a good crop from the grapes and from the garden. We all look forward to seeing you before too long . . .

Mykel folded the letter carefully and slipped it into his tunic. He couldn't help but worry about Viencet. His younger brother had always wanted a "good" place without too much study, without too much work, and without too much risk. From what Mykel had seen, unless a man came from wealth, such positions didn't exist.

Outside the small headquarters building, the fall wind moaned.

Mykel looked at the unfinished court-martial orders. Finally, he picked up the pen.

36

On Quinti morning, Dainyl stood on the stairs leading down to the main floor of the house. Someone was pounding on the front door—practically at sunrise, no less.

"Dearest! Would you . . . I'm not exactly . . ." called Lystrana from the breakfast room.

In his undertunic and trousers, Dainyl made his way to the door and opened it. Standing there in the fog and chill was Adya—one of Zelyert's older assistants. Behind her waited Zelyert's personal coach.

"Marshal . . . the Highest regrets the intrusion, but he requests your immediate presence at the Hall of Justice. He said to tell you that it's of the greatest importance."

"Come in out of the chill. Let me grab my tunic and gear, and I'll be with you in a moment." Dainyl closed the door behind Adya, then hurried to the breakfast room.

"What is it?" Lystrana's eyes narrowed.

"The Highest wants me at the Hall of Justice as soon as I can get there. His carriage is waiting outside." Dainyl shook his head. "I don't like it. Not when you're leaving for Dereka this morning. I'll take one of your cases with me. If I can't meet you at the Table, I'll just take it to Dereka. Jonyst and his driver can get it to you."

"Maybe I can get to the Table while you're still there." Lystrana smiled nervously. "I'll try. I might wait a bit."

"I'll do what I can." He embraced her, tightly, for a long moment, then stepped away and walked swiftly back to the foyer and up the steps to their bedchamber, where he finished dressing. When he came back down, wearing his flying jacket and carrying the heavier of Lystrana's cases, Lystrana was standing in the foyer, talking to Adya.

". . . leaving for Dereka this morning . . ."

". . . so sorry . . ."

Lystrana handed a large chunk of bread to Dainyl. "At least eat this on the way."

"I don't know if the Highest . . ." Dainyl grinned.

"He'll have to deal with the crumbs," suggested Adya.

After giving Lystrana a last kiss, with the bread in one hand, the case in the other, Dainyl followed Adya out to the carriage. With the case and two alectors, the carriage was cramped, but better than most hacks.

"Do you know what this is all about?"

"No, sir. All I know is that he had a recorder with him, a woman. I don't know her."

Either Sulerya or Delari, then. If either were in Elcien, matters in Blackstear or Lysia were not good. Dainyl frowned. The odds were that the recorder was Delari, since Sulerya had support from Eighth Company and close to a battalion of Cadmians. Had the ancients or the Reillies overrun

Blackstear? Zelyert wanted to use Myrmidons, and quickly, or he wouldn't have roused Dainyl out so early.

Once the carriage pulled up to the Hall of Justice, Dainyl got out and lugged the case up the stone steps, across the receiving hall, and back down the inside staircase to the lower level. Adya stayed with him.

The High Alector of Justice had obviously sensed Dainyl arriving and stood in the doorway to his private study. "What's the case for, Marshal? Weapons, by chance?"

Dainyl shook his head. "Gear for the Regional Alector of Dereka."

"That may have to wait." Appearing as grim as Dainyl had ever seen him, Zelyert stepped back to let Dainyl enter the study, then closed the door. Beside the small conference table stood a tall and angular woman in the green of a recorder. Deep circles ringed her eyes, and her entire being radiated exhaustion.

"Delari." Dainyl inclined his head.

"I see that you are now marshal. The High Alector did not tell me that."

Zelyert gestured to the chairs around the table. "We might as well sit. Delari has had some exhausting times." He waited until everyone was seated. "If you'd tell the marshal what you told me."

"We've lost use of the Table at Blackstear. We've lost the entire building. Forces of Myrmidons from Ifryn came through the long translation tubes, and they kept coming. They had lightcutters, and they overwhelmed the guards."

"They can use the Table there as an entry to any Table," Zelyert pointed out. "Every Table chamber could be a battlefield."

As if most of the chambers weren't already, reflected Dainyl. "When . . . how?"

"Yesterday," replied Delari. "I managed to use my Talent to conceal the hidden chamber. They've already started fortifying the Table building, using lightcutters to cut stone to seal windows. Early this morning, while they were recovering, I slipped out with Talent cover and got to the Table. I had to use the Table to kill three of them before I could translate here."

"How many Myrmidons are there?" asked Dainyl.

"No more than twenty, right now. From what I overheard, they lost forty to take Blackstear."

"If you act quickly, before they get reinforcements," suggested Zelyert, "you can stop them. I know you don't want to move Myrmidons out of Elcien, Marshal, but I don't see that we have any choice."

Dainyl didn't either. "What sort of weapons did they have besides lightcutters?"

"Sabres. Not all of the lightcutters worked," replied Delari. "Long translations are hard on the crystals."

Dainyl turned to Zelyert. "How many Myrmidons are there, or were there, on Ifryn?"

"There were twelve companies, eight with pteridons."

"Were the foot companies the same size as the flying companies?"

"They're larger—sixty rankers."

"It sounds like one entire foot company, no more than two. They knew which Table to target and trained for it." Dainyl turned back to Delari. "What was the weather like?"

"It was cloudy and cold, but I don't think it was snowing."

"Is the Table still activated?"

"Yes."

Zelyert frowned.

"Do you know if they had any Table engineers with them?"

"I don't think so. They didn't seem to know anything about the Tables, except as transport."

Dainyl turned to Zelyert. "Do you have any lightcutters here? I'd sent some under seal."

"They're in the storeroom."

"Good. I'll need three."

Delari's eyes widened.

So did Zelyert's. "I need a marshal, not a missing commander."

"You need to isolate the Ifryn Myrmidons in Blackstear before anything gets worse. If I can do that, then you can handle them at leisure—or even let them all freeze. Delari and Chastyl will be able to tell if I'm successful."

"And if you're not?" asked Zelyert pointedly.

"Then all the Myrmidons in the west won't be enough to stop them," replied Dainyl.

"Do you know Table mechanics?" asked Delari.

"Enough to inactivate the Table," temporized Dainyl, standing to forestall more questions. "The lightcutters?" He didn't like revealing skills the High Alector didn't know he possessed, especially as neither Duarch remained Talent-augmented, but stopping the consternation and disaster angry Myrmidons from Ifryn could create was more important. The more authority he had, the more he had to reveal about himself, and the less he could keep to himself.

"How—?" began Delari.

"We'll worry about that once we get them isolated." Dainyl looked to Zelyert. "Highest, if you could have someone bring the lightcutters to the Table chamber, please?" He'd tacked on the "please" because he could sense Zelyert's growing irritation. The High Alector had no business being irritated, but there was no point in not trying to mollify him.

"I will." Zelyert left the study first. He was still angry.

Dainyl picked up the case.

"Marshal . . . do you know what you're doing?" asked Delari quietly. "You could get stranded in Blackstear, and with the Ifryn Myrmidons as angry as they are, even you . . ."

"Unfortunately, I do know. Sulerya taught me, and you're the only recorder I'd tell that to." He began to walk toward the Table chamber.

"I never thought it would be like this," Delari said quietly.

Neither had Dainyl, for all that he had learned in the past two years. They walked without saying more to the Table chamber, where Delari opened both doors for Dainyl. Lystrana had not arrived, and that was probably for the best.

Chastyl glanced from Delari to Dainyl, and then to the case. His eyebrows rose. He looked even more exhausted than did Delari.

"That's for the new RA in Dereka," Dainyl explained.

"I hadn't heard . . ."

"My wife. She'll be here later to translate there."

"Do you think . . . ?" began Chastyl. "With Blackstear . . . ?"

"Better now than later," replied Dainyl. "That's why it's important to get Lystrana to Dereka. It's been without a regional alector for too long. If I get back in time, I'll go with her and then translate back."

Another expression of puzzlement crossed Chastyl's face.

"I have a task in Blackstear. You and Delari will need to monitor the Tables."

The door to the Table chamber opened again. The High Alector stepped up to Dainyl and handed him the lightcutters—in their holsters.

Dainyl fastened one holster to his belt on each side, and slipped the third inside his tunic. "One way or another, this will be quick." He stepped onto the Table.

As he did, a young alector in a blue tunic appeared on the mirrored surface beside Dainyl, his eyes wide. Dainyl stepped around the youth and concentrated on the dark depths beneath the Table, sliding downward and . . .

. . . into the chill purple duskiness. He focused all his attention on the black locator, by far the hardest to discern, and extended a Talent link.

Around him flashed lines of pinkish purple, and in the distance—except it was a distance with no direction—he sensed a vague amber-green force, links of a type. The translation tube shivered, once and then once more, as if the ancients were forging those links with a massive Talent hammer.

Dainyl redoubled his concentration on Blackstear. He felt the locator approach—it was never that he approached it—and the silvered-black barrier dissolved before him.

He held full shields, and his hands went to the lightcutters at his belt.

Five Myrmidons in the gray and green uniforms of Ifryn lifted lightcutters. Dainyl sensed their shields, and fired at the two with the weakest shields, using Talent to break an opening in each shield. Both Myrmidons fell, dying.

". . . High Alector!"

". . . get help!"

Lightcutter beams from the remaining three played across his shields, but Dainyl managed to hold them firm. He focused on the Myrmidon heading for the doorway, cutting him down—and exhausting the charge in one of his own lightcutters. He dropped the useless weapon and yanked the one from inside his tunic, even as he focused on the undercaptain who reached for a riflelike lightcutter.

Dainyl lashed out with Talent at the other remaining ranker, throwing him against the stone of the wall, then flared a bolt of Talent, not at the heavily shielded undercaptain, but at the weapon, which felt like a miniature lightcannon.

The weapon's power crystals exploded, and the undercaptain staggered back.

In the alector's moment of surprise Dainyl struck with both lightcutters and Talent. For the first onslaught, the junior officer's shields held, but not for the second.

Dainyl did not even leave the Table, but probed with his Talent, weakened, for the tiny octagonal crystal within the Table that would put it into an inert state. He offered a small Talent pulse and could sense the Table reacting.

Even as the door to the chamber opened, and a blast of light and heat flared against his weakened shields, Dainyl was concentrating on the darkness beneath, and sliding through the mirrored surface of the Table . . .

. . . into the welcome chill of the translation tube.

For a timeless but apparently long moment, he did nothing, before forcing himself to focus on the brilliant white locator of Elcien. His thoughts and Talent felt sluggish.

Slowly . . . slowly . . . the locator vector neared him, and finally, the white-silver barrier shattered away from him in large fragments.

He stood on the Table, taking two staggering steps to keep from falling. Frost and cold mist wreathed him, something that had not happened since he had first learned to use the Tables. Deliberately, carefully, Dainyl stepped down. His legs were wobbly, and he had to lean against the Table. Blackness swam around him, and he put his head down to keep from losing consciousness.

"Are you all right?" asked Delari.

". . . took a lot . . . of Talent . . . empty stomach . . ."

After several moments, Dainyl straightened. He didn't see Zelyert, but Adya was standing in the corner of the chamber. He realized he was still holding the lightcutters. It took a deliberate effort to holster them.

"Sir? What should I tell the High Alector?"

That alone told Dainyl that Zelyert was still angry. Still, until he regained his Talent-strength, Dainyl had best not show his own anger at the self-centered arrogance of the High Alector. He forced a smile. "You can report to him that the Table at Blackstear is inactive—"

"We can confirm that," added Chastyl. "It's off the grid."

"—and that there are five less Myrmidons from Ifryn at Blackstear. Where can I get something to eat, quickly?"

"You can sit down in my study, sir," offered the assistant. "I'll get you something."

Neither Chastyl nor any of the guards said a word as Dainyl followed Adya out of the Table chamber, with Delari behind him. Dainyl looked to see if Lystrana's case was still set against the wall and was reassured to see that it was. He winced as he saw the blue tunic folded on top of the neat pile of garments in the corner of the chamber. His stomach turned. Yet he had done exactly the same thing. He'd even sought out alectors whose only offense was that they had broken the rules in an attempt to survive. The fact that a whole world might die if entry from Ifryn were not restricted didn't take away those deaths.

"This way, Marshal . . ." prompted Adya.

Dainyl followed, almost blindly, finally sinking onto the hard wooden chair set at the corner of the small writing desk in a truly tiny study.

Delari remained standing, her back against the stone of the wall. She did not speak until Adya was well away. "How did you manage that? It's impossible to translate from an inactive Table."

"There's the slightest delay between the Talent command and when it starts powering down. You just can't hesitate. Not in the slightest."

She shook her head. "I wouldn't want to try that."

"You shouldn't. It's not your line of work."

"What are you, Marshal—Myrmidon, flier, officer, assassin, Table mechanic, recorder?"

At the moment, he felt more like an assassin. "I'm just trying to do what has to be done." *And not liking it in the slightest.*

Adya returned with a mug of cider, a wedge of cheese, and half a loaf of dark bread. "It's not fancy . . ."

"It looks wonderful." Dainyl looked up. "Has my wife arrived yet?"

"Sir?"

"Didn't anyone tell you? She's the new RA for Dereka. She's scheduled to translate there later this morning."

"I'd heard that she . . . but . . . after all this?"

"It's probably safer right now than it will be in a day or so, even with one Table off the grid," Dainyl pointed out.

Adya looked to Delari.

"He's right about that."

"Let me check on your wife," offered Adya.

"Tell her I'll be with her as soon as I can," replied Dainyl with a mouthful of bread and cheese.

In moments, or so it seemed, Dainyl had gone through all the bread and cheese, as well as drained the large mug of cider. He could feel his light-headedness begin to recede.

"Zelyert is afraid of you," Delari said. "That's why he's avoiding you. You may have as much Talent as he does, and he's the most Talented of the High Alectors."

Dainyl didn't feel all that Talented. He just felt tired. He also wondered how many more alectors would die at his hand or through his orders.

Less than a tenth of a glass later, as Dainyl was beginning to feel he had regained some of his strength and Talent, Adya returned.

"Your wife is down the corridor, outside the Table chamber. She's waiting for you."

"Thank you very much." Dainyl rose.

This time Delari did not follow him as he walked back to the Table chamber. She headed in the direction of Zelyert's private study.

Lystrana stood outside the outer door to the Table chamber. "I'm glad to see you."

"I'm glad to be here to see you," he replied. "I can translate to Dereka with you, but I'll have to return immediately. I'll have to take First Company to Blackstear."

She glanced at the weapons at his belt, then raised her left eyebrow, as if to ask what had been going on.

"Trouble in Blackstear. We need to get you to Dereka." He really didn't want to explain more, given where they were. He opened the doors for Lystrana, and she carried the smaller case through the foyer and into the Table chamber.

Chastyl looked up. "Do you think this is wise?"

"She has to get to Dereka. It's calmer now," Dainyl replied. "It won't stay that way." He walked over to the wall and picked up the case he had left there, then joined Lystrana on the Table. "If the High Alector asks, I'll be back very shortly."

The recorder looked as though he wanted to protest, but he refrained.

Dainyl nodded to Lystrana, then waited a moment, until she began to fade and drop into the Table. Only then did he concentrate on the dark tube beneath.

In the purpled shadowy chill, he thought he could sense a warmer purpleness, but he did not dwell on it, concentrating instead on the crimson-gold locator of Dereka.

While the flashes of purple were fewer than when he had translated to Blackstear, there were far more than there had been even a few months before, and the amber-green links reverberated in the immeasurable distance.

He was surprised to find the locator flashing toward him, the silvered crimson-gold barrier dissolving away from him.

Belatedly, he strengthened what shields he had left as he emerged practically on top of Lystrana. He had to step sideways to avoid crashing into her.

Four alector guards, tired-eyed but alert, watched the Table, but their eyes flickered toward Jonyst.

The recorder nodded. "Marshal of Myrmidons and the chief assistant to the High Alector of Finance."

Dainyl stepped off the table with the heavier case and set it down, taking the second case from Lystrana.

Once they were off the Table, Lystrana murmured, "You never told me why you're headed north, besides trouble."

Dainyl set the smaller case down. "Myrmidons from Ifryn stormed the Table at Blackstear."

Jonyst looked up from where he stood at the end of the Table. "I couldn't help but overhear, Marshal. The Table at Blackstear has gone inactive."

Dainyl smiled politely. "I know. That's why we'll be able to handle them with a company, but we'll need to put the Table back on the grid before long."

Lystrana's eyes widened and dropped once more to the lightcutters at Dainyl's belt.

He nodded, very slightly. "Later." He raised his voice. "Jonyst, Lystrana is taking over as the new RA for Dereka."

The recorder smiled broadly. "That is good news for those of us here in Dereka. I was wondering when the Duarch would replace Yadaryst."

"Would it be possible for your driver to get her and these cases to her headquarters?"

"Guersa would be pleased to help with that. I'll have her come to carry the other case."

Dainyl turned to Lystrana and hugged her. He didn't like doing it in public, but the way matters were turning out, he had no idea when he'd see her again. "You be careful."

"You're the one who needs to be careful. The green is stronger. Not much, but it is. Please be careful," she whispered in his ear before they broke apart.

"I will."

Dainyl stepped back onto the Table, concentrating.

The purple chill barely bothered him as he linked with the white locator of Elcien and then flowed through the mist of silver and white.

He was off the Table before Chastyl spoke.

"That was quick, Marshal. I haven't even had time to pass the word to the High Alector." His smile was quick, but held a hint of a grin.

"I'd guess you won't have to," replied Dainyl. "I can tell him what he needs to know."

With a nod, he left the Table chamber, wondering if Zelyert had left the Hall or if he remained in his study. He also couldn't help but worry about Lystrana's words about the Talent-green of the ancients being stronger.

Delari stepped into the corridor from Zelyert's study as Dainyl neared. "The Highest would like to speak to us."

"I'm certain," Dainyl replied dryly, moving into the private study behind Delari and closing the door.

"Where did you go, Marshal?" Zelyert remained standing.

"To Dereka and back. I chose to escort the new RA. I admit to a certain proprietary interest in her safety, but knowing she is safe in Dereka will allow me to concentrate without distractions on resolving the difficulties in Blackstear."

"Since it took little time," Zelyert replied, "that is acceptable." His voice hardened, a touch. "We can't leave the Table inactive. When the Archon shifts the Master Scepter, that will put too much stress on the grid. We don't know when that will be, but it won't be all that long."

"I know. But without a Table, when I take First Company to Blackstear, it won't take that long to flush them out."

"You think you should leave Elcien? You personally?"

"It will be quicker if I go. If you don't want me to, I'll send Alcyna. If I go, though, I should be able to return by the Table. We'll have to leave Myrmidons to guard the Table, and we'll have to take most of those lightcutters you have under seal. I don't imagine the Myrmidons from Ifryn will have left either guards or weapons."

"When would you leave?" pressed Zelyert.

"This morning," replied Dainyl. "We'd overnight in Klamat and attack tomorrow morning."

"You don't think any of them will escape?"

Delari laughed. "It's already winter there. The harbor's frozen in, and so is the river from Klamat. There's nowhere to go and no way to get there."

"I'll have Seventh Company shift two squads from Tempre here to cover dispatches and emergency transport. It would help if one of your assistants could translate the orders to Tempre . . ." Dainyl went on to offer a brief outline of what he planned, trying not to be too specific, but also including the need for fully charged lightcutters for the Myrmidons to use inside the Table building.

He wasn't looking forward to frigid cold-weather flying—or what waited at the end of the flight.

37

A wind that sounded far more like winter than fall whistled outside the headquarters building. Mykel stood as Rhystan walked into the study, carrying a rifle.

"I have this feeling . . ." offered Mykel.

"It's worse than that. This is what third squad found with the dead Reillie." Rhystan handed a Cadmian rifle to Mykel. "Take a close look."

Mykel took the weapon, turning it and examining it closely. There was neither a maker's mark nor a serial number on the rifle, yet it was almost brand-new, with few scratches on the stock or barrel, and clearly a Cadmian rifle, made in either Faitel or Fordall. "Another contraband weapon. How many do you think they have?"

"Who knows?" replied the older captain tiredly, letting himself slump slightly in the chair. "I'd say a lot. Maybe even enough to arm all of them. I wouldn't wager against their also having enough ammunition as well. They're already gathering to the west of Wesrigg. The scouts say that they've got more than a thousand men."

"How could they come up with that many after all these years?" Mykel sat on the corner of the small writing desk.

" 'Men' is a relative term. Their women ride and shoot as well as the men, and that's with hand-forged, single-shot weapons. The boys—and the girls—can shoot before they're grown. They do tend to use the girls more as long-range snipers. Our big advantage has been in weapons and tactics.

Now they've got better weapons than they ever had, and a larger force."

"They're still angry with us, and with Majer Hersiod," Mykel added. "Do we know where they're headed?"

"After us."

"I don't think that they'll attack directly. They never have. They'll feint, then get us to follow them and set traps and ambushes all along the way."

"That points to Borlan eventually. There's a bridge there, and Iron Stem and Wesrigg are pretty poor. If they wipe us out, they can loot Borlan and retreat into the Westerhills for years."

"But they'll want to hit us first, or make us chase them?"

"Either way, we'll end up chasing them," Rhystan pointed out.

"How good is Nineteenth Company?"

"What do you have in mind?"

"Ride in force out the high road to Wesrigg," Mykel said. "The road's open enough that they'd have trouble ambushing us. If they attack, then we'll do whatever's necessary. If not, we'll start after them. They'll ride like the storms. That's when we'll back off with Third Battalion, and set up along what looks to be their planned track southward. We'll have Hamylt pursue—at a leisurely and careful pace."

"And you'll have Hamylt chase them toward us?"

"That's the hope."

"You don't like playing others' games, do you?"

Mykel never had. "I don't know if it will work, but let's see what else the scouts can find out."

"The local inholders won't like us pulling out the patrols against the predators."

"They'd like it even less if the Reillies and the Squawts came in and took over Iron Stem," Mykel replied.

Rhystan laughed ironically. "They won't see it that way."

He was doubtless right about that, Mykel thought. "Just get all the scouts together, along with the company commanders, say, in a glass, and we'll go over things. Maybe some of them have already noticed small things that will make it clearer."

"Could be." Rhystan sounded less than convinced.

Mykel was the one to laugh, so dour had Rhystan sounded. "You may be right, but we can hope."

"Just so long as we don't rely on hope, Majer."

After Rhystan left, Mykel stood and stretched, thinking.

Were the manufactories in Faitel producing rifles for the Reillies and the Squawts? Why? It almost seemed like the alectors were out to destroy both the hill peoples and the Cadmians. Rachyla had said that the alectors had their own purposes, and the soarers had indicated the same. What had the soarer "said" exactly on that night in Hyalt?

He concentrated, bringing back the words, more like thoughts planted in his own mind.

The invaders, the ones you call alectors, will kill you if they sense what you are. They wish no rivals to their ability . . . They will bleed the world dry long before its time.

Were the Cadmians rivals to their ability? Had Mykel and Third Battalion been too effective in dealing with the rebel alectors in Tempre? Or was something else happening, as had occurred with the rebel alectors in Hyalt and Tempre?

38

Alcyna looked up as Dainyl stepped into her study.

"We have a problem," he announced, brushing unruly black hair back off his forehead. "Foot Myrmidons came through the Table from Ifryn and stormed Blackstear. They hold the Table building, but the recorder escaped, and the Table's been temporarily inactivated. The High Alector wants us to take it back so that the recorders can reactivate the Table before the Master Scepter is transferred."

"That soon?" Alcyna's eyes widened only slightly.

"I don't know. I don't know that it could be more than weeks or a few seasons at most. Zelyert doesn't know, either. That's why he's worried about the Table."

"When did all this happen?"

"Yesterday. The High Alector found out early this morning."

"I can't say I'm totally surprised," Alcyna replied. "There or Soupat would be logical. They're the most isolated. Do you want me to take First Company to Blackstear?"

"Not this time. The Table's been inactivated. That means they're trapped there, but the High Alector wants the Table back on the grid as soon as possible. We can't do that until we retake Blackstear. While I'm gone, you're in command here." Dainyl smiled wryly. "Why don't you work out a plan for Seventh Company—and some of Fifth, if necessary—to deal with something like this happening elsewhere? Like in Soupat. You've already pointed out that there's nowhere else more isolated in the west than Blackstear. In the east, they might target Prosp, but if they do, Brekylt and Noryan will have to deal with it. At least for now."

"You don't think the Ifryn Myrmidons were sent information by Brekylt?" asked Alcyna.

"It's possible, but I don't think so." Dainyl paused. "Do you?"

"No. That's not his way. He'd have no control," she pointed out. "When are you leaving?"

"In a glass, if we can manage it."

"That's pushing it. You have cold-weather gear?"

"In my study. I stopped and picked it up on the way back from the Hall of Justice."

"You would." Alcyna laughed sardonically. "I hope you get back before anything else happens. I'd rather not deal with the Highest. He's not all that fond of women."

"I'd rather you didn't have to, either. I'll be back to you before I head out." After a nod to her, Dainyl left her and walked down the corridor toward Captain Ghasylt's study. He'd noted the captain had been there when he'd first entered headquarters.

Ghasylt immediately stood as Dainyl appeared. "Marshal, sir?"

"We're leaving for Blackstear—all of First Company—in one glass. A company of foot Myrmidons from Ifryn stormed the Table in Blackstear. The recorder escaped, and the Table is shut down. That leaves the rebel Myrmidons trapped in

Blackstear, but the recorders can't reactivate it until we retake it from them."

"It's winter up there already, sir," Ghasylt said, his voice even.

"I know. It still has to be done. That's one reason why I'm coming with First Company."

The company commander nodded. "We've got two fliers from third squad out on dispatch runs. They won't be back until late this afternoon."

"That's fine. They can fly urgent dispatches until the squads from Seventh Company get here tomorrow afternoon. Then they can fly to rejoin us."

"A glass might be pressing it, sir. We'll have to make sure everyone's got all their cold-weather gear."

"Do the best you can. I'll have to get mine together as well."

"Sir . . . ?"

"Yes."

"You don't have to say if you can't, but for a company of Myrmidons to take a long translation to Acorus . . . I mean, most of us have never even seen a Table . . . it'd seem to me that things aren't good on Ifryn." Ghasylt shifted his weight from one foot to the other, but kept his eyes on Dainyl.

"I honestly don't know," Dainyl replied, "but my judgment would be the same as yours. There have been more wild translations and refugees coming through the Tables. Some of them have come through armed and firing weapons and had to be killed. I'd imagine conditions on Ifryn are anything but good and getting worse, but the Archon has said nothing to anyone here."

"Thank you, sir."

"I wish matters were different, Captain, but Acorus won't last long either, if thousands of alectors translate here in the next few weeks."

Ghasylt's eyes widened as he understood the implications of Dainyl's words. "No, sir, but it seems a terrible waste."

Dainyl nodded. "I don't like it, either. All we can do, right now, is keep matters from getting worse. That's probably all anyone can do."

"We'll be ready, Marshal."

"I'll join you shortly." Dainyl turned.

A terrible waste. Ghasylt's words ran through Dainyl's mind as he headed back to his study to go over the last-moment preparations for the immediate deployment. For the past few years, Dainyl and Lystrana had talked about what might happen, and how Efra and Acorus could not take all the alectors living on Ifryn and how many would die in the long translation and how many would become wild translations and die. In a sense, the words had been just that—words. Now, real alectors and alectresses and children were dying, even before Ifryn died. Yet, as Khelaryt had said, what could he do to save them without dooming all alectors?

Why had it come down to this? Could the Archon not have planned better? Did the Archon and the High Alectors regard the majority of alectors in the same fashion as alectors viewed the indigens? Or was it inevitable so long as the oldest alectors drew so much lifeforce? Or was it that no one wanted to consider events before they drew near, when it was too late to even mitigate the situation?

39

There is no higher calling for a people than to create beauty and structure where it has not existed previously. In its time, every world in the endless universe will be formed, will exist, and will perish. Some will perish even before their creation is complete, and others may endure the long life of the universe. Upon many of those worlds, there will be no life. Upon others, that life will consist of lichens, algae, and other minute forms that will never progress toward intelligence. Upon still others, there will be animal and plant life, but sentience will not appear.

Only upon a comparative handful of worlds will sentience appear, and in many cases, with the advent of technologies that enable widescale warfare, will come a decline that will destroy that sentience before it has barely begun to learn what intelligence is and could be. That occurs all too often because sentience without individual and societal self-mastery enables destruction more readily than creation.

Sentience rewards those who possess it and master it—with creations of beauty and joy, with an understanding of what the universe is and will be, and with mastery of the worlds in which those intelligences find themselves. Yet, at the same time, sentience exacts great demands upon any world on which it arises and upon any society that reveres sentience.

What do all these possibilities have to do with being a responsible alector? Everything, for the thinking alector must understand that sentience of a lasting nature is rare, and that no price is too high to pay for the perpetuation of a society that enshrines sentience. We must never forget that we, too, as a society will be called upon periodically to pay the price in blood for our way of life, and that at such times, not all will survive. Should we forget that price, and what it entails, all that we are, and all that we represent, will perish as surely as will we. . . .

Views of the Highest
Illustra
W.T. 1513

40

Two solid glasses of flight had brought First Company eastward over a lower section of the peaks of the Coast Range and then northward, roughly following the high road from Elcien to Harmony. The pteridons flew at an altitude of a thousand yards, high enough to afford the Myrmidons a view of the terrain ahead and low enough that the pteridons did not use an inordinate amount of lifeforce— nor did the fliers have to contend with the colder air that would have surrounded them at a higher altitude. Flying was cold enough, because they were under a high layer of clouds that blocked direct sunlight, and left the world beneath them looking winter-brown and gray, although there was technically still a week left in fall.

Each Myrmidon had also been supplied with two lightcutters, in addition to the pteridon-powered skylances, for use inside the Blackstear Table building. Zelyert hadn't been happy about that, either.

As Ghasylt had announced to the company, the northward flight, especially as they neared Blackstear, would make a winter Spine run seem warm. Dainyl was flying wing on the captain, if in the second seat harness behind Halya, one of the younger members of the company, normally in second squad. As marshal, he did not rate a pteridon, scarce as they were, but he still missed being the one who actually flew the pteridon.

From behind Halya, Dainyl studied the high road below and to his left. While there was an occasional wagon or rider, most stretches of the road were empty, except for the five vingts or so on each side of a hamlet or town. The horizon to the north was a featureless gray, and that worried Dainyl because it suggested one of the northern blizzards might be brewing.

The wind had begun to shift, from the northeast to the northwest, and the air felt slightly warmer. Slightly warmer meant only that the air would freeze unprotected skin in perhaps a tenth of a glass rather than in moments. It also indicated a greater likelihood of a storm.

Another third of a glass passed before Dainyl could see Harmony almost dead ahead, where the two high roads crossed, and where the one First Company had followed turned from a northeast direction to due east, running straight as a rifle barrel for three hundred vingts from Harmony to Soulend. The other high road ran to Klamat, some 270 vingts north of Harmony. Beyond Klamat no high roads ran. From there First Company would have to fly across the frozen Moors of Yesterday to Blackstear.

From nowhere, a howling wind buffeted the pteridon, and the Talent creature's left wing went up, and the right dropped, more than forty degrees. Even before Dainyl caught the sense of command from Halya to the blue-winged creature, the pteridon had righted itself. Even after they were level, the wind raked across Dainyl's face like miniature daggers with ice-fiery points, then fell off until the pteridons were flying through absolutely calm air.

Dainyl glanced ahead.

The featureless gray looked more like a wall of clouds. He judged it to be a good twenty vingts away. What bothered him more than even the wall-like appearance of the clouds was the growing hint of blackish green behind the clouds.

The light strengthened as the fliers continued northward, passing Harmony, and changing course so that they flew due north, following the high road that led to Klamat. Dainyl glanced up. The higher clouds that had been above them had thinned, but the sky still held but the barest hint of green, lost in a silver-gray sheen, although the air around Dainyl seemed to become both grayer and greener with each vingt flown.

He looked ahead once more. Now the clouds had become more distinct, showing a wall of dark gray for the first few hundred yards up from the ground, and then turning positively black for the next several thousand. Under the leading edge of the storm, Dainyl could see a line where the ground and trees had begun to turn white from snow that fell in sheets.

"Marshal!"

Dainyl turned his head.

Ghasylt had eased his pteridon closer to that of Halya and Dainyl. "We can't fly through that!" The captain gestured toward the dark wall of the storm.

"Turn back to Harmony! Land at the local Cadmian garrison there!" Dainyl called back.

"Harmony Cadmian garrison! Yes, sir!"

Ghasylt banked his pteridon into a descending right-hand turn.

As Halya followed, an unseen force pressed the pteridon downward, into a dive.

Dainyl could sense the increased lifeforce draw as the

pteridon struggled to avoid losing more altitude, and as the wings beat faster. He watched as the forests flanking the high road drew closer and closer.

The pteridon was less than fifty yards above the tops of the fir trees before Halya managed to level out. They had lost over a thousand yards in altitude in the space of moments. Slowly, the pteridon began to climb until, once more flying wing to Ghasylt, they followed the high road south back to Harmony at an altitude of roughly five hundred yards.

Dainyl swallowed. He'd never felt that severe a downdraft, not in all his years of flying, but he'd flown mostly in the south. He glanced back at the rest of the company. While the other fliers seemed to have hit the same downdraft, they had not lost as much altitude, probably because their pteridons had not been carrying double.

To the north, behind First Company, the clouds continued to darken, advancing inexorably southward. The advance fliers had not seen the storm rising. From where had it come? Had the ancients something to do with it?

Dainyl shook his head. Storms happened, even unforeseen ones. They could only get to Blackstear when they could.

41

Lazy flakes of snow drifted past Mykel's face as he rode westward on the high road from Iron Stem to Wesrigg. Beside him rode Rhystan, with Sixteenth Company immediately following. Behind Sixteenth Company rode the other companies of Third Battalion. Nineteenth Company brought up the rear. They had already been riding for two glasses along the westbound high road. The snow had become even more intermittent with each vingt they traveled. To the north of the road, at times, Mykel caught sight of a stream or creek, and for a time a small dam and a lake behind it. He thought that might be the reservoir for Iron Stem and for the ironworks.

Now, in the distance ahead, Mykel could see that white covered the more distant summits of the Westerhills, the legacy of the storm that had swept through the Iron Valleys late on Quinti, leaving less than a span's depth of snow on the ground, and nothing but a slight layer of slush on the high road. The wind had shifted once more, back to the northeast, becoming colder, but promising clearer skies. Mykel had already seen breaks in the clouds, and glimpses of the deep silver-green that marked a winter sky.

"This isn't going to melt quickly," observed Rhystan, "except on the high road. The back roads will be muddy, where they aren't frozen."

"They won't be that bad, and it's not that deep. Besides, it will make tracking the Reillies and Squawts easier. Hamylt will have to be careful he doesn't close too quickly."

Rhystan nodded. "Looks like it's a lot deeper to the west, up in the hills."

"If they retreat there, we'll leave them for now. We can wait in Wesrigg for a few days if we have to and see what they do."

"They could wait all winter."

Mykel shook his head. "No, they can't. They've pulled everyone from their hill steads. They can't hold a force that size together for long. They'll either have to attack or disband."

"If they disband . . . then what?"

"We wait until they gather again in the spring, but I don't think that's what they'll do."

"Why not?"

Mykel didn't answer what he felt—that something more was happening, that the soarers or the alectors—someone—wanted the Cadmians under attack and reduced in strength and ability. "They won't have gone to all this trouble to pull together, just to give up. The leaders who called them together would lose too much influence."

"Have to wonder how many bad decisions have been made for reasons like that," mused Rhystan.

"More than anyone would like to think." Mykel laughed.

Over the next glass or so, Mykel began to feel a growing sense that they were being watched from the woods that lay behind the snow-covered fields and meadows bordering the road. Yet the scouts riding ahead of the column had yet to report seeing anyone, and they had seen no one on the road, and no sign of any travelers. The roadside steads gave way to occasional meadows set between stretches of woods, and then to unbroken stretches of trees, beginning about fifty yards back from the high road itself.

Mykel shifted his weight in the saddle. "Rhystan . . . send some scouts out on the south side of the road ahead. Rifles ready. Have them look for signs at the edge of the woods there."

Rhystan half turned in the saddle. "Kursolt, Alberut, Wersylt . . ."

As Rhystan instructed and ordered the scouts, Mykel studied the woods, probing with both his eyes and his Talent. Ahead, perhaps in the trees on the lower part of the hill that climbed away from the shoulder of the roadbed, he could sense someone. Where the trees began was a good ten yards higher than the road, and there were perhaps as many as two or three men, but he could not place where they were—as if they had some sort of partial Talent shield. He frowned. They'd let the road scouts and the vanguard pass, and that meant they were looking either for information or to attack the main body of the column, but with only a handful of men, that didn't make sense, not unless they didn't expect any pursuit.

". . . check the south side of the road, all the way up to that hill. Keep your eyes sharp and your rifles ready," Rhystan finished.

"Third Battalion! Rifles ready!" Mykel ordered as the additional scouts rode forward. "There might be snipers or Reillies somewhere ahead," he added in a lower voice to Rhystan as he took out his own rifle.

He studied the hillside ahead on the south side of the road. It bothered him, but he could only sense a few people, and fuzzily at that. He couldn't very well order the battalion to fire until he knew what was there. They might well be shooting at innocent foresters or peasants.

The morning was silent, except for the sound of the Cadmians.

Mykel strengthened his shields, knowing *something* was

going to happen, but not knowing exactly from where it would come.

Crack! Crack!

The first shot hammered Mykel back in the saddle, twisting his left shoulder from the force on his shields. He forced himself erect and lifted his own rifle, aiming toward the faint flash from where he thought the sniper had fired. He willed the shot home as he squeezed the trigger.

He could sense death . . . the shriveling of lifeforce. As the Talented Reillie died, the Talent screen vanished, and Mykel could sense more than thirty riders in the trees.

"Rhystan. A squad and a half of Reillies ahead of the scouts! Sixteenth Company! Forward!" As he gave the order, Mykel urged the roan forward, flattening himself against the gelding's mane and neck. At least the slope was gentler, taken from the east, than it would have been had he waited until they were directly north of the hill.

"After the majer!"

A ragged volley of shots spewed from the trees. Behind him, Mykel could sense injuries and at least one ranker's death. He managed to get the rifle back in its case and get his sabre out before he reached the trees, where he used his Talent-sense to guide the roan around the thinner pines at the edge of the woods and then to his right.

The snow, light as it was, had flattened the undergrowth, and he could see two Reillies ahead, on foot behind the trees, swinging their rifles toward him.

He urged the gelding to the left, around a larger fir, and then forward—only to see a fallen trunk. The gelding recovered enough to jump the trunk, but all Mykel could do was hang on. The Reillies' shots went over his head.

One scrambled to the left and out of sight. The other one tried to bring his rifle up.

Mykel was on top of him before he could fire. One slash was enough, awkward as it was, to cut deeply into his neck. Mykel barely managed to hang on to the blade as the roan kept moving past the dying man.

Behind him, Sixteenth Company followed, scattering into the trees.

"Sabres!" came Rhystan's command.

Mykel caught a flash of red and brown to his left and turned the gelding. The Reillie jumped to the side and tried to bring the rifle to bear, but Mykel was faster, although he had to lean to his right to avoid a heavy tree branch, and slashed with the sabre, using the momentum of his mount to augment the force of the blade.

As the Reillie went down under the sabre, Mykel's stomach turned. He'd realized, after he'd delivered the fatal cut, that the Reillie had been little more than a girl. *She was shooting at you and your men*, he reminded himself.

He saw green and red ahead, but reined up when he realized that the Reillie slumped against the ancient pine was dead. He could only hope his Talent had been accurate, and that there were no more Reillies. Fighting more than a squad of Reillies in the frigging trees was stupid. He just hoped Sixteenth Company casualties weren't too high.

He reined up, looking around. From what he could sense, only Cadmians remained in the woods.

"Sixteenth Company! Back to the road! Re-form on the road." Mykel turned his mount back northward. He repeated the command as he rode, whenever he saw one of his men. In less than a tenth of a glass, he was on the hillside slope overlooking the high road, where the rest of Third Battalion and Nineteenth Company remained, holding the road. Behind them were the supply wagons and the rear guard.

Fortunately, there were no more shots. Unfortunately, it was more than half a glass before all Sixteenth Company was back in formation on the road. Mykel could only feel a slight soreness in his shoulder, but it was in the back of his shoulder blade, more from the twisting impact of the bullet against his Talent shield than from an impact or an actual wound.

Rhystan reined up on the south side of the road. "Squad leaders. Report!"

"First squad, two dead, two wounded, one seriously."

"Second squad, two dead, one wounded . . ."

"Third squad, one dead, no wounded . . ."

All in all, Sixteenth Company had lost only five men, and neither fourth nor fifth squad reported any casualties. Mykel hadn't expected many, since the fighting had largely concluded before they had reached the area where the Reillies had set up the ambush.

After they resumed riding, Mykel looked to Rhystan. "Do you have any idea how many we killed?"

"Ten, maybe fifteen, but that's a guess. How many did you take out, Majer?"

"Three." Mykel grimaced. "One was still a girl."

"They shoot as well as their brothers and fathers, sometimes better."

"I know, but I don't like it."

"Women fly with the Myrmidons. That captain of the Myrmidon Seventh Company is tougher than most of the alectors she commands. That's how I saw her, anyway."

"She's formidable." Mykel hadn't cared at all for the way in which Captain Lyzetta had studied him, not in the slightest.

"I still don't see why those Reillies didn't fire a full volley when we charged," said Rhystan. "They could have dealt us far greater casualties if they had."

"Two reasons, I'd guess," Mykel replied. "First, they were planning to shoot directly down on the road, so they had to turn, and it was a longer shot, and they weren't really prepared for it. Second, old habits die hard. They're used to single-shot weapons. You need staggered fire with them or you're defenseless if everyone's reloading at once. They probably haven't practiced that much with their new Cadmian rifles, and they might not have that much ammunition."

"We won't be that lucky again."

"They'll still be slower than we are for a while," Mykel said. "That's another reason why we need to clean them up as quickly as we can."

Rhystan shook his head. "You did Hamylt a favor, you know?"

"What? Giving the Reillies the idea that we'd come after them into the trees?" Mykel had almost said "stupidly," but he'd realized before he spoke that there was no point in undermining himself when the casualties had been low, probably no higher than they would have been had he and Sixteenth Company not charged into the trees. "I'll have to tell him not to do it, because he won't have a battalion behind him in case things don't work out." He paused. "Then, they might do more to provoke him."

"True."

They rode westward for another glass, and the clouds overhead began to break, providing intervals of sunlight, but there was no sign of any more Reillies.

"You think the main body is still west of Wesrigg?" Mykel finally asked.

"They could be anywhere around here," Rhystan replied, "but I'd say so because there's an old road that leads back toward that town that's off the road between Dekhron and Iron Stem. Sudon—that's it."

Mykel nodded. "So they can take it to Sudon or take the south fork to the bridge across the Vedra to Borlan. And they won't have to fight through us to get to the road."

"Right."

Somehow, Mykel doubted that anything would be that simple.

42

First Company had left Harmony before sunrise on Sexdi and flown for over a glass before the orange-white light of the sun had cascaded across the forests and the scattered holdings that flanked the high road north to Klamat. Under a clear silver-green sky, below the pteridons, everything was white—except for the high road, which was already a dark gray as the snow had begun to melt. Dainyl had always marveled at how the eternastone intensified the light and heat of the sun, so that the roads were clear long before anything else had begun to melt.

With the help of a tailwind, by slightly before midday they reached Klamat, where they stopped briefly, then left the guidance of the high road behind, flying directly across the whiteness of the snow-swept Moors of Yesterday.

"Much better today, sir," Halya called back.

"Much," Dainyl agreed.

He'd sent a message by sandox from Harmony, saying that the weather had delayed their flight to Blackstear, and Alcyna would probably receive it late in the day. Dainyl hoped that First Company would hold Blackstear by then, but in case they didn't someone should know the reason why they were running late.

The night before, Dainyl and Ghasylt had discussed their planned approach to the Table and the options they would use. From what he had seen so far, it appeared as though the sky over Blackstear was going to be clear, and that First Company would fly in from the west-southwest.

Another three glasses or so passed, and in the distance ahead, Dainyl could make out a change in terrain, where the moor gave way to the band of forest south and east of Blackstear.

Before that long, Dainyl could see the area more clearly. The plateaulike hill on which the Table building sat was covered with snow. He could barely make out the depression in the snow where the stone road wound toward the harbor. Only the snow-covered flatness between the hills to the west of the Table structure revealed where the river ran. The roof of the warehouse and the tops of the bollards on the harbor piers provided the sole indication of where the edges of the small harbor ended and the frozen ocean began. From the handful of dwellings clustered behind the pier warehouse rose thin trails of white smoke. East and south of the Table building was the evergreen forest Dainyl recalled, stretching into the distance, although so much snow had fallen that it was hard to make out the green under all the white. The open tundra to the north was an expanse of white that melded with the darker white of the frozen ocean.

"Edge closer to the captain!" he called to Halya.

"Yes, sir."

The pteridons closed, and Ghasylt looked up.

"Head west! For the approach!" Dainyl called out across the space between the pteridons.

Ghasylt nodded and banked into a gentle left turn, straightening on a course slightly north of west. The fliers of First Company followed. After a good five vingts Ghasylt began a wide turn back toward the northeast, straightening up so that the pteridons were aimed directly at the Table building, with the white sun falling directly on the backs of the Myrmidons.

The approach minimized the glare for the Myrmidons and would make it difficult, if not close to impossible, for the Ifrits holding the Table to see the approaching pteridons against both the sun and the glare off the new-fallen snow.

Dainyl neither saw nor sensed anything out of the ordinary until they were less than a vingt from the Table building when several figures in green and gray scrambled out onto the north portico.

A line of intense blue-green light flashed past him. It had to be some kind of lightcannon, but he'd never seen anything like it. Clearly, it was something the fleeing Ifrits had brought with them—probably the weapon Delari had described.

"Skylances! Fire at will!" Dainyl yelled.

Ghasylt echoed the command, and the blue flare of skylances crossed the scattering of blue-green rays coming from the north portico of the Table building.

"Drop altitude and take evasive action!" Dainyl called to Halya. "That's a lightcannon! Bring us in as low as you can!" He realized after he gave the command that the weapon was probably better termed a light-rifle, but he wasn't about to change command terms in the middle of an attack.

Halya said nothing, but the pteridon sideslipped and dropped off to the left, then dived in toward the ground, leveling off less than twenty yards above the snow.

As late as it was in the afternoon, with the sun low in the sky, Dainyl hoped that glare and sunlight would make it even harder to aim the handheld lightcannon, but even as he thought that, blue flame filled the sky to the right, above, and behind them. He sensed the loss of a Myrmidon, but not of a pteridon.

Halya's skylance flared toward the portico, and blue flame flared, then splashed away from one of the stone pillars. Another line of blue-green angled off Dainyl's shields, and he staggered in the harness, just before Halya pulled up, barely clearing the roof of the Table building.

Dainyl looked back to see how the remainder of First Company was faring. Skylance beams outnumbered the light-rifle beams, and he could no longer catch a glimpse of any of the gray and green uniformed Ifrits.

By the time Halya and Ghasylt had completed their turns and were flying inbound once more on another pass, the light-rifle fire from the portico had died away.

Dainyl called to Ghasylt. "Have first squad set down on the side of the building, where they can't fire at us without exposing themselves. Have the rest of the company circle and provide cover."

"Yes, sir! First squad . . ."

Halya didn't even ask, but set her pteridon down less than three yards from the marble wall that was the west side of the building.

"You stay here with your skylance ready. Fire at anyone who so much as sticks his head out."

"Yes, sir!"

Dainyl eased out of the harness and slipped off the pteridon. He immediately found himself in waist-deep snow, yet he was almost beside the building. No one was firing at him. The outside north portico was empty.

The four remaining pteridons of first squad had landed, and the Myrmidons had their skylances covering the north portico. From what Dainyl had seen and could now confirm, the Ifrits had ripped out stones from an outer terrace—or somewhere—and hurriedly blocked windows and the entrance to the south portico. They had retreated inside, and getting in—or getting them out—was going to be more than a little difficult. Absently, he wondered why inactivating the Table had not killed some of them, as had happened in Hyalt. Was it that he had not totally destroyed the Table, and there was a residual link?

Had he known that, he might have destroyed it—but then that would have created a whole set of other problems.

Slowly, still holding his shields and lightcutters, he moved through the snow toward the stone base of the portico, trying to keep himself shielded by the stone from a direct shot by the light-rifle. A skylance flared, and blue flame wreathed one of the stone columns.

Dainyl could sense pain . . . injury . . . but not death. His right shoulder was almost against the marble as he moved through the snow, still powdery, but heavier than he had thought. He was thankful that the air was still. As he neared the edge of the portico, he staggered and nearly fell as the toe of one boot struck the first of the stone steps hidden by the snow.

He extended his Talent-senses, trying to determine who might still be hiding or waiting behind the pillars on the portico above. From what he could sense, no one remained out in the open air, but at least two were close to the entrance, although Dainyl was not sure whether they were in the entryway arch or just inside. Still, he should be able to get up to the portico, taking cover behind one of the columns, without exposing himself.

As he started up the snow-covered lower steps, he found himself joined by three rankers from first squad. He hadn't even heard the orders.

"Take cover," he ordered, keeping his own head low as he edged up the steps and came up directly behind the column to the right of the open space flanking the center of the steps leading down to the snow-covered road to the harbor.

Dainyl strengthened his shields, then eased the barrel of the lightcutter around the stone, and fired, using Talent to direct the blast at the entry arch and the Ifrit flattened on the left side.

The Ifrit's shields held, but barely, and Dainyl fired again.

The second blast went through tattered shields, and the alector fell. The second alector retreated inside the building.

"Cover me!" snapped Dainyl, moving as quickly as he could across the stone tiles that held patches of packed snow in places.

A single flare of green-blue flashed by his shoulder, then broke off as the blue beam of a lightcutter returned fire.

The heavy doors clunked shut.

With the doors closed, Dainyl made it to the side of the

archway without coming under more fire. He passed three sets of boots and tunics, and there might have been others.

"We need a pteridon at the front of the portico! They've closed the doors."

Almost as soon as he called, Halya appeared. Her pteridon used claws and tail to balance so that Halya could point her lance directly at the doors. "What do you want?"

"At my signal, full fire at the door."

"Standing by."

Dainyl moved along the wall to the far west edge, holding his shields, and creating a Talent funnel toward the lock plates. "Now!"

Hsssttt! The odor of burning wood and hot metal filled the chill air.

"Do you need another blast, sir?"

Dainyl extended a Talent probe, checking the door, and feeling it move. "No . . . that's fine. Move to the side, so that they can't fire at you when I open the door."

"Yes, sir."

The pteridon's wide blue wings spread, and with a brief burst of Talent, it lifted itself a good ten yards to the east.

He looked back in the direction of the three Myrmidons behind columns at the edge of the portico, then called, "Join me, but stay clear of the center here." He moved back to a position beside the doors.

One of the Myrmidons—Saedryk—made his way from pillar to pillar along the west side, coming to a halt against the marble wall to Dainyl's right.

The other two Myrmidons eased into position on the east side of the archway.

"Now what, sir?" asked Saedryk.

"We open the doors and go in, yard by yard, until we finish them off, or they surrender." They wouldn't surrender, Dainyl knew, but he had to allow for the possibility. "I move forward, and you provide covering fire, and then I cover you while you catch up."

The Myrmidon nodded.

Dainyl reached out and took one of the door handles, pulling the right-hand door as far open as it would go, roughly to a forty-five-degree angle from the wall. Then he stepped around it, but kept himself shielded from direct fire from inside the building. From there, he extended another Talent probe, past the archway and into the square foyer. It was empty, but two Ifrits were using doorways farther down the corridor as cover.

Dainyl fired two quick blasts down the corridor, then rushed through the archway, taking cover against the south wall of the inner foyer, to the right of the square arch that separated the foyer from the corridor beyond. Belatedly, a single blast of a lightcutter—not the light-rifle—flared past the foyer archway.

Once more he eased the muzzle of the lightcutter barely around the edge of the wall, and fired a quick blast down the corridor, using his Talent to direct it at the nearer Ifrit.

There was a dull thud and a clatter as the alector toppled half out of the doorway and onto the polished green marble floor of the corridor. Dainyl replaced the exhausted lightcutter with the replacement from inside his cold-weather flying jacket.

Then he repeated the process with the second Ifrit.

Before he could call for the other Myrmidons to join him, the light-rifle fired from the far end of the corridor, scoring the stone of the archway, and leaving the odor of melted stone.

Dainyl snapped off a quick shot, then bolstered his shields and sprinted for the first doorway. Again, the light-rifle fired, but late enough that Dainyl's shields only had to deflect a glancing blast at the last moment, just before he jumped over the boots and tunic of the dead and vanished Ifryn Myrmidon and into the small side chamber.

He couldn't help but note the body on the floor—that of a gray-haired lander woman, sprawled beside a small desk. He hadn't really thought about the fact that Delari must have gotten some help from landers—and probably restricted to the upper level.

Dainyl forced that thought from his mind and returned his attention to the corridor that led to the staircase down to the Table chamber. There couldn't be that many of the Ifryn Myrmidons left. If there had been twenty and Delari had killed three, and the initial assault by First Company had taken out another three, and he had killed another two, in addition to those he'd killed earlier, that meant only seven or so remaining, probably no more than ten or fifteen. That assumed, he told himself, that they did not have an engineer who had gotten the Table back in service.

But . . . if they had, there would either be more resistance—or far less.

Dainyl took a deep breath, sending out another Talent probe, and lifting the lightcutter.

Yet another Ifryn waited in the next doorway along the corridor.

Dainyl used his Talent to direct the lightcutter beam, and the alector collapsed.

Abruptly, another alector sprinted from the last doorway. Dainyl fired once more. He did not miss.

Dainyl paused, taking a deep breath. Using so much Talent was tiring.

The upper level was empty.

He called to the three. "You can join me." Then he moved to the next doorway, glancing in. This time, the body was that of a young lander woman—unclad. He did not look back as he hurried to the next chamber, the last one on the upper level . . . and thankfully empty except for a circular conference table and chairs.

As he waited for the three Myrmidons to rejoin him, he kept Talent-checking, but the staircase to the lower level remained clear. He also checked the two lightcutters remaining with power. One was fully charged, the other less than half.

"Sir . . . you're doing all the work," offered Saedryk as he dashed into the conference room.

"That might change when we head down to the lower level," Dainyl pointed out, breaking off as the other two Myrmidons joined them.

"It's clear to the end of the corridor," he said, after another Talent check. "Let's go."

The landing at the top of the steps was empty, and as he stepped through the archway into the foyerlike space that was the landing, Dainyl glanced to his right where an archway led into a small library—empty, although two chairs lay sideways on the green marble.

He moved forward, stopping short of the steps and the staircase on the east side of the landing. The steps led back to the north, paralleling the landing foyer. Even so, the Table chamber lay under the main upper level, dug into the hillside—as were all Tables.

As he stood back from the side and the top of the steps, a blue-green line of light flashed up the staircase and struck the east edge of the stone frieze on the south wall—a simplistic but elegant rendering of the Black Cliffs as seen from the sea to the north, looking southward. The steps down to the Table chamber were narrower than Dainyl remembered. While that would make it easier for the remaining Ifrits to fire at him, it also meant he could concentrate his Talent shield into a smaller area.

Dainyl extended another Talent probe. From what he could tell, there were two Ifrits in the doorway at the bottom of the staircase, and the door to the Table chamber was open. He looked to the three Myrmidons. "Get as flat as you can around the top of the stairs. When I signal, I want the three of you to fire down the staircase. Then I'll give a second signal. I'll want two separate shots. Don't worry about aiming, except in the general direction of the bottom. Then I'll head down."

"Ah . . . then what, sir?" asked Saedryk.

Dainyl smiled. "Then you listen for my next orders."

He waited for the three to creep into position, standing back somewhat. When they were ready and looking at him, he first focused a Talent shield, one that would direct their lightcutter discharges to a point. Then he raised his hand. "Now!"

The three blue beams fused, and with the impetus of Dainyl's Talent, sliced through one of the Ifrits.

"Now!"

The second beam was equally effective.

Before Dainyl could move more than two steps, blue-green beams flared up the stairs, and boots thudded on the steps. Dainyl fired three times, and the Myrmidons kept firing.

A single Ifrit reached the top of the steps, holding a light-rifle aimed at Dainyl.

Before he could speak, Dainyl enfolded him with Talent shields.

The light-rifle exploded under that pressure, and for a moment Dainyl could only see flashing stars. When he finally released the shields, there was no sign of the last Ifrit except a circular pile of black ash and dust, half of which began to vanish.

"What . . . what was that?"

"Talent shield," Dainyl replied, absently, still trying to determine if anyone remained below. He didn't think so, but he wanted to check again.

Then he started down the steps, cautiously, well aware that his shields were far weaker than he would have liked.

He did not have to worry. There was no one left in the Table chamber, only empty uniforms and boots. He walked back to the door. "There's no one left. Saedryk . . . would you go out and have Captain Ghasylt join me here."

"Yes, sir."

"Meya and Tueral, you can come down and join me."

Meya was the first down, and she stepped over and around the gray and green tunics and the sets of scuffed boots. Once she reached the doorway, her eyes traversed the chamber, stopping to fix on the Table. "That's a Table?"

Dainyl nodded. "It's not operating now."

Tueral looked from one pair of boots to the next as he descended, then finally to the marshal. "There were nine of them here." Unlike Meya, he avoided looking at the Table.

While the three waited, Dainyl holstered his lightcutters and reflected. Once they had gotten into the Table building, while progress had been slow, it had been steady, and without additional Myrmidon casualties—except for the effort exacted on Dainyl himself. He was close to being unsteady on his feet.

He looked across the Table chamber and up the steps, seeing the green and gray tunics and boots lying everywhere. His lips tightened, but he said nothing. He felt light-headed, and forced himself to sit on the edge of the Table.

A tenth of a glass later, Ghasylt stepped into the chamber.

"Meya, Tueral . . . if you'd wait at the top of the steps," Dainyl said quietly. He did not stand.

Ghasylt surveyed the chamber, but said nothing until the Myrmidons had left and climbed the stairs. "Congratulations, Marshal."

Dainyl shook his head. "It's not something I liked doing, but there's no way we could risk them learning how to activate the Table again and create an open translation tube here from Ifryn."

"Would it have been that bad?"

Dainyl understood what Ghasylt meant. "Acorus can take another thousand alectors—or could before we started accepting them months back. At the last count, we'd accepted more than four hundred survivors. There are over five thousand alectors left on Ifryn for whom there is no room on either Efra or Acorus—not without dooming everyone on both worlds."

"Is that a really hard number?"

Dainyl shrugged. "Probably not to the last alector, but the Duarch is convinced that it's close. So is the senior alector in Lyterna, and he's studied it for decades."

"How did we . . ." Ghasylt shook his head. "Sorry, sir. It's just . . ."

"They weren't that different from us, and we had to kill them."

"Yes, sir."

"I don't know how it got this bad, Captain. I only know that it is."

Ghasylt remained silent.

Dainyl looked at the captain. "Once I get my strength back, I'll reactivate the Table and translate to Elcien. You're going to have to keep guard on the Table all the time, no less than four Myrmidons. If another force slips through . . ."

"Someone else will have to do what we just went through," the captain finished. "None of us want that."

"No. We'll probably have to ferry a bunch of guards up here, and I'd guess that Seventh Company will have to bring them."

Dainyl had the feeling that no one had ever anticipated

needing large numbers of Myrmidon or other alector guards in Blackstear. If it weren't for the need to keep the Table active while the Master Scepter was being transferred, he would have recommended shutting it down. He might anyway.

43

Dainyl stepped up onto the Table in Blackstear, concentrated, and dropped through the mirrored surface into . . .

. . . the chill purple dusk of the translation tube. As he focused on finding the Elcien locator wedge, he realized that he did not sense the greenish Talent forging—if that were what it had been—by the ancients. He did sense an amber-green "presence" somewhere beyond, so great that it felt as though it loomed over all of Acorus.

He pushed that thought aside and Talent-linked to the brilliant white locator of Elcien. Even as it neared him, he could sense even more purplish flashes—and what he could only have described as purplish explosions. Those had to be failed translations.

How soon would the Archon transfer the Master Scepter? Could it really be a season away, with all the unrest and the desperation on Ifryn? Or was that what the Archon wanted in order to reduce the number of alectors drawing higher amounts of lifeforce from Efra and Acorus? Or was he trying to stretch out the time Ifryn could last through such manipulations?

With all too many questions swirling through his mind, Dainyl slipped through the white-silver barrier and . . .

. . . onto the Table at Elcien, holding what Talent shields he had remaining, barely enough to stop the weakest of lightcutter bolts.

Chastyl looked up, and a smile crossed a face worn with worry, and showing dark circles under his eyes. "You put it back on the grid! I'll have to let Delari know. She'll be pleased."

Dainyl offered a wry smile as he stepped off the Table, ignoring the guards. "You'd best wait a moment until I tell the Highest. I think he'd like to know."

Chastyl's smile faded, but he nodded. "You're right. He was in his private study. There's more trouble. He'd better tell you."

"Thank you. I'll try to be quick so that you can tell Delari. Just give me a few moments."

Chastyl gave Dainyl a sympathetic smile, but said nothing.

Dainyl made his way out through the foyer and down the corridor. There, he opened Zelyert's door without knocking, knowing the High Alector was alone.

The Highest looked up, his face twisted in annoyance. "What took you so long?"

Dainyl took the seat across the table from Zelyert and settled into it. He was tired and ached all over, and he would have liked to have seen Zelyert do what he'd done. "I sent a message by sandox on Quinti, but it might have been delayed. We ran into a blizzard that was too heavy to fly through and too big to fly around. We had to wait it out overnight in Harmony."

"I suppose you couldn't help that." The High Alector's tone reflected a combination of grudging acceptance and frustration.

"That kind of weather isn't something I could do anything about." Dainyl paused. "Blackstear is in our hands, and all of the invaders are dead."

"That's one problem taken care of, but I'd hoped you'd be quicker."

"I take it that there's more trouble."

"The same thing has happened in Soupat. Another group of Myrmidons from Ifryn. Nomyelt was killed when he tried to shut down the Table. His assistant translated to Ludar. We got word late yesterday. The Table's still on the grid, and it's beginning to get increasing numbers of long translations. The Duarches are extremely worried."

Dainyl couldn't say he was surprised. "If it had to happen anywhere else, that would be the most likely." Before Zelyert could say more, Dainyl asked, "What is the situation at Hyalt?"

"The Duarch Samist has indicated that Hyalt is heavily guarded and that matters are under control there. It's not a problem. Nor is Tempre. What do you intend to do about Soupat?"

Dainyl bristled inside at the quick assignment of responsibility to him. Table security hadn't ever been a primary Myrmidon duty. In fact, usually the only Myrmidons who ever even saw a Table were the marshal and submarshal. He kept his voice pleasant as he replied, "Whatever is necessary. I asked Alcyna to draw up a plan for what to do if we had to handle another situation like Blackstear. The Cadmian Sixth Battalion, Mounted Rifles, has been operating there for the past two seasons, but they've already suffered heavy casualties, and I assume you'd rather not get them involved unless it's absolutely necessary."

"An astute observation, Marshal."

"I'll go back to headquarters and see what else we have available."

"What you have available?" Zelyert raised his eyebrows.

"Unless you want me or Delari to inactivate Blackstear again, First Company will have to guard it until we can get more guards there, one way or another. Guarding it day and night will take almost all the Myrmidons from First Company. So they can't be used to fly guards up there, and the harbor is already frozen in. That means using Myrmidons from somewhere else, like Second Company in Ludar." For most tasks Dainyl wouldn't have considered Second Company, but even Samist and Brekylt had a clear interest in keeping too many refugees from Ifryn from arriving on Acorus. Still . . . he'd rather not rely too heavily on Second Company.

Zelyert was silent for a moment, clearly taken aback. Then, he said, "I'll have to talk to Delari."

"I'll see what we can do." Dainyl turned and left, without

asking Zelyert's leave. He did close the door behind him . . . and quietly.

He found Delari in Adya's study, seated on one side of the small writing desk. Adya was not there.

Delari stood and turned. "Dainyl . . . Chastyl told me that Blackstear's back on the grid. I was getting together some things before I returned."

"You'd better wait until Zelyert talks to you. He's not happy."

"You don't sound very encouraging." Her voice was cool.

"You'll pardon me if I'm not, Delari. The only people alive in the Table building in Blackstear are my Myrmidons. The intruders killed everyone else, and we ended up having to kill all of the intruders. That's not exactly encouraging." He cleared his throat. "I have one question. Then I have to get back to work on what to do about Soupat. When the Table is powered up, it's almost impervious, isn't it? Except to a direct Talent thrust, I mean. You could drop a timber or something on it, and nothing would happen—unless the timber were Talent-guided?"

The tall recorder frowned, then nodded. "That's supposedly so. I wouldn't want to try it. Do you have something in mind?"

"Not yet," Dainyl temporized. "I wanted to know because we may have to use more force in Soupat."

"You can't do what you did in Blackstear?"

"I think it's unlikely. They're already getting more translations, and the weather and geography won't limit them to the Table building. But we'll have to see." He managed a smile and a nod before taking his leave.

An icy rain was falling across Elcien when Dainyl left the Hall of Justice looking for a hacker. Because it took a while to find one, he was glad for the cold-weather gear he was still wearing.

From the outside, through the cold rain, headquarters looked deserted when Dainyl got out of the coach and walked through the gates and then into the entry foyer.

Squad leader Doselt was handling the duty desk, one of his

extra responsibilities when all of First Company was gone, and he looked up as Dainyl entered headquarters. "Sir? The rest of the company?"

"They're still in Blackstear. I came back by Table. Is Seventh Company here?"

"Two squads, sir. Undercaptain Asyrk is in charge."

"Good. I'll want to see him later. Is the submarshal in?"

"Yes, sir."

"Good. Thank you."

Dainyl walked down the corridor to Alcyna's study, stepping through the open door and taking the chair at the corner of her table desk, motioning her to keep her seat.

"You look tired, Marshal. How did it go?"

"We hold Blackstear. The insurgents, refugees . . . whatever you want to call them, they killed everyone at Blackstear. We stormed the building, killed all of them, and First Company is now guarding the Table there."

"You were successful." Her voice was level.

"For the moment. As soon as I returned by Table, less than a glass ago, the Highest informed me that another group of Myrmidons from Ifryn has taken over the Table at Soupat. He doesn't want the Cadmians there involved. They wouldn't do well if the intruders in Soupat are as well armed as the ones in Blackstear were."

"How did you know that was going to happen?" asked Alcyna.

"I didn't. It seemed logical that attacks would be made where we couldn't respond quickly, except through the Table, and there aren't that many alectors here on Acorus who are Table-trained. Certainly not enough to mount that kind of a counterattack."

"They must have counted on that."

"I'm certain that they did. Have you got a plan for dealing with Soupat?"

"I have three options. None are that good. Seventh Company is already understrength. Majer Keheryl insists that Samist wants two squads of Second Company in Ludar at all times . . ."

"So we're looking at two squads from Seventh Company and three from Fifth Company?"

"So long as First Company is tied up with Blackstear, that's the best option."

"What about tactics?"

"What else is there but using skylances and going in the way you did in Blackstear?"

"Aerial bombardment," suggested Dainyl. "Drop as many large boulders as necessary on the Table building to seal it enough so that even if the Table remains working no one can get out of the Table chamber. That way, it remains on the grid, but we don't have to guard it. Then we patrol the area from the air and flame down anyone who doesn't belong."

"That's drastic."

"It's realistic," he countered. "And it risks fewer Myrmidons and pteridons."

A knock on the door broke the momentary silence.

"Marshal, sir," said Doselt, "the High Alector sent his carriage and a request that you return to the Hall of Justice immediately."

"I'll be there in a moment." Dainyl looked at Alcyna. "It's getting late, but you need to remain here until I know what else has gone wrong and what we'll have to do. Make sure Asyrk stays, too." He rose from the chair.

"I had that feeling." Alcyna stood. "The best of luck with the Highest."

Dainyl nodded.

As he left Alcyna's study and walked back down the corridor toward the entry foyer, he realized that he'd been in Elcien for over two glasses and that he was still wearing the cold-weather flying jacket and had the heavy gloves tucked in his belt.

He did not speak to the driver of the Highest's coach on the return to the Hall of Justice, thinking instead about possible adaptations of the tactics he had ordered to bring down Hyalt. He also had to wonder why Samist had garrisoned Hyalt immediately upon the return of its Table to active status, yet the Duarches had done little to preclude a takeover at Soupat.

When Dainyl made his way from the coach back down to the lower level at the Hall of Justice, he found the door to Zelyert's private study was open. Zelyert did not rise from behind the table, but gestured for him to enter.

"You requested my return?"

"You'll translate back to Blackstear. So will Delari. Detail four Myrmidons to remain there. She'll inactivate the Table and only activate it periodically to receive translations and messages on a schedule. It's far from ideal, but it's the best we can do." Zelyert cleared his throat. "Now that you've had a chance to consider our other problem, what do you suggest for Soupat?"

"Take out the refugees and make sure that no more of them arrive."

"Do you have a plan for that?"

"Yes, sir. I'll translate back from Blackstear once I brief the Myrmidons there, and I'll translate to Tempre early tomorrow morning and take the half of Seventh Company that's there to Soupat. Submarshal Alcyna will follow with the three squads of First Company once they return here. If we need more support, we'll pull two squads from Fifth Company in Dereka."

"You aren't tasking Second Company at all?"

"Majer Keheryl has informed us that Duarch Samist requires a minimum of two squads in Ludar at all times. If what we've planned is insufficient, we'll request two additional squads from Ludar."

"You handled Blackstear with one company. That's four squads. You're suggesting close to two companies—and before, you were reluctant to send any away from Elcien. What changed your mind?"

"The location, the weather, and the timing all favored us in Blackstear. None of those will favor us in Soupat, and there are already more armed refugees there. I was reserving Myrmidon companies for contingencies—such as these."

"You don't plan to inactivate the Table yourself?"

"It was touch and go last time, sir. The alectors in Blackstear didn't know about inactivation. The ones in Soupat do. Otherwise, they wouldn't have killed Nomyelt. It also suggests that they might well be able to reactivate the Table as well. I don't see any point in taking that kind of risk for something that won't be effective for more than a glass or so, if that."

"That makes some sense." Zelyert's tone suggested Dainyl had other ulterior motives.

Dainyl did. He knew he would be close to exhaustion before the day was over and that his ability to raise full Talent shields was compromised, and probably would be for several days.

"Who will be here in Elcien—Myrmidons, that is?"

"The assistant operations director—that's Captain Zernylta—and two squads of Seventh Company commanded by Undercaptain Asyrk."

"I'm glad to see you do not have the Myrmidons totally abandoning Elcien." Zelyert's deep voice verged on the sardonic.

"We do the best we can, sir, but eight companies does not constitute a great force for an entire world, especially when three of them may be loyal to others. That is one reason why I've also had to rely on the Cadmians, but I doubt that they would be effective in Soupat."

"You'd best find Delari and return to Blackstear."

Dainyl inclined his head at the dismissal, then turned and departed. At times, Zelyert still remained more than a little enigmatic, but at the moment, Dainyl was scarcely in the mood for conversation. After he translated to Blackstear and then back to Elcien, he would still need to go back to Myrmidon headquarters and finish working out the details with Zernylta, Alcyna, and Asyrk.

Then he needed some sleep, and sleeping alone in the big bed at the house, he knew he would miss Lystrana.

44

Third Battalion had reached Wesrigg late on Septi. The hill town was little more than a hamlet, except for the chandlery, some shops, and two inns catering to travelers. Most of the shops on the short stretch of the high road that served as Wesrigg's main street had been shuttered, a clear sign that the townspeople had been aware of trouble.

Mykel and the company officers shared rooms at the Red Ox and the Yellow Jug, with Mykel and Rhystan at the Ox. The men had slept in storerooms, stables, and haylofts, out of the elements, but with little comfort. Mykel hadn't been able to do more than that, but he had made sure they all were fed and dry.

After an early breakfast, provided by an innkeeper fuming behind his polite demeanor, Mykel and the other officers gathered in the front parlor, such as it was, to receive the reports from the scouts.

Most had found little, but the Fourteenth Company scout, one of the last to return, reported, "There's a company of Reillies on the ridge south of the road, just east of Wesrigg. Leastwise, it looks like a company. They're mostly in the trees, but you can see a few."

"Could you tell if there were other Reillies or Squawts around?" asked Mykel.

"Was still pretty dark in the trees, sir, but I don't think so. More than a hundred yards away, and you could hear birds, and there weren't any other tracks at the edge of the woods. Also, the cots between them and the town had their shutters open, and fires in their chimneys."

"Sounds like a lure, some kind of trap," opined Culeyt.

"We'll act as if we don't know they're there," said Mykel. "If they're setting up snipers in the woods, we won't see anyone, and we'll withdraw if they start firing. If they're partly formed up, then they'll fire some and back off, trying to pull us into the woods again. I think we can turn things on them in that case. We'll go to staggered firing lines and rake them. They'll either charge or retreat. If they retreat, no one is to follow them. Let them go. We'll get them another way." His eyes moved from officer to officer. "Is that clear?"

"Yes, sir." The response was murmured, but not resentful.

"Good. Go get your companies formed up. We'll move out in half a glass." Mykel started to follow the others, but the innkeeper stepped up.

"Majer . . . there is the matter of settling . . ."

"We agreed on the golds," Mykel stated. "I don't carry

them with me. No officer does. I'll have them sent to whatever factor here in Wesrigg you name."

"They'll take a cut."

"No. They get paid for the service. If they try to take more, send me a note, and I'll take care of it."

"Sir . . . you say that . . ."

"Innkeeper . . . with a battalion of Cadmians this close to Wesrigg, it won't be a problem. If it is, then the factor is a Code-breaker, and you should know how the Duarches and the Cadmians feel about that."

The innkeeper stepped back. "I'll be taking your word on that, sir, and thank you."

The man was less than totally pleased, but not angry. That would have to do.

Rhystan was waiting as Mykel stepped out of the ancient Red Ox and into the stable yard. "Do you think the Reillies will still be there?"

"I'd guess that they will. If they hadn't wished to be seen, they wouldn't have been."

"But why are they being so obvious?"

"I wish I knew." Under the long slanting rays of a sun that had barely cleared the trees on the low rolling hills to the east of Wesrigg, his eyes took in the slumped roof line of the stable, sagging like a sway-backed mare. "The only thing that makes sense is the losses that Fourth Battalion took. Somehow, they think that, if they can do the same to us, the Duarches will back off on strictly enforcing the Code."

"So they can log every old tree for timber and burn the rest for charcoal?" Rhystan snorted. "I've seen what they've done on their steads. That's why they have to move so often. They wear out the land."

"They don't like outsiders telling them what to do." Mykel laughed. "None of us do."

"There's a difference . . . ," Rhystan began, then shook his head.

"There is. You know it, and so do I, but how do you explain it? Anyone who doesn't understand before you start talking won't agree when you're done."

"I suppose that's another reason why I'm still a Cadmian," Rhystan said.

Mykel hadn't thought of it in those terms, but he realized he would have said the same thing a year before. Now . . . after discovering his Talent, having listened to ancient soarers—and Rachyla—he wasn't so sure.

He eased those thoughts aside as he stepped into the stable to check his gear and saddle the roan.

Slightly more than a half glass passed before the battalion was formed up on the main street between the inns and the muster reported to Mykel, long enough that the sun, shining through clear air, had warmed the air so that his breath no longer created a white cloud when he spoke. "Third Battalion! Forward!"

Mykel rode with the vanguard and Undercaptain Fabrytal, only a quarter vingt back of the scouts, close enough that Mykel could order them back once the Reillies were spotted—if they were still there.

As Culeyt's scout had reported, a score of Reillies waited on the low hill east of Wesrigg and south of the high road. They had ridden around the area enough that they had packed down or scraped away most of the snow.

"Scouts back!" he ordered. "Third Battalion, rifles ready."

From their languid demeanor, to Mykel it was clear that the Reillies wanted to provoke the Cadmians into pursuing them into the woods, and that idea had probably been strengthened by seeing Mykel's impetuousness of the previous day.

He eased the roan forward slightly, then took out his rifle, checking it once more.

The Reillies were still a good five hundred yards ahead, roughly sixty yards to the south of the shoulder of the road. They began to form into a rough line so that they approximated a formation by the time Mykel was some three hundred yards from them.

The first shot came from the insurgents when the Cadmians were little more than a hundred yards away.

"Third Battalion! Halt! Staggered firing lines! Stand by to

fire. Fire at will!" As Mykel finished the command, he lifted his own rifle and fired once, willing the bullet home, targeting the Reillie whose mount was slightly forward of the others. The man sagged in the saddle, then fell. Mykel fired once more, then again. All in all, he emptied his magazine. Then he reloaded, and fired again.

The Reillies picked up the pace of their firing, but the years of training Mykel had insisted on began to show as more and more Reillies fell. Mykel finished the second magazine and quickly reloaded, but before he could fire, the Reillies rode back into the woods, at an angle to the southeast.

"Cease fire! Cease fire!"

Mykel could sense the line of snipers to the east along the south side of the high road.

"Third Battalion, to the rear, ride!"

Mykel brought the battalion to a halt a half vingt west, in front of the snow-covered fields and meadows of a smaller holder, an area where it would be hard for anyone to approach without being immediately obvious from a distance. "Captain Rhystan!"

While Rhystan rode to meet him, Mykel used his Talent to try to get a better sense of where the insurgents might be.

Rhystan reined up. "Yes, Majer?"

"I'm putting you in charge of the battalion, and I'd like your steadiest squad to accompany me. They have snipers in the woods. I'm going to use their tactics against them. We'll ride back, but stop short of where they were. I'll pick them off, starting with the closest, one at a time."

"I believe, sir, that I mentioned my reservations about the commanding officer going off alone . . ."

"I'm not going that far. I don't intend to go more than five or ten yards into the trees, if that. Your squad will be just inside the trees, just to the west of where I am. From what I can tell, there's a larger body another vingt east, but I don't intend to get too close to them. There's no one deeper in the trees behind the first three or four snipers. The entire battalion will be on the road, a half vingt or so behind the squad supporting me."

Rhystan waited.

"If we take out the snipers for the first vingt, then the battalion can move eastward, following the squad with me. If there's any sign of a massed attack, I'll ride back to the squad, and we'll rejoin you and the battalion."

"You're trying to get them to attack?"

"I want them off-balance. If I can create the impression that we can beat them in the woods, they'll be far less likely to try too many ambushes on Hamylt. Or . . . they'll offer a pitched battle, and we won't have to spend days or weeks dealing with them."

"They lose too many, and they'll back off, sir, and we'll still do that."

"That could be." Mykel smiled coldly. "Then we'll have to pick them off one at a time."

"I have to point out, sir, that you're running an unnecessary risk."

"Your point is taken, Rhystan. I'll try to be very careful, and I'll stay close to your squad. Which squad?"

"Second squad, sir. They're ready."

"We might as well start, then."

Rhystan raised his hand, and second squad eased out of the column and along the shoulder of the road, hard-packed gravel better than many of the back roads in Corus. The squad reined up short of the two officers.

"We're going to ride to the edge of the trees," Mykel said. "I'll be barely into the trees, but I want you thirty yards back of me, right at the edge of the trees. You're to keep an eye out for other Reillies while I'm looking for snipers."

Mykel turned to Rhystan. "I'd like the column back about two hundred yards from second squad. That way, no one's really in range of more than one sniper at a time, if that."

Rhystan nodded.

"We might as well get started." Mykel realized he'd repeated himself, but there was no help for that. He turned the roan southward, angling toward the trees, moving at a slow walk, his Talent-senses extended.

For the first hundred yards along the tree line, he could sense nothing except Sixteenth Company's second squad behind him. Then, perhaps forty yards ahead through the trees, was a Reillie. Feeling the man's nervousness, Mykel halted the roan behind one of the wider-trunked pine trees. He spent several moments using his Talent to scan the area somewhat farther into the trees before he rode, slowly, forward and to his right.

The Reillie kept looking, turning his head from side to side, but not that far to the rear, as Mykel eased the roan slowly closer, raising his rifle.

Crack.

At the sound of the old fallen branch snapping under the hoof of the roan, the Reillie jerked around. He barely had half lifted his rifle when Mykel's shot went through his forehead.

The sound of the single shot echoed through the trees, then faded.

Mykel continued onward, slowly, moving somewhat to the north and nearer the road so that Rhystan's men could see him, at least intermittently.

The next Reillie sniper was closer to the road, directly ahead, and Mykel reined up, lifting his rifle, then leaning slightly to his left and firing.

After the single shot reverberated through the morning, a cascade of powdery snow slithered off a fir branch and down across Mykel's neck. He couldn't help wincing at the jolt from the cold down his back.

Slowly, he eased the roan forward.

Almost a glass passed, and he killed three more Reillie snipers. Ahead, he could sense a larger grouping of riders, still several hundred yards away to the southeast, and farther back into the heavier woods, if up a gentle slope. Mykel doubted that it would be wise to proceed much farther, and he was disappointed, and concerned, that there had been little reaction to his removal of the snipers. But then, did the Reillies really even know what he had done? All they had heard had been occasional shots.

Mykel eased the roan to a halt, right behind the trunk of a giant pine. He realized that an uneasy feeling had been building, and that there was an area ahead and to his right where he could sense nothing . . . nothing at all. Could it be the doing of one of the soarers or their predatory creatures?

Or was it a Reillie with Talents like his own?

He didn't want to move until he had some idea what he was facing, yet he knew that remaining where he was left him somewhat exposed, and he didn't like either possibility.

The faintest of sounds brought his head around, and he tried to strengthen his shields, but two shots hammered at them, throwing him back, and then *something* slammed through them, aided by the greenish feel of Talent. The missile—a crossbow quarrel—had struck his left shoulder, practically yanking him out of the saddle.

The Reillie stepped from behind a fir less than ten yards away and deliberately lifted a rifle. Mykel managed to grab his rifle with his left hand and fire first, awkwardly and one-armed, willing the bullet straight into the tree directly behind the Reillie, since he had doubts about using Talent successfully directly on the Reillie.

The insurgent pitched forward, a look of astonishment frozen on his face. Mykel fumbled his rifle back into the case and turned the roan back toward second squad. He could feel blood oozing out around the quarrel, and a dull throbbing.

The thirty yards of riding felt like three hundred.

"It's the majer . . ."

"Something got him."

"It's a frigging iron quarrel."

Mykel was feeling light-headed by the time he reached the vanguard of the battalion. He was looking for Rhystan when he could feel himself lurching in the saddle. He tried to grasp the roan's mane . . .

45

Dainyl slept well for the first part of the night, restlessly for the early morning glasses, and rose well before dawn. Even after taking his time to wash up, dress, and walk through the chill morning to the Hall of Justice, carrying a small amount of gear in a kit bag, it was still well before sunrise when he stepped onto the Table and dropped through its mirrored surface into the purpleness of the translation tube.

As he Talent-linked with the blue locator that was Tempre, he was aware that he no longer even felt the chill of the tube and that he sensed fewer of the purplish streaks and flashes than he had the evening before.

In the distance that might be immediately outside the tube or a continent away, he could still feel the amber-green that he had once thought to be a chain of massive Talent links.

Then, he was through the silvered blue of the barrier at Tempre and . . .

. . . standing on the Table in Tempre. He stepped down onto the polished floor stones.

A young-looking recorder in green appeared from the hidden chamber, bowing. "Marshal Dainyl, sir?"

"Yes?"

"We're honored to see you here in Tempre. How might we help you?" The recorder's eyes only met Dainyl's for an instant.

The recorder was not being evasive. Rather Dainyl could sense fear and great apprehension. Great apprehension? Who had told the recorder about him, and what had they said?

He smiled. "I'm here to see Captain Lyzetta of the Myrmidons. If there is any transportation—I'd prefer not to walk."

"Sir, I am most certain that the regional alector's coach will be ready for you. He has already arrived this morning. He left word soon after he came to Tempre that you were to be accorded every courtesy."

The recorder meant what he said. That bothered Dainyl more than the alector's fear. "That is kind of him. I have to confess I don't know the new RA."

"Senior Alector Byrnat. He was appointed two weeks ago by Duarch Samist."

Dainyl thought he had heard the name, and that Byrnat had been some sort of special assistant to Samist, but he didn't fully trust his memory. "He has served the Duarches well."

"Yes, sir."

With a last smile at the nervous recorder, Dainyl stepped through the doorway and into the outer corridor. He could not help but note the new oak door, reinforced with iron, and the freshly mortared stonework that replaced what had been destroyed in the fight over the Tempre Table weeks earlier.

The two guards outside stiffened. "Sir."

"Carry on." Dainyl made his way to the end of the corridor and up the stairs to the main level. From the southwest corner of the building he had come to know too well, he walked quickly along the wide west corridor toward the front and then around to the main entry hall.

The few individual alectors and alectresses in the corridor all nodded respectfully—and gave him a wide berth.

". . . he the one?"

"He's the new marshal . . . you know . . ."

Whatever they "knew," Dainyl didn't hear, but as the recorder had said, there was a coach waiting, and he was at the stone-walled compound—completed less than a year earlier for the now-disbanded and disavowed Alector's Guard—in less than a quarter glass.

The coach stopped outside the gates, where Dainyl stepped out. The sun was just rising over the top of the hills, and its long orangish white rays angled through the bare branches of the trees to the east of the compound.

"Will you need me to wait, sir?"

"No, thank you."

Dainyl walked through the open gates and into the courtyard, glancing around, and seeing two duty pteridons at the east end.

"Marshal!"

Dainyl turned to see Captain Lyzetta striding across the courtyard toward him. As she neared and then halted before him, Dainyl could clearly see the resemblance to her father. Although she did not have Khelaryt's extreme height and breadth, she was almost as tall as Dainyl and broad-shouldered, with the strong features of the Duarch. Unlike her father, she moved with a fluid grace that disguised her size, rather than a muscularity that emphasized it.

"Marshal, sir. You're here early, even before muster." Her eyes dropped to the gear he carried.

"Matters compel it, Captain. How are you finding Tempre?"

"Now that we've managed proper length beds for everyone, it's quite comfortable. There's far more space than we need."

"I've spent more time with your father, recently," Dainyl began.

"How is he?" Lyzetta's words were guarded.

"You can communicate with him now."

"Sir?"

"He's no longer shadowmatched."

Lyzetta paled. "Then it's been decided?"

"Decided, but not implemented. The Master Scepter will go to Efra. We don't know when."

"He's still . . . Duarch?"

"Khelaryt is still far more Talented than any of the other High Alectors."

"More important, sir, so are you, and you stand behind him."

The words took Dainyl by surprise. "I do stand behind him, Captain, but you give me far too much credit, and too much Talent."

"I think not, sir."

"Be that as it may," Dainyl went on quickly, seeing that his protests would avail him little in changing her mind, "we have a difficult situation. You knew about Blackstear?"

"Only that First Company was dispatched there, and that was why Asyrk took squads to Elcien."

"A company of foot Myrmidons from Ifryn chanced the long translation. Two-thirds of them perished, but the remainder stormed the Table in Blackstear. The recorder killed several and escaped. We took the Table back. While we were doing that, another company took Soupat." Dainyl paused and studied Lyzetta. While she seemed concerned, she was not shocked. "You anticipated this?"

"Not exactly, sir. I did question the idea that Ifryn would die quietly, and that there would be an orderly series of translations to Efra and Acorus. Given the nature of alectors, even of steers, that seemed unlikely." She shrugged. "What puzzled me was why so many waited so long. It seemed obvious that attempting the long translation before anyone truly worried about excess lifeforce use on Efra or Acorus would offer a better chance of survival."

Dainyl laughed, sharply and harshly. "The majority of people, especially those who are privileged, even in minor aspects of their lives, do not believe that the worst will befall them. When they learn that the most successful possibility is perhaps one chance in two of surviving the long translation, they have a tendency to wait until it is clear that they have no other choices. Then . . . they have almost no chance unless they are among the chosen few."

"My father made that choice early. I think you would have, sir."

"I have not been faced with such a choice, and until one is, it's difficult to judge how I or anyone might react. Remember, too, that such choices affect all the ones you love. Will your husband or wife survive? Will the children? How will you react if told that one of you will die immediately on a long translation?"

"You've thought much about this."

Not so much as I should have. "Enough to know that it's not simple." He cleared his throat. "About the mission . . . so long as these insurgents hold the Table, they will accept unlimited numbers of refugees, too many, even within weeks. We cannot shut down the Table without taking the Table building. With the numbers they already have, we could suffer prohibitively high casualties attempting to storm the structure. Oh . . . there's also a Cadmian battalion there, and I don't want them close to what's happening."

"I can see that, sir."

Many Myrmidons wouldn't have, Dainyl knew. "Our strategy is simple enough. It has two facets. First, use enough blasting powder and heavy boulders to bring the Table building down on the Soupat Table. Second, destroy any rebel or refugee alectors we find."

"Sir? *Our* strategy?"

"I'm coming with you. Submarshal Alcyna will be bringing three squads from First Company and will join us within a day or so, but they're still in Blackstear. I'd like to leave as soon as possible."

"Won't we destroy the Table as well?"

"According to the recorders, there's a good chance we

won't, but if we do, we do. We'll need the Myrmidons more and more in the weeks ahead. How soon will you be ready?"

"We should be able to manage in a glass, sir. Do you want the duty dispatch flier to fly with us or do the run to Salcer, Ludar, and then to Elcien?"

"This takes precedence over routine dispatches."

"Yes, sir."

"The other aspect of this mission is that no one else besides yourself in Seventh Company should learn that the invaders are Ifryn Myrmidons. Only tell them that they are invaders from Ifryn who will threaten the very existence of Acorus if they are not stopped. Should anything occur to me, you are not to discuss it with anyone else except Submarshal Alcyna, the High Alector of Justice, or the Duarch of Elcien."

"Yes, sir."

Dainyl forced a smile. "I will need to fly with someone."

"We can manage that, sir."

Dainyl had no doubts that Lyzetta could manage a great deal more—and that she would have to in the days ahead.

46

Mykel could hear the faint squeaking of the wagon wheels. The noise was almost welcome as a distraction from the burning in his shoulder. His eyes did not seem to want to open, but he persisted in trying until he could see—hazily—that he was lying on a pallet looking up at the canvas of one of the supply wagons. As smooth as the high road was, the slightest of jolts sent waves of agony through him.

As he dropped into darkness again, his eyes closing against his will, his fading thought was that even a crossbow bolt shouldn't have been that bad.

The heat and agony came and went. At times, he dropped into darkness where he felt nothing, only to find himself back in fire and pain.

Finally, he managed to succeed in opening his eyes once

more. From what he saw—the grayish walls, and the narrow window—Mykel thought he was on the bed in the senior officers' quarters in Iron Stem.

"What day . . . ?"

"He's awake . . . Get the captain . . ."

Mykel closed his eyes for a moment. At least, he thought it was a moment before he opened them.

Rhystan was sitting on a stool beside him. "Majer . . ."

"I know," Mykel replied, aware of the raspiness in his voice. "I . . . shouldn't have been leading from the front. I shouldn't be doing scouting . . ."

"No . . . you shouldn't, and you won't be for a while. You shouldn't even be alive, let alone talking. The healer had to cut the frigging quarrel out of you."

"That's why it hurts . . ."

"She said she tried not to cut too much muscle, but it's going to be a long time before you use a sabre. There was also something on the bolt."

With all the fever and pain he'd felt, Mykel didn't need to hear more about that. "The Reillies?"

"They took off, didn't even look back."

"Good. You must have handled . . . the battalion well . . ."

Rhystan snorted. "I didn't have anything to do with it. When you rode out of the trees with that thing sticking out of you . . . someone yelled, and they hightailed it off."

"Where are they?"

"They headed west. They're camped ten vingts beyond Wesrigg."

". . . doesn't make sense . . ."

"It didn't seem to. Not until I sent out some of the scouts to talk to people—and I had one take the golds to that innkeeper. I thought he might say something."

"Did he?"

"Not much." Rhystan grinned. "He asked if you were still alive. When Meurgelt said that you were, and that you would recover, he got real quiet."

"I'm glad you're . . . confident."

"Someone has to be." Rhystan's smile dropped away. "It seems that you killed the Reillie who shot you, and that he was the local commander or battleleader or whatever, and now they have to go through some sort of ritual to select another. It's likely to take a few weeks. That's the good news."

"And?" Mykel was still feeling light-headed, but he knew Rhystan well enough to know that there was more.

"The first duty of the new leader is to avenge the death of the old one."

"That's not so bad," suggested Mykel. "We won't have to chase them."

"You haven't heard it all, Majer. The man you killed was a Reillie. The Squawts and Reillies may sometimes fight among themselves, but they like outsiders less, and there's a good chance all the Squawts will join the Reillies in attacking us. So far, only a handful have been with the Reillies."

". . . have to take more time," murmured Mykel.

"Another few weeks, at most, enough to gather another thousand men, women, and youths."

Mykel had to wonder why, but he didn't feel like asking.

Rhystan went on inexorably. "It seems that by attacking their battleleader, man-to-man, you threatened something. No one wants to say what it might be, and maybe they don't know, but you've apparently gotten them to agree on something for the first time in centuries."

". . . problem is," said Mykel, forcing himself to articulate as clearly as he could, "what they're agreeing on is getting rid of the Cadmians."

"And you, Majer."

"I'd better heal quickly, then," Mykel said with a cheerfulness he scarcely felt.

47

Less than ten vingts north of Soupat, the air a thousand yards above the rolling desert hills was warm, verging on hot and uncomfortable—even in early winter. From the second harness behind Alynt, one of the younger rankers in Seventh Company, Dainyl studied the valley ahead.

The eternastone of the high road glistened like silvered water in the late afternoon sunlight, a shimmering markerstick running due south toward an irregular oval of green—the oasis that sustained Soupat and made possible the tin and copper mines, as well as the goldenstone quarries. In addition, Soupat provided a central gathering and distribution point for the desert nuts, so highly valued by the landers and indigens. Dainyl found the nuts filling, but not that delectable, but if landers wanted to pay exorbitant amounts for them, that was their business.

As the two squads of Seventh Company flew closer to Soupat, he saw that the solid green he'd seen earlier was but an illusion created by the spreading foliage of the iliaki trees that lined every street and lane clustered around the central spring, now walled and contained in goldenstone marble. Despite their lush appearance from the air, Dainyl could remember the one time he had touched one of the triangular leaves and come away with a slash across his fingers. The leaves were more like razor-edged flexible glass than the leaves of trees like oaks or apricots—or even the dried needles of pines or firs. Tough as the trees were, they still required some minimal water, and there was not even that more than a vingt away from the natural springs in the center of the oasis. Grass was sparse, tan most of the year, and tough.

"That must be Soupat, sir," Alynt called back.

"That it is," returned Dainyl. "The alector's complex is on the northwest edge." He looked for the three buildings that sat on a low flat rise less than a half vingt from where the iliaki trees ended. "We'll be avoiding that for now."

Lyzetta began to lose altitude, angling down and eastward, well away from the three alector's buildings and toward the small local patroller station on the southeast side of Soupat, beyond the fringe of the tree line.

"Lances ready!" came her order.

Alynt's lance was out with the others. Without a lance, Dainyl concentrated on raising and holding Talent shields around them.

The patroller station consisted of two small buildings, one a barrackslike structure and the other a stable, separated by twenty yards, with a flat expanse of reddish sandstone to the east, intermittently covered with knee-high dunes of fine sand, and a low hill to the northwest, barely more than ten yards high, just enough so that the alector's complex was most likely out of sight for anyone at the patroller station. Dainyl couldn't help but wonder if the location had been a subtle statement of lander defiance.

As the pteridons began to descend, a single patroller rushed out of the barracks, rifle in hand. When he caught sight of the pteridons—and the Myrmidons with their lances—he lowered his rifle and watched as the pteridons began to land on the sand-strewn flat. Two remained circling, acting as scouts and surveying the area.

Dainyl dismounted quickly and walked toward the patroller. After having flown for most of the day, he was unsteady, his legs protesting at the first few steps, but he continued until he reached the man, who wore a short-sleeved light gray uniform shirt with matching trousers. His belt was brown leather, and from it hung a truncheon.

"Sir?" The local's voice was uncertain, filled with a combination of curiosity and bewilderment.

"I'm Marshal Dainyl, commander of the Myrmidons."

The patroller's eyes widened as he took in the green-edged gold stars on Dainyl's tunic collar. "Yes, sir. Whatever you say, sir."

"Have you seen anyone from the regional alector's grounds in the last few days?"

The sense of bewilderment grew, even before the patroller replied. "No, sir. Haven't seen anyone at all. We don't see many alectors in town most days, anyway, except on market day, and then only one or two."

"Consider yourself fortunate," Dainyl replied. "We'll be using your post here for the next few days. It could be as long as a week."

"This post? Whatever you want, sir, but we barely have enough room for the ten of us."

"Do you have a wagon or cart here?"

"Yes, sir."

"We may need to borrow that as well." Dainyl offered a smile. "What about the Cadmian Battalion? Where are they?"

"They took over the old barracks at the mines."

"The copper mines? The ones to the southwest?"

"Yes, sir."

"Marshal!"

Dainyl turned to see Lyzetta gesturing to him, still mounted on her pteridon. "Excuse me," he said to the patroller before hurrying back to the captain.

"A group of insurgents are riding from the alector's compound. They have a wagon with them. What are your orders, sir?"

"That means they saw us, and they want supplies before we put them under attack, or they want us to think they want supplies. If it's a trap, they'll be carrying a weapon like a rifle, but it's more like a small lightcannon." Dainyl paused. "Here's what we'll do. Have one squad lift off immediately and circle high enough to be out of easy range, as if you're observing them preparatory to an attack. While they're doing that, the other squad will make a low pass, just above tree level coming in right inside the north tree line. I'll lead with Alynt—"

"Sir?"

"I can hold heavier shields than anyone else. We'll make a pass almost at tree height. That will make it hard for them to aim at us. If they have heavier weapons in the compound, they may not be able to depress them enough to hit us. But warn the first squad, the one climbing and circling, to be careful and stay well back. If they see anything dangerous or strange, they should break off."

"Yes, sir. If you're taking the attack, I'll have Undercaptain Resya follow you, and Buorl and I will rejoin squad one. I'll keep them clear but visible."

"Good." Dainyl hurried back toward Alynt, where he climbed back into the second seat and strapped himself into the harness. "We're leading squad two. Wait for Captain Lyzetta and Buorl to lift off. Resya and the others will follow us. Once we're airborne, head northeast, over the little hill there, and then stay low, right above the iliaki trees."

"Yes, sir. Is that what they're called?"

"It is. The leaves are knife-sharp." Dainyl watched as the first two pteridons lifted off, then waited until they were high enough to be visible from the alector's complex. "Now!"

The pteridon eased into the air, rather than exploded, and barely cleared the hill, then dropped into level flight about thirty yards above the tallest of the iliaki trees.

After they had covered a hundred yards, Dainyl called out, "A little more to the west. You can see them on the paved road down from the complex."

"Got them, sir."

The pteridon eased slightly to the left, barely banking at all before leveling out once more.

Dainyl glanced back over his shoulder. Four other pteridons followed. "Skylances ready!"

"Lance is ready, sir."

Dainyl could sense, rather than see, the townspeople looking up in the heat of the late afternoon as the five pteridons swept above the trees, in a triangular formation, their wide leathery blue wings beating evenly, heading northwest. Soupat proper was two vingts across, give or take a few hundred yards, and it seemed as though only moments passed before Alynt and Dainyl were leaving the trees behind and heading directly toward the small party of alectors in gray and green uniforms. Because they were a third of the way down the sloping slope to Soupat, the pteridon was flying toward them almost on the same level.

"Stand by to fire . . . fire!"

The blue skylance beam flashed toward the lead rider, who had turned his mount before Alynt fired, and missed by less than a yard. The blue beams from the other pteridons flared among and around the refugee Myrmidons.

Alynt fired again, almost on top of the party.

"Break left! Now!"

As the pteridon banked southward and down, the thin line of blue-green from the wagon behind the three riders confirmed Dainyl's suspicion that the "food sortie" had been an attempt at a lure.

"Hard right and come up over the slope from the west!" Not for the first time since he'd been promoted out of flight status, Dainyl heartily wished he were the one doing the flying. "Be ready to fire as soon as you clear the crest!"

Alynt didn't waste time replying, but complied.

Another light-rifle beam flared toward them, slamming into Dainyl's shields, and jolting him back in the harness, but the shields held—at least long enough for Alynt to drop below the rocky ridge to the southwest.

Dainyl took a deep breath. He couldn't absorb or deflect more than another one of the light-rifle shots . . . if that.

Alynt brought the pteridon back around to the north, then dropped even lower so that they appeared from the west, behind the refugee alectors. One of the other Seventh Company Myrmidons had incinerated the small rear guard.

Alynt shifted his lance, getting off two blasts from the skylance and taking down the remaining two riders slightly ahead of the wagon.

"Fire on the wagon! Now!" With the wagon and the two-horse team less than fifty yards away to the left—and the alector's compound a good five hundred yards up the road—Dainyl wanted to finish off the diversionary—or lure—force and get the Myrmidons back to the patroller post.

As Alynt triggered the lance, Dainyl used his Talent, in an effort to funnel that force into a needle point—not at the alector who held the light-rifle, but at the weapon itself.

A gout of flame erupted from where the wagon had been, with enough force to throw the pteridon to the right.

"Return to base! Return to base!" Dainyl didn't know who would hear it, but it was more than time to clear the area.

At that instant, a line of deep greenish blue flared above Dainyl—clearly the heaviest lightcannon he'd ever encountered, with so much power that he could feel it sucking lifeforce—from somewhere—and shaking the air. His shields, strong as they might be for an alector, would shatter in instants under that kind of focused lifeforce.

"Lower! As low as you can keep us without hitting anything!" he yelled at Alynt. "Straight south and circle the town back to the patroller station."

The Myrmidon said nothing, but the pteridon dropped even closer to the rocky and sandy ground, then angled even farther westward to drop behind a ridge that Dainyl realized was actually half rock and half sand dune.

Dainyl looked back, squinting to block out the orangish glare from the sun setting behind the southernmost peaks of the Coast Range. He could see three pteridons following them, but not the fourth. Although the road descending from the alector's complex was dotted with wide black splotches, he had no idea which splotch represented what, except that he was fairly certain that the large one in the center was what remained of the wagon, the horses, and the alector with the light-rifle. Whether the fourth pteridon was taking another route or had been a casualty he wouldn't know until the two squads returned and landed at the patroller station.

Once Alynt landed, Dainyl scanned the sky, now turning into the purpled dark green of twilight. He saw no pteridons at all and could only hope that Lyzetta had seen the massive beam of the green-blue lightcannon and ordered first squad well away from the weapon.

Rather than wait, hoping Lyzetta would indeed bring first squad back safely, Dainyl strode past the patroller barracks and began to climb the low hill. He wanted another look at the alector's complex.

He reached the hilltop, mostly rock, with red sandstone boulders scattered about, and a kind of dried thornweed in the few places where there was even a semblance of sandy soil. From there he studied, as well as he could in the fading light, what lay across Soupat from him.

Abruptly, he sensed Talent, and turned, taking a deep breath as he saw the first pteridon sweep in from the southeast and settle down. Then another followed. When they all had landed, there were eight on the ground—Lyzetta's pteridon, and three remaining from first squad joining the four from second squad.

Dainyl started down the hill.

Losing two pteridons within the first glass or so of arriving in Soupat wasn't exactly what he had planned, but if he'd counted correctly, the Ifryn refugees had lost more than ten Myrmidons and one light-rifle, and he'd managed to keep them from leaving the compound in large numbers—he hoped.

Lyzetta was waiting for him beside her pteridon.

"What was that greenish blue beam, some new form of lightcannon?" she asked.

"I suspect it's something they brought with them from Ifryn. I wouldn't be surprised if someone hadn't raided an arsenal of forbidden weapons." How things had changed, reflected Dainyl. Until the past year, there had been no weapon on Acorus that could destroy a pteridon. Then, Rhelyn—or more probably High Alector Ruvryn's engineers—had come up with the lightcannon used at Hyalt, which had taken out pteridons from both Seventh and Fifth Companies. Now, the insurgent Myrmidons had something that made both the Myrmidons' skylances and Rhelyn's weapons look childlike in comparison.

Of equal, if not greater, concern to Dainyl was the ravenous use of lifeforce by the weapon. If the battle for Soupat lasted longer than a few days, the impact on Acorus would be great enough that the world would be able to support far fewer alectors. A few weeks, and . . . who knew?

"You don't think it was used on Ifryn?"

"Ifryn would already have used all of its lifeforce, and the Master Scepter would have been—" Dainyl broke off his words and shook his head.

"What?"

"It's only a guess, but Ifryn was supposed to have lasted years longer than it has. There have been two revolts against the Archon, from what I've heard, and they were put down savagely."

"You think they used this . . . lightcannon?"

"I don't know, but it would explain a lot."

"What do we do about it?" asked Lyzetta. "We've already lost one pteridon and flier to it, and you lost one to the smaller weapon. That lightcannon will destroy anything it hits. The only advantage we have is that they don't seem to be able to use it often."

"From where they have it, they can't fire it too low, not unless they move it, and that would allow us to use the strategy we'd already planned." He smiled grimly. "I have an idea."

48

Sometime before muster on Octdi morning, Mykel managed to get himself propped up in the quarters bed, although it took him some time because each movement of his upper body sent waves of agony through him so great that he felt light-headed. He moved slowly, not because of the pain, but because he couldn't see the point in fainting and falling on the floor. That wouldn't help his healing in the slightest. He supposed he should have slept longer, but the intermittent burning in his shoulder had made that more than a little difficult.

He couldn't see his shoulder, but he did use his Talent-senses for a moment to study the wound, not that he understood what they showed him. He had to stop almost immediately because he could feel himself getting weaker, even with that minimal effort. He did try to wiggle the fingers on his right hand, and they did move. That was somewhat encouraging.

There was a perfunctory knock on the quarters door before a ranker appeared with a tray. "Sir . . . you hungry?"

"I think I could manage something, thank you."

"Here you go, sir." The ranker—Mykel finally recalled his name, Einsyl—eased the tray down in front of Mykel.

Mykel was surprised by the egg toast, perfectly golden brown, the fried apples, and particularly by the small pitcher of berry syrup, accompanied by two mugs, one of cider and one of ale. He doubted he'd ever had a more appetizing breakfast prepared by Cadmian cooks. "Thank you,

Einsyl . . . and thank the cooks for me. It might be a day or two before I can do it personally."

"Yes, sir. I will, sir." Einsyl inclined his head, then backed out of the quarters.

Eating left-handed, balancing a tray on his lap, was awkward, but Mykel had to admit he felt better after he finished. He drank both the cider and the ale. The liquids, especially, seemed to help the light-headedness.

Outside the window, he could hear morning muster, and what he did hear convinced him that the entire battalion, less scouts or a few others, remained in Iron Stem.

Shortly afterward, Rhystan entered the quarters. "You look better this morning, Majer." He smiled wryly. "You're only as pale as an alector, rather than a corpse."

"You're cheerful this morning. Have the Squawts and Reillies picked their new battleleader and left the hills to wreak vengeance on me and all Cadmians?"

"No word on that." Rhystan bent down and took the breakfast tray, setting it on the small writing desk, then sat on the stool beside the bed. "They're still having their big meeting. We have another problem."

That didn't surprise Mykel. He only wondered what the new problem might be. "What is it?"

"I think it's your absence."

That did surprise Mykel. "*My* absence?"

"In the last day or so, the attacks by sandwolves and the other predators have been increasing around Iron Stem. It's almost as if they know you're not there. The head of the outholders was here last night . . ."

"Croyalt?" asked Mykel.

"Right. He said not to lose men fighting them and let the inholders take their losses. The big danger was the Reillies."

"That's easy for him to say," Mykel replied. As he recalled, Croyalt hadn't said anything about the Reillies. He'd told Mykel to leave well enough alone, and to depart from Iron Stem, if he could. "Did he say any more about the Reillies?"

"He said that they knew how to call the sanders . . . but he didn't say who these sanders were."

Mykel realized, belatedly, how that tied to the Reillies.

"They're the other predators, the ones that look like little stone men. They're very hard to kill. The Reillies probably called them up when Hersiod took on the miners."

"Why is it that the more I hear about Iron Stem the less I want to be here?"

"Because you're a sensible Cadmian, and nothing sensible is going on here," Mykel replied. "None of it makes sense. The outholders want the inholders to lose their livestock. The inholders hate the outholders. The people in the town hate the ironworks, but want every coin they can get from it. No one likes the dreamdust, but they don't seem to do anything about it. Hersiod's sent here to protect people, and he immediately kills hundreds. The alectors want more iron and coal, yet they seem to be going out of their way to antagonize everyone who might help them produce it. At the time they need it most, for whatever reason, the weather turns bad, and the rivers run high and flood out the loading piers in Dekhron." Mykel took a slow deep breath. "There's probably more that I don't know."

"That's enough."

"What about the ironworks and the mines? Any new problems there?"

"No problems there at the moment, not that anyone's brought to my attention."

"On the patrols where the sandwolves and sanders show up . . . concentrated fire is the answer, and they shouldn't corner the sanders—the small sandy figures."

"Makes sense. Anything else?" asked Rhystan.

"If I think of anything, I'll let you know."

"Take it easy, Majer. You need to rest and let that shoulder heal."

Mykel remembered what he'd wanted to ask. "Did the healer ever say what was on that bolt?"

"No, sir." Rhystan offered a wry smile. "She did say that no one ever lived after they'd been wounded with one with grooves like that on it."

"Good fortune. There's always a first time."

"Yes, sir." Rhystan's tone was polite, but barely short of openly disbelieving.

Mykel laughed. He couldn't help it, and the pain from the laughing didn't stop him—just shortened how long he laughed.

"I'll tell the men you're doing much better."

"I'll be up in a day or so."

"Don't push it, sir." Rhystan nodded and slipped out of the quarters.

Mykel forced himself to lie back against the pillows. He didn't like the idea that the sandwolves and the other predators might know about him. He couldn't believe that they could sense that, but he could easily believe that the soarers might know, and that suggested that they were behind those attacks. What he didn't know and couldn't understand was why. The one soarer had once told him that the Cadmians—he started to shake his head, but the jabbing pain from his shoulder halted the gesture uncompleted—not the Cadmians, but he, personally, was an ally of the soarers against the alectors. What was happening suggested that the soarers didn't like what the Cadmians were doing. But why? How could he find out?

Mykel had no answers, not yet.

After a time, he found his eyes were closing.

49

The patroller had been right. The station quarters were very tight, even though all the patrollers had disappeared into the twilight by the time the Myrmidons had finished settling their pteridons for the night. Dainyl's sleep on Septi night had been fitful, with visions of baleful light-cannon incinerating pteridons and their fliers in brilliant blue-green incandescence, followed by scenes of women and children being executed on Tables of immense size and scope. What was worse was that in one of the dreams he was the one ordering the executions, even as tears streamed down his cheeks, tears that burned like flames eating away his visage.

Just before dawn on Octdi, when he could sleep no longer, Dainyl dressed and washed up, then walked up the low hill that sheltered the patroller post to take another look at the RA's complex. In the gray predawn light, he could see nothing moving outside the structures. He turned and studied the hills beyond the settled area, looking for the rockier locales. After a time, he walked back down. He thought his stomach was settled enough for some travel rations.

Lyzetta was waiting for him. Her violet eyes studied him, but she said nothing, just nodded.

"How was your night, Captain?" he finally asked.

"I've had better, sir. I've had worse, too."

"After we eat, gather the fliers together, and we'll go over how we'll implement what we discussed last night. After that, we'll have them gather the boulders and stockpile them. There's a deeper valley about a vingt and a half to the north of the ridge where the RA's place is. The valley's across the high road to the east from there. We'll put the boulders there. While you're doing that, I'll need Alynt to fly me out to the mines so that I can talk to the battalion commander."

"I'll let him know. You think this will work?"

"It will work." How long it might take was another matter.

Once the Myrmidons had eaten their rations and gathered together in the sunlight outside the barracks, Dainyl took out one of the sheets of paper he'd found in the barracks and began to sketch, using his own grease marker. When he finished, he had a crude side view of the low stone ridge on which the regional alector's buildings were set. "I'd like each of you to take a quick look. That's a rough sketch of the east and west approaches to the ridge. You can see that if we fly low enough, we're not exposed to the lightcannon until we have to climb over the edge of the ridge. After that, if we fly directly toward the buildings, we'll be exposed long enough for that lightcannon to target us. It's less than half a vingt from the edge to where they're dug in, but that's too much exposure."

There were several nods, especially from those fliers in second squad.

"The tower where they have the lightcannon isn't that

high," Dainyl went on. "That means they can't see when a pteridon approaches until we come up over the edge." He paused. "We aren't going to fly that distance. How big a boulder—or a rock—can a pteridon carry?"

"For short flights, twenty to thirty stone," offered Lyzetta.

"If we try to drop something that big on them," ventured Alynt, "won't we be as vulnerable as clipped-wing fowls?"

Dainyl shook his head. "What happens if a pteridon flies up to the edge of the ridge out of sight, then pops up for a moment and lets that huge stone go . . . on an arc, with all the speed of flight behind it? Then it drops back out of direct sight. No pteridon will come up in the same spot as the one before, or any other one. It's sort of like that lander bowling game, except the objective is to throw the boulders at the buildings and keep doing it until we flatten them. The buildings are stone-walled, but the walls aren't that thick. They were designed to last against weather, not against pteridons bombarding them with stone missiles." For the moment, Dainyl did not mention his other idea.

"We're going to miss some. It could be most of the time," pointed out one of the Myrmidons whose name Dainyl couldn't remember.

"We'll get better," Dainyl said.

"What if they turn that lightcannon on the boulders?"

"They'll just waste power. It's not designed for that." Dainyl could see that some of the Myrmidons didn't understand exactly how much force would lie behind a thirty-stone boulder propelled by a pteridon that could cover over seventy vingts a glass. "Have any of you seen what happens when a large boulder rolls down a mountainside?"

"Yes, sir. It happened in Coren last year, after the fires and all. It flattened one of the cottages, and it had thick stone walls. Maybe they were as thick as the ones in the RA's buildings."

"The boulders your pteridons will be tossing will be moving about twice as fast." Dainyl didn't know that for certain, but he had to say something. "We do have to locate a number of boulders first, the rounder the better. Sharp-edged ones will tend to dig in. Captain Lyzetta will tell you where to stockpile them. Take care to stay well away from the target. Then, once we have enough to begin operations, I'll go over with each of you how I want you to approach the RA's complex, based on the approach of the previous pteridon."

"Prepare for liftoff in a quarter glass," said Lyzetta.

While the others moved to their pteridons, Dainyl motioned to Lyzetta. "Late this afternoon, we'll have to watch for First Company. We don't want them flying into that lightcannon."

"You don't think we'll take out the complex today?" Lyzetta raised her eyebrows.

"I'd be surprised."

"Ah . . . sir . . . what if they've used lifeforce the way they did in Hyalt, and all the boulders pile up?"

"Hyalt was different. It was built into a cliff. Here, the buildings are out in the open on a flat surface." Dainyl laughed. "If they try to use lifeforce, it will take longer, but it will work out the same in the end. They can only coat the outer walls. That will stop skylances, maybe even something like their lightcannon, but it won't add that much strength to the stone behind the coating. It's like taking a lander bullet with a shimmersilk tunic. You get bruised with the first bullet. It gets worse with the second . . ."

"I hadn't thought about that, but it makes sense." Lyzetta nodded. "What do you plan to do during the bombardment?"

"Watch from behind a thick pile of stone, close enough so that I can see how matters are going, and where I can signal you or the squad leaders when I need to. If I fly with anyone, it only reduces what they can carry and their maneuverability, and with that lightcannon, that's not something I'd want to do."

"I'll have the second seat put on my pteridon then, after you get back from the Cadmians."

Dainyl didn't argue. He wouldn't be spending much time on a pteridon once he finished meeting with the Cadmian commander.

In less than a quarter glass, he was airborne, seated behind Alynt as the Myrmidon directed his pteridon southward, across dry and sandy hills, following the paved road that led to the mines, and then to the only occasionally used goldenstone quarries.

From the air, the copper mine looked more like an oval, with a road wound around its edge down to the lowest level. Farther to the west were the works for the tin mines, which looked deserted. The barracks and other buildings were on a low mesa to the east of the copper mine pit. Dainyl could see two companies of Cadmians formed up to the north of the buildings.

"Set down where the Cadmians are, but not too close!" he called forward.

The Myrmidon eased the pteridon into a glide downward, and warm air rushed past Dainyl's face, comfortable enough, but hot enough that he wondered how the indigens dealt with the heat in the heart of summer. Alynt landed his pteridon with a gentle flare.

By the time Dainyl was out of the harness and standing on the sandy ground, a Cadmian undercaptain had ridden up.

"Marshal, sir . . . ah . . . what can I do for you?"

"Is Majer Juasyn still the battalion commander?"

"Yes, sir. He should be here in a moment." The undercaptain glanced back over his shoulder. "He's riding here now, sir." He eased his mount back slightly.

Juasyn rode toward Dainyl with the ease of someone who had spent a great deal of time in the saddle, reining up short of the marshal. He was a smallish and dapper black-haired man with a thin mustache. His eyes were light brown, but penetrating. "Marshal, sir. Welcome to Soupat mines. I must say that I never expected you here. What can we do for you, sir?"

Dainyl smiled politely. "I'm afraid that we can't offer you support in your efforts against the mountain brigands, and for the next few days, possibly a week, our actions will create some difficulties for you and the mine. The regional alector's compound in Soupat has been taken over by some insurgents, and we will be using pteridons and skylances, as well as other methods, to return it to control of the Duarches. Unfortunately, that will require that none of the mine wagons will be able to travel the high road north until we finish the operation. It will also require that you keep your men out of Soupat until further notice."

"Yes, sir." Juasyn cleared his throat. "We have been told that the High Alector of Engineering expects no delays of any sort with the production and shipment of the copper . . ."

"I'm certain of that," Dainyl replied, "but he will be even more distressed if the wagons and horse teams are destroyed by the weapons likely to be employed over and around the high road north of Soupat. If anyone questions you, tell them that you felt it unwise to dispute your overall commander." Dainyl grinned. "And two companies of pteridons and skylances."

Juasyn bowed slightly, a glint in his eyes. "Thank you for that clarification, sir."

Dainyl could sense the officer's concealed amusement. "If you have problems with supplies or other items, we will be operating out of the patrollers' station on the southeast side of Soupat, and you can contact me or the senior officer in charge there."

"Might I inquire as to whether we might be of assistance, sir? I would not wish to be presumptuous . . ."

"Your courtesy and kindness is appreciated, Majer, but the insurgents are using weapons similar to skylances, and I would prefer not to expose your men to such weapons, except in extreme circumstances. If we do need your assistance, you will be the first to know." Dainyl smiled. "I appreciate the offer."

Juasyn nodded. "We will be happy to do what we can."

"Thank you. How are your efforts against the brigands going?"

"We have managed to reduce two of the larger bands into scattered groups small enough that they pose far less of a threat. The one matter that is of some concern is how so many of them managed to obtain Cadmian rifles and ammunition."

"I'm afraid I can answer that, Majer. Last year, an assistant engineer reported that a large number of rifles, thousands in fact, were flawed and scrapped. They were not. He diverted them for a great number of golds. While he was discovered and executed, we're still finding the rifles in places we never expected." If Ruvryn had been behind the weapons being made and shipped to indigen insurgents, Dainyl wondered, why would he have allowed them to go to the mountain brigands? Or had lander golds diverted them without alector knowledge? Everywhere he turned, there was something else that seemed to make no sense.

"Like Soupat, sir?"

"Unfortunately." Dainyl paused but briefly. "If you do not have any more questions, Majer, I need to be returning to our efforts against the insurgents."

"Yes, sir."

Dainyl nodded, then turned and climbed back into the harness and second seat behind Alynt. The pteridon launched itself into the wind, then swung northward.

50

Even with the tireless pteridons beginning to gather stones less than a glass after sunrise, it was past midmorning before there were enough of the huge stones piled in the desolate valley, more like a collapsed sinkhole. After returning from the mines, while the Myrmidons were completing the task of ferrying their makeshift ammunition to its staging point, Dainyl had located a rocky outcrop to the north of the target ridge, a vingt away, which was as close as he could get with adequate protection should the massive light-cannon be turned on him. The lower south side of the outcrop was covered in powdery sand, almost dunelike.

Another half glass passed before all the fliers gathered around Dainyl. He looked over the Myrmidons. "If you want to survive this, you have to make sure that the rebels have no idea where you'll appear for the few moments it will take to release your boulders." He smiled. "I assume each of you knows the day and the month you were born? It's very simple. You note where the pteridon in front of you goes over the ridgeline. The first time you angle to one side fifty times your birth month. If you were born in the third month, that's 150 yards. The second time, it's fifty times your day of the month. Alternate sides, but not evenly."

"Sir . . . I was born on the fortieth of ten month."

"You'd better cut those in half," Dainyl said with a laugh. "The reason I want you to base the deviation from the previous flier on your own birth dates is so that whoever aims that lightcannon will be facing a different distance each time. You'll have to adjust early because you still want to come up over the ridge facing the buildings. That's so you spend as little time as possible where they can fire at you.

"Captain Lyzetta will direct you as to which of you are to attack from the east and which from the west." That would keep the defenders from focusing on one side or the other.

"The marshal will be watching this operation and advising us," Lyzetta added. "I'll drop him at his observation post. When I get back, I expect everyone ready to fly. For now, second squad will attack from the west, first from the east."

Dainyl followed her to her pteridon, mounting after she did.

"How do you intend to signal me?" Lyzetta asked as she fastened her harness.

"I'll move to the back side and wave my jacket. Or fire a lightcutter into the air, if I need something urgently. You'll have to watch occasionally, but not much will happen for a while."

"You think that they'll just let us roll rocks at them and do nothing?"

"I don't think they'll realize the danger at first. That big lightcannon can't be easy to move, and they don't leave its protection while we have pteridons and skylances."

"I hope you're right." She turned to face forward in her harness, and the pteridon was airborne, moving in almost a low glide out of the sinkhole valley and across the high road, turning slightly southward, and then climbing gently up the long rugged incline leading to the ridge point Dainyl had earlier pointed out.

"Land on the back side. I can climb up the last fifty yards. That way they won't know from where I'm watching."

Lyzetta eased the pteridon down, but the north side was so uneven that its crystalline talons crunched into the rock, and it kept its wings spread to maintain balance while Dainyl dismounted.

After a quick wave, Dainyl clambered up the steep and stony slope until he reached the top. From there, he took a careful survey before slipping from behind one outcropping and moving forward to another, and then another. His final vantage point was a hundred yards higher than the flat ridge that held the alector's complex, but both were actually outcroppings on a larger underlying ridge.

Dainyl wished he were close enough to use his lightcutter or even Talent, but a vingt was too distant for effective use of either. He tried to find a comfortable position behind the rock shield from which he could watch the coming bombardment.

Lyzetta began the first run, her pteridon barely above the ground, certainly not more than twenty yards, so close that it seemed that the tips of the long blue leathery wings nearly touched the uneven stony prominences that rose in places. Then, she was up over the eastern edge of the ridge, the boulder arcing across the hard ground toward the middle building before catching something and skid-rolling sideways.

From that one pass, Dainyl had the feeling that it was going to be a long day.

The next pteridon followed her, rising over the eastern ridge edge some seventy yards to the south of where Lyzetta had released her boulder. The Myrmidon managed a touch more lift, arcing the stone almost to the base of the easternmost building, before it slammed into the building wall and lifted a small plume of rock dust.

The following pteridon came in from the west, and its boulder rolled past all the buildings and down the eastern slope.

The Myrmidon on the fourth pteridon—from the east—had no better aim than his predecessor, and his weapon dug in a good fifty yards short of any building.

Two more passes went by before another boulder shuddered into the main building, but it hit with enough force that Dainyl could see the entire structure shiver.

As Dainyl watched, he could see that about one in three or four missiles actually contacted the buildings, and only half of those impacted with great force, and so far, the defenders had not opened fire on the attacking pteridons. He doubted that would continue, especially if the Myrmidons and their pteridons became more accurate in their bombardment.

Another set of passes by both squads resulted in four more strikes against the stone and masonry construction, and a pall of sandy dust was beginning to enshroud the complex.

After the first pteridon lofted its heavy stone at the beginning of the third run, the light-rifle flashed out at the second Myrmidon, if nowhere close to the pteridon.

Lyzetta must have passed a shift in directions because the next set of pteridon passes came more from the northeast and northwest—the southern approaches were too exposed—and the light-rifle beams did not anticipate any of the pteridons. Four more of the heavy stones slammed into the buildings, and the dust thickened. While Dainyl hadn't planned that aspect of the attack, the dust aided his forces far more than the defenders, since the pteridons were changing positions constantly and the buildings remained fixed targets.

Suddenly, from somewhere behind him, Dainyl could sense a growing sense of amber-green—the Talent of the ancients—but he was certain that there were no portals on the ridgeline. The amber-green wavered, and then strengthened.

Abruptly, one of the ancients hovered beside him, almost at his shoulder. *You must crush them.*

"I know that." He hated being told the obvious, even by an ancient. "I'm doing the best I can."

It would be far easier if you linked directly to this world.

"I don't know how," he pointed out, trying to see when and where the next pteridon would loose its heavy stone.

You know how. You wish to remain as you are. If you do not change, Talent-strong as you are, you will perish. Once more, there was the impression of certainty, finality, and sadness.

"Why are you so interested in me? Why did you heal me

before? Why don't you destroy me the way you have so many others?"

We only destroy those who attack us. You have not. You have a ????? with those landers who also have ties to the world.

Dainyl had no understanding of the word or phrase she used. He frowned as he watched the pteridon on the attack run loose a stone that rolled between the three buildings without touching any of them, coming to rest a good hundred yards to the west.

The light-rifle fired by a defender missed by a wide margin.

Another pteridon flashed up on the west side of the alector's ridge, then dropped out of sight. That stone rolled or slid into the westernmost building, and a puff of dust or sand or crushed stone rose skyward. "Better . . ."

"Exactly how am I supposed to change?" Dainyl had asked the question before, but the soarer of whom he had asked had simply told him he had been shown.

You have the strength and ability to link your lifethread to this world. All you lack is the will. There was the sense of an ironic laugh. *We will provide the desire. You had best know what to do when that time comes. It will not be long.*

What was "long" to creatures that seemingly outlived alectors?

You see so much, and yet you learn so little.

With that, she was gone.

The last thing he needed was to worry about the undefined threats of an ancient when refugee Myrmidons were using weapons that, if not stopped, would destroy Acorus long before its time.

Another stone hit the outbuilding to the west, and a corner crumbled slightly, with a small cascade of stones spilling onto the ground of the ridge.

Following six more passes at the buildings by both squads, there was a break, since the pteridons needed to gather more of the heavy stones. Some of the rock dust cleared, enough that Dainyl could see that the eastern wall of the center structure was severely damaged and sagging inward around a gaping hole.

In less than half a glass, the bombardment began again.

This time, two of the light-rifles began firing, but after both squads had completed their run, none of the pteridons had yet been hit, and there were two more places where parts of the building walls were sagging, and the dust had begun to rise once more.

Lyzetta had just finished her next pass—successfully directing a near-spherical boulder into the middle building, and shaking down more of the eastern wall—when Dainyl sensed the heavy lightcannon begin to operate even before he saw the intense blue-green beam sweep the eastern approach to the RA's complex. He could feel the weapon sucking lifeforce from *somewhere.* That meant it had a shielding mechanism of some sort, or all the alectors in the complex would be dead or dying.

The lightcannon kept trying to track the pteridons—and missing—all through the next run. Even so, the weapon was having one effect—the accuracy of the boulders went down, with only two hitting the buildings.

In some ways, Dainyl wished he had the numbers a commander like Majer Mykel had. For Dainyl, every pteridon was valuable—and irreplaceable. The majer could afford to lose scores of troopers to gain an objective. Dainyl had to weigh every possible loss. But then, that was because there had never been that many pteridons on Acorus, and they'd effectively been invulnerable.

Lyzetta had delayed the next run of the pteridons. Then, suddenly she and another Myrmidon, separated by a good hundred yards, managed simultaneous appearances directly north of the buildings. By the time the lightcannon had swung north, cutting through the dust and turning the larger particles into minute burning points of light, the two pteridons had dropped below the edge of the ridge. Lyzetta's boulder had struck the northwest corner of the large middle structure with enough force, combined with the earlier damage, that the entire corner slumped into rubble.

The lightcannon flicked off.

Another pair of pteridons attacked from the southwest, but

there was no reply from the defenders. Dainyl knew that they were waiting, probably picking a spot and hoping to trigger the weapon if any pteridon appeared there, instead of chasing the pteridons.

He just hoped Lyzetta understood that as well.

Four more pteridons appeared and lobbed or threw boulders before the lightcannon flashed once, narrowly missing the fifth. The central structure was sagging on two corners, and Dainyl had to wonder why the defenders did not move the heavy lightcannon. Or was it tied to something?

He shook his head. Of course, it was tied to the Table. That was the only source of lifeforce that wasn't strictly local. Did that mean that the lightcannon remained virtually invulnerable, like the Table, so long as the Table was powered?

He had no way of knowing that, and if that happened to be true, then his strategy was the only one that had a chance of working.

The bombardment came to a halt once more, while the pteridons gathered more boulders. This time there was a longer break, doubtless for the Myrmidons to stretch their legs and eat. Dainyl glanced at the sun—and was surprised to realize that it was well past midafternoon.

He took a long swallow from his water bottle, finishing it off.

Close to a glass passed before Lyzetta initiated the next run.

The lightcannon did not fire for the first three pteridons.

Then, a ball of blue-green fire exploded on the west edge of the ridge. Dainyl *knew* the explosion was the result of the lightcannon striking one of the second squad pteridons.

The defenders had calculated well—or had been lucky. Either way, it didn't matter. Seventh Company had lost another pteridon and Myrmidon.

Dainyl watched the next few pteridons closely, but the lightcannon did not fire, and more boulders battered the structures. If the defenders got more accurate, he'd have to come up with something else, but until they did, what the

Myrmidons were doing was the best approach he could come up with.

He glanced to the northwest. Before too long, the three squads from First Company should be arriving—if they hadn't run into other difficulties.

51

By a glass before sunset, the structures on the top of the ridge were closer to resembling piles of rubble than the buildings that they had once been, but Dainyl had the feeling that despite the outer appearance, the lower levels were not that badly damaged and that the Table was still receiving alectors from Ifryn. The lightcannon was still operating and had claimed one more pteridon. At that point, Dainyl had signaled Lyzetta to pick him up, and then had ordered a withdrawal to the patrollers' station, leaving two pteridons flying surveillance, both to watch the complex and to intercept and warn First Company—assuming that Alcyna did in fact arrive with the three squads.

Neither Lyzetta nor Dainyl spoke until she had landed the pteridon and dismounted from the harness, stretching her long legs.

"This has been a hard day."

"These are hard times," he replied, thinking about all the pteridons and Myrmidons lost in the past seasons.

"Was it planned this way, sir?"

"Was what planned this way, Captain?"

"The secondary world being set up as a target for the desperate from Ifryn. The lack of pteridons and effective weapons to combat the numbers of alectors trying to escape Ifryn."

"I don't think so. Not in that way. The Archon wouldn't want Acorus to exhaust its lifeforce. He'd want another world ready when Efra fails. But . . . he didn't want either world strong enough to resist him and those around him when he transfers the Master Scepter. That's just a guess on my part, but I imagine once the decision was made, probably several years back, the Archon began sending his own people, more than a few shadowmatched for loyalty, to Efra to ensure his reception. Some have been sent here, too, I suspect." He paused. Had Zestafyn and Kylara been such? Was that why they'd been removed? While Zestafyn's death—since he had been Khelaryt's unofficial intelligence chief—made sense in terms of his role in uncovering the engineering misfeasance, why would anyone bother with his wife, who had no such role, unless something else had been involved?

"Marshal?"

"Just thinking." He forced a smile. "You'd better have your Myrmidons get some food and rest. Tomorrow could be another long day."

"They can't hold out that much longer, can they?" asked the captain. "What if they decide to abandon everything tonight and scatter into the hills or try to take over Soupat?"

"Then we bury the complex tomorrow so deeply that it can't be used anytime soon, and start to hunt down any troublemakers. I don't think the Duarches will bother, not right now, anyway, with a comparative handful of refugees—if we make sure no more come through." Dainyl tried not to think of what would happen if someone tried to translate to a buried Table.

"What do you think will happen tomorrow, sir?"

"We'll either find an abandoned complex, or they'll have figured out some new weapon or way of using that lightcannon—or both—and we'll have to figure out something else."

Her eyebrows lifted. "Blasting powder?"

"I've thought about it, but we don't have the right containment to blast through unbroken stone, and it would take longer than we have to create that kind of weaponry." Dainyl also didn't want to be the one who demonstrated that kind of weaponry with landers around.

"There's no other solution besides force?"

"If we allow Acorus to admit every alector who wants to come, in less than a generation, if not in a few years, we won't have a world that will hold life. On the other hand, they're fighting for their very lives. Do you see a solution, Captain?"

"Couldn't we find a way . . . ?"

Dainyl laughed. "Asulet and the lifeform specialists have worked for over a thousand years. They'd like nothing better than to have a better solution. So would your father."

"There must be . . ."

"Generally, I've found that when we say that there must be a solution or a way, that means that we can't think of one, but we don't want to accept the situation that faces us." Dainyl knew he was no different. The ancients had suggested that he had to change, and Dainyl had twice dismissed their declaration. But . . . what if they were right?

"Pteridons to the north!"

Both Lyzetta and Dainyl turned and watched as the three squads of First Company swung eastward and circled around, well clear of the RA's complex, to set down farther to the east.

Alcyna was in the second harness of the second pteridon, and she unharnessed herself quickly and walked across the sand-swept ground toward Dainyl, where she stopped. "First Company reporting, Marshal."

Dainyl noted that Lyzetta eased away gracefully. "Thank you. How was the flight?"

"Long. We all appreciated the warning about the lightcannon." The briefest frown crossed her brow.

For that moment, Dainyl was aware of just how small she was for an alectress. Most of the time, her sheer energy conveyed an impression of far greater height and presence.

"How did they get it here?" Alcyna asked.

"I'd judge that they carried the crystals and components here through the long translation. How many they lost to get it here I wouldn't want to speculate. They probably had the strongest Talents do it, and had spares. It's nothing like the ones Rhelyn had. It's far more powerful, and they're tapping the Table and translation tubes to power it."

Alcyna winced. "Even Brekylt and . . . some of those around him aren't that stupid."

"Or that desperate." Dainyl gestured toward the low hill to the northwest of the patroller station. "We can get a view of the complex from the top of the hill."

"That might be a good idea."

Once they were away from the other Myrmidons, Dainyl glanced at Alcyna. "You're worried. I don't think it's about Soupat."

"No. Brekylt sent me a dispatch. It was Talent-sealed. Someone had opened it and resealed it. I doubt anyone besides me or his chief assistant would have caught the difference."

"Zelyert?"

Alcyna gave a low and rueful laugh. "Possibly. It doesn't matter. He'll know by now."

"What are you going to do?"

"That's one of the things I like about you. You don't ask the inane questions like 'Do you want to tell me?' You know I wouldn't mention it if I didn't. Brekylt was like that, too."

Dainyl kept walking, listening.

"It was a simple note, really," Alcyna went on. "Not that what was behind it was simple at all. He just wished me well in Elcien. He wrote that I had great ability and should be rewarded with a position that offered me the ability to command without having to compromise with those who did not understand and never would. That was all."

"That was almost an offer of command if you return."

"He didn't go quite that far. He never does."

"But you know that, and he knows that you do," Dainyl pointed out.

"Shastylt truly underestimated you. So does Zelyert."

"You don't want complete command?"

"Of course, I want to be in command." Her eyebrows lifted and her lips quirked into a sardonic expression. "I also don't want to be a mere tool if there's any alternative, and Brekylt is looking for tools. Even Noryan knows that."

"How long before Brekylt declares the east independent of the Duarches?"

"Just before the Master Scepter is transferred, when no

one can really do anything. Efra will take all the effort and power the Archon and those with him have. Once Brekylt consolidates his power and controls the Tables in the east, the Archon will have to recognize him as the equivalent of a Duarch."

Dainyl frowned. "I'm new to the deeper levels of this sort of plotting, but it seems that all the refugees from Ifryn might well be another means to keep matters unsettled enough that the High Alectors didn't get ideas like Brekylt has—or make implementing them more difficult."

"I wouldn't be at all surprised. It's aimed as much at the Duarches as at Brekylt, though."

That was certainly true. "What else should I know about what's happening in Elcien?"

"Doubtless there's something, but what that might be . . ." Alcyna shrugged. "Zelyert has yet to talk to me since I arrived in Elcien."

Dainyl sensed both the truth and a certain frustration behind her words.

She gestured toward the northwest. "It looks as though your bombardment is working, but . . . it's been hard on the pteridons."

"The two squads from Seventh Company started out one short, and we've lost four," Dainyl admitted.

"You knew this wouldn't be as easy as Zelyert thought, didn't you?"

"I don't think he cares what it costs."

"You're right about that." After the briefest of pauses, she asked, "How much damage do you think you've done?"

"Less than it looks. In a bit, I'm going to try something else."

"Dropping a large boulder from overhead?"

"That's the idea. It's not practical for most Myrmidons." He snorted. "It may not be practical for me."

"You have blasting powder, don't you?"

"Some . . . but the more I've thought about it, the less I think it's practical."

"And you still don't like giving ideas to the indigens?"

Dainyl couldn't help but think of Majer Mykel. "Some of

them already have it figured out. They just fear the consequences."

"Those are the dangerous ones."

Not wanting to discuss that particular matter further, Dainyl turned. "I need to get ready."

"Of course."

They began to walk down the hill.

"How is Lystrana doing in Dereka?"

"I have no idea, except that she arrived safely and the recorder was pleased. I haven't exactly had access to a Table here."

Alcyna's laugh was rueful. "I'm sorry. Sometimes, it seems . . . you know what I mean."

"We take the presence of Tables for granted."

"We couldn't hold even Corus together without them."

"We may not be able to even with them," Dainyl replied sardonically.

When they reached the station area, Dainyl found Ghasylt talking with Lyzetta.

". . . hands-on commander . . . knows what a pteridon can do . . . what it can't . . ."

Both looked up.

"Captain Ghasylt, is Halya available for a short flight . . . with a passenger? I have one more tactic I'd like to try."

"Yes, sir. I believe she's . . . over there. Halya!"

In less than a quarter glass, Dainyl was standing beside Halya's pteridon, explaining. "We're going to lift a large boulder very high in the sky, after twilight, but while there's light in the sky, and then we're going to drop it. You have a good idea of how much your pteridon can lift, I take it?"

"Yes, sir."

"Then we should get airborne. We'll head toward the sinkhole valley to the north, just to the east of the high road. There we'll see which boulder looks best. Then, we'll head north and circle west, climbing as we go. I'd like to be at least two thousand yards up before we start to come south over the RA's complex."

"We can do that, sir."

Dainyl was more than a little amused by the alectress's cheerful confidence.

At the supply valley he had Halya's pteridon pick up the largest and most spherical boulder that she felt confident the creature could carry. Even so, he had to wince at the Talent/lifeforce draw that it took for the pteridon to get into the air and slowly climb out.

They continued to climb for a good four vingts before Dainyl called forward. "You can swing back south now."

"Yes, sir."

At two thousand yards above the rocky hills to the north and west of Soupat, Dainyl could sense that the pteridon was close to its limits. He waited until the battered buildings came into clearer view, the stones golden red in the indirect light diffusing from the setting sun.

"A touch more to the right!"

The pteridon banked ever so slightly.

"Just a bit more."

The pteridon centered on a course that would carry them directly over the center building, the one that held both the lightcannon and the Table.

From what Dainyl had seen earlier, they were above the range of the heavy lightcannon, even assuming that the defenders had a way to aim it directly overhead. That was the advantage that using altitude to accelerate impact weight had. The disadvantage was that Dainyl's Talent only extended perhaps fifty yards below them, but what he planned was to have the pteridon release the boulder and guide it through a Talent-tube pointed at the main structure.

It couldn't hurt to try, and it might shake up the defenders, even if it failed.

As they neared the buildings, the blue-green beam of the lightcannon stabbed toward them, but only creating a faint bluish haze that did not quite reach the pteridon. As quickly as it had appeared, it vanished.

"A little longer!" Dainyl called. "Have the pteridon release it when I call 'Drop!' "

"Yes, sir."

Dainyl began to form the Talent-tube he needed—and the pteridon dropped a good fifty yards before stabilizing in flight.

"Sorry, sir! Don't know what happened."

Dainyl did, but he could explain later. "Keep it level for a few moments longer." He was trying to mentally gauge the arc toward the building, taking into account their own momentum.

"Drop! Now!"

Dainyl could feel himself pressed into the saddle by the combination of stress on his Talent-tube and the upward movement of the pteridon when it lost the drag of the boulder.

He'd tried to impart a Talent-affinity in the boulder, as well as guiding it, in the few instants before it was out of his Talent range.

From far beneath, he could sense an effort at a Talent shield. Then a puff of dust rose on one side of the building, and stones cascaded down onto the ground.

"You hit the building, sir!" Halya exclaimed. "You hit it."

The boulder had struck the building, but had missed the lightcannon, either because his aim had been inaccurate or because the defenders had managed to shield the weapon. His smile was rueful. From the altitude from which they'd dropped the boulder, he should have been happy to have gotten even close to the building.

Like it or not, First and Seventh Companies were going to have to continue the close-in and tiresome business of lofting and bowling heavy boulders at the buildings on the ridge until the defenders surrendered, fled, or died.

"Take us back down to the patroller station, but keep us well away from that lightcannon!"

"Yes, sir!"

The pteridon continued south for almost two vingts, only gradually descending until they were well south of Soupat. Then, Halya circled eastward in a swift descent, coming in and flaring at the edge of the flat sandy expanse to the east of the patroller station.

Once the pteridon folded its wings, Dainyl unfastened the harness and dismounted.

"Sir . . . ?" offered Halya.

"Yes?" Dainyl looked forward at the Myrmidon, who was inspecting her skylance.

"My skylance is exhausted, but we didn't use it."

"No. That sometimes happens when the pteridon is having trouble drawing lifeforce. That was also why when I used Talent to try to guide the boulder, we lost altitude." Those were both reasons why Dainyl wasn't about to suggest repeating the effort—or that anyone else try it.

"Oh . . . tell Captain Ghasylt that you're not to fly for the first glass tomorrow. It will take your pteridon that long to recover."

Halya's eyes widened slightly. Then she nodded. "Yes, sir."

Dainyl turned and began to walk—slowly—toward Alcyna, who was waiting near the station. He was as exhausted as the pteridon was.

52

By Novdi morning, Mykel did manage to walk to the officers' mess for breakfast, although his legs were unsteady by the time he seated himself.

One of the orderlies hurried over. "Sir? Cider? Ale?"

"Both." He smiled. "They seem to work better together."

As the ranker hurried toward the kitchen, Culeyt and Fabrytal turned from the side table.

"It's good to see you up, sir," offered the undercaptain.

"It's good to be up." *Unsteady as I may be.* Mykel suspected that Fabrytal worried because Mykel had been riding with Fifteenth Company just before he had undertaken his less than successful effort against the snipers.

The ranker orderly returned with two mugs. "Here you are, sir. Breakfast'll be here soon, sir."

"Thank you."

Before Mykel had taken more than a single swallow of the ale, Rhystan stepped into the mess.

"Might I join you, sir?"

"Please do."

"You're still pale," Rhystan said quietly as he eased his chair into place across from the majer.

"I feel pale, but I'm stronger, and it's important for everyone to know I'm on the mend." Mykel kept his own voice low. Why he felt that way, he couldn't have explained. "How have the attacks by the sandwolves and sanders been going?"

"More of them," admitted Rhystan, "but I passed on your advice to the other officers and made sure they told their squad leaders. The squads are doing better. The inholders are losing some livestock, but not as much, and we didn't lose any men yesterday."

"You think it will get worse."

"I do. The outholders have been quiet, but that won't last, either."

"What about the miners and workmen?"

"No one's saying anything."

"The Reillies?"

"The scouts report that they're still meeting. The locals say it takes almost a week for the burial ceremonies, and another two or three days to select a successor. The Squawts have a council meeting or whatever they call it on Duadi."

"That gives us some time."

"You mean," Rhystan parried, "it gives you time to recover. It's not enough. It's going to be weeks, if not months, before you can use that arm again."

"I'll just have to use my brain more."

"I believe I suggested that, sir."

Mykel caught the humorous glint in Rhystan's eyes. "You did. I'll even write up your evaluation with a commendation for providing invaluable advice." He managed a grin.

"I'll take that, sir. I'd appreciate it even more if you make sure you're around to do the writing."

"I'm working on that. Have we had any dispatches or orders from the colonel or from the Marshal of Myrmidons?"

"Nothing yet, but we won't get another sandox coach here until . . ."

"I know. They don't travel here on the end-days." Mykel

smiled as the orderly set the breakfasts before him and Rhystan. "I have to say that it looks good." But then, after not being sure that he'd recover from what he'd been through, anything looked good.

He took another swallow of ale.

53

Octdi evening had been warm enough, but the wind rose through the night, and by Novdi morning a hot gale was whipping sand at the buildings and the pteridons. When Dainyl looked outside, he could barely see the outline of the stables. Whether he liked it or not—or Zelyert and the Duarches did—until the wind and blowing sand subsided, no one was going to fly anywhere.

Before long, other officers joined him, and Dainyl, Alcyna, Ghasylt, and Lyzetta stood in what had been a very compact squad room. The chairs were too small for comfortable sitting, except perhaps for Alcyna, but Dainyl knew she would never sit while others stood.

"This isn't good," offered Alcyna. "Sandstorm or not, they can still use the Table."

"They aren't too likely to go anywhere, are they?" asked Ghasylt.

"They could build up their forces and try to take another Table," the submarshal replied.

"That would be harder. All the other Tables have been warned," Dainyl said. "I don't like it, either, but there's little enough we can do about it."

The thin walls of the building shuddered, and more grains of fine sand seeped through the cracks around the shuttered windows and slowly tumbled down, adding to the small piles growing on the floor against the outer wall.

"This is winter," Dainyl said. "I can't imagine what it's like in the summer."

"I don't wish to, thank you," replied Alcyna.

"The sand won't hurt the pteridons," added Ghasylt. "They could use the rest."

Although it was more a recharging of lifeforce, Dainyl knew, Ghasylt was basically right.

"Seventh Company's, too," added Lyzetta. "I need to check with the squad leaders. I think we got in a little local food last night."

"That'd be good," added Ghasylt.

Both captains departed, Ghasylt slightly after Lyzetta.

"She reminds me of someone," murmured Alcyna. "I can't say whom, though. I feel I should."

"That's not surprising," replied Dainyl, "given how few alectors we have on Acorus, and how many you've met."

"How diplomatic of you, Marshal. By the way, has it occurred to you that there's no one really in command of the Myrmidons?"

"It has. I'd hoped this would be over somewhat sooner, and one of us could return to Elcien."

"You also didn't want me to remain in Elcien with Zelyert," suggested Alcyna. "I can see that, but what about the other companies? Don't you worry that he'll send orders to them directly?"

"That's possible, but Majer Keheryl will plead necessity to avoid them, and Fifth Company is too far away to react immediately. Sevasya won't do anything against the interests of Khelaryt, and Captain Elysara will consult with Asulet. Besides, I have my doubts that Zelyert will want the Myrmidons to do anything until he knows what will happen here."

"Can this be the same officer who sought obedience to authorized orders from all Myrmidons?" Alcyna's voice was light, almost but not quite mocking.

"Exactly the same. I'm just having more difficulty in knowing what an authorized order might be." *And what it might cost us all.*

"There's nothing worse than uncertainty in command," parried Alcyna.

"Except absolute certainty that's wrong. That was what Shastylt offered."

"You're suggesting something close to treason, Marshal."

"I'm suggesting nothing. I'm still obeying orders. But I can't help but wonder about the infallibility of a system that knows that thousands of alectors will have to die for a small number to live, and that has known that it must be so for thousands of years—and has done little to avoid it." Dainyl shook his head. "I've known it, too. It's different when you see them die, and when you've even killed some of them."

Alcyna looked squarely at him. "If you had been in charge of the Myrmidons who took Soupat Table, no one would have been able to do anything until it was too late. You've known who Noryan was for seasons, but you let him be. There are others as well, knowing you. You respect courage and ability. Those who are fleeing Ifryn now generally lack both foresight and ability, and courage alone is merely stupidity."

"What about those who lacked the power and access to the Tables on Ifryn until now?"

"Some are stupid, and some are without courage, and some are merely unfortunate victims, and every world has all three. You cannot have a strong society if you pander to the unintelligent, the willing weak, and the unfortunates. The universe does not reward compassion, only survival and success."

"You're quoting *Views of the Highest.*"

"Sometimes they're right." Alcyna's lips quirked into an ironic smile.

For all of her words, and her cynicism, Dainyl could sense that, deep within, she was as troubled as he was.

Outside, the wind moaned. Grains of fine sand oozed through the cracks in window frames and shutters and dropped to the floor, building miniature dunes against the outside walls of the patroller building.

54

Slightly past midmorning on Londi, the wind began to die away. Within a glass, Dainyl could see the hills around Soupat once more. Everything was coated with fine sand, but as Ghasylt and Lyzetta reported, the pteridons were untroubled and ready to fly.

The greatest difficulty facing the Myrmidons was getting the sand out of the riding gear. The skylances were sealed units, and untouched by the powdery sand, but little else was. A glass later, all five squads of pteridons were lifting off, heading out to begin finding and stockpiling boulders. Almost three glasses went by before they had gathered enough to begin their bombardment, an understandable delay given the coating of sand on the southern sides of the valleys and hills.

During this time, the Myrmidons observing the buildings held by the Ifryns reported no outside activity except on the top of the central structure, where the sand had been shoveled away even as the observation pteridons were taking to the air. That area was where the heavy lightcannon was located, and clearly the Ifryn refugees wanted to have their main weapon in readiness before Dainyl's pteridons could attack in force. There were no tracks in the sand on the ridge or on the road down to Soupat.

Once more, after briefing the Myrmidons from both companies, just before midday, Dainyl took his position as an observer on the higher ridge, although the climb up from where Halya landed him was more treacherous because there was far more of the powdery sand that made crossing smooth sections of rock treacherous. He assigned Alcyna the task of questioning the locals about recent events in Soupat.

Lyzetta and the two reduced squads from Seventh Company began the bombardment from the west. The captain's first boulder plowed to a halt a good twenty yards from the easternmost building, raising a large cloud of sandy dust. The next pteridon was from First Company, and the boulder lobbed from the northwest barely managed to travel thirty-odd yards before rolling to a halt well short of anything remotely resembling a building.

Lyzetta's second flier was on-target with a cylindrical boulder that hit on its side and rolled across the flat, striking the easternmost building. Stones and masonry flew everywhere. Dainyl only wished that it had impacted the central building—the one holding the lightcannon. Two more First Company pteridons flung boulders from the west, but neither rolled close to any structure, although they raised more of the sandy dust that seemed to hang in the still air, creating areas of haze across the ridgetop.

A beam of brilliant blue-green lashed eastward, barely missing the third pteridon from Seventh Company. The heavy lightcannon hummed so loudly that Dainyl could hear it from his position more than a vingt away, and the sand dust in the air sparkled and burned, leaving a swath of clear air for a moment. Once the beam vanished, more of the dust began to swirl into the space that had been clear moments before.

The boulder released by the pteridon targeted and missed by the lightcannon arced up and onto the ridge, then tumbled eastward until it clipped the northeast corner of the easternmost building, but only a handful of stones fell. Still, the eastern building, the smallest of the three, appeared so damaged that Dainyl doubted it would be that long before it collapsed in upon itself.

One after another, using various launch points, the next four Myrmidons guided their pteridons into position and released more of the heavy boulders. Three missed, and the fourth did minimal damage to the westernmost building.

After a brief pause, two more Myrmidons attacked, simultaneously, one from the west and one from the northeast. The lightcannon did not even attempt to fire at either, but neither was successful in inflicting additional damage on the structures.

Dainyl had the feeling it was going to be a long day, perhaps even a long week, and a week was not something he or the Myrmidons could afford.

For the next two glasses, the maneuvering and bombardment efforts continued, with the sand and dust rising into an ever hotter day, and with some improvement in accuracy, especially on the part of the Myrmidons of First Company. By midafternoon, one in three boulders was striking one of the buildings, and perhaps half of those inflicted some damage. The heavy lightcannon continued to stab intermittently through the sand and dust, trying to destroy pteridons, but only turning airborne particles into momentary flashes of fire or light and creating momentary swathes of clearer air.

After a break by the Myrmidons for food and gathering more boulders, during which Halya brought two water bottles to Dainyl, along with some field rations, the attack began again.

The break had clearly helped, either in focusing the Myrmidons, or in letting some of the sand and dust settle to afford a better view of the targets. The first two pteridons were successful in casting their boulders directly into structures. Unfortunately, the structures were the two outbuildings, rather than the central one, but the eastern building shuddered under the impact, and a good section of its north wall sagged almost to the point of collapse.

The next pteridon, coming from the west, rose well above the ridgeline and used both sets of talons to propel an even larger boulder directly at the central building.

Dainyl winced even before the lightcannon swung from the east and fired, slamming into the side of the pteridon and turning both pteridon and Myrmidon into a glaring blue explosion that roared through the afternoon air.

Dainyl blinked, and almost missed the impact of the overlarge boulder delivered by the Myrmidon and pteridon who had just perished. Inexorably, it rumbled toward the western wall of the center building, crashing into it with enough force that Dainyl could see the entire building shudder and a course of stones fly off the top of the north side wall.

For all that, Dainyl would have preferred less impact and not losing the Myrmidon and pteridon.

Another pteridon released a boulder from the northeast, one that slammed into the north wall of the smaller eastern building. First, the northwest corner crumpled, then the northern wall, followed by the northeast corner. Dust shot up from the middle of the smaller structure as the remainder of the building imploded into a pile of stone. Dainyl did not see any alectors leave the collapsed structure, but he doubted that there had been many within, not after the damage inflicted on the previous day.

Three more pteridons released their boulders before the lightcannon attempted to fire again, and two struck—one hitting the central building, if indirectly, because it had actually struck one of the boulders that had earlier smashed against and into the lower wall, but still widening the gap and dislodging more stones from the wall above. The second boulder shivered the western building.

Another glass passed, with more boulders missing than hitting, but without any more Myrmidon casualties.

In late afternoon, after yet another break for replenishment and rest, the attack resumed once more. As before, the first pass resulted in more strikes, and the western building was close to collapsing. Even the main structure was showing significant signs of weakness. The southern third of the west wall was leaning outward, so far that it looked as if it might topple any moment, and the northeast corner was so battered that Dainyl could see light halfway down the stone courses. The southern side would not be nearly so damaged because the pteridons could not make a southern approach without totally exposing themselves to the lightcannon, but one intact wall would not hold up an otherwise collapsing structure.

The second pteridon in First Company's third pass lingered above the ridgeline far too long—and another explosion of blue flame filled the west side of the ridge.

Dainyl's eyes flicked back to the east, where the lightcannon had swung, as if the Myrmidon aiming it had decided that a Seventh Company pteridon might attempt to push the limits of an attack while the lightcannon was still focused westward.

The lightcannon struck just as the pteridon had released its boulder, and the stone absorbed the energy, one side melted into an instant glaze.

Dainyl stared for a moment. From what he could tell, both pteridon and rider had survived. He shook his head. They had been extraordinarily fortunate—unlike those destroyed by the lightcannon earlier.

The sun was getting close to the top of the higher peaks of the Coast Range, and Dainyl could sense that pteridons and Myrmidons were getting tired—and sloppy. And that could only lead to more costly casualties.

From his viewpoint, with the real troubles yet to come, he needed to minimize casualties as much as possible, and he doubted that his failure to close the Soupat Table and destroy all the Ifryn refugees was causing that many additional problems elsewhere. Even if it were, there wasn't much else he could do besides what he was doing.

Whether the Duarches and the High Alector would understand that was another question.

He dashed from behind cover and to the back side of the ridge, raising his jacket, and waving it, then firing the light-cutter. It was time—if not past time—to call off the attacks for the day.

55

Mykel sat and looked at the battered wood of the writing desk in the study, then looked up and out through the window at the gray sky, before his eyes dropped to the blank paper on the desk, useless for him at the moment. Although it was Duadi, he had decided to wait another few days to send a report to Colonel Herolt. His arm was immobilized in a splintlike dressing that left him unable to write. If he did dictate a report for Rhystan to draft, he wanted to report that while his shoulder had been injured, he was on the way to recovery. Another reason was that he had little to report, except that the Reillies and Squawts were likely to pose a threat, but had not yet moved, and that the threat from the sandwolves and sanders had increased slightly.

"Majer?"

Mykel looked up at the ranker standing in the door.

"Got something for you, sir." The Cadmian's hands were empty.

"Yes?"

"It's outside, sir, at the gates. One of the factor's men said something about half a silver."

Mykel almost laughed. "That's what they charge if it doesn't come by sandox." He had to fumble with his wallet, because it was on his belt on the right. He hadn't thought about that when he'd gotten dressed that morning, not when dressing had been such an awkward and laborious effort. Finally, he extended a half-silver coin. "If you'd take care of it."

"Yes, sir."

Shortly, the ranker reappeared with an envelope and handed it to Mykel.

"Thank you." Mykel would have liked to have given him a copper, but that wouldn't have done at all, not within a military organization.

"My pleasure, sir." The ranker smiled, then inclined his head in respect, and left.

Mykel looked down at the heavy paper of the envelope, stiff in the fingers of his left hand. On the front was his name, with the words "Commanding, Third Battalion, Cadmian Post, Iron Stem" written beneath in a script he did not recognize. On the back was an ornate seal he recognized, but it was above the phrase: Amaryk, Factor in Tempre for Seltyr Elbaryk. From Rachyla? But not in her hand? Or some sort of notice of something ill happening to her?

Mykel fingered the envelope with his left hand, then transferred it to his right, barely able to hold the heavy paper of the envelope as he used his belt knife in his left hand to slit the paper, avoiding breaking the seal. There was an inside envelope, blank on the exterior, but not sealed. He extracted the single sheet of paper, opened it, and laid it on the writing desk.

Major Mykel,

I trust that you are recovering from your injuries, severe as they may have been.

Matters here in Tempre are proceeding as expected, and Amaryk is proving to be adept in forging the alliances necessary for commercial prosperity.

As once noted, daggers have more than two edges.

Mykel frowned. The handwriting was Rachyla's, yet she had not signed it. And how had she known he had been injured, let alone that he was recovering? There was no way a message could have reached her in time for her to write and send back the letter.

There was only one explanation, and that explained all too much. While he could not sense anything she felt or sensed, despite his Talent, she could sense at least something of what he felt, and perhaps more. He shivered slightly. How much had she felt? How much did she know of his feelings for her? Was that why she had risked touching his hand in Tempre? In the hope he would sense or realize her feelings? She was sending him messages on two levels—one formal and proper—and one suggesting a deeper and more personal concern. Did the phrase about "more than two edges" suggest that his injuries cut her?

Mykel eased back in the armless chair, very carefully, thinking. She was conveying, as best she could within the limits of her situation, her interest in him, as well as her inability to accept him at present. Was it just because his position and social status were insufficient?

He laughed, softly and not quite bitterly. Just?

His thoughts went back to their last meeting. He had mentioned hope, and she had said hope was for children. He paused. That wasn't quite what she had said. She had said that hope was for children who did not realize that the faults and the status and the reputation of their parents could blight their future. Yet she had reached out to him, if formally.

He sat there for a time, still holding the unsigned missive. Children . . . Rachyla wasn't just thinking about herself. She was thinking about children, about, in a way, what she had suffered because of her father's failings and her mother's abandonment. She could not accept a mere majer's suit, not and remain in the south of Corus, and she would not doom a child to a life where that child was forced by birth to be subservient to those with whom she had been raised. Those were the messages she had sent, and given the indirect nature of the world in which she had grown up, she was clearly suggesting that she cared, but that she could do little about it unless he could do better by her. Somehow . . . he had to cut her loose from her prison.

Yet . . . what could he promise? He had no commercial prospects, and from what he had seen, he was not by nature a factor, even had he the golds to launch such a venture. He'd been promoted early to majer, and it was unlikely that he would ever become a colonel. Even if he did make the rank, it would not be for years, and there was no guarantee that Rachyla would be there for him by then. Would she accept him as a majer, living near Elcien or Faitel?

He shook his head again. That was most unlikely, given the luxury in which she had been raised.

Yet . . . she knew what his limitations were. She was far too intelligent not to, and she had mentioned them more than once. But she had earlier made certain that she had been sent to Tempre as Amaryk's chatelaine, and now she was informing him that she knew of his injuries when there was no way that she could have.

His eyes dropped to the letter once more, and he smiled. For all her protestations against the vanity of hope, she had hopes as well, and those hopes included him . . . and she wanted him to know that.

His smile faded. No matter what she wrote, no matter what they both wished and hoped, there would be no prospects at all if he did not find a way out of the situation in which fate and Marshal Dainyl had placed him—and one in which he had to find better solutions than always risking himself.

56

Duadi morning had come far too early for Dainyl, since he had awakened well before dawn. While the other alectors slept, he had thought . . . and thought some more. He did not wish to lose more pteridons, but he also could not afford to take a week to reduce the Soupat alector's complex to rubble, and the way matters were going, it might take that long. Losing two pteridons a day for who knew how many days more wasn't acceptable, either.

Finally, after an informal morning muster, he met with Alcyna and the two company commanders outside the dilapidated patroller's barracks, just as the sun edged over the sandy rolling and rocky hills to the southeast. Alcyna stood slightly back of his shoulder.

"We need to change the attack strategy some." Dainyl studied both Ghasylt and Lyzetta. They looked more tired than he felt, and every bone in his body ached. That was more from sleeping on a hard floor on a partial pallet, because none of the patroller beds were long or wide enough to fit even an alector of Alcyna's diminutive stature, although she was only slightly taller than almost all indigens and most landers. "I'd like to try varying the attack numbers, having two pteridons attack on one side, then several single attacks, interspersed irregularly with dual attacks."

"Anything to keep them from predicting when and where the next pteridon will appear," added Alcyna in a quiet voice.

"We can do that," replied Ghasylt.

Lyzetta nodded.

After the captains left, Dainyl turned to Alcyna. "We're running out of time."

"Better that than pteridons, sir."

But Dainyl knew they were running out of both.

For the third day running, nearly two glasses passed before Dainyl was in position and the pteridons began their passes at the regional alector's complex. As on previous days, few local inhabitants were out in the streets or lanes, and despite the warmth of the day the majority of homes, especially those to the northwest, nearer the bombardment, remained shuttered. Dainyl had seen no sign of the Cadmians of Sixth Battalion, and that was also for the best.

The sky was a dusty beige-silver, with but the slightest trace of green, except near the northern horizon. As he watched the pteridons release their boulders, Dainyl wondered if that beige-silver was the way it looked all the time during the intense heat of summer.

Both companies completed their first set of passes and part of the second before the lightcannon fired even once. That first shot was nowhere close to the single pteridon, but once more the power of the weapon created brilliant burning sparkles in the air and left a clear swath through the dust and sand raised by the bombardment.

The second bombardment run continued, and Dainyl noted that the lightcannon was not firing so often as on the previous days. In fact, it only fired three times at the next fourteen pteridons. He also sensed what he could only have described as a Talent-vibration each time the beam winked out.

After a slight break, First Company began the third set of runs with two pteridons, one from the west-southwest and another from the northwest, both delivering substantial boulders. One missed the central building, but the second slammed into the southwest corner of the smaller western building.

Dainyl watched as the corner shuddered and then toppled outward, stones flying in a long slow arc. Then the ends of the western wall crumpled into a heap in the center, leaving the northwest corner as a triangular battlement—but after a moment it imploded in toward the center of the structure, and the remaining walls collapsed, with sand and dust exploding skyward.

A single alector scrambled away from the rubbled ruin, sprinting toward the remaining battered building.

Battered the surviving structure might have been, but after three more glasses, with a break for replenishment and rest, the Myrmidons had still not been able to inflict any more significant damage on the central building. In fact, Dainyl had the sense that the boulders piling up around its walls might now actually be providing a measure of protection.

The lightcannon fired erratically, but despite the feeling of instability Dainyl sensed, the actual blue-green beam was as powerful as ever, and those aiming it were getting closer and closer to bringing down another pteridon.

The pteridons were getting tired. That Dainyl could tell. Many more passes, and the lightcannon would start taking them out. He studied the flat area around the remaining building on the ridge, littered as it was with boulders, not huge, but a number large enough for cover. He'd already seen that the lightcannon did not have the power to stop or destroy the boulders, only to glaze one side.

After another moment of thought, he edged back from cover and partway down the backside of the ridge before signaling Lyzetta. While he waited for her, he checked the light-cutters at his belt. Both were fully charged. Two would have to do.

Before that long, Lyzetta made a low approach and landed. Rather, her pteridon balanced on the slope while Dainyl scrambled into the second harness.

"Here's what I need," he called forward to the Seventh Company captain. "Set me down on the east side, below the ridgeline, low enough that they can't see me from the central building. Then make one or two more passes, but make them from due east, and don't come above the ridgeline—just lob boulders over the edge as well as you can, and not too often. Don't expose yourself. Give the same message to Captain Ghasylt. I don't want anyone exposed."

"Sir . . . ?"

"I need to get close enough to check out some things." That much was true, but that was only the start—unless things were worse than he thought, in which case he had no compunctions about withdrawing as expeditiously as possible. "I'll come back as close as I can to where you drop me and signal for pickup."

"Yes, sir."

The pteridon turned and glided down the east side of the ridge, almost into the sinkhole valley, before turning back west, but remaining barely a handful of yards above the uneven and rocky ground on the east side of the ridge that held the regional alector's complex. Once more, when the pteridon landed, it balanced with tail and talons until Dainyl was clear.

He took a deep breath once Lyzetta and her pteridon were away, then looked at the seventy-some yards of steep and rocky incline before him. He began to climb, extending his Talent-senses to make certain he did not face snipers, even though there had been no evidence of them previously.

He angled his way up the slope, using his Talent to guide him, so that he would reach the area directly behind the rubble of the smaller eastern building, where he would be seen so easily from the remaining building. There were no boulders or other types of cover above where the slope flattened out—not until within fifty yards or so of the first pile of rubble.

Dainyl stopped short of where he could be seen, then came up the last part of the slope at a sprint, holding his Talent shields as well. He had covered almost a hundred yards before the first light-rifle fired past him. He angled to his right, then back left, before skidding to a halt behind the first boulder he reached. He had to tuck himself tightly together to keep all of his body behind the stone. Somehow, the stones that had looked large while being flung seemed all too inadequate to conceal an alector.

Another light-rifle beam flaring overhead emphasized that point.

Keeping low and out of sight, he tried to breathe deeply and let his body recover.

From what he could tell, he still had a good three hundred yards to go before he reached the area where there were numerous boulders for cover. He extended his Talent, trying to locate the next nearest patch of cover. Ahead and to his left was a slight rise, slightly less than a yard, but high enough to have slowed and stopped one of the boulders launched at the buildings of the complex.

Dainyl coiled his legs under him, strengthened his shields, and sprinted again.

The lightcannon hummed above him, not aimed at him, but somewhere beyond. As close as he was, Dainyl sensed the definite growing instability of the weapon, an instability that suggested a failing crystal in the power or control system. He also had the feeling that one of the Myrmidons had appeared more than he had ordered, perhaps to draw fire from him. It had helped, because there was only a single light-rifle shot, and that was a belated one as he drew up behind the rocky escarpment that was little more than knee high and the boulder that had half climbed it and stuck.

Could he do something about the failing crystal—before the

refugees noted it and replaced it? He couldn't count on there only being one crystal. Surely, they had at least one spare and were trying to make each crystal last as long as possible.

After several more deep breaths, he used his Talent to chart a path back to the right toward the larger of two boulders fifty yards away.

Then he began another dash. He managed to make it almost to the boulder before the light-rifle slammed into his shields, and he staggered behind cover. This time, he had to wait longer, and he took a long swallow from his depleted water bottle.

The lightcannon hummed overhead again, only briefly.

Dainyl winced, but relaxed when he realized that it had missed whatever had been its target. He forced himself to wait as he used Talent to chart his next dash—this time to the pile of rubble that had been the eastern building.

Two light-rifle shots went past him but barely grazed his shields on the dash to the fallen structure. Once there, Dainyl was happy to be able to stand, rather than having to squeeze into the most compact form he could imagine to avoid getting hit. Slowly, he worked his way northward and then to the west, easing around the mass of fallen stone and masonry, which was still close to three yards in height in places.

He could also sense that there had been more than a few alectors in the structure, and he could see treated shimmersilk uniforms protruding from the heaped stones in places. There were also other garments as well, all remnants of alectors who had died, far more than he would have guessed—and the eastern structure was the smallest of the three. How many alectors had used the Table in an effort to escape Ifryn—only to die under his bombardment?

Dainyl had to force those thoughts out of his mind, as he looked westward. With less than a hundred yards between the fallen building and the central structure, its walls battered, but still holding together, there was more than a little cover in the field of stones and boulders between the two buildings.

He had worked his way halfway across the field when he realized that the light-rifle was no longer firing at him. He knew he was close enough to the central building that the heavy lightcutter could not be depressed enough to aim at him without hitting the building itself. But now, even the light-rifles could not be used unless those firing them wanted to chance the weakened outer walls of the structure.

A lightcutter beam flared over his head, reminding him that there were weapons that could be used against him. He peered around the side of the boulder and caught a glimpse of a gray and green uniform behind an embrasure on the second level. Lifting his own lightcutter, he fired, adding a touch of Talent-direction. Then he sprinted for the next boulder, one a few yards short of the eastern wall of the building.

Crouching there, he caught his breath, still holding his shields, and began to extend a Talent probe into the building.

There had to be some sort of Talent link between the light-cannon and the Table. Otherwise, the lifeforce demands would have killed everyone in the buildings. He probed farther, almost at the limit of his Talent, before he discovered a node, or something like a lifeforce reservoir. There was a Talent "valve" between it and the lightcannon.

Dainyl nodded. Now . . . if he could use his Talent to "open" that valve full and let all that force out at once, it should overload the control systems of the lightcannon. Without the lightcannon operating, even if Dainyl had to accompany every pass, the Myrmidons could come close enough to destroy the building at will, and in less than a day.

He fumbled, seeking the tiny Talent links that had to hold the "valve" together.

Another lightcutter beam splashed against the stone above him.

His forehead and neck felt damp, and he realized he was sweating. Alectors seldom did. Dainyl couldn't remember the last time that had happened.

Then, he discovered the key link, and Talent-twisted. The lifeforce reservoir collapsed, and all the compressed and stored lifeforce flooded through the link to the lightcannon.

Dainyl could feel the explosive force building and wedged himself between the foundation and two large boulders.

The entire structure shuddered, and stones and rocks began to rain down everywhere around the building. Even more ominous, Dainyl could sense a void, a deep pinkish purpleness that began to suck lifeforce. He reinforced his own Talent shields, hoping they would hold against the void.

The ground trembled, then shuddered with the impact of more stone and sections of the building cascading down. Dainyl huddled under stone and his own shields, hoping both held against the explosions and the seeking hunger of the lifeforce void.

Struggling to hold his shields and his mind, he closed his eyes, but his Talent told him of each alector who died, one after the other, scores of them, if not more, as the void he had inadvertently released sucked the very life out of all those in the structure beside him. The sucking dark pinkness pressed against his shields, gnawing, trying to erode his defenses.

Abruptly, another, far larger explosion shook the ground, and more stones cascaded everywhere. Dainyl felt his whole body being bruised from the impacts on his shields, but the life-seeking void was gone. Dainyl had no idea what it had been, except that it had been some sort of feedback from or reaction to the destruction of the lifeforce reservoir.

He wanted to shake his head. If such weapons had been used on Ifryn, no wonder people were trying to escape. No wonder the world had exhausted its lifeforce far earlier than projected. And the Archon had allowed—or not halted—such weapons?

After several moments, slowly, he began to climb out of his protected position, careful not to touch or dislodge any stones that might fall. His shields were shredded, and his entire body was trembling. When he stood clear of the enormous rubble pile, he sat down on one of the smaller boulders and forced himself to use what Talent remained to him.

Deep in the pile of stone beside him, he could still sense the Table. He sensed no other lifeforce at all. None. In places, amid the stone, the afternoon light glinted on shimmersilk tunics of green and gray, empty shimmersilk tunics.

He rose to his feet, stiffly, and began to move away from the ruined structures.

He had walked a quarter of a vingt before a pteridon appeared and flared to a landing before him. From her harness on the pteridon's neck, Lyzetta looked down at him. "Marshal, sir? Are you all right?"

Was he all right?

What an inane question, although she could not have known that. All right, when what he had done had just extinguished the lives and hopes of hundreds of alectors, people who had been caught in forces beyond their control and who had merely wanted to survive? He couldn't even claim that he was like them, not after what he had done.

"Sir?"

"I'm in one piece, Captain. Thank you." He cleared his throat of some of the sand and dust that he had not realized coated it. "All the refugees are dead. All those who were in the complex anyway. Some might have escaped during all the attacks, but there won't be many, and there's little point in trying to find them."

"They're . . . all dead?"

"That lightcannon was a lifeforce weapon. When it exploded, the backlash sucked the life out of everyone in the building. I barely escaped, and that was because I was outside, and it didn't last any longer."

"That's . . . a lifeforce weapon?"

Dainyl nodded slowly. "That's where it got its power. That's why we had to destroy it. If they'd kept using it . . ."

This time Lyzetta nodded. "You'd better climb up, Marshal. You look like you might fall over."

Dainyl wasn't that exhausted . . . except inside.

57

Dainyl and First Company were up before dawn on Tridi, preparing for the long return flight to Elcien. Dainyl would have preferred to have given the company a day of rest, but he'd been out of touch too long. Had any true disaster occurred, Zernylta would have dispatched one of the Myrmidons from Seventh Company, but that didn't mean that one wasn't about to occur. If it hadn't, First Company could have at least Quattri off.

Dainyl stood in the dimness outside the patroller barracks, facing Alcyna. "You should be able to finish up here today. You know what to do."

"Use Seventh Company to pile enough rocks on everything that even if anyone could use the Table—assuming it's still in operation—there's no way for them to get out."

"The Table's still in operation. With the number of long translations it's accepted recently, if it had failed, there would have been a much, much larger explosion."

"How will you explain closing off use of a Table to the High Alector and the Duarches?"

"As the only alternative when the Archon is allowing lifeforce-destroying lightcannon to be translated here. Do you see any way we could have taken the Table without even greater losses?"

Alcyna met his eyes. "Sir, I still don't see any other way that anyone could have taken the Table against those weapons without destroying most of the lifeforce balance on Acorus, if not even more."

"If we'd fought them with the same kind of weapons, the result would have been disaster," agreed Dainyl.

"Neither Zelyert nor the Duarches will wish to hear that."

Dainyl didn't want to dwell on that. "Tomorrow morning, fly back to Tempre with Seventh Company and use the Table there to translate back to Elcien as soon as you can."

"Yes, sir." She paused. "What do you think will happen now?"

"Brekylt will find some reason to provoke a break with the Duarches. Khelaryt won't wish to accept it. I have no idea what Samist will do."

"If he can't bring down Khelaryt, he'll ally himself with Brekylt and try to take over all Corus from the east."

That sounded all too likely, but Dainyl didn't say so. "I'd better get moving. It's a long flight."

"I'd suggest giving Ludar a wide berth, sir."

"We definitely will." With a nod to Alcyna, Dainyl turned and hurried across the sandy space that held six fewer pteridons than it had three days earlier. Six irreplaceable pteridons, more than twenty percent of the force he had brought to Soupat. He climbed into the harness behind Halya.

"Ready, sir?" she asked after he finished strapping himself in place.

"Anytime."

"First Company! Lift off! By squads!" ordered Ghasylt.

The pteridon eased off the ground, rather than exploding into the air, another sign that the Talent creatures were as weary as the Myrmidons who flew them.

As they flew past the ruins of the regional alector's complex, Dainyl took in the destruction, the three piles of rubble in which more than a hundred alectors had died, possibly nearer two hundred, all of whom had died either at his hand or through his orders.

Yet . . . with their use of a weapon like the heavy lightcannon, and their willingness to flood Acorus with more alectors than it could support . . . what else could he have done?

The fact that he could find no answer did not help the way he felt.

58

All too often, both less perceptive alectors and the vast majority of steers consider the ideal ruler or administrator to be a paternal figure, one steeped in care and love, and one who shows benevolence toward all under his administration. Such an idealization of a ruler is mere wish-fulfillment, for a "good" father is one who will do all that he can to ensure the survival of all of his offspring. A good father has sufficient offspring to assure his heritage is carried on unto the generations. And a good father will place his offspring above the needs of the offspring of others and of a society as a whole. Thus, a society comprised of "good" fathers will in fact populate itself into a crisis of insufficient resources and a shortage of lifeforce.

A ruler who follows the tenets of such a "good" father will

doom his people to destruction. Yet, any ruler who states that too many offspring are not in the interest of all or who acts directly to assure that there are not too many mouths to feed will find those under his rule becoming angry and rebellious. Any ruler who would openly choose who can breed and who cannot will find himself needing to muster and apply more and more force to his people with each passing year until his rule collapses from lack of advancement and investment or from outright rebellion.

What is to be done, then?

The wise ruler advises and admonishes quietly, but does not apply force directly in attempting to reduce the number of offspring, whether of alectors or steers. Because he controls privilege and position for alectors, he can limit their numbers to some degree, but that will prove insufficient over time, because few alectors perish from natural causes.

Thus, he prepares his chosen cadre and sequesters resources for the time when all will collapse into anarchy, assuring each and every alector that each is indeed part of that cadre, but keeping the actual cadre far smaller and known only to himself until the proper time has come when he must allow to perish those who were so unwise as to breed themselves into death.

Then, once more, he must begin anew, always preparing for the inevitable overbreeding and the collapse that will indeed follow. . . .

Views of the Highest
Illustra
W.T. 1513

59

The three squads of First Company with Dainyl had flown tiredly into Elcien just after sunset on Tridi, and Dainyl had dismissed them, putting them on flight rest for both Quattri and Quinti. He had spent three glasses drafting his report to Zelyert, and then retired to the house that felt so empty without Lystrana. He'd even been exhausted enough to sleep most of the night dreamlessly. Most of the night.

He still woke before dawn.

A half glass before morning muster at Myrmidon headquarters, he appeared at the Hall of Justice. Zelyert was not there, but at an early meeting with Duarch Khelaryt. Since the High Alector was expected within a glass, Dainyl sought out Chastyl, to see what the Recorder of Deeds might be able to tell him.

He found Chastyl in the Table chamber.

"Marshal! Can you tell me—"

Dainyl gestured for Chastyl to join him outside.

"I don't know that I should leave the Table chamber, Marshal," protested the recorder, glancing around the room at the five guards armed with lightcutters, all watching the Table. .

"A few moments won't matter. If you like, we can retire to the foyer. It's early enough that we're unlikely to be disturbed."

"The foyer . . . ah, yes, that's close enough." Chastyl's face was drawn, and the circles beneath his eyes were darker than ever.

"Exactly what has been happening with the Tables?" asked Dainyl when the two were alone, at least for the moment, in the small foyer between the corridor and the Table chamber.

"We've been getting more long translations. Too many, and most of them were in uniforms and armed. There have been fewer yesterday and today. I don't know why. Perhaps you do."

"Can you tell which Tables were receiving them?"

Chastyl shook his head. "We can tell which Tables are operating, and with their energy levels, we can guess."

"I'll be reporting to the High Alector when he returns. Soupat Table is sealed off, but still operating."

"Sealed off?"

"We brought the buildings down around it, and a weapon backlash wiped out the rebels holding it. There's so much stone and rubble over the Table that I'd be surprised if anyone can even enter the Table chamber, by translation or otherwise. They certainly won't be able to leave it."

Chastyl shook his head once more. "I had wondered . . . when the translations dropped off. There was also a huge surge of some sort of energy."

"That was the weapon's backlash. I thought you'd like to know." Dainyl offered a professional smile. "What about the Tables in the east?"

"They're reporting too many unauthorized translations, but they all have retained control of their Tables."

Or they're reporting that way. Dainyl did not voice the thought. "What about Dereka and Lyterna?"

"Jonyst is fine, and so is Myenfel."

That wasn't quite what Dainyl wanted to know, but he let it pass. "Is there any word . . . any indication about future . . . Table instability?"

"No . . . we've heard nothing about any decisions from Ifryn."

That was what Dainyl had feared. The Archon was going to bleed Ifryn to the last dram of lifeforce, or close to it, before transferring the Master Scepter. "Thank you. I'd best be leaving you to your duties."

"You will be reporting to the High Alector?"

"That's why I'm here." With a smile he tried to keep from being too wry, Dainyl nodded and stepped back, opening the outer door to the foyer.

Zelyert had still not returned.

So Dainyl made his way to Adya's chamber.

She stood as she saw Dainyl in her doorway. "Marshal . . . what can I do for you?"

Dainyl smiled and stepped into her tiny study, leaving the door ajar enough so that he could hear when Zelyert returned. He sat on the stool, the only furniture for visitors. "I'm waiting for the High Alector. I thought you might be able to tell me about anything I should know that happened while I was in Soupat."

The alectress frowned, momentarily. "I don't know . . ."

"No secrets," Dainyl reassured her. "Do you know what's happening in Alustre?"

"We haven't heard anything, except that there was some road damage along the Northern Pass, and the High Alector of the East was sending some of the road-building equipment to keep a cliff from collapsing and blocking the pass."

Dainyl managed to nod and avoid a frown. Cliffs usually didn't collapse in fall or winter, but in spring. "Did High Alector Ruvryn say anything?"

"His assistant said that after the problem in South Pass they didn't want any problems in the north."

South Pass. Dainyl had to struggle for a moment before he recalled that Alcyna never had gotten a clear answer as to why the repairs on the South Pass bridge were taking so long. But with what Adya had just told him, it was obvious that Brekylt would be able to deny any easy land access to the east in a matter of days. "What did the Highest say?"

"Nothing that I recall, sir."

Adya was telling the truth, and that disturbed Dainyl. Was Zelyert thinking about backing Brekylt—and Samist?

Both Dainyl and Adya looked up as a deep voice inquired, "Is the marshal still here?"

"Thank you." Dainyl smiled at the assistant and stepped out into the corridor. "Yes, sir. I've been waiting for you."

Zelyert gestured for Dainyl to join him. "Close the door."

Dainyl followed Zelyert into the private study and eased the door shut behind him.

The High Alector seated himself. "What did you do in Soupat, Marshal?" Zelyert's deep voice was deceptively mild.

Even before he finished seating himself, Dainyl could sense an anger verging on rage behind the even words. "What I was able to do, Highest." The honorific might mollify Zelyert, although Dainyl had the feeling that little would. He extended the report he had labored over the afternoon and night before. "This provides all the background and details. In effect, we brought the complex down around the rebel refugees and destroyed their weaponry before it destroyed Acorus. We also destroyed all of them."

Zelyert took the report and laid it on the table without looking at it. "It would have been a great deal more beneficial to all of us had you not taken so long. A great deal more beneficial to all of Acorus."

Dainyl had to wonder what it was about alectors such as Shastylt and Zelyert. Did the fear of losing power or prestige drive them all to the point of total unreasonableness? "We arrived on Septi night and began our attacks on Octdi morning. We lost two pteridons almost immediately. They possessed portable light-rifles that often can destroy a pteridon, and a lightcannon from Ifryn that instantly obliterated anything in its path or range. Despite that, we managed to destroy their weapons, and most of them with the loss of only six pteridons."

"*Only* six? You lost almost a third of a company against these . . . refugees?"

"They weren't refugees, sir. They were trained Myrmidons with weapons superior to ours. The heavy lightcannon was actually linked to the Table itself. You find another Myrmidon who actually has delivered you those kinds of results, and I'll be pleased to hand over command." Before Zelyert could speak again, Dainyl added, "The Archon is either sending alectors like that against us or allowing them access, in order to channel the most enterprising and bold here, so that he won't have to deal with them on Efra. I wouldn't be surprised if he's holding off transferring the Master Scepter until he can use us to purge all those he doesn't want with him."

Some—but not all—of Zelyert's anger vanished. "A lightcannon linked to the Table? You're certain of that?"

"Recorder Chastyl noted the energy backlash through the Table when the lightcannon failed. At the time, he did not know what caused the surge. I only told him it was a weapons backlash."

"I'm beginning to see why Shastylt found you . . . difficult . . . Marshal."

Dainyl was getting greater confirmation of why Shastylt had wanted to find a way to replace Zelyert and why Khelaryt did not trust Zelyert. "I have always done the best I could under the circumstances."

"Commensurate with your own self-preservation."

"I could not continue to serve were I dead, sir."

Zelyert laughed, deeply, but harshly. "Sometimes, the dead serve better than in life."

"That may be, but you will pardon me if I avoid proving such."

Zelyert looked long at Dainyl.

Dainyl met his eyes, and did not look down. He also held his shields ready.

"Did Adya tell you about the Northern Pass?"

"Only that Brekylt is sending road repair equipment to deal with a cliff that has not toppled and likely will not. That will give him the ability to cut off the east from all easy land access and heavy equipment transport. He's doubtless used the flood in unauthorized long translations as a rationale to build up the guard at all Tables in the east. If any of the refugees from Soupat escaped with equipment through the Tables, he will have that as well."

"And you could not hurry your attacks?"

"Had we done so, you would have no pteridons left from those who attacked. We lost only a few more than a squad."

"Could you not have captured that weapon?"

"I know of no way, even afterward. But . . . if I had, there would likely have been no point in doing so. Or in stopping the insurgents."

At that, Zelyert frowned, but the expression was one of puzzlement, not anger.

"It drew so much lifeforce that any extensive use would soon render Acorus in a lifeforce deficit, if not worse."

"So . . . that was what you meant . . ." The Highest nodded. "The Archon wishes to further weaken us, so that we will be in no position to challenge Efra in the years ahead."

Dainyl was glad not to have been the one to voice the sentiment.

"What do you think we should do next, Marshal?"

"Request Third and Fourth Companies fly to Dereka to deal with the growing threat posed by the ancients."

Zelyert's eyebrows rose. "Exactly how do you propose to

get those orders to Submarshal Noryan? Hand-carry them into Alustre?"

"No, sir. By sandox coach. I doubt that Brekylt will stop such transport immediately."

"Do you expect that to work?"

Dainyl smiled. "One way or another, it will achieve a purpose, and I see no point in waiting."

"No. I suppose not." Zelyert offered a sardonic smile. "Do you think the ancients pose such a problem? Really?"

"Does it matter, sir?" Dainyl did not want to come close to answering Zelyert's question. "They've certainly created problems in the Iron Valleys."

"Go ahead. It can't hurt to anticipate Brekylt." Zelyert stood. "But I'd hope you will keep all the pteridons you can close at hand."

"I have been," Dainyl replied, "and I intend to keep doing so." *Until we need them for matters of the greatest import.*

As he left the Hall of Justice, he reflected on one thing. He trusted Zelyert even less, and he'd trusted the High Alector of Justice little enough before.

60

After leaving the Hall of Justice, Dainyl had gone to Myrmidon headquarters. He'd checked the schedules, and spent a glass with Captain Zernylta learning everything affecting the Myrmidons that had occurred in his absence. Little of import had—except he had gotten a formal note of acceptance of rank by Majer Sevasya.

Elcien and Ludar appeared ominously quiet, given the attacks on the two Tables and the pending transfer of the Master Scepter, a transfer no one discussed. There was a dispatch from Colonel Herolt that reported increased unrest in the Iron Valleys involving the indigens, but no immediate hostile action against the Cadmians and some increased casualties in

Soupat, but the Soupat report clearly dated from before Dainyl's attack there.

As for Iron Stem, Dainyl felt that he had the best battalion commander there in Majer Mykel, but if the ancients became more involved, even the majer might have difficulty. Still, there wasn't much he could do about that.

After catching up with Zernylta, he drafted the orders to Submarshal Noryan. Noryan would either obey them and deprive Brekylt of the two companies of Myrmidons, or would refuse, and in doing so, effectively declare that he was supporting Brekylt in rebellion against the Duarches. Then, Dainyl had no way of knowing what Captain Josaryk would do. Sevasya might be able to keep Fourth Company there, even if Noryan stood by Brekylt.

Perhaps Dainyl should have recommended a more patient approach, but from what he had seen, waiting tied Khelaryt's hands more than anyone else's. Brekylt continued to build support while professing to be an administrator loyal to the Duarches. Yet, because everything was so subterranean, Khelaryt could not remove Brekylt, not without the support of Samist, and even then, such an action would be perceived as high-handed, particularly by the engineers, who comprised the largest single group of alectors besides the Myrmidons.

The other worry Dainyl had was the problem of lightcannon. Until he'd seen them in action in Soupat, he hadn't realized how destructive of lifeforce they truly were. The ones Brekylt had sent to Rhelyn in Hyalt—which Dainyl had destroyed—had used storage crystals, and that had disguised the amount of lifeforce use. Widespread use of lightcannon would be even more destructive than pteridon against pteridon.

Dainyl finished drafting the orders for Noryan, sealed them personally, and had Zernylta deliver them to the sandox coach dispatcher. Next came his contingency plans. Those took most of the afternoon.

Alcyna arrived at headquarters late in the afternoon, walking straight into Dainyl's study and dropping into the chair across from him.

"You're tired," he said. "Did you have any problems on the way back?"

"No. The problems were before we left."

"Some alectors who escaped before everything exploded?"

"They weren't the problem." Alcyna shook her head. "Several of the alectors' dwellings away from the compound have visiting 'relatives,' mostly alectresses and a few infants and children. I didn't press. There weren't that many, probably less than the Ifryn Myrmidons killed in the takeover."

"The locals, then?"

"Exactly. The council wanted to know who was going to pay for the mining and quarrying now, and when the golds would arrive. I told them to send the charges to the High Alector of Engineering. It's his responsibility, and to mine only what had been ordered. The council head wasn't happy with that. Then the nut growers wanted to know who was going to buy their surplus."

"Surplus?"

"Apparently, one of the assistants to the RA had a small side business. I have no idea where he was selling them or why."

"Brekylt. Rations. Nuts keep."

"You're more cynical than I am, Marshal."

And getting more so with each day, reflected Dainyl. "What else?"

"Hidden whining about use and damage to the patroller barracks. They're so polite. They bow and scrape and are so reasonable. 'Most honorable alector' . . . 'highest of the high' . . . I heard more new titles in the days since you left than in all the years in the east."

"Do you think we've blocked access to the Table there well enough?"

"Unless you're a snake or an ancient. Supposedly, they can go through rock."

"Neither is a problem in Soupat," Dainyl said dryly. "I've sent orders to Noryan to deploy Third and Fourth Companies to Dereka to deal with a possible ancient threat."

"He's not likely to get them."

"I sent them by sandox coach. I thought it was worth a try."

"At what? Forcing Noryan into a corner?"

"We're all in corners. I'd rather see him in ours, or not in Brekylt's."

"Is there really an ancient threat?"

"Yes. Zelyert doesn't understand it or think that there could be."

"I think we outnumber them," mused Alcyna. "A few of those light-rifles might have helped."

"They might, but . . . we don't have them."

"Do you think they'll actually attack? The ancients, that is?"

"I don't know what they'll do, but I can't believe they won't do something, and do it at the worst possible time for us."

"You believe that, don't you?" she asked.

"Yes."

"That's frightening."

Dainyl didn't understand that. Everyone had beliefs.

"Marshal. One reason I'm here, rather than in Alustre, is because I saw one thing. You don't always have the best strategy. You're far from the best politician. But when you say that something is going to happen, you're very seldom wrong. Information is power, and in that respect, you're the most powerful alector on Acorus."

To Dainyl, the fact that she believed that was chilling. "Now that we're both frightened, what else do we do? Did you see the High Alector?"

She shook her head. "Chastyl said he was at a meeting. He didn't say where, and he wasn't happy admitting that."

Ludar? That was Dainyl's first thought.

"What will you do next? What do you want me to do?"

"Find out what you can and help me keep us from sending Myrmidons where they don't need to go. I'm going to Dereka tonight."

"Lystrana might have some good ideas." Alcyna paused. "Alectresses tend to support you more than do alectors. Why do you think that's so?"

Dainyl hadn't noticed that, not exactly. "I could guess. Why do you think so?"

"You're more interested in solving the problem and getting

the task done. You only want power as a tool. Most alectors want power to prove they're the most powerful. Alectresses are more interested in results than power. Power is nice, but results count and last longer."

Dainyl couldn't disagree with her conclusion. "Go get some rest," he finally said. "I'll see you later tomorrow. There are multiple reasons I'm going to Dereka. I hope to be back before midday tomorrow."

"Yes, sir." Alcyna rose. "Some sleep on a decent bed would be good."

After she left, Dainyl thought again about her comment about alectresses. It had taken him aback, slightly, but he'd thought about it, and there was more than a little truth in it. Most of his promotions and appointments had gone to alectresses. He'd always trusted Lystrana, from far before they fell in love—or he had fallen in love with her. And he was always asking what kind of power other alectors sought, and why. That Alcyna had recognized it so quickly—and used it to remind him that he should stay task-oriented—was another confirmation of the submarshal's abilities.

Less than a glass later, he took the duty coach back to his house to pick up some clean uniforms, and then had the driver take him to the Hall of Justice.

Zelyert was not in the Hall itself, nor in his private study, and Dainyl made his way to the Table chamber, carrying a small bag of uniforms and personal gear. Dainyl couldn't help but force himself to step onto the Table. Smiling at Chastyl was even harder. "Oh . . . when do you expect the Highest back from Ludar?"

The momentarily frozen expression and the inner shock were enough to confirm that was indeed where Zelyert was.

"He didn't say where he was going, sir, or when he would return."

Dainyl nodded. "If he asks, tell him I'm in Dereka, arranging for some matters we discussed."

"Yes, sir." The words concealed another feeling of puzzlement.

That was fine with Dainyl. He concentrated on the darkness beneath the Table and felt himself slip through the mirrored surface and . . .

. . . into the cool purpleness of the translation tube.

He concentrated on the crimson-golden locator of Dereka, to the exclusion of all else, until the locator neared him.

The number of purplish flashes and streaks were far less than when he had translated to Tempre a week before, but the looming, yet distant feel of amber-green power remained, like a cliff overhanging all the Tables, held back only by some unseen and unsensed force.

The immensity of that force was so great that he remained immobile as he flashed through the silvered, crimson-gold barrier and . . .

. . . took a staggering step.

"It's the marshal!"

As he took another step to catch his balance, swinging the gear bag slightly, Dainyl recognized Jonyst's voice.

The Recorder of Deeds looked far older than the last time Dainyl had seen him. His face was lined, uncharacteristically for an alector, and the streaks of white in his black hair were wider and far more pronounced.

Dainyl recognized none of the guards, but his Talent-sense registered that two had translated recently from Ifryn. He did not comment upon that as he stepped off the Table.

Jonyst stepped forward with a smile. "Guersa's still on duty. She will be more than pleased to take you to the RA's quarters. I assume that's where you're headed?"

"Tonight. Tomorrow, I'll be checking on Fifth Company."

"I'd thought you might be doing that."

Dainyl inclined his head to the doorway that framed the staircase leading up to the elegant library. "Do you have a moment?"

"So long as we leave the doors open."

"We can do that." Dainyl led the way.

As he stepped into the paneled spacious library, for a moment he was startled at the darkness outside the wide windows overlooking the main boulevard. He should not have been. Dereka was more than 1,100 vingts east of Elcien, and its sunset came earlier. Sometimes, though, he was still taken by surprise by the time effects of Table translation. He set his bag on a carved chair pulled away from one of the tables, on which were several stacks of papers.

"What did you want to talk about?" asked Jonyst, standing just beyond the top of the staircase, where he could hear an alarm from below.

"I'm worried about the ancients." Dainyl saw no reason to be indirect with Jonyst. "I can occasionally sense something that feels like them when I'm translating, and there's been a great deal more activity with their creatures in the Iron Valleys."

Jonyst nodded slowly. "You're more perceptive than most, Marshal. The Table monitors sometimes show flickers of another kind of Talent energy." He shrugged wearily. "We can't tell where it's located, or what it might do, if anything."

"I thought you might have some thoughts, since this was once a city of the ancients."

"Thoughts? I have more than enough of those. What I do not have is any solid indications."

"Did you know that Brekylt is moving heavy road-building equipment to forestall weather damage in the Northern Pass?" asked Dainyl.

"I cannot say I am surprised. What will you do?"

"Try to reduce the resources under his control."

"I assume you don't intend to fight pteridons against pteridons. That would only increase his power."

"I can't do much if he suborns some of my commanders and turns them against us, but I'm not about to begin anything like that."

"You already moved Seventh Company, and Eighth Company cannot be suborned," observed the recorder. "I still don't see how you persuaded Samist to appoint Lystrana RA here."

Dainyl smiled. "I think, once Captain Fhentyl took over command of Fifth Company, and it became clear that Dereka Table would not suffer any mishaps, Samist hoped that I would be splitting my attentions and time."

"That alone tells me that he's a slender brace for Brekylt."

"Unless . . . unless he is convinced that the ancients will strike here."

"That's why . . . ?"

Dainyl nodded. He was only guessing, but little else made sense.

"I will keep my eyes and Talent looking, Marshal." Jonyst glanced at the steps down to the Table. "You know where to find Guersa."

"I do. Thank you."

Dainyl picked up his bag and walked to the ramps that led down to the main entrance.

Guersa smiled when she saw Dainyl step out through the archway. He had no idea why he'd recalled her as a redhead, since she was a very blond lander, but perhaps it was the hint of freckles or the broad smile that had colored his recollection.

"Marshal, sir. To the RA's quarters or the Myrmidons?"

"Tonight . . . the RA."

Dainyl had no idea if Lystrana was actually in her quarters, he realized, as he entered the coach, but Jonyst would have known if she had left Dereka. Besides, Lystrana didn't like the idea of using the Tables that much as her pregnancy advanced.

The coach pulled away from the ancient-built structure and turned south onto the main boulevard. It felt good to sit, even on the hard bench seat.

After less than a quarter glass, the coach drew up outside the quarters, a small separate wing behind the main building. When he stepped down onto the stone mounting block, Dainyl realized that while the main structure bordered an area low in lifeforce, although not dead as Jonyst had suggested, the quarters wing had been built in an area displaying no overt diminution of lifeforce.

"These are the RA's quarters, sir."

"You brought her here last week?"

"Yes, sir."

"Thank you." Dainyl smiled and slipped her a gold. "My thanks for helping her when I could not."

"Sir . . . you don't . . ."

"It's my pleasure, Guersa. Thank you."

"Thank *you,* sir."

Dainyl carried his small bag to the archway, where an iron grillwork door served as an additional protective measure for the heavy oak door behind it.

He tugged the bellpull.

Shortly, a lander girl opened the oak door, but not the grill. Her eyes widened as she took in Dainyl's uniform. "Oh . . . you must be . . . the marshal . . ."

"Marshal Dainyl. I was hoping my wife might be here, although I didn't have a chance to let her know I'd be arriving tonight."

"Please come in . . . sir. She said you were welcome anytime. She is dining with . . . some of her staff in the . . . I'll tell her." She turned a heavy lever and the grillwork lock clicked open.

Dainyl stepped into the foyer and waited for her to relock both doors. He stood in the foyer while she scurried off, taking the white-walled corridor through the right archway.

Lystrana appeared, wearing a pale but rich blue shirt, accented with a lighter green vest and matching trousers. The garments were loose, because even from across the foyer Dainyl could sense the strengthening but not yet separate lifeforce that was their daughter.

For a moment, neither spoke.

Then, they were in each other's arms, a tangled mass of emotions with the need to reassure themselves that the other was indeed there.

Lystrana broke away, with a smile. "Have you eaten?"

"Not since breakfast."

"Then come and join us. You can leave your bag here. Jylena will take care of it. We've just been served, and there's plenty, and I'm certain that Garatyl and Dyena will be honored to dine with the Marshal of Myrmidons."

"I could use something to eat." Dainyl grinned, setting his bag on the small carved bench on the left side of the foyer.

"Would you like to wash up? There's a guest facility right here. It's closer."

Dainyl took advantage of the offer, vaguely bemused by the green marble sink and facilities.

Lystrana was still waiting when he emerged.

He offered his arm, and she took it, guiding him down the corridor to the first archway.

"How much should I tell them?" he asked in a low voice.

"No more than you'd tell Zelyert. They should know that."

The dining room was large, a good ten yards in length and close to eight in width, with a nutwood table, so dark it was almost black, and polished so that it reflected the light from the brass wall lamps. The floor was goldenstone, also polished to a gloss. The table was now set for four at one end, two across. One of the settings was untouched.

Both younger alectors were standing. Garatyl was slender, painfully thin for an alector, and was half a head shorter than Dainyl. Dyena was taller, not quite Lystrana's height, and muscular. Her eyes were golden-flecked violet, and her aura was a slightly deeper purple that suggested she might have been translated to Acorus while her mother was still carrying her unborn.

"Dyena, Garatyl, my husband, Marshal Dainyl."

Both bowed.

"We're honored," offered Dyena, her words echoed by Garatyl.

"I apologize for disturbing the meal. Please sit down." Dainyl stood for a moment, allowing Lystrana to seat herself. It was her honor, and position, as the RA.

The hint of a smile crossed her lips, and one eyebrow lifted ever so slightly as Dainyl slipped into the seat at one side of the table, across from Lystrana and with Dyena to his right.

Lystrana lifted her goblet, bearing only cider, Dainyl sensed. "To your safe arrival, dearest."

Dainyl lifted his goblet in return. "To yours as well, if belatedly."

All four took sips. Dainyl did not recognize the pale amber wine, save that it was the best he had tasted in weeks.

"I had hoped you would be able to come to Dereka before too long," Lystrana said, "but I had no idea how long the difficulty in Blackstear might last."

"It wasn't the difficulty in Blackstear that delayed me so much as what happened after that in Soupat. Two companies of Myrmidons from Ifryn—or their survivors—assaulted the Table there . . ." In between bites of his dinner, Dainyl gave a cursory description of what had happened, although he did include a mention of the lightcannon and the damage it could have created. As he spoke, Dainyl realized that most of the foot Myrmidons had to have been already involved in the two attempts. That meant that order on Ifryn was already close to gone, and that it couldn't be that long before the Master Scepter was transferred. He should have realized that sooner, but he'd been so tied up with details . . . or was it because he hadn't really wanted to accept that Ifryn was truly dying?

Both the younger alectors had to concentrate to keep from displaying a combination of astonishment and disbelief.

"I have the feeling," Lystrana said dryly, "that the actual circumstances were worse. I don't believe you mentioned losses."

"Six Myrmidons and pteridons from our forces. Somewhere over a hundred on their side, almost all of that from backlash from the explosion of the lightcannon."

"But . . . why?" asked Garatyl.

Dainyl looked to Lystrana, wondering if it would be better if she or if he explained.

She nodded to him.

"Ifryn is dying. There are more alectors on Ifryn than Efra and Acorus can take, even combined. The more knowledgeable junior Myrmidon officers on Ifryn have come to realize that they will not be included in those allowed to make the long translations. Faced with certain death, they attempted to force their way here."

"That . . . it can't be," protested Garatyl.

Dainyl had forgotten how sheltered some of the younger alectors were.

Dyena looked hard at the other assistant. "Didn't you believe Silyrt? About the Table guards? About all the shimmersilk garments that they carry away? Why is every Table heavily guarded?"

Garatyl shook his head. "But they must have known it would come to this. They must have. How could they not?"

"What makes you so certain that they didn't know?" Lystrana's voice was both cool and sympathetic. "Even *Views of the Highest* alludes to it, in talking about there being too many alectors over time."

"That makes it worse."

Dainyl agreed with that, but then, after Dramur, he'd seen that was how the High Alectors thought and acted.

Abruptly Garatyl turned his eyes to Dainyl. "Marshal, sir . . . ?"

"You'd like to know how I could possibly kill all those innocent alectors?" Dainyl's eyes fixed on the young alector. "My choices are limited. If too many alectors flee here, Acorus itself will die in a double handful of years, if not less. Some of the recorders have been allowing the best of the unauthorized refugees to remain and live. That's charitable, but it has reduced the additional numbers that can be accepted from Ifryn. Also, the weapons they were using would have destroyed so much lifeforce that, within years, Acorus might die. I cannot be merciful to a few hundred, even a few thousand alectors, if it will doom Acorus and everyone now living here."

"There must be . . ."

"I've discussed it at length with the senior lifeforce alector in Lyterna and with the Duarch of Elcien, as well as with the knowledgeable recorders. None of them see any alternatives. Neither do I." After a silence that continued to grow, Dainyl cleared his throat. "I must apologize for being so blunt."

"You might also consider, Garatyl," Lystrana added, "that Dainyl has been marshal for less than a season, and submarshal for less than a year before that. He had no knowledge of what was planned, nor any way to affect it. As a matter of fact, neither did the Duarches. What was planned was determined by the Archon in Illustra centuries ago. All we can do is manage the situation as we can."

"It's . . . horrible."

"We can all agree on that," Lystrana said. "Will you refuse

to have children so that, thousands of years from now, this will not happen again? Or . . . who will you order not to have children? On what grounds? How will you punish those who have too many children? And if you do not, how well will you sleep, knowing that each additional child shortens the time before what you are hearing about happens again?"

Garatyl looked haplessly from the RA to the marshal, and then to Dyena. Finally, he just shook his head.

"I think we should defer any more discussion on this until tomorrow," Lystrana said. "It's best if you have some time to think it over."

Dyena nodded strongly.

"I'm sorry . . . ," Dainyl mouthed silently to Lystrana.

"Don't be," she said quietly.

Garatyl merely looked bewildered, while Dyena covered a brief but knowing smile with her napkin.

"Now . . . ," declared Lystrana, "it's time for you two to talk. Dyena . . . where did you grow up?"

"I was born here in Dereka, only three months after my mother translated here from Ifryn . . ."

Dainyl took a larger swallow of wine than he should have, far larger, as he sat back to listen to what the two assistants had to say.

The remainder of dinner was far more cheerful, if forced at first.

Two glasses later, Dainyl sat on the edge of the triple-width bed. "I'm sorry about dinner. One thing led to another."

"I told you not to be sorry. Garatyl is the youngest and newest assistant. He has to understand how the world is, not how he thought it was. How else will he learn?"

"He didn't seem to understand how much lifeforce a light-cannon consumes. It's terrifying, and so is the fact that Brekylt and Rhelyn seem willing to use them. I have nightmares about it." Dainyl looked at Lystrana in her nightgown, her figure clearly showing her advancing pregnancy.

"How could you not?" she said, drawing back the covers. "I do. I was so happy when Kytrana was conceived. Now, there are times when I wonder if . . ."

"Don't even mention something like that. All people go through hard times."

"Not like facing the death of a world and asking how and why we are fortunate enough to survive and they are not. Not like killing people so that others will live, or knowing that if you do not, none will survive."

Dainyl slipped under the covers, putting his arms around her.

She was even colder than he felt.

61

Getting up the next morning was difficult, perhaps because the time was effectively two glasses earlier for Dainyl. On the other hand, he consoled himself, he could talk to Lystrana over breakfast and not hurry off. Unlike their house in Elcien, the quarters did not have a sun porch or a courtyard, and the breakfast room was a modest nook off the kitchen with but a pair of high windows that offered no view. Even so, as he sat down across from her, he could see that the sky was gray, and threatening snow or an icy rain.

Lystrana held a mug of steaming cider up to her chin, inhaling the warm vapor. She studied him. "You still have that greenish Talent aura about you. It's faint, but it's still there."

"It is?" Dainyl hadn't thought about it in weeks.

"Someone would have to get close to you." She smiled fondly. "Far closer than I'd appreciate. I don't think it's going away, or not anytime soon."

"All because of Rhelyn." He shook his head. The ancient's weapon had started it, but his own contacts with the ancients hadn't helped any—except, without them, he'd likely have been dead. Still, there wasn't anything he could do about it, and so long as it remained faint . . .

After a moment, he asked, "How have things been going here?"

"Very quiet. There was a backlog of decisions on land use, and I probably didn't make anyone very happy."

"Oh?"

"I limited additional croplands to those who wanted to build extensions to the aqueducts and to those who could prove that their water usage would not deprive anyone else of water."

"Doesn't that reward those with golds?"

"Absolutely. But it also requires them to spend them. The others didn't want to spend a copper but wanted the water. Nothing that creates crops or lifeforce is free." Her lips curled into a gently humorous smile. "I believe you made that point last night."

"Young Garatyl was appalled."

"At his age, he should be. It's hard to teach concern when people are older."

"You know I don't like what I did at Soupat . . . but they were trying to send hundreds of alectors here." He poured a mug of ale. His stomach was slightly unsettled, as it was more days than not in the morning. After a small swallow, he went on, looking to the archway and lowering his voice. "Maybe the ancients are right. Maybe we should look into changing how we link to Acorus. Wouldn't that reduce the lifeforce needs? Wouldn't it prevent or at least delay what's happening on Ifryn?"

"I don't know." Lystrana frowned. "There must be some reason why it hasn't been tried."

"Asulet said it was possible, but that anyone who tried it would end up as little more than a Talented lander." Dainyl shook his head. "And that one early alector tried it and wanted to change back and couldn't . . . and ended up as a wild translation." He paused, thinking. Majer Mykel was a Talented lander, as Talented as many alectors, and he did not require the kind of lifeforce draw that an alector did. But then, he would die within sixty or eighty years, a mere fraction of an alector's life span.

"That shouldn't have happened."

"Oh, it didn't happen that way, according to Asulet. He couldn't change back here, and he tried a long translation to Ifryn and ended up wild."

"I'm certain that's what they told Asulet," Lystrana said.

"Oh . . . of course. Any lander showing up on a Table in Ifryn would be destroyed before he could explain."

Dainyl took another sip of ale. Assuming Asulet was correct, and alectors could link to Acorus directly, and not through the Master Scepter, but the cost was a shorter personal life span. Just what was a longer life span for a few alectors worth, compared to all the other lives, and the death of a world?

"What are you thinking?"

"About choices. About the costs of what we have." Yet . . . what could he do? He couldn't force all the other alectors to link directly to Acorus—even if he knew how. And that would only turn them all into landers, and more alectors would arrive from either Ifryn or Efra, once the Master Scepter was transferred.

"It's not a choice we have, Dainyl. Even if it worked, we'd be Talented landers. How long would we last? What about Kytrana? Would you do that to her?"

He shook his head. "I'm not one for useless or empty gestures. But . . . how can I not think about it?"

She smiled sadly. "Knowing you, you can't. But you can only do what you can. That's all any of us can."

"I suppose so." He took a bite out of the omelet, not so tasty as those fixed by Zistele and Sentya. "Brekylt is moving heavy road equipment to repair possible damage to the Northern Pass."

"Suitably modified, I trust," replied Lystrana, taking another sip of her hot spiced cider. "Heavy weapons, in effect."

"I've ordered Third and Fourth Companies here." Dainyl shrugged. "I have no idea what Noryan will do."

"Noryan? Or Brekylt?"

"I think there's a chance Noryan will follow the orders."

"But you think Brekylt will stop him somehow?"

"I think Brekylt will try, if he finds out. I sent the orders by sandox. It's worth the effort to reduce his power." He looked down at the half-eaten omelet that he knew he would not finish. "Have you sensed anything like the ancients? Have there been any reports of anything odd?"

Lystrana cocked her head, then replied, "Some of the northern holders in Aelta reported greenish lights on the top of the Aerlal Plateau last week, but only for one evening."

"Do you know if there's been anything like that reported before?"

"No. There's no record of that. I had Dyena check. Jonyst has no record, either, and his records go back farther than those of the RA. What do you think they plan?"

"I don't know. I only know that they do. I can still feel the sadness and the finality of what the one ancient conveyed. And her words—that we would have to change or die." Asulet had also mentioned that the ancients were Talent creatures, and that suggested that they could survive when alectors might not . . . so long as there was lifeforce.

"I'm sure that they would have acted before this, had they the ability to do something that drastic."

"I'm sure you're right, dearest."

"Dainyl . . . don't humor me. You don't believe that for a moment. I know that. I won't change your feelings, but I am asking you to consider the facts. They've been here for longer than we have. Dereka was one of their cities, perhaps their only great city, and it was abandoned. As individuals, they're more powerful than pteridons, but we can build weapons that can destroy pteridons. Don't you think that if they could destroy us—or force us to change—they would?"

"It would depend on the costs, I suspect," he replied dryly, before finishing the ale. "I know that what you say makes more sense than what I feel, but you didn't feel the absolute certainty behind her words."

"You can't do much until they act, if they do, or until you can discover what they plan."

"No. But that's another reason to bring Third and Fourth Companies here. If Noryan will."

"If he can."

Dainyl nodded. "I'll be checking on Fifth Company before I head back to Elcien."

"Will you be here tonight?" she asked.

"I don't know. I'm leaving what I wore yesterday."

"I'll have them cleaned."

"Thank you. If nothing else happens, I should be here tonight, but Zelyert was in Ludar yesterday, and that could mean more complications."

"When you're ready to leave, I'll have my driver take you around. I don't have to go anywhere until this afternoon."

"Thank you." Dainyl just looked at her, trying to push away all the concerns for a few moments, before he finished eating and dressing and began what might be a very long day.

62

Quinti morning, Mykel dressed himself completely, although getting on his boots one-handed was a time-consuming effort, and his forehead was damp by the time he finished. He sat on the edge of the narrow bed and blotted his forehead, waiting until he cooled off some before heading to the small officers' mess for breakfast.

Rhystan, Culeyt, Hamylt, and Fabrytal were all there and eating when he stepped through the archway, offering a cheerful, "Good morning."

"Good morning, sir."

Since they had filled one table, and looked to be finishing, Mykel settled himself at the smaller adjoining table.

An orderly hurried up with two beakers, one of ale and one of warm cider, setting them before Mykel. "Here you are, sir. Breakfast will be right here."

After the ranker had scurried off, Mykel said dryly, "Amazing how quick they are when they realize you're going to be around for a while." Even as he said it, he knew it was unfair. "They've been good all along."

"They should be," suggested Fabrytal.

"None of you have had any more trouble with the dusters, have you?"

"No, sir," replied Culeyt. "We've been sending occasional patrols at night up the road a ways, and word must have gone out."

"The men have been good about not going out alone," added Hamylt. "That's helped."

"If you'll excuse me, sir?" asked Fabrytal. "We've got an early patrol."

Mykel nodded.

In what seemed like moments, the mess was empty, except for Mykel and Rhystan, who moved to the seat across the table from Mykel.

"You do look better," Rhystan said quietly.

"You say that with surprise," Mykel replied with a laugh.

"I would suggest you wait a few days before you undertake more strenuous efforts."

"I'll take your advice on that." While Mykel had thought about accompanying one of the companies on patrol, he had already decided against it—for Quinti, at least. "I had thought to take a ride through Iron Stem itself. Just Iron Stem," he added quickly, before Rhystan frowned. "I'll need to ride some each day."

"With escorts, I trust?"

"One or two should be sufficient in town."

Rhystan nodded. "That might be for the best."

"Trouble?"

"Not yet. But word about you is spreading, and if you ride out . . . it can't hurt."

"What sort of word?" Mykel tried to keep his voice even.

"Oh, the usual, whenever you're around." There was a slight edge to Rhystan's words.

"Rhystan . . . you know who I am. I'm a junior majer who got lucky a few times and is trying to learn how to be a better commander without inflicting unnecessary casualties on his men and officers."

"That's one reason why you're effective." The edge had vanished from the captain's speech. He laughed softly. "The only illusion you have is that you're just another officer."

Mykel wasn't going to get into that. He stopped as the ranker returned with a platter.

"Here you are, sir."

"Thank you." Somehow, it reassured Mykel that the egg

toast was slightly overdone. He took several bites before he spoke again. "What about the Reillies?"

"The big meeting is tomorrow. Then, there will be another feast and celebration."

"And then we'll start to have trouble?"

"They could decide to wait."

"You don't think they will."

"If they know you're riding around, it might slow them down."

Mykel didn't even pretend to understand that. He was a junior battalion commander who'd already made too many mistakes. Yes, he had Talent, just enough to keep getting himself in trouble. Why would his presence slow any Reillie or Squawt down? "Sympathizers or spies in town?"

"Relatives, most likely."

"You're not patrolling today, right?"

"Tomorrow. You want to ride out after muster?"

"I'd thought so."

"I'll have your mount saddled and two rankers standing by." Rhystan rose from the table.

"Thank you. I'd appreciate that."

Mykel finished his breakfast, then had to struggle into his riding jacket, fastening it over his splinted hand, right arm, and shoulder. He took his time making his way to the stable. If there were any dispatches, they wouldn't come in until later.

Scoryt and Gamail stood in the courtyard with their mounts and Mykel's roan.

"Morning, sir."

"Good morning." Mykel took the reins, but managed to mount one-armed, and not too awkwardly. The effort sent a spurt of pain through his injured arm and shoulder, but it subsided once he was in the saddle.

He eased the roan forward and then out through the gates, such as they were, before turning south on the high road, heading toward the center of Iron Stem, with the green tower behind him. The wind was icy, coming out of the north. With each gust came miniature snowflakes, carried with enough force that Mykel could feel each one that struck the unprotected section of the back of his neck.

The windows of the small school were shuttered, but a thin line of gray smoke angled from the single chimney. Intermittent tiny drifts of snow had piled against the low walls of the park south of the school. The narrow windows of the dwellings beyond were mostly shuttered, but Mykel did not see any smoke from their chimneys.

Only a few women and small children were about on the streets around the dingier buildings nearer to the ironworks. A single small boy looked at Mykel, his eyes widening as he looked at the loose sleeve of the riding jacket that should have held a healthy arm.

The one benefit of the chill north wind was that the air, cold as it was, held none of the acrid bitterness he had so often breathed in nearing the ironworks. He slowed the roan slightly to allow one of the black iron wagons onto the high road in front of the three of them. As always, despite the wind and snow, mals were working in the loading yard to his left, lifting the iron pigs onto the transport wagons. Beyond them, to the west, the blast furnaces were roaring, as if trying to hold the chill of the oncoming storm back with the heat of burning coke.

The inn was also shuttered, but smoke rose from both the main chimney and the kitchen chimney. The town square was close to empty, with only a small cart at one end, and a youth calling out, "Hearth coal! Copper a stone! Hearth coal!"

Mykel doubted whether the cart could have held more than four or five stones of coal, probably grubbed from the roadsides and leavings around Iron Stem. He rode on toward the cart.

The youth took in the uniform riding jackets of the three Cadmians. "I wasn't doing nothing wrong, I wasn't, sirs . . ."

"I never said you had, young fellow," Mykel replied.

A figure rose from behind the cart, a woman in a patched woolen coat, narrow-faced and gray-haired. Mykel could sense the decay and the age enveloping her. She would not live long.

"He's a good boy, sir, my grandson, he is."

Mykel laughed, then fumbled under his jacket, coming up with a half-silver. He tossed it in a gentle arc toward the youth, who caught it, almost reflexively. "That's for you, young fellow. Use some of that coal to keep yourself warm." He turned the roan, noting the ice rimming the water in the trough below the public fountain.

Behind him, he couldn't help but hear the words of the old woman.

"Keep that coin . . . boy! Luck, if you ever saw it. That there was the one they call the Dagger . . . Rose from the dead, they say, with a crossbow bolt through his heart. Broke the steel in half and pulled it out."

Within himself, as he looked northward, into the wall of gray that promised even heavier snow, Mykel winced. Luck from a coin he'd tossed? Risen from the dead? With an injured arm and a wound less than a month old?

63

Dainyl arrived at the Myrmidon compound on the south side of Dereka less than a quarter glass past morning muster. Captain Fhentyl rushed out to meet him, almost before Dainyl had taken a handful of steps away from the coach and through the outer gates.

"Marshal! We'd thought you might be here more often, but we'd heard nothing." Fhentyl offered a sheepish smile, followed by an apologetic shrug.

"Much as I would have liked to visit Dereka, I've been in Blackstear and Soupat."

"We heard about those. I'd thought . . . if you needed us . . ."

Dainyl laughed heartily. "You don't know how close you came to being needed this time, Captain. But after the losses you took at Hyalt, I didn't want to call you in unless absolutely necessary. That's because I may need you again before too long."

"Yes, sir." Fhentyl paused. "Word is that you had a rough go of it in Soupat."

"We did. The insurgents brought a lightcannon powered by lifeforce. It cost us six pteridons and Myrmidons—and the RA's complex in Soupat. None of the insurgents escaped, and there were close to two hundred." Dainyl wasn't about to mention the handful of women and children who had survived. The disruption and confusion might serve to protect them so long as everyone believed the attackers had all perished.

"That's as many as all the Myrmidons on Acorus, sir. Some said that they were Myrmidons from Ifryn."

"Some were. The Archon had four full companies of foot Myrmidons on Ifryn, each with sixty rankers. Because a number didn't survive the long translation, we don't know exactly how many Myrmidons were involved. In Blackstear they killed everyone but the recorder. In Soupat, they did the same. But that's over now."

"Do you have any duties for us now?"

"I'd like you to run occasional patrols of the high road to the west, and the sections of the aqueducts in the lower section of the Upper Spine Mountains. If your scouts see anything unusual, they are not to approach too closely." Dainyl offered a crooked smile. "There have been reports of actions by the ancients that could lead to hostile efforts, and I'd rather have the information about what they might be doing, rather than lose any more pteridons or Myrmidons."

"Yes, sir."

"Since I'm here, I'll also make a quick inspection."

By the time Dainyl had completed his inspection of the compound and was in the coach headed back to the recorder's building, a cold drizzle had begun to fall, and the wind was colder. He had the feeling that the rain would be turning to snow before long.

Jonyst was actually in the library, rather than in the Table chamber, when Dainyl arrived there. "Marshal."

"Recorder. Is there anything I should know? Or that you think I should?"

"The number of attempted translations from Ifryn has dropped off considerably," Jonyst said. "We've only received two since last night. Both were wild, and very weak."

"It could be that those with sufficient Talent and desperation have already tried."

"Or that the Archon is taking tighter control of the Tables prior to transferring the Master Scepter."

Or both, thought Dainyl. "You will watch for Talent efforts by the ancients?"

"That we can do."

Dainyl walked down the staircase from the library to the Table chamber. Jonyst followed.

Once there, Dainyl stepped onto the Table, concentrating on what lay beneath.

The purpleness of the translation tube seemed more like a faint haze, and the Table locator vectors appeared dimmer, if still distinct. The amber-green presence of whatever the ancients had created was far stronger, a deeper green, yet seemingly no closer.

Dainyl focused on the white locator of Elcien.

As the locator neared him, two things became more obvious. The translation tube felt smaller and its "walls" more porous, and the purple flashes of unsuccessful long translations had increased, but each was less powerful than those of days and weeks previous.

He stood on the Table at Elcien, shields firm, but the guards were far less nervous than they had been in recent weeks. More telling, Dainyl did not see Chastyl.

With a pleasant smile, Dainyl left the Table and the chamber, but did not go far, since Zelyert stood in the entrance to his private study.

"Marshal, a moment of your most valuable time, if you would." The High Alector of Justice retreated into the study, leaving the door open.

"Of course, sir." Dainyl closed the study door after he entered, if warily. Zelyert seemed to become more and more angry and hostile each time he met with Dainyl. Dainyl remained standing since Zelyert had not seated himself.

"What did you discover, if anything, in Dereka, Marshal?"

"Fifth Company has recovered from the Hyalt effort and is ready to support us in whatever may be necessary. The ancients massed a great amount of Talent a week or so ago on the heights of the Aerlal Plateau, so much that it was noted from Aelta. Recorder of Deeds Jonyst confirmed that a number of the insurgent Myrmidons attempted to use the Tables to flee and were unsuccessful."

"While you have been . . . traveling, Marshal, the High Alector of Engineering has lodged a number of complaints with both Duarches that your efforts disrupted copper and tin production at a critical time. The Duarches are not pleased."

Dainyl suspected that Samist was the one not pleased, rather than Khelaryt.

"If the High Alector of Engineering had been more careful in overseeing his engineers so that they had not produced thousands of rifles and other pieces of equipment that ended up in the hands of all sorts of indigen rebels, he would not have to be so worried. Even the mountain brigands southwest of Soupat have new unmarked Cadmian rifles. If the RA of Soupat had been more diligent in guarding his Table, there also would have been less disruption. I did not cause the disruption, yet I am being faulted for taking less than a week to resolve it? Oh . . . and I fail to see how I could have disrupted tin production, since those mines were closed well before the Myrmidons arrived."

"More is expected of a Marshal of Myrmidons than a submarshal or a colonel."

Dainyl was seething, so much that he knew Zelyert had no trouble discerning it. "How did you find Ludar, Highest?"

"Marshal, Ludar was most informative, particularly since I did not have to deal with the presumption of subordinates."

"I can understand that, Highest," Dainyl replied, his tone polite. "Presumptions and questions by those who must bear the burdens and resolve the difficulties can be particularly annoying." He shouldn't have pressed that point, but Zelyert was beginning to behave just as Shastylt had, and Dainyl had the feeling that superiors who became excessively secretive were engaged in matters that were not necessarily in anyone's interest but their own, and certainly not in the interest of their subordinates.

"You are most presumptive, Dainyl."

"I suppose that is because, Zelyert," Dainyl replied, emphasizing the personal name, "I'm getting exceedingly tired of resolving problems that no one else could at less cost than anyone else could and then being condemned or condescended to because matters did not go as you would have wished. The more I do, the less happy you are, as if you wished I would fail and have been disappointed when I did not."

"I could crush you." The statement was arrogantly matter-of-fact.

"Perhaps you could," replied Dainyl, although he had his doubts that Zelyert was that much more powerful, "but what is the point of that? Everyone knows you're powerful. Then who would you find to resolve the difficulties you face?"

Dainyl could sense Zelyert beginning to gather Talent-strength and he added, "Is that your answer, Zelyert? Destroy me because I have the honesty and audacity to suggest you might be mistaken? Then who will do what you need done? Unlike the others who might replace me, I'm not scheming for your position, and you should be wise enough to see that."

"You are an arrogant imbecile."

Dainyl laughed. "I'll admit to arrogance. What alector isn't, at times? I'll even admit to making mistakes, but why are you attempting to destroy me? It won't solve your problems."

Zelyert continued to marshal Talent force, as did Dainyl.

"Destroying a presumptuous subordinate is never wrong."

"What do you gain? Either way, you lose. If I defeat you, you lose. If you destroy me, you lose, because there isn't anyone left who can do what I can, and you will need me and the Myrmidons." He smiled. "At least, in the near future."

Before Zelyert could say more, Dainyl inclined his head. "I have no interest . . ." He strengthened his shields and took two steps forward, sensing that Zelyert had no intention of listening to reason.

He was within a yard of Zelyert when he was stopped cold by the sheer ferocity of the barrage of Talent against his shields.

Dainyl could barely even stand against the bolts of Talent, let alone attack, and he could feel his shields being eroded.

"You're nothing," Zelyert said. "A trace stronger than many alectors, but hardly anything to worry about."

The superior brute strength of Zelyert's Talent pressed

Dainyl back, enshrouding his shields with purple. Dainyl interlocked shields within shields, but still found himself being pressed backward, toward the stone wall behind him.

Another bolt of Talent energy shivered his shields, adding to the purple aura of air in the study.

Something about the purpleness nagged at Dainyl as he shored up his shields, trying to stand against the onslaught . . .

Then, he had it. Talent didn't have to be purple!

Dainyl extended a probe to the greenish blackness that lay beneath the Table, not all that far away.

His shields strengthened, and the pressure against him subsided. Rather his own strength, aided by what he drew from beneath, balanced that of the High Alector.

"You're a tool of the ancients . . ." gasped Zelyert. "Anyone can see it . . . the green."

"I'm no one's tool." Dainyl opened the channel wider, allowing more of the greenish Talent-strength to flow into his shields. Then he was the one to step forward, pressing Zelyert backward.

Zelyert extended his own Talent probe, toward the Table itself.

Dainyl enveloped it with the greenish black, squeezing it off short of the Table.

The room exploded into an inferno of unleashed Talent.

Dainyl hung on to his shields—and the link to the blackish green below. The entire Hall of Justice shuddered . . . and purple and green darkness slammed into Dainyl, hurling him against the wall.

Then . . . there was only darkness.

64

For a time, Dainyl lay on the stones of the private study. Every muscle and bone ached. Then, there was chill—cold compresses on his forehead. He managed to open his eyes.

Adya was kneeling beside him, applying the compress. "You're alive."

"After a fashion," Dainyl whispered.

"I didn't think anyone . . ." She lifted the compress.

Dainyl sat up, then slowly stood. Dizzy as he felt, he immediately sat down in the chair before the table. Only then did his eyes go to the High Alector's garments, lying on the stone floor. Empty.

"You're . . . green," Adya said.

"I feel green," Dainyl offered dryly, although he feared he knew what she meant.

"Your Talent . . . it's more like greenish purple, with some black," she explained.

"It's been like that ever since Hyalt. Rhelyn—he was the RA and the recorder—wounded me with one of the weapons of the ancients." Dainyl offered a hoarse laugh. "I've been tinted green ever since."

"They say the ancients . . ."

"Their Talent is green. It was a weapon forged by their Talent."

Her mouth opened. "The records say . . ."

"What do they say, Adya?" Dainyl forced himself to be patient. He needed time to recover, and he didn't need anyone upset.

"The green alector . . ." She stammered. "I don't recall. I only heard the Highest mention it once. He said something about it being a time of danger for everyone."

Dainyl had a good idea that Zelyert had said much more. He also doubted that Adya would tell him. Not at the moment. "Zelyert was angry even before I returned from Dereka. Do you know why?"

"No, sir. He'd been at the Palace, and he was short-tempered when he returned. He didn't say why. He told Dalyrt that he'd have to take the petitions in the Hall today. The way he said it no one wanted to ask why."

"He was in Ludar yesterday. What sort of mood was he in when he came back?"

"I couldn't say, sir. He came back after I left for the day. Dalyrt was the one who had to wait."

Dainyl was still light-headed, although he could feel some Talent-strength returning. "Could I persuade you to get me something to eat and drink?"

"Yes, sir. I can do that."

Her acquiescence was frightening, almost as though she couldn't wait to leave the study.

Dainyl took a deep breath. He had to get his thoughts together. He supposed he needed to tell Khelaryt. But what could he, what should he tell the Duarch? And was it wise to appear Talent-tinged in green in the Palace?

Could he conceal some of the green? Turn it inside, and leave the purple outside?

He concentrated, attempting not to change what he was, but only the outward radiation of the mixed Talent he seemed to embody. By the time he finished, he was even more light-headed, and he lowered his head into his hands for several moments, straightening up only when he sensed Adya returning.

"You're looking much better, sir. Most of the green's faded. Not all, but most." She carried a wooden tray, on which were a small loaf, a wedge of white cheese, and a beaker.

"I'd think it should fade over time." Dainyl was beginning to have doubts about that. Exactly what had been in the weapon Rhelyn had used? Or had the ancients' healing of him made him more susceptible to showing the green? It couldn't just have been the result of his recent drawing on the black-green Talent. He'd had a tinge of green before.

Dainyl ate the entire loaf of bread and the cheese and drank the whole beaker of cider. He did feel more clearheaded when he finished, and far better than he ought to have, given what he'd been through.

Adya stood waiting, as if fearful of leaving.

Dainyl didn't even know the protocol for seeing the Duarch. In the past, he had only responded to requests and sent reports, but what had happened merited more than a report, and it couldn't wait, especially if what he feared might be happening.

"Adya, is the Highest's coach here?"

"Yes, sir. I think so."

"I'll need a ride to the Palace."

"Let me check, sir."

No sooner had Adya scurried off again than Chastyl appeared in the doorway. "Might I come in?"

Dainyl nodded.

The recorder's eyes dropped to the shimmersilk garments still on the floor, then he looked at Dainyl, clearly comparing the marshal's plain blue and gray shimmersilk uniform to the richer raiment of the late High Alector. "Ah . . . who . . . will you . . . ?"

"I have no idea, Chastyl. I asked Adya to find the coach so that I could report Zelyert's unfortunate death to the Duarch."

"You . . . intend to do that personally, sir?" The recorder's tone suggested the lack of wisdom in such a course.

"How else? If the Duarch finds my self-defense unacceptable, what would be the point of telling him indirectly? Indirection has never been my strength, Chastyl."

"Ah . . . no, sir. I've observed that."

"What should I know, Chastyl? You had something to tell me, I'd wager."

Chastyl's eyes dropped once more to the garments that had been Zelyert's, as if the recorder could not believe what had happened. "Ah . . . yes, sir . . . I think, sir. You'd mentioned that you'd thought that the Highest had gone to Ludar. He did, but he was furious when he returned, the kind of anger he walled away, but so great not even his Talent could hide it."

"Do you know why?"

"No, sir. When he left the Table, he said, 'Beware those who know everything and understand nothing.' That was all, except for one thing. Almost as an afterthought, he added, 'The marshal knows nothing, yet understands almost everything. That makes him all the more dangerous.' After what's happened, I thought it might make sense to you."

"I'll have to think about that. I appreciate your letting me know." Dainyl had the feeling he did in fact understand. That suggested even more that he needed to talk to Khelaryt before anyone else did.

"If that's all, sir, I'd better be returning to the Table."

"I won't keep you. Thank you." Dainyl managed a smile he hoped was pleasant as Chastyl inclined his head and backed out of the study.

As though she had been waiting in the corridor, which she had been, Adya stepped into the doorway. "The coach is ready for you, sir."

"I appreciate your finding that out for me." Dainyl stood and walked deliberately to the inner stairs and up them.

A cold mist filled the air and continued to seep out of the low-lying clouds as Dainyl left the Hall of Justice and walked down the wide stone steps to the waiting coach.

"To the Palace, sir?"

"The Duarch's entrance, please."

"Yes, sir."

Dainyl climbed into the coach. Was he the imbecile Zelyert had suggested, or merely foolhardy, as Chastyl had hinted? Neither, he tried to convince himself. Fleeing or delaying would only make matters worse, not only for him, but for Lystrana and Kytrana.

The coach ride was short, and in fact, Dainyl could have walked the distance, but somehow walking up to the Palace did not seem to fit the occasion—and riding was quicker, if not by that much. He stepped out of the coach onto the wide marble mounting block.

"Would you like me to wait, sir?" asked the driver.

"I'd appreciate that." With the mist thickening, Dainyl glanced from the Palace to the north, where a wall of gray bore down on Elcien, the first of many winter fogs, he suspected. Then he turned and strode through the archway and past the pair of guards armed with lightcutter sidearms. As he had suspected, Bharyt appeared almost immediately.

"Marshal Dainyl . . ." The functionary's forehead creased into a puzzled frown. "I do not recall . . ."

"I was not summoned, nor do I have an appointment, Bharyt. I'm here to see the Duarch on a matter of great urgency."

"Might I tell him in general terms?" asked the slender alector, his words more suggestion than question.

"This time, no. I'd also suggest that you would not wish to be the one to do so," Dainyl replied.

Bharyt stood for a moment, then nodded. "I will tell him that you're here, sir."

Dainyl watched as the other alector turned and made his way along the corridor flanked by goldenstone marble columns, goldenstone doubtless quarried generations upon generations earlier in Soupat. Bharyt vanished through one of the doors, then, after several moments, reappeared and walked swiftly back until he faced Dainyl.

"He will see you."

"Thank you."

As he followed the functionary, Dainyl's boots clicked on the green and gold marble tiles, a sound muted somewhat by the gold-trimmed dark green velvet hangings. As they neared the library, Bharyt stepped back and motioned to the door. "You may go in."

Dainyl opened the door, stepped into the library, and closed the door behind him. He was well aware of the finality of the metallic *click* of the latch.

The Duarch was not seated at his desk, but stood before the oak shelves on the inside walls, as though he had just replaced one of the leather-bound volumes. Standing, he remained a towering presence, but his shimmering black hair was disarrayed, and there were circles under the deep violet eyes. While the Duarch still radiated Talent, Dainyl noted that now that the shadowmatch was gone, Khelaryt's Talent seemed only slightly more impressive than Zelyert's had.

On the Duarch's desk was a single large crystal, absolutely clear. Beyond the desk and crystal, through the narrow floor-to-ceiling windows on the outer walls, the sunken garden looked gray, half-veiled by the mist that was rapidly being replaced by a full-fledged fog.

"Sir." Dainyl bowed, then straightened, waiting.

"You haven't seen the crystal before, have you? It's useful for turning malign Talent energies against the user . . . or for identifying strange energies. As you know, it was not necessary . . . earlier." Khelaryt smiled, warmly, although the warmth was even more superficial than on their past meetings. "You have an urgent message?"

"More like unfortunate news, sir. On my return from Dereka, after I had inspected and briefed Fifth Company, High Alector Zelyert summoned me to his private study, charged me with incompetence, and then attacked me."

Khelaryt nodded slowly. "Since you are here, and he is not, the outcome is obvious. I cannot say that I am surprised that he would act so. I am mildly astonished at the outcome. You apparently have some abilities beyond the apparent."

Dainyl decided to ignore that point. "I have also learned that he has been traveling to Ludar and that he has been in rather close touch with High Alector Ruvryn. You are doubtless aware of that, but you may not be aware that even more Cadmian rifles manufactured in Faitel have turned up, this time in the hands of the mountain brigands to the southwest of Soupat, and that Ruvryn has apparently attempted to blame a delay in copper shipments on the events in Soupat. He also charged me with delaying tin shipments when he had already closed the mines some time earlier. At least, those were the offenses which Zelyert laid at my feet."

Khelaryt had not been watching Dainyl, but the crystal, which had turned a misty green from its previous clear color.

"Very interesting. Your Talent is mixed, as if you were part ancient and part alector. That cannot be, of course. There are warnings about green alectors . . ."

"You know the reason for that, sir. When I was wounded in Hyalt . . ."

"That is certainly part of the reason, Dainyl. Tell me. Do you wish to be Duarch? High Alector of Justice?"

"No, sir. I have no desire to be Duarch. I'm too direct, and I know too little. Lystrana would be far better at it than I."

Khelaryt glanced at the crystal, clear once more. "My daughters have been in touch recently. They both have sent the same message. Both urge me to trust you and to use you as necessary. On the other hand, every single High Alector, except Chembryt, distrusts you. Who should I believe?"

"Yourself, sir. Others can only advise you, and all have their own interests at heart."

"And you do not?"

"I have my own interests as well, sir. I'd like to think that they are far less injurious to you and to the fate of Acorus."

"What *are* your interests, Dainyl? To be High Alector of Justice?"

"I had not thought of that until this morning, sir, after I was forced to deal with Zelyert." Dainyl smiled apologetically. "He accused me of being an imbecile and arrogant. I suppose that I am ignorant and arrogant, because my feeling has always been that the duty of the High Alector of Justice is to be just and because I believe that I certainly could handle the duties of being High Alector of Justice at least as well as Zelyert did."

"What would you do if I did not name you High Alector?"

"Continue to do my best as Marshal of Myrmidons. Resign if you requested it."

Khelaryt laughed ruefully. "Zelyert was the imbecile . . . or the arrogant one. You are one of the loyal ones. You did not seek Shastylt's title and responsibilities. You only sought to do what you thought best. In the end, that made you a threat to both of them. That has all too often been the case." He laughed again. "As matters now stand, I am the only one to whom you do not pose a threat." Khelaryt paused, frowning.

Dainyl managed to keep a pleasant expression on his face as he realized that despite the Duarch's words, Khelaryt was concerned about Dainyl being a threat.

"In time, anyone can be a threat, but your loyalty says much about you," the Duarch continued. "I believe you understand that as well. But you cannot remain as Marshal of Myrmidons."

"Sir?"

"There is no one among the High Alectors who is strong enough to be your superior, Dainyl. We are not exactly blessed with an abundance of alectors with ability and great

Talent." Khelaryt frowned again. "The green sheen to your Talent poses another problem, but for the moment, we will avoid that problem by noting that you will be occupied in learning your new duties as High Alector of Justice. During that time, meet with Alseryl and Chembryt personally, so that they will have no reason to bring up the issue of green-tinged Talent before me. You will also need to brief your successor as marshal. I assume that Submarshal Alcyna meets your requirements."

"There is no one else qualified, sir." Dainyl was having difficulty in grasping Khelaryt's matter-of-fact handling of what had happened. He also had no idea who could become the next submarshal.

"That seems to be the situation facing both of us, High Alector of Justice." Khelaryt added, "It has always been difficult to find those with both integrity and ability. So often those with the greatest ability lack integrity and those with integrity lack imagination."

"Since I've never been a High Alector," Dainyl replied, "what do I do now? Is there any formality, documents . . . ?"

"I trust you will not object to a lack of ceremony. It has been some years since a High Alector has been replaced, and now does not seem a time for celebration. If you will wait a few moments, I will sign a writ making the position officially yours."

Khelaryt sent a Talent pulse, and the library door opened.

Bharyt stood there. "Most High?"

"Marshal Dainyl is the new High Alector of Justice. If you would prepare a writ immediately for me to sign . . ."

"Yes, sir."

As soon as the door closed behind Bharyt, Khelaryt moved to the desk, then settled himself behind it. He gestured to the chairs on the other side. Dainyl took one.

"I understand that the insurgents in both Blackstear and Soupat were led by Ifryn Myrmidons. Is that so?"

"Yes, sir."

"The late Zelyert was not terribly specific, but I was under the impression that you actually inactivated the Blackstear

Table and still translated away from it and then returned to Blackstear with First Company and destroyed the invaders to the last alector."

"That's generally true, sir. But I didn't translate from an inactive Table. There's a short time between when a Table gets the Talent signal to inactivate it and when it responds. I was standing on the Table when I sent the signal, and I translated that instant."

"Rather amazing feat, I'd say. You translated in, killed enough rebels to allow you to inactivate the Table, and then departed."

Dainyl shrugged. "It had to be done."

"You didn't do the same in Soupat."

"No. It was clear that they knew more about Tables. Blackstear may even have been a diversion."

"I had wondered about that. I don't suppose we'll ever know for certain."

"I'd doubt it, sir."

"What do you intend to do about the east?"

"Nothing until I know more," Dainyl replied. "I don't know how Brekylt intends to establish his independence from the Duarches or what exact role Zelyert and Ruvryn played in his schemes or whether they were only apparent allies with their own separate schemes. I'm troubled by the number of Cadmian rifles produced by the engineers and sent to rebels and insurgents all throughout western Corus and Dramur. To me, it seems obvious that Ruvryn wanted to weaken the Cadmians. Almost all the Cadmian companies are significantly understrength. The Myrmidons have been weakened, if not to the same degree, and largely, once more, in the west. My assumption is that these are all part of a design to make it difficult for the Duarches to maintain order and control west of the Spine of Corus, let alone deal with Brekylt's efforts to set himself up as an equal to you and Samist."

Khelaryt laughed. "For an alector who professes to know little, you have a better understanding of what is transpiring than do most of the other High Alectors."

"They must know, sir. They just refuse to talk about it or admit it."

"That is a difference without a distinction, Dainyl. Knowledge unexpressed is no different from ignorance."

Dainyl thought it worse, because the ignorant had the excuse of not knowing. The High Alectors' only justification was fear and self-interest.

There was the slightest knock on the door, and Bharyt stepped inside bearing two small scrolls. "These are old-style writs, sir, but they were the most convenient."

"Tradition can always be useful, particularly in times of change." Khelaryt held out a hand.

Bharyt crossed the room, passing the pair to the Duarch. "One for the High Alector, to be posted in the Hall of Justice, and one to be posted here in the Palace."

"Even in these times, there are some traditions to be followed," murmured Khelaryt.

Bharyt looked to Dainyl. "Sir, there is another tradition . . ."

Dainyl nodded for him to continue.

"The day after a new High Alector of Justice is seated, he personally receives petitions in the Hall of Justice. He is expected to show mercy where possible, and more than usual."

"Zelyert often heard petitions. Is that not expected? Or is it the greater degree of mercy that is the tradition?"

"The mercy," replied Khelaryt, signing and sealing one scroll, and then the second, using several of the books on the table to pin down the corners of the scrolls so that the wax could harden and the ink dry. "What else will he need?"

"Highest Dainyl can use the same seal. It's a seal of the office, not the individual," replied Bharyt, "but he should find official garments in green and purple, at least for public appearances. We might have some that would fit . . . it has been a time."

"Do what you can." As Bharyt departed the library, Khelaryt turned his gaze back on Dainyl. "I'll expect you at the second glass of the afternoon tomorrow, after you hold your morning audience for petitioners, for a greater discussion of matters. For now, you should return to the Hall of Justice and establish your presence. Then you will need to deal with the Myrmidons. I will communicate your status to all the recorders and the other High Alectors."

"Do I need to present myself to Duarch Samist?"

"That would be politic, but I would judge you have a day or two, and I would send a written request asking his indulgence for you to call on him at his convenience."

"Is there anyone else?"

"Had you not already established yourself with Asulet, that would have been necessary. As it is, you have spent more time with him than most High Alectors." Khelaryt smiled and gestured toward the door. "Best you get on with the politics that you love so much."

Dainyl caught the humor behind the words and did not conceal his smile. "I fear I have never hid my dislike of empty and misleading words and gestures." He stood.

"They are misleading, but seldom empty," replied Khelaryt. "You should remember that, High Alector."

"Yes, sir." Dainyl accepted the mild rebuke, inclined his head, then turned.

He did not hear the latch of the library door click as he shut it behind him, and he paused for a moment. Was the *click* a device to unnerve those coming into the library to see the Duarch?

Bemusedly, he shook his head. That was certainly possible.

As he crossed the entry foyer of the Palace, toward the coach waiting beyond, Bharyt stepped forward. "I took the liberty of placing some tunics and trousers that might fit in the coach."

"Thank you, Bharyt."

Outside, the fog was far thicker than earlier, and Dainyl could not even see the Hall of Justice to the north.

"Highest? Back to the Hall, sir?" asked the driver.

"Yes, please." Dainyl stepped up into the coach and closed the door. Clearly, the driver had either asked Bharyt or seen the purple and green garments laid out on the other bench seat.

The ride back was slower, short as it was, because of the

fog, and because the driver had to wait at the boulevard for several carriages to pass.

When the coach came to a halt at the steps of the Hall of Justice, Dainyl opened the coach door.

Before he could gather up the High Alectors' raiment, the driver called down, "Sir . . . in this wet and damp, best you send someone up for the garments."

Dainyl considered the words and then nodded. While he preferred to handle personal matters himself, somehow, it wouldn't have been exactly decorous to return as High Alector of Justice with an armful of garments proclaiming the change. "I will, thank you."

He hurried up the steps and then took the concealed staircase down to the lower level, not that he needed to worry that much, because the Hall was empty of petitioners, and Dalyrt had left the dais already.

Adya, Cartalyn, and an assistant Dainyl did not know stepped out into the corridor. "Sir?"

"The Duarch was most understanding." Dainyl handed the scroll to Adya. "This should be posted somewhere."

"Sir?"

"Oh . . . I'm sorry. It's the writ of my appointment as High Alector of Justice."

She bowed her head. "Highest . . ."

" 'Sir' will do. Oh . . . there are some garments—the official garb of the High Alector of Justice—in the coach. Could you have someone bring them down?"

"Patrylon," Adya told the alector standing at her shoulder, "you can do that, and I'll post the writ."

"Thank you both."

Adya scurried down the corridor in one direction past the Table chamber, while the stocky Patrylon marched toward the staircase. Cartalyn followed Patrylon.

Dainyl looked into the private study. Thankfully, someone, probably Adya, had removed Zelyert's garments and boots. He stepped inside and surveyed the chamber. Besides the table and the three chairs, there was little enough in the manner of furnishings, just a single low bookcase of three shelves. He scanned those volumes that displayed titles on the spine, although most did not: *Views of the Highest,* looking so newly bound that Dainyl wondered if Zelyert had ever lifted it off the top shelf; *The Administrator; History of Inefra; The Code of Laws . . .*

Clearly, Zelyert had kept all personal items elsewhere, and Dainyl had no idea where that might have been.

He Talent-sensed someone approaching, straightened, and turned as a slender but tall alector appeared in the open doorway. Dainyl recognized Dalyrt, although he had never formally met him, because Dalyrt had substituted for Zelyert as administrator at the last administration of justice at Myrmidon headquarters.

Dalyrt bowed deeply. "Highest."

Dainyl could sense a buried combination of consternation, puzzlement, and resentment, but decided against commenting. "A simple 'sir' will be more than sufficient, Dalyrt. I certainly didn't expect it, but one refuses the Duarch at greater risk than I was prepared to undertake." *That should add to your confusion.*

"I can see that might pose a problem, sir." Dalyrt's voice was deep, as Zelyert's had been, and even smoother and more polished.

Dainyl instantly distrusted him, but kept the feeling well behind his shields. "The Duarch, even in these troubled times, is a formidable presence, with great experience in being able to determine whom to trust and to support. He is far more practiced in not revealing that experience than are most High Alectors, unless he chooses to do so. I am deeply convinced that he seeks the best for all alectors, and I worry that those who might oppose him do not see all that he does."

"Yes, sir." Dalyrt's puzzlement grew.

"Power not only corrupts, Dalyrt. It also blinds."

"Yes, sir. I stand to do your bidding, and I will certainly follow your guidance and heed your advice."

So long as it seems to benefit you. "Thank you."

Dalyrt bowed and stepped back into the corridor.

No sooner had Dalyrt departed than Chastyl appeared.

"Congratulations, sir."

"Thank you, Chastyl."

"Just let me know anything I can do . . ."

Dainyl had the feeling that he would get little done for the next few glasses except to meet with the immediate staff of the High Alector and accept their congratulations and profession of loyalty and support. It was hard to ignore their unvoiced concerns about the green component of his aura and Talent—especially when Asulet's warning remained in the back of his mind.

He also needed to try on the garments sent by Bharyt. That bothered him more than a little, because it meant taking off the uniform he had worn for almost all of his adult life—not that he would ever shed the heritage of being a Myrmidon.

65

It was slightly before midafternoon on Quinti when Dainyl finally took the coach to Myrmidon headquarters, feeling slightly uncomfortable in his garb as High Alector of Justice. In the end, he had found two older sets of garments—not that the lifeforce-treated shimmersilk had aged in the slightest—which suited him far better than the others. Unlike the others, they offered an almost Myrmidon cut to both tunic and trousers. The tunic and trousers were green, and the purple trim was limited to the tunic cuffs and collar, and to single thin strips down the outside of the trouser legs. He still wore his black Myrmidon boots—and intended to keep doing so.

When Dainyl stepped through the archway into Myrmidon headquarters, Captain Ghasylt was standing by the duty desk, talking to Undercaptain Chelysta. Both had worried expressions, and Ghasylt had just gestured toward the entrance.

"Good afternoon," Dainyl said.

Ghasylt looked up and took in the tunic and trousers, his

eyes widening only slightly, although the shock was far more obvious to Dainyl's Talent than to his eyes. After the barest hesitation, the captain replied, "Congratulations . . . Highest."

"You looked worried there, Ghasylt."

"Yes, sir. When I saw the High Alector's coach drive in . . ."

"I would have been concerned, too." Dainyl smiled. "Is the submarshal in her study?"

"She was a moment ago," added Chelysta. "She was reviewing next week's flight schedules."

"I need to see her. Thank you." Dainyl walked down the corridor. Behind him, he could make out the murmurs, enhanced by his Talent.

". . . never thought he'd become Highest . . . too honest . . ."

". . . stronger . . . can't you sense the Talent?"

". . . sort of green . . ."

Dainyl eased open Alcyna's door and stepped inside, closing it behind him.

Alcyna looked up from the flight schedule she held, took in the green and purple, then stood, leaving the schedule on the desk. She nodded slowly. "Congratulations, Highest."

" 'Sir,' please."

"I said Zelyert underestimated you. I assume he decided you were a threat and created a reason to attack?"

"Generally, yes. He complained that we took too long in Soupat, that we delayed copper shipments, as well as tin shipments from closed mines, that we lost too many pteridons, and that it was all my fault. I told him if he could find any other Myrmidon who had been as effective that I would happily resign. Because he had no answer he attacked. That was early this morning. I had to spend some time with the Duarch and then with the staff at the Hall of Justice before I could get here." He smiled wryly. "I did want to tell you that you don't have to go back to Alustre to get command."

"To get command?" Alcyna raised her eyebrows.

"Effective immediately, you are the Marshal of Myrmidons." He extended the green-edged gold stars that he had taken off so recently.

Alcyna did not move to take them. "There has never been an alectress who commanded the Myrmidons. What will the Duarch say?"

"I already told him, and he agreed." Dainyl reached forward and laid the stars on the bare wood of the table desk beside her. "There may be a personal reason there."

"His daughter?"

"Daughters," Dainyl said.

"There is another besides Sevasya?"

"Captain Lyzetta." Dainyl smiled ruefully. "I didn't know she was Khelaryt's daughter until after I promoted her." He almost mentioned that the shadowmatch had prohibited the Duarch from mentioning or contacting either daughter, but refrained, realizing that he had never discussed that aspect of the shadowmatch with Alcyna.

"I'm very glad I decided to come to Elcien," Alcyna said. "Do you know what else Brekylt said about you?"

"I'm certain he said a great deal."

"He said that you had the instincts for doing the right thing, and that it would either be your death or the death of those who opposed you, and that he preferred not to engage in those kinds of battles."

Dainyl laughed. "He would give me too much credit, even while he was sharpening a knife." After the briefest of pauses, he added, "Marshal Alcyna, I'd like to request that you assume command of the Myrmidons and that you put on the insignia of your rank."

"Yes, sir. With pleasure." She half turned and lifted the stars off the table.

Dainyl watched as she replaced the silver stars on her collar with the gold stars. Then he motioned for her to take her seat and settled into the chair in front of the table desk.

"Now . . . who would you suggest as your replacement as submarshal?" he asked.

"At the moment, I would prefer not to name a replacement, sir."

Dainyl thought he understood why, but still felt he had to ask. "Why is that?"

"Submarshal Noryan would be the logical choice, assuming that he shows his loyalty to the Duarches."

"You wish to wait to see his reaction?"

"We would have to wait until he has a chance to receive orders. If they're not delayed, the orders should reach Noryan in Norda on Decdi or Londi, no later than Duadi." Alcyna smiled politely and added, "As I recall, there was no official submarshal in Elcien when you were the head of operations for several months."

"That's true, but all you have now is an assistant chief of operations."

"Zernylta is doing well at that. In another year, I could promote her to majer, and make the position of operations chief that of either majer or colonel."

That certainly squared with where Dainyl had been headed as marshal. "What other changes would you suggest for Myrmidon operations or headquarters?"

"We need more trainees and the ability to call them from Transport immediately."

"You don't think we should skip the time spent as a sandox driver?" Dainyl didn't, but he wanted her reaction.

"No, sir. First, until they work with either sandoxen or pteridons, there's no way of telling whether their Talent is strong enough and suited to Talent creatures. Second, there's too much power involved with being a Myrmidon. Sandoxen have some of that power, and being a driver for a time makes younger alectors aware of that power, and it also gives them the sense that it is both a duty and a privilege to be a Myrmidon."

Dainyl nodded, but his thoughts strayed to the Myrmidons from Ifryn. Were they as dedicated as the alectors and alectresses he commanded? Or had it been that conditions had become so bad on Ifryn that the desire for sheer self-preservation had overwhelmed their sense of duty? Or had they simply felt betrayed?

"Sir?"

"I was thinking about the Ifryn Myrmidons."

"I've thought about them as well."

"Did you ever talk to Noryan or Veluara about it?"

"Noryan didn't want to say much. He only said that the Ifryn Myrmidons had once held the ideals that we do, and that they did no longer, and that there was little point in talking about it."

"Why did you replace the original with Noryan?"

"Why not? The original one had been caught abusing a local boy. The child wasn't that badly hurt, and with some Talent manipulation, I managed to erase or blur his memories. But that meant he wasn't suitable to be a Myrmidon. Noryan was."

"You just executed him?"

"It was better than he deserved. If he'd had to go through a court-martial and an administration of justice, he would have been found guilty and had his lifeforce ripped out. We don't know if he had tried to abuse others, and trying to dig that up would have made matters worse. I didn't want to see any Myrmidon paraded in front of other alectors as that decadent."

Alcyna was telling the truth, and Dainyl could see that she believed she had acted as well as she could have under the circumstances . . . but it still bothered him, not that he could see any point in taking the matter any further.

"Did you know about that before you promoted me to submarshal here in Elcien?"

"I knew who Noryan was, but not why you made the substitution. It bothered me, and it still does, but we've all done things that could have been done better, and I had the feeling that you were treading a narrow path with Brekylt." He still wondered what her relationship with Brekylt had been.

"That's a charitable description." Her laugh was throaty, nervous. "He was worse than Shastylt. From what I saw, anyway."

"We need to go over my perceptions of the Myrmidon companies and their needs, and your thoughts and reactions to each," Dainyl said mildly. "I have the feeling that after tomorrow I'm going to be occupied with a few other concerns."

"Tomorrow, sir?"

"That's when I have a long meeting and discussion with Khelaryt."

"I think I'd rather be marshal, at least so long as you're High Alector of Justice."

As he gathered his thoughts to begin briefing her on insights and observations he had not previously shared, Dainyl could not help but wonder how long he might be High Alector.

66

By the end of Quinti, Dainyl had found a green jacket, similar to a flying jacket, that matched the High Alector's tunic and trousers. He needed one and felt that it was inappropriate to wear a Myrmidon flying jacket or cold-weather coat. He also still carried both lightcutters, unnecessary as he thought they might be, on his belt as he stepped onto the Table in Elcien.

He half smiled. One advantage of being High Alector was the closeness to the Elcien Table.

"Sir?" inquired Chastyl, hurrying into the Table chamber, followed by Adya.

"I'll be back very early tomorrow. I am taking the petitions in the morning."

"Yes, sir," replied Chastyl.

Adya said nothing, but the disapproval in her face mirrored her internal feelings. Apparently, she and Chastyl felt that High Alectors were only supposed to use the Tables to travel to and from Elcien and Ludar.

Dainyl concentrated on the darkness beneath the Table and felt himself sliding through the silvered surface of the Table and into the coolness below . . .

. . . where he found that his perception of the translation tube alternated between two views. One timeless instant, the tube appeared narrow and solid, its "walls" deep purple, the next instant, little more than a misty and insubstantial cylinder perched parasitically upon a deeper greenish black

extension—almost an underground high road, one that was part of the rock and yet separate from it.

Reaching out with a Talent probe that appeared as much green as purple, he linked to the crimson-gold locator that was Dereka. As soon as the link was complete, he flashed through the faintest mist of silver and golden red.

He stood on the Table in Dereka, belatedly realizing that he had not even checked on the purple flashes or on the amber-green creation of the ancients, whatever and wherever it might be.

The five guards stationed around the Table leaned forward, although they did not raise their lightcutters.

"Highest?" Jonyst's eyes widened, and he bowed. "Highest . . . might I ask?"

"High Alector Zelyert met an untimely end. He attacked a loyal subordinate for no reason other than the subordinate's effectiveness. The Duarch was pleased to offer me the position."

"I see. Congratulations." The recorder inclined his head slightly, and Dainyl could see that Jonyst's hair had gotten more of the streaks of brilliant white. As the recorder straightened, Dainyl also noted that his face had become even more haggard.

Dainyl stepped off the Table. "A moment, if you would." He nodded to the staircase, gesturing for the recorder to go first.

When they were in the library on the next level, Dainyl glanced around. Although there were papers on two of the tables, no one else appeared in the room.

"Jonyst . . . you're wearing yourself out. Can't your assistants help?"

The recorder shook his head. "Ilerya and Wasen are helping as much as they can, but someone has to monitor the guards, and that leaves Whelyne and me. Otherwise, they'd let anyone translate here." He lowered his voice. "Except those who would be most useful."

"The ones who can help you or Acorus?"

"Yes, Highest."

"If you must use a title, just use 'sir,'" Dainyl said tiredly.

"I've been High Alector for less than a day, and . . ." He decided against saying what he might have. "I'm not much for titles based on position, rather than accomplishment or ability."

"You never were."

"Have you noticed anything new or different about the Tables or the translations?"

"We're still getting fewer long translations, and the majority of them are wild."

That made an unfortunate kind of sense to Dainyl.

"It can't be that long before the Archon acts," the recorder suggested.

"I've thought that before, but I think he'll squeeze as much lifeforce out of Ifryn as he can, and that may take longer."

Jonyst raised his eyebrows. "Your predecessor would not have said that."

"I know. I'm less indirect, and it may be my undoing." With barely a hesitation, Dainyl went on. "Is it possible to borrow your coach and driver for a short ride?"

Jonyst smiled. "A High Alector who asks and means it is welcome to all that I can supply. Mostly."

Dainyl smiled in return. "That last word shows you're a wise and cautious alector."

"Cautious. Were I wise, I'd no longer be a recorder."

"I'm glad you are. I'll see you or Whelyne in the morning." With those words, and a smile, Dainyl turned and headed for the ramps to the lower level and the main entrance.

Guersa stared as Dainyl approached the coach.

"Guersa . . . not that much has changed. The Duarch only promoted me."

"Ah . . . yes, sir . . . I mean . . . I've never driven . . . a High Alector . . ."

He opened the coach door. "There's a first time for everything. I'd just like to see my wife."

"Yes, sir. We can do that."

As he stepped inside the coach, he heard her murmur, "High Alector in Dereka . . ."

When he settled onto the bench seat, he realized that only in coaches had he been alone since he had left breakfast that morning. Would every day as a High Alector be like that?

The sun was dropping behind the Upper Spine Mountains when Guersa brought the coach to a halt outside the RA's quarters.

"Will you need me in the morning, sir?"

"I think not, but thank you." Dainyl nodded politely, then turned and walked up the stone steps. To the fading sound of hoofs on stone as the coach pulled away, he tugged the bellpull.

After several moments, Jylena opened the door, and like Guersa, stared for a long moment through the grillwork.

"I was promoted," Dainyl said dryly. "I'm still married to the regional alector."

"Oh . . . yes, sir . . ." She released the lock on the grill door.

Dainyl had not even taken two steps into the small foyer when Lystrana appeared, clad in an outfit similar to what she had worn the day before, except the colors were reversed with the vest of light green and the trousers and tunic of the rich blue.

She stopped and looked at him, then smiled. Her eyes were sad.

Dainyl eased forward and put his arms around her. "It's all right."

Jylena had finished closing the doors and eased away down the right side corridor.

Lystrana stepped back, still holding his hands. "He attacked you, didn't he?"

"You saw it coming?"

"I thought it might, but not yet. You're getting more powerful, dearest." She frowned. "You've also got more green about you. It was fading." She glanced around. "Dinner will be the two of us this evening. Why don't we go to the study? I had them plan for later."

Dainyl offered her his arm. As they walked, he let his Talent sense Kytrana, a growing Talent presence. He worried about her, and about Lystrana. Alectors' children, for all their strength, needed every moment of their eight months within their mothers.

"I could sense that," Lystrana said. "I'm fine."

"Can I help it if I worry? Wouldn't you?"

"At times I worry enough for both of us, dearest." When she stepped into the study—a small room with only two narrow windows, but with an entire wall of bookshelves, half empty—Lystrana stepped away from him. "Do you like the garments?"

"You look good in them, but you always do."

"Your mother sent several sets by sandox. They arrived yesterday. She even sent a short letter, admonishing me to stay away from Tables from here on in."

"I'd agree with her," Dainyl replied, "and we don't often."

"I like yours, too." Lystrana grinned. "They aren't typical for a High Alector . . ."

"They're more traditional. Bharyt found some for me, and I liked these better than what Zelyert was wearing."

"That's because they're far more like a uniform, and you'll always be a Myrmidon, no matter what happens."

Dainyl wouldn't have contested that.

"There's something else. The green—it's now part of your Talent, and it's even stronger within you. How did that happen?" Lystrana settled onto the short settee to the left of the floor-to-ceiling built-in bookcase.

"When Zelyert attacked me . . ." Dainyl stopped. "I think I'd better start from the beginning. After breakfast, I inspected Fifth Company and then took the Table to Elcien . . ." He went on to describe the events of the day, including how he had been forced to call up the green Talent from beneath the Table, all the way through to his arrival in Dereka.

"Your ability to use the ancients' form of Talent . . . it can't be just because of the wound from Rhelyn's weapon," she said.

"I think it's partly that, and partly because they healed me." He moistened his lips. "I also have the feeling that all really Talented alectors could do it. Otherwise, why would the ancients have been telling us that we have to change?"

"I don't like that at all."

"Neither do I. I'd rather not talk about it anymore. I don't know that there's anything more to be said, anyway. I'm looking forward to dinner, and I'm happy that you don't have any company tonight—except Kytrana."

"So am I." Lystrana smiled.

67

Mykel sat behind the writing desk in the dilapidated study of the run-down garrison in Iron Stem. His shoulder was sore. He was tired, and it was still a glass before midmorning.

For an instant, a flash of green—Talent-green—seemed to surround him, but it was gone almost before he had recognized it. Then . . . from somewhere came a deep and distant rumble, not one that he heard with his ears, but one that he perceived.

"Loryalt!" he snapped.

Within moments, the undercaptain stood in the study doorway.

"Put everyone here at the garrison in combat duty status. Immediately. Have them saddle their mounts and stand by for orders." According to the schedule, only Sixteenth and Fourteenth Companies were out on patrol. "In the courtyard."

"Yes, sir. Any other orders?"

"Not yet. I'll know more in a bit." *You hope you know more.*

Loryalt hurried off. "Muster for ride-out! All companies!"

Mykel had certainly felt and sensed something, and that it meant trouble. If it didn't, he could always claim he wanted to see how fast the battalion responded. That would be better, embarrassing as it might be to him personally, than the unnamed danger he sensed was about to strike Iron Stem. It had something to do with the soarers. At least, he thought it did.

For a time, he sat there, but could not think of what more he should be anticipating. Then he began to hear mounts and men out in the courtyard. Finally, because sitting and thinking was doing him little good, Mykel stood and struggled into his riding jacket one-handed, fastening it over the arm in the bound sling, leaving that sleeve empty. Then he walked quickly toward the courtyard. He was opening the door when the ground began to tremble.

He staggered for a moment, then ran into the center of the

courtyard. "Away from the buildings! Get away from the buildings."

While the buildings swayed, and several windows broke, and an old shutter crashed to the stones, in several moments the shaking of the earth stopped. Lazy flakes of snow drifted out of the gray sky, so at odds with the feeling of doom that he sensed, even after the apparent earthquake.

"Majer, sir!" Loryalt rode toward him followed by the other four officers.

Mykel surveyed them. "Fabrytal. Fifteenth Company is to patrol the area around the ironworks. Shoot anyone who doesn't obey, and anyone who looks like he's looting."

"Looting, sir?"

"This earthquake and whatever else has happened might have wrecked houses or even the ironworks. Those orders are for all companies. Loryalt, Seventeenth Company has the area around the town square. Dyarth, you've got the area to the east of the square. Hamylt, you and Fourth Battalion have the area north of the ironworks and around the garrison. Leave two squads here in case someone gets ideas."

"Yes, sir."

"All of you send back scouts with reports of what you find."

The chorus of "Yes, sir" was ragged, but firm.

"Go!" Mykel wanted to ride out to get a better view of what had happened. Instead, he forced himself to walk to the front of the headquarters building. There, he stood outside, watching as the companies rode out.

"Sir?"

Mykel turned to see a ranker bringing a tall stool with a back. He didn't know the man, but thought he had to be from Fourth Battalion.

"If you're going to wait here, sir, this might help."

Mykel couldn't help smiling. "Thank you."

He set the stool under the eaves that formed a slight roofed area over the front entrance and settled down to wait.

In less than a quarter glass, a mount galloped back toward the gates, then slowed to a walk as the ranker guided the horse into the garrison. Mykel recognized the Cadmian—Jasakyt, the lead scout from Fifteenth Company.

"Jasakyt! Over here!" called Mykel.

The scout turned the chestnut toward the majer, finally reining up less than three yards from Mykel, who had stood and stepped forward. "Sir . . . the dam for the ironworks must have burst. There's water half a yard deep in places around the ironworks. Some of the furnaces exploded, it looks like. A few of the houses are burning. Before I left, the company had to shoot some of the mals from the ironworks."

"Tell Undercaptain Fabrytal that he's to keep order at all costs. The water will subside before long, and there will be more looters then. Tell him he can break the company into half squads, but no smaller."

"Yes, sir."

"If anything changes, especially for the worse, I'll need to know."

"Yes, sir."

"On your way . . . and thank you." After Jasakyt rode out, Mykel walked out to the gates, now guarded by a squad from Fourth Company.

"Sir!"

"I'm just looking." Mykel took several more steps, until he was partway into the high road, then looked south toward the center of Iron Stem. Through the intermittent snow, he could see several patches of orangish red, but the distance and the snow blocked any clear view. After a moment, he turned and walked back to his self-appointed post.

Not more than a few moments later, another scout rode back up the road and through the gates. One of the guard detail apparently told the rider where Mykel was, because the scout rode directly toward him.

Mykel stood once more and waited.

"Sir . . . Seventeenth Company has established order around the town square. Some of the men from the ironworks tried to break into the chandlery and the inn. Three of them ignored the undercaptain's orders and were shot. They're dead. The others scattered. Everything is quiet now."

"What about the buildings?"

"One of the houses caught fire. The locals look like they've saved the ones around it, but that house is going to burn to ashes."

"Thank you. You can return to your company. If anything changes, have the undercaptain let me know immediately."

"Yes, sir."

Once more, Mykel settled onto the high-backed stool. The dam that served the ironworks and the mine shouldn't have burst. Even if it had, there shouldn't have been enough water to flood the section of Iron Stem around the works—not unless the stream flowing into the lake created by the dam had also flooded. But how likely was it that an earthquake and a flood would occur at once?

Not at all likely . . . unless the soarers were involved. But why would they do something to Iron Stem? He frowned. It wasn't Iron Stem; it was the ironworks.

He looked to the south, where the glow of the fires around the ironworks diffused through the snow. He couldn't do any more by riding out, but he would have liked to. Maybe he wasn't cut out to be a battalion commander. Or . . . he hadn't gotten used to delegating.

He shook his head. That wasn't it at all. He *knew* he could do a better job than any of the officers under him—except perhaps Rhystan—and Mykel didn't like the idea of things not being done well.

A crooked smile twisted across his face. He could imagine what Rhystan would say about that—that it was Mykel's job to make sure his officers did learn how to handle things in the best possible fashion. Rhystan was right about that, too.

68

Dainyl had taken the Table back to Elcien early on Sexdi to spend some time going over the procedures for the petitioners' hearings. As a senior Myrmidon he was familiar with the Code and knew where to find most sections, but what he did not know was how often the hearings changed things and on what basis. After less than a glass of studying the records of previous hearings, the answer was clear. Very seldom had the High Alector, or his designee, changed sentences. The most usual change was a reduction in the penalty. Very occasionally, a sentence was voided.

Dainyl snorted to himself as he stood and adjusted his tunic and the purple robe used by the High Alector at the hearings. It wouldn't be difficult to show some mercy, although from what he'd read, he had the feeling few of those who appealed deserved it.

"Sir?" Patrylon stood in the study door. He would sit below Dainyl to document the decisions handed down by the new High Alector and handle the details.

"I'm ready." Dainyl picked up the symbolic Mace of Justice. Unlike the one used in the administration of justice, this one had no power.

As he left the study and began to walk toward the steps up to the receiving hall, he felt a distant flash of unseen green. He frowned.

"Sir?" asked Patrylon.

"Something . . . we'll have to check on it later."

A line of petitioners had already filled the hall when Dainyl followed Patrylon to the dais. On the raised green marble platform were two stone tables, one on the lower level, with a stool behind it, and a wider one on the next level, half a yard higher, with a stone chair set behind it. Dainyl was gratified to see that there was a thick cushion, if in green that matched the marble.

He stood behind the upper stone table, holding the Mace of Justice, while Patrylon declaimed. "Petitions will be received. Justice will be done, in the name of the High Alector and the will of the Duarches."

Dainyl sat down in the cushioned stone chair, setting the Mace to his right on the table.

"Highest and Most High." A heavyset man stepped forward and handed his petition to Patrylon.

In turn, after reading it, and jotting down some notes, Patrylon handed it to Dainyl. There were two parts to it. The first was a decision handed down by the local alector in Arwyn, and the second was a single written sheet appealing the decision. The local alector had fined one Doveilt five golds for overgrazing his pastures and for allowing the waste products of his sheep to foul the stream. The decision noted that previous fines of three silvers and a gold had failed to encourage Doveilt to rectify the situation. Doveilt had written that he was a poor man, and that five golds was more than he made in a year.

Dainyl understood that five golds was the yearly pay for a starting indigen laborer, but if Doveilt had enough sheep that fouling a stream was a problem, he was making more than five golds. More than a gold and a half in fines already paid suggested something else entirely.

Dainyl looked down from the dais at the beefy man. "You're Doveilt?"

"Yes, sir, Your Highest."

"How many sheep do you have?"

"Ah . . . I have a flock, sir."

"How many are in the flock?"

The man shifted his weight, his eyes not meeting Dainyl's. "Mayhap fifteen, sir."

The man was lying about that.

"How much do you get for each one when you sell them, a ewe, that is? And for those you keep, how much wool do you get?"

"I don't sell them, sir. Just shear them."

Dainyl waited.

"A good year I get a quarter stone a head in raw wool."

"What's the price range for that?"

"For a quarter stone, could be two silvers, three in a good year." Doveilt was clearly puzzled at the questions, as was Patrylon.

"That means that from your flock you'd make between five and ten golds each year, and you lied about the number of sheep in the flock. How many do you really have, Doveilt?"

The herder swallowed. "Sixty-two, when I left, sir."

"Consider yourself fortunate that I don't have you flogged

for lying. I will charge you a gold for wasting my time and that of those who have had to wait. Pay it to my assistant now."

The herder swallowed, but placed five silvers on the stone table before Patrylon.

"Next petitioner," Patrylon called out, then handed the petition up to Dainyl.

Dainyl scanned the papers. Mylesh had been sentenced to five years in the gravel quarries for adulterating spirits in a tavern he owned. The tavern-keeper had used hempseed, pepper, soot, and salt, as well as powered acidstone, to adulterate the ale, and powdered lead to sweeten spoiled wine.

"You're not Mylesh." Dainyl studied the round-faced and mid-aged indigen woman.

"No, Most High. Mylesh is my husband. He is working in the gravel quarries. For what he did, that is too much. I know he was wrong, but to condemn a man to die crushing rocks for such a little thing. I beg you for mercy, Most High."

"Enough powdered lead in wine will kill a man's brains," Dainyl said mildly. "As a tavern-keeper, your husband knew that. If he did not, he should have. How long was he a tavern-keeper?"

"All his life, as was his father before him."

"I cannot grant mercy to a man who granted none to his patrons, and should have known better. Dismissed." Dainyl only hoped someone in the hall had a petition worth considering.

"Next petitioner."

A haggard and thin-faced woman stepped up. Behind her, Dainyl noticed several men who eased away from the line of those waiting.

Patrylon glanced over the sheets she handed to him, and then passed them up to Dainyl.

He read through them quickly. Quiona was a widow whose husband had been a fuller's assistant in Tempre. He had been killed when the Alector's Guard had chased a thief from the market and the thief had grabbed him from where he had been washing the front window of the shop and thrown him in front of the horses to slow pursuit. The thief had been caught and executed for the murder and for his thefts. But since the thief had no legal property, the widow could not make a death claim. She had appealed to the regional alector—Fahylt—for a widow's pension. Fahylt had denied it because there was no provision for a pension in such a case, citing the fact that the Guard was only doing its duty.

Dainyl looked down at the sad-eyed woman. "You are Quiona?"

"Yes, Highest." Her voice trembled.

"I know your husband died under the horses of the Guard, but you are not that old. Why do you need a pension?"

She turned slightly and, with her left hand, drew back a scarf to reveal a withered right arm. "No one will offer me a job that will feed my children."

"How many children do you have?"

"Only two, Highest. They are three and six. Gabraal said that a man should only father those children he could feed . . . but I cannot . . ."

"Patrylon," Dainyl said quietly.

The assistant looked up.

"I hereby grant Quiona of Tempre the standard widow's pension for a woman whose husband has been wrongfully killed by the acts of those carrying out the will of the Duarches . . ."

Dainyl could sense the confusion from the assistant.

"The Regional Alector Fahylt had created the Alector's Guard in contravention of the will of the Duarches. Therefore, any death of an innocent man created by their direct actions is in fact wrongful and requires compensation."

"Thank you . . . Highest . . . thank you." Tears streamed down the woman's cheeks.

"Next."

Joronyl was appealing a finding that had fined his factoring establishment five golds for false measures on a shipment of cotton. His carefully written petition claimed that he had not known that the measures were off, and that even so, the difference was slight, so slight that other factors who had bought from the same lot had not been cited and fined by the trade inspectors.

Dainyl looked down at the factor. "How do you compare in

size to the other cloth factors in Elcien?" As he finished the question, Dainyl could sense the puzzlement from both Joronyl and Patrylon.

"I'd be one of the smaller ones, Highest."

"How did it come that you were fined five golds?"

"That's the thing, Highest. I bid on the bales, and you take what you get. Maybe they were a little short, but sometimes we all get short bales. I don't see the inspectors at Falest's or Caturyk's warehouses, but every time there's a lot that goes to all of us, it'd be my place they come to first. If it's not short for them, it oughtn't to be short for me."

"If I understand you, Joronyl, you're claiming that the cotton shippers often send short bales, and you don't know that until you've bought them."

"Not like often, Highest. Sometimes." A fine sheen of sweat had begun to appear on the factor's forehead.

"And you resold the cotton, claiming it met measure?"

"It was only off a bit, Highest, and all the other factors been doing the same."

That, unfortunately, rang all too true. Still . . .

"I cannot reduce your fine, Joronyl, on the grounds that others have gotten away with cheating customers and that you got caught. Dismissed."

Even so, that petition bothered him, because it suggested the same pattern that he'd observed in Dramur. The larger factors got away with practices not allowed for the smaller factors, and yet when alectors attempted to step in and require the same standards of everyone, the landers and indigens complained—or those with golds did.

The first petitions were a rough indication of the way the morning went. Dainyl found that in only about one in six cases could he even consider changes to the decisions—and that was being merciful. He did reduce some fines and commute two sentences to time already served.

By the time Patrylon announced that the time of petitions was over, Dainyl had looked at more than twenty of them, and there were still petitioners waiting. He worried about leaving them unheard, but he had the feeling that if he stayed beyond noon, word would get out, and every day would bring more petitions. Also, it had been clear that some of the petitioners had heard of a new High Alector and were hoping to get a better decision.

Still, Dainyl took a deep breath once he was headed back to the small study beneath the Hall of Justice. He was more than glad to take off the heavy purple hearing robe as soon as he entered the study and did not fully close the study door behind him.

Outside in the hallway, he heard voices. He used his Talent to catch their words.

"How did it go?" murmured Adya.

"The Highest has a very good grasp of justice," replied Patrylon, before lowering his voice and adding, "He's not patient with fools, either."

"You like that . . ."

"It's different . . ."

Their voices faded as they walked farther from his door. Zelyert had clearly presented his warm voice and sympathetic demeanor to the petitioners, even while denying their petitions, seeming to do so reluctantly. That was something Dainyl could not do . . . and did not intend to. Justice was justice, and at times it needed to be tempered with mercy, but false sympathy was a form of corruption, no matter how politic it might be.

He was tempted to take the coach to check on Alcyna, but that would only suggest a lack of faith in her ability. He also pondered the green flash, but did not know what he could do about it, since he did not know where it had taken place or even what it meant, except that it involved the ancients—and that could mean another problem.

Instead, he summoned Adya.

He waited until she was seated before he spoke. "Several matters came up this morning at the petitioners' hearings, but one suggested that we have a much larger problem."

"Yes, sir?"

"One of the smaller cotton factors was fined for being short on measure. He insisted, and he clearly believes this to be true, that the larger factors are often short, but are never fined."

"That's very possible, sir. The inspectors are landers and indigens. They can be bribed, and they probably are. For a time, High Alector Zelyert enforced a more stringent effort in dealing with such." Adya shrugged. "As fast as he removed the old inspectors, and sent them to the gravel quarries, the new ones would soon end up taking bribes. Those who were honest either had great misfortunes befall them or soon left for other occupations. The High Alector attempted to raise the stipends of the inspectors, but that did little except increase the price of cotton, and many factors closed their warehouses and moved to Ludar or Southgate."

Dainyl said nothing for a moment. Adya believed what she said.

"Were you here when that occurred?"

"It was the first task I undertook for High Alector Zelyert."

Dainyl had the sudden feeling that Adya had asked for the task, perhaps for the same reasons that he had been interested in the matter. "How long did the effort go on?"

"Five years, sir. We lost a third of the cotton and wool factors, and a fifth of the other factors, and the merchants of Elcien sent a petition to the Duarch. They did not address the bribery outright, but they did say that under the conditions imposed by the High Alector, they could no longer do business in Elcien."

"And everything went back to the way it had been?"

"Not quite. The worst cases disappeared. The factors know that if there are too great a number of abuses the High Alector can always make matters hard on them. It has become a tacit compromise. Minor shading of the standards and rules, if done quietly and if products are not adulterated, is occasionally accepted. More than that risks greater costs and oversight."

"I see. I trust we do not accept such . . . laxity in goods for Myrmidons and Cadmians."

"No, sir. That's understood. One beef supplier provided maggoty meat. The High Alector had him flogged to death on the main wharf."

Yet they would cheat each other?

"What we buy is little compared to what they sell to each other," explained Adya, understanding his unspoken question. "They can accept our standards because we pay well and punish severely. They do not pay each other well, and they do not wish to be punished severely."

That was a balance of sorts, but not one of which Dainyl approved. Still . . . until he understood more, it would be best not to try to change matters. "Thank you."

"You are welcome, sir."

"I'll doubtless have more questions, although I hope they'll become fewer."

After Adya left, Dainyl looked at the schedule Patrylon had left on the Table early that morning. He had petitions the next morning as well, and a meeting with Chembryt at the second glass of the afternoon, and another meeting on Octdi afternoon with Alseryl, the High Alector of Transport. Dainyl had no doubts that Alseryl was going to complain about Alcyna's requests for more recruits.

Then he drafted once and rewrote twice the necessary letter to Duarch Samist, requesting a meeting to pay his respects. By the time he finished that and gave it to Patrylon for dispatch to Ludar, he was hurrying out to the coach in order not to be late for his meeting with the Duarch.

When he arrived at the Palace, Bharyt conducted him immediately to the library where Khelaryt was seated behind the table desk.

The Duarch gestured to the chairs, and Dainyl took one.

"We have a number of items to discuss, Dainyl. First is the issue of Ruvryn."

Dainyl nodded. The more he'd learned about the High Alector of Engineering, the less he cared for the alector, but he wanted to hear what Khelaryt had to say.

"Did you know that he is Paeylt's son?"

"No, I did not." That explained a great deal, such as why Asulet was handicapped in dealing with Paeylt. Dainyl had always wondered why the senior alector in charge of the underground city of Lyterna had not acted more decisively against an alector who was but the senior engineer in Lyterna. The fact that Asulet had only said Paeylt and Ruvryn were "related" clearly indicated Asulet's reluctance to admit he could not overcome such nepotism.

"You have had some concerns about Ruvryn as well, did you not?"

"Yes, sir. Do you know why he has taken such steps to weaken the Cadmians? I can understand why he would wish the Myrmidons weakened, especially if the Duarch Samist is considering an alliance with Brekylt against you, but why the Cadmians?"

"You are referring to all the Cadmian rifles that have been diverted to various indigen rebels and insurgents?"

"And to the seltyrs of Dramur as well."

"He has avoided discussing those matters, and since he reports directly to Samist, I cannot press him too hard. What I have observed, though, is that he feels the Cadmians create officers who are disciplined and less inclined than most indigens to seek golds at all costs. He sees this as a possible threat."

"They are disciplined in carrying out our requirements and tasks, and they are a threat?"

"Upon several occasions, junior officers have improvised the equivalent of cannon. A few have suggested larger bore rifles. Explosive devices have been used against insurgents. As you are well aware, alectors are few in number. Should the Cadmians turn on us with weapons such as those, we would have great difficulties. Ruvryn believes that they should be kept understrength and that thoughtful and disciplined senior officers need to be monitored closely."

Dainyl nodded slowly. Another aspect of the intrigue among High Alectors had become clear. "Then I think I can say with some confidence that Ruvryn was working closely with former marshal Shastylt. Shastylt applied modified shadowmatches to several Cadmian majers and a colonel to the end of increasing Cadmian casualties in Dramur."

"I cannot say that surprises me."

Dainyl had the sense that Khelaryt did not totally disapprove, and that meant Dainyl needed to be very cautious. "There is a delicate balance there."

"I would agree, but I would suggest that Ruvryn is not always against our interests."

"I will keep that in mind, sir."

"There is another aspect of matters of which I have not apprised you," Khelaryt said quietly. "Why do you suppose that Majer Sevasya is stationed in Lysia?" He smiled. "Thank you for her promotion, not that she had not deserved it years before."

"As you said, sir, she deserved it." Dainyl had wondered why she had been stationed in Lysia ever since he had become submarshal and discovered that Sevasya was Khelaryt's daughter. "I assume there is another reason besides her being remote enough that it would be difficult to influence you, sir, but I do not know what it is."

"The dual scepters are often considered as legendary or mythical. They are not."

"One of them is in Lysia, then." Dainyl frowned. Where else would the other be? "Is the other in Dereka?"

Khelaryt had not been at all surprised at Dainyl's first conclusion, but he could not conceal his concern about the second one. "How did you know that?"

"I did not know it until you raised the issue of the dual scepters. Only then did it make sense that Jonyst had to be the other guardian, given who he is and the stress he has been under lately. Also, it was once a city of the ancients. There must have been some reason dealing with Talent for why they located a city in a place not ideally suited to their . . . physical needs."

"There was indeed. It is one of the major lifeforce focal points of Acorus. I can only surmise that Samist also agreed to the choice of Lystrana as regional alector because she would certainly not wish the scepter compromised, nor would you."

"No, sir."

"The entire translation tube network on Acorus—as well as the long translation tubes—owe their stability to the existence and the placement of the two scepters. It is an unspoken rule that they be left alone, where they are. They are not where they might seem to be, and that is all you need to know."

Dainyl nodded once more.

Khelaryt continued to bring up various items, from the timing of the meetings with his High Alectors to the limitations of the great ships of the ocean and the intricacies of their schedules.

Finally, he paused and looked at Dainyl. "Do you have any other questions?"

"One, sir. I spent my first morning receiving petitions, as you know, and one of them came from a small factor—"

Khelaryt laughed, but the sound was more mournful than the hearty and humor-filled guffaws Dainyl had heard before. "The bribery of the merchant inspectors, no doubt. The small factors cheat, and they get caught, but the large ones do not because they bribe the inspectors. Yet, if we do anything . . ."

"I fear I have trouble understanding this." What Dainyl feared was that he did in fact understand it.

"Golds rule the indigens and landers in trade. They have no sense of ethics, only a desire to amass the largest amount of gold possible and to live in the greatest luxury. Your most honest steers are Cadmians. That is because treachery there will kill too many men. Otherwise, they would be like all the others, and often, the senior officers are."

Always the golds, reflected Dainyl. That was the weakness of landers and indigens. But then, the love of power, to the equal exclusion of practical sense, was the weakness of alectors.

"That will have to be all for now," announced the Duarch, standing abruptly.

Dainyl rose quickly. "I appreciate your time and the information."

"Just remember, Dainyl, to make sure that you understand how something came to be before you attempt to change it. I will see you at next week's meeting of the High Alectors."

As he left the Palace, Dainyl couldn't help but recall the

Duarch's last words. *But what if you do understand and no one wishes to change a course for disaster?*

He also still worried about the green flash. Was it connected to the green Talent force he had perceived when he had been traveling between Tables?

69

Once it was clear that the initial chaos had passed, Mykel immediately sent off a dispatch rider to Dekhron with an initial report on the damage to Colonel Herolt and a copy to the Marshal of Myrmidons. One of the river tugs could get the dispatch to both far faster than the next sandox coach would.

Although all of his company officers had reported that they had established and were maintaining order throughout Iron Stem, Mykel decided that he needed a firsthand view of what had happened. Even so, he waited until well past midafternoon before he finally mounted the roan and, in the company of fifth squad from Fifteenth Company, began his inspection tour. The light snow had long since ceased, but the sky remained covered with featureless gray clouds.

"It's pretty bad around the works, sir," offered Vhanyr, the squad leader, as he and Mykel turned their mounts south on the high road.

"How many houses damaged?"

"Hard to tell, sir. The water's down, now. Ironworks got hit the hardest."

"That's not surprising. Their dam was what broke."

"It's worse than that, sir. You'll see."

Mykel knew he would, but he studied the area adjoining the Cadmian garrison. The school to the immediate south of the garrison appeared untouched, as did the smaller dwellings. Beginning some two hundred yards south of the school, large puddles remained on both sides of the road, and less than a quarter vingt beyond that the watermarks on the houses were nearly a yard high, and still damp.

The doors of some of the lower hovels were open, and women were still sweeping out water and setting chairs, stools, and other furnishings on porches or other raised areas. Mykel didn't see bedding, which suggested that while the water had gotten into the houses, it hadn't been high enough to damage everything. He doubted that the furniture had been set out to dry, given the chill of the day, but probably to clear the floors so the water could be swept out.

As Mykel neared the works, he could see more damage, and higher watermarks. A heap of brick and ashes was all that remained of one small house, and several sheds had been flattened. Bedraggled chickens squawked and fluttered away from the road, and two boys struggled with ropes to drag a pig toward a sagging fence.

Once past that section of houses, Mykel turned his mount onto the road heading to the works, covered with a thin film of water. The water in the loading yard of the works was boot deep, and occasional gusts of warm damp air mixed with the colder winter air.

Mykel reined up well short of the fallen wall stones that had marked the boundary between the loading areas and the works itself. He looked westward, at the steam that sifted upward out of the heaps of rubble that stretched more than a vingt westward. He had not realized that the works was that large—almost a half vingt north to south, and three times that from east to west. Not a chimney remained standing, nor was any structure intact.

Groups of men and teams of the draft horses were working, dragging equipment from fallen buildings, digging a channel, and pulling down a tottering wall. Mykel found it hard to take in the scope of the destruction.

A figure in a splattered coverall turned and walked toward the Cadmians from the wreckage of what had been the works headquarters building. After a moment, Mykel recognized the engineer. "Curosyn?"

"The same, Majer." His eyes lingered on Mykel's empty sleeve for but a moment.

"The earthquake and flood—it did all this?"

"Combine cracked furnaces, water, steam, molten metal, partly cured coke, and that's what you get. It'll be months, maybe years, before we can put everything back together. This is a works, not just furnaces. The coking ovens pretty much exploded, and the furnaces did too after the earthquake cracked them. Molten metal, coke, limestone—it's a mess. Some of the coal piles feeding the ovens caught fire. It may be weeks before some of them burn out. We must have lost a hundred men from the fire, explosions, and the steam."

"I'm sorry to hear that. I don't imagine there's much we can do."

"Just keeping order was a help. The High Alector of Engineering won't be happy with this." Curosyn gestured toward the devastation. "Excuse me, Majer."

"We'll talk later." Mykel turned the roan.

As he rode back to the high road, he could sense the heat at his back.

"We'll ride through the town square and then east," he told Vhanyr.

The buildings around the square, on slightly higher ground than the works, seemed largely undamaged, although Mykel could make out several missing shutters on the inn, and one window with batting or fabric behind the shutters, suggesting that the glass had broken.

Despite what Curosyn had said, Mykel had his doubts that the earthquake and flood had created all the damage. The green Talent flash suggested that the soarers not only had been involved, but that the destruction had been planned—and possibly even abetted or enhanced around the ironworks. The destruction in the rest of Iron Stem had been modest, at least in comparison. But why the ironworks?

He hadn't the faintest idea, and all he could do for the moment was to keep order and hope that the Reillies and Squawts didn't move up their attacks on him and the Cadmians.

70

Septi morning found Mykel back behind the small writing desk. Iron Stem was quiet, according to the reports from all the patrols, although there were still fires in parts of the ironworks, and probably would be for days. One of Rhystan's scouts reported that the Reillies were still gathered south of Wesrigg, but that there were signs that they might move out before long, and some of those signs were weapons being cleaned.

Mykel looked at the map spread before him. From where the Reillies were situated, they could take one of two easily traveled routes, the farm road to Borlan, or the high road to Iron Stem. If they took the Borlan road, Third Battalion could take the high road south, and then the cutoff through Sudon to the ridges overlooking the farm road. The valley there was narrow, and if Fourth Battalion sealed the road to the north . . .

All that was theoretical, unless the Reillies did decide to attack, rather than disband and head into the hills to their homes for the winter.

Finally, one-handed and slowly, he refolded the map. What he ordered the battalions to do would depend on what the Reillies did. If he were more calculating—like an alector—he would have just attacked the Reillie encampment, with all the women and children. Tempting as that was, he felt that he had to let them make the first move. After that . . . he shook his head.

He took out the unsigned letter from Rachyla and laid it on the wood, reading the few lines carefully once again, although he already knew every word. Should he reply?

There was no question about that. The real question was how to frame the reply in a fashion that only Rachyla would understand fully, since Mykel could hardly count on his missive reaching her unread.

In the end, writing his response was physically laborious

and required using his left hand. More than a glass passed before he finished. Then he read it over, slowly and carefully.

Lady Rachyla,
It has come to my attention that rumors may have circulated as to my recent injuries. I would have written sooner to assure you and the most honorable Amaryk that Third Battalion remains in good order and strength despite a number of strange occurrences in Iron Stem, which include a flood and an earthquake. These resulted in severe damage to the ironworks, and with the existing damage to the piers at Dekhron, that may well affect the price and availability of worked iron for some time, as well as other metals, and for coal as well. These facts might be of interest to you and your family, since they are matters of substance and affect power.

I would also convey my best wishes to the most worthy Amaryk and to your aunt, with my hopes that all of you are well, and that you may all realize your own deepest hopes in these troubling times.

I also must apologize for the penmanship of this letter, but because of the nature of the injuries to my arm, it will be some time before grace returns to the form of my correspondence, but I have been assured that it will, as surely as both edges of a good and ancient dagger can cut sharply, yet serve high purposes for both factors and their families.

He would have liked to have said more, but he had to assume that anything he sent would be read. He hoped that the reference to the ironworks and trade would at least partly mollify Amaryk and Elbaryk, if either did indeed even see the missive.

He addressed it to the Chatelaine Rachyla, in care of Amaryk, Factor for the Seltyr Elbaryk in Tempre. Later in the day, he would ride into town and take care of getting it sent.

"Sir?" One of the Fourth Battalion rankers stood in his doorway. "One of the outholders to see you."

"Have him come in, if he will."

"Yes, sir."

Shortly, the tall and muscled outholder walked into the study.

Out of courtesy, Mykel stood. "Outholder."

Croyalt looked at Mykel, taking in the arm still bound in the sling. "So it's true, is it? You took on a Reillie sniper squad and the warleader and took them all down, and killed him after you took a crossbow bolt?"

"I didn't get all the snipers," Mykel replied.

Croyalt laughed, a booming sound that filled the small study. Then he asked, "How many?"

"Five snipers."

"Most Cadmians don't get one in a career. No wonder they . . ." He shook his head.

Mykel wondered what the outholder had been about to say.

Croyalt looked squarely at Mykel once more. "I have to congratulate you, if reluctantly. I am told that you deployed your entire force immediately after the flood and earthquake to keep order, and that your men took care of looters and other thieves in the only way that they should be handled."

"Keeping order is one of our assigned duties, Outholder Croyalt."

"So I've been told, but you're the first from headquarters who seems to understand that."

Mykel waited. He had the feeling that was not why the outholder had come to see him.

"I also thought you should know that both the Reillies and the Squawts have declared you a blood enemy of their peoples. They will begin their efforts against you and your forces on Decdi."

Mykel smiled. "I'm sorry for them, then."

"Sorry for them? They must number four times your force."

"All that means is that four times as many will die, and there's no need for it."

"Majer . . . maybe not for you, there's no need for it, but for them, they live for fighting. You and the alectors want to turn them into upland farmers or growers, or foresters or whatever. They do those things to support themselves until it's time to go into battle."

"Most of them don't make good Cadmians. We've tried."

"Of course they don't," snorted Croyalt. "They're not soldiers. They're warriors."

What could Mykel say to that? The world didn't need warriors. Even as he was beginning to understand the need for soldiers, he saw no need for the kinds of people Croyalt called warriors. What was the point of fighting for the sake of fighting, whatever the rationale?

"They fight for honor, and to prove their bravery," Croyalt added.

"I hear what you say, Outholder, and I do appreciate your explanation. But I think it's a poor excuse for a man who has to prove bravery by killing anything, whether it be an animal or another man. We may have to slaughter animals to eat, and I may have to kill Reillies and insurgents and sandwolves to keep order and protect those who cannot protect themselves, but I see no honor in the act of killing anything, even if it is necessary."

Croyalt opened his mouth, then closed it.

Mykel waited for a moment, then added, "I do thank you for coming, and for the information about the Reillies and the Squawts. I don't mean to offend you, and I trust you will take my words as a statement of what I believe and not as an attack upon you."

The outholder nodded slowly. "You just might be right in pitying the Squawts and Reillies." He smiled, an expression that Mykel's Talent interpreted as one embodying elements of sadness and chagrin. "I'll be seeing you, Majer."

"Until then, Outholder."

Mykel did not settle back into his chair for several moments.

71

There were far fewer petitioners in the upper Hall of Justice on Septi, and Dainyl and Patrylon finished well before noon.

"Word gets out quickly," Dainyl said once they were headed down to the lower level.

"The number of petitioners will go up again next week, sir," replied the younger alector. "There are those who have studied what you have said, and they will bring petitions crafted along those lines."

That hardly appealed to Dainyl. "I suppose Dalyrt should accompany me one of these times, so that he knows how I judge."

"He has studied my notes, but that is a matter for each High Alector to decide, sir."

"Notes help, but experience is invaluable," Dainyl replied with a laugh. "It's also more costly."

Patrylon nodded.

Dainyl could tell that the young alector did not exactly agree. Like many of the assistants to High Alectors, Patrylon believed that knowledge and Talent would suffice in any situation. The two certainly granted an alector an advantage, but if Dainyl had not been through his experiences with the ancients, he would have died at least twice already. He wasn't about to mention those, but most of the High Alectors had the same mind-set as Patrylon, and the only real experience they had was in maneuvering around the Palaces of the Duarches, the Hall of Justice, and the Engineering Hall. Sometimes, he wondered if he had that much more, but whatever he had was greater than the others, and certainly more recent.

"Will you be receiving petitions on Duadi, sir?"

"I assume so, but anything could happen between now and then." Especially since his orders to Noryan should have arrived on Londi—if they arrived. If they didn't, that would also create problems, if of a different nature.

When they reached the lower corridor, Dainyl said, "I need to see the recorder. You'll take care of sending the changes in those decisions to the affected alectors?"

"Yes, sir."

Leaving Patrylon, Dainyl slipped into the Table chamber.

Chastyl hurried over. "Yes, sir?"

"I noted something yesterday morning, just before we heard petitions. It might have been connected with the Table. Did anything unusual happen?"

The recorder frowned. "There was something. It was like a Talent wave in the translation tubes, but it was momentary, and none of the other recorders have reported anything."

"I wondered."

"Sir?"

"Yes?"

"The arrangement with the Table in Blackstear?"

Dainyl thought for a moment. "It will have to remain as it is. The Myrmidons don't have enough pteridons to ferry guards up there, and there's no other way to get them there in winter. I'll keep reviewing that, though, and I appreciate your bringing it up."

"Yes, sir. Thank you."

"Thank you, Chastyl." Dainyl offered a smile before slipping out through the small foyer and returning to the small private study. He left the door ajar and sat down behind the table desk.

He needed to consider exactly what issues he wished to bring up with Chembryt . . . and how. He also needed to convey, indirectly and firmly, that he stood behind Khelaryt. Dainyl wasn't that supportive of Khelaryt's views on the Cadmians, but given what Dainyl had seen of Brekylt and his methods, and Ruvryn, he didn't have any alternative to backing Khelaryt.

Less than a glass later, he was in the coach—his official coach as the High Alector of Justice—on his way to the Palace to meet with Chembryt.

The coach came to a stop at the lower level of the north wing of the Palace. Dainyl stepped out, feeling almost underground with the columns and stone rising above him into the upper levels. He walked through the columns to the lower archway, past the two guards with their jagged shortswords, rather than lightcutters—a clear sign that the lower level was not considered as vital as other levels of the Palace. While they stiffened as he walked past, their inspection and interest was clearly cursory.

Chembryt's study was in the northeast corner, and a single assistant sat in the outer study.

"Highest . . . he is expecting you." The eyes of the young

alectress remained slightly downcast as she stepped toward the paneled golden oak door and opened it.

"Thank you," murmured Dainyl as he stepped past her, maintaining his shields, as had gotten to be a firm habit after the events of the past year.

She closed the door behind him. Unlike Khelaryt's study door, it did not *click* warningly, but his boot heels did echo on the stretch of green and gold marble floor between the door and the thick green carpet.

The study was larger than the one Dainyl now had at the Hall of Justice, but by only a third. The walls were paneled in golden oak, and rich deep blue hangings, trimmed in crimson, framed the single window. The oblong table desk was also oak, and clear of all papers, with two oak armchairs on one side and one between it and the wall. On the paneled wall above and behind the single chair was a painting of the Palace, a good two yards in width and little more than half that in height, showing it from the north, as it might have appeared in spring years before. Under the window was a single bookcase, filled to overflowing with ledgers. The one window looked out into a small courtyard that held little more than a white marble table and bench, and a raised green marble planter three yards in length and less than one in width, holding low plants with fading gold blossoms.

Chembryt stood before the table desk, to the side of the chair nearest the window. He inclined his head in welcome.

"I appreciate your taking the time to see me," offered Dainyl.

"You do me the honor of calling on me, and it is always an honor to receive the High Alector of Justice."

"It's equally an honor to be received by the High Alector of Finance," replied Dainyl.

Chembryt gestured to the chairs in front of the table desk, then seated himself in one.

Dainyl took the other, turning it slightly so that he could look directly at the older High Alector.

"If I might note," began Chembryt cautiously, "your Talent and shields bear a certain tinge. Green, I believe."

"Unhappily, yes," agreed Dainyl. "You might call that a combat injury. It occurred in the Hyalt operation last harvest . . ." He went on to explain how Rhelyn had used the ancients' Talent weapon against him, finally concluding, "I had hoped the effect would fade, and at times it has seemed to, but then it returns. The Duarches are both aware of it, and it has not seemed to trouble them."

"It does give you a dangerous aura, and that is not all unwelcome for the High Alector of Justice, not in these days and times. I had heard you have been receiving petitions . . ."

"I have. Necessary and informative as it is, it is also discouraging to see the pettiness behind so many of them."

"The steers can be petty, and many are." Chembryt laughed. "If we're being honest, though, I'd have to say that so are some alectors."

"But it's usually not over golds."

"No. That's true. It's more likely to be over who controls what resources or what land."

"That sounds very familiar," suggested Dainyl. "That was what happened last year in Coren and in a few other places."

"It will be a growing problem in years to come as there are more and more steers, and more alectors. They only think of golds, and we want matters our way and tend not to think of why they think of golds."

"Why is that, do you think?"

"They have so many children. How could they not think of golds? They must feed and clothe them, teach and train them." Abruptly, Chembryt shook his head. "I must confess that I miss your wife, not that I begrudge her the fortune and recognition of being regional alector. She was the best chief assistant I ever had. That's saying quite a bit, you know."

Dainyl smiled. "I've known for many years that she was extraordinarily capable."

"Everyone thought that the only reason you became operations chief for the Myrmidons was because Shastylt wanted whatever information she might pass to you—and because you could rely on her."

"I've always been able to rely on her," replied Dainyl. "Her judgment is excellent."

"That may well be, Dainyl, but it is clear from even casual observation that you have more Talent-strength than did either Shastylt or Zelyert. Yet neither of them recognized that. Nor did I when you appeared before the High Alectors not that long ago. Now, even behind shields, you approach Khelaryt in strength."

"Lystrana counseled me early to develop shields first, and I did." Dainyl shrugged. "I found it useful." He paused. "There is no way . . . I would not wish to be presumptuous or ingenuous . . . but I have no interest in becoming Duarch. I have even less interest in having Khelaryt replaced, or in seeing more power in the hands of Samist or Brekylt."

"I had wondered . . ."

"Wonder no more." Dainyl laughed. "I'm a Myrmidon, and I prefer to avoid indirection in all its forms. Lystrana could tell you that, if she has not already."

"She has mentioned that." Chembryt pursed his lips. "How did you manage for Lystrana to be appointed regional alector?"

"I asked. I actually asked for her to become regional alector in Tempre, but she was offered Dereka. The choice was hers."

"So she said."

"I could not ask her to do that which was not in her interest and nature."

"I can see that."

There was a silence.

"What information might I provide?" Chembryt's eyes held a twinkle. "That you have not already discovered?"

"How did Ruvryn manage to conceal the diversion of enough golds to produce over five thousand Cadmian rifles to ship to indigens and landers across the western half of Corus?"

Chembryt pulled at his chin. "You phrased that inquiry in a rather interesting fashion, and one that supposes that such rifles were in fact produced and diverted."

Dainyl laughed. "I've already documented over three thousand. Ruvryn has avoided any direct answer, and it appears that neither Shastylt nor Zelyert wished to dwell on the matter. At least, I never received a satisfactory explanation. Why, I cannot say, but the fact of the production and diversion is not up for question. Nor is the production of a number of portable weapons based on road-building equipment that were used against Myrmidons by Regional Alector Rhelyn. Both of those bring up the question of how such enterprises were paid for."

"Simply put, the funds were requested for other purposes, in a number of accounts that had been inflated for years. When we discovered the irregularities, we originally supposed that the diversions had gone entirely into the heavier lightcutting weapons, especially after the unfortunate events involving Zestafyn. Until she was given some clues, even Lystrana could not deduce what was occurring, and then only after looking at the internal records of the High Alector of Engineering."

"Was Zestafyn only what he was supposed to be?"

Chembryt smiled. "That is another interesting question. You might wish to clarify it."

"I have the feeling that he was more. Otherwise his wife would not have been able to kill herself with a weapon she did not have, supposedly in sorrow over his death, but in fact even before she could have known about it."

"It is rumored that she was not unfamiliar with those connected to the Archon, but there was never any proof. I assume that is what you were asking."

"I said I was poor at indirection," Dainyl replied with a laugh.

"What else would you like to know?"

"I think you have been more than kind," Dainyl said, "and I will save other inquiries for the time when I know enough to ask." That was more true than Chembryt would have guessed, Dainyl judged, and he did not wish to admit too much ignorance, nor to press at the moment. "I thank you for your kindness."

"And I appreciate your forthrightness. Khelaryt is fortunate, indeed."

"I'm fortunate that he is Duarch."

"We both are." Chembryt rose.

Dainyl stood, and the two High Alectors laughed.

72

Since he did not have to receive petitions on Octdi, Dainyl spent the first few glasses of the morning going over the master ledgers of the High Alector of Justice. He learned little, except that the golds allotted to the Cadmian Mounted Rifle Regiments had been decreased each year for the past three years. There was a discretionary account for the High Alector of five thousand golds, but no details on the expenditures. On what had Zelyert spent five thousand golds every year? Or had he?

He finally summoned Adya and had her sit down at the table in his private study.

"The High Alector's discretionary account—on what are those funds spent?"

"The Highest is only accountable to the Duarches for such a discretionary account."

That told Dainyl less than nothing, since any of the High Alectors were accountable only to the Duarch to whom they reported. "Are there any records of that account?"

"I do not know, sir. Luftyne would be the only one who could answer that."

At that moment, there was a knock on the study door.

"The Marshal of Myrmidons is here, sir," offered Patrylon.

"Have her come in." Dainyl stood and looked at Adya. "We'll finish this after I talk to the marshal—and bring Luftyne."

"Yes, sir."

Behind the pleasant tone, she was worried. That, Dainyl could sense, but not why.

Alcyna stepped into the small study and inclined her head. "Highest . . ."

"You can close the door." Dainyl gestured to the chairs.

Alcyna took one. "This is a very modest study."

"Your study has a far better view," he replied with a smile. "I assume there's a problem, since you hurried here."

"Yes, sir. We got a message from the Cadmian commander in Iron Stem. It was addressed to you as Marshal of Myrmidons. I took the liberty of opening it." Alcyna placed the dispatch on the table. "There was an earthquake and a flood. The dam west of Iron Stem burst, and the ironworks has been almost totally destroyed. Nothing else was severely damaged."

"The ancients," said Dainyl.

"How can you surmise that? He never mentioned them."

"An earthquake and a flood that destroy only the ironworks? In one of the towns closest to the Aerlal Plateau, where there have been increasingly frequent reports of the ancients' creatures? When Ruvryn has been pressing for production of more iron and copper?" Dainyl frowned. "You better send a dispatch to both Duarches and to Ruvryn . . . if you haven't already. Just the facts, and nothing about the ancients . . . but note that it is unusual for damage to be so severe in one area while yards away there was little."

"I left Zernylta to draft them while I briefed you. I'll add that observation."

"Ruvryn will try to blame us, either for lack of timely warning or for being the cause of the problem. It might be best if you told him you were sending the message on the chance that he had not already heard from his engineers. Oh . . . if you have not already considered it, send a note thanking Majer Mykel for his thoughtfulness in keeping you informed."

"I had thought to do so." She frowned. "I cannot say I have ever seen a Cadmian dispatch directly to the Myrmidons, even a copied dispatch."

"He is the only Cadmian officer I know who ever has."

"Trusting a Cadmian can be dangerous, sir."

"No more dangerous than trusting Samist or Brekylt. Besides, receiving and encouraging information is not quite the same as trusting."

Alcyna nodded, if dubiously.

"Have you heard anything from Submarshal Noryan?"

"No, sir. But it is not likely that he would have received your orders yet."

That was all too true, and there was little to be done there until Dainyl knew how Noryan would react. Or Josaryk, for that matter, still in Lysia, presumably.

"What do you recommend we do about Iron Stem?" asked Dainyl.

"Send two pteridons from Tempre on a reconnaissance."

Dainyl nodded. "Also have them check the Vedra at Dekhron. Is there anything else?"

"When will you release the Myrmidons from duty in Blackstear?"

"Whenever you can spare enough pteridons for two or three days to ferry five or six alector guards up there—assuming we can find any."

"I can spare two trainees more than the squad of Myrmidons. Can you find three more guards, sir? If so, we can ferry them up in the morning, weather permitting. At dawn."

"Plan on it, then. I'll talk to Chastyl." Dainyl smiled. "Is there anything else?"

"Not at the moment, sir." Alcyna returned the smile.

Once Alcyna left, Dainyl walked to the Table chamber looking for Chastyl, but only Diordyn, his assistant, was there.

"When he returns, tell the recorder I need a moment with him."

"Yes, sir."

He returned to his study, only to find Adya standing in the corridor with a wiry alectress who carried two ledgers, one heavy and thick, and the other slim. From the dark purple of her aura, Dainyl judged she was possibly the oldest assistant serving the High Alector of Justice.

"This is Luftyne, sir," said Adya.

"Highest." Luftyne bowed.

" 'Sir' will do." Dainyl closed the door and walked to the table, seating himself and waiting for them to sit down.

"How might I serve you?"

"There is a discretionary account of some five thousand golds . . ." Dainyl waited.

"That is the amount for the year, Highest. At the moment, the balance is slightly over five hundred. That is not unusual, since it is so close to the end of the financial year."

"Is it possible to determine where the golds in the account went?"

"That depends. If you as High Alector draw the golds personally, the ledgers will only show that the golds were paid to you. If you transfer funds to another account in Justice, say to the Marshal of Myrmidons, then the ledgers would show that."

"I'd like to see the records for that account for the past few years."

"Yes, Highest." Luftyne glanced to Adya. "According to the Code of Accounts set forth by the Duarches, discretionary accounts may only be reviewed by the chief of accounts, the High Alector who has control of the account, and the Duarch to whom that High Alector reports."

"By your leave?" offered Adya.

"By my leave," Dainyl replied.

Only when the study door had closed behind Adya did Luftyne open the smaller ledger and set it before Dainyl. "Did you wish me to explain from the beginning of this year?"

"First, let me ask something. Could I spend all the golds in this account on myself?"

"Yes, sir. As High Alector, you receive two thousand golds a year. For a High Alector, that is often insufficient, particularly if one must host the Duarches often."

Dainyl hadn't even thought about entertaining—or that it might be part of the position of High Alector. But then, who had paid for the time when Brekylt had hosted him and Alcyna?

"As you will see, sir, High Alector Zelyert drew only a few hundred golds for personal use, but his predecessor drew a great deal more. That was many years ago, of course."

"Perhaps you should go over the expenditures for this year."

"Yes, sir. There are only a few expenditures every year. The first use of funds did not occur until the third of Duem, and that was a transfer of two hundred golds to the High Alector personally, with the note that it represented coming travel and entertainment expenses."

"Are there any expenditures or transfers of funds to other High Alectors?"

Luftyne frowned, fleetingly, before she replied. "There was a transfer of two thousand golds to the High Alector of Engineering on the thirty-third of Duem. That was for engineering services and equipment." Luftyne laid the ledger flat and pointed to the entry.

Dainyl scanned the page, noting that the next entry on the fifteenth of Quattrem was a transfer of one thousand golds to the Marshal of Myrmidons' account for "expenses relating to Dramur." Other entries of smaller amounts ranged from ten golds for a matched pair of bays for the High Alector's coach to thirty golds for shimmersilk for ceremonial garments. In mid-Octem, Zelyert had also transferred five hundred golds from the discretionary account to the Hall of Justice operating account for paying and equipping the new Table guards.

Finally, Dainyl looked up from the ledger. "I'll need to study this in greater detail, but that will do for now. Thank you." He still needed to think out what he was going to say when he met with Alseryl later in the day.

"Whatever the Highest requires." The accounting chief rose, bowed, and backed out of the private study.

Before Dainyl had a chance to puzzle through the implications of what the discretionary ledger had revealed or to think about how best to deal with Alseryl, Chastyl knocked.

"Come in." Dainyl did not stand.

"You wanted me, sir."

"Yes. You'd asked about the Blackstear Table. The Myrmidons can ferry five guards up tomorrow morning. The marshal will supply two Myrmidon trainees, but that means you'll need to designate three other guards to go to Blackstear. They'll need to be at Myrmidon headquarters a half glass before dawn, dressed in heavy-weather gear. It's a long flight and a very cold one."

Chastyl swallowed. "Sir . . . we're stretched thin here."

"I'm sure you are, but there are very few times that the marshal will be able to do this." Dainyl smiled. "I'm certain that you can work this out."

"Yes, sir." The recorder bowed. "How long will they be there? Would both alectors and alectresses be acceptable?"

"They could be there for the rest of winter, and for Triem and possibly Quattrem. If they're qualified, I'm sure Delari would not have any problems."

"There will be three guards at Myrmidon headquarters, sir."

As Chastyl departed, Dainyl could sense both frustration and relief. He closed his private study door. He needed some time to think.

73

While Mykel had hoped to ride with one of the Third Battalion companies on Sexdi or Septi, the ironworks disaster precluded his even considering going on a patrol until Octdi. He had ridden through Iron Stem a number of times, and he had dispatched his letter to Rachyla through the wool factor, although whether she would receive it and how she—or Amaryk—would take it he could not predict. He had cut back on patrols to allow greater rest for the men, and particularly for their mounts, in the event that Croyalt's information proved to be accurate. He could not dispense with them entirely, not when the sandwolves seemed ever more daring.

A half glass after morning muster, under a clear sky with a penetrating chill wind blowing out of the northeast, Mykel was riding across the garrison courtyard toward Undercaptain Dyarth and Thirteenth Company. His arm was still in the sling, and bound, under his winter riding jacket, not because of the arm itself, but to reduce pressure on the injured shoulder.

"Sir?" Dyarth turned in the saddle.

"I'll be accompanying you today, Undercaptain."

"Yes, sir."

Mykel waited, his roan slightly back of the undercaptain's chestnut, while Dyarth received the reports from his squad leaders. He eased his mount beside the chestnut when Thirteenth Company began to ride toward the gates.

Once on the high road, Mykel turned his mount northward. His eyes lingered on the green tower just to the west. Not for the first time, he wondered why the windowless towers had even been built, but that mystery was one that could wait.

They had traveled half a vingt north on the high road before the undercaptain spoke. "Sir . . . do you plan any changes to the patrol route or operations?"

"No, Undercaptain. I'm just here to observe." Mykel wasn't all that sure he'd be much good at more than that, but he'd spent far less time with Thirteenth Company than some of the others. Besides, he'd wanted to get another look at the area to the northeast of Iron Stem, the area patrolled by the company—partly in response to inholder complaints about sandwolves.

"Do you think that we'll be seeing more and more of the sandwolves?"

"I think it's likely, but I can't tell you why." Mykel couldn't, not without revealing far more than he felt safe doing. The increased sandwolf attacks were a way for the soarers to put pressure on the alectors, as had been the attack—and it could have been nothing less—upon the ironworks.

"Right north of town, once you get past the hovels, there's nothing here except dry grasslands." Dyarth gestured at the sparse grasslands stretching away on both sides of the high road. There were but few structures anywhere, and most looked to be either abandoned or storage huts of some sort. "You can ride vingts and not see anyone or a proper house."

"It looks desolate, all right." Mykel's Talent told him that there was more life than met the eye. "But there has to be more than we see, or the holders wouldn't be here, and the sandwolves wouldn't have enough to eat."

"Can't be too much, sir, or they wouldn't be raiding the inholders."

"I don't know about that. The outholders seem to be a pretty tough group. Maybe the sandwolves find the pickings easier close to town."

Dyarth frowned, then replied, "That could be, and they

want us to take care of the problem so that they don't have to work as hard as the outholders."

The patrol followed the high road four vingts north before turning eastward on one of the holder access lanes, although it was almost a true road, wide enough for two mounts comfortably abreast, unlike many, which were barely able to handle a single mount or a narrow cart.

To Mykel, the farther north and east they rode, away from the high road, the more the air smelled and tasted metallic, as if a cold and rusty sabre had been laid on his tongue and he'd inhaled deeply.

The patrol had covered another two vingts, and the winter sun was well clear of the Aerlal Plateau, whose cliffs ran like a wall across the eastern horizon, when Mykel began to sense a faint violet-gray—the aura of sandwolves—as well as something else, a blackish gray that he had not sensed before. His best judgment was that the sandwolves and the other creatures were at least half a vingt ahead, probably in the vale to the northeast of the lane that followed the ridgelines of the hills.

"There's something ahead," Mykel said quietly. "I'd suggest ordering 'ready rifles.' "

"Yes, sir." Dyarth turned in the saddle. "Company! Ready rifles!"

"Ready rifles!" echoed the squad leaders.

The blackish gray aura grew stronger, but not that of the sandwolves, as Thirteenth Company followed the holders' road.

Then, as the road edged more to the north and to the side of the ridge, Mykel caught a glimpse of animals below, creatures he'd never seen before.

"We'll need to halt at the curve in the lane ahead," he told Dyarth. "That will give us the best vantage and the high ground."

"Ah . . ."

"For whatever those are, and the sandwolves that are stalking them," replied Mykel, still watching the black-coated animals a good two hundred yards downslope.

"Company! Halt!"

The creatures did not startle, although several glanced up the slope toward the Cadmian force as the troopers reined up.

A pair of males edged toward each other. Mykel assumed they were males from the curled black horns that glittered cruelly on the front edges, as if they had been sharpened like a sabre. Black wool of some sort covered their two-yard-long bodies, and wide and thick shoulders added to their massive and menacing aura. Abruptly the two broke off whatever dispute or dominance conflict that they had barely begun and turned.

Mykel could sense the gray-violet aura of at least one sandwolf even before the creature appeared out of the brush to the east of the small flock. Its long crystal fangs were evident from where Mykel watched as it broke into a run toward one of the smaller black-coated creatures trailing the others.

A large male charged from the flock toward the sandwolf. Mykel didn't think that the smaller creature—although it wasn't that much less in size and perhaps even closer in weight—had much chance against the sandwolf and its fangs. Yet, a moment before the two met, the black male lowered his shoulders and horns, and then twisted his head.

The sandwolf barely let out a howl as it was lifted off the ground and then flung aside, partly disemboweled and dead before it could have realized what had happened.

Mykel swallowed. He could sense more sandwolves, not all that far to the east. He and the company might well seem an easier target than the giant horned killer sheep. "Stand by to fire! Sandwolves! To the south."

"Staggered line abreast! Stand by to fire!" echoed Dyarth.

Mykel wasn't certain how they had managed it, but less than a hundred yards downslope and to the south of the company appeared a pack of the sandwolves. They were moving at full speed, and that was faster than a galloping horse.

"Fire at will!" snapped Dyarth.

Behind the sandwolves, Mykel could sense one of the sanders, but what could he do? Could he will the bullets of another Cadmian to a target?

"Over there!" he called to the ranker slightly behind him. "The sander, the small figure. Fire at it."

"Yes, sir!"

As the man fired, Mykel concentrated on him, his rifle, and the bullet in the chamber. The shot went wide, and Mykel concentrated once more as the ranker fired. All the shots in the magazine missed, and Mykel could feel that it had taken some effort from him.

As the Cadmian reloaded, Mykel decided to concentrate on the bullet alone.

The third shot struck the sander in the shoulder, twisting it down. Mykel could feel the loss of lifeforce and death. Immediately the creature began to disintegrate. Several of the sandwolves had gone down as well, but with the death of the sander, the pack broke and turned.

In moments, the Cadmians were once more alone on the herder's road. Below them, the black creatures grazed, as if nothing had happened.

"That was strange," Dyarth said, reining up beside Mykel. After a moment, he went on. "Is there any reason not to continue the patrol, sir?"

"I think continuing the patrol would be a good idea, Undercaptain. I don't think we'll see any more sandwolves very soon, but you never know."

"Yes, sir." The undercaptain turned in the saddle. "Company! Double column! Forward!"

Mykel and Thirteenth Company only rode another vingt, down through a shallow vale and up onto another ridgeline, before Mykel saw five riders headed toward them. As they drew closer, he recognized the first rider—Outholder Croyalt.

"Have the company halt."

"Company! Halt!"

Mykel rode forward to greet the outholder, reining up yards short of the older man.

"I heard rifles, Majer."

"We ran across some sandwolves—and some other creatures," Mykel replied. "Black and wooly, and the males have sharp curled horns."

"The nightsheep." Croyalt nodded.

"You call those sheep?"

"They have a coat—the wool's more like armor. I'd wager it would make a sturdy cloth." The outholder laughed. "It won't happen in my lifetime, though. You can't domesticate them, and the flesh is poisonous to nearly any animal. Nightsheep can eat anything that's green, but they seem to prefer the quarasote."

Mykel had never heard of quarasote. "What's that?"

"It's a spiny bush that grows in the colder and drier places, mostly near the base of the plateau, but there's some almost everywhere. The older branches will cut through leather, and just about anything else. The scrats eat the seeds, but not much else besides nightsheep will browse on the shoots. Even they prefer the new growth. There's not much quarasote here. That's why we usually don't see them here." Croyalt smiled. "You're fortunate. Not many outsiders do."

"They're dangerous. I saw one gut a sandwolf."

"That's why we leave them alone. They don't attack unless provoked."

"Where did they come from?"

"They've always been around, but they usually stick close to the plateau. This is as far west as I've seen them." The outholder studied Mykel, seemingly taking in his still-injured arm. "You're riding patrols with the Reillies and Squawts likely to come after you in two days?"

"All the more reason to do so, while we can. There were reports of more attacks on the flocks of the inholders."

Croyalt snorted. "They always want someone else to do the hard work of protecting them. They leave the town, and most of them are helpless."

Mykel sensed that the holder's contempt was far stronger than his words. "Some people are like that."

"So they are, Majer." Croyalt nodded briskly. "We need to be moving, and I imagine you do as well. Good day." The holder eased his mount off the lane, as did the four behind him, three men, and a blond woman who looked like Croyalt, except that she reminded Mykel of a soarer as well, although she was almost as tall as Croyalt and Mykel could sense no overt Talent in her. Still, her aura was so dark it might as well have been black, and there were definite streaks of green in it.

Once Thirteenth Company was riding again, more to the southeast, Mykel could make out a holding, with a large house and outbuildings, well to the east. Ahead was a lane leading off the road they were taking that presumably led to the holding. Mykel wondered if it was Croyalt's, or if the outholder had been visiting someone. Sooner or later, he'd find out, he supposed.

In the meantime, he needed to see if he could determine a better way to use his Talent on the bullets and weapons of his men—or at least those close to him. He'd fired a rifle one-handed a few times, but that wasn't a good plan for an officer who was charged with commanding a battalion—especially one who might be facing forces twice his in number before long.

The air still had a metallic feel, and the wind was stronger—and colder.

74

Dainyl was in the coach at a quarter past the first glass of the afternoon, heading toward the Palace for his meeting with the High Alector of Transport. Once more, he stepped out on the lower level, but this time he headed to the northwest corner of the Palace.

As he entered the paneled outer study, Dainyl could see immediately that Alseryl's spaces were effectively the mirror image of Chembryt's.

The alector assistant seated behind the small desk jumped to his feet. "Highest, High Alector Alseryl is expecting you." He took two steps to the door and rapped. "High Alector Dainyl." After a moment, he opened the door, bowing and stepping back.

"Thank you." Dainyl maintained full shields when he stepped into the study.

The assistant closed the door as Dainyl crossed the green and gold marble floor.

Alseryl's study was also paneled in golden oak, with crimson-trimmed deep blue hangings framing the single window, except the window was on the left. The oblong table desk held four neat stacks of papers. An oak armchair was set at each corner of the inner side of the table desk, while the third was behind the desk, centered on the painting of the Palace—one that showed the Palace from the south, clearly in full summer. There were no bookcases.

Alseryl stood directly behind the table desk, using it as a barrier between him and Dainyl. His welcoming nod was less than perfunctory.

"I appreciate your taking the time to see me," offered Dainyl.

"I could do no less." Alseryl seated himself.

Dainyl took the chair closest to the window, moving it slightly so that Alseryl would also be looking toward the window when he faced Dainyl.

"I am normally most politic, Dainyl. You might call it indirect, but among High Alectors, indirection will usually suffice. With you, I cannot be certain of that, not with your . . . background. So I will be less indirect, much as that pains me." Alseryl smiled.

Dainyl disliked the expression, because it conveyed trust, honesty, and concern, and behind the smile were none of those.

"First, I can see that your Talent carries a tinge of green, and that is not normally acceptable for an alector, much less a High Alector, let alone the High Alector of Justice. I can understand the regrettable nature of the injury, and the service performed, but green is green, especially in these times."

"True enough," countered Dainyl, "but both Duarches are aware of the injury and its causes, and the green that resulted has not greatly troubled either."

Those words created a momentary, if hidden consternation, but Alseryl smiled quickly. "I am glad to hear that. As you may know, High Alector Zelyert had great concerns about the future of Acorus, and about the need for a strong framework to ensure that we do not become a mere tool of the Archon or a dumping ground for those who have fallen out of favor in Illustra. You have already demonstrated that you are cut from the same shimmersilk as Zelyert in the matter of restricting long translations by those who would weaken Acorus and shorten the years of useful lifeforce." Alseryl smiled once more, this time condescendingly.

Dainyl nodded. "I believe I have."

"In the other matter, however, your actions, however well intended, have proved less than satisfactory in assuring a framework on which we may build a strong Acorus."

Dainyl had a strong suspicion where Alseryl was heading, but he offered a frown meant to convey worry and concern. "I am glad you are being direct, Alseryl, because I had thought my actions were totally in line with preserving the Duarches."

"It has come to my attention that you informed both Duarches of the pending transfer of the Master Scepter to Efra. In doing so, you reduced the Talent force available to each. Could you explain how reducing the power of the Duarches strengthens Acorus?"

Alseryl couldn't be that stupid. That meant more was at stake. "As you well know, Alseryl," Dainyl replied, "I am a Myrmidon, and I have spent all of my adult life as one, or preparing to be one. In dealing with conflicts and opponents, a Myrmidon learns that there are many kinds of strength. An alector who has massive Talent, but who is unable to use that strength except as another wishes, is often weaker than one with lesser Talent and more flexibility. The shadowmatches prevented either Duarch from considering what might be the best course for Acorus were the Master Scepter *not* to be transferred here. My goal was not to weaken either Duarch, but to give them greater applied strength to deal with the difficulties ahead. In fact, whether you were aware of this or not, Zelyert was pressing me to reveal the transfer to Khelaryt for some time before I did." Dainyl let the truth of that escape.

For a moment, just a moment, Alseryl was silent. "I find that hard to believe, despite your apparent honesty, but perhaps that is because of the greenish tinge to your Talent, a tinge always associated with wildness and rebellion in the past, although you certainly have been the model Myrmidon for many decades, always serving, following orders effectively, and never questioning the reasons behind those orders."

While keeping his shields fully in place, Dainyl had been absorbing the Talent impressions of the chamber. He observed that there was a Talent concentration behind an apparent boss in the crown molding at the top of the paneled wall that held the painting of the Palace, and that power was similar to what he had sensed with Rhelyn's portable lightcannon. Doubtless it was aimed at him—or whoever was seated before the desk. It was positioned high enough and the chairs were set far enough back that the energy would not threaten Alseryl.

"Any alector who has perception is cautious when caution is merited. I have observed that some who had the greatest reasons to be loyal have not been so, and some who seemed less supportive of the Duarches have been far more loyal. Seldom is what one sees all of what is."

"The truth goes beyond mere vision. That is true." Alseryl nodded.

"So does reality, and what is includes more than what many would call the truth."

"For an alector reputed to be direct, your words are somewhat obscure, Dainyl."

"All I was suggesting is that each individual's idea of truth does not usually encompass all of reality." Dainyl shrugged. "Although many have claimed that knowing the truth will set a thinking being free, I've found that such 'truths' reflect a selective vision of the world. Selective visions restrict freedom of action, and such restrictions also reduce an alector's capabilities."

"That sounds perilously close to rejecting the views and guidance of the Duarches and the Archon in favor of your own predilections."

"I must not have made myself clear, Alseryl. The more one

perceives, the more ability one has to carry out the policies of the Archon and the Duarches." *Or to understand why they should not be carried out.*

"That is an intriguing observation."

"How have you found working with the other High Alectors?" asked Dainyl. "I have yet to even meet Jaloryt and Zuthyl."

"We all share the concerns of the Duarches and the Archon. Jaloryt is faced with the unenviable task of making sure that the pursuit of golds in trade by the steers does not reduce the world's lifeforce. Zuthyl has his difficulties as well."

"What of you? Have the problems with the South Pass required great adjustments in the sandox routes?"

"Some adjustments, but not great ones. The greatest difficulty has been, as I am certain Marshal Alcyna has conveyed to you, the increased requirement for Myrmidon trainees from our sandox drivers and assistant drivers. It seems rather strange that the requirements have increased so dramatically recently, coincidentally, as it were, with two new marshals."

"They have increased dramatically," Dainyl replied, "but the increase resulted from higher casualties, and those casualties, as I am certain you are aware, resulted from the increased activity of the ancients and from the late Rhelyn's attempt to use unauthorized translations to attempt to create an independent Duarchy in Hyalt. Of course, Brekylt's misreading of the situation compounded matters as well, but that has been resolved for the time being."

"Oh?"

"The Alector of the East and I had a lengthy conversation several weeks ago, and he understands quite thoroughly my views and my support of the Duarch Khelaryt."

"I am glad to hear of that support."

"My support of the Duarch has never been in question." Dainyl smiled. "But then, I'm sure you understand that."

"That is true. Khelaryt is fortunate to have a High Alector of Justice so devoted and supportive."

"Is that not the duty of a High Alector?"

"It is indeed." Alseryl smiled once more. "And it has been

a pleasure to learn how seriously you take that duty." He rose, almost languidly.

"As it has been for me, to hear your words and observations." Dainyl stood and inclined his head just slightly. "Until later."

He could feel Alseryl's eyes on his back as he left the paneled study.

While he walked down the columned Palace corridor, out toward the waiting coach, Dainyl had no doubts as to where Aseryl stood, and that was with Ruvryn and Samist, even though Aseryl reported directly to Khelaryt. The hidden lightcannon in Alseryl's study suggested strongly that Aseryl was allied to Ruvryn and had been for some time.

He didn't know whether to hope that the Archon moved the Master Scepter soon or whether it would be best if he had more time. He shook his head. Just what could he do until they acted?

75

Outside the headquarters building, intermittent gusts of wind rattled the narrow window of the study where Mykel sat, studying the map spread across a writing table desk small enough that both ends of the map drooped over the sides of the desk. Although it was close to midafternoon, Mykel had been studying the maps since early on Novdi morning, trying to develop a better sense of how to use the roads and terrain to trap the Reillies and the Squawts.

Rhystan appeared in the doorway. "Sir, Jasakyt has just ridden in. He's got news about the Reillies. They're getting ready to move." The captain paused. "What about the other scouts?"

"They're farther west and south. I can't say when they'll be back. Gather the officers in the mess. Jasakyt can tell us all at once. We'll have to brief Loryalt when he returns."

Rhystan nodded, then left.

Mykel stood and rolled up the large map, one-handed and

awkwardly, before tucking it under his left arm and leaving the study. Croyalt had been right, not that Mykel had doubted the outholder, but the fact that such information was widespread meant that any failure by Mykel and the Cadmians would spark even greater insurgency in the west of Corus. With the regiment significantly understrength, the last thing the Cadmians needed was to fight more insurgents.

Mykel was the first in the officers' mess. He set the map on one end of the large table and looked up as Culeyt appeared.

"We're getting word on the Reillies, sir?"

Mykel nodded.

Shortly, Dyarth and Fabrytal joined them, followed by Captain Hamylt and Undercaptain Sendryrk of Fourth Battalion. The last to arrive were Rhystan and Jasakyt.

"We might as well sit down," said Mykel, following his own suggestion. "Jasakyt, tell us what you found out."

"Yes, sir." The lanky scout remained standing. "The Reillies are breaking up from that big gathering they had. The only ones that are leaving are the older women and small children, and a handful of graybeards. They look to be heading back into the higher hills to the west of Wesrigg. Yesterday, a bunch of Squawts rode in, but most of them rode out early this morning. Two heavy wagons came in late yesterday, too."

"Supplies or ammunition," murmured Culeyt.

The wagons bothered Mykel, because they suggested an outside provider of provisions or ammunition. While he hoped that such a provider was not an alector, if he had to wager, he would have bet that the provider was either a rebel alector or one of the High Alectors with the goal of weakening the Cadmians. Otherwise, the earlier smuggling of Cadmian rifles to Dramur, and even the creation of the Alector's Guard in Tempre, made little sense. And Mykel was quite certain that the alectors seldom acted without a definite purpose.

"What about mounts?" he asked.

"They've got more mounts than possible fighters, sir." Jasakyt stopped for a moment, then added, "The younger women carry rifles, too, and so do the older boys. It's hard to tell, but some of the young ones might be older girls. They all dress the same, and their hair's about the same length."

"So we have to shoot women and girls, too?" asked Fabrytal.

"If you don't," replied Mykel, "they'll shoot you." He glanced at his own shoulder. "They don't care much for any of us. As I can tell you."

There were several chuckles from the officers.

"How many Reillies are there?" asked Mykel.

"I couldn't get a good count, sir, but somewhere over five hundred of fighting age. If you count the young ones with rifles, might be as many as eight hundred."

That was more than Mykel had left in Third and Fourth Battalions combined—and didn't include whatever force the Squawts added. "Did you get any idea of where they're headed?"

"They sent a party, not sure you could call 'em scouts, down that southeast road, the one that leads to the west of Sudon toward Borlan. No one was headed toward Iron Stem."

That made sense to Mykel. The locals were going to force a confrontation. They knew the Cadmians would likely have to protect Borlan, and if Mykel didn't, they'd take the bridge across the Vedra and raid the town. He'd thought that was the most likely possibility all along.

"It's already winter in the hills, and they want to fight now?" asked Dyarth.

"Why not?" replied Rhystan. "They like to fight, and the harvesting and gathering's done. They're used to the snow, and we're not. Besides, we don't have any snow on the ground here, not yet. So, if we chase them back into the hills, we're at a disadvantage, and they can scatter."

"We don't let them scatter," said Mykel. "We have to win decisively, or Third Battalion or some other Cadmian battalion will be fighting the same people next summer and fall. Do any of you want that?"

The murmured "no, sir" gave an answer, although Mykel would have wished for a slightly less resigned tone from his officers.

He leaned forward and unrolled the map. "Here's what we're going to do."

76

Dainyl had finally taken the Table from Elcien to Dereka a glass before noon on Novdi. He'd felt guilty about leaving early, although the Hall of Justice was largely deserted by then, since most alectors in Elcien regarded all of Novdi as a full end-day and not the half end-day practiced by the Myrmidons. He'd arrived in Dereka a glass past noon, local reckoning, but Jonyst's second driver had been glad to take him to the RA's complex. He still found the ancient construction odd, with the extended quarters for the RA running practically to the outer wall, and effectively splitting the rear courtyard in two. Once more, he also wondered why the original structure had been built half over a Talent-dead area. Had the builders not considered it? Or had the area not been Talent-dead? Or had they been less perceptive?

As Dainyl left the coach and walked up to the outer door under a sky covered with high gray clouds, he tried to put aside his worries. At the moment, there was little he could do, and worrying wouldn't help. For all that, he couldn't stop the broad smile when Lystrana opened the door herself.

"I thought it might be the High Alector." She opened the iron gratework door and stepped back.

"The High Alector is in Elcien. Your husband is here." Dainyl gently wrapped both arms around her.

"Is that a promise?" Her words were muffled against his shoulder.

"So long as the regional alector doesn't show up. After I tell you one thing."

"Just one thing?"

"One of the dual scepters is somewhere in Dereka," Dainyl murmured in her ear. "The other is in Lysia."

Lystrana stiffened. "How did you . . ."

"Khelaryt told me. That's why Sevasya—"

"And Jonyst . . . and the separate building here for the recorder. It has to be there somewhere."

"That's what I thought." He kissed her neck. "That's all, but I wanted you to know."

"So you'll stop being the High Alector now?"

"I can manage that."

For a time, they held tight to each other, before Lystrana freed herself. "I need to breathe . . . and close the doors."

"Let me." Dainyl closed and locked both before turning back to her.

"You're still carrying that greenish Talent. Is it stronger when you haven't eaten?" She paused, then asked, "Have you eaten?"

"Enough for now. I'm not hungry."

"Come and tell me what's happened. I'd like to sit down. We can use the sitting room. I hadn't realized how isolated an RA could be." She headed across the foyer, but before she reached the archway, she winced, ever so slightly.

"Is something the matter?" Even with Talent, Dainyl couldn't tell whether the pain came from Lystrana or their daughter.

"Kytrana's upset," Lystrana admitted.

"Is she . . . ?" Dainyl didn't know quite what to ask.

"Growing pains. It happens. Sometimes they sense things. It doesn't have to be bad. It can even be a strong feeling."

"Like seeing your husband?"

"Or hearing about a scepter." She nodded. "But it takes her a while to settle down."

"When does it look like?"

"Not until the middle of Duem, maybe Triem—three months from now." She stiffened, almost imperceptibly.

"Why don't we take a coach ride? Might that not help?"

"Using the coach for personal ends?" Lystrana raised her left eyebrow. "On an end-day?"

"Isn't one of the drivers on duty? He'd rather be driving than sitting doing nothing."

"She," corrected Lystrana. "It's still personal use."

"Have you actually toured Dereka since you got here?"

"No. I haven't had time."

"Don't you think you should? You are the RA, you know? Do you want the reputation of being aloof?" Dainyl grinned.

"Or not knowing where things are?" His stomach growled.

"You need to eat," she replied. "Go get something from the kitchen. I'm sure you can find something. I'll let Dunneta know we'll need the coach."

"Yes, dear . . . and regional highest." He grinned.

"Go."

Dainyl went.

He found some white cheese and some flaky rolls. Only after he'd eaten three rolls and a goodly amount of the cheese did he admit to himself that he had been hungrier than he'd thought.

"So . . . you'd eaten enough?" Lystrana stood in the doorway to the expansive kitchen, furnished with two large porcelain stoves, a large water cooler for the cheeses and other items, and a fully-stocked walk-in pantry larger than their kitchen in Elcien. She wore a light jacket over her loose but heavy tunic and vest.

He shrugged. "I was mistaken."

"You're still carrying that Talent-green."

"I don't know what to do about it. I've been shielding it as much as I can."

"You'll think of something. The coach is ready when you are."

Dainyl swallowed the last of the cheese, chasing it down with sweet cider, then used the kitchen sink to wash his hands. "I'm ready."

They walked out to the private entrance—the only one Dainyl had used—where the coach was waiting.

Lystrana stopped and looked at the driver. "Drive us north along the boulevard, Dunneta. We'll go all the way to the north end of the city."

"Yes, Highest." The darker-skinned indigen woman nodded.

Dainyl opened the coach door for his wife, then joined her, sitting beside her on the narrow bench seat. The seat cushion was at least yielding.

As the coach pulled out through the gates, Dainyl glanced back through the opening in the goldenstone walls at the massive structure. "Do you really need a building that big?"

"No. When it was built, the idea was that there would be an

administrative center in the middle of Corus, one to match Alustre in the east."

"It didn't work out that way. Was that because of the lack of water?"

"That . . . and no alectors wanted to live here. It makes most alectors uncomfortable."

"Does it bother you?"

"At times. By the end of the day, though, both Dyena and Garatyl can't wait to leave. Going back to the quarters is a relief for me. It's strange how such a short distance makes such a difference." Lystrana eased down the coach window on her side. "Would you?"

"You're hot? It's chilly here, far cooler than in Elcien."

"Pregnancy makes even alectresses a great deal warmer, dearest."

Dainyl eased his coach window down, and surreptitiously fastened his jacket.

Behind the RA's complex, to the east, Dainyl caught sight of the narrower gray eternastone aqueduct that ran northward, parallel to the paved yellowstone boulevard. He glanced farther north along the boulevard, catching sight of the gold eternastone building of the recorder, and the larger one to the north of it. Beyond both rose the green eternastone tower, and the aqueduct of the ancients that ran westward to the Upper Spine Mountains, paralleling the main eternastone high road, although the road had been built by alector engineers to follow the aqueduct.

"Who uses the other ancient building?"

"It's used as a warehouse. No one really wants to live or work in it. Half is for grain and crop storage, and it does seem to preserve them better than most granaries."

Dainyl glanced past Lystrana to look at the shops on the west side of the boulevard, realizing that the boulevard was really three streets—the main one in the center, down which they drove, and narrower ones on each side for pedestrians and street merchants, separated from the wider center section boulevard by two yards of raised stone.

The shops were of yellowstone, with roofs of split dark slate and narrow windows that required less wood for their shutters. As gray as Dereka often seemed, Dainyl couldn't help but feel how dark the insides of those structures would be, especially for landers and indigens without an alector's night sight.

Ahead loomed the ancient aqueduct, but before the coach reached it, they crossed the eternastone high road that began in the west at Elcien and spanned the continent to end at Alustre in the east. To the north of the high road, the boulevard became eternastone as well.

As they passed under the arch of the ancient aqueduct, Dainyl looked up, studying it with both eyes and Talent. There was indeed a faint Talent residue—an amber-green within the very stone—and he wondered how many thousands of years before it had been built.

He shook his head.

"What is it, dearest?" asked Lystrana.

"Oh . . . just the aqueduct . . . and the goldenstone buildings. The ancients are small, tiny compared to us, yet they built all this who knows how long ago, and they still stand. They have at least one city with soaring towers on the Aerlal Plateau, where pteridons cannot even venture. Yet most of the High Alectors dismiss them as little threat at all."

"It isn't just the aqueduct, is it?"

"The ironworks and the dam that served it were totally destroyed this past week, by a directed flood and an earthquake. Earlier, the Vedra flooded and ripped out all the piers in Dekhron and Borlan. I've seen them destroy two pteridons. Noryan watched them destroy another pair. But they aren't a threat." Dainyl couldn't keep the bitter irony out of his voice.

Less than half a vingt north of the aqueduct, Dereka ended. There were no more dwellings or shops, only the high road heading north to Aelta, and off to the northeast some thousand yards, the gray walls of the Cadmian compound.

"You can head back south now, Dunneta!" called Lystrana.

The driver guided the team around the turnout and headed back southward.

"How is Kytrana feeling?" asked Dainyl.

"She's settled down. The coach ride was a good idea."

"I do have some, you know," Dainyl replied with a laugh. "Does Dereka seem to upset her? Or your headquarters?"

"I haven't noticed that. Not yet, anyway. I'll watch for it, though, as I get nearer to term. If need be, I'll have meetings and see people in the quarters."

"Good thought." Dainyl cleared his throat, trying not to shiver.

"You can close the window partway, dearest."

"I'm all right."

"I'm not so hot as I was."

Dainyl eased the window up a third of the way, ignoring his wife's smile. As the coach neared the center of Dereka, he tried to get a better feel for the small city. It was as though a darkness lay beneath it. Not the darkness of horror or evil, but more the darkness that underlay the translation tubes . . . yet . . . it wasn't quite the same.

"You have that look. What are you thinking?"

"There's more here than meets the eye, or even Talent."

She nodded. "I've felt that as well, and it's not just the Talent-dead areas. It's like a presence . . . someone or something that departed, and yet hasn't."

Was that it? Dainyl wasn't certain, but he didn't have a better description.

Once they had passed the RA's complex heading south, to the west Dainyl saw the next walled enclosure and the two-story structures within. "Have you visited the engineers?"

"Once. Thuvryn was polite, but little else."

"Thuvryn? Is he related to—"

"He's Ruvryn's nephew, and even less pleasant than his uncle."

"So far, I've found Ruvryn to be less unpleasant than Alseryl. I met with Alseryl yesterday, and he was thoroughly unpleasant. He's also allied with Ruvryn."

"That doesn't surprise me. A hungry grass snake has more sense and ethics."

"Matters could come to a head this week. Noryan should finally receive my orders to bring Third and Fourth Companies here to Dereka."

"Will he do it? Will Brekylt let him?"

"That's what we'll find out."

"Does Khelaryt know?"

"I never mentioned it to him, and he never asked directly."

"That's probably for the best, since only you and Chembryt truly support him. What will you do if Noryan refuses?"

"I don't know that I can do anything, except tell Khelaryt. I thought it would be best to see if I could remove the Myrmidons from the east before Brekylt made an open break. If it doesn't work, we're no worse off than we are now."

"Until Samist and Brekylt order them against you."

"They might not. I don't think any of us want Myrmidon to fight Myrmidon."

"That would mean that Brekylt will have neutralized the Myrmidons, and Khelaryt will lose."

Left unsaid was the implication that Dainyl would also lose.

"I can hope we don't have to fight, but . . . you're right."

She nodded sadly.

Neither spoke as the coach carried them along the yellowstone road that had replaced the boulevard once they had left the houses and buildings behind, since the Myrmidon compound was almost a full vingt south of Dereka.

"It looks almost forlorn out here," observed Lystrana. "Today, especially. Gray walls, gray buildings, gray skies . . ."

"Maybe that's why the ancients left."

"I don't think so . . . but I doubt that we'll ever know that."

Dainyl couldn't help but agree. Yet there was something deeper about Dereka, and that bothered him, especially since he'd been the one to maneuver Lystrana into becoming RA. He hoped he didn't regret it.

77

After an early breakfast with Lystrana on Londi, Dainyl used her coach to travel the short distance to the recorder's building in Dereka. He would arrive in Elcien a good glass earlier than usual, but he could not help being apprehensive and wanting to be in the Hall of Justice, for all that he knew Noryan would likely not receive his orders until later in the day and decide well after that—if the orders reached him at all.

For the first time since Dainyl could remember, Jonyst was not the one on duty in the Dereka Table chamber. Instead, a stocky alectress with violet eyes—but black wavy hair—stood there with a welcoming smile. Behind her were four guards, but after they took in his purple-trimmed greens, their eyes and concentration turned away.

"Good morning, Highest."

"Good morning. You must be Whelyne. Are the Tables operating as they should be?"

"At the moment, yes, sir."

"Have you been seeing greater or fewer wild translations? Or unauthorized ones?"

"The unauthorized ones have dropped off to almost nothing, sir. Wild translations are fewer, but not by that much."

"I see." He nodded. "Thank you." That confirmed for him that the Archon had clamped down on Table access, and that the majority of wild translations were authorized but undertaken by those without sufficient Talent control to reach Acorus safely. Then, it could be as simple as the fact that few alectors with Talent and knowledge enough to try the Tables were left on Ifryn.

He stepped up onto the Table and concentrated, sliding down through the silvered surface.

The translation tube was more like being in a purple-shaded early twilight than the near-total darkness he recalled from his first translations from Lyterna, less than a year before. Around him, in the mild chill, he could sense an intermittent streak of purple, and then another. The looming presence of amber-green energy was stronger and more distant, a combination that unsettled him.

He concentrated on the white locator that was Elcien, and extended a Talent probe, trying to ignore the fact that it was more green than purple in the translation tube. Before he could fully finish that thought, he was flashing through the white-silver barrier and . . .

. . . standing on the Elcien Table, his shields strong and firm.

Chastyl stood in one corner of the chamber. "Sir."

"Good morning, Recorder." Dainyl stepped off the Table. "Are you still getting wild translations from Ifryn?"

"Yes, sir."

"How many compared to a few weeks ago?"

"It's hard to say, sir . . ."

Dainyl looked hard at the recorder.

"A few less."

"And how many authorized translations?"

"None, sir . . . except some of the wild ones. One had a document. It looked genuine."

Dainyl smiled and projected both warmth and reassurance. "Thank you, Chastyl. I appreciate your keeping track of those."

On his way down the corridor to the small private study, he paused at the open door to Adya's even smaller space and peered in.

The chief assistant bolted to her feet. "Sir, you're here early this morning."

"There's quite a bit to do." He offered a smile. "Adya . . . I'd like to see any dispatches or messages dealing with Alustre or the Myrmidons—immediately."

"Yes, sir. I haven't seen any this morning yet."

"Whenever you do, bring them immediately."

Adya nodded.

Dainyl was grateful that he did not have to receive petitions again until Duadi. He could use the time to get a better grasp on the Justice operations. So far he'd found little beyond intimations that Zelyert had been maintaining communications with the High Alectors under Samist. Still, the fact that Zelyert had quietly pressed Dainyl to reveal the fact that the Master Scepter would be going to Efra suggested that Zelyert had truly wanted Khelaryt's shadowmatch, and his artificially enhanced Talent, removed. In hindsight, it was equally likely that Zelyert had not expected Dainyl to survive that revelation.

Once in his study, he began to look through the older ledgers. He had not found anything more than suggestive when Alcyna arrived, slightly past midmorning.

She stepped into the small study, closed the door, and inclined her head in respect. "I thought you'd like to know that the guards were transferred successfully to Blackstear, and that all of First Company's squads are now at headquarters—except for the dispatch fliers, of course."

"That's good to know. Thank you." Dainyl gestured to the chairs.

"We have another problem, and it's one for the High Alector." Alcyna seated herself.

Dainyl didn't like that at all. "Which is?"

"Majer Sevasya sent a message noting that she is not receiving equipment and resupply either by sandox or by ship. Currently, the situation is not critical, but she felt I should know and requested I inform you."

Sevasya had to have learned of his elevation to High Alector through the Tables—and that probably meant from Delari or her father. Dainyl looked across the study table at Alcyna.

"How soon do you think we'll know about Noryan?"

"Not until Tridi at the earliest."

"I'll have to suggest that Alseryl include a special shipment on the next of the Duarches' vessels to make the south run to the west. We may even have to supply Myrmidon guards."

"Do you think that's their purpose . . . to weaken us more by diluting our forces?"

"It could be, but we could half the time required for the Myrmidons we send."

"By flying a messenger the last legs? They'd be over the east."

"They could stop in small towns where there aren't any alectors, or few of them."

She nodded. "Let me see what I can work out."

"I'll bring it up before the Duarch when we meet tomorrow. Alseryl will try to find a way out, but if I'm firm, he'll have to agree, because he won't want to openly defy Khelaryt."

"That doesn't mean it will happen."

"No. But it means that if he disobeys the Duarch or stalls

and delays too much, I can act. Then, that might be what they want, as another example of Khelaryt being unreasonable, or having unreasonable High Alectors."

"He'll stall and try to have Ruvryn or one of the others remove you in the meantime."

"That's likely. I'd be surprised if anything happened immediately."

She nodded slowly. "But when it does . . ."

"We'll need to be ready." Dainyl offered a smile he wasn't certain he felt. "Is there anything else?"

"We did receive a report from Cadmian Colonel Herolt, noting 'great damage' to the ironworks in Iron Stem. The remnants of Fifth Battalion are regrouping in Northa, but the colonel pleads difficulty in recruiting to bring the battalion up to full strength. The Sixth Battalion in Soupat is having much greater success, and casualties are now minimal—"

"Does that suggest something?" asked Dainyl.

"Unfortunately, it does." Alcyna's words were dry.

"Perhaps you should visit the colonel. I question whether he might be partly shadowmatched."

"If he is, then what?"

"Can you remove it?"

"If it's not one of the complex ones."

"If it is, let me know. What about Seventh Company? Do we have any reports from Second Company?"

"Captain Lyzetta has managed to obtain two replacement pteridons from Lyterna, which brings her closer to full strength."

Dainyl wondered how she had managed that, since he'd been told earlier that Captain Elysara had been under orders from Asulet not to release any of the pteridons sealed in timeless sleep in Lyterna.

"I understand that Lyzetta once served under Elysara," volunteered Alcyna.

"That might explain a few things." But only a few, since Elysara would still have to have gotten permission from Asulet, and the de facto Duarch of Lyterna had very firm ideas.

Dainyl frowned. He needed to visit Asulet, and he should have done so earlier. He could use the Table after Alcyna left. "Second Company?"

"As always, all is well with Second Company, except that they're useless save for carrying dispatches."

"And as a personal guard for the Duarch Samist," noted Dainyl. "What about Majer Sevasya? Have we heard anything about how she is handling Josaryk?"

"No. Not yet." Alcyna's words were guarded.

"I take it that Josaryk doesn't care much for the majer."

"They have a different view of the world. Sevasya is older than you are, you know?"

Dainyl hadn't known, but it didn't surprise him. "Is it fair to say that Captain Josaryk is somewhat more impressed with himself than he should be?"

Alcyna laughed. "Noryan was always telling him not to take himself so seriously." The laughter vanished. "That was hard when Brekylt invited him to sail on the sound with him."

"So Josaryk is on friendly terms with the Alector of the East."

"He thinks so."

Dainyl understood. Josaryk might pose as great a problem as Noryan. "Is there anything else I should know, or any questions you have?"

"Is there any hint about when the Archon might act?"

Dainyl shook his head. "I can't believe it will be that long, but I've thought that for weeks." He stood.

So did Alcyna.

After she left, Dainyl made his way to the Table chamber.

Diordyn glanced at the High Alector.

"You can tell Chastyl I'm going to Lyterna. I might be back in a glass." Dainyl stepped up onto the Table, then concentrated, feeling himself drop through the silvered surface and . . .

. . . into the purplish half-light of the translation tunnel. A purpled explosion flashed past him, so close that he could sense the death-agony. In the blackish green that underlay the tube, streaks of amber-green flashed, far more than he had ever sensed.

He extended a Talent probe to the pink of Lyterna, and almost as soon as he was linked, he was through the silvered-pink barrier.

Myenfel looked up from where he stood beside the outer door to the Table chamber. "Highest . . . what a surprise!"

As he stepped off the Table, Dainyl could sense that while the six guards—all older alectors and alectresses with hair either pure white or black streaked with white—might have been surprised, the recorder was not, although he did appear pleased. "Matters have been rather confused in Elcien, and I came to pay my respects to Asulet as soon as I could."

"I am certain he will be as pleased as I am. It has been decades since the High Alector of Justice has been here."

That did surprise Dainyl.

"Viora? The Highest should have an escort. Would you?"

Viora led him out of the Table chamber and along the narrow corridor to the steps carved out of stone that rose to the main gallery east of the Council Hall and past the grand pteridon battle scene mural that had become more and more prophetic in the past months. After two more turns, Viora and Dainyl were in the gallery with the niches that held ancient specimens of life—and the spare pteridons.

Viora halted at the first door, half-open to Asulet's study. "He should be here in a moment, Highest."

"How long have you been here?"

"Long enough that I've lost count. It's not as though it matters as much here."

Dainyl couldn't see living for decades in a place where one seldom saw the sun, and not unless one made a special effort.

Asulet appeared from a side corridor and walked toward them. He wore nondescript gray garments, and as he neared, Dainyl detected the faint hint of an odor not totally pleasant.

"Dainyl, while I am delighted to see you, you would have to arrive while I was working on the environmental systems, the less pleasant side of them, in fact." He gestured for Dainyl to enter the study.

Dainyl followed, closing the door behind him after entering the windowless, oak-paneled study. Asulet walked to the wide table desk of ancient oak and sank into one of the two oak armchairs.

Dainyl took the other chair. For the first time since he had met Asulet, he could actually sense weariness. "You're tired, aren't you?"

"I am. After centuries, the years do add up, I have to admit." Asulet took a slow breath.

"I apologize, but I had thought you should be apprised of several things, and I also thought I should pay my respects—as High Alector of Justice—before matters become even more complex."

Asulet smiled. "I forgot to offer my felicitations. Congratulations on becoming High Alector. You've worked at keeping the green in check—but not hard enough."

"With the ancients active everywhere . . . that's been difficult." He paused. "What would happen . . ." He stopped. "You'd said that the ancients weren't that different from pteridons and other Talent creatures, but are they that different from us?"

"You're worried about the green taking over and making you an ancient?" Asulet laughed.

Dainyl flushed. "Put that way, it sounds stupid."

The older alector frowned. "The ancients, from what I've been able to determine, are close to pure Talent, but not totally. Pteridons are close to the ancients in the proportion of Talent composition, as opposed to lifeforce. We are far less so, even the most Talented of us." He shrugged. "Probably someone like you has enough Talent that the Talent side of your being might be equivalent to the amount of Talent in an ancient, but you'd lose the more physical lifeforce side of what you are. That's assuming anyone could even make such a transformation. It certainly couldn't happen naturally. I've already told you what could happen if you get too green. Even so, the green Talent alone wouldn't change you. It might make other alectors wary."

"What I have made Zelyert more than a little wary."

"I presume he attacked you?"

"He did. He said that I was presumptuous . . ." Dainyl paused. "Did you know that the Duarches are no longer shadowmatched?"

"Has the Archon announced where the Master Scepter is destined?"

"No, but enough evidence has appeared that it became clear to both of the Duarches that the decision has already been made to transfer it to Efra."

"And the Duarches have not been replaced by wardens?" Asulet raised his eyebrows.

"I doubt the Archon knows that the Duarches know. Besides, with all the Tables guarded, exactly how would he enforce that?"

"You had a hand in it, didn't you?"

"Zelyert pushed me into a situation where I had the choice of revealing it within weeks or telling Khelaryt immediately. I chose the time, rather than letting circumstances choose it."

"I'm surprised you're still with us."

"I almost wasn't. He shredded my shields and threw me into his bookshelves—and then sent me as an urgent envoy to Samist."

"Who was relieved, I imagine."

"Exactly."

"Then Zelyert had to try to remove you himself, since the Duarches didn't." Asulet fingered his long chin. "Most interesting. What do you want from me?"

"I thought you should know. Any insight, any advice would be welcome."

"You seem to have done well enough without it." Asulet smiled.

"That was the easy part, I think," replied Dainyl. "Will the Archon really attempt to send wardens or forces here?"

"It's never been tried before. In the past, the transfer has gone from one world to another, without a third world being involved. The problem was that the Archon and those closest to him have been through three such transfers, and the life-force demands have gotten greater with each."

"The Archon felt two worlds were necessary." Dainyl paused. "It was all a farce, wasn't it? Acorus was never intended to receive the Master Scepter."

"Perhaps later, if a better world could not be found after Efra."

Dainyl sat silently for a time. Finally, he spoke. "Did you *know* that?"

"I was never told. No one was, so far as I know. But those of us with more open minds, or those who were out of favor, we were the ones sent here, and we had a much harder time of it. There were years when no one translated from Ifryn here."

Dainyl shook his head. "It all seems . . . not exactly pointless, but what difference does it make if Brekylt creates his own Duarchy in the east?"

"Would you want someone like Rhelyn using lifeforce weapons and squandering the future? Brekylt would have even fewer compunctions than he did."

"So the best course is to support Khelaryt?"

"Have you ever doubted that?"

Dainyl had, especially after meeting Samist, who had seemed reasonable, but . . . the Duarch of Ludar clearly supported Ruvryn, who was anything but reasonable, and Dainyl had come to distrust those he had met who served Samist. "It seems like choosing the lesser of evils."

"Much of life presents that choice." A sadness permeated the elder alector's voice. "We do what we can. I can't offer you much more insight than that, and you seem to know more about what is happening than do I."

"I'd better get back to Elcien."

Asulet rose from his armchair. "Give my best to Lystrana. It's about time her abilities were recognized. How is she finding Dereka?"

"Cold . . . but she's . . . reluctantly glad to be there." Dainyl stood as well. How had Asulet known of Lystrana's appointment, but not about how she had received it? Of course, the Duarches announced appointments, but not what was behind them.

"It's a good place for her to be now, and she'll make a good regional alector."

"I thought so."

"You were right. You'd best be returning, though."

"I suppose so." Dainyl nodded and turned.

In the end, as he walked back to the Table chamber, he had to wonder where the certainty in his life had gone. Little more than a year earlier, he'd been a Myrmidon colonel with a clear view of the world and the future. Now . . .

78

Mykel stood on the porch of the inn in Sudon, waiting for one of the rankers to bring his mount. He'd always preferred to saddle and groom his horse, but trying to do so now would have been difficult—and foolhardy. He still was uncomfortable in relying on others, perhaps because he wasn't certain he had a good feel for the balance between what was wise and necessary and what was arrogance and an abuse of position. For a battalion commander to insist on doing too much personally was stupid, but so was flaunting power, and easy as it was to say those words, Mykel had seen too many officers slide into arrogance.

He glanced at the sky. The clouds were lower, but seemed thinner, and the wind had shifted so that it blew more strongly and warmly from the southwest. If the warmth continued, some of the side lanes and less-traveled back roads would turn into quagmires, and that could prove a problem.

Murthyt—the senior squad leader from Sixteenth Company—and a ranker Mykel didn't immediately recognize rode up to the front of the Red Pony, with Mykel's mount between them.

"Here you are, Majer."

"Thank you, Murthyt."

"Vakyn did the hard work, sir."

Mykel smiled. "Thank you, Vakyn." He mounted, one-handed and awkwardly, then settled himself in the saddle before riding out into the square and reining up. "Officers front!"

Rhystan was the first to ride up, followed by Dyarth. Shortly, the other three joined them.

"We'll ride out to the east side of the valley and form on the ridge, immediately behind the trees on each side," Mykel announced. "Sixteenth Company will take the low hill at the north end, just over the crest and out of sight. Fourteenth Company will take the high ground on the southeast end. No one is to begin firing until Sixteenth Company does. Is that clear?"

"Yes, sir."

"Good. Let's ride out."

The officers rode back to their companies, all but Rhystan, since Sixteenth Company led the column.

Mykel and Rhystan rode side by side on the narrow road westward out of Sudon. The provisions and ammunition wagons were next to last, but with Fifteenth Company bringing up the rear behind them. Mykel thought that the Reillies could arrive in the valley by a glass before midday if they pressed, but it was more likely to be early afternoon. Still, he didn't want to be caught off guard, and he didn't want to press the mounts.

A good half glass passed before Rhystan spoke. "You're quiet this morning, sir. Do you think they'll follow the road?"

"With Reillies, who knows? If they do stay with the road, we'll be positioned on higher ground and set so that they can't flank us. If they don't, either they'll go more west, and we won't see them, or they'll be in the woods and in the deeper snow on lower ground." That was the best plan that Mykel had been able to develop.

"You're thinking that position will matter with them?"

"There's close to sixty vingts between the valley and Borlan. If we can crush them early, that's for the best. I'm trying to set it up so that even if we don't get a decisive battle, they'll take heavy casualties trying to come to grips with us."

"Won't they back off?"

"They might." Mykel grinned sardonically. "But they won't be able to get my head and blood unless they close with us."

"You think the Squawts have joined up yet?"

"No." Mykel had the feeling that the Squawts would let the Reillies take casualties for a while before joining battle. "But I could be wrong."

"About that, I'd agree, sir."

"What don't you agree with, Rhystan?" Mykel kept his tone light.

"I have trouble with the idea that they're all so upset at your killing their leader that they'll ride out in early winter just to try to kill you in return. We've got better arms and better training and more ammunition, and they've almost never won a big battle against us."

"They think they did. They believe that they destroyed half of Fourth Battalion. Why should another battalion be any different? Besides, they seem to like to fight."

Rhystan shook his head. "My head tells me that, but my feelings have a hard time understanding."

"It was that way in Dramur, too. I never could understand why the seltyrs risked everything when they already had almost everything." Because of Rachyla, he could understand, even feel, that people did feel and act that way. He still had trouble understanding *why* they did.

More than a glass went by before Mykel called a halt at the top of the gentle downgrade into the valley—more like a vale little more than a vingt wide at the bottom with a narrow stream, its edges frosted in ice, meandering through the bottomland.

He turned to Rhystan. "Make sure that you don't leave any obvious tracks."

"We can manage that, Majer." Rhystan turned. "Sixteenth Company! Forward!"

Mykel eased the roan to the south side of the road, angling behind the copse of trees that overlooked the valley.

"Fourteenth Company! Forward!" Culeyt nodded to Mykel as he rode past, leading his company toward the rise at the southeastern end of the valley—overlooking the road to Borlan.

Mykel watched and said little as Seventeenth Company wound its way to the south and downhill to the lowest section of trees overlooking the road. Thirteenth and Fifteenth Companies set up slightly behind him, shielded from the road below by the trees.

It was close to a glass before midday when Bhoral rode up to Mykel, who had long since dismounted and tied the roan to a low and thick limb of a fir.

"Sir! We've got the scout reports from Captain Rhystan. Sixteenth Company is in position. They've seen Reillie outriders, but not the main force."

"Thank you, Bhoral." Mykel took a swallow from his water bottle, then walked forward toward the edge of the woods overlooking the southwest-facing snow-dotted meadow. Across the valley, more like a vale, was another meadow between the trees, but since it faced north and was shaded largely by the towering pines, the snow was drifted and knee deep in places.

Mykel walked back to the roan. He hated waiting, but an officer who couldn't wait as needed was borrowing trouble, if not worse.

A quarter glass passed before Bhoral returned. "Captain Culeyt reports that Fourteenth Company stands ready in position."

One glass passed, then another.

Shielded by the trees, Mykel stood and watched the road to the north. Several riders appeared, riding slowly. Then, a larger group followed, several hundred yards behind. Mykel kept waiting, hoping that Rhystan would wait until the last possible moment before opening fire.

Abruptly, the Reillies turned eastward, off the road, moving toward the trees that held Sixteenth Company.

Finally, a puff of smoke rose from the front of the hillside trees sheltering Sixteenth Company. A second followed. Two of the leading Reillie riders were cut down immediately. The volleys continued, and despite the scattered bodies falling from mounts, the Reillies poured into the valley.

A mass of riders—close to company size—charged the hillock and the woods. The shots from Rhystan's men ripped through the Reillies, and more and more of them fell. Yet they pressed toward Sixteenth Company, coming within thirty yards before breaking.

Rather than continue to face the withering fire from the trees on the knoll, they turned and galloped south, to the narrow snow-covered meadow, where the remaining riders—less than thirty—turned and rode up the slope.

"Sir . . . they're riding straight up through the snow on the west."

Mykel had already seen that. He turned to Khaerst, the messenger mounted beside him. "Ride to Undercaptain Loryalt. He's to have his best marksmen ride forward to pick off those that they can, but he's not to pursue under any circumstances." *Not through the knee-deep snowdrifts on a north-facing slope.*

"Yes, sir. Pick off those they can, but don't pursue." Khaerst spurred his mount out along the tree line and then onto the road downhill, before cutting back to the south and the lower hill where Seventeenth Company was drawn up.

Mykel glanced back to the northern end of the vale, but the road there was empty, except for fallen mounts and men. The bulk of the Reillie force had turned back.

Then he watched as a half squad of Seventeenth Company rode downhill and formed up into a rough firing line. With the wind blowing away from him, he could not hear the shots, but he did see the results as a number of Reillie mounts went down in the snow. At least ten Reillies fell as well, presumably from the shots.

Less than a half glass later, the valley was empty of Reillies, except for the scattered handfuls of dead and wounded.

Mykel and his officers remained mounted, in a tough circle on the section of the road above the valley, as he received the casualty reports—eleven Cadmian casualties against more than seventy deaths for the Reillies. That was acceptable, but not decisive, reflected Mykel. Still, gradual attrition of the enemy with minimal Cadmian losses wouldn't defeat the insurgents, and with the coming snows and cold of late winter, a war of attrition would become less and less practical.

79

On Duadi morning, accompanied by Dalyrt and Patrylon, Dainyl once more made his way up to the Hall of Justice to hear the petitions of the disaffected and aggrieved. The first petitioner was one Rexana, an older indigen woman. She claimed she had been robbed at the Eastern Market Square in Elcien. While a patroller was citing her for having a cart that did not meet standards of cleanliness, a common thief had run off with her cash box, and the patroller had just watched, and then added to her fine because she had left him to chase the thief.

"Do you know who the patroller is?" Dainyl asked.

"How would I be knowing that?" claimed Rexana. "He was one of the new ones, not like old Gievat, who knew what was important."

"I cannot remedy a wrong if I cannot ascertain if it took place and who committed it," Dainyl pointed out. "You bring me his name, and justice will be done."

"I'll be back, Highest, that I will."

Dainyl couldn't help but remember the painting by Jeluyne—in the art exhibit in the Duarch's Palace months before—that had depicted a scene all too much like Rexana's testimony. Were the patrollers really that inflexible? He had the disturbing feeling that they were, but he couldn't do that much to help the woman without more information. Still . . .

He leaned forward and murmured to Patrylon, "Make a note of patroller inflexibility."

"Yes, sir."

Dainyl also noted the mixed feelings of puzzlement and condescension from Dalyrt, but decided that the dais was not the place from which to explore them—or that, even if he did, Dalyrt would understand.

"Next!" declaimed Patrylon.

The second petitioner was also a woman, a much younger one, named Erlyna. She had a bruise on one side of her face.

Patrylon handed Dainyl the petition and several sheets from the justicer of Elcien.

According to the justicer's decision, rendered five months earlier, one Tehark of Elcien had beaten his wife Erlyna repeatedly. The justicer had granted her both a divorcement and the dwelling, as well as custody of their three children, and required Tehark to pay one gold a month. According to the petition, Tehark had left Elcien, but he had refused to pay the golds, and he had returned in the night two months ago, and broken down the door and raped her and beaten her. The patrollers had been unable to find him—except it was thought that he had been the one to kill a patroller. He had been sentenced to death in absentia. Two nights ago, he had returned and assaulted her once more and vanished into the night.

"Did Tehark assault you two nights ago?" Dainyl hated to ask the question, but he needed to sense her answer and truthfulness.

"Yes, Highest. He hurt me. There are bruises . . ." She started to unfasten her jacket.

"That will be enough. I can sense the truth." Dainyl dropped his eyes to the papers, trying to think. What good was a judgment that seemingly could not be enforced? With an alector, it would not have been a problem, because there were so few that they could not have escaped, but there were more than two million landers and indigens just in the western half of Corus, and unless they were willing to turn in malcontents like Tehark . . .

He looked up and studied Erlyna. Her jaw trembled, and Dainyl could sense she was close to tears. "Has anyone seen Tehark besides you?"

"No, Highest. He's too clever." She sobbed once. "He's strong. He's almost as big as you are, Highest."

An indigen that big should stand out, and yet no one could find him. "What do you do?"

"I'm a weaver."

Dainyl took a slow deep breath. "Be it decreed that the life of one Tehark, formerly of Elcien, is hereby forfeit, and that any who bring him or his body to the Hall of Justice shall receive ten golds, and no questions shall be asked, except to verify the identity of Tehark."

Erlyna's mouth opened.

"I cannot find a man who does not wish to be found and who hides among his own disreputable kind, but those who are disreputable may wish to enrich themselves at his expense."

Dainyl turned to Patrylon. "Have copies of the decree sent to all patroller stations and have them posted in the market squares."

"So be it," announced Patrylon.

The remaining petitions were somewhat less vexing and included reducing the levy of an excessive fine for failure to maintain the proper sand and water barrels for fire suppression. The others, Dainyl saw no reason to change.

Promptly at midday, Dainyl vacated the dais. He already understood that remaining a moment longer merely encouraged more people to come late in hopes of waiting less time for their petitions to be heard.

Once Dainyl was in the lower corridor, Dalyrt cleared his throat.

"Yes, Dalyrt?"

"That woman who was beaten, sir? We haven't used a decree like that in decades," ventured Dalyrt.

Dainyl turned to him. "Perhaps we haven't. Do you have a better idea for those like this Tehark? He's assaulted and beaten her, probably killed at least one patroller, and we've been able to do nothing in more than half a year. We're supposed to provide order. I could have made another judgment against him, but what good is a judgment that cannot be enforced?"

"Does that not appeal to the indigens' greatest weakness, sir, their love of golds?"

"Have the other appeals—to their sense of fairness, for example—been effective?"

Dalyrt did not meet Dainyl's eyes. What exactly had Zelyert been doing as High Alector? Wasn't the High Alector supposed to foster justice?

Dainyl did not go directly to his study, but to see Adya first. "Do we have any messages from the east or from the Marshal of Myrmidons?"

"No, sir," replied Adya. "The only message is one from the Duarch's chamberlain."

"Bharyt?"

"Yes, sir. He wanted to remind you of the meeting with the Duarch."

Dainyl scarcely could have forgotten, considering he needed to confront Alseryl about the supplies to Lysia.

"Oh . . . I gave Patrylon a note about patroller inflexibility. There have been two cases brought to my attention involving the Eastern Market Square where patrollers were so concerned about cleanliness that they ignored more significant theft."

Adya nodded, but Dainyl could sense something more. "What is it, Adya?"

"It has always been a problem keeping the market squares clean, sir, particularly the eastern one. At one time, the stench was . . . overpowering."

"We wouldn't want that," Dainyl agreed. "But about the theft . . . ?"

"No matter what any High Alector has done, the theft remains. If there are more patrollers, it becomes more hidden, and the cost to the Hall of Justice and the Duarchy rises."

"So we maintain enough patrollers to keep theft from being rampant and have them concentrate on those matters where their efforts seem to yield results?"

"That has been the past policy," Adya said carefully.

"Thank you. I will consider whatever I decide in light of the experience of others." So far as Dainyl was concerned, that didn't necessarily mean following such precedents, but he would need to be careful in whatever changes he undertook and how he structured those changes.

He offered a smile before heading back to his study—and perhaps another half glass of work in the time until he had to leave for his early afternoon meeting with the Duarch.

Before that long, he had taken the coach to the Palace and was stepping through the archway into the entry foyer—just slightly before the glass appointed for the meeting of the High Alectors and the Duarch.

Bharyt, as always, stood waiting.

"Good afternoon, Bharyt."

"Good afternoon, sir. Moryn will escort you to the conference room." Bharyt inclined his head slightly. An unsmiling alector in dark gray trimmed in green stepped forward.

"Are any of the others here?"

"The High Alector of Transport, sir."

"Thank you."

Bharyt nodded slightly in reply.

Dainyl followed Moryn through the columned section of the entry foyer and down the high-ceilinged corridor, past the closed library door where Dainyl had always met with the Duarch, and to the conference room. The only other time that Dainyl had been in the conference room was when he had briefed some of the other High Alectors on the events in Hyalt.

Alseryl stood beside the circular table in his shimmersilk greens. He glanced at Dainyl and smiled faintly. "You affect an older style, in your greens, as well as in other matters."

"The older styles seem to suit me best, Alseryl. They do most Myrmidons, I would judge."

"Ah, yes, always the Myrmidon."

"I find that preferable to other possibilities," replied Dainyl with a laugh.

"I can see that—the comfortable confines of regulation and certainty."

"And the understanding that while power is necessary to maintain what is right, it does not make right."

Before Alseryl could respond, the door opened once more, and Chembryt stepped inside.

"Good to see you both, you especially, Dainyl. I heard that you decided to employ financial incentives to bolster adherence to justice."

"You obviously have better information than some in the Hall of Justice, although that is changing," replied Dainyl.

The faintest hint of a frown crossed Alseryl's forehead.

Immediately behind Alseryl came Khelaryt, and Chembryt stepped aside in deference to the Duarch.

Khelaryt gestured to the comfortable chairs around the circular table. Chembryt seated himself easily, as did Dainyl. Alseryl hesitated slightly, then sat. The three High Alectors in shimmersilk greens were loosely clustered around the half of the table facing the Duarch, who smiled warmly as he settled into his chair.

While Dainyl was aware of the Talent forces swirling behind the shields of those in the room, he was aware that now neither Chembryt nor Alseryl could have prevailed against him, even together. He also realized that for all the Talent-strength manifested by Khelaryt, there was what he would have called an uncertainty behind that power, and that made no sense to him.

"This meeting will have to be short," began Khelaryt. "If you would begin, Chembryt . . ."

"Yes, sir. As I mentioned at the last meeting, we face a significant financial shortfall. The annual budget is roughly one million five hundred thousand golds. The deficit for the past half year was close to one hundred thousand golds and was covered by transfers from the Duarchy's reserve account, but we cannot continue to do that for more than three years before it will be exhausted, and either trade tariffs will have to be increased or some other form of tariffing will need to be instituted. Or expenditures by entities under the various High Alectors will need to be reduced." Chembryt cleared his throat, then continued. "The largest single deficit was incurred by Engineering, totaling close to sixty thousand golds, while Justice incurred a thirty-thousand-gold deficit, and Transport one of ten thousand."

"How much of those deficits represent onetime expenditures?" asked Khelaryt.

"Very little, I would judge, but you should ask the other High Alectors, sir."

Khelaryt looked to Dainyl. "Justice?"

"I cannot answer that for all items, sir, but part of the deficit resulted from the need for additional Table guards. Once the Master Scepter is actually transferred, the majority of those expenditures should not be necessary on a continuing basis. Likewise, there was more construction of new facilities for Cadmians and Myrmidons than normal. Also, operational costs were higher than budgeted because of unrest related to the transfer of the Master Scepter . . ."

"I beg your pardon, Dainyl," said Alseryl, "but could you explain that?"

"The costs were an extension of events on which I briefed the High Alectors when I was Marshal of Myrmidons," Dainyl replied. "First, RA Rhelyn destroyed the local Cadmian garrison in Hyalt apparently because one of the local Cadmians noted the buildup of his rebel forces. At the time, that destruction was blamed on local insurgencies, and a Cadmian battalion was dispatched with two local trainee companies to subdue the supposed insurgents and to build a more secure local compound. Then, in support of Rhelyn, RA Fahylt created his own mounted rifles in Tempre, and the Cadmians were required to take action to subdue and destroy them. In the course of those efforts, disloyal alectors under Fahylt attacked the Cadmians and inflicted casualties on men and mounts. Both had to be replaced." Dainyl smiled. "None of these events would have occurred had it not been for actions among alectors related to the pending transfer of the Master Scepter. The same is true for the additional Myrmidon costs related to defeating the attacks on the Tables at Blackstear and Soupat. I trust that satisfies your inquiry."

"More than sufficiently," interjected the Duarch. "Please continue with your analysis of which costs were onetime, and which may be ongoing."

Chembryt smiled at Dainyl.

"The costs of the transfer of Seventh Company to Tempre were mitigated by the construction of facilities by the former RA, although some additional construction will be required to modify the facilities for pteridons. Activities by the ancients, almost completely in areas adjoining the Aerlal Plateau, have increased casualties and operating costs for the Cadmian Mounted Rifles, and I cannot say whether those types of costs will continue. . . ." When he finished Dainyl inclined his head.

"Thank you," replied the Duarch. "Alseryl."

"Yes, sir. Virtually all of the deficit incurred by Transport related to two basic causes. First was the scheduled overhaul and refit of the *Duarches' Honesty*. We had budgeted for that, but overall operating costs were increased when the road through the South Pass was blocked. We have had to arrange for transport of goods by other routes, and by sending more by sea, and then trans-shipping them. We also have been tasked with recruiting, training, and replacing more sandox drivers as a result of higher Myrmidon casualties, and we have had to make two special ocean transports in support of Cadmian deployments."

"Special?" queried Chembryt. "Are not such deployment transport costs part of your budget?"

"Historically, we have budgeted for one or two. There have been four in the past year." Alseryl coughed slightly.

"Have there been any additional transport costs incurred as a result of increased engineering and artisan output?" asked Dainyl.

Alseryl paused, and Dainyl could tell that the inquiry had caught him unprepared.

"Have there?" prompted Khelaryt.

"Yes, sir. Perhaps twenty percent or more of the deficit occurred from that source."

"Could you provide some details?" asked the Duarch. "What sort of output and to where?"

"I could not, sir. I do not keep track of all the items in a ship's hold or in the cargo section of a sandox carriage. I can say that there was a greater weight and volume of iron pigs coming down the Vedra to Faitel, and more finished products shipped from Faitel."

"What about the floods on the Vedra?" asked Dainyl. "Will those have an impact on future expenditures?"

That question puzzled Alseryl as well, but because—Dainyl suspected—it sympathetically implied that Alseryl would face costs beyond his control.

"Replacing the piers at Dekhron and Borlan, and repairing those at Tempre, will add between two and five thousand golds to our construction outlays."

"I think we have a picture of what we face. I don't see any point in attempting to make changes in your operations until after the Master Scepter has been transferred. After that, some economies may well be necessary, and I ask each of you to consider what might be practical for your area of responsibility." Khelaryt paused only long enough to signify that the budget matters were closed, then asked, "Do any of you have any other matters?"

Chembryt shook his head.

Alseryl remained silent.

After a moment, Dainyl spoke. "I have one slight difficulty. I've been informed by the commanding Myrmidon majer in Lysia that certain critical military goods have not reached Eighth Company there. It appears as if that aspect of ground transport faces some difficulty. I'd like to request that a consignment of such equipment and supplies be included on the next vessel to take the southern route. To ensure its safety, we would be willing to send a small Myrmidon detachment with it."

Khelaryt remained impassive.

"You must know, Dainyl," replied Alseryl, "that such cargoes are determined months in advance. With the small number of powered ocean transports, our flexibility is very limited."

"That I understand, but we are not talking a significant fraction of even one ship's cargo capacity."

"You may be High Alector of Justice, Dainyl, and I understand your concerns about proper supply of your Myrmidons, but supply should be carried out through the proper distribution system by the Alector of the East. If you have a problem, shouldn't you be taking it up with him first?" asked Alseryl, his voice mild.

Dainyl could sense a certain buried glee.

"The Alector of the East has been requested to supply such, but he has replied that he lacks those particular items and supplies. Since he lacks them, and apparently will for the foreseeable future, I'm making the request of you."

"That seems reasonable, Alseryl," suggested Khelaryt.

The High Alector of Transport nodded. "Given the critical nature of the supplies and equipment, I suggest that you do supply Myrmidons as guards."

"I will have Marshal Alcyna work with your assistants to make the arrangements."

"If there is nothing more . . ." Khelaryt's words were not a suggestion.

The Duarch departed immediately, followed by Alseryl, who clearly displayed a mixture of pique and buried elation.

Chembryt and Dainyl walked down the corridor toward the Palace entrance with greater deliberation.

"You know that shipment of goods will be dispatched and require guards at the time when you most need Myrmidons?" Chembryt laughed.

"That thought had occurred to me, but the Duarch would prefer to hold Lysia, and that would be difficult for the Myrmidons without supplies and equipment."

"How is Lystrana finding Dereka?"

"Somewhat stressful at times, but she's pleased not to have to worry about disappointing you by not being able to use the Tables." Dainyl smiled.

Chembryt wasn't about to say more, at least not in the Palace where every word could be, and usually was, overheard, and Dainyl didn't want to say more, because he still knew too little about the interplay between High Alectors.

80

Mykel rode forward, just enough that he had a vantage point from behind the trunk of the leafless oak tree. He glanced to the east where Selena had just risen, to join Asterta low in the sky, then back to the north, watching the valley. In the darkness of Tridi before dawn, he doubted that any of the other Cadmians saw what he did, what with the night sight that accompanied his still-increasing Talent.

If you have so much Talent, how did you manage to get wounded so badly? Because he'd relied on it exclusively just before he'd been shot, because the dead Reillie had had Talent as well, and because Mykel himself had been struck with bullets, Talent, and the crossbow quarrel.

Explanations were all well and good, but he still felt almost helpless in a battle situation. If he had been able to use his rifle effectively, he knew he could have reduced the casualties suffered by his men—as well as cut down the number of enemies. *But with every battle where you lead the fight there's a greater chance of getting killed.*

Mykel concentrated on what was about to happen to the north, where Hamylt was making his first attack in an attempt to get the Reillies to attack and chase elements of Third and Fourth Battalions into range of the main Cadmian body.

The sound of rifles echoed through the gray before dawn, continuing for a quarter glass before ceasing almost instantly. Hamylt had either run out of ammunition or the Reillies were mounting a counterattack.

As the darkness lightened into gray, the only sounds from the north were muffled yells and commands from the insurgents' camp.

"Sir?" Loryalt eased his mount toward Mykel and the roan. "Any word?"

"No. Hamylt's attacked once, but there wasn't much of a Reillie reply."

"Do you think they slipped away?"

That was certainly possible, but Mykel had the feeling that wasn't the case.

Then, from farther north, came another volley of shots . . . and then another. This time, scattered shots replied.

"There are some Reillies there. They're shooting back."

"Sir?"

"At Hamylt. He's made two attacks. That's what it sounds like, anyway."

Loryalt frowned. "You've got better hearing than I do, sir."

"Practice," replied Mykel. He *thought* that Hamylt had attacked successfully and withdrawn, but he saw no riders on the road to the north heading in either direction.

"You still want us to stand by?"

"The Reillies usually make some response. Let's see what it is."

"Yes, sir." Loryalt eased his mount through the trees to the southwest.

Mykel returned his full attention to the road and the valley.

The sky lightened into pale gray, and then, with the edge of the sun peering over the hills to the east, to silver-green. And still no riders appeared. Out of the silence, three or four, perhaps as many as a score of shots echoed from the area of the bridge, and then the Fourth Battalion squads galloped back toward Third Battalion, riding hard, faster than Mykel had expected.

Mykel could sense the Reillies and Squawts before he could see them, but within another fraction of a glass, even the shortest-sighted of the Cadmian troops lined up in the trees on the knoll overlooking the road could make out the horde moving toward them. The Reillies had not taken just the road, but were riding through the orchards, across the frozen fields touched with white, so that they formed a front nearly half a vingt across, only roughly centered on the road.

The middle of that front was extended slightly, into a point of mounted riders that, had it been extended, would have centered itself on Mykel. More than coincidence, that suggested to Mykel that the Reillie he had killed earlier was not the only insurgent with Talent.

Mykel fumbled out his rifle, left-handed, and laid it across his knees. Then he waited until the riders were only a little more than a hundred yards away before he issued his orders. "Third Battalion! Fire at will!"

"Fire at will!"

"Fire at will!"

The commands echoed from the company officers to the squad leaders, and shots rang out, flashing from the trees into the uneven front of the Reillies and Squawts. Despite the accuracy of the Cadmians, and even with bodies falling and mounts going down, the insurgents rode up the gentle slope toward the Cadmians.

A greater number surged toward the center. Mykel felt that all of them were riding directly toward him, but he left the rifle across his knees.

From somewhere came a tendril of Talent—greenish brown Talent from the center of the attackers.

"Aim for the center! Aim for the center!" Those commands

came from his right, where Rhystan and Sixteenth Company were set up.

Within moments, Loryalt issued the same orders.

Mykel eased his mount back slightly, trying to use the oak for greater cover. His eyes dropped to his rifle. *Not yet.*

Three riders crashed through the low leafless bushes on the lower section of the slope, less than fifteen yards below Mykel. They bore long blades, swords that looked too long to use effectively in the brush and trees, but Mykel knew that while he could not have handled such a blade, they certainly could.

"He's up there! Right behind the oak! The priest-killer!"

"Death to the priest-killer! Avenge Kladyl!"

The cracking of brush behind Mykel was followed by a command, "Fifth squad! Charge!"

"Third squad! Forward!"

Cadmians in maroon cold-weather jackets rode past Mykel on both sides, rifles sheathed and sabres out, sweeping down toward the oncoming Reillies.

"To the priest-killer!" came the call.

The Cadmians cut deep into the mass of the Reillies, driving them back, then swinging aside to allow another set of rifle volleys to decimate the front lines of the attackers.

From the left, a single rider burst through the thinnest part of the line of Cadmians, laying one aside with the outsized blade, urging his mount uphill toward Mykel. His long blond hair streamed back over his broad shoulders. A thin aura of Talent enshrouded him.

Mykel could feel at least two bullets strike the rider, but the young Reillie ignored them as he flattened himself against the mane of the white horse he rode.

Two Cadmians urged their mounts forward. Mykel could sense that they would be too late. His left hand lifted his own rifle, and he swung it up and toward the Reillie, concentrating on the youthful face of the attacker.

The Reillie straightened in his saddle and lifted the massive blade, almost like a metal bar, bringing it forward for a killing blow.

Mykel fired, willing the bullet into the Reillie's forehead.

The rifle slammed back against Mykel's arm and side, and he struggled to bring it forward and up.

The youth stiffened, and an incredulous look froze on his face, before he plunged forward in the saddle. His face reminded Mykel of his own younger brother.

Mykel managed to lever his own rifle high enough to slide the Reillie's falling blade away from him, as the white horse swung away and to a halt, the body of the Reillie who had looked like Viencet half hanging out of the saddle.

Suddenly, like a spent wave, the Reillies and Squawts receded, quickly flowing back to the north and west, leaving the bodies of men, women, boys, and girls—and their mounts—strewn on the hillsides, fields, and even the narrow road that eventually led to Borlan.

"Third Battalion! Hold your position! Third Battalion! Hold!" Mykel tried to boost his order with Talent.

"Hold position!" The order reverberated across the knoll.

Watching as the last of the attackers vanished into the wooded area to the west of the orchards to the north, Mykel slowly eased the rifle back across his legs, then glanced to his left, in the direction of Loryalt and Seventeenth Company. Seventeenth Company was re-forming. To the right, so was Sixteenth Company.

Mykel glanced at the white horse, shuddering and still panting, somehow entangled in the bare branches of a smaller tree. He was glad he could not see the face of the young Reillie.

"Majer? You all right?" Rhystan reined up beside Mykel.

"I'm fine."

The older captain's eyes took in the rifle across Mykel's knees. "How much use did that see?"

"One shot." Mykel nodded toward the white horse and the dead Reillie.

"You killed him, didn't you? One shot, one-handed, with your left hand."

"He was younger than my brother Viencet," Mykel replied.

"Nothing short of killing him would have stopped him."

"I know." Mykel had to wonder if anything would stop the hill insurgents, other than their total destruction.

81

Dainyl had only had to receive petitions for a glass and a half on Tridi morning, for which he was thankful, since he hadn't gotten as much sleep as he might have liked. While he'd spent Londi night in Elcien, he had taken the Table to Dereka on Duadi night. He and Lystrana had enjoyed a quiet dinner alone together, but Lystrana had slept restlessly. Even in his sleep Dainyl had sensed her discomfort—and Kytrana's stirrings. Given his own restless sleep, he wasn't that displeased in the fall-off in petitioners and his being able to leave the Hall of Justice by late midmorning.

Dainyl had been in his study less than a quarter glass after the hearings, looking over local regional Cadmian garrison reports, seeking a hint of where else the ancients might be undertaking whatever they were doing, when Chastyl appeared with an unfamiliar alectress.

"Sir?" asked the recorder.

Dainyl set aside the reports and gestured for the two to enter. He remained seated.

Chastyl let the alectress enter first, closing the door behind them. "This is Vyane. She's the assistant recorder in Lysia."

Vyane was a good head shorter than Dainyl, but not nearly so slender and petite as Alcyna. Her eyes were a deep purple, but her skin bore the slightest tinge of almond. She inclined her head. "I'm Sulerya's assistant, Highest. If at all possible, she would request that you come to Lysia. So would Majer Sevasya, although she has made no request."

"For how long might the recorder require my presence?" Dainyl understood more fully—after Khelaryt's revelation about the scepters—why the recorder would not leave Lysia.

"She did not say, but I doubt that it would be that long. Certainly no more than the day, and perhaps less."

"Did she indicate why my presence might be required?"

"No, sir, only that you would find it vital and necessary."

Dainyl could sense the truth behind the words, and the cryptic nature of the message chilled him. He could also see that the message was a shock to Chastyl. He looked to the older recorder. "Has anything unusual happened with the Tables this morning?"

"Not that I know, sir."

"I'll go now." He stood, donned his jacket, and checked the lightcutters he still wore at his belt. Then he followed Chastyl and Vyane back down the corridor.

He stopped and peered into Adya's small study. "I'm headed to Lysia. I might be gone much of the day."

"Sir?" The question suggested that such Table travel might be unwise.

"There are important reasons for it. If Marshal Alcyna seeks me, tell her where I am and my expected return."

"Yes, sir."

Dainyl was the last through the small foyer and into the Table chamber. It was definitely crowded, with Diordyn, Chastyl, Vyane, Dainyl, as well as the five guards and the Table itself.

"You first." Dainyl nodded to Vyane.

The assistant recorder stepped up onto the Table, faded into a misty figure, then vanished.

Dainyl followed her onto the mirror surface, concentrating as he dropped . . .

. . . into the purpleness of the translation tube where he concentrated on the orange-yellow locator for Lysia and linked. Now was no time to linger in the tube. The locator sped toward him, and then he was through the silvered barrier . . .

. . . and standing on the Table, by himself. He glanced around, then nodded as Vyane appeared behind him.

The assistant recorder looked stunned to see Dainyl there in front of her.

Dainyl smiled at her, then stepped off the Table, moving toward Sulerya.

The Recorder of Deeds for Lysia had dark circles under her eyes. She did not speak, but gestured to the open entrance to the hidden rooms off the Table chamber, then turned to Vyane. "We won't be that long."

"Yes, Recorder."

Dainyl followed Sulerya, noting again how deftly she employed her Talent to manipulate the mechanism to seal the stone doorway behind them. Sulerya sat down heavily in one of the chairs in the study that was far smaller than the one of the High Alector of Justice in Elcien.

"Why did you request my presence?"

"The grid is . . . they're making adjustments somewhere on Ifryn . . . and it's making translations here unpredictable."

"I noticed. Preparations to transfer the Master Scepter?"

"That would be my guess, but it could be a result of the rapid decline in lifeforce on Ifryn."

"Is that the only reason you requested my presence?"

"No. Noryan is dead. So are about half the Myrmidons in Norda. We found out just before I sent Vyane for you."

"When?" The single word was harsh.

"Last night—or very early this morning. Brekylt learned somehow that you'd ordered Noryan and Josaryk to Dereka, and when he discovered that Noryan was planning to obey, he and a squad of personal guards—assassins, in truth—used the Table to travel to Norda in the middle of the night. Most were killed in their sleep."

"Most?" There was something in her tone that bothered him.

"One attempted to use his pteridon to escape. One of Brekylt's assassins used one of those lightcannon on him."

"They took a lightcannon to Norda?"

"Or it had been shipped there earlier in preparation and hidden," suggested Sulerya.

"That's not at all good. Those shred lifeforce. Even the ones with storage crystals draw down lifeforce." Another thought struck Dainyl. "Someone had to have told Brekylt, someone who knew how to use a Table. He couldn't have found out soon enough, otherwise."

"Dubaryt."

"Is he the recorder?"

Sulerya nodded. "He's always been Brekylt's creature."

"How did you find out?"

"One of his assistants. She'd only made one or two translations, but she slipped onto the Table after the assassins left while Dubaryt was Talent-locking the chamber. She almost didn't make it here. Dubaryt may have tried to reach her inside the tube. She collapsed, and she's sleeping right now. If you want to talk to her . . ."

"Does Sevasya know yet?"

"I've told her, but she already knew some of it. She has had a few problems of her own."

"She didn't want to summon me?"

"You're the High Alector, and she doesn't trust the marshal."

Dainyl could understand that. "The marshal and Noryan have turned out to be far more trustworthy than others." In fact, it appeared as though the submarshal had paid for his loyalty with his life. "I'd better see Sevasya."

"Vyane can—"

"I can find my way, and you may need her."

"Thank you."

Dainyl started to turn, then stopped. "I saw your father not that long ago—on Londi."

"How was he?"

"In good health, but tired."

Sulerya nodded. "He has worked too hard for too many years. We see each other seldom, usually only through the Tables." The momentary wistfulness left her face. "Sevasya could use your advice and help."

"Then I'd better go and provide them."

The door to the hidden chamber opened, and Dainyl stepped out, just in time to see a creature appear on the Table. It had the head of a pteridon, the lower legs of sandox, and ropy arms that held lightcutters. Two guards triggered their lightcutters, and the creature collapsed, but did not disintegrate.

"You're still getting wild translations," he said, turning back toward Sulerya.

"There are fewer, but they're more bizarre."

Dainyl nodded and left the Table chamber, following the corridor to the staircase—also cut through solid stone—that he took up to the doorway leading out into the walled courtyard beyond. The mild sun and moist air reminded him that even winter in Lysia was warm, and he unfastened his shimmersilk green jacket as he crossed the courtyard, skirting the immaculate pteridon squares and then stepping through the archway into the headquarters building.

The duty officer jumped to her feet. "Highest!" Her eyes darted down the corridor.

"I'm here to see the majer. Is she in her study?"

"Yes, sir, Highest."

"Thank you." Dainyl turned left and walked to the second doorway, opening it and stepping inside.

A Myrmidon captain was bound with shimmersilk ropes and tied to a chair. Dainyl could sense the darker purple aura of an alector born on Ifryn.

Sevasya stood by the narrow window, thinking, but her eyes immediately turned to Dainyl. "Highest!"

"I understood that you are facing some difficulties. I can see that Captain Josaryk—this is Josaryk, is it not?"

"It is."

"I can see where his loyalties lie." Dainyl looked to the majer. "How did you find out?"

"He tried to suborn the wrong Myrmidon. I've been watching ever since."

Dainyl could see the weariness in her eyes. He looked directly at Josaryk. "Why?"

"The Duarches are weaklings. Only Brekylt can save Acorus."

"Even if that were true, you owed your allegiance to those Duarches. You could have left the Myrmidons and become an assistant to the Alector of the East. Why didn't you?"

The captain's eyes flickered, but he did not answer.

"Might it be that you wanted the pteridons, and that suggests that the Duarches are not that weak. When will Brekylt declare that he is Duarch of the East?"

"I know nothing of that."

"What did Brekylt promise Duarch Samist?"

"I have no idea what you're talking about."

"Or Ruvryn?"

Josaryk closed his mouth.

Dainyl turned to Sevasya. "Do you need to know anything else?"

"No. He's revealed what he knows, and it's not all that much. He was supposed to fly Fourth Company back to Alustre this morning."

"Did Sulerya tell you about Noryan?"

"Yes."

Dainyl unholstered the lightcutter.

"You can't do that," said Josaryk.

"I can. The Marshal of Myrmidons can't, but the High Alector of Justice can." Dainyl lifted the lightcutter and aimed it, focusing his Talent into a thrust that opened a wedge in Josaryk's shields. Then he fired.

The Myrmidon barely had the chance to look surprised.

Dainyl turned to Sevasya. "Do you have enough trainees for the pteridons of the rebels?"

"Yes, sir."

"And an undercaptain we can promote to command? Who'll be loyal and can command?"

Sevasya nodded. "Waelstyr. He's solid, and Fourth Company will follow him."

"Let's see the next one of the rebels."

"That's Undercaptain Staetyl." Sevasya turned and left her study, walking to the south end of the building and down the steps to the lower level.

Staetyl's eyes widened as Dainyl followed Sevasya into the narrow cell. The undercaptain stiffened. "You may execute me, but that will not change matters."

"I believe that's the point," Dainyl replied. "You and Josaryk and Brekylt wanted to change things to have your own Duarchy. That's not an acceptable change, especially when you try to implement it through mutiny." Dainyl could sense that Staetyl had been born on Acorus, but birthplace was no indicator of treachery, one way or the other.

In the end, Dainyl executed all eight of the mutinous Myrmidons, disliking each killing more than the previous one. But as High Alector, he needed to make a statement that disloyalty had a high and immediate price. And Sevasya, Alcyna, and he—and Khelaryt—needed the pteridons without going through the lengthy process of transferring each from a living flier.

After he finished the distasteful task, he and Sevasya stood in the entry foyer of the Myrmidon building.

"By definition, as senior Myrmidon, you're now the acting submarshal of Myrmidons in the east," Dainyl said. "Marshal Alcyna will make the rank permanent. For now, Seventh Company will remain in the west, and Third Company is officially in mutiny."

"Yes, sir." Sevasya's smile was simultaneously rueful and grim. "Has the Alector of the East made any statements or taken any other action against the Duarchy?"

"He's said nothing, and he'll doubtless claim that he's done nothing. If a recorder's assistant had not escaped, and if you had not caught Josaryk, we wouldn't even know about the attempts to subvert the Myrmidons."

"Might I ask what you intend to do? Do you have any orders for me?"

"I don't propose invading the east for now, but even if I did, I'd still have to report these events to the Duarch and request his approval. So, the next step is to inform the Duarch. Then we'll see. At the moment, I can't even confirm where the pteridons of Third Company are. Your orders are simple. Maintain Lysia as part of the Duarchy, reporting to the Duarch of Elcien. Use whatever force you must. I'm in the process of arranging resupply directly by ship." Dainyl inclined his head. "Unless you have any more questions, I'll be returning to Elcien."

"No, sir." Sevasya smiled. "I'll be most happy to maintain Lysia for the Duarch."

"I thought you might."

Dainyl hurried back across the paved courtyard and down the stairs cut from the stone itself back to the Table chamber. When he stepped into the Table chamber, he looked for Sulerya. She stood at the end of the Table itself.

"You'd best make the translation quick, Highest," said Sulerya. "Those energy pulses are continuing."

"Thank you—for the information and the warning. As acting submarshal, Majer Sevasya has orders to maintain Lysia loyal to the Duarch of Elcien."

"You have an interesting way of phrasing things, Highest." Sulerya's green eyes twinkled.

"I'm certain that the Duarch of Elcien wishes to maintain the Duarchy," replied Dainyl, stepping onto the Table. "As does the senior alector of Lyterna."

He concentrated on the darkness beneath, and slipped . . .

. . . into the cool purpled light. There he concentrated on the white locator that was Elcien, and then he was through the silvered-white barrier.

One of the guards gaped as Dainyl stepped off the Table.

Chastyl turned, paused for just a moment, then spoke. "Highest . . . I'm glad you're back."

"Because of the fluctuations in the tube?"

"Yes, sir. We've had several more wild translations. *Very* wild. Oh . . . sir?"

Dainyl stopped.

"You might wish to know that High Alector Ruvryn appeared while you were in Lysia. He went to the Duarch's Palace. He did not ask where you were, and we did not volunteer that information."

"Thank you. Keep me informed as you can. I'll be at the Palace for a time." Dainyl left the chamber at a fast walk, hurrying into Adya's study. "Is the coach back?"

"Yes, sir. It's standing by."

"I'm headed to see the Duarch. I'll be back when I can get here." Dainyl wasn't about to send a written message about Brekylt's treachery or a verbal one unless he delivered it personally.

Dainyl hurried up the hidden stairs and then through the Hall of Justice and down the outer steps to the coach. The lowering clouds promised some sort of cold rain, but none was falling as he climbed into the coach.

While he rode the short distance to the Palace, he tried to anticipate what might happen next. Brekylt still had close to three hundred alectors, more than enough to replace all alectors in the east who might be loyal to the Duarchy, particularly since Brekylt had been filling positions with those loyal to him for years. With the pteridons of Third Company, and the lightcannon Ruvryn and the engineers at Fordall had created, Brekylt was in a good position to defy the Duarches. And . . . if Samist backed Brekylt . . .

Dainyl shook his head. He'd have to leave that to Khelaryt.

Bharyt stepped forward even before Dainyl was fully through the archway from the entry rotunda at the Palace. "Highest . . ."

"Bharyt, I haven't been summoned, but I have urgent news."

"He is meeting with High Alector Ruvryn, sir."

"He should know this news before that meeting is over. Is there any way you could ask him to step out? I promise that it will only take moments."

"I think I can manage that, sir. For you. He is in the conference room."

Dainyl followed the Palace functionary down the column-lined corridor he felt he had walked too often recently.

Outside the conference room, Bharyt stepped to the door, opened it just slightly, and sent the quickest of Talent pulses. Then he stepped back.

In moments, the Duarch stepped out into the corridor. His eyes went from Bharyt to Dainyl. A steely purpled darkness hovered around him. "You knew I was in a meeting?"

Bharyt eased back several yards.

"Yes, sir. When I heard with whom you were meeting, I felt it was imperative you know this. Brekylt and his assassins murdered Noryan and half of Third Company this morning. They also got one of those lightcannon and used it to kill one Myrmidon trying to use a pteridon to escape. Officially, Third Company has mutinied. Effectively, it belongs to Brekylt. Fourth Company is in Lysia, under the overall command of Majer Sevasya. Eight Myrmidons in the company, including Captain Josaryk, attempted mutiny. They're all dead, and Majer Sevasya had enough trainees to replace them. She is acting submarshal. In addition, there are energy fluctuations coming from Ifryn that may affect the translation tubes, but it's not possible to tell the cause or whether the fluctuations will abate, or worsen."

"You're quite resourceful, Dainyl. Only losing one company out of four . . ."

"Two out of eight, possibly, sir. And the spreading of lightcannon worries me. They can draw down lifeforce quickly."

"True. Is that all?"

"That's all for now. I can provide details as you wish. I wanted you to know as soon as possible."

"Thank you. The details will have to wait." Khelaryt nodded and turned, reentering the conference room.

Bharyt escorted Dainyl back down the corridor. Neither spoke.

Just short of the archway leading out to his waiting coach, Dainyl stopped, then turned. "Thank you, Bharyt. I appreciate your help and forbearance."

"You are welcome, sir."

Dainyl nodded and hurried back out to the rotunda. "Myrmidon headquarters."

"Yes, sir."

Dainyl half climbed, half jumped up into the coach, then sat back trying to think how he should handle the situation in the east. Despite the assassinations, there was no real proof of an actual attempt by Brekylt to seize power.

Once the coach pulled up outside the gates, Dainyl hurried through the almost-freezing drizzle into Myrmidon headquarters. He barely nodded at the duty officer—Undercaptain Chelysta—as he turned left and went down the corridor to the marshal's study.

Alcyna stood abruptly as Dainyl barged in and shut the door behind him.

"Sir?"

"I was summoned to Lysia, but Sulerya's assistant didn't let me know why. There, I found out that Noryan got the orders we sent, but someone let Brekylt know. Brekylt took a team of assassins to Norda and murdered Noryan and half of Third Company in the middle of the night, more toward this morning. They used a lightcannon as well. The rest threw in with Brekylt. So you've got a mutiny of Third Company. Josaryk attempted the same thing in Lysia, but Sevasya caught him and the seven others. They're all dead, but Sevasya had enough trainees to replace them. In effect, she's acting submarshal."

"The ones in Lysia are all dead?"

"I executed them. Both Josaryk and Staetyl were quite certain that the Duarches are weaklings and that only Brekylt is fit to govern Corus."

"Were they shadowmatched?"

"No. They really believed it."

Alcyna shook her head. "Unless you have objections, I'll appoint Sevasya as submarshal."

"I'd hoped you'd see it that way."

"Who else is there? Fhentyl and Lyzetta are too junior, and Elysara is committed to stay at Lyterna." She paused. "What will the Duarches do?"

"What can they do? Officially, we've had a mutiny and an attempted mutiny, nothing more. Brekylt will deny everything, and he'll claim the Myrmidon problems are all because the Myrmidons lack effective leadership or something like that."

"The implication will be that alectresses can't lead." Alcyna's voice was cold. "He won't say that, of course. Not in public."

"And I'll be at fault for choosing you."

"It's a wonderful pattern," Alcyna said. "Shastylt, Zelyert, and Brekylt all create this mess, and then when everything's falling apart, and you and Khelaryt put in some alectresses to try to undo the damage, we all get blamed for all the problems they created."

"Of course," replied Dainyl. "There weren't any problems until all these alectresses started ordering alectors around."

Alcyna snorted, her eyes flickering to the window and the gray drizzle beyond. "What will you do?"

"Whatever I can to put an end to it. But I'd like a glass or two to think about it."

"Sir?"

"Yes?"

"There is one other thing. I had one of the fliers ferry me over to see Colonel Herolt first thing this morning. I'd just gotten back when you arrived. You were right. He had a partial shadowmatch."

"What did you do?"

"I thought about removing it, but that might make matters even worse. Shastylt put in a suicide link."

"So that if anyone tried to remove it, he'd suicide?"

"More like he'd do something so risky he was bound to die."

"What did you do?"

"Just added a modification, so that he can't order anything that might endanger the survival of an entire company. If he feels that way, he has to defer to the site commander." She shrugged. "I thought it was worth a try. If it doesn't work, then we're not that much worse off, since he can't really issue direct orders to his battalion commanders anyway."

"That had to be Shastylt."

"He didn't want the Cadmians to be too effective."

"I think he was afraid of them if they had good leadership at the top. From what I can tell, strange things happened to bright captains. Very few ever became majers."

"But why?"

"Can you imagine two thousand Cadmians with explosives and large-bore weapons?"

"They couldn't do that much damage against lightcutters."

"I wonder," mused Dainyl. Inside, he didn't wonder at all. Majer Mykel's battalion had used rifles to destroy close to fifty alectors armed with lightcutters in a single afternoon, and the Cadmians had incurred only moderate casualties. Dainyl understood Shastylt's fear, yet he also recalled the ancient's words about Acorus needing both alectors and landers. And much as he might wish otherwise, he could not forget that he owed his life to the majer.

Alcyna looked at him sharply. "You know something."

"Shastylt was half-right. The Cadmians could be very dangerous, but killing off the obviously bright officers won't solve that problem. Sooner or later, officers who are even brighter and who can see what happens to obviously bright officers will hide their brilliance and bide their time and get promoted, and then it will be too late."

"You would see that."

Dainyl ignored the reference. "I need to get back to the Hall of Justice."

He had to do something about Brekylt, before the Alector of the East split Corus into civil war and deployed lightcannon against the Myrmidons.

82

Late into the day, and then into the early evening, Dainyl remained in his private study beneath the Hall of Justice. There was no word from the Duarches, and no word from Brekylt. Nothing changed so far as the Tables were concerned—the energy fluctuations continued, but neither increased nor decreased in amplitude or frequency.

Theoretically, Dainyl could recommend that the Duarches order the Myrmidons to attack Brekylt, but it was highly unlikely Khelaryt would agree to that since the Duarch had not summoned him back to the Palace. Duarch Samist would oppose such an effort. Even if the Duarches were united in that, Dainyl had real doubts about such a strategy's success. Second Company would not obey that order, and sending First Company east would be foolhardy, since that would leave Elcien unprotected against Second Company. Fifth and Seventh Companies could be sent east, and perhaps the reconfigured Fourth Company. Sixth Company *might* comply, but Eighth Company was tied to Lysia. Four companies against one weren't bad odds, except for several problems. First was the distance. The closest company to Alustre was Fourth, and it was a long day's flight from Lysia. Sixth Company was more than two days away, and Fifth and Seventh were at least three days' flight from Alustre. Add to that the fact that Brekylt had lightcannon and had no compunctions about using them—and Dainyl had no idea how many or where they might be. Nor did he know where Third Company was. Finally, in all probability, most of the alectors in the east probably supported Brekylt. And the situation was bound to get worse. Unless Brekylt was stopped, it was only a matter of time before Corus was split into factions, and Brekylt still might use the lightcannon, threatening everyone's future in a form of lifeforce blackmail.

Dainyl had an idea, but whether it would work was another question. That was what he needed to find out.

Finally, he stood, leaving the platter that had held a casual meal of bread, cheese, and cold sliced ham on the table. He checked the charges in the two holstered lightcutters, then donned the green jacket and walked out of the study and down the corridor to the Table chamber.

Diordyn was sitting on a stool between two guards. The other two guards stood on the far side of the Table. All watched the Table. Against the inner wall, Dainyl saw a small bundle of folded clothes, and a set of delicate shoes.

"Highest? To Dereka?" asked Diordyn.

"I'm going to test some things." Dainyl stepped onto the Table, concentrating on the blackness beneath the purple of the translation tube.

He slipped into the purple-shaded twilight of the translation tube, letting his Talent-sense range beyond the tube itself, even deeper. After a moment, he focused on dropping into the greenish blackness beneath the tube.

There was an instant flash of green, and he was beneath the translation tube. He could sense, not just the single "line" of the translation tube above him, but also a web of interconnected blackish green with points of brilliant amber-green. He was both within that web and yet able to view it from without.

One of the blackish green points seemed not too "far" from the amber locator of Hyalt. Dainyl extended a Talent probe, but one sheathed in green. This time, he was aware of his own motion, rather than feeling that the destination approached him. He came to a halt with the silver-green above him, not breaking or flashing through a barrier.

Did he have to concentrate on leaving, in a fashion similar to what he did when entering a Table?

Carefully, he visualized rising through soil or rock or what might be there. He could feel himself moving upward, and darkness—the true darkness of night—rising around him.

But he was still somehow linked to the blackish green web. He looked down, abruptly aware that he could see with both eyes and Talent, and saw that the lower part of his trousers and his boots were "buried" in red stone. He concentrated on moving upward.

Suddenly, Dainyl stood on a rocky uneven surface, and a cool wind blew around him. He had to take a quick step sideways to avoid falling. He was perched on a large chunk of sandy rock. Carefully, he eased himself off the rock and onto the narrow ground between two boulders that were parts of a rocky jumble.

Where was he?

He glanced up, but clouds covered most of the night sky, although he caught a quick glimpse of the green disc of Asterta before the smaller moon was covered by a fast-moving cloud. He looked to his right, down a long slope toward a ruined compound of some sort, and the town beyond. It was familiar . . . Hyalt!

He took a deep breath, even as he turned to the west, where he could barely sense the RA's complex, still being repaired and rebuilt.

He'd done it. Once, at least.

He'd also learned that the ancients' web allowed more freedom in exiting, but there was also the problem of figuring out where he was headed before he got there.

He felt a drop of rain on the back of his neck, and to the south, lightning flashed, and a rumble of thunder followed.

He didn't sense a green point or locator, but he could sense the darkness beneath the ground. Could he link to the blackish green web from where he stood? He might as well try. Dainyl concentrated once more, thinking about the blackness beneath.

Nothing happened, except that several more drops of rain pattered down around him.

Would a more direct Talent link work?

He extended a link, trying to emphasize the green, but the blackish green of the web eluded his probe.

A few more raindrops pattered down, several striking his hands and head, and another bolt of lightning flared to the south, followed by a long rumbling roar of thunder.

It had to be possible, because he'd seen the ancients vanish. But how?

Dainyl attempted to meld a focus on the dark green web with a more diffuse, almost misty green linkage . . .

. . . and he found himself connected to the web and sinking through the sandstone and soil, his vision being cut off and replaced solely by Talent perception.

This time he attempted to create a mental "map" of the locator wedges "above" him with the interlocking web that he could sense fully, even while being within one of the "strands." Immediately, he noted that every locator wedge was situated above a point where three or more of the web strands—although they were far wider than strands—connected. Ley nodes—that was what ley nodes were.

He located the sullen red wedge that was Soupat, but concentrated on the green node closest to that. Once more, he felt himself moving along the ley lines, until he reached the node.

Deliberately and gently, he eased himself from the node upward.

He emerged beside a pile of rocks. He glanced around, trying to orient himself. He was to the east of a fallen building on the low mesa that had held the RA's complex in Soupat.

"The ancients! Run! Run, if you value your life!"

A spade—or some other implement—clattered against stone, and the sound of boots on stone faded away in the damp night air.

Dainyl could sense that there had been two men. His eyes and Talent revealed an opening in the half-collapsed stone wall to his right.

Scavengers—looking for whatever they could find in the ruins.

He laughed softly.

Overhead, the sky was clear. The rain that had begun to fall in Hyalt had long since left Soupat, and both Selena and Asterta shone down on Dainyl.

Dainyl Talent-sensed the blackish green of the web below

and concentrated on replicating his early effort of melding focus and diffuse linkage.

Even more easily, he dropped into the web below.

He started to orient himself for the return to Elcien when he became aware of a growing sense of amber-green surrounding him—and what he could only have described as pressure. It could only be the ancients.

Should he resist? He decided against resistance, although he could not have explained why, and let himself follow the pressure toward another ley node, one of a handful that showed a golden green.

He emerged in a chamber that was walled in amber-green stone—it had to be in one of the towers on the plateau, because he could feel his breathing was more labored, and the air was almost frigid.

Hovering before him were three of the ancients—all looking like winged miniatures of lander women.

You do not belong traveling the web—not as you are. It will hurt you more than you can imagine.

Hurt him? By making him more "green" or in some other way?

The conflict between what you were and what you will be can destroy you.

"You're saying that I'll change whether I wish it or not."

Actions change one. Desires in conflict with actions make such change difficult. Sometimes that conflict can also kill.

Dainyl realized he could not sense which of the ancient soarers "spoke."

"I need the web. If I do not use it, you will suffer as much as everyone."

?????? was the response.

"One of my . . . kind . . . wishes to start a war, one that will expend lifeforce that will weaken the entire world. Without the web, I cannot stop this."

Do what you think you must, but you have been warned. Go. Behind the words was a link-reminder, or something similar, that called up an image of the massive concentration of

humming green Talent/lifeforce. There was also a sense of indifference to his warning that accompanied the implied threat of the concentrated green lifeforce.

Go.

Dainyl decided that further "discussion" was definitely unwise. For the third time, he melded focus and diffuse linkage and . . .

. . . found himself back in the blackish green web. He concentrated, this time on the white locator for Elcien and found himself sliding into the translation tube.

For the first time ever, within a tube, he could sense his own motion, and not the illusion of the locator moving to him. There was no barrier, not even the faintest hint of silver-white . . .

. . . as he appeared on the Table.

One of the guards fired his lightcutter, then a second.

Using his shields, Dainyl deflected the bluish beams, almost absently.

"Stop! It's the Highest."

Belatedly, Dainyl could sense the greenish aura around himself, strong enough that it was visible to eyes as well as Talent-senses.

"Sir?" Diordyn swallowed as he looked at Dainyl.

"Some strange things are going on between Tables," Dainyl said tiredly, trying to defuse the concerns of the assistant to the recorder. "They're not going to get better soon, either." He straightened. "It doesn't help when you shoot at someone who's trying to solve the problems."

"I thought . . . you were going to Dereka . . ." stammered Diordyn.

"It doesn't matter what you *thought,*" Dainyl replied tartly. "It matters what you do." The sudden realization of the inadvertent irony of his words, echoing what the ancients had said to him, took away the edge of his anger at being a target. He focused on Diordyn. "Dereka is going to have to wait. Tell Chastyl—or leave word with him—that I'll need to talk to him."

"Ah . . . yes, sir."

As Dainyl left the Table chamber, not only could he sense

the continued shock within Diordyn, but he could hear the murmurs from the guards.

". . . green . . ."

". . . lightcutter like it wasn't there . . ."

". . . why he's the Highest . . ."

After he left the Hall of Justice, Dainyl took the coach back to his dwelling. He wasn't about to use the Table to travel to Dereka. Had he done so, Lystrana would have immediately discerned what he had in mind—and both she and Kytrana would have been mightily disturbed at the increasing amount of green that permeated his Talent.

He stiffened on the bench seat of the coach. The attitude of the ancients gnawed at him. He'd tried to point out the dangers of lifeforce loss, and the three ancients had clearly dismissed the threat as trivial. Trivial? What were they doing that made lightcannon trivial?

He couldn't help shivering, but it was just the result of a long and tiring day, and the chill of a night in early winter, wasn't it?

83

Dainyl did not sleep well, but forced himself to eat a hearty breakfast before he left for the Hall of Justice in the coach that he had arranged for the night before. He wore the green jacket over his official garments and carried four lightcutters, two in holsters at his belt, and two tucked inside his jacket. He still worried about the ancients' diffidence toward him, as well as about their casually chilling warning—and the fact that the green aspect of his Talent had faded not in the slightest overnight.

At the same time, he knew he had to do something about the deteriorating situation facing him—and all of Acorus. He'd focused too closely on Brekylt and those who followed him, assuming that Brekylt had merely wished to become Duarch of the East. That *might* have been acceptable, had Brekylt limited his efforts to less devastating weapons. The fact that he had not, and that neither Samist nor Khelaryt had reacted, could only mean that Samist was truly behind Brekylt and that Khelaryt felt powerless against the two.

Even if Brekylt were not the principal cause of the deterioration, after what Dainyl had seen at Soupat, with the depletion of lifeforce by the heavier lightcannon, and the widespread distribution and use of such weapons by Brekylt and his allies, Dainyl had to do something. He was in no position to attack Samist or Ruvryn, but at the least he could deal with Brekylt and reduce the lifeforce depletion.

Not only did he truly fear for the future of Acorus, both for himself and Lystrana, and especially for their daughter, but he felt as though he might be about the only one who fully understood what the use of lightcannon truly meant.

Early as it was—a good half glass before morning muster at Myrmidon headquarters—the corridors and studies beneath the Hall of Justice were empty, except for Adya's study.

Dainyl peered in at his chief assistant. "Good morning, Adya. Any messages?"

Adya stared at him for a moment, then shook her head quickly. "No, Highest."

"I'll be gone for a time." With that, he headed down the corridor toward the Table chamber.

Dainyl had barely stepped out of the entry foyer when Chastyl stepped forward. "Highest."

"Good morning, Chastyl. Did you get my message?"

"Just that you wished to talk to me."

"Something is happening between the Tables."

"The energy fluctuations—"

"No. There's some sort of green Talent. It's irregular, but it's there. The ancients are massing forces, somehow." Dainyl laughed ruefully, extended his left arm, and looked at it. "I should know."

"I don't know what we can do . . ."

"I don't either, but I'd like you to get word to Myenfel and Sulerya. I'll let Jonyst know."

Chastyl moistened his lips. "Is using the Tables wise . . . after yesterday, sir?"

"Wise? No. Necessary, yes." Dainyl eased past the recorder and the guards and stepped up onto the Table.

He cleared his mind and used the melding-focus technique. After a moment, he slipped downward and . . .

. . . through the purpleness of the translation tube into the blackish green of the web beneath. With the complexity of the web, Dainyl felt it took longer to find both the dark gray of the Alustre locator and then the ley node that corresponded to it.

The near-distant **humming** *of the ancients' Talent concentration or device felt higher-pitched, but Dainyl wasn't certain whether the frequency had shifted or his perceptions had changed. Either way, there was little enough he could do about it at the moment.*

The transport/translation was swift, but as he neared the node and locator above it, Dainyl tried to focus on breaking out well away from the Table, visualizing and extending himself . . .

. . . to find himself in the corridor outside the Alustre Table chamber, where he quickly used his Talent to conceal his presence. He needed to do better in the future—if he could.

One of the alector guards stationed outside the doors to the Table chamber—less than ten yards away—turned. "There's Talent there." He raised his voice. "Whoever it is, I'll fire."

Dainyl dropped the sight concealment.

"It's him!"

Both attempted to fire lightcutters.

Dainyl brushed away the energy beams, then turned them back on the guards. Both fell.

He just looked for a moment at the fallen pair. He'd never been able to do that before. He'd seen the ancients do it, but he'd never seen an alector do it. He hadn't thought about killing them, not precisely, but turning their energy back. Was he becoming as callous as he felt Brekylt was? He pushed away the thought. He needed to find Brekylt, especially if the Alector of the East had put out word that Dainyl was to be killed on sight.

He walked quickly to the stairs and then up to the next level, using sight concealment as he neared the section of the building frequented mainly by landers—and alectors of lesser Talent.

Two landers walked out of the second doorway. Neither looked back.

"Something's going on," said one.

"No one's talking. Not the alectors, anyway."

"Haven't seen many today . . ."

The two turned down a side corridor, but Dainyl kept moving, trying to remain near the center where someone was less likely to step out of a doorway and run into him, since he should be invisible to all but those with Talent.

He knew from past experience that there was a direct set of stairs to the alectors' level, and that it was in the middle of the building. After searching that part of the building, Dainyl used his Talent-senses to locate the back staircase to the uppermost level, and to release the Talent lock on the lower door. Shields firm, he opened the door and stepped through into a small foyer.

The single alector guard in black and silver whirled, lifting his lightcutter.

Dainyl dropped the sight concealment. "I wouldn't, if I were you."

"Highest . . ." The guard's eyes flicked from Dainyl to the door through which he had entered.

"I'm looking for the Alector of the East."

"His study is on the next level."

"I know."

"You can't go up there . . . sir."

"I wasn't aware that a mere senior alector could prohibit a High Alector from doing anything." Dainyl stepped forward.

"Stop, sir." The guard's finger tightened on the firing stud.

Dainyl reached out with his Talent, shunted the energy aside. The guard paled, then stepped back. Dainyl walked past him, reaching out and taking the lightcutter and slipping it inside his jacket before he started up the narrow staircase. At the top was another door, but without a guard.

After walking ten yards to his right in the direction of Brekylt's formal study, his boots clicking on the silver and black marble of the corridor floor, it became clear that there were no alectors anywhere nearby. In fact, as he discovered by Talent and looking into study after study, no one at all was there.

Dainyl hurried back along the corridor and down the stairs, noting that the guard had also vanished, and made his way under sight concealment back toward the Table chamber.

All that remained of the two alector guards were their black and silver uniforms and their boots. That no one had checked on the guards suggested strongly that Brekylt and those closest to him had left Alustre. Even so, as he opened the door into the Table chamber, he strengthened his shields. The chamber itself was empty, but Dainyl could sense Talent concealed within the hidden recorder's chambers.

He moved toward the section of the stone wall that was the hidden door, extending a Talent probe to release the lock. The door slid open, revealing a younger alector in the green of a Recorder of Deeds. His face was stern, and his violet eyes hard.

"Recorder Retyl?" asked Dainyl politely.

"You're not the Highest! You're an abomination!" Retyl fired a blast of Talent.

Dainyl deflected it and stepped forward, using his shields to block the recorder's access to the Table. "Where is Brekylt?"

Retyl backed away.

Dainyl forced his shields around those of the recorder. "Where did he go?"

"I'll never tell you, abomination."

Dainyl contracted his shields more.

The recorder swallowed, then lashed out with all his Talent, dropping his own shields.

Dainyl was a fraction of an instant too late, and the recorder's Talent force rebounded from Dainyl's shields and slammed back into the recorder, who smiled in the instant before his form shattered to dust under the impact of his own powers.

Retyl's reply, and his actions, suggested strongly that Retyl had known where Brekylt was or had gone. That meant Brekylt had used the Table to go somewhere. The most likely destinations were either Dulka, where he had been building a force, or Ludar. Until Dainyl knew more—and could prove it—he didn't want to travel into Ludar, and that left Dulka.

Dainyl turned, as if to climb onto the Table, before shaking his head. He didn't need the Table to access the deeper web. He concentrated on it, finding himself dropping . . .

. . . simultaneously through and past the purpled translation tube down to the deeper blackish green web. Above him, he could sense from outside the contractions of the translation tube, those seemed stronger and more frequent.

Just how long would it be before the Archon transferred the Master Scepter?

Dainyl caught himself. He could still end up trapped in the ancients' web if he didn't concentrate on the task at hand. He searched for the maroon and blue locator of Dulka, and then the green node corresponding to it.

He flashed toward it, coming to a halt, hovering above it and below the translation tube and the locator. Carefully, trying to keep a link to the ley line, he focused on moving upward through the stone and angling in the direction that led to the RA's study.

Then, suddenly he could see clearly, if still linked below, and found himself in one of the redstone corridors. He nudged his way along toward the steps leading up to the RA's complex. Ahead at the archway at the base of the stone stairs were two alector guards in black and silver shimmersilk.

Both raised their lightcutters.

Dainyl strengthened his shields and . . .

. . . found himself standing on the redstone paving of the corridor, as though reinforcing his shields had cut the link to the ley node below.

"It's the Highest of Justice! Pass the word! Heavier weapons!"

The blue energy from their lightcutters flared around his shields. A second blast flared around him from behind.

Dainyl had hoped to link to the ley node, but how could he when holding stronger shields cut him off?

The guards fired again. This time, Dainyl diverted the energy back at them, boosting it with his own Talent. Both went down, sprawling on the redstone floor.

Dainyl turned in time to see his attackers from the rear dart into a side corridor.

Then two more guards spilled from the RA's staircase, and one carried a riflelike device. He immediately leveled it at Dainyl and fired. A bolt of blue-green flame slammed against Dainyl's shields with enough force to reverberate through him.

Dainyl swung to face the new attackers, marshaling Talent force, concentrating on the light-rifle, and struggling to divert those energy bolts back at the guard who was firing it. Even as he moved forward, the second and third bolts began to fray at his shields.

Trying to hold the shields, he Talent-reached for the ley node and the green Talent force that it held. Then, he could feel a well of Talent, and he focused it into a narrow line, directly at the light-rifle.

The corridor exploded into light, so bright that Dainyl could see nothing. His eyes burned, then watered. Flashing points of light filled his field of vision. He blotted his eyes with the back of his hand, but that didn't help much. The air around him was stifling, and there was an odor of ash and molten metal.

After several moments, he still could not see, but his Talent-sense gave him a feel of the corridor. He was the only one in it. He took one careful step forward, and then another. By the time he neared the archway to the staircase, his eyes were providing a blurry picture. One side of the stone archway had been melted to the point that thin rivulets of stone had run down the wall and then cooled and hardened.

Dainyl did not see or sense anyone on the stone stairs or on the landing at the top of the stairs. He started up, warily, but no one approached. The landing was empty, as was the corridor beyond.

His eyesight had begun to improve, and he could also sense a greater concentration of Talent farther beyond, in the direction of the RA's study. He stood for several moments, then moved down the corridor, unholstering both lightcutters and holding them ready. As easy as he tried to make his steps, he still felt his boots sounded like thunder on the redstone tiled floor.

An alector guard peered out of a doorway ten yards ahead.

Dainyl fired, and the alector dropped.

The concentration of Talent ahead remained constant, and Dainyl sent out a Talent probe.

"It's an ancient!"

Smiling mirthlessly at the exclamation that showed how little the speaker knew about the ancients, Dainyl continued his approach to the RA's study. He could detect two sources of Talent within the outer foyer to the RA's study. One was that of an alector, somehow partly shielded, and the other source was a lightcannon—but one without storage crystals. Dainyl stopped. He really would have preferred to sprint away from the lightcannon—really more like a roadcutter—that would suck lifeforce from the entire area. The shielded alector had to be an alector, possibly even an engineer—in one of the insulated suits.

Dainyl stopped dead, carefully extending a Talent probe to the lightcannon. It would be hard for the alector in the suit to detect because Talent and lifeforce insulation worked both ways.

The energy already stored for discharge was massive.

Dainyl eased back a step, then another. There was no sense in trying to face something that obliterated rock walls scores of yards high and deep.

"There he is!"

With the words, a bolt of greenish blue slammed into his shields from behind.

He concentrated, trying to hold his shields and at the same time attempting to use Talent to discharge energy from the lightcannon in a fashion that would destroy it while inflicting damage on everyone and anything but himself. The energy patterns had more than a few locks within the mechanism, and he was trying to manipulate them from more than ten yards away, strictly applying Talent.

Another light-rifle bolt battered him, and the alector controlling the overpowered lightcannon began to wheel it forward to where it could fire at Dainyl.

Dainyl realized he wasn't going to have time to manipulate the lightcannon's controls. He slammed a Talent blast into the control crystal, then dropped to the floor and contracted his shields, hoping he could protect himself—remembering to close his eyes.

The entire stone structure shuddered. Light flared through his closed eyelids, and his body skidded across the redstone tiles back toward the stairs. Stones and other heavy objects slammed into his shields, and kept striking.

For a moment, Dainyl lay stunned on the hard redstone tiles. Then he rolled over and staggered to his feet. The north end of the upper level of the RA's building was gone, as was the entire roof. The south end was heaped with rubble.

Dainyl could sense, through shields that were but a fraction of what they had been moments before, that a small circular area around where the lightcannon had been was lifeforce-dead. After a moment, he turned and made his way, half climbing over stone and wood rubble, toward the staircase that would get him lower and closer to the ley node below.

Twice, on the way down the stairs, he nearly lost his balance on the stone chunks that half filled the staircase and nearly tumbled down. Beyond the bottom landing, the corridor leading back to the Table area was clear of rubble, but the walls were riddled with cracks, wide enough in several places to admit lines of sunlight.

Then he heard voices ahead.

"He's still alive, just ahead . . ."

"Should have killed him . . ."

"Where's the other lightcannon? Get it here!" The voice was unfamiliar, certainly not Brekylt's. Might it be Quivaryt?

"Hurry! We've almost got him."

"We can't let him escape."

Why was there such urgency about that? Dainyl set that question aside and Talent-groped for the ley node below him. He hoped he could link because what shields he did have left wouldn't stand against a lightcannon—or even one of the light-rifles.

His Talent felt weak, limited.

What about letting the green attract the green?

As he tried to meld and create that necessary diffuse link, he added a sense of similarity . . .

. . . and he dropped through the stone toward the blackish green of the ley node below.

The ley web was cool, welcoming.

Yet Dainyl couldn't seem to locate the ley node that matched the crimson-gold of the locator for Dereka, and his entire body felt as though it were turning to ice.

In desperation, he jabbed a Talent link at the Dereka locator . . . and slowly, glacially, it neared him. He toppled through the silvered barrier . . .

. . . going to his knees on the Table. For a moment, he remained there on his knees.

"Don't fire! It's the Highest! He's hurt."

Dainyl eased himself to the side of the Table, getting his legs out from under himself. He sat on the edge, trying to recover some strength.

Whelyne walked around the end of the Table. As she studied him more closely, her eyes widened, and her mouth opened. "Highest . . . what . . . ?"

". . . Jonyst . . . around?"

"No, sir."

"Tell him . . . that Brekylt has left Alustre . . . There are lightcannon and light-rifles in Dulka . . . and the ancients are massing some kind of green Talent force." He forced a smile. "Do you think Guersa could take me to the RA's quarters? I need some rest."

"Yes, sir. I'm certain she could." Whelyne added, "Do you need help?"

"Let's see." Dainyl stood, slowly. His knees felt wobbly, and his calves were weak, but he walked slowly to the archway out of the Table chamber and up the stairs into the spacious library. The afternoon sun poured into the room, giving it a sense of warmth.

"I'll walk down with you," Whelyne said.

"You don't need to . . ."

"If Jonyst found out I hadn't, sir . . ."

Dainyl understood that. He was also grateful for her presence.

When he stepped out of the recorder's building on the lower level where the coach waited, Dainyl could tell he wasn't going to walk that much farther, not the way his legs alternated between feeling like jelly and as though they would seize up in cramps any moment.

"Guersa . . . you'll need to take the Highest to the RA's quarters. He's been in some sort of . . . battle."

Dainyl could sense that Whelyne had almost said a "Talent battle."

"I can do that."

Dainyl did take Whelyne's arm and assistance to climb into the coach. "Thank you. You'll tell Jonyst?"

"I will, Highest. You need to get well."

For several moments after the coach pulled away and headed south on the main boulevard, Dainyl just sat on the hard bench seat of the coach. For the first time in his life, or at least in a long time, he realized, he'd faced an array of weapons that could kill him—regardless of the Talent of the alector who held them. What was worse was that Ruvryn and Brekylt—and Samist—seemed intent on manufacturing and distributing them widely. Didn't they understand the implications? Or were a few years of power more important to them than the future of both indigens and alectors?

He had recovered slightly—just slightly—by the time Guersa eased the coach to a halt outside Lystrana's official quarters.

He opened the door and stepped down as carefully as if he were an older alector close to losing all his lifeforce—and maybe he had come that close—then made his way to the doors.

Fortunately, the house girl opened the door quickly.

"Oh, Highest . . . she's still at work."

"That's all right. I've had a hard day, and I need some rest."

"Oh . . . yes, sir." Jylena fumbled the ironwork door open.

"Thank you." Dainyl forced himself to smile politely as he entered. Then he walked along the inside hallway that seemed endless, slowly making his way to the bedchamber.

He could only manage to remove his boots before the walls began to strobe and swirl around him. With the last of his strength he took two steps from the chair to the bed, half climbing, half falling onto it as his eyes closed and a blackish green swept over him.

84

In the orangish light preceding twilight, Mykel reined up outside the small shedlike barn, taking in the other outbuildings and the larger barn that would hold many of the men. He turned to Rhystan, who had ridden in beside him. "It's not much, but it's better than bivouacking in the open or in woods. After you get your companies set, we'll meet here. By then, the last of the scouts should be back. If you'd pass the word to the other officers?"

"We'll do that." Rhystan turned his mount, and he and Culeyt rode toward the barn.

Rather than dismount immediately, Mykel made another tour of the area, looking and saying little. The main house was shuttered tight, and he couldn't say he blamed the family.

He rode past the provisions wagons, lined up on one side of the barn. The ammunition wagons were farther away, next to a shed, but a five-man guard was already on duty. Beyond the barn, the stock pond had ice around the edges, and a guard to keep Cadmians from using or defiling it. To the northeast of the stock pond, another hundred yards away, was the southwestern base of a low hill that rose a good fifteen yards above the rest of the holding. The upper section was bare black rock, almost polished-looking. Mykel studied it for a moment, thinking that it reminded him of something, but what it was he couldn't say.

He took his time with his survey, then rode back to the shed barn. After dismounting carefully, he tied the roan to a fence post. Although he could now use his right hand, he still could not lift his forearm, and the sling remained a necessity. By the time he had carried his saddlebags and bedroll into the shed—one-handed—and found a corner that looked dry and less drafty, he heard voices. He walked back outside.

Jasakyt and Coroden had dismounted and tied their mounts.

"Afternoon, Majer," offered Jasakyt, the Fifteenth Company scout.

"Majer, sir." Coroden inclined his head.

Mykel could see others approaching—Rhystan and Loryalt on foot, Culeyt and the other two undercaptains riding, followed by three more scouts. He moved back in front of the shed and waited. Once they all were present, he cleared his throat. "Let's have the scouts' reports."

The first was Coroden from Fourteenth Company. He swallowed and began. "Most of the tracks lead down that lane that circles around the hill. . . ."

By the time all five scouts had reported, the sun had dropped below the tree-lined western horizon, and the northeast wind had picked up. Mykel fumbled his jacket closed. It appeared likely that the Reillies and Squawts were preparing to move first to the southwest and then intercept the Borlan road another ten vingts to the south. Their strategy looked to be direct and simple. Keep threatening Borlan and force Mykel to try to stop them so that they could attempt to kill him and destroy Third Battalion.

As a Cadmian commander, Mykel couldn't risk letting the hill barbarians loose on Borlan. "We'll leave at dawn. We should be able to reach the hills to the north of the flats across the river from Borlan."

"Yes, sir." That came from the three undercaptains. Rhystan and Culeyt only nodded.

"That's all for now," Mykel went on. "I'm going to walk through the camp."

The scouts and undercaptains and Culeyt departed immediately.

Rhystan waited, then turned to Mykel. "Do you think you can get them to fight us?"

"Sooner or later. I'd prefer sooner, and we'll have to make it costly for them."

"You already have, sir, but that doesn't seem to be stopping them."

Mykel was well aware of that. From the latest reports, the Reillies had left close to four hundred on the field in three encounters, yet they were regrouping. From the two Cadmian battalions, thirty men had been killed outright in the second skirmish, with another ten dying later of wounds, and fifty wounded. "Some people can only accept things their way. They'd almost rather die than change."

"Almost?"

Rhystan's tone was wry, but Mykel could sense the deeper feelings behind it.

"I know. I'm going to walk through the camp for a bit. Do you want to join me?"

"It might be best if I didn't, sir."

"Then I'll see you later." Mykel smiled and turned to his left. Less than ten yards toward the barn, he dodged a half-frozen hole that contained water and worse, heading for the closest company—Thirteenth Company.

"Sir!" Dyarth stiffened as he saw Mykel.

"I'm just looking around, Undercaptain. How are your wounded doing?"

"We lost one, sir. The others look to make it."

"Good. Just keep up the good work." Mykel offered a smile he hoped was encouraging and sympathetic, then moved on.

As he neared the cookfires to the south of the main barn, the odor of wood smoke grew stronger. From the edge of Fourteenth Company, he could hear voices from a group of rankers.

". . . puts on his pants like everyone else, bleeds like us, too . . ."

". . . rode out of that forest with an iron bar through his chest . . ."

". . . dagger of the ancients . . ."

Mykel managed not to wince. When he stepped away from the cookfires, in the growing darkness he looked toward the lone hill, a hill that seemed cloaked in a black and amber-green.

. . . Learn what you must know . . .

Were the soarers calling him?

They always had a reason. He turned toward the hill, following an old and overgrown path. He glanced toward the holder's dwelling, where the shutters remained tight, although a healthy line of smoke issued from the main chimney.

The upper part of the hill was surrounded by a wooden plank fence, old enough that several of the planks had fallen and not been replaced. Likewise, the gate half hung from a single iron hinge. Mykel stepped around the gate and continued up the gentle slope of the path.

The soarer hovered over bare black stone short of the highest point of the low hill, clearly waiting for Mykel.

You have become more perceptive.

"You summoned me."

Invited.

Mykel received the impression of humor. He waited.

What do you intend to do about the invaders?

"What do *you* intend? It's clear that you planned the attacks to destroy Fourth Battalion. Why? You said that we weren't the problem, but the . . . the Ifrits were."

That is not quite true. They are the greater danger. They will destroy the world for all life, all but the lowest forms. But a herding dog who follows such an invader is also a danger.

"So I'm a danger, now?"

Not you. Not so far. The one bound by the Talent of the Ifrits. We had him destroyed.

That had to be Hersiod. "So why didn't you just kill him and not all the innocent rankers and miners?"

Not all of them were innocent. A single death would not have brought you here.

Him? In some fashion, they'd created the carnage so that he would be sent? "How did you know they would send me?"

They know you have Talent. Before they kill you, they wish to use you against us. If we kill you, then they risk nothing. If you weaken us, it costs them nothing. That is obvious. The soarer radiated bitter humor. *They do not understand the choices they have forced.*

"Why are the Reillies so intent on destroying me?" Mykel thought he might as well ask.

You have Talent. Only their high priest and his assistants may have Talent. You also support the Ifrits, and they have Talent. For the hill peoples, that is wrong. It is an affront to their god. It matters little that such a god does not exist.

"What do you want of me?" *And my Talent?*

?????

"You would not have invited me if you didn't have some reason."

We have our reasons. We wish you to survive and return to the one to whom you are tied. That will benefit all the world. Avoid the Ifrits until you know that matters have changed greatly enough that they will no longer attempt to kill you.

"That's easy enough for you to say. You can soar and disappear into rock."

Have you ever tried?

Mykel blinked. The soarer had vanished.

After trying to locate the soarer with his Talent-aided senses, Mykel finally turned and began to walk down the path. The Reillies and the Squawts were out to kill him. The alectors were out to kill him, as Rachyla had said, once his usefulness was over. He had Talent. That he knew, but how to use it effectively was something he still had not mastered. And now the soarers were suggesting that he could soar and disappear into the rock.

He stopped and concentrated on the ground beneath the hill, using his Talent.

Somewhere beneath him lay a blackness, of the same sort he had sensed in Hyalt. That suggested the soarers used it, or drew on it, as a form of transport. He tried to reach it . . . somehow. For a moment, the sky seemed to swirl around him. He stumbled, then caught himself.

There had to be a way. He shook his head. That would have to wait.

He smiled as he recalled what else the soarers had said—that he was tied to Rachyla and that would benefit all the world? The tie was obvious, but benefiting the world?

He snorted.

85

Dainyl felt a warm hand on his forehead.

"Dearest . . . dearest . . ."

". . . be all right." His words came out mumbled.

"I'm sure you will be, but you need rest."

He opened his eyes, taking in the darkness beyond the bedchamber windows. Then he realized that Lystrana had undressed him and put him in a nightshirt, as well as propped two pillows under his head, and folded the counterpane across his chest. "Thank you."

"It was the least I could do." Her perfect violet eyes showed concern.

Dainyl could sense the deeper worry. "I just need rest. Quivaryt . . . he had a lightcannon of the roadcutting kind. They tried to use it against me." Even those few words left him light-headed, yet he *knew* he hadn't taken any physical injuries, not beyond some bruises, anyway.

Lystrana didn't bother to hide her feelings. "That's . . . awful. It's appalling. They suck lifeforce from everywhere."

"Lightcannon and light-rifles . . . they're showing up everywhere. They should know better."

"They should." She eased a tray in front of him. "You need to eat. You had almost no lifeforce when you got to Dereka." She handed him a beaker of ale. "Start with this."

He sipped it slowly, then stopped. "How did you know?"

"Jonyst sent his assistant to tell me. They got worried after they saw you."

"I hope I didn't disrupt your afternoon."

"Keep drinking. No . . . it was already late. Even Jylena noticed how pale you are. She said you were so pale you were green."

"I suppose I am." He took another sip of the ale. "No matter what I do . . ."

"And the soup in the cup."

"Yes, dearest." After setting down the beaker on the tray and sipping some of the soup, he said, "I think Brekylt must already be in Ludar. He's left Alustre, and I don't think he was in Dulka."

"There's not much you can do about that. Not in your condition. Besides, if the Myrmidons are needed, you have a marshal in Elcien to command them."

"I'll be better tomorrow."

"I'm sure you will be," she said soothingly. "You just need rest and nourishment. Please drink some more."

Light-headed as he was, Dainyl could still recognize the placating tone. He went back to the ale.

"And a little cheese." She slipped a small sliver into his mouth after he'd taken another swallow of the ale.

"They'll destroy Acorus to rule it for but a few years," he added, realizing his words were not as logical as he would have liked. "You know what I mean."

"I do." She picked up the beaker of ale and held it so he could grasp it. "You need to drink more—and have some of this." She eased something into his mouth.

He chewed the morsel of what felt like paté. "Not bad."

"Some more." Lystrana eased more of the paté into his mouth.

"It won't be that long before the Archon transfers the Master Scepter, and they're squabbling—"

"You can't do anything about it, dearest, unless you eat and rest and get stronger."

While her words made sense, Dainyl couldn't help but say, "I don't have time to wait to get stronger." He yawned.

"You need a good night's sleep."

That was a good idea, but there was so much he had to do, so very much.

"Just rest . . ." Lystrana's voice was soothing.

He closed his eyes.

86

In the grayness before dawn, Mykel stood in the corner of the shed and loosened the sling. He tried to lift his arm. Sweat beaded on his forehead, and lines of pain shot across his chest, but he could lift it a span or more. The day before, nothing had happened. Had his momentary link to the darkness helped speed healing? That might be, and there might be other things his Talent would allow him to do . . . but those didn't seem too helpful at the moment when he was responsible for two battalions and had to stop over a thousand Reillies and Squawts from killing him and his men, not to mention from sacking Borlan.

He stepped out of the shed into the chill air, carrying his gear. Someone had groomed and saddled the roan, for which he was grateful, and tied it to the nearest fence post. Fastening his gear behind the saddle was time-consuming, but easier than it had been. He mounted as quickly as he could and rode toward the barn where the battalion's companies were forming up. There, he reined up beside Bhoral.

"Morning, sir. The scouts aren't back yet," offered Bhoral.

"Let me know." Mykel rode toward Rhystan, who turned in the saddle and looked closely at Mykel, then nodded.

"You're inspecting me like you might a new mount," Mykel observed.

"Yes, sir. I'm glad to see you're looking better."

Mykel laughed. "I'm happy to know that I pass inspection. How are the men?"

"They're happy. The night was cold, the ground hard, but they got to fill their bellies."

Mykel couldn't help but smile at Rhystan's wry assessment. "Good." He eased the roan along toward Seventeenth Company and Loryalt.

In the end, the entire battalion moved out half a glass before sunrise, riding for more than a glass on the Borlan road, a packed clay track that would turn to a quagmire in heavy rain. The road wound through a wide valley filled with stubbled fields and meadows whose grasses had been cut, leaving a short tannish thatch. Occasional apple and plumapple orchards dotted the low hills. As the sun rose into a clear silver-green winter sky, the air warmed enough that the breath of men and mounts no longer steamed, and a slightly warmer breeze blew out of the southwest.

Mykel watched the road as well as the higher hills to the west. More than a vingt ahead, on the western side of the road, was a heavily wooded hillside. Mykel glanced at it, then glanced back. Even though he sensed no Talent emanations, there might be men there. He turned in the saddle. "Bhoral!"

"Sir!" The battalion squad leader rode forward.

"Send out some scouts and some men to check out the forest on the hill up there—the one on the right side. Just half a squad. I want them to go at least a hundred yards in a line abreast, and I want them close enough to see each other. If they run into Reillies, they're to withdraw."

"Yes, sir!"

The Cadmians rode forward of the battalion and toward the wooded area that had drawn his attention. No one shot at the ten Cadmians as they neared the woods and then spread into a line abreast and started into the trees. Mykel kept watching, as did Rhystan and Bhoral.

A single shot echoed down the road from the wooded area, followed by several more. Shortly, a handful of Cadmians rode out of the trees, and turned their mounts back toward the company. Hundreds of mounted insurgents poured out of the forest, and swept along the road, northward toward the main body of the battalion.

Mykel turned his mount, standing in the stirrups. "Sixteenth Company! Wide front, staggered firing line! Centered on the road! Fourteenth Company! On the right, wide front . . ."

By the time Mykel finished both bellowing orders and sending Bhoral and his messengers to pass them along to the companies in the rear, Rhystan already had Sixteenth Company in position, and Fabrytal had Fifteenth Company on the left, and Culeyt had Fourteenth on the right, both angled forward slightly to allow somewhat of a cross fire. Seventeenth Company was behind the center, and Thirteenth was moving forward onto the higher ground off the road to the east, from where they could rake the Reillies if they continued their attack.

By now the Reillies were less than half a vingt away.

Rhystan rode up to Mykel. "Majer . . ."

"Since I'm not that good with a rifle right now, you'd appreciate it if I didn't make a target of myself in the front rank?" Mykel knew Rhystan had a point. "I'll move back a rank or two, but I need to see."

"Yes, sir."

Mykel could detect the relief in the captain's voice and bearing as Rhystan turned his mount back south to face the oncoming Reillies. Mykel eased his mount back into the formation of Sixteenth Company so that there were two staggered ranks before him.

"Rifles ready!" Mykel ordered. "Hold your fire!"

When the Reillies reached a point two hundred yards out from the Cadmian formation, Thirteenth Company opened fire—as ordered. Reillies and Squawts began to fall, but the losses barely slowed the charge.

The Reillies formed a tight spearhead of riders aimed at the center of the Cadmians—and at Mykel. He could sense the faintest of Talent probes, clearly trying to fix his location. What sort of beliefs were they when people insisted that only their leaders could use certain abilities and when they were determined to destroy anyone else who showed such abilities? He laughed, low enough that only he could hear the sound. The alectors believed that way, as did the Reillies, and probably, were Talent widely enough spread among landers, so would they.

He forced himself to wait until the Reillies were only about seventy-five yards away before standing in the stirrups and ordering, "Open fire! Fire at will!"

Mykel dropped back into the saddle. He hadn't wanted to be a target, but he had wanted the orders heard. Besides, the Reillies seemed to know where he was anyway.

Under the withering fire, Reillies and mounts dropped, and other mounts fell over the fallen. And still, the hill riders kept coming. Mykel slipped his rifle out of its case and laid it across his thighs. If necessary, he could get off a good shot or two, one-armed or not.

Of the attackers' first wave, less than a score reached the battalion's first rank. Half of those were cut down before they could bring their oversized blades to bear. A handful of Cadmians had to use sabres, but in moments there were no more Reillies within twenty yards.

"Battalion! Reload! Now!" The order was probably unnecessary, but some might need the reminder.

The thunder of hoofs increased as another wave of hill riders pounded toward Third Battalion. Once more the concentrated fire from the Cadmians ripped through the Reillies.

Over the haze of dust and smoke, Mykel could tell that Dyarth had brought Thirteenth Company closer to the road, where they continued to deliver a punishing cross fire at the trailing section of the Reillie attack.

This time, the Reillies turned, veering toward the west, and riding through a low vale between hills, avoiding any of the roads or lanes.

In less than a quarter glass, Third Battalion remained alone on the Borlan road.

Mykel rode forward, easing the roan through the ranks of Sixteenth Company. He only saw a handful of wounded and one empty saddle, but that was only one squad. The road to the south was littered with the bodies of men and mounts, and Mykel reined up, trying to survey the carnage, as well as get a rough count of the Reillie casualties. He guessed there were well over a hundred dead and wounded, just on the road.

Bhoral rode up beside the majer. "What about their wounded?"

"Take their rifles and ammunition—and the good mounts. Shoot anyone who resists, but leave the others alone." Mykel didn't feel particularly merciful. From what he could tell, killing Reillies didn't make an impression. Perhaps leaving a large number of the wounded fending for themselves would. Then, he wasn't certain anything would have an effect on the Reillies, except killing them all, and he wasn't willing, prepared, or equipped to undertake butchery of that extent, the late Majer Hersiod's words notwithstanding.

Mykel looked down at the rifle. He hadn't had to fire it—this time.

87

Dainyl looked up from the breakfast tray that Lystrana had brought him and that he had finished to the last morsel. "Thank you." He sat up straighter in the wide bed. "I suppose I'd better get dressed."

"You're not getting dressed—not to go off anywhere. I don't care if Khelaryt might get assassinated in the next glass, or if Brekylt becomes Archon of Acorus, or if the world is crumbling into dust around us," stated Lystrana, her voice rising slightly, "you are not going anywhere today. Until you recover your strength, you're not going anywhere."

Dainyl realized she was right. He was too tired to argue, and if he couldn't do that . . . "Yes, dearest."

Lystrana smiled at him fondly. "If you're that acquiescent, you may be here a week. You were almost as green as you say the ancients are when you got here last night."

"And this morning?"

"You're not much better."

"Asulet said it wasn't reversible," Dainyl admitted.

"You skipped over that. All you said was that you had to keep it in check."

Dainyl couldn't help frowning. Was that what he had said?

"Those were your words," she said.

"I thought you understood."

"I do now." She paused. "Do you have to use the green Talent?"

"I wouldn't be here and alive, weak as I am, if I hadn't."

"I was afraid of that."

"I've been traveling the ways of the ancients," he admitted. "They lie beneath and outside the translation tube, but I don't have to use a Table. That was necessary, because the recorders in Alustre and Dulka, certainly Ludar, are allies of Brekylt."

"I think you'd better tell me just what you've been doing." Lystrana's voice was firm.

"It started two days ago, when we discovered that Brekylt had murdered Noryan and Josaryk had mutinied . . ." Dainyl told her everything, from what had happened in the east, to his discovery and ability to use the web of the ancients, to his conversation with them, and through his attempt to track down Brekylt and his near collapse on the Table in Dereka.

"It might be easier for everyone," she said dryly, "if they made you Duarch."

"That won't happen. Before long, everyone will be after me, and Acorus will be awash in lifeforce-destroying weapons—and that's if the ancients don't come up with worse. I can't tell you how much their attitude conveyed how little what I was attempting mattered."

"They're as arrogant as Samist and Brekylt, it sounds like."

"It wasn't arrogance. It was an absolute certainty, combined with an overwhelming sadness. And there was something else, too," he mused. "I didn't catch it at the time, but you know how they've told me before how I—or we—had to change or perish? Well . . . now their attitude was more like . . . we've told you, and you haven't listened, and we're sorry for you, and please go on and do whatever meaningless task you have in mind."

"Do you really think they have that kind of power and ability?" asked Lystrana.

"I didn't. Now . . . I have to wonder." He took a last sip of the beaker of ale. "I still can't believe that Samist and his supporters are using lightcannon."

"It's the invulnerability of arrogance. We're powerful. We're so powerful that nothing can truly hurt us. That's the way they think."

"But more than a few of them have died."

"Of the higher alectors, none except Zelyert," she pointed out. "And that's in over a hundred years. They've gotten into the habit of believing that it can't happen to them—or here."

"If I could have reached Brekylt . . ."

"If you had, and if you'd killed him, the others would have dismissed it as Brekylt's weakness." Lystrana glanced to the door. "It's time for me to go to the hearing."

"Hearing?"

"I'm presiding over a hearing. One of the landholders built a dam on his land that collapsed and flooded a small town east of Aelta. Five indigens were killed. He claims it's not his fault, even though the stream was listed as one that was not to be channeled or dammed."

"That should be interesting."

"I know. It's almost absurd, when you've been trying to preserve the entire world, but life does go on. At least, I have to hope that it does." Her smile was faint and rueful.

"I am going to get dressed," Dainyl said, adding quickly, "but I won't go anywhere."

Lystrana looked at him.

"I do need to think over some things, and I don't think well in bed." He grinned at her.

She finally smiled back. "I'll see you later, dearest."

Dainyl watched her go, sensing both her aura and that of Kytrana. He wished he were stronger, but there was no help for that, and he was definitely going to have to find ways to accomplish what he wanted—other than by direct force.

He looked at the empty beaker, then set it and the tray on the table beside the bed. He did need to think—on more than a few things.

88

On Sexdi morning, after breakfast, Lystrana shook her head as Dainyl checked the lightcutters and their holsters, then donned his green jacket.

"You're still far from recovered," Lystrana said.

"I know, but I'm well enough to travel, and Khelaryt needs protection. I'll see Fhentyl first and have Fifth Company fly to Elcien today. Then I'll take the Table to Tempre and give the same orders to Seventh Company. After that, I'll translate to Elcien."

"You're not directly in command," she pointed out.

"No, but they won't want to disobey me, and I'll merely order them to report to the marshal in Elcien. I'll be there before they are—"

Lystrana sighed. "Do all High Alectors start believing they're invulnerable?"

"This one certainly doesn't, but if I don't show up before long, that will encourage Samist and Brekylt."

"Not if they see you in the shape you're in."

"I'll have to make sure that doesn't happen, won't I?" Dainyl grinned.

"That might be wise, dearest—along with all the other caution you can manage." She stepped toward him, then kissed him gently on the cheek. "The coach is waiting outside."

Less than half a glass later, he was stepping out of the coach at the gates to the Myrmidon compound south of Dereka. Occasional flakes of snow swirled out of a light gray sky, but not enough to provide the thinnest layer of white on the ground. "I won't be long."

"We'll be here, Highest," replied the driver.

Dainyl turned and walked through the gates and across the stone-paved courtyard to the headquarters building. Captain Fhentyl was waiting for him in the entry foyer.

"Highest." The captain bowed slightly. Although Fhentyl's greeting was more than polite, Dainyl could sense a wariness behind the greeting.

"Captain. I have orders for you. They're very simple. Fifth Company is to deploy to headquarters in Elcien and to await further orders from the marshal."

Fhentyl nodded, and Dainyl could sense his relief.

"You're to fly out today. If you have difficulties or weather problems, you can stop in Tempre. Seventh Company will be joining you as well. It's possible that the Alector of the East is trying to subvert the Duarchy. He murdered Submarshal Noryan and about half of Third Company, and it appears he is supported by High Alector Ruvryn."

"Sir?" Fhentyl was actually surprised.

So was the duty officer at the desk less than five yards away, an undercaptain who had been listening while trying not to show that she was.

"This happened late on Duadi or early on Tridi. Also, the commander of Fourth Company attempted a mutiny, but Majer Sevasya stopped that, and she's now the acting submarshal. We don't know how Duarch Samist sees matters, but it's prudent to provide additional support to Duarch Khelaryt."

"I can see that, Highest."

"There is one other matter of which you should be aware. High Alector Ruvryn and Brekylt have been building and distributing more lightcannon, like those used in Hyalt."

"I had wondered if we would see more of them." Fhentyl shook his head.

"I need to be on my way, Captain. Good flying."

"Thank you, sir."

Dainyl turned.

Fhentyl walked back to the RA's coach with him, through the chill and gusting winds. "Will we see you in Elcien?"

"I'll be there, but you'll be dealing with Marshal Alcyna." Dainyl opened the coach door and stepped up and into the coach.

Even the intermittent snow had ceased by the time he reached the goldenstone building that held the Table. He did not see the recorder's coach, but Jonyst was in the library.

The older alector turned and smiled. "You're looking better than Whelyne described you, if more green and not so well as I'd prefer."

"You're looking whiter-haired than I'd prefer," countered Dainyl.

"We do what we can," replied the recorder dryly. "You should know that the tube fluctuations have not subsided. They're slightly stronger, in fact."

"How long do you think it will be?"

"A week, perhaps a few days less."

A week before the Archon began the transfer? That didn't give Dainyl much more time. "I'm headed to Tempre and then back to Elcien."

"You shouldn't have any trouble with the Tables. Not yet." Jonyst led the way down the stairs to the Table chamber.

Dainyl followed, then moved directly to the Table and onto it, hoping that a simple Table to Table translation would take less effort. He concentrated . . .

. . . and dropped into the purpled Talent light of the tube. For the first time, the purple felt slightly slimy, but he pushed that thought away and concentrated on the blue locator of Tempre, ignoring the still-present amber-green force of the ancients that continued to loom over both the tube and the deeper web.

He was clearly aware of his own progress, and he sensed himself moving toward Tempre, rather than having the feeling that the locator was moving toward him. He brushed through the misty silvered-blue barrier and . . .

. . . stood solidly on the Table.

Chyal looked up from one end of the Table, flanked by two guards. He bowed immediately. "Highest."

"Recorder." Dainyl stepped off the Table. "Do you think I might borrow the RA's coach for a quick trip to the Myrmidon compound and back?"

"No, sir." A faint smile crossed the young recorder's lips. "No one is using it. A mason's wagon smashed it, and it is being repaired. There are several hackers there, however."

"That will be fine. I hope no one was injured."

"One horse was bruised and slightly cut, but no passengers or drivers."

"Has the number of wild translations decreased recently?"

"Yes, sir. There were only two all of yesterday, and none today . . . so far."

Dainyl nodded. "I should be back before long. Thank you."

He made his way out of the chamber and out into the lower stone corridor. Once he had climbed the corner staircase to the main level, he walked to the front of the building. Both the handful of alectors and landers in the corridor nodded politely, but gave him a wide berth.

Within a quarter glass a local hacker had dropped him at the compound that had once housed the Alector's Guard of Tempre. As Dainyl stepped out of the coach, he couldn't help but note the clear silver-green sky—and that it was earlier than when he had left Dereka. He wondered if he'd ever really get used to traveling faster than the sun.

He was through the gates and a good third of the way across the courtyard toward the section that held the headquarters area when Lyzetta hurried across the courtyard toward him.

"Highest!"

"Captain. How are you . . . and Seventh Company?"

"Well, thank you, sir, and closer to full strength."

"That's good. Did you hear about Submarshal Noryan?"

Lyzetta's cheerful smile faded. "Yes, sir. We got the dispatch late yesterday, about him and Sevasya. It's hard to believe."

Dainyl could tell that it was no surprise at all to the captain, but he merely nodded in response. "All of Seventh Company is to fly to Elcien immediately and report to the marshal."

"Yes, sir. We can do that."

"Brekylt has access to more lightcannon, and they've been used in Norda and Dulka in the last few days. Right now, we don't know if there are others or where they are, but they'll turn up here in the west before long. Will you have any difficulty in getting to Elcien today?"

"No, sir."

"Oh . . . Fifth Company may have to overnight here tonight. They're flying to Elcien."

"That won't be a problem." Lyzetta gestured at the stone structures surrounding the courtyard. "There's enough space for four companies here. I'll tell the staff." She paused. "Is there anything else we should know?"

"Only that the next few weeks will likely be very uncertain and that every Myrmidon needs to be particularly careful." He smiled. "I'll be returning to Elcien now."

"You're leaving so quickly?"

"I've been in Dereka, and there was no reason to send someone else to give you the orders, but I do need to get back to the Hall of Justice."

The coach ride back to the RA's building and the translation back to Elcien were uneventful, but by the time Dainyl sat down behind the table in his small study in the Hall of Justice his legs were slightly shaky.

He didn't have time to think about that because Adya appeared, holding an envelope. "One of Bharyt's assistants just delivered this, Highest."

Dainyl took the envelope and opened it, reading it quickly. "The Duarch has invited me for a private luncheon today."

"That could be very good or not so good, Highest."

"Possibly both," Dainyl suggested. "I'll have to go to find out. Make sure the coach is standing by. Oh . . . will you send a quick message to the marshal, requesting her to come here at her earliest convenience?"

Once his chief assistant had left, Dainyl closed his eyes and leaned back in the chair. Lystrana had definitely been right.

He actually managed to get a short semi-nap before Alcyna arrived.

"If you will pardon the observation, Highest," she said, after settling herself into the chair across from him, "you've looked a great deal better than you do now."

"That's why you're here. I had an . . . encounter with two lightcannon in Dulka and more than a few lightcutters in Alustre. Brekylt has left Alustre, and he's not in Dulka."

"You think he's in Ludar?"

"That's my best judgment, but I can't prove it. I've ordered Fifth and Seventh Companies here to Elcien to report to you for further orders."

"We'd better set up more patrols, then."

"Some of the recorders also think that the Archon will transfer the Master Scepter within the next two weeks."

"That explains Brekylt's actions, then."

"I thought so," replied Dainyl, stifling a yawn. "I'm having lunch with the Duarch. Is there anything I should know?"

"Sevasya set up her own patrols and found a group of alectors in black and silver using a sandox team and coach to advance on Lysia. She regrets the loss of sandoxen and the coach."

"No regrets about the alectors?" Dainyl couldn't keep the sarcasm out of his words.

"She didn't convey any." Alcyna gave a small laugh. "I can't imagine why not."

"What more should I know?"

"There have been no dispatches at all for the last two days out of Ludar, but the dispatch fliers delivering messages there say that they have observed nothing out of the ordinary."

"Has anyone seen Ruvryn?"

"No."

"How are the Cadmians doing?"

"Sixth Battalion has destroyed a number of the mountain nomads. Third and Fourth Battalions have had conflicts with the Squawts and Reillies and have inflicted severe casualties."

"You know more than that," suggested Dainyl.

"Some of my sources suggest the Reillies have taken some sort of belief-oath against the Cadmians. It's unlikely that the Cadmians will prevail without killing virtually all the Reillies."

"You don't think that's likely."

"Not before full winter sets in."

Dainyl nodded. If anyone could deal with the Reillies, Majer Mykel could. But . . . as he was learning, sometimes even great ability wasn't enough. "Anything else?"

"Not that you don't already know." She paused, then said, "Try to get some rest before you meet the Duarch."

"I will. I'll let you get back to headquarters."

With a nod and a brief smile, she rose and made her way from the study.

Dainyl leaned back in his chair, as much as he could with its straight back, and closed his eyes, trying to think about what he should say to the Duarch, and what he should not. He wasn't certain how long he half thought and half dozed before there was a knock on the study door.

"Yes?" His Talent-strength had to be returning, because he could sense Adya beyond.

"The coach is waiting, Highest."

Had he dozed that long? "I'll be right there." He stood and stretched. His legs did feel steadier.

He opened the door. Adya was waiting.

"Is there something I need to do before I go?" he asked.

"Oh, no, sir."

Dainyl laughed. "You wanted to make sure the overtired High Alector did get to the coach."

Adya blushed, the first time Dainyl had seen that.

"I'm on my way, and thank you." He turned toward the staircase.

Outside, before he entered the coach, Dainyl looked up, absently realizing that the sky was a clear and deep silver-green—as opposed to the clouds he had left behind in Dereka.

At the Palace, the seemingly omnipresent and imperturbable Bharyt stepped forward to greet Dainyl as soon as he stepped through the archway. "This way, sir. The Duarch will be joining you in the sunroom. He often eats there." Bharyt turned.

Dainyl walked beside the functionary. "I imagine matters have been quiet here recently."

"For a Duarch, quiet is often as bad as overt alarm, sir."

"Sometimes worse, I've found."

"That is also possible."

Bharyt escorted Dainyl to the very last door on the right side of the corridor, opening it and gesturing for Dainyl to enter. "The Duarch should be with you momentarily, sir."

"Thank you." Dainyl walked forward into the chamber, a modest room ten yards by fifteen, set to take advantage of its position on the southwest corner of the Palace. The high and wide glass windows to the south overlooked a courtyard garden and offered a vista across the shore park to the Bay of Ludel. The west windows overlooked the same garden, but beyond the walls stretched the western section of Elcien, dwellings and buildings interspersed with trees, none high enough to block the sweeping view of the city.

Next to the south window, a table was set for two, with china and crystal and pale green linens and napkins. On a side table were several bottles of wine.

"Greetings, Dainyl."

Dainyl turned at the warm and hearty words of the Duarch,

who had entered by a side door. "Greetings, sir." He bowed his head momentarily.

"We might as well sit." Khelaryt gestured to the chair at the table that faced east, while taking the one that faced west.

As Dainyl seated himself, a steward in pale green appeared, who immediately poured a colorless wine into the goblets.

"It's a Vyan Alte . . . very subdued but full," said the Duarch, lifting his goblet.

Dainyl lifted his.

They drank, and Dainyl had to agree with the Duarch's assessment.

"The Vyan Alte is somewhat like you," Khelaryt said, setting his goblet on the table. "There's a great deal more there than is immediately apparent."

"Should I be flattered or concerned by that comparison, sir?"

"Perhaps you should tell me." Khelaryt leaned back slightly as the steward reappeared and eased a small plate before him, then another before Dainyl. On it were three thin circular slices of something white with the slightest hint of tan. "These are hearts of bosquite. One of the few delicacies from the Dry Coast." He speared one and ate it slowly.

Dainyl followed his example. The bosquite combined fruity and nutty tastes, albeit with the crunchiness of a not-quite-ripe melon rind. That could have been why the slices were cut so thin.

"I saw Captain Lyzetta recently." Dainyl decided against being too specific. "She is a good commander, not that I would expect otherwise."

"I'm happy to hear that, and I appreciate your letting me know." Khelaryt sipped his wine. "You have been absent in recent days, Dainyl, and I have heard some disturbing news."

"You should have, sir. The High Alector of Engineering has been building and distributing more lightcannon since I last mentioned this to you. The Alector of the East and most of his close supporters have left Alustre." Dainyl finished the appetizer.

The steward replaced the plates with small and delicate cups of steaming soup.

Khelaryt picked up the cup in a hand that dwarfed the delicate porcelain and sipped the soup.

Dainyl enjoyed the seed-gourd bisque far more than the bosquite.

"I assume you have responded to these events. Exactly how, might I ask?"

How? Besides nearly getting myself killed? "I personally destroyed at least one lightcannon in Dulka and removed the Recorder of Deeds in Alustre after he admitted his support of Brekylt against you. Majer Sevasya is now acting submarshal of the Myrmidons and has both Fourth and Sixth Companies firmly under her control in Lysia. Both Fifth and Seventh Companies are already flying here to reinforce First Company."

"You did not inform me of these?"

"I was somewhat injured, Highest, and only returned from my efforts this morning. Had I not been invited here, you would have had a request for me to brief you by now."

"How did you like the bisque?"

"Very much," replied Dainyl.

"It's one of my favorites." Khelaryt paused as the steward removed the cups and placed a plate before each alector, each holding a juvenile oarfish glazed with lemon-citron. Then he cut a section of the fish with his fork and ate it, clearly savoring the oarfish.

Dainyl took a smaller bite. The glaze was excellent, mellow and tangy simultaneously, but he'd had more than enough fish in his tour at Sinjin, although that had been decades earlier.

"Duarch Samist has sent a dispatch saying that unfriendly forces had destroyed a large section of the RA's complex in Dulka," Khelaryt said mildly, "and asking if I knew anything about it. How would you suggest I respond?"

Dainyl ate another small bite of oarfish before speaking. "You could reply that the forces were only unfriendly to those who oppose the continuation of the Duarchy as it is now constituted, and that the destruction was the result of the explosion of a lightcannon employed against those loyal to you and the Duarchy."

Khelaryt laughed. "That is true . . . if not exactly in the fashion that Samist would appreciate." After his last bite of oarfish, he asked, "Were there other lightcannon in Dulka?"

Dainyl finished his own fish before replying. "I would judge so, although I was forced to withdraw before confirming that."

"You . . . withdraw?"

"Some lightcannon are too powerful for the most powerful of alectors, and I am not one of them."

"If you are not, I would wish to know who such individuals might be."

"You, sir, are clearly one."

"You're sounding like Zelyert, Dainyl."

"I would not wish to do so, but you are the most powerful of alectors that I know."

The steward removed the fish plates, replacing them with larger platters holding chiafra—mint-minced beef mixed with creamed white cheese and parsley, rolled in thin pastry tubes and covered with an almond sauce—accompanied by spears of something green and jellied-looking. Then he replaced the goblets and poured a maroon-reddish wine into each new goblet.

Dainyl couldn't help but look hard at the jellied spears.

"Those are jellied prickle—it's a lander delicacy," Khelaryt offered.

While Dainyl had always liked chiafra, he personally preferred it with a richer brown sauce. As for the prickle, it tasted like a combination of rancid oil and sawdust, delicacy or not.

"Tell me, Dainyl. What is your best judgment as to what will happen next?"

"I believe we're getting very near to the time when the Archon will transfer the Master Scepter. Brekylt has begun to move forces westward, perhaps in support of Duarch Samist."

Following Khelaryt's example, Dainyl sipped the red wine.

"Why do you believe the transfer is imminent?"

"Because wild translations have dropped considerably and

because the recorders have been reporting strange fluctuations of a type they've never known before from the Tables." Dainyl took another bite of the chiafra. He wasn't about to eat any more of the prickle.

"That could be coincidence."

"That is always possible," Dainyl conceded.

"Your actions suggest you believe the danger is here in the west, yet Brekylt's power lies in the east."

"His base of power lies in the east," replied Dainyl. "Outside of Lysia, though, his support there is so strong that he has no fear of losing it. In addition, it is clear that Ruvryn and the engineers support him. Given that, it may even be that Samist supports him . . . or that he may be doing Samist's bidding."

"That is a serious charge. You are as much as saying that Samist will attack me."

"Yes, sir. I am."

"Is that why your wife is in Dereka, Dainyl?" Khelaryt's voice was smooth.

Dainyl was not deceived, sensing the anger behind it. "Not exactly, sir. Long before I became even marshal, I was worried about conflicts in the west. I also wished my wife's abilities to be rewarded, and you may recall that I mentioned the extent of those abilities."

"That you did," grudged Khelaryt.

"I might also add that I am here, and I have never shied from danger."

"There is that."

"And she *is* carrying a child."

"All that would be mere rationalization in other alectors, Dainyl, but even suspicious as a Duarch must be, I concede your loyalty, if only from the injuries and risks you have taken. Will you return to Dereka tonight?"

"Certainly not tonight. It is unlikely I will travel to Dereka often, if at all, until these matters are resolved."

Khelaryt nodded, and Dainyl could sense a certain satisfaction behind the pleasant facade.

"You will definitely enjoy the dessert," the Duarch said. "It is an old favorite of mine as well. Did I tell you that once I fancied that I could have been the best pastry chef in Illustra?"

"I can't say that I'm surprised, sir." Dainyl smiled politely.

Khelaryt had the information he wanted, whatever it had been, perhaps only a confirmation of Dainyl's loyalty, and little more of import would be said or asked, for which Dainyl was grateful, although he would certainly remain on his guard.

89

Dainyl slept uneasily. On Octdi night, he'd debated returning to Dereka, but he'd decided against it because his Talent-strength was returning, and he had the feeling that traveling the Tables—or the ancients' web—might not only reduce his strength but also provoke some sort of attack that would only weaken him and leave him less able for the inevitable attack on Elcien by Brekylt and Samist.

On Novdi morning, he woke before dawn, drenched in sweat. He'd had dreams of battles, with pteridons fighting pteridons and lightcannon turning the sky into a web of crisscrossing lines of blue flame, of ancients taking an oversized beaker and pouring green fluids down his throat until he burst . . . and of amber-green barriers walling off the sun itself and soarers hovering around him chanting, "Change or die . . . change or die."

Still, after a shower and a breakfast of egg toast and ale, he felt better physically. In fact, for all of the disturbance of his dreams, he felt that he was close to full Talent-strength.

He did find a hacker and was at the Hall of Justice well before anyone, except for those on duty in the Table chamber. Once in his study, he went over the latest reports from Alcyna. Her Myrmidon scouts had reported seeing, from a distance, a number of pteridons in the air around Ludar. Two of the Duarches' massive seagoing vessels had been at the piers in Ludar on Septi. Since those vessels were under the control of Alseryl, and since no one had seen Alseryl for several days, that suggested that the High Alector of Transport had allied himself with Samist.

Dainyl had not mentioned the possible alliance, but on Octdi morning he had sent a message to Khelaryt noting the ships' location and Alseryl's absence. There had been no response throughout Octdi, and none was waiting at the Hall of Justice. In fact, Dainyl had received no communication of any sort from the Duarch since their private lunch meeting.

Just because Dainyl *thought* Samist, Brekylt, Ruvryn, and Alseryl were planning an attack on Elcien—or on Khelaryt himself—Dainyl couldn't very well order an attack on Ludar. He had no real proof of anything except that Ruvryn's engineers had built lightcannon and that Brekylt and the RAs in his area of administrative oversight had used them.

He was still wrestling with what he could order besides patrols and observations when he sensed Chastyl outside his study door. "You can come in, Chastyl."

The recorder opened the door and stepped into the study, closing the door behind him. "Sir . . . I've been noting something. It might mean something, and it might not."

Dainyl nodded for him to continue.

"Since about midnight, we have seen absolutely no wild translations. I checked with some of the other recorders. They haven't seen any, either."

A chill ran through Dainyl. "You're certain of that?"

"Yes, sir."

"Tell me, Chastyl . . . have you noticed anything else out of the ordinary? Or the absence of something normal?"

The recorder pursed his lips, then tilted his head. His forehead furrowed. After a moment, he replied, "Outside of that, I cannot say that I have, Highest."

"If you do, please tell me immediately—and thank you for telling me about the wild translations . . . or rather, about their absence."

After the recorder left, Dainyl sat in silence. There were only three possible reasons for the sudden elimination of wild translations, and all of them suggested that the transfer of the

Master Scepter was imminent, possibly within the next day, if not already under way. Yet there was little more he could do, beyond what he had already put in motion.

He felt as though both his hands and legs were tied, or that he'd been chained in an underground cavern with unbreakable Talent chains. No matter what he felt, he couldn't offer more evidence than he had, and couldn't prove anything, and he didn't have the authority to order further action without effectively becoming a rebel himself.

Finally, he got up and walked to his chief assistant's study.

"Adya . . . make sure that the coach is standing by for me. I may need it at any time."

"Yes, sir."

"Thank you." Dainyl returned to his study and looked at the ancient stone wall opposite him. How had it all come to this?

Less than a quarter glass later, Chastyl appeared at his door once more, this time with a young and wide-eyed alector. "This is Balyt. He says he was sent from Lyterna."

Dainyl gestured them both into the study.

Chastyl closed the door carefully, but stood back as Balyt stepped forward.

"I'm Balyt, Highest," stammered the young alector.

"Yes?"

"I'm the most junior of Myenfel's assistants, and that's why he sent me. They're fighting, sir. It's awful. It's all over Lyterna."

"Who's fighting, and why are you here?"

The young alector straightened. "Paeylt and the engineers tried to storm the upper levels. Asulet blocked them and sent me to Myenfel through the hidden ways. Paeylt's killing all the old alectors and anyone who won't pick up a lightcutter for him. Myenfel's got the Table chamber blocked, but he doesn't know how long he can hold it."

Dainyl rose. Maybe he could at least do something in Lyterna.

"Ah . . . sir . . ."

"What?"

"Asulet and Myenfel sent a message." Balyt fumbled and

pulled a folded sheet of paper from his pale green shimmersilk tunic, extending it to Dainyl.

Dainyl unfolded the sheet and read it. Then, short as it was, he read it again, his eyes running over the words and letters.

> Dainyl,
> The time is upon us, and Paeylt will attempt to take Lyterna. Whatever you may do, leave the Hall of Justice and do not attempt the Tables or come to Lyterna until it is all over.

The signature was that of Asulet, and Dainyl could even gain a Talent-sense of the ancient alector tied to the words and paper.

"Did either Myenfel or Asulet say anything?" pressed Dainyl.

"Oh, yes, sir. Asulet did, sir."

"What did he say?" Dainyl was trying to control his exasperation.

"Ah . . . sir . . ."

"What?" snapped Dainyl.

"Asulet . . . he said that you'd better know what he meant . . . and that if you didn't . . ." Balyt's voice trailed off.

"And if I didn't . . ."

"Then . . . then . . . you deserved whatever happened . . ."

Whatever happened? Dainyl disliked those words. He looked at Chastyl. "Is there any change in the Tables?"

"There are more . . . Talent waves. At least, there were right after Balyt arrived."

"Once the Archon starts to transfer the Scepter . . . how long will it take?"

"I cannot say. The translation would seem immediate, but time passes to others . . . outside the tube. It could be several glasses, or it might be longer. Days, conceivably. I know of no records, Highest."

"Go check the Table right now and report back immediately."

"Yes, sir." Chastyl scurried out, leaving the study door ajar.

Dainyl turned back to Balyt. "Does Paeylt have any other weapons besides lightcutters?"

"They're not like the ones the Myrmidons sometimes carry, sir. They're bigger, like rifles, and the light-flame is blue-green. It's much stronger."

Had Paeylt been the one who developed them? He could have gotten or brought the designs from Ifryn.

"Who was winning?"

"I don't know, sir. Asulet had done something that blocked Paeylt from the upper levels, and that was why Paeylt was killing anyone who wouldn't tell him what Asulet had done. That's what Myenfel said. But no one knew what he'd done. Even Myenfel didn't."

That gave Dainyl some hope.

Chastyl burst back into the study. "Highest . . . I've never seen anything like it."

"Like what?" Couldn't anyone describe *what* was happening?

"The whole Table is flashing, between brilliant purple and black-purple."

Dainyl jumped to his feet. "It's time to clear the Hall of Justice . . ." Before he could say more, a wave of blackish purple washed over him, and the entire Hall of Justice strobed between purple and green, and then between black and purple.

Diordyn pounded on the door to the study, then burst inside without waiting for an acknowledgment.

"Highest! They're moving the Master Scepter! No one should use the Tables! The flashes from the Table killed the guards."

Dainyl rushed into the corridor. "Clear the Hall! Get everyone out of the Hall. Right now! Leave everything!"

Adya appeared instantly.

"Adya. Get everyone out of here and out of the Hall of Justice above. Don't tell anyone up there why. They're moving the Master Scepter, and the Table's giving off killing Talent. Send a message to the Duarch. You take it personally to Bharyt, not the Duarch. Tell him that the Archon has started to transfer the Master Scepter."

"Me, sir?"

"You. I've got to get to Myrmidon headquarters!"

After those words, Dainyl bolted for the stairs, sprinting up and out of the Hall and down the stone steps to the coach, barely noting that the sky was a cold but clear silver-green.

"Myrmidon headquarters! As fast as you can!" He jumped into the coach and closed the door behind himself, all in one motion.

As the coach clattered down the boulevard toward Myrmidon headquarters, Dainyl found himself worrying more about Lystrana than what was happening in Elcien—although she was certainly far safer in the RA's complex in Dereka than she would have been in the Duarch's Palace. He also found himself looking out the coach window into the clear silver-green sky to the south, seeking the pteridons that would surely be headed toward the Duarch's Palace.

As soon as the coach came to a stop outside Myrmidon headquarters, Dainyl was out the door. "Stand by here!" he called to the driver over his shoulder as he ran up the steps of the building.

He burst through the doors and into the front foyer before the duty desk.

"Highest?" asked Undercaptain Yuasylt.

"The marshal?" Dainyl didn't finish the question. He could sense Alcyna hurrying down the hallway toward him.

Alcyna stopped in midstride as she saw Dainyl.

"The Archon is moving the Master Scepter," he said. "The Tables are throwing off killing energy. We'd best expect an attack anytime."

"It's already under way. I sent a messenger to the Hall."

"I was already on my way here. Go on." Dainyl motioned for her to continue.

"The patrols have already reported a force of sandoxen and unmarked coaches moving toward us from Ludar. There are heavy wagons as well, and alectors in black and silver. They're less than fifteen vingts away. There's a formation of pteridons, circling to the south, east of the bay, and the two ships to the south-southwest are making full speed for Elcien."

Dainyl forced himself to take a slow deep breath. From all that, it was clear that the attackers hadn't known exactly when the Master Scepter would be moved, or they would have timed their assault to the exact moment.

After a pause, he asked, "What have you planned?"

"Once the ships get closer, Seventh Company will deal with them. Captain Lyzetta has developed something special. Fifth Company will deal with the ground forces, and First Company will lead the attack against the pteridons, possibly with two squads from Seventh Company, as well as the others once they've sunk the ships."

Alcyna made it sound so simple, and so easy.

Dainyl almost laughed, realizing that when he'd been submarshal and marshal, he'd done the same. "How close are the ships?"

"A quarter glass in flight time."

"Have Lyzetta take them out now."

"Before they do anything?" Alcyna raised her eyebrows. "Do we know—"

"Can we risk waiting?"

The marshal gave a brisk nod. "If you'll excuse me, sir."

Dainyl nodded, then walked to the back of the foyer and through the door to the rear courtyard. From there, he surveyed the pteridons on their squares, and the Myrmidons standing by, waiting for orders.

Alcyna crossed the courtyard.

Dainyl watched as she spoke to Captain Lyzetta, then stepped away.

Shortly, two squads of pteridons lifted off, led by Lyzetta. Four of the Talent creatures carried slings. In those slings were large metal cylinders that radiated Talent energy. Dainyl felt limited and helpless, just watching, but what else could he do now, except watch?

Alcyna walked back across the courtyard to Dainyl. "I'd prefer to wait until their pteridons commit, and until we see how Lyzetta's scheme works."

"Do you know what's in those cylinders?"

"I can't claim I understand totally. She said that it combines something like a lightcutter with lifeforce-coated crossbow quarrels and Talent-boosted blasting powder." Alcyna smiled ironically. "She said she got the idea from you."

From him? "It's supposed to sink the ships?"

"She didn't say. She just said that they should take care of the ships."

Dainyl looked southward, but the pteridons were out of sight.

"You actually look worried, Highest," offered Alcyna.

"I am."

A single pteridon swept in over the southern wall, flared against the north wind, and settled onto the landing stage. As he accompanied Alcyna toward the raised stone stage, Dainyl recognized the flier—Vorosylt from First Company's second squad.

Vorosylt had dismounted, but remained beside his pteridon. "Marshal . . . Highest . . . the pteridons are forming and heading northward toward Elcien. They're about twenty vingts south right now."

Less than a third of a glass away, thought Dainyl.

"How many?"

"More than a company. Might be two."

"Stand by, Vorosylt," ordered Alcyna, "Captain Ghasylt and all of First Company will be lifting off in a moment." She turned, but the captain had clearly seen the incoming scout and was running across the courtyard.

"Marshal, do we lift off?" asked Ghasylt as he halted before Alcyna, looking down on her.

"This moment. Intercept and destroy the attackers."

"Yes, sir!" Ghasylt turned, loping across the courtyard toward his own pteridon, waiting on the first row of stone squares. "First Company! Lift off by squads! First squad!"

Alcyna hurried toward the west side of the courtyard, directly toward Fifth Company. She had not covered ten yards when the pteridons of first squad rose, springing into the air and spreading their blue leathery wings, climbing out northward into the wind and then banking into an eastward turn over Elcien before heading southward. Once all of First Company was airborne, Fifth Company followed. In less than a tenth of a glass, only two squads of pteridons remained in the headquarters courtyard—both from Seventh Company.

Alcyna and Dainyl stood beside the empty flight stage.

"I'm holding the last two squads for a bit, to see where they're needed," offered Alcyna. "If we don't get a report in a quarter glass, I'll send them to defend the Palace."

Dainyl could feel Talent forces of some sort from the south, and he turned. Scattered quick lines of blue and blue-green light flashed skyward.

"Lightcannon . . . those must be coming from the ships," said Alcyna.

Dainyl snorted. There was the proof he had not been able to provide, proof that Alseryl had defected, proof that Samist and Brekylt were working together against Khelaryt. Both he and Khelaryt had been so worried about pteridons versus pteridons—and now look what they had.

He and Alcyna stood by the flight stage . . . waiting.

They could have waited inside, out of the chill, but to Dainyl that wouldn't have felt right.

"Why did he let it happen?" Alcyna looked at Dainyl.

"Khelaryt?" Dainyl shook his head. "I can only guess that he was so worried about the lifeforce losses from direct fighting against them that he hoped they'd feel the same way. I've warned him about it. All the lightcannon and light-rifles show that they don't care."

"I've known that about Brekylt for years. Khelaryt should have."

How many alectors *should* have known over the years?

A dull muffled *boom* rumbled out of the south, and the walls of the compound and the buildings shook.

"That had to be one of Lyzetta's devices," Dainyl declared.

"From more than ten vingts away?"

A smaller explosion followed.

Dainyl kept studying the sky. There were no more lightcannon or light-rifle beams. Either the two squads of Seventh Company had been destroyed or the ships disabled. He wanted to believe the latter, but worried that it might be the former.

Alcyna walked from the flight stage toward the remaining two squads of Seventh Company. Once more Dainyl followed, feeling even more helpless. Yet . . . what could he do?

Alcyna had the situation in hand—as much as anyone could. Even if he had gone back to the Table in the Hall of Justice, nothing he could have done through the Tables or the web of the ancients would affect the battle around Elcien. And he certainly didn't want to be in the Palace at the moment.

"Lift off! Defend the Palace!" ordered Alcyna.

The remaining nine pteridons spread wing, and in instants the courtyard of Myrmidon headquarters was empty.

"Now . . . we wait. Again." Alcyna's voice was simultaneously dry, yet weary.

Dainyl had always disliked waiting.

Another wave of purple-black Talent washed across Dainyl, and then the ground shifted underfoot, enough that he had to take two steps to keep his balance.

Alcyna turned to him. "What was that?"

"Something from the transfer—that's what it felt like the first time," he replied. "It killed all the guards in the Table chamber."

"I wondered . . ."

"Why I'm here?" Dainyl asked. "The Tables aren't usable, and even if they were, what could I do with them to change this?" He gestured skyward, then paused.

Four pteridons were flying toward the headquarters compound. But whose pteridons? His hands went to the lightcutters at his belt. Watching the Talent creatures near, he waited.

One pteridon swept in, coming for a landing, the first indication that the four were from those companies loyal to the marshal and the Duarch. As it touched down, Dainyl recognized Undercaptain Asyrk. The next two fliers were also from Seventh Company. The last pteridon carried no Myrmidon.

Dainyl jumped onto the flight stage. This time Alcyna followed him.

Asyrk looked down without getting out of his saddle and harness. "One ship destroyed, sir. The other's a flaming wreck. Fifth and First Companies have engaged two companies and the ground forces beneath them, but the sandoxen and coaches are carrying lightcannon."

"Are you the only ones left from your squads?" Dainyl

looked at Asyrk, sensing the truth of the undercaptain's words, as well as a combination of apprehension, devastation, and sadness.

"Yes, sir. Each ship had a lightcannon and light-rifles. Some of the squad took hits so the captain could deliver her weapon."

Dainyl turned to Alcyna. "I'll take the pteridon. If another comes in without a Myrmidon . . ."

Alcyna offered a grim smile. "I thought you might."

"You've developed the plan. I can't add to that, and I might help in the air."

"I can't deny that. Good luck, Highest."

Dainyl smiled wryly. Her use of his title was as much disapproval as acceptance. With a nod, he dropped from the platform and loped across the courtyard to the flierless pteridon. Once there, he vaulted into the saddle and quickly fastened the harness, then turned to Asyrk. "Lift off!" Belatedly, Dainyl checked for the skylance and was relieved to see it in its holder.

The pteridon was airborne, climbing into the north wind.

Right turn . . . tight . . . south.

Dainyl took a quick survey of the sky over Elcien, but saw only the two squads from Seventh Company in formation above the Palace. His eyes went to the Hall of Justice, and he swallowed as he sensed the entire structure swathed in purple Talent—a force that felt *slimy* from even a vingt away and from his five hundred yards of altitude.

To the southwest he saw smoke rising from a fiery shape on the waters of the bay, the smoke being carried southeast by the wind. To the west of the smoke and fire was a widening oil slick.

Lyzetta . . . dead . . . killed defending Elcien . . . and her father.

As the pteridon leveled out heading south, Dainyl could see scores more pteridons swirling around in aerial combat, with occasional skylance discharges and even more occasional bolts of lightcannon flashing skyward. The lightcannon blasts were coming from the high road, or close beside it, less than ten vingts south of the bridge that spanned the channel separating Elcien from the southeast shore of the bay.

The lightcannon were a problem that he just might be able

to remove, and should. They were a threat to the future of the world and a threat that neither Khelaryt nor Samist should ever have allowed to continue and grow.

Down . . . fifty yards, above the high road.

The pteridon swept down, and the road flowed by beneath them.

Dainyl eased out the skylance, preparing for what was to come. Even from more than three vingts away, he could make out the lead lightcannon, both with his eyes and his Talent, so great was the lifeforce stored in the long flat wagon on which it was mounted.

Lower . . .

Dainyl felt as though the pteridon's wings were only yards above the trees that edged the fertile fields flanking the high road, but the lower he flew, the less likely they were to be spotted until the last moment.

He strengthened his shields and lowered the tip of the skylance.

The alectors in black and silver on the modified sandox coaches turned, raising their light-rifles. Thin lines of blue-green flashed against his shields.

Dainyl could feel the outer edges of his shields fraying, but not badly, not yet, and he aimed the lance, not at the lightcannon itself, but at the heavy-bodied wagon beneath it, filled with crystal storage cells.

The lightcannon was swinging toward him.

Dainyl raised the lance and triggered a quick blast, Talent aimed at the cannoneers controlling the weapon. While their shields absorbed most of the blast, one of them was thrown off, and the second lost his grip.

Drawing even more on the pteridon's lifeforce, and his own Talent, Dainyl triggered the lance, using his Talent to keep the blue flame-light focused on the wagon.

Hard left!

The pteridon banked eastward at his command.

CRUMMPTTT!

Even the pteridon was thrown sideways, and then upward, and its lower wingtip sliced through a tree limb.

Level . . . stay low.

For a moment, Dainyl wasn't sure whether he'd remain airborne, but the pteridon managed to right itself, even as he could feel the heat behind him, the result of the enormous release of lifeforce.

Two smaller explosions followed, and from the bluish feel to the second, he was certain it had been one of the pteridons following him.

Right . . . and climb fifty yards . . .

Dainyl glanced westward and slightly back, catching sight of the still-climbing pillar of flame—and two smaller columns of smoke and fire, one of bluish flames, short of where the heavy lightcannon had been.

The high road around where the one lightcannon had been was a mass of flames, and the trees and winter-dry grass on both sides of the road had begun to burn. Unfortunately, he also saw that another lightcannon—set up on a knoll to the west of the high road—was still firing at the pteridons above. Dainyl glanced upward. Between the girths and straps on the underside of Brekylt's pteridons were swathes of black and silver shimmercloth—clearly there for easier identification by those firing the lightcannons from below.

Right . . . steady . . . lower . . .

Another set of blue-green lines flashed past him, some hitting his shields, as the pteridon sped just south of the line of flames that marked the high road and toward the remaining heavy lightcannon.

Dainyl twisted in his harness and aimed the skylance, triggering it twice.

One of the light-rifles exploded, the flames enveloping the alectress who held it.

Returning his concentration to the heavy lightcannon ahead, Dainyl eased the pteridon lower, so close to the ground that Dainyl felt the tops of the trees in the woods to the south were higher than he was. Even as the pteridon closed to less than a vingt from the lightcannon, the alectors firing the weapon continued to concentrate on the pteridons overhead.

The guards between Dainyl and the lightcannon turned abruptly and leveled their light-rifles at him. Before they could fire, he triggered two quick bursts, Talent-aimed at their weapons. One light-rifle exploded, then the second.

The heat rose past Dainyl as the pteridon swept over the explosions and flame, and he felt as though he had flown through a furnace. Ahead was the heavy lightcannon. Once more, he Talent-guided a long bolt at the cart beneath the lightcannon, boosting the power of the bolt with his Talent and lifeforce from the pteridon.

For a moment, the pteridon lost altitude, one wingtip almost brushing the top of a hedgerow.

Left! Hard!

The pteridon banked, gently at first, as it struggled to hold and then gain altitude, and then more steeply.

The lightcannon flared into energy, and the explosion flung the pteridon farther southward. Dainyl could sense the Talent creature drinking in the dispersing lifeforce and getting stronger, righting itself. While the pteridons could take concentrated lifeforce when it was unattached or directed, as at an administration of justice, that happened so seldom that Dainyl was taken aback for a moment.

Climb!

As the pteridon circled upward, Dainyl tried to make sense of the melee above him, but before he could pick a target, one of the black and silver pteridons wheeled away from the pack and toward him, angling down in a high-speed dive.

Dainyl triggered his skylance, but the blue flame cascaded off the other flier's shields. Those shields were far stronger than those of any Myrmidon Dainyl had ever encountered—and of a deeper purple, suggesting a Myrmidon from Ifryn.

The return blast flared away from Dainyl's shields, and Dainyl could sense the surprise from the other flier, even from more than a hundred yards away. The other flier banked to the east and started a climb.

Dainyl followed, his pteridon gaining quickly on the other. Rather than trigger the skylance from a distance, Dainyl waited until he was less than fifty yards away. Then, as he triggered the skylance, he drove a Talent wedge through the other's shields.

Both pteridon and rider flared into blue flame—and once more, Dainyl's pteridon fed on some of the dispersing lifeforce. Dainyl checked his altitude—more than a thousand yards aboveground so far.

A skylance bolt slammed into his shields from behind.

Dainyl darted a glance back. Another pteridon was diving directly toward him.

Dainyl sent a command—and an image. *Straight up, over . . . and down.* The image was a loop that would bring him and the pteridon above and behind the attacker, above because of the climb, and behind because the maneuver essentially stopped nearly all forward motion for a moment. It took more lifeforce and Talent, but Dainyl's pteridon had that to spare.

The attacker never saw the bolt that blew him out of the sky—and destroyed his pteridon.

Another Ifryn Myrmidon came out of a wingover headed for the shoulder of Dainyl's pteridon, a position from which Dainyl could not turn enough to physically aim the skylance at the attacker.

Dainyl waited for several moments, using his shields to deflect the blue flames, until the attacker was closer, then twisted the lance as far back as he could, then triggered it, using his Talent to direct the energy through the other flier's shields. Blue flame exploded into the sky.

Climb!

The pteridon responded immediately.

Within moments, Dainyl was a good three hundred yards above the others—except for one other pteridon, bearing the black and silver, which was a good hundred yards even higher.

The flier carried no skylance, but something different, a device that looked from a distance like a short lance mounted on a light-rifle frame. Dainyl immediately reinforced his shields, barely in time before a bluish purple beam slammed into those shields, with enough force to lift both Dainyl and his pteridon slightly.

Hard right, dive. Then left, climb, loop, and half roll! Dainyl followed with the image of the maneuver.

Another blast of bluish purple flared past Dainyl's shoulder, but missed even his shields, for which he was grateful. Then Dainyl and his pteridon were directly under the silver and black flier, who had begun to bank westward.

Dainyl corrected, and his pteridon came out of the roll, opening its half-furled wings, directly above and behind the flier with the light-rifle lance.

Dive! Dainyl wanted to be as close as possible, suspecting that the flier was Talent-strong, but a comparatively inexperienced flier.

His quarry tried to turn, twisting his body, only when Dainyl was less than thirty yards away.

The Talent-boosted skylance bolt slammed into the modified weapon.

Hard left!

From the force of the explosion from the weapon, so violent that it obliterated both rider and pteridon, Dainyl's pteridon went through an unscheduled roll, losing at least five hundred yards of altitude before recovering. Dainyl barely managed to hang on to the skylance, and his stomach was in his throat by the time the pteridon was level, heading toward yet another hostile pteridon.

Dainyl's Talent-boosted lance bolt took out both flier and pteridon.

Another pteridon dived toward him . . .

Dainyl reacted . . . and kept reacting until, abruptly, there were but three remaining black and silver pteridons. All three broke away simultaneously and flew southward, trailed by four pteridons without fliers.

Dainyl checked the distance—too far to catch them until they slowed for landing, and that was likely to be in Ludar, two glasses later in the day.

After slipping the skylance into its holder, he banked the pteridon and began to search for any remaining officers. He did not see Ghasylt, but he did fly by Undercaptain Ghanyr—if just high enough that the wing vortices did not entangle—and called out, "Back to headquarters! Pass the word to First Company!"

"Yes, sir!" Ghanyr raised a hand in salute.

Dainyl began to climb, looking for Fhentyl or another officer from Fifth Company. Finally, he spotted the captain and winged into a bank, coming out beside Fhentyl. "Return to headquarters!"

After sensing the captain's surprise, Dainyl realized that Fhentyl had not seen him join the Myrmidons, but the captain nodded.

Dainyl raised his arm in acknowledgment, then banked the pteridon back toward Elcien.

After several moments, he glanced back over his shoulder. The remaining pteridons were formed into two wedges, with two pteridons trailing. A quick count showed thirty-one pteridons, one of them without a flier. Assuming that none of the Seventh Squad pteridons guarding the Palace had been lost, the three companies had lost more than a third of their strength, and the attackers had lost all but seven out of something more than thirty.

In less than a season, the Myrmidons had lost almost half their pteridons . . . and for what?

Fires raged across the fields and woods around where the ground forces and lightcannon had been, and thick grayish white smoke, with thinner areas of black, billowed skyward. Dainyl scanned the bay below, but there was no sign of the vessel that had been a column of flame—except for a rough oval of floating items and a slick spreading across the gray-blue waters.

After another quarter glass, as he neared the channel south of Elcien, ahead, he could see the nine pteridons from Seventh Company still circling the Palace. He altered course to intercept them. When he neared the Palace, he looked past it toward the Hall of Justice—still enshrouded in the slimy purple Talent-miasma. He kept his shields up, just in case one of the Myrmidons might fire, but while he could sense skylances leveled at him, no one fired as he eased toward them, both hands held high.

He finally eased the pteridon toward one of the undercaptains, coming close enough so that their wings would have interlocked, had Dainyl not been higher and slightly to the rear, in order to call out his orders. "Return to headquarters! Pass the word!"

After a moment, the undercaptain replied, "Return to headquarters! Yes, sir."

Dainyl banked back to the west and brought the pteridon down in a steep descent. He swept in over the southern wall, flared, and let the pteridon settle onto the flight stage. For a moment, he remained in the harness.

Alcyna walked at a measured pace from the headquarters building, then stopped and waited several yards from the raised stone platform.

Carefully, Dainyl released the harness and dismounted, then took the steps down the flight stage.

"You were victorious, I take it."

"Only after a fashion. We lost something like twenty pteridons and Myrmidons. By my count, they had Second and Third Companies. Three of them escaped. There were another four pteridons without fliers."

Alcyna looked at Dainyl. "You can't destroy a pteridon with a skylance. Did they shoot down their own pteridons with lightcannon?"

Dainyl swallowed. In the heat of the battle, he hadn't even considered that. "No. Well . . . it's possible that they might have hit some of their own. They were heavy lightcannon. Each one was powered by a wagon full of lifeforce crystals . . ."

Alcyna's white face turned even more pale. "*You* destroyed almost twenty pteridons?"

"I didn't seem to have much choice. They were trying to destroy ours, and they had light-rifles in the air and on the ground." Dainyl stopped speaking and watched as the pteridons that had followed him began to land, one after the other.

"Neither of the Duarches will be happy."

Dainyl agreed with her on that. Anything that pleased Khelaryt certainly wouldn't have pleased Samist, and the reverse was certainly true. Since neither had totally triumphed, neither would be pleased.

He turned and walked across the courtyard, not that he really had anywhere to go at the moment, not with the Table in the Hall of Justice pouring out a purple miasma of deadly Talent, but he didn't wish to note which faces were among the missing, particularly those from First Company.

Inside, the duty desk was held by Doselt, the administrative squad leader.

"Highest, sir?"

"First, Fifth, and Seventh Companies have returned. Casualties were high. The marshal will be able to fill you in."

Dainyl turned and walked down the corridor to the empty study that had been his when he'd been submarshal. He left the door slightly ajar and sat down behind the empty table desk.

He'd tried to keep it all from coming to what had just happened. He'd warned Shastylt. He'd warned Zelyert. He'd warned the Duarch and kept him informed. He'd stopped Rhelyn and Fahylt. He'd kept more than half of the Myrmidons in the east loyal. And what had Khelaryt done?

The High Alector of Justice looked out the window in the direction of the Palace.

90

Some time after Dainyl had entered the empty submarshal's study, perhaps a half glass later, Alcyna stepped into the study and quietly closed the door.

"We lost Ghasylt and Yuasylt, Lyzetta and one of her undercaptains, and two of Fhentyl's undercaptains."

"I'm sorry about that," Dainyl replied quietly.

"I've done a quick debriefing," Alcyna went on. "According to Chelysta, Ghanyr, and Asyrk, you destroyed all the lightcannon and light-rifles and something like twenty pteridons. By yourself. All by yourself. All by your frigging self."

"I didn't keep count," Dainyl admitted. "I tried not to get our Myrmidons into the mess. It would have been much better not to be on the defensive, but Khelaryt wouldn't respond. I had to do something."

The marshal shook her head. "You went after Brekylt, didn't you?"

"In both Alustre and Dulka." He laughed ruefully. "I didn't have a pteridon. They do make a difference."

"For you. Not necessarily for everyone."

There was a sharp and hard rap on the closed door.

"Marshal! Highest! There's a messenger here from the Duarch."

Alcyna and Dainyl exchanged glances.

"You said he wouldn't be pleased," Dainyl finally said, standing.

Alcyna opened the door.

Doselt stood there. "He doesn't look happy."

"Let's go see what it's all about," suggested Dainyl.

As he and Alcyna walked down the corridor toward the entry foyer, Dainyl looked toward the front entrance, where a green dispatch coach waited.

The alector who awaited them wore dark green. His face was grim, and his eyes twitched. He did not look at Dainyl as he stepped toward Alcyna. "Marshal . . . you are summoned to the Palace immediately—"

Dainyl stepped forward. "No. The marshal acted under my orders. If there is a summons, I will take it."

"But, Highest . . ."

"I will accompany you. I will be most happy to explain matters to the Duarch, but I will not have my subordinates summoned and questioned for my orders."

The alector glanced across the faces of the Myrmidon officers. His shoulders slumped. "As you wish, Highest."

"I need a moment with my officers," Dainyl said. "Wait. I'll follow you in my coach."

After a moment of hesitation, the messenger nodded, then turned.

Once he was out of the building, Dainyl faced Alcyna. "If anything happens to me, fly all the Myrmidons to Lyterna and place yourself under the command of Asulet. If he has not survived, then you will be the senior alector. Take control of Lyterna and defend it."

"Do you know what you're doing?" asked Alcyna, her voice low.

"No. I know what I should have done, and I know what I won't do. Widespread use of lightcannon will destroy Acorus and all of us. Unless he changes his mind, Khelaryt is unwilling to accept or understand that. He is more worried about pteridon fighting pteridon than about a weapon far more deadly and dangerous." *And I still don't understand why.*

"He'll kill you."

"He may, but he needs to hear what is, not what he wishes to hear, and a good Myrmidon offers his best judgment." Dainyl walked toward his still-waiting coach.

"To the Palace." Dainyl was tired, almost exhausted, when he climbed into the coach and closed the door. Yet the summons to the Palace was an order, and one that obviously indicated that the Duarch was displeased. But why? Because of the losses the Myrmidons had taken in repulsing the attack and destroying most of the attackers? Or because Dainyl was supposed to have let them destroy Elcien without a fight in order to avoid pteridon fighting pteridon?

He sat back on the hard bench seat and closed his eyes for a time, just gathering himself together. Then, as the coach neared the Palace, Dainyl looked to the Hall of Justice, partly because he wondered how long the transfer would take and partly because he worried about the conflict within Lyterna, yet there was no way to discover how Asulet and Myenfel had fared against Paeylt without the use of the Tables.

He still recoiled from the purpleness around the Hall, stronger than before, yet paradoxically, he could sense a stronger presence of the blackish amber-green of the ancients beneath and around it.

Do you dare? Did he not dare?

He extended a Talent probe—one of green—to that well of lifeforce/Talent, touching it, but not drawing from it. *Not yet.*

He held that tie after the coach halted in the entry rotunda and he stepped out and through the archway into the entry foyer. He also held full Talent shields. The messenger had to run from the dispatch coach to catch up to Dainyl, then abruptly stopped behind him in the foyer.

The functionary who greeted Dainyl was not Bharyt, but a younger alector—the stern-faced Moryn. "Highest . . ." His eyes flicked to the messenger.

"I intercepted the summons," Dainyl stated firmly. "The marshal acted under my orders, and I will see the Duarch. If he is displeased with my actions, he can summon the marshal later."

After the briefest of pauses, Moryn replied, "He will see you in the conference room. This way."

Dainyl nodded and followed the functionary down the long columned hallway.

Moryn opened the door. "He will be with you shortly, Highest."

Dainyl had his doubts about that and settled into one of the chairs. He waited a good half glass before the door from the private library and study opened.

Khelaryt stepped into the conference room. Talent and anger swirled around him, but he closed the door gently, if firmly.

Dainyl stood, inclining his head slightly. "Most High."

The Duarch took two steps into the room and stopped, looking down on Dainyl.

"I am less than pleased with you, Dainyl. Why did you not bring the news about the transfer of the Master Scepter personally? Why did you decide whom I would summon?"

Dainyl eased away from the chair and the table. "Because Elcien was under attack, sir. I could do nothing about the Master Scepter, and two companies of pteridons loyal to Samist, two ships fitted with lightcannon and loyal to Alseryl, who decided to betray you to Samist, and sandoxen and lightcannon under Ruvryn—they all were headed here to attack Elcien."

"All because you angered the Duarch of Ludar, and Brekylt and the other High Alectors. That was your doing." Despite the dark reddish purple of the anger roiling within the Duarch, his deep voice was mild.

Dainyl strengthened his tie to the black amber-green beneath Elcien.

"And you continue to employ that improper Talent."

"I have always supported you and the Duarchy, no matter what the nature of my Talent may be," replied Dainyl calmly. "Even when others have not."

"Did I give you orders to attack? Was that support? Did I tell you to sacrifice scores of pteridons? Was that support?"

"We did not attack, sir. We defended Elcien against attack. We would have lost even more pteridons by not responding."

"Why did you fight pteridons against pteridons?" asked Khelaryt.

"I was not aware that we had any choice, sir."

"The responsibility of the High Alector of Justice is to avoid such wasteful conflicts."

"I thought that was your responsibility, sir. By refusing to see what has developed, and by refusing to act against disloyal High Alectors when you had the power to do so, you ended up with only me supporting you. These events have angered you, and now you wish to take that anger out on me."

"*You* were supposed to stop the disloyalty. You failed me and the Duarchy."

Dainyl just looked at the Duarch. "I did not fail you, Khelaryt. I may have failed the Duarchy." Had the Archon selected Khelaryt as a figurehead shadowmatched and conditioned not to use force just so that there would not be a violent war? Was that how Dainyl had failed? In not understanding the true power basis of the Duarchy?

"You want to be Duarch, don't you, Dainyl?" Anger and sadness mixed in Khelaryt's words.

"No. I never aspired to be Duarch. I still do not."

"And yet you have destroyed the Duarchy. Why?"

Because I was trying to save it in the only way I knew how.

"Why?" demanded Khelaryt. "You must answer for it."

"Because you were too weak to save it."

"Weak? Without that green abomination you would not have the strength to stand in the same chamber with me or any other true alector."

"What do you intend to do now?" Dainyl asked.

"I need do nothing. I am the Duarch." Khelaryt meant every word he spoke.

Dainyl steeled himself, opening the channels to the well of amber-green beneath Elcien, letting it pour into him.

Take care with what you do.

The words, seemingly from nowhere, gave Dainyl pause.

"You cannot stand against a Duarch," Khelaryt said, smiling winningly. "You will not."

Dainyl struck, with all the power of the web beneath the world, all focused into the narrowest blade, a tiny spear of infinite power.

For an instant, Khelaryt looked stunned.

Then . . . there was only dust and a set of shimmersilk garments fluttering to the green marble floor.

Dainyl stood there, stunned himself, both at what he had done, at the ease of his action, and at the fact that Khelaryt had been, impressive as he had seemed, little more than a figurehead, a placeholder, in case the Archon had decided to move the Master Scepter to Acorus. Was Samist also a placeholder, or had he been positioned for a stronger role?

After a time, Dainyl stepped out of the conference room, green light radiating from him.

Moryn turned and looked at Dainyl. Then he paled and swallowed. He bowed deeply.

Dainyl looked hard at the functionary. "The Duarch of Elcien is dead. Announce mourning. A great alector has died. I will convey the news to the Duarch Samist personally. Tomorrow, most likely by pteridon, since the Tables are blocked."

"You are not claiming . . ." stammered Moryn.

"I am the High Alector of Justice, and for now, I intend to remain so. It would be presumptuous and premature to do otherwise."

Moryn bowed again as Dainyl walked past him. Dainyl felt as though the Palace had become a prison, confining him. But then, hadn't it been just that for Khelaryt? For that reason alone, even if it were offered, he would not be Duarch. Behind him he heard Moryn and another voice.

". . . let him leave?"

". . . *look* at him. You try to stop him if you wish. No one has ever crossed him and lived . . . No one ever will. Not now."

No one ever will. Not now. Those words rang in Dainyl's ears as he walked down the corridor and out to the waiting coach.

He looked to the driver. "Myrmidon headquarters, please."

The driver did not look in Dainyl's direction. "Yes, Most High."

Dainyl did not bother to correct him as he climbed into the coach.

After he closed the door and leaned back, a sad smile crossed Dainyl's face.

Had Khelaryt always been that way, and Dainyl just hadn't seen it? Or had losing the shadowmatch and the power it held unbalanced him? Or had the Archon planned it all that way from the beginning? The more Dainyl discovered, the less he knew. And the less sense anything made. Khelaryt's youngest daughter had given her life for her father, and it had meant nothing, not so far as Dainyl could tell. More than thirty Myrmidons and pteridons had perished, and Dainyl wasn't certain their loss changed anything.

When the coach reached Myrmidon headquarters and Dainyl entered the building, he discovered that Alcyna and all the officers were waiting in the foyer and around the duty desk, Their eyes fell on him, and not a one looked directly at him for more than an instant.

Alcyna looked at Dainyl, then squinted, looking slightly away. "You're back. You're . . . different. What happened?" Alcyna glanced toward the corridor leading to her study.

Dainyl shook his head. "The Duarch is dead. I told the acting chief assistant to prepare mourning for a Duarch and great alector."

At the indrawn breaths from the officers clustered behind the duty desk, Dainyl paused. "He had failed as Duarch, and he knew it, and he could not accept that." That was true enough. Khelaryt had never really tried to defend himself, not that it would have made any difference, Dainyl knew. He also knew that Khelaryt had known that as well, but had not wished to admit it.

Dainyl nodded toward Alcyna's study.

Neither spoke until she closed the door.

"Now . . . what do you plan to do?" asked Alcyna.

"*We* attempt to reach an agreement with Samist. They destroy the lightcannon, and I remain as High Alector of Justice, and you become the next High Alector. There *will* be a vacancy."

Her mouth opened, but she said nothing, closing it. Finally, she spoke. "After all this . . . when you could be Duarch . . . and you'd let . . ."

"What do you suggest I do?" asked Dainyl. "The only force to balance them is the Myrmidons. I want Acorus safe for everyone. It won't be safe for anyone, and it won't last long enough with lightcannon and light-rifles everywhere."

"You're the only force. Don't you see? You're the only frigging force that can stand against Samist! *You* destroyed twenty pteridons. You destroyed the Duarch . . ." Alcyna's voice died away.

Dainyl understood. Now . . . she feared him, and was truly appalled at the words that had spilled from her lips.

"No . . . we're the only force," Dainyl replied quietly. "If anything happens to me—and it could because no one is indispensable or invulnerable. Khelaryt thought he was, and so did Zelyert. If anything happens to me," he repeated, "they still have to deal with you, and we can set it up so that if anything happens to you, they'll still have to deal with Sevasya."

"When . . . how?"

"Tomorrow morning. If the Tables are still blocked, we'll take pteridons. Fifth Company, I'd suggest."

"I suggest you go by pteridon regardless. They won't deal with you. Khelaryt wouldn't, would he?"

"No," admitted Dainyl. "But I have to try."

"They'll have more lightcannons. Not that it will do them any good." Alcyna laughed, softly, bitterly, almost under her breath.

Dainyl doubted her assessment. Samist would not react as Khelaryt had, nor would Brekylt. If Dainyl had to lead a battle, it would be worse than what had happened in the skies south of Elcien. And he was tired. Bone-tired.

91

Mykel rode northward, with Fabrytal beside him, and a squad from Fifteenth Company behind them. The sun had barely cleared the old oaks on the east side of the narrow lane, and although the sky remained clear, his breath—and that of his mount—steamed in the shadows cast by the trees.

Another wave of the unseen purple-black flashed through the skies, or so it seemed to Mykel. He'd been sensing such flashes for almost a day, but no one else had noticed them. Was he losing his mind? Was it some sort of delayed poisoning from his wound? It couldn't be that. While he would bear scars for the rest of his life, the wound itself had healed cleanly, even if he had a ways to go in regaining the strength and mobility in his right arm and shoulder. But purpled flashes? Was it from something the alectors were doing?

Mykel glanced back in the direction of the Aerlal Plateau, although he could not see it because of the trees. He *felt* that it had somehow become amber-green, yet when he had glimpsed it, the distant ramparts had only appeared dark gray.

"Do you think it'll be long before they attack, Majer?" asked Fabrytal. "It is Decdi."

"I'm not sure I'm the one to ask," replied Mykel, with an ironic laugh. "I thought they would have attacked long before this, but I doubt they would care whether it was an end-day or not."

"They must have a reason, sir. Everyone has a reason," suggested Fabrytal. "Sometimes they believe in the worst ones the most."

Mykel smiled at that. Certainly, that was true enough. The seltyrs of Dramur had almost everything, and yet they'd precipitated a revolt out of a need for . . . what? Wanting to prove that the alectors couldn't tell them what to do? Wanting to be able to treat their women like slaves?

Yet many women, like Rachyla, were far more perceptive

than the seltyrs. Thinking of her, he wondered if she had even gotten his last missive to her. They both had hopes, but . . .

He snorted softly. No matter what the soarers told him about finding or returning to the one to whom he was tied, it wouldn't matter much unless he were wealthy and prosperous—or more powerful than he was ever likely to be.

Mykel rode without speaking, following the lane along the eastern side of the hills for nearly a vingt before turning westward through a vale between a pair of hills. Ahead, at a wide spot beyond the crest of the lane, waited Jasakyt, Coroden, Culeyt, and Loryalt.

"Seems strange not to see Captain Rhystan," said Fabrytal.

"He'll do fine holding the bridge." *If the Reillies ever get around to it.*

Shortly, Mykel reined up beside the group, then looked to the scouts. "What are they doing now?"

"They've got some big ceremony going, sir," reported Jasakyt.

"Another one?"

"This one's different . . . seriouslike. No beer, no wine. Solemn."

Put that way, Mykel liked the picture even less. "Any sign of mounts being readied to ride out?"

"They've got grindstones out, and they're sharpening those big blades of theirs," added Coroden.

"That sounds like tomorrow," offered Culeyt.

Loryalt nodded.

Mykel looked at the Borlan road on the far side of the valley, beyond the swampy ground bordering the stream, then to Culeyt. "You'll be here. If they stay on the Borlan road, don't engage them. Don't fire a single shot."

"Yes, sir."

"If they do come this way against you, you'll have to hold them, at least until we can swing up the road and hit them from the south."

Culeyt nodded. "We can do that."

"If they don't come at you or if you turn them back and they follow the road toward Borlan"—Mykel gestured to the south—"I want you to swing in behind them, but not too close, not so that they stop and fight you. It's only two vingts from here to the bridge causeway, and I think once they see the open bridge they'll move on toward it and Borlan."

Mykel certainly hoped so. He hadn't been pleased to find the lane that might offer another route for the hill people. It hadn't been on any of the maps, and yet it was traveled enough that it had been around for a long time.

He should have known better than to trust maps, but then, there were more than a few things he should have known better about—like chasing down Reillies single-handed, or falling in love with a seltyr's daughter.

92

Dainyl and Alcyna lifted off from the Myrmidon headquarters at dawn on Decdi, and still the Hall of Justice was suffused in Talent force, with pulsations of purple and black all too apparent to Dainyl. Somewhere in the depths, as well, Dainyl had sensed the amber-green of the ancients, implacable and distant, yet somehow nearer and stronger. Or was that just his imagination, playing on his fears?

He doubted that, because even Alcyna had looked away from the Hall as they climbed out, carried southward by the wide-winged and tireless pteridons. Behind them flew the thirty-seven remaining pteridons of First, Fifth, and Seventh Companies. Strapped into a second lanceholder, on the left side of the pteridon's thick neck, was a white banner of truce, to indicate that Dainyl wanted to talk.

The waters of the Bay of Ludel were a hard blue-gray, seemingly without waves. The wind was little more than a light breeze, although the air was chill enough to remind Dainyl that it was winter, despite the cloudless sky.

By late midmorning, after three glasses of steady flight under a silver-green sky that now bore a hazy sheen, Dainyl could make out the dome of the Engineering Hall in Ludar to the south. A thousand yards beneath the wings of the pteridons ran the great high road—empty of riders, sandoxen, or wagons. On most Decdis, the high road carried only sparse traffic, but there was usually some. Today, there was none. Several vingts to the west of the high road was the Bay of Ludel, which extended some three vingts to the south of the west side of Ludar. The great piers were empty of all vessels.

Dainyl had not taken notice of it before, although he had not overflown Ludar that often, and not for years, but the Engineering Hall was on a low ridge, one perhaps not even noticeable from the ground, that was the southeasternmost extension of the rocky hills forming much of the western boundary of the bay. Immediately south of the Engineering Hall was the long structure of the Palace of the Duarch of Ludar. Once more, Dainyl could not help but smile at the domes and curves of Ludar, and the green gardens and trees, the beauty of a city well planned—and its construction well executed. The streets and boulevards surrounding the Engineering Hall and the Palace were empty as well.

Dainyl reached forward and pulled out the white flag and unfurled it, a banner a good yard wide and three long, large enough to be seen from a distance, bracing it against the holder. Then he called to Alcyna, "I'll lead the way with this. Have everyone else stand off! They'll have lightcannon, and they'll fire if everyone follows me."

"Yes, sir." Alcyna raised her arm in acknowledgment, then raised her voice. "Bear off! Bear off! The Highest will bear the truce flag in. Pass it back!"

Dainyl began a gentle descent from a thousand yards, reaching five hundred at the point where he crossed the northern boundary of Ludar, on the north side where the city truly began, when a beam of deep blue flared upward from the Engineering Hall. While he could not prove it, Dainyl suspected that Ruvryn, or Paelyt, or their engineers had designed that particular lightcannon and perhaps all those in Ludar to draw from the Table under almost any circumstances, just as the invaders in Hyalt had.

After reinforcing his shields, Dainyl tried to lift the truce banner higher as he descended even farther, to less than three hundred yards above the ground.

Yet another blast flared upward, this time clearly in his direction, despite the long white banner that had to be clearly visible from the Engineering Hall.

He was less than half a vingt away when the third blast came within yards. He could sense the ripping of lifeforce from somewhere—but through the Table. Extending a Talent probe, he tried to study the Engineering Hall, but could only sense the purple miasma centered on where the Table was. The lightcannon had fired from beyond the edge of that.

Did he want to keep trying to persuade them to talk? His eyes angled back toward the truce banner.

Another bolt of lifeforce energy slammed against the edge of his shields. Dainyl dropped the truce banner, letting it flutter toward the ground. Samist, Brekylt, and Alseryl had attacked Elcien without provocation or warning, and now they did not even wish to talk, as they continued to use weapons that would lay waste to Acorus long before its time.

Down . . . and right . . . just above the water. The pteridon complied, half furling its long leathery wings and dropping like the predator it was toward the winter blue-gray waters of the bay.

Dainyl hoped he could deal with the lightcannon. No one else would even have a chance against a weapon like that, possibly even more powerful than the ones of the day before—or of the one in Hyalt. He would have little enough chance if the blue blasts struck him and his shields directly.

Once he was but ten yards above the water, Dainyl made a complete course reversal, turning back to the southeast on a heading centered on the Engineering Hall. He glanced back to the northeast, where the other pteridons circled, well out of the range of the lightcannon. With relief at not having to worry about them for the moment, he eased out the skylance, and at the same time began to probe for the ancients' web. It had to be near the Table.

Finding that blackish green web took longer than he had thought it would, for it was deeper beneath the soil and rock. He was almost at the edge of the bay, north of the piers that had held the oceangoing ships of the Duarchy days before, when he finally located and Talent-linked to the web.

The pteridon swept between the twin green towers at each end of the long causeway, from which the piers jutted out into the bay, and toward the Engineering Hall.

He was less than half a vingt away from the Hall and the lightcannon when light-rifles began to fire at him. His shields, boosted and bolstered by the lifeforce/Talent of the ancients, frayed slightly at the edges, but were more than adequate.

In quick bursts, he triggered the lance, taking out each light-rifle whose energy he could sense, but he was almost over the Hall—and he could not sense the lightcannon, not until he was past it.

Banking the pteridon right, toward the Palace, he could sense an enormous buildup of energy behind him.

Down . . . as low as possible!

The pteridon skimmed across the gardens, its wings seemingly spans above the bushes, and its wingtips occasionally cutting through the ends of tree limbs.

SSSSsssssss!

The deep purple-blue energy that seared through the air passed less than two yards above his head, and less than half that above the pteridon's crest.

Around the Palace . . . keep low.

More light-rifles began to fire as he swung around the Palace, but Dainyl ignored them as he completed the turn and headed back for the Hall—less than three hundred yards away.

He immediately triggered the lance, focusing it on the stone terrace on the south side where he knew the lightcannon was mounted, pouring Talent force into that narrow beam.

Right! Steep bank!

The weapon itself exploded into a shower of metal and crystal, killing the alectors who had been firing it, but some sort of insulation had blocked and diverted the boosted skylance beam from the storage crystals and the link to the Table. Still, his attack had stripped away most of the Talent camouflage.

The pteridon straightened out on an easterly heading, and

Dainyl waited several moments before turning back toward the Engineering Hall. When he did, from a vingt away he could see two more lightcannon, both mounted on the north terrace, but one on the east end and the other on the west. Each was sending occasional bolts of dark blue light toward the Myrmidons. Since the Myrmidons were well north of Ludar, those bolts were only a warning—and more wasted lifeforce energy.

If he didn't shut down the lightcannon, it would make little difference who "won," because everyone would lose.

On his third approach to the Engineering Hall, Dainyl concentrated on linking to the energy of the web well beneath Ludar. The pteridon was barely clearing the low trees and the topiary of the Duarch's gardens as it swept toward the north terrace and the lightcannon.

More light-rifle fire centered on Dainyl, and a blast of blue force passed so close overhead that the heat and power shook the pteridon. Dainyl's shields were strained, and sweat threatened to run into his eyes.

He aimed the skylance, not at the lightcannon's discharge formulator, but at the heavy cable at its base, a cable he could not see, but only sense with his Talent, for all the energy it carried. Then he triggered it, pouring energy from the pteridon and from the amber-green in the depths, guiding it with his Talent.

Left! Hard! . . . Keep low.

The pteridon made more of a sweeping turn than a steep bank, but it couldn't bank more steeply, not without digging a wingtip into shrubbery or trimmed lawn of the gardens only yards beneath them. Dainyl kept pouring energy into the cable.

CRUMMPTTT!

As the pteridon was being hurled toward the ground, Dainyl threw all his own Talent and whatever else he could draw into shields and protection. In addition to his own shields, for a moment, he was surrounded in amber-green.

Then he was rolling across a stretch of lawn, ending up with his back against a hedge.

Link to the web! Link yourself to the web, or you will die.

Dainyl rolled away from the hedge and struggled to his knees. That was an effort because the very ground beneath his feet was swaying, and a deep set of groans issued from deep within the earth itself. He turned his head, and then his body, trying to see where the soarer was who had spoken.

One of the ancients hovered beside him, but she was not facing him but the pteridon that had struck the ground almost a hundred yards away and was struggling to right itself with what looked to be a broken wing. Dainyl had never seen an injured pteridon.

An intense line of brilliant amber-green flared from the ancient to the pteridon, so bright that Dainyl blinked and then closed his eyes momentarily against the glare. The green vanished, and a pillar of blue flame flared upward, so hot and intense that Dainyl threw up both arms to shield his face.

In moments, the flame had vanished, leaving only a circular blackened patch in the expanse of grass—and ashes where a tree and another section of the hedge had been.

A pteridon gone—like that.

Dainyl staggered to his feet, turning to the soarer, who seemed to be fading.

Link or die . . . That message carried both an imperative and sadness.

Then she was gone, as if she had never been there, as if she had died and never existed. That was what Dainyl felt.

He looked northward, into the sky, his mouth open. More than a score of ancients had appeared in the midday sky, hovering, each one close to a pteridon and Myrmidon. Dainyl *knew* what was going to happen.

He turned, looking for another pteridon, for anything, for some way to stop the coming carnage in the sky.

The sky exploded in blue flashes.

He had not taken a dozen steps before the sky was empty—both of pteridons and of ancients—and a wave of what he could only describe as death and sadness swept over him. In an instant, less than an instant, the ancients had destroyed thirty-nine pteridons.

He shuddered.

Beneath him, coming from the web of the ancients, was that menacing cold and amber-green force that he had been sensing through his Table travel for months, looming over Ludar, as if it were a massive wall of rock ready to crush the city—yet it was rising from beneath Ludar. At the same time, the shuddering and shaking of the earth did not die away, but became stronger, the vibrations quicker and more intense, so much so that Dainyl had a difficult time maintaining his footing on the manicured lawn of the Duarch's garden.

He turned back southward, looking at the massive oblong structure that was the Palace of the Duarch, as the entire building began to vibrate—and to sink into the very ground.

Abruptly, he felt weak, disoriented, as if he were going to collapse. What was happening?

The purpleness that had shrouded the Engineering Hall and the Table contracted, writhing against something, then exploded outward into a fine mist that seemed to evaporate like fog.

Dainyl swallowed inadvertently and forced what little Talent he seemed to have left, and it was all green, toward the web beneath, trying to link with it before he lost all consciousness.

Yet making that connection seemed impossible, as if each time he reached forth to link the web twisted away from him.

Faint stars flashed before his eyes, and his legs felt like jelly, almost unable to support him.

Around him, the rumbling increased, and the ground no longer shook, but began to heave, sections of the turf rippling until the lawn looked like a green ocean. Dainyl staggered, trying to maintain his footing, even as he could sense an enormous pressure within the Engineering Hall.

The Table! All the energy within it was about to explode.

Lystrana . . . Kytrana . . . he *had* to get to them, to Dereka.

With a last effort, he pressed his link to the web, letting himself be suffused in amber-green, and feeling himself sink downward, even as the Table and the Engineering Hall exploded in a deafening roar.

Downward . . . through an amber-green that no longer felt so menacing, toward the web itself . . .

93

As Culeyt had predicted, the entire mass of Squawts and Reillies began to ride out of their encampment at dawn on Decdi. Before long, according to the scouts, they were riding—or flowing—down the Borlan road toward the bridge. Mykel had moved the three companies he had with him into the prearranged positions, while he took up a vantage point in the center of the companies, concealed over the crest of several grassy knolls to the east of the flat bluffs, less than half a vingt from the Borlan road. The section of road directly to the west of Mykel was also about half a vingt to the north of the causeway approaching the bridge, a graceful arched eternastone structure wide enough for two wagons abreast, or five riders comfortably.

In the early chill, Mykel was grateful that the low morning sun offered some slight warmth on his back as he waited beside the roan for the next set of reports from the scouts. After a time, he readjusted the sling on his right arm. He'd taken to not wearing it for short periods every day, but he was likely to be in the saddle for a long time in the day ahead. Fabrytal stood beside Mykel.

After a time, the undercaptain cleared his throat. "Sir?"

"Yes, Fabrytal?"

"You know the ground was shaking early this morning just before dawn?"

"I know. I felt it." Not only had Mykel felt it, but he'd also sensed a wave of green Talent, seemingly radiating from the Aerlal Plateau, or at least from that direction. "It lasted for more than a quarter glass." The earthquake—or whatever it had been—had felt much like the one that had leveled the ironworks earlier. What else had the ancient soarers done? Would it affect the battle ahead? How?

Mykel couldn't help but worry about the River Vedra, so much so that while the Cadmians were forming up, he'd ridden to the edge of the bluffs to check the water level. The river had been no higher—or lower—than the day before. Since the bluffs were a good thirty yards above the river, Mykel felt slightly reassured. But only slightly. Still, it seemed unlikely if not impossible that enough water could flow down the Vedra to wash over the top of the bluffs, particularly since the volume of water would flood the lower land to the east on the south side of the river west of Dekhron and be lost long before it reached Borlan. For all that, where the soarers were concerned, Mykel had learned not to discount anything. Something was going to happen.

He smiled ruefully. That didn't mean it would happen to him. He wasn't exactly the center of the world for either the ancients or the alectors. "Sometimes those things happen. We're on high ground here."

"What about the Reillies? It's been over a glass. It doesn't take that long to cover four vingts."

"Except at a very slow walk," Mykel pointed out.

"Majer, sir!"

Mykel turned, raising his left arm and watching as one of the scouts rode toward him, up the narrow space between where Seventeenth and Fifteenth Companies were drawn up. The Cadmians were all dismounted, but still in a loose formation by squads.

Coroden reined up. "Sir, the Reillies and the Squawts . . . they all just stopped. Couldn't be more than a vingt from us. One of their leaders rode out in front, and jumped and stood on his saddle. He was wearing green, all green. Even his face was painted green."

"Are they still there?"

"Yes, sir. They've been there for nearly half a glass. That was when I'd left. It looks like they're all praying, but they've got their blades out, or the captain might have been tempted to ask to attack."

Mykel didn't like that at all, especially not with the rumbling in the ground, and the Talent he'd felt before dawn—not when the soarers had suggested they didn't care much for Cadmians who acted as hunting dogs for alectors. "Tell him to hold. He's not to attack except if he's attacked. Otherwise, he's to follow the battle plan, unless I send other orders."

"Yes, sir."

"Have him send word if or when the Reillies start to move again."

Coroden nodded, then turned his mount back down the slope, heading toward the back lane that paralleled the Borlan road.

"Praying to their gods?" asked Fabrytal.

"Goddesses," replied Mykel. "If they're green, they have to be praying to the ancients."

"Are the ancients all women?"

"I don't think anyone knows for certain." Mykel pulled out his water bottle and took a swallow, thinking. He'd never seen a male ancient.

The entire mass of hill riders had stopped dead—less than a vingt from Mykel's Cadmians and less than two from the Borlan bridge. And they hadn't disbanded. They hadn't made camp. They just prayed and waited. *For what?*

For a sign from the ancients? For the ancients to attack and destroy the Cadmians?

Another glass came and went, without either a messenger or any sign of the Reillies and Squawts. The light breeze that had blown out of the northeast died away. So still was the air that, despite the chill, the day felt far warmer than it actually was.

"Majer!"

Mykel turned and caught sight of Coroden riding hard from the back lane and across the winter-browned grass of the slope up toward him.

"They're moving, sir," the scout reported, even before fully reining in his mount and coming to a stop short of the majer. "They didn't even look at the side lane. They're pouring down the Borlan road, sir. The captain's waiting for them to all get past before he follows, but there's got to be close to two thousand of them."

"Thank you. Tell him to follow more closely. He's to attack as soon as he hears us begin to fire."

"Yes, sir."

"Go." Mykel gestured with his good arm. "Be careful on the ride back."

Coroden turned his mount and headed back down the slope.

"Third Battalion! Mount up!" Mykel half jumped, half climbed up into the saddle of the roan, an awkward but effective mounting for a man with a single usable arm.

"Mount up!" The command echoed across the slope of the knoll.

While the three companies were forming up, Mykel rode to the top of the knoll and looked to the northwest, but he did not see any sign of the Reillies and Squawts. Uneasily, he rode back down on the east side, toward his men, but only far enough that he could still watch the road without being silhouetted against the sky.

As the companies finished mounting and re-forming, the ground began to shiver, and then to rumble. The high haze in the silver-green sky became even more silvery. Mykel sensed violent pulses of brilliant amber-green energy flowing somewhere in the ground, not beneath him, but both to the north and south. *What* were the soarers doing?

Fabrytal rode forward toward Mykel. "Fifteenth Company, mounted and ready, sir."

"Thirteenth Company . . ."

"Seventeenth Company . . ."

The three undercaptains looked at Mykel.

"Sir?" Loryalt finally asked. "Is that the Reillies?"

"No." Mykel shook his head. "It's the ancients."

The three officers exchanged glances.

A roaring, rushing sound filled the air, coming from the south and east. Mykel turned the roan toward the bluffs overlooking the river. He could sense water, knew it was crashing downstream, but his mouth still dropped open when spray spewed up the side of the bluffs to the south, turning into a thick fog. Even from half a vingt away, Mykel could feel that the water was warm—even hot.

"Sir!" shouted Fabrytal. "Here they come."

Mykel turned the roan. The river would have to wait.

A mass of mounts and men rode down the road, and then rode away from it, aimed directly at the knolls behind which the Cadmians waited.

"Battalion forward. Re-form just below the top! Staggered firing lines!"

"Battalion forward . . ."

After initially riding forward of the battalion, Mykel turned back and reined up on the crest of the knoll, letting the Cadmians ride past him. The three companies slipped into the positions Mykel had planned.

By that time, the Reillies were less than a half vingt to the west. There was no strategy, no flanking maneuvering, no attempt at a cross fire—just a swarm of hill riders with green-painted faces riding full speed toward the Cadmians.

Mykel waited until the foremost of the hill riders were less than a hundred yards away. "Open fire! Fire at will!" He glanced to the south in the direction of the Vedra. A thick fog rose over the river, and some of it had begun to roll northward. The line of fog was high enough to be seen above the tops of the trees and the bluffs, and followed the course of the river.

He forced his concentration back to the flat below and to the east of the knoll.

Already, scores of Reillies were dead and dying, and yet the flow of riders went over and around the fallen.

From their slight elevation on the upper section of the knoll, the Cadmians continued to fire down on the flat. Occasionally, Mykel could feel a Cadmian fall, but few of the Reillies and Squawts were using rifles. Most were carrying their overlarge blades. Some of the blades dripped green as well.

Mykel glanced to the northwest, catching sight of maroon and gray uniforms—Fourteenth Company riding toward the Reillies and Squawts. Even as the shots from Culeyt's men began to rip into the rear of the attackers, not a one turned. All of them pressed forward.

The charge had begun to slacken, if less than fifty yards from the base of the knoll, as more and more riders were slowed by fallen riders and mounts.

Then, a group of close to fifty riders coalesced at the base of the knoll, right in the center, and redoubled their efforts, riding straight uphill toward Fifteenth Company—and Mykel.

"Fire! At the center!" ordered Fabrytal, standing in the stirrups at the front of the company.

Seeing the undercaptain so openly ordering his company, Mykel winced.

The concentrated fire from Fifteenth Company reduced the number of riders in the oncoming advance charge to less than half those who had started up the slope, but there were still fifteen or twenty who neared the front line more than forty yards ahead of the main body.

Fabrytal's sabre flashed—once, twice, perhaps again—before he was surrounded.

The first lines of Fifteenth Company struck back, and the rest of the Reillies went down, one way or another.

"Dress those lines!" Senior Squad Leader Chyndylt's voice penetrated the chaos, and Fifteenth Company responded.

While the continued fire from Third Battalion had taken its toll on the attackers, they still rode forward.

Mykel calculated the distances and the speeds, noting how the attackers were bunched in the middle, then called out his own orders, boosting them with his Talent. "Fifteenth Company! Rifles away! To sabre! To sabre! Seventeenth Company! Thirteenth Company! Keep firing!" To offer the example to Fifteenth Company, he raised his own sabre, if left-handed. After a moment, he shouted, Talent amplifying it, "Fifteenth Company! Charge!"

"Charge!" echoed Chyndylt.

Clearly, the Reillies had not expected the Cadmians, with their smaller sabres, to charge, but those smaller sabres could be—and were—far more deadly in confined quarters, with riders and mounts pressing on all sides.

The Reillie and Squawt riders broke off, despite shouts and orders from somewhere.

"Fifteenth Company! Withdraw and re-form! Withdraw and re-form!"

Mykel was relieved to see that most of the company did ride back up the slope, already littered with bodies.

From the west, Fourteenth Company continued to rake the Reillies with rifle fire, but the warleaders or priests in the front seemed ignorant of or indifferent to those losses as the much diminished mass of hill riders regrouped into a rough series of lines and once more charged toward the bulk of Third Battalion.

Another concentration of Reillie riders formed a wedge aimed at Mykel. In between the grunts, the screams of men and mounts, and the continuing rifle fire from Fourteenth Company, he could hear the shouts of the attackers.

"To the priest-killer . . ."

"For Kladyl!"

At those words, Mykel did his best to gather and strengthen his Talent shields around him, but he remained behind the center of Fifteenth Company.

From beyond the swirl of attackers and Cadmians below him, Mykel could sense a focus of Talent somehow being directed at him, and he raised his sabre, if left-handed, trying to infuse it with what Talent he could. As he did, a line of greenish flame arced toward him, a crossbow bolt coated in Talent.

Amber-green flared before Mykel, and he rocked slightly in the saddle at the impact of bolt and sabre. His eyes still watering from the last Talent impact, he tried to get a clearer view of the battle beside and below him.

Thirteenth and Seventeenth Companies remained on the fringes of the attack, but Loryalt had angled his lines downhill on the north side to give his men clearer shots at the Reillie center. Mykel did not see Dyarth, but Thirteenth Company also continued to fire telling shots into the mass of hill riders.

He took a quick look at his sabre, but it seemed undamaged by the Talent-bolt, if slightly discolored.

A loud shrieking series of yells presaged another charge up the hill at Fifteenth Company. This onslaught was formed like a blunt wedge, and Mykel had a good idea why. When the attackers reached the first line of Fifteenth Company, nearly half had gone down wounded or killed, but they had shielded the older and more seasoned Reillies who spurred their mounts through the center of third squad, striving to reach Mykel.

"The priest-killer!"

"Avenge Kladyl!"

Much as his instinct was to charge down toward them, Mykel did not, instead, waiting, rebuilding his Talent shields. A squad of Fifteenth Company angled southward, trying to cut off the Reillies who were cutting their way through the center of the company, but a handful of Reillies surged past them before the squad intercepted those following.

Only when those few riders were within a handful of yards did Mykel urge the roan forward, waiting until he was almost upon the four riders to do his best to stiffen those shields.

The combination of his shields and momentum were enough to unhorse two of the riders and push the others away, where they were cut down by the near rankers of Fifteenth Company.

Mykel reined up. Although there were less than half of the attackers left, he wasn't about to go charging into them.

He could sense another blaze of green Talent being readied, centered on yet another group of riders who appeared, riding from the northwest side of the mass of Reillies, led by two men clad totally in green, their faces painted green as well. A faint green aura surrounded them.

"Aim for the greenies! Aim for the greenies!" Loryalt's voice bellowed forth across the hillside.

The renewed fire from Seventeenth Company cut down close to a third of the attackers within moments.

Mykel had the feeling that all the Reillies and Squawts below had stopped—and were watching—as if all those in the world around him had decided to hold their collective breaths. Except that they hadn't stopped. The remaining attackers had re-formed around the green priests, and the entire body was aimed at the northern edge of Fifteenth Company.

Seventeenth Company had swung southward.

"Charge!" ordered Loryalt.

Mykel could see that the Cadmians would not be able to cut off the leading section of the attackers. He turned the roan and reined up. Holding tight to his shields, he did what he had winced to see Fabrytal do. He stood in the stirrups, trying to anchor himself and the roan to the very ground, and to whatever lay beneath it, trying to drive pylons of Talent to bedrock.

Fire from the Cadmians to the south redoubled, ripping into the body of Reillies and Squawts for several moments, then died away as Seventeenth Company's rankers hurled themselves into the northern flank of the attackers.

The riders leading the green priests had fallen, leaving the priests alone and isolated from the remainder of the Reillies.

Still, they charged forward up the gentle slope toward Mykel, their mounts moving apart so that they would strike at him with their green-stained blades simultaneously, one from each side.

At least one bullet struck the one on the left, but he barely winced as he readied his oversized blade.

Mykel Talent-reached for greenness . . . for strength.

Both blades slashed toward Mykel.

Just before both touched the edge of his shields, Mykel grasped, with his Talent, *something*, an extra bit of Talent, a sense of amber-green. His shields flared, and the blades rebounded, and exploded into lengths of burning molten iron. In instants, both priests were human torches, and both they and their mounts were flung sideways from Mykel, tumbling into heaps that flamed skyward.

A wailing groan rose from the remaining attackers.

Mykel dropped back into his saddle, breathing heavily and watching as the Reillies and Squawts broke, as what had seemed a single immovable mass fragmented . . . and then dissolved. Riders turned their mounts back toward the northwest, to the west, anywhere there appeared to be no Cadmians.

"Third Battalion! Hold! Hold position! Fourteenth Company! Hold!" Mykel tried to project the last order through his clearly weakened and waning Talent.

There was nothing more to be gained by chasing the survivors down, not when they were scattering as individuals fleeing for their lives. The Cadmians wouldn't catch that many, and butchering fleeing riders, many of whom were little more than youths, would only sow unnecessary hatred. The Reillies and Squawts had been decimated enough to weaken them for a generation, if not longer, and that was enough for Mykel. The slope and the flat below were littered with the bodies of men, women, boys, and girls, hundreds of them, if not more than a thousand.

Equally important, the Cadmians had taken enough losses already, and there was little point in adding to them.

But the feeling of greenness persisted, and Mykel was aware that the Cadmians near him, indeed all of the survivors of Third Battalion, were turning to him. The haze of greenish light intensified.

Then, hovering beside Mykel, was a soarer. Sadness radiated from her, a sorrow that enveloped him in melancholy.

The towers have fallen. Ludar and Elcien and Faitel are no more.

"No more?" Mykel realized his words sounded inane. "How? What did you do?"

We did what needed to be done. The Ifrits are no more. The future is yours.

His? Landers? What was he supposed to do?

Go to Tempre. A wry undertone shaded the sadness behind her words.

"Tempre?"

But the soarer had vanished.

The air was still, and then the silence vanished, and Mykel could hear the sounds of the aftermath of a bloody battle—moaning men, wounded mounts, cries for help. He could smell blood and death. Dumbly, clumsily, he sheathed the sabre he still held, the muscles in his left arm protesting and threatening to cramp if he did not do so.

He glanced around. Rankers were staring at him, many openmouthed. Others looked to their comrades, questioningly. Mykel suspected that not all the men had been able to see the soarer, but more than a few had.

Loryalt was the first officer to reach Mykel. "Sir . . . are you all right?" There was an awkward pause. "What was that? Was it really an ancient?"

"It was. She . . . said that the . . . alectors are gone." Mykel had a hard time saying that, but he could not deny the sadness or the truth that had accompanied her words.

"They're gone." Loryalt's tone was between incredulity and disbelief.

"That's what she said." Mykel gestured southward toward the steaming fog that still rose from the Vedra. "They boiled the entire river. I'd hate to think what else they did." He straightened in the saddle. He needed some time to think. "I'm all right. How is Seventeenth Company?"

"Eight dead, seven wounded, sir."

"Have your men reclaim what they can from the fallen in ammunition and rifles and blades. We'll need every shell we can find."

"Sir?"

"If the Duarchy has fallen, ammunition won't be easy to come by."

"Yes, sir." While Loryalt's face held the question of what the Cadmians were to do next, he did not ask.

"We'll gather the officers later."

"Yes, sir." Loryalt turned his mount, then looked back at Mykel, his expression one of worry, awe, and fear.

Mykel forced a wry smile.

Chyndylt rode toward Mykel, reining up. "Sir?"

Even if he had not seen what had happened, Mykel would have known what the senior squad leader's presence meant. "Undercaptain Fabrytal?"

"Yes, sir. They got him on that first big charge. He took out a bunch of them."

"I'm sorry." Mykel was sorry, knowing that, in a way, he had contributed to Fabrytal's death, merely by the example of his own actions. Few Cadmians had Talent, and Mykel had survived too many ill-advised excesses in battle only through his Talent—and that had set a poor example, even if he had cut more than a few battles short with his efforts. "You're undercaptain now, Chyndylt."

"Yes, sir."

"As I told Loryalt, have your men collect every scrap of ammunition they can and every weapon . . ."

Mykel gave the same orders to Zendyr, the senior squad leader of Thirteenth Company who would have to take Dyarth's place, and to Culeyt, who was the last of the officers at the battle to report. Then he sent off a messenger to find Rhystan and request that the senior captain rejoin the main body. He could only hope that Sixteenth Company had not suffered casualties from the steaming water of the river.

As he watched his men pick up the fallen weapons and ammunition, take care of the wounded, and seek spoils from the fallen Reillies—trying to ignore the looks from the rankers whose eyes seemed to linger on him—Mykel sat tiredly in the saddle, looking out across the carnage, knowing that there were close to a thousand bodies lying on the winter-tan grass, staining it with dark splotches that would vanish under the winter snow that would fall in the days or weeks to come.

In one year, or in ten, would anyone know that hundreds had died on the hillside because of . . . what? Because the alectors of Corus had wanted order, no matter what the cost, and the hill people wanted the absolute freedom to kill and pillage?

The soarer had said that the Ifrits were no more. What had the ancients done? How had they destroyed Elcien and Ludar? And Faitel, his own home? What had happened to his family? Sesalia and her children—and Viencet? Could the soarer have lied to him?

He shook his head. For whatever reason, the soarers did not lie.

But why had the soarer appeared to him? In front of everyone? And directed him to Tempre? Then, where else could they go? Nothing in the Iron Valleys would support even the reduced Third and Fourth Battalions. Nor would Borlan.

He continued to watch over the quick and the dead, and those who were living and would not survive that much longer.

94

Link to the world. ***Change or you will die . . . Link to the world . . . Change or you will die*** *. . . As Dainyl grappled with the web of the ancients, trying to orient himself, those words rang through his mind. Never . . . never had he really believed that the ancients had that much power . . . even though he had felt the certainty behind them . . . and the sadness . . . that incredible sadness.*

In the dark amber-green of the web, he forced his sluggish thoughts back to what he had to do. He had to get to Dereka. He had to . . .

He struggled and fumbled, his thoughts freezing once more when he realized that some Table locators were gone—the white of Elcien, the brilliant yellow of Ludar, the brown of Faitel. He finally extended a Talent probe, one of pure green, green without his even trying, toward the web node that seemed to be closest to the crimson-gold locator that was Dereka.

For a timeless moment, nothing happened, and then he began to move. As he neared the node, he could feel that the Tables were . . . dead.

Not exactly dead . . . because they still held energy, but it was as though each locator existed independently. Instinctively, Dainyl understood that the Tables were now little more than portals for the deeper web, and each held a residual purple sliminess that he had never sensed until the Archon had begun to transfer the Master Scepter. The translation tube that had linked them, once lying on top of the web like a parasite, was gone. So was the long tube to Ifryn—except it should have been the tube to Efra now.

He extended a Talent probe upward, away from the inert Table, trying to leave the web. Slowly, agonizingly slowly, he could feel himself moving upward until . . .

. . . he found himself on the library level of the recorder's building. Papers were stacked neatly on the tables—except for one pile half strewn across the green and gold marble floor. Beside the papers was a set of shimmersilk garments—recorders' greens—and a pair of boots.

Jonyst? Or Whelyne? Dainyl swallowed. Lystrana! Could that have happened to her? He had to get to the regional alector's!

He glanced around the library. It was empty. He hurried down the staircase to the Table chamber, almost stumbling, as something caught at his boots. He steadied himself on the oak door frame and surveyed the chamber. The only signs of alectors were four sets of shimmersilk garments and matching boots.

He turned and started to take a step back up the stairs. He stumbled again, because his trousers had slipped enough that his boot heels had caught them. His shimmersilk greens, which had been snug before, were loose, and too long, although his boots seemed to fit. He tightened his belt, rolled up the jacket cuffs and the trouser cuffs to keep from tripping on them, and then climbed the steps again.

He hurried down through the building, seeing no one, only scattered sets of shimmersilks and boots, lying in rooms, in the corridors, but the building was empty of anyone, including landers and indigens.

How many more? Had any alectors besides himself been able to survive? Where were they? Could Lystrana have survived? She knew about the possibility of linking. He'd talked to Lystrana about the ancients' warning, about linking directly to the world. He could only hope that she had remembered. She *had* to have remembered.

When he went down the last ramp and out through the main entrance, he found that the rotunda was empty of the coach or any drivers. Certainly, he could walk south to the RA's complex. He took a deep breath and followed the stone-paved side lane toward the boulevard, but before he was more than a few paces away from the rotunda, as he turned the corner, the late, late afternoon sun struck him full in the eyes. It was so close to setting behind the mountains that its normally white orb had shifted toward the orange.

After a moment, when his eyes readjusted, he realized that the space west of the main boulevard was filled with landers and indigens. Some were shouting. He thought he heard some cheers. Quickly, tired as he was, he shielded himself with Talent as he moved toward the east side of the boulevard. He still needed to get to Lystrana—and Kytrana.

As he neared the boulevard, he could see that most of the indigens still remained on the west side, away from the section reserved for riders and coaches, although Dainyl saw neither. His Talent concealment shield seemed to be working, because no one noticed him. If they did, no one said anything.

He turned south and picked up his pace. He'd walked less than a hundred yards when he realized that his boots were loose. Not badly, but they were slipping on his feet somewhat. He concentrated on walking—and listening.

". . . closed the counting house . . ."

". . . be back . . . all too soon, if you ask me . . ."

". . . tell you. They're all gone."

"Syphia said that when the ground rumbled and the air turned green, then the one she worked for, she vanished, turned into dust, and her clothes fell to the floor. Ha! Good cloth. Leastwise, she brought it home . . ."

". . . see that big fellow there . . . he's gone now . . ."

". . . don't look for what isn't there, Fharyd. You might find it."

". . . still say . . ."

Dainyl kept walking, as fast as he could. He thought about running, but the RA's complex was too far, and he'd end up walking before long anyway.

He glanced to the west side of the boulevard once more. Some few shops were closed, but they might have been anyway, since it was Decdi and some crafters and merchants weren't open on the end-day. But if all the alectors—or most of them—had vanished, why wasn't there more unrest, more disturbance?

He shook his head. Why would there be? Even in Dereka, there weren't more than a hundred alectors, if that, and outside of tariff collection overseers and a few handfuls of supervisors, how much direct contact did indigens and landers have with alectors?

In Elcien and Ludar, things would be different . . .

He almost stopped walking, because he doubted that there was anything left of Ludar. The city had been disintegrating before him when he'd escaped, and there was no Table left. That suggested the Tables in both Ludar and Elcien had exploded, and they were used enough that the explosion might well have leveled everything for hundreds of yards. The landers and the indigens there wouldn't have escaped.

Ahead, on his left, he could see the open gates to the RA's complex, the ironwork showing a hint of orange from the setting sun. He hurried toward them, then turned and walked across the paved courtyard toward the main entrance. The sound of his steps echoed in the courtyard.

The columned entryway was empty as well. Beyond, halfway across the high arched entry hall, he saw a long-haired figure sprawled on the green and gold marble. As he neared her, he could sense she was dead. From the waist up, she was—or had been—a young alectress. Below the waist, she was foreshortened, smaller, more like an indigen.

Had she tried to link to the world—and failed?

Dainyl shook his head again and hurried toward the rear corridor that would lead to the RA's quarters. Then he stopped. Lystrana wouldn't have been in the quarters when whatever the ancients had done had occurred. She would have been in the RA's study.

He'd never been there, but all of the regional alectors had studies on the upper level. He headed up the center staircase at the back of the vaulted entry hall. Just beyond the landing at the top of the marble staircase was another set of shimmersilk garments, but they had belonged to an alector.

Dainyl had no idea where her study might have been. So, with dread, he quickly surveyed each and every chamber on the upper level. He found another score of shimmersilks, but none that were hers. Even in the RA's main chambers in the southwest corner, he found no sign of her, except for a slightly disarrayed stack of papers on the table desk that was clearly hers.

In the growing gloom of twilight, he took a deep breath. She still might be all right. He turned and headed back down to the lower level and the rear corridor that led to the RA's quarters. His boots clicked on the marble, the only sound he heard beside that of his own breathing.

The door from the complex to the quarters was ajar, and unlocked. Dainyl moistened his lips and stepped into the small foyer. He glanced around. No lights were lit. He saw no one and heard nothing.

"Lystrana!"

The only reply was silence.

Slowly, he walked down the main hallway. There were no shimmersilks in the hall or in the larger front foyer. The outside door to the entrance Dainyl had always used was locked. He unlocked and opened it. The ironwork door beyond was also locked. He closed the inner door and locked it.

"Lystrana!"

Then he went from room to room, searching each, even the closets, and the pantry off the kitchen. The quarters were untouched, as if she had walked out, and left the door ajar.

He stood in the hallway outside the bedchamber, then stepped inside. Using a flick of Talent, he lit the old-fashioned oil lamp, thinking that he might see more in the light, that his night sight might have missed something.

He studied the sitting area of the bedchamber, looking closely at everything, trying to catch a glimpse of anything that might give him an idea of where she might be or what had happened. He found nothing—not a piece of clothing out of place, not a bloodstain, a spilled glass . . . nothing at all.

Finally, he moved to the dressing room, where he also lit the lamp.

As he looked up, he saw a motion out of the corner of his eye. He turned quickly, throwing up shields, even before he confronted the image in the wall mirror. The figure was somewhat shorter than Dainyl, with a lightly tanned face, brilliant green eyes, a strong nose, and hair that was several shades darker than iron-gray—not the color of an aging lander, but a vigorous healthy gray. The image wore shimmersilk greens with rolled-up jacket sleeves and trousers that were too large.

Dainyl raised a hand. So did the image.

The image was his. He was the image, and he looked like a lander with dark gray hair, if somewhat larger than the tallest of landers he had seen. No longer a black-haired and white-faced alector, he was a lander with Talent.

A lander with Talent? He shuddered. He'd been warned, but he still couldn't believe it had happened.

Finally, he turned away from the image that was him—and wasn't. He still had to find Lystrana. At the worst, he had to *know*.

Slowly, painstakingly, he began to study the dressing chamber, fearing he would find crumpled shimmersilk, and hoping that he would not. He checked the garments hung there, but all that she had brought still looked to be there, save perhaps one, possibly two, and her toiletries were laid out on the dressing table.

Finally, he left the dressing room and the bedchamber, and lit the lamps in each room in the quarters, studying each one, and then snuffing the lamps when he finished in each. He found nothing.

He took a deep breath.

He needed to go back to Lystrana's study in the main building. Perhaps he had overlooked something. He forced himself to walk deliberately back through the rear corridor and back to the upper level.

Once there, in her study, he lit the wall lamps and went back over every span of the space. Again, he found nothing, but it was at least two glasses before he returned to the quarters, having found nothing that indicated what had happened to Lystrana—or even where she might be. He had found none of her shimmersilk garments left and crumpled. He would have recognized them. He would have Talent-sensed that they were hers. He still had his Talent. But what had happened to her?

He locked the doors behind himself, and then went to the

kitchen, where he forced himself to eat some bread and cheese, the only thing that was there that he could eat without preparation.

Where was she? What had happened to her? How could he find out?

As the darkness dropped across Dereka, he lay there alone on the triple-width bed in the bedchamber, too worried to sleep, and too exhausted to move.

95

Late in the day, after Fourth Battalion and Sixteenth Company had rejoined Mykel and Third Battalion, and after the Cadmians had done what they could to reclaim weapons and ammunition, and after Mykel had had a chance to gather his thoughts together, he assembled the officers and Bhoral on the north causeway to the bridge over the Vedra.

For all the flood, the bridge itself—and its eternastone supports—remained untouched and secure. South of where they stood on the approach to the bridge, below the bluffs, steam and fog still rose from the river, and the warmth from the river air mixed with the chill of the growing wind out of the northwest.

As he waited for Zendyr to join them, Mykel was all too conscious of the covert looks from the officers, particularly from Loryalt. Most of them, with the exception of Hamylt, seemed to be studying him when he was not looking directly at them.

"Sorry, sir," offered Zendyr, hurrying up.

"Someone has to be last," Mykel said lightly. He waited a moment. "Any more reports on the Squawts and Reillies? Are they regrouping?"

"No, sir," replied Chyndylt. "Jasakyt checked that out. They've all headed north. They're pretty much making their separate ways. It looks like they just fell apart after you stood up to their warleaders."

"Priests," murmured Loryalt.

"How do we stand on supplies, Bhoral?"

"We picked up some from the locals and from what the Reillies discarded. Maybe five days, eight on short rations."

Mykel nodded. "There's not that much left in Iron Stem, and no more ammunition, and winter's coming on. We've also accomplished what we can as far as our orders go." *And we have the pay chests and what's left in them.*

Zendyr and Bhoral nodded. A faint smile crossed Rhystan's lips. Hamylt glanced from Mykel to Rhystan. Sendryrk looked at the ground.

"We're going to Tempre," Mykel said. "We'll have to ride, because after that flood of steaming water, there won't be anything left that can take us by river. Tempre's halfway to Elcien, and they've got a good barracks in Tempre, enough for all of us there, and there might even be ammunition in the armories there."

"Leastwise, in the one that's locked underneath," suggested Bhoral. "The Myrmidons didn't even know it was there, but they don't use ammunition anyway, not for those lances of theirs."

"Sir?" offered Loryalt. "The ancient . . . I mean . . . does . . . well . . ."

Mykel had hoped to avoid dealing with what the soarer had said. "For better or worse, she indicated that the alectors were gone and that we should go to Tempre. Going to Tempre makes sense even if she hadn't said it, and even if there are alectors somewhere."

"Sir?" asked Sendryrk. "Begging your pardon . . . but what if the colonel sends orders to Iron Stem?"

"The orders will find us, and if they do before we can get word to him, we'll certainly obey them. But we have a responsibility to the men as well, and I don't see how we could take care of them in Iron Stem through the winter, not without additional provisions, and there's no way to get them to us, not for a long time, with all the damage on the river."

"You're thinking that there's more trouble than just here, sir?" asked Zendyr, the new Thirteenth Company undercaptain.

"That's pretty clear. You saw the steaming river, and that boiling water went a long ways. Elcien, Ludar, and Faitel have been destroyed. How much other destruction there is besides, I don't know. We certainly can't do any more here, not until spring, if then, even." He turned to Rhystan. "Captain, you've scouted Borlan."

"They've got a couple of chandleries where we can get more supplies, and the inns aren't full."

"We'll spend tonight there and head out in the morning. Pass the word. They've got a quarter glass to mount up and cross the bridge."

"Yes, sir."

Rhystan waited until the other officers had left before easing closer to Mykel. "You know more than you've said. The ancient?"

Mykel nodded. "It's not anything I can prove yet, but there's trouble all over the west of Corus. I don't think we'll be getting orders anytime soon." *Maybe not ever.*

"That's why you're picking Tempre? Or because of the ancient?"

"Both. If things get back more to normal, it makes sense, and I can explain it to the colonel. If they don't, cities like Tempre will need protection, and there'll be a place for us."

Rhystan offered a wry smile. "I'll make sure the senior squad leaders know."

"I'll talk more to all the officers on the ride to Tempre," Mykel added.

"They'll understand."

Mykel hoped so.

As he walked back to where the roan was tied, he could only hope that, somehow, his family had escaped the disaster that had struck Faitel, whatever it had been. But there was a cold numbness inside that told him not to expect too much.

He also hoped fervently that Rachyla had escaped any harm.

96

Early evening seven days later found Third and Fourth Battalions camped at the way station to the west of Krost. Mykel and the officers stood around the dying cookfire. Although the evening was chill, the wind had died away. Overhead, the tiny green disc of Asterta neared the zenith. Selena had set at twilight.

"The alectors are all gone, every last one," said Loryalt. "That's what they were saying in Krost."

"Where did they go?" asked Hamylt. "They couldn't just disappear."

"Why not?" countered Culeyt. "That factor in Krost said he watched one turn to dust. All that was left were his clothes."

"It doesn't seem right," murmured Sendryrk.

"It didn't seem right that a flood destroyed the ironworks and little else," replied Rhystan. "Or that the entire River Vedra boiled. But it happened."

"Who'll need us now?" asked Zendyr.

"Tempre will need us more than ever," suggested Mykel. "It's a trade city, and there's no one to protect it now."

Rhystan and Culeyt exchanged knowing glances. Chyndylt nodded, while Sendryrk looked from face to face.

"Without the alectors and the Myrmidons, who will protect the factors and the merchants? Brigands and bandits—and insurgents—could almost walk in. We're going to offer them a deal, a very good deal. We'll protect Tempre and the surrounding area, at least to Krost and the Vyan Hills, and they'll pay us."

"Why would they do that?" asked Hamylt skeptically.

"Because I'll tell them the alternatives," Mykel said. "They'll listen."

"They'll listen to you now," pointed out Rhystan. "But how will you make sure that they keep listening?"

"That's simple enough. They don't trust each other. We'll

have to collect a tariff in order to make sure we get paid; so we'll take charge of all the things the alectors used to do and fund them out of the tariffs. They get to keep making coins, and we keep order and protect them, and it won't cost them much more than before . . . and a great deal less than having to raise and train their own army."

"They won't like that."

"They'll like it a lot better than what else could happen," suggested Mykel.

"So we'll be running things . . ."

"I think the majer will be running things," said Culeyt, "and we'll help him. Unless you have a better idea. We'll do a lot better than having to fight rebel alectors and seltyrs in Dramur, or fighting off those sandwolves in Iron Stem when half the people could have cared less."

"We'll have to run road patrols to keep off the brigands, and probably take over supervising the patrollers," Mykel said. "If we do, we'll be able to get more recruits."

"What about the men?" asked Sendryrk. "What if they don't want to stay?"

"For now, if anyone asks, tell them that we have to find out whether there is a Duarchy. The rules stay the same until we know. If everything does change, they'll be told the new rules, and they can make a choice then. Right now, what we're doing is getting them all closer to wherever their home might be, and doing it a lot safer than on their own. That's true for all of us."

That got a round of nods.

"Why don't we go to Elcien?" asked Hamylt.

"Because there isn't any Elcien," Mykel replied.

"Because that ancient told you that?" Hamylt did not quite sneer.

"The soarers boiled the river and created earthquakes and destroyed the ironworks. I'm inclined to believe them. In addition, the factors in Krost confirmed that all the alectors there died."

"What about Ludar?"

Mykel looked hard at Hamylt. "The word is that it's gone as well. What are you asking, Hamylt? Are you asking why I'm in charge?"

"I guess I am."

"Because I've done a better job. I didn't get most of Fourth Battalion killed. I didn't lose most or all of my company the way a lot of captains have, and I've stuck my own neck—and shoulder—out for my officers and men. Now . . . exactly what have you done?"

"I just asked."

"So did I," replied Mykel. "I understand when people ask questions about things they don't know. I understand when people ask questions when they don't understand something. But when someone asks questions to cause trouble, I don't like it. I don't like troublemakers. There's a reason for that. We're still two hundred vingts from Tempre and more than seven hundred from what's left of Elcien or Ludar. We have a responsibility to the Cadmians out there." He gestured toward the way station. "At the very least, we need to get them to a place like Tempre, where, if things are falling apart, they can make a choice that means something. Now . . . are you going to cooperate with me and the other officers? If you're not, I'll make an exception. You can walk out of here with the clothes on your back and your personal gear." Mykel's voice was like ice, and he found himself projecting a sense of power.

Hamylt stepped back. "No, sir. I was out of line. I was worried."

Mykel could sense the captain's fear, and he tried to project reassurance. "We're all worried, but sticking together is the best way to get through this. I don't want to coerce anyone. I think you all ought to talk it over without me around." He offered a smile, then turned and walked away from the way station out to the west through the calf-high tan grass that scraped gently against his gray trousers.

He finally found himself on a rise some hundred yards from the way station, looking westward in the general direction of Tempre. Had he pressed too hard, based on what he wanted, and on what the soarer had told him? Didn't they understand, that as a force, they could establish themselves in an even better position than they'd had as Cadmians?

But was he the right person to lead them?

He laughed softly. If he weren't he'd find out quickly enough.

Half a glass passed before he sensed someone coming through the grass. He turned and watched as Rhystan neared.

"What did they decide?" he finally asked.

Rhystan laughed. "The choice was between flogging Hamylt on the spot or tying him to a post in the way station and leaving him. Chyndylt told him that if he ever said a word against you, he wouldn't wake up the next morning—and that he didn't care if they hung him for it. Culeyt asked him if he'd slit his skull and poured out his brains—or if he really wanted to oppose someone favored by both the ancients and his men. Even Sendryrk said something about how casualties had gone way down since you'd taken over, and asked how many officers he'd known who fought injured and one-armed. Lor̂yalt asked him why he didn't want to follow an officer who'd faced down High Alectors for his men and who'd won doing it."

"That doesn't tell me whether they thought it was a good idea." Mykel looked to the older officer.

"Of course they did. They're troopers, Majer. Where else are they going to be troopers? Where else will they find a commander they trust?"

"What about Hamylt?"

"He'll be all right. It was a good thing to get things out in the open. I told him that. I also told him you don't hold grudges so long as people do a good job."

"I try not to," Mykel replied.

"You do better than most, better than I do." Rhystan paused. "You handle the seltyrs and traders right, and you could be the Duarch of Tempre, Majer," suggested Rhystan.

Mykel shook his head. "How about just the Protector of Tempre?"

"You can't do that and command in the field, you know?"

"Are you volunteering to be the field commander?" countered Mykel.

"Absolutely. It's got to be better than being a captain or a majer."

"You'll need a title. How about 'Colonel'?"

"How about 'Arms Commander'?"

"That's a good title." Mykel laughed.

So did Rhystan.

97

In the late evening, Dainyl sat in the kitchen of the deserted quarters of the abandoned RA's complex. When the locals had begun to plunder the main building, they had seen him, and left him alone. Then, some of the local landholders had taken charge and posted their guards, again avoiding him, as he had avoided them. That would not last much longer, he knew, but what remained in the quarters was all that he had left of Lystrana—and Kytrana—for all that he had searched.

It had been almost a week since the world had changed. He had traveled the webs of the ancients, and discovered that Ludar had been destroyed, and that the stone isle on which Elcien had been built had sunk so far into the Bay of Ludar that only the tips of the towers remained above the water. Most of Faitel had been destroyed, possibly because of the lightcannon that had been built there. Lyterna was deserted, except for the upper sections, sealed behind some sort of barrier he could not penetrate. He had roamed the streets of Dereka, using his Talent as concealment, but he had found no sign of Lystrana there, either—nor in the abandoned Myrmidon compound.

Nowhere had he found signs of alectors, nor of pteridons.

Yet . . . he *knew* that he would have known if she had died. But was that knowledge rational? Or was he deluding himself, hanging on to hope that had no basis in reality?

Soon, he would have to venture forth. That he knew. But he would not until he had to.

A green radiance spilled around him, and he stood . . . turning.

A soarer appeared, carrying a bundle. Dainyl could sense not just the soarer but another lifeforce.

Take her . . .

"Take who?" The alector who was now lander, who had been a High Alector of Justice, looked at what the soarer carried—a child.

She is your daughter. You, the few who linked to this world and changed, and the handful of landers with Talent must make sure that she and the children like her live and prosper. They are the only hope for the future.

"My daughter? Kytrana died. She and Lystrana died." The words were cold, angry. "What you did killed them." He wasn't sure, but he *had* to know.

We did not. She did not die from the change, but there was not enough lifeforce for her and the child. Not to remain as you do. The soarer looked at him evenly.

Dainyl *knew*. After a moment, he asked, "She did this . . . knowing . . . ?

She loved you and this world enough to give you a daughter. Her child and her child's children must come to learn what you know—and more. When the barriers fall, the Efrans will return, and we will not be here to help those children of your children's children.

"How could that be? You defeated them . . ."

We did not defeat them except on this world. We made it so that they could not draw their lifeforce from this world. We have blocked their long tubes between worlds. For now. It cost us most dearly. There are some handfuls of us remaining, but thousands of us died so that the world would not.

Take your daughter. Care for her.

"How can I care . . . ?"

Leave here. Go to the Iron Valleys. Do not use the webs with your daughter. When you reach the Iron Valleys, find the nightsheep. They should suit you, who were once a herder of men. You will learn how the nightsheep can sustain you. Now . . . take your daughter.

Dainyl extended his arms.

The infant looked up at him with eyes greener than the lifeforce of a soarer. The fuzz that covered her head was gray—dark gray, like his.

When he looked up, the soarer had vanished.

He looked down at Kytrana, for it was his daughter, with the same lifeforce for which he had searched. Tears streamed down his face. He had lost . . . so much . . . but not everything. He had Kytrana . . . and an unspoken promise.

He *would* find his way to the Iron Valleys. He could not stay in Dereka, for all too many reasons, not the least of which was that the soarer had told him to leave. One thing he had learned—far too late—was disregarding the ancients was most unwise.

98

After Third and Fourth Battalions had taken possession of the compound that had once held the Alector's Guard, and later the Myrmidons, Mykel had immediately established road patrols and had paid a friendly visit to the small headquarters of the local patrollers, with an armed squad mounted outside. He had also made certain that Amaryk's villa was safe, and had ridden by several times, although he had not seen Rachyla.

In less than a few days, the majority of the scattered brigandage on the roads near Tempre had vanished. Mykel knew that the brigands had only moved farther away, but in time, he had plans to deal with that as well.

The travelers and refugees who dribbled into Tempre confirmed what the soarer had told him, but there was no news from as far away as Southgate or the towns of the north—or Dereka or Alustre in the east—and nothing more about Faitel. In all cities nearer to Tempre where there had been alectors, nothing remained except empty shimmersilk garments and boots.

A week later, Mykel had sent out invitations to all of the seltyrs and large factors in Tempre, requesting their presence on the following Duadi in the large conference room of the structure that had once been the headquarters of the regional alector. Each invitation had been delivered by two squads of armed Cadmians.

He had not heard from Rachyla, nor had he expected that he would, much as he might have hoped to, but he forced himself to bide his time as he readied for his "proposal" to the seltyrs and factors. He wanted to be in the greatest position of strength possible in dealing with Amaryk, since he was Rachyla's de facto guardian.

While Mykel still had trouble lifting his arm above his shoulder, even before Duadi he was able to move around without the sling, and he made a practice of riding through Tempre with only a pair of Cadmians accompanying him.

When Duadi came, he stood by the conference-room door and greeted each man who entered. When it appeared that no others would appear, he nodded to the two Cadmians, who closed the double doors to the oak-paneled room. Mykel moved to the low dais at one end, from which he'd had all chairs and the low table removed. Then he turned and surveyed the seltyrs and, in some cases, their representatives. He'd already noted those who had not appeared. He would have to call on them personally. One way or another, they would agree.

"I invited you all here to formalize what I have already been doing in Tempre, and that is providing order and keeping the peace. In simple terms, I am proposing that you accept my role as Protector of Tempre and that we develop and agree to the structure and the tariffs necessary to fund it . . ." Mykel talked for a quarter glass. Then he waited.

"Aren't you being terribly presumptuous?" That came from Gheort, Seltyr Asadyl's heir second, beside whom sat young Amaryk—Rachyla's cousin of sorts, for whom she was chatelaine.

"I'd suggest that I'm being terribly practical. The alectors are gone. So are the Myrmidons and pteridons. All that remains are their garments and boots. There has been no sign of any living alector in almost a month. But there are more and more reports of brigands in the areas we have not patrolled.

Do you have the coins and the expertise to train a force able to protect you? Less than a month ago, we destroyed a force of over two thousand Reillies bound on sacking Borlan. Could any of you manage that? Without us, they will be back."

"Why should we accept an arrangement such as yours? We've languished too long under the alectors," pointed out another seltyr.

"There are several reasons," replied Mykel reasonably. "First, it makes sense. Second, you really don't have a choice, not one that won't cost you personally and disastrously." He smiled and held up a hand, projecting absolute power and assurance. "Hear me out. Here are some of the reasons this makes sense. None of you trust each other, not for long, and not when coins are at stake, and you'd end up spending your coins fighting each other. I'm not interested in being a trader. In fact, I'm interested in all of you prospering, because a city or a land doesn't run without tariffs, and one cannot collect tariffs from the poor. Likewise, the more prosperous you are, the less of your total earnings need to be tariffed. If you were to attempt to maintain the peace and order without me, it would cost you far more, and that's even if you could avoid fighting each other. I may not be so old as some of you, but I've been in enough lands to know what works and what does not. In addition, by having an armed force in place, and one composed of battle-trained veterans, you will discourage anyone from taking advantage of you. By accepting a Protector of Tempre, you will be setting up the framework that will allow an area where you can trade with far less fear of brigands or loss to raiders and one that will expand as others see the advantage."

"How large an area could you protect . . ."

"Why should we trust you . . ."

"What protections would we have . . ."

Mykel noted that Amaryk occasionally murmured words to Gheort, asked no questions, but listened intently as Mykel replied to the inquiries.

When the last of the questions died away, Mykel smiled

again, then looked at Gheort. "Would you care to offer the first draft of the agreement, or would you prefer that I do?"

"Several of us will present a draft to you by Septi." Gheort's voice was cool, and Mykel sensed the calculation behind it.

"It seems to me," Mykel replied politely, "that I have laid out the duties required of the Protector of Tempre clearly, as well as the level of tariffing required. Those duties and powers cannot be less. Nor can the costs of operating what will be a government. What would be most helpful is a structure of how you suggest tariffs be structured, in a way that is fair to you, as well as to smaller merchants and crafters, and a listing of what you believe to be the rights of all who live in Tempre."

Surprisingly, that statement elicited nods from most of those present. Even Amaryk nodded.

Mykel listened as they left, but heard only a few scattered comments.

". . . going to be Protector . . . like it or not . . ."

". . . might work . . . can't hurt to try . . ."

". . . who does he think he is?"

Mykel smiled at the last.

Once the front courtyard was empty, Mykel walked up the wide stone center steps to the upper level of the building and to the corner study that had once been the regional alector's, and where cases of files remained, with judgments and reasons for them. He had the feeling that he'd find them very useful—assuming matters did work out.

Rhystan was waiting.

"How was your morning?" asked Mykel.

"Sendryrk caught the brigands who'd been lurking to the west of the piers. Most of them used to work the river."

"Could we put them on some sort of work gang to rebuild the damage? We'll need the piers before too long."

Rhystan laughed. "You're already acting like the Protector of Tempre."

Mykel sank into the overlarge chair that had been used by the regional alector and looked at Rhystan. "They'll agree.

They won't be totally happy, but they'll all see that the alternatives are worse."

"That's more encouraging than in some places."

Mykel laughed. "We're just giving them back a familiar structure. They'll complain, but they'll adapt to it."

"Just so long as you're strong and fair."

"So long as *we* are. You're going to need some more recruits. We'll need to fill out Fourth Battalion and add at least one more battalion. That will give some heft to the Southern Guard." Mykel had wondered about the name, because there were other parts of Corus more to the south, but Tempre *was* south of the Vedra, and anything that was had always been considered "southern." He also had to look ahead.

"Two more by the end of next year," suggested Rhystan. "More than that if you want to expand the area we protect."

"We really need to include the whole square—Krost, Syan, Hyalt, and Tempre—and probably Borlan," mused Mykel.

There was a knock on the door. "Sir?"

"Yes."

"Do you know someone called Viencet? He claims he's your brother."

"He probably is," Mykel replied. "I do have a brother named Viencet." *Or I did.*

Rhystan put a hand on the hilt of his sabre.

Mykel stood and moved beside the wide table desk. "Have him come in."

The door opened.

The young man who walked into the study was clad in shabby work trousers, boots almost without soles or heels, and a stained brown jacket. His long blond hair was bound up behind him in a sloppy braid.

Mykel immediately sensed that he was indeed Viencet. "Viencet . . . I wasn't sure . . . I heard about Faitel . . ." He smiled warmly. "It's so good to see you."

"Mykel . . . Mykel . . . I knew you'd make it." Viencet straightened. "You'll put things right for me, won't you?"

"What about Mother? Father?"

Viencet shook his head.

"Sesalia . . . the children?"

"They were all too close . . . half of Faitel . . . it exploded . . . there's a big lake filled with black water. It steams."

Mykel stood silently for a time. He'd had that feeling, and he'd tried to push it away. Now, all he had left of his family was the last letter from his mother . . . and Viencet. Finally, he asked, "How did you . . . ?"

"I was in Naerton . . . not more than a hamlet . . ."

"A work gang?" asked Mykel.

"You would ask that. Your own brother."

Rhystan edged forward.

Mykel repressed a sigh. He'd been glad to see Viencet—for a few moments—until he realized that nothing had changed.

"I need coins, Mykel. Surely, you've got silvers. You're in charge."

"I think we can find you a job here in Tempre, Viencet. There's a lot to be done. Or you can join the Southern Guard."

"You'd . . . make me work? Your own brother?"

The outrage flowed out, so obvious to Mykel's Talent-senses that it turned his stomach. He took out his wallet and handed over four silvers. "That's what I have, Viencet. You may have it all. None of us has been paid in more than a month. Before long, we'll be back on a better schedule, but for now, that's all there is."

"You should make all the fat merchants pay." Viencet stuffed the four silvers into his wallet.

"They can't pay because I need coins or you do."

"But you're in charge!"

"I have to work within the rules, Viencet. Everyone does." *And you never saw that, or wanted to.*

"You could change them. You've always been good at that." Viencet smiled hopefully.

Mykel could sense the calculation behind the smile. "No. I've been able to work within the rules, and sometimes improve them, but even when you're the one who sets up rules, you need to follow them."

"You're just like Father and Sesalia. There's always a reason. You've never understood. You never will."

"Viencet . . . I think you'd better go. Anytime you want me to help find you a position, I'll be here."

Viencet's eyes widened. "You'd turn me out . . . like that?"

"You want everything handed to you. You always have. I'm here because men trusted me, and some even lost their lives following my orders. You don't even want to work for coins. How can I ask men to follow me and then turn around and give you coins for doing nothing? Tell me, Viencet."

"But I'm your brother."

"You are. That's why you should know better."

"Some brother you are."

"I think you'd better go," Mykel said again. "If you want to earn your coins, I'll be here."

"I'm sure you will be, in your cozy study, while I'm in some hovel." The sense of entitlement and anger was even more violent than Viencet's words.

"That's your choice."

Without another word, Viencet turned and walked out, leaving the door ajar behind him.

Rhystan closed it, silently.

What had happened to Viencet? He'd always been self-centered, but . . . now? Mykel walked to his right and looked out the window, watching, as Viencet slouched out the main entrance below and to his left, then walked across the front paved area, spitting once on the stones. He did not look back. Before long, his brown jacket disappeared into the park across the boulevard.

Mykel turned.

Rhystan smiled sadly. "We all have some in the family like that. My cousin Vyrn would have said the same things. He did. He came to my father and told him that he had to take care of him, that my father owed it to his older brother."

"He's the only one left . . . but . . . what else could I do?" If he'd taken Viencet in, Viencet wouldn't have changed. He'd just have spent silvers and then golds—or Mykel would have had to have thrown him out later.

Rhystan said nothing, but Mykel understood what Rhystan felt as though he had, and the answer was that Mykel, being who he was, could have done nothing else.

Mykel forced a rueful smile. "Worrying isn't going to get us through the next week. Can we cut back on the boulevard patrols now?"

"I was going to suggest that. Loryalt also thought that we ought to arm the local patrollers with truncheons as well as those shortswords. There are times when you need force, but you don't want to run someone through. They'll let a cutpurse or a grifter go rather than do that."

"We could try that . . ."

Rhystan stayed for another glass before leaving, and Mykel continued to work on trying to figure out how to structure the tariff agents so that they didn't divert coins, but so that he didn't have to pay people to watch other people.

Abruptly, Mykel got up from the table desk and walked to the window. He could feel . . . something. Outside, the sunny morning had given way to a gray and cloudy afternoon, one that threatened snow or a cold rain.

A carriage rolled up to the entrance, but so close to the steps and mounting blocks that Mykel could not see who stepped out. One of the factors?

He turned, wondering even if whoever had come was there to see him, but why else would anyone come at the moment?

He looked out at the clouds, but it would be a while before it rained . . . or snowed.

"Majer, sir?" said Roryn, one of the wounded rankers who was serving as an orderly in the outer study. "There's a . . . someone . . . You'd better come out, sir."

Who could it be? Certainly not Viencet. Not so soon, and not in a carriage. Possibly one of the factors or seltyrs trying to cut a deal of some sort? That was most likely. He squared his shoulders and took a deep breath, then stepped to the door and opened it.

Rachyla stood there.

He stood there, frozen. He had hoped so much . . . yet until he was Protector of Tempre . . . a man of power and substance . . . he would not have dared to approach her, not until he was certain he could fully protect her.

"Won't you ask me in?" Her voice carried a trace of humor, but behind it was a tightness. Apprehension?

"Certainly. You're always welcome." Mykel bowed, then gestured for her to enter. Why had she come? Amaryk?

He closed the door.

She walked to the window and gazed out, not immediately looking at him.

As always, he could not sense what she felt, and that worried him.

"You have a good view from here, Majer. Or should I say, 'Protector'?"

"I don't think that's been settled, Lady."

She laughed, and melodic as the sound was, Mykel thought he heard nervousness in it. Rachyla, nervous?

"They're always self-centered, and often fools, but they are not complete idiots. They would not tell you, but already they had worried about how to protect themselves. Gheort had looked into expanding his private guards, but the cost would have destroyed him had the others not done the same. They will send you a document, and it will try to protect all that they wish, but so long as you are close to reasonable, they will accept your terms and changes."

"Were you sent to tell me that?"

"No one sent me." Rachyla turned from the window. "Once . . . once . . . someone of great power came to me and offered an apology and asked a favor." There was a pause. "I . . . I would do the same."

"You do not owe me any apologies, Lady. I will do you a favor, if I can."

She stepped forward and extended the sheath that held the dagger of the ancients. "Would you take this back? Or take back the words with which you called me an enemy?"

"I don't have to, Lady. I never was your enemy. You declared that you were mine, and I was forced to acknowledge that, against my will and my desires. I am not your enemy, and you have never been mine. That I will affirm. If you still wish, I will take the dagger, but only if you wish."

"Then . . . I will keep the dagger . . . for now." She slipped the dagger into her belt and took another step closer.

Mykel forced himself to keep from swallowing.

"You understood my words when you last left Tempre, didn't you? Your letter seemed to indicate that."

"I believe so. Especially those about children. That is one reason, one hope, behind my attempt to become Protector of Tempre. That and your message about my injuries. How did you know that?"

"I felt something the first time, in Dramur. It was worse when you were injured here. The pain was almost unbearable this last time." Rachyla offered a low laugh. "You think of me often, don't you?"

"Yes."

"I had . . . thought so . . . hoped so."

Mykel waited. He wanted to hold her. More than anything.

"Even Amaryk cannot complain about my wedding the Protector of Tempre. In fact, he said that he would not oppose such a marriage."

"Your marriage?" Mykel *thought* he knew what she meant, but after so long, he feared that he might be disappointed.

Rachyla lowered her eyes and then her head. "Mykel . . . do not make me beg. I will if I must, but . . ."

He remained motionless, mute. She had never used his name, not alone, not without a title. "Lady . . . you do not have to beg. From me, you will never have to beg."

"I am no lady—" She looked up.

The shock of seeing those deep green eyes so close went through him like a blade, as did the warmth of her presence.

"If you wed the Protector of Tempre, and he loves you, how can you not be a lady?" *My lady.* He smiled, then took her hands in his, and gently, he bent and kissed her cheek, daring no more.

She turned her head. "For so long . . . I had so hoped . . ."

This time, their lips touched.

Outside, the first snowflakes of winter began to drift by the window.

EPILOGUE

Dainyl stood in the doorway, listening, as Lystrana hovered beside the railed bed set in the small room. Outside, the wind whispered, and heavy spring snow fell across the holding he had begun to build, not that he had ever expected to be a herder, but the nightsheep were more tractable than pteridons, and only those with Talent could manage them. Only a former alector to whom the soarers had given the specific knowledge on how to turn that wool into a fabric softer than linen, yet more durable than shimmersilk, and more precious than gems.

He listened to the lullaby.

Londi's child will know fair faces.
Duadi's child will form life's graces.
Tridi's child will cross the years,
but Quattri's must conquer fears.
Quinti's daughter will prove strong,
while Sexdi's will set right from wrong.
Septi's child will find new lands,
but Octdi's will meet their hard demands.
Novdi's child must find the able,
while Decdi's child will yet rule the Table.
You, precious child, I praise the most,
for you will be the future's host,
to raise bright banners high
under the green and silver sky.

Dainyl waited until she turned. "You have to go, don't you? Again."

The soarer who had been his wife nodded. *I cannot come often, for the lifeforce and the web are weak, and weaker still for me here. They will be for many years, but they will recover, now.*

Soarers did not cry, but he felt the sorrow as she turned from the bed and the sleeping child.

In moments, she was gone.

Dainyl slipped out of Kytrana's chamber and outside onto the narrow porch. There, for a time, he stood looking eastward through the darkness in the direction of the Aerlal Plateau. Although it was shrouded in clouds, he could sense its solidity, and the flickering presence of the remaining ancients, a presence that included one who had been an alectress, and one who had survived through her Talent and bequeathed most of her lifeforce to her daughter.

The ancients had made their choice, and in turn Lystrana had made hers, for the sake of Kytrana—a soarer's choice.